The music echoed their surging desire . . .

They faced each other on the floor, and she met his eyes, a kind of challenge. Then the dance began.

It was wild, as always, and the haunting whine of the pipes underscored the pace of the music. When it came time for the two of them to take their turn in the circle, they had become strangely mesmerized, caught in some dark attraction that was more than the music, more than the physical magnet of opposite sexes.

She and Royce Campbell danced forward, then away from each other. She felt the blood pumping from her heart, her lungs ached for air, but it was glorious. Her hair was flying, her body, too, and her very soul screamed with joy. Her fiancé was all but forgotten, and the past, too. Even the future did not matter, because all that mattered was Royce Campbell and this dance. . . .

Flames of Desire

Flames of Desire

by
Vanessa Royall

A DELL BOOK

Published by
Dell Publishing Co., Inc.
1 Dag Hammarskjold Plaza
New York, New York 10017

Dell ® TM 681510, Dell Publishing Co., Inc.

ISBN: 0-440-14637-2

Printed in the United States of America
First printing—June 1978

For Ellen and Jonathan

Flames of Desire

PROLOGUE

The mead shop in the village of Lauder had a clay floor, shuffled to dull gloss by two centuries of topers. It was just elegant enough for such activity, too: a bar, a couple of battered tables, a soot-ridden hearth. Here one might quench a throat parched by the long trek from Edinburgh. Many men stopped at this inn on their way to meet Lord Seamus MacPherson, political leader and member of the Scottish Parliament, at his nearby Coldstream estate. Here stopped young Alan MacTavish one day, late in the Year of Our Lord 1774, and here he drank ale and whiskey in quantities insufficient to prevent him, after a time, from remounting his chestnut stallion, but certainly adequate to loosen his tongue, which declared a passionate hatred of England. And *he* was *friend* to Lord MacPherson, the hitherto irreproachable statesman? Many heard MacTavish on that cold afternoon, and now the peasants of Lauder possessed a secret they did not desire.

Such secrets are not long kept.

December now, and getting colder. The logs in the fireplace crackled but cast little warmth around the small taproom. Two weather-beaten peasants sat at a table, drinking mugs of stout, now and then staring covetously at the buxom, bold-faced barmaid. She pretended not to notice, feigning a coy innocence that had ceased to be convincing years before. But she was the landlord's wife and he was asleep or maybe drunk in the back room of the inn, so the men were content to snicker over lascivious possibility, both of them hinting of such experience with the barmaid on stolen nights in years past. But they held their tongues.

The landlord was mean, and a brawler. Besides, this kind of secret was not important enough to tell.

Then the three turned expectantly as the tavern's wood-and-nail door swung open. A tall, saturnine figure entered out of the dusk, trailed by a blast of wind, a cloud of brittle snow. Had he been an ordinary pilgrim, stopped along the road for food and drink, the men would have stared and measured him, given him the eye. Instead, the two drinkers turned quickly away, hunching down over the table, studying their mugs. This arrogant man with the dagger at his belt and the hint of menace in his slightly narrowed eyes was not the kind you look at long unless you want to fight. Even the barmaid, who had known hard men, stifled a gasp and seemed to shrink away. The stranger allowed himself a smile, half amused, half contemptuous. He had a face of sharp angles and predatory, hawklike eyes.

"Whiskey. Fast," he demanded, and strode to the bar. A black cape billowed as he moved, and he seemed larger than he was, his dark face accentauted by a tricornered hat. He did not wear the kilts of Berwick Province, but rather knee breeches and glossy boots, stylish cloak and silk cravat: the fashion now in Edinburgh and London. He smiled his unsettling smile once more—a momentary grimace of flashing teeth, slitted eye—and the barmaid nervously poured the strong whiskey from cask to mug, discarding any thought of "cheating the measure," a trick that had brought many extra pound into the landlord's till. This was not a man one crossed in any way.

"Ah, enou', m' lassie," he said now, reaching for the mug, taking it and her hand, too, for a long string of seconds. Then he released her, grinning. She stared stupidly at her hand, rubbed it on her skirt.

"T' England and the Act of Union!" he said, raising his mug and turning toward the two men at the table. His smile was still in place and it held more than a hint of clever malice now. Now they knew he was an Englishman after all. They must pretend to welcome him as a fellow citizen, but it would be more like offering grudging obeisance. He would make them drink with him against their will; they dared not refuse a toast to the Act of Union, which, under Queen Anne in 1707, less than seventy years before, had combined Scotland and England into what was called Great Britain. But the King was George III and his throne was in London. A thing of bitterness still to many of the Scots, a passionate and patriotic people.

"T' England an' the Act of Union," the two men muttered, hunched over the table.

The tall man drained the pewter mug in one long draft, returned it to the bar, and from a calfskin pouch at his belt took out a gold sovereign, far more than the drink was worth. He held it before the barmaid's eyes, held it in the flickering light so that even at the table the peasants could see it clearly. He laughed aloud at the flashing greed that rattled in the room.

"Aye, 'tis yours, m' bonnie," he hissed softly, " 'tis yours indeed," leaning across the bar and cupping her right breast in his hand. It was a gentleman's hand, well-shaped, strong, but the fingers were long and cruel. The barmaid winced, her mouth and eyes flew wide open with pain as he ground her nipple between thumb and forefinger. But she made no sound and did not move, as if either would invite greater agony, or worse. . . .

"See, lads," smiled the caped man, turning. But the peasants concentrated on the pattern of the grain in the wooden table. This amused him. "Ah, lads, *lads*," he said, turning back to the barmaid. "Ye've nithin' t' fear o' Darius McGrover, y' ken it, do ye na?" But then he snarled and those pincerlike fingers closed a final measure. The barmaid yelped, a sound of pain and fright, a sound that Darius loved. Master of His Majesty's Secret Offices, Darius had heard—and caused—such sounds of pain in dungeons and cellars throughout the Empire.

Slowly, grinning, Darius removed his hand. The men did nothing. There was going to be trouble now and they knew it. One of them glanced at the door, as if it were a way out. The barmaid rubbed her savaged breast, her mouth open in a soundless grimace of pain. Darius made a sound something like laughter and slammed the sovereign down on the bar, a ringing gold disk on dark wood.

"Wouldna ye like t' 'ave it?" he asked, and from the unnecessary thickness of the accent they could tell he was mocking them even in speech. He was an Englishman, the lord. They were serfs, the appropriated, the dispossessed.

They hated him then with a sullen fury that only accentuated their impotence. He felt it like a burning pall in the room. It did not bother him. In his business he was used to it, even amused by it. It meant nothing in the end, when accounts were settled. Aye, a seditious traitor running in the back alleys, free to sow dissension and discord, was sure to be proud and defiant. But on the rack, where the screws were turned, he would sing quite another tune. Darius knew. It was his profession to reduce men to their lowest common denominator: fearful husks in terror of death and pain. When he distilled from them this final essence of themselves, he learned the truth. Always.

"I require information," he said softly to the three of them, "about a young man called Alan MacTavish. A big, rangy lad, insolent of expression, with a shock of yellow hair, and a mount perhaps, of chestnut hue."

The barmaid looked quickly at the two men, saw the greed and fear fighting in their eyes, on their faces, saw the quivering pulse of greed in their twisting hands. They looked back at her, eyes moving from her face to the gold piece on the bar.

Darius waited awhile, took another slow swallow of whiskey directly from the bottle this time. "Well? Are you ready now to accommodate me? This MacTavish, you may know, is quite clearly a traitor to the King and the Empire. Have you seen him here? Has he passed by?"

Now he spoke slowly, almost as if bored, with the refined diction of the highest class. He spoke as if he had all the time in the world, and something played around his mouth that was like a smile, but not quite.

The barmaid and the two peasants twisted and suffered before him. Certainly, MacTavish had passed this way, had ridden on to see Lord MacPherson. But MacPherson was highly respected, and he was the most powerful lord in Berwick Province. There were many things he could do to them, should it be learned that any of them had spoken out of turn. He might even send against them his hot-tempered son, fiery Brian, and that would be no treat. They were caught betwixt unknowns of equal menace. But Darius was right here before them, with his hand on the dagger at his belt.

"You know this MacTavish fellow is a Rob Roy, *do ye na*? And I'm sure you do not wish to be accused yourselves of harboring or assisting one of them."

The men bowed their heads quickly and the barmaid stifled a gasp. The Rob Roys were a secret, outlawed political faction, whose goal it was to repeal and abnegate the Act of Union, to make Scotland entirely independent once more. Many Scots cheered them silently, but to raise one's voice in their behalf was to invite the hangman's noose. Or worse.

"I see," McGrover was saying, nodding, with that unspeakable smile. "You are afraid of MacPherson, are ye not? But do not be. The King will protect you from the ravaging of his bloody ilk, should he be in it with MacTavish. Ah, I know them, too," he went on, in response to their sudden, surprised glances. "I know the lord and his bloody son, and I've seen that wench, his daughter, Selena. You know her, too, I'm sure, don't you, lads? A fine blond beauty with that proud body and those haughty breasts? But ye'll nivir 'ave 'er," he muttered coarsely, lapsing back into the idiom to enhance the sexual connotation of his words. "But I intend to. An additional prize, a bounty, you might say, when I complete the mission that brought me here."

Envy showed in the barmaid's eyes at mention of Selena's name, the envy of a rough peasant woman whose knowledge of life included raw whiskey, winters of black bread, crude grapplings with drunken, brutal men, a knowledge of these things which stood against the reality of a noblewoman's life: fine gowns, handsome men who took you in soft beds, servants to light the fires, sweet wine. She was on the verge of speaking when, suddenly, one of the men could no longer bear the pressure. Lurching sideways from his chair, he scuttled crablike, half running, half crouching, toward the door. The movement was so unexpected that even Darius was taken aback. For a tiny spasm of seconds it even seemed as if the man would escape. Already his fingers fumbled at the leather loop of latchstring. In a flashing instant, Darius made his decision. His hand was at his belt and then high in the air, the bladed point of the dagger poised between his fingers, just as the barmaid's nipple had been. Then his arm swung down in a smooth arc of blinding speed. Silver flashed through the mead shop, fast as light. The peasant stiffened at the door, slumped forward, fell. In a moment blood formed at the corner of his slack mouth and ran down his chin in a thin red line. The hilt of the dagger protruded from his back.

Darius walked over to the body, kicked it, bent, and eased the weapon slowly from the man's body, drawing it out with exquisite slowness, almost a parody of sensual disengagement. He wiped the bloody blade on the peasant's rude cloak, stood up.

"I believe you will now speak to me of MacTavish and the MacPhersons," he smiled. Brandishing the unsheathed dagger, he advanced toward the barmaid. The peasant at the table shivered, his mouth working soundlessly. The barmaid made a sound deep in her throat, an indeterminate gurgle, somewhere between a sob and a moan. It was not loud but it was loud enough. The dirty, hanging curtain in the doorway behind the bar, which separated the taproom from the rest of the inn, was shoved aside by a brawny arm, and the landlord's heavy face poked in. Still half-asleep, a mean mouth, pouchy, lethargic, hung-over eyes.

"What're ye moanin' aboot, woman . . . ?" Then he saw Darius and the dagger and the dead man at the door. He was a big man himself, and although startled, his eyes showed no fear.

"Ye're welcome t' the money, mate," he said, his eyes narrowed and crafty, as if ready to make some move. "There's precious little o' it, truth t' tell."

The barmaid shook her head. "MacTavish," she bleated. " 'E wants t' know on MacTavish and the MacPhersons."

The landlords's eyes fell upon the gold sovereign on the bar. Instantly he understood the proffered transaction. His face brightened, then darkened quickly in contempt. Grunting, he cuffed the woman soundly on the side of the head. Off balance, she half spun and crashed into a row of bottles, one of which fell and shattered on the hard, slick floor. The strong smell of smoky whiskey rose in the room.

"Fool woman! If ye'd o' told 'im, a man'd be alive and there'd be gold in my pocket."

Darius smiled, a real smile this time. It was going to be easy now. "It is an affair of His Majesty's Secret Office. I seek information regarding Alan MacTavish." He gave the description again, asked when and in which direction the young man had passed.

"Treason, aye!" the landlord muttered, turning to his wife. "An' this one time o' all times ye kept yer mouth shut? An' get us wrapped into a treason business? Oh, I vow, ye're goin' t' get the beatin' of yer bloody life . . ."

"Well?" Darius prodded.

"Aye!" the landlord hastened to explain. "Aye, 'e were 'ere 'bout a fortnight past. 'Ad 'im many a pint, an' were talkin' of the Rob Roys an' glory an' the King. A young man's ravin', seemed t' me then. If I'da ken, I'da . . ."

"Save your good intentions, man. 'Tis too late now. In which direction did he ride?"

"Southeast to Coldstream Castle. But I know more . . ."

"What's that?"

" 'E told me 'e were goin' t' meet MacPherson. 'E said that Lord MacPherson were a bosom friend o' 'is."

"He did?"

The landlord nodded, crafty and conspiratorial.

"What else do you know?"

The landlord chuckled, pleased with his wisdom and indispensability.

"I know 'he's aboot t' marry 'is daughter off t' a rich man. The lord is. Ye ever seen 'is daughter? She's a . . ."

Darius made his unsettling grimace again. "I've seen her before, many times, in Edinburgh at the Christmas balls. You might even say I've watched her grow."

His cold laugh was like chunks of ice rattling in a bowl.

"No, they will not save themselves by marrying her now. Nor will they save her, either."

For just a moment, his eyes took on a faraway glint of anticipation and pleasure, then he returned to the taproom. "All right," he snapped. "I must go now. But of course you understand that I can return at any time?"

They all understood.

Darius turned and walked across the room; the cape billowed and flowed. He stepped across the body at the door.

"You'd best get rid of this man," he ordered, nudging the body idly with the toe of his black boot. "If I hear nothing of this, there will be three more sovereigns delivered here by messenger. But if not . . ."

The landlord was already protesting his loyalty to King

and Crown when Darius pushed open the tavern door with
an insolent crash. It was fully dark now and snowing heavily, but he left the door ajar and disappeared into the darkness. The entering wind chilled the mead shop and fanned
the embers in the fireplace, cheerlessly glowing the logs.
After a little, the barmaid arose and pulled the door shut,
while the landlord and the other peasant wrapped the dead
man in his own tattered cloak.

"Ground's too cold t' bury 'im," the landlord decided.
"We'll take 'im an' throw 'im in the Teviot River. There's
ice in 'er this time o' year batterin' enou' t' 'ide a dagger's
prick."

Heavily, with much panting and cursing, the landlord
got the body up on the back of the other man, opened the
door again, and the two of them lurched into the swirling
snow, vowing oaths against the devil and the darkness.
Once more the barmaid grabbed the latchstring and drew
the door to. Caught wind died out in the tavern. Rubbing
first the side of her head and then again her stinging breast,
she padded dimly back to the bar, her simple mind a jum-
ble of confused and conflicting impulses. She had done a
stupid thing and now she had to face a beating. But maybe
he would be too tired when he got back from the river. She
poured herself a glass of whiskey and set it on the bar.
Darius. The dagger slashing through the air. That cruel
smile. And Selena, of the high and mighty MacPhersons,
who would know that smile, too. Now she was massaging
her breast again, in an oddly rhythmic manner, and there
was a flush on her face that had nothing to do with the
waning fire. The gold coin caught her eye, and for a moment she dreamed of being a high lady like Selena Mac-
Pherson, whom men would embrace sweetly, not curse and
whip, and whose lives were lived in the luxury of towered
mansions. But then she remembered Darius again, and she
no longer wished to be Selena.

"Traitors," she murmured, and knocked back a slug of
the drink.

Wrapped in his cape, within a shroud of swirling snow,
Darius rode. The puzzle was coming together in his predatory mind; the plan was forming. He must get MacTavish

now. MacTavish was the next link in the chain. MacTavish would sing long and loud, sing quite a pretty tune. MacTavish would be a whole ensemble, a whole choir.

And Darius would conduct.

Part One

Scotland, 1774

CASTLE HOME

Selena MacPherson stood atop the highest watchtower of Coldstream, in Berwick Province, Scotland, on the North Sea. The estate had been in the hands of her ancestors at least as far back as William the Conqueror, and the keystone in the arch at the castle's outer wall read "Anno Domini 1152." Stealing away, she had climbed the dangerous, swaying ladders this morning, to be alone. She wanted to think back upon those seven centuries, to find in them, as she had so many times before, the steadiness and strength to sustain her in a time of troubles. She had need of that support today, although she did not yet know why. Something was wrong, perhaps many things. Sean Bloodwell was one of them, to be sure; because of him, a crisis impended between her father and herself. Father was worried, too, she could tell, and not just over this business with Sean. There was more to it. Selena didn't know what, and she watched sadly as his gloomy preoccupation cast a pall over the usually effervescent preparations for their annual Christmas trip to Edinburgh. Even Brian, her fiery, high-spirited older brother, was curt, distant. Throughout the long month of December, a vague disquiet, a growing sense of unease, had settled over Coldstream Castle, and on this very morning of the journey, with the grooms already harnessing six gleaming bays to the carriage in the courtyard far below, a shadow of fear, of imminence, enveloped her.

It was all so complicated. In the beginning she had more than invited Sean Bloodwell's attentions—as what young woman would not?—and she had been pleased with her success at turning his head. But it had soon become evident that Sean was unlike Selena's usual beaux, and now she realized that what had seemed to her a quality of shyness, of reserve, was actually a sense of dignity and certainty unusual in a man of twenty-four, and a steely seriousness of purpose as well. He had told her that he intended to ask her father for her hand. That was serious indeed! She had never intended to let the flirtation go that far, especially now, with the ball approaching.

Because just last year, at the Christmas Ball in Edinburgh Castle, she had fallen in love with Royce Campbell. They had been alone for only a short time, to share kisses, caresses—Selena had fashioned dreams, to which he'd listened—and it had been enough. She had been caught in a whirl of emotions that, until Royce held her in his arms, had seemed dim and unreal. But no longer. Need and want, desire and ecstasy, beat in her blood, and now with the long year finally drawing to its close, she would see Royce again.

She was almost positive he would remember her.

And this time she would be all of eighteen, surer of herself. Brian would not interrupt them, this time, and she would make certain Royce was invited directly to Coldstream after the holiday. And this time . . .

Soft possibility wrapped itself about her like a cloak, and she could almost feel herself in his embrace. Then a gust of wind blasted cold against the battlements, snapping the pennants like the rigging on a ship.

This time *what*, Selena? Because if Sean had already spoken to Father, she might never be able to win her desire.

"An opportunist, and that's but the start of it," she'd once overheard Father say of Royce Campbell, while talking politics with some of his political and parliamentary friends who were always stopping at Coldstream. "Too rich and too bold. Too unpredictable for . . . for our purposes. I'd use him if I needed him, but the price would be high. Not a true patriot, by any means. Has trouble looking for a place to light, that's the way I read the lad."

There had been much nodding, affirmative and judgmental, as the bowl went round again, as the thick smoke of the pipes swirled slowly upward to the flaming tapers on the castle wall.

Remembering, Selena hugged herself against the chill, and pulled more tightly about her the lush traveling cloak of muskrat pelt. Her large violet eyes glimmered with inner conviction, and, almost defiantly, she shook her rich, wind-tousled mane of golden hair. A young girl, slim but strong of body, ripe for the future, not yet old enough to believe that she would ever die, Selena stood upon the battlements of her ancient home.

Father would simply *have* to dissuade Sean, or at least put him off for a time. He *must!* That was all there was to it; her whole life and happiness depended upon it. She knew Father would move heaven and earth for her, if he had to, and she loved him still with a residue of childhood's trusting affection. But his feelings toward Royce Campbell indicated a favorable reception to Sean Bloodwell's overtures. The only advantage she had in convincing her father was the fact that Sean was not of the nobility. But that was something Father did not seem very concerned about anymore. Selena wondered why.

Sometimes, when she was younger, she'd found herself wishing that she had been born a commoner, like one of the rowdy peasant girls in Coldstream village. They seemed not to have problems. They seemed happy enough teasing and being chased by the rough, grinning, open-faced boys of the countryside. And more, too. On festival days, when Selena accompanied Father and Brian on ceremonial visits to the common, she saw the boys and girls sneaking off, two by two, edging into the dark grove of shielding trees hard by the graveyard. And she could hear, even over the tumult of the revelers on the green, the giggling and laughter down among those trees, then the long silences, and now and then a moan so delicious one could fairly shiver with the pleasure that gave rise to it. *Gave rise*, indeed! She blushed, in spite of the cold, recalling the lewd, good-humored chatter of the scullery maids at Coldstream, *their* ribald idea of the measure of a man.

A peasant girl, at eighteen, would have had more opportunity to make her own appraisals of a man, Selena had often thought. But, oddly, it didn't seem to matter anymore. With Sean, she felt cherished and protected, and that might have been more than enough had she never experienced anything else. But with Royce Campbell, last Christmas at Edinburgh Castle, she had known something more, something wild, almost dangerous. The very air encircling their embrace had crackled with delicious tension. It had been like bobsledding in the Lammermuir Hills in winters long past; you went over the crest and dropped down and down, forever down, into the bright, blinding fever of depthlessness.

Selena drew back and pulled herself out of the memory of that fall. She was not sure Royce would even be in Edinburgh this year. Last April, she'd heard that he'd left for India, and there'd been no news since. And then there was Sean Bloodwell to consider, and his hopes. And Father, with his responsibility for the future of the MacPherson family. And all the rest of it. Once again, for just an instant, she envied the peasant girls. Being of the nobility was like being locked in a tower forever. So she thought that morning, on her remote watchtower, as she began to realize that her life was not entirely her own.

Then, far below, she saw her father stride out of the main hall and look about. One of the coachmen raised an arm up toward the tower on which Selena stood, for Lord Seamus MacPherson lifted an arm as well, to beckon his daughter down. They would be leaving for Edinburgh now. She saw his mouth open as he called to her, and in a few moments the sound carried up: "Selena. We're ready. Come down and let's be off." In spite of the distance, she read in his voice that tone of worry that had been so much a burden to him lately. Why didn't he open up and tell her what the trouble was? It had to be more than Sean Bloodwell alone—assuming Sean had even *spoken* to him yet! She would have been willing to give everything (Royce Campbell excluded) to restore her father's smile and customary cheer.

Waving her response, she stepped back toward the trapdoor, where the ladder was. Then, on impulse, she looked out once more over the North Sea, tumbling in winter fury, and her gaze drifted over the buildings and gardens and fields of Coldstream. This was home, and for no reason she could fathom there came into her mind a sudden premonition: *Look long, Selena MacPherson. You may never see these sights again.*

The force of the feeling was momentary but overpowering. "Rubbish," she steadied herself. "We'll return, as always, with the New Year."

But she was shaken. Within an instant, her spirit had been rendered as barren as the sere, burnt plains of Northumberland, across the English border, which she could see from Coldstream Castle. Upon this tower, in centuries past, men of Scotland had stood vigil against the swarming armies of English kings. Thank God, she thought, the Act of Union had put an end to all that fighting and death. Now there was naught to be seen but a single hawk, hunting far above those fields of ancient England, with its black, angular wings outstretched, coasting on the morning wind. The hawk held steady for a minute, drifting, then swooped, silent and deadly, toward some quarry in the dark December hills of Selena's beloved Scotland.

She shuddered for that nameless prey, turned, and climbed down the ladder, following the intricate corridors and passageways of the castle, which had been her playground since childhood, and which she knew as well as her own image, reflected in a glass. The heels of her new boots echoed on the old stones, and as she passed the chambers, the halls, the great rooms, she felt again that intimation of finality, of leave-taking, as if she were passing in review before the place in which her life had been spent. All the servants had gathered at the entrance to the main hall to see them off. She bade them farewell, they gave her Godspeed, and she climbed into the glistening, rust-colored carriage with Brian and her father. The coachman cracked a long, black whip, and the bays moved off, their hooves ringing on the stone.

Edinburgh was a long day's journey, and for a time they rode in silence, wrapped in furs against the cold, staring moodily at the passing landscapes. The frozen road, scarred and potholed, slammed again and again beneath the wheels of their coach; the passengers jounced and swayed against the sides of the carriage, and tried to avoid colliding with each other.

This is the fifth time, Selena was thinking. She had been fourteen and Mama had still been alive when, for the first time, she'd been permitted to make the trip and to wear one of the exquisite gowns fashioned just for her by Coldstream's seamstresses, to attend the great banquet, and then to dance at the Christmas Ball itself, with the glittering decorations, tangy punch, heady music, and, of course, the young men of the great families of Scotland. Selena had been a bit nervous, that first year, but she ought not to have worried. In the years that followed, she attracted all the attention any girl could have wanted, and she'd overheard some of the old dowagers talking, saying: "Have you see that horrible crowd of boys around the MacPherson girl? One would think she fancied herself a princess, holding court. Well! Do you know what I think . . . ?"

Holding court. A princess. Selena rather liked the idea. She had grown more practiced and regal each year. Until last year, when Royce Campbell appeared; under his frank, appraising gaze, she'd once more felt like a fourteen-year-old school girl, giddy with a bright, flashing surge of magnetic heat.

Royce Campbell. His image swept over her, held her, as the horses trotted along to their first stop, at the mead shop in the village of Lauder. This year. This year they would be alone. Brian would not come barging along—as if he hadn't known she and Royce were there!—and this year there would be the place and the time to give him all that he wanted, because that was what she chose to give. And after that? After that didn't matter. Yes, it did, Father. Sean. *Don't think about it. Not yet, not now.* There had to be a way to have what you wanted without disappointing those who loved you in different ways.

There in the rocking, swaying coach, Selena made tight fists, concentrating, and pressed her eyelids closed. Brian, trying to doze, paid her no heed, but when she opened her eyes, her father's glance was puzzled.

"Christmas wish?" he asked, with the hint of a smile.

Selena nodded, although *wish* was a pale word indeed for her secret aspiration. She looked away, and her mind returned to last year's ball, when her life had changed so greatly. All the girls her age, and most of the women right on up to ninety, were abuzz with the news of that holiday week: Sir Royce Campbell would attend the ball. The news flew up and down the long corridors of Edinburgh Castle, in which the revelers were traditionally ensconced. The news was passed down long tables in banquet rooms, spread in the salons, pavilions, and courtyards. It was an event.

Selena had heard a great deal about Royce Campbell.

Not yet thirty, this reckless son of Scotland's most fabled Highlands clan roamed the world at will, his fleet of fast ships available for any purpose to anyone who met his price, whether king or merchant or bloody mercenary with a steel knife in his teeth and a hunger in his belly for stolen gold. News of his exploits, both martial and amorous, were stock-in-trade at the great ports of the British Isles, Edinburgh and Liverpool, London and Southampton. In his personal flagship, the *Highlander*, it was said, he had ravaged pirates and privateers in the West Indies, had made the seas in those regions virtually his own private domain. He had been to Asia, India, Africa, and seen everything, and somewhere behind the stories of adventure and plunder was the half-heard whisper of a woman, Royce Campbell's woman, more sensual and beautiful and mysterious than other women—of course, for a Campbell, she would have to be—remote as royalty, passionate as sin, the peerless perfection of her sex: fire and ice.

Selena refused to believe those stories. After all, he had been unaccompanied at the ball last year, had he not?

There had been no preliminaries, no explanations. Selena had seen him first, a lean, dark-skinned, black-haired stallion of a man striding toward her across the glittering ballroom in Edinburgh Castle. She had known immediately who he was, not only from the stories, but also from the manner in which men and women alike turned to follow his passage, almost as if it were royalty that moved in their midst. A smile passed over his mouth, half amused, half ironic, a smile that obscured more than it revealed, and kept secure the detachment he seemed to be guarding, as if his thoughts were like those of no other man. The smile flickered again when he saw her, a smile that was at once for her and because of her, as if he frankly invited feminine lures without permitting himself to become entranced by them. Ah, that was it. The smile was a challenge. And Selena just seventeen.

At first, when she saw him start across the floor in her direction, she could not believe he was coming to talk to her. Surely, there must be some mistake. Her breath caught and she felt her skin grow warm in the anticipation of something she could not name. Beside her, she felt Sean Bloodwell, her escort for the evening, and the man with whom she believed herself in love, grow tense with a kind of quiet readiness, like an animal exposed to the possibility of attack.

And everyone seemed to be watching. The whole world seemed to be watching.

Then Royce Campbell was standing before her, smiling that smile, bowing slightly. His skin was tanned deeply by wind and sun, and his eyes were a shade of blue so pale they seemed translucent. When he smiled, she saw his teeth were strong and white and even.

"I am Royce Campbell," he said formally, bowing slightly. Then he offered Sean Bloodwell his hand. It was taken courteously, as was Sean's way. His looks were of a different kind—a lighter complexion, reddish-blond hair, a more open expression—but they were two strong men who regarded each other in cool appraisal. It would almost have seemed they were evenly matched, in spite of the fact that Sean was five years younger. But, of course, there was no contest taking place, was there?

"My apologies, my *lady*, for approaching you without first having been presented," Royce said to her, in a tone that held no hint of an apology, "but I wish to pay my respects to your father. I had heard that he might have need of such services as I might be able to provide. . . ."

Father? *Father* had need of the kind of services Royce Campbell was said to deliver?

". . . and I have been unable as yet to locate him at this . . ." he waved his hand icily, indicating the crowded ballroom ". . . this most elegant affair," he concluded.

He smiled again, this time with a perceptible touch of mockery. There had been a cold, strange tone as he pronounced the word "elegant," much like the intonation he'd used when addressing her as "my lady." Selena was surprised into irritation. Wasn't the Christmas Ball the most exciting social affair in all Scotland? Didn't Royce Campbell think so?

"Father has been delayed," she said, recovering. "He remained at table to talk with certain gentlemen. I'm sure he'll be joining us directly."

Again, that smile, but less blatant this time. "Politics can be a dangerous business, young lady."

"So can privateering," Sean interjected coolly, with a touch of his own irony.

Selena knew everyone was watching. The two men measured each other.

"Ah, yes, *that* Bloodwell," Royce said, as if recalling a fragment of idle information. "The ambitious young man with all the collieries and textile mills. Have you won yourself a title yet?"

Sean flared, but resisted the bait. The fact that his father had been a commoner, albeit a wealthy and powerful commoner, made him overly conscious of class distinctions. After all, times were changing, and the rising entrepreneurs could buy and sell half the nobility on a quiet afternoon.

"I expect," he said grimly, "that it does little good to discuss genealogy with a pirate."

Royce Campbell laughed good-humoredly. "Pirate? Bloodwell, what *have* you been hearing? I am a capitalist, like yourself. I offer my services for whatever the market will bear, as do you. And, just between you and me and the MacPherson beauty here . . ." he glanced at Selena, and it seemed that he actually winked, as if they were sharing a joke ". . . a title and a ha'penny will buy you all of a piece of stale bread."

Sean looked at him, not knowing how to take the remark. Campbell seemed serious now, but to Sean an elevation to the peerage possessed the aura and significance of a sacred relic. To doubt the value of title would be like doubting the True Cross or the worth of Scotland itself.

"I do not know of stale bread," he began doubtfully, as if some slight might have been conveyed by the phrase.

"No matter. I meant nothing." Royce turned back to Selena and looked directly into her eyes. "Perhaps I might have a dance later?" he asked. It was a question, but it had not been pronounced as a question. It had been more like a command, softened by the casual intimacy of his smile and the flattery of his attention. Her throat was dry, and she could hear her heart drumming dully beneath the bejeweled bodice of her long white satin gown. It took all the willpower she possessed at that moment, but she met his ice-colored eyes with her own wide, violet ones. She'd learned as a little girl that other women envied her those eyes, and now she would use them as they were meant to be used.

"Perhaps you may," she replied, flashing him a look she meant to be that of an older, experienced woman weighing an impudent request.

But he laughed! Right there in front of everybody.

"I shall present myself, then, at the appropriate time." He bowed to them both. "Lady MacPherson. Mr. Blood-well."

With that, he turned away and moved off, only to stop in the middle of a group of women a short distance away and to be immediately encircled by them, and then by their male companions.

Selena tried to make light of the encounter, to tell herself it meant nothing, but her young heart was in a tumult all its own.

"I believe you've made another conquest," Sean said. His voice was unconcerned, but his eyes were narrowed.

She heard him from a distance. All she could think of at the moment was the sudden feeling that had come upon her when Royce Campbell had looked into her eyes, the strange, tingling way her body was still reacting.

"What?" she heard herself asking.

"I said, I believe you've made another conquest."

Selena was momentarily flustered. "Oh, no, all he wanted was to speak to Father. Perhaps Sir Royce intends to offer a business proposition of some kind, shipping, or some other such . . ."

"No, Selena. Like many of the old nobility, your father's fortune is his land, granted to the MacPhersons long ago by an act of royalty. New enterprises, such as my own, coal and cloth, require men like Campbell—hopefully more reputable—with ships to transfer raw materials to our factories, and finished products to markets all over the world. So if he really does have business with your father, you can wager it's of another kind. . . ."

"*Really*? You don't believe . . . ?"

"He wouldn't be good for you, Selena."

"*What?* Oh, no, it's not . . ." Confused, she was also flattered, that he would acknowledge her appeal to a man such as Royce Campbell, that he might even be jealous of more than the other man's genealogy.

Sean was smiling, but he spoke seriously, as always.

"There's no doubt he's exciting, and brave as well. But, Selena, that kind of man makes everyone he meets rather like himself. And I would not want you that way."

What way? she wanted to ask. But it was far more prudent to drop the matter. Beside her, Sean seemed suddenly tense, and a cautioning look appeared on his handsome face. She followed his glance to a curtained archway not far from where they stood. A man stood there, had probably been there for some time. He was watching them closely, yet without seeming to, and his eyes moved casually over the ballroom crowd without actually settling upon anyone for longer than a moment. He was thin and dark, hawklike in black evening dress, and he had the thinnest, meanest, most beaklike mouth Selena had ever seen. She suppressed a shudder, and suddenly the memories returned. She had seen this man before, every year since she'd been fourteen, when first she'd come to the ball. He was always there, like an apparition. His body exuded a fierce energy, more of resolve than of actual strength, a cruel body that possessed an intensity of passion known to few. Now the man let his glance linger on them for a long moment, altogether without embarrassment, then he broke it off, and strolled, as if bored, down along the side of the ballroom. People seemed to stiffen slightly as he passed by them, and afterward they seemed nervous, unsettled, like buoys bobbing in the wake of a boat.

"Who is that man?" she asked Sean, when hawkface was out of earshot.

"That is Darius McGrover, an agent of the Crown. Where he walks, no man is safe."

"But whatever is a man like that doing here?"

Sean chose his words carefully. "There is much afoot, Selena. I know more of it than I wish, and you already know all you need."

"But I don't know anything. I . . ."

"That is exactly what I mean."

"Well, Father is a member of Parliament, and we have nothing to be worried about."

Then the orchestra began to play, and the dancing commenced. The evening became a gay whirl of dances, chatter, wine, and punch, as the young men of Scotland

sought her attention for a moment, one after another of
them pouring out, for her approval, the tumbled tales of
adventures they meant to undertake as soon as they could.
They would go to America and straighten out those rebels
who were caterwauling in a place called Massachusetts. Or
they would go to India, and seek out treasures in the dark
interior. Or they would sail for China, to come back twenty
years from now hardened and wise, having tasted of delights unknown in Edinburgh. She listened to them. She had
known most of them since childhood, and they amused her.
Now and then one of them, noting Sean was her escort, and having heard of her father's high regard for
Bloodwell, would make veiled reference to the supposed
deficiencies of his paternity. But they never made so bold
as to remark upon it to his face because, although he was
not known for his temper—he knew his superiority and tolerated the young men—it was clear that he was a match
for any man in the room, with the possible exception of
Royce Campbell, whose notoriety put him in a special class
of his own. And it was a fact of life in these modern times
that the wealth of the land nobles was being eclipsed by
young, savvy men like Bloodwell. It was best to stay on the
good side of them. Fortunately, such politics did not pre-
clude flirting and dancing with young ladies, no matter
whom their escorts happened to be.

In spite of its natural conservatism, Scotland had been
for many decades in a state of high and unresolved passion.
The Act of Union, a cherished goal of the English, had
required the support of many Scots. In manner of reward,
the Crown had approved "enclosures," which took from
the peasants their time-honored plots of land, their "commons," and enclosed them into the already vast estates of
the rich, the nobles. The peasants, deprived both of home
and land, migrated to the burgeoning, squalid cities of
Perth and Dundee and Glasgow, there to become virtual
slaves in the textile mills that processed wool from the
sheep of the rich, the same sheep that now grazed fat and
unrestricted over the lands that once had been the peasants'
homes. Or the poor were impressed by starvation and necessity into the coal mines of Argyll and Aberdeen. Scotland and the world had entered a new age, and few knew
yet what that age held for them. Even Sean, otherwise so

certain, had his doubts. "Of course, the workers have a terrible life," he said, "but they agree to work for me for a certain wage, and I pay them that. If it weren't for men like myself, they would all starve."

Something about this reasoning did not make sense to Selena. It was as if a part of the equation had been left out, whether by accident or intention, and she did not yet have the experience to know what it was, nor to act upon her compassionate instincts. She knew that the country was in a state of profound transition, and the Empire as well (Father had told her as much), but the form of the future had not yet taken shape. This was a simmering time, a time of reassessments. Thus the young lords eyed Sean Bloodwell warily, unsure if he were the representative of a new kind of nobility which had not yet assured its ultimate place in society, or merely an upstart. They eyed him warily, just as they watched Royce Campbell with a measure of envy and not a little wonder. He seemed the adventurer of old, a throwback to the era of Raleigh and Drake, bound to no man but his King. And there was, it seemed, some doubt about that loyalty, too.

The orchestra began another dance, and once more the circle of young men drew near to ask her favor.

But they dropped back suddenly, as Royce Campbell himself approached, bowed, and offered his arm.

"I believe I was promised."

She took his arm and they went out onto the floor. Neither of them spoke. She could see Sean watching, his eyes alert, his face impassive.

The ball was well along by now, and the people, into the spirit of the dance (and many of them well into the spirits, too), shouted down the orchestra, which had commenced yet another minuet. First there was a call here and there from around the ballroom, then more joined in, and then finally everybody entered the clamor. Nothing would do but the Highland fling, and the white-haired old conductor, shaking his head and smiling, motioned the bagpipe players forward.

The major requirement in dancing the fling was energy—it was a dance that could go on and on—and Selena had always loved the freedom and excitement of it. You could really *dance* the fling. You could put your whole body into it.

That could not but impress Royce Campbell.

They faced each other on the floor, and she met his eyes. He bowed in a kind of challenge. Then the dance began.

It was wild, as always, and the ever-strange, haunting whine of the pipes underscored the pace of the music. About then, dancers shouted and leaped, whirled and spun. Selena could not remember a time when she had felt as unfettered, nor danced as well. All around the ballroom the dancers flashed, and when it came time for the two of them to take their turn in the circle, they had already become strangely mesmerized by motion and music, caught up in a dark attraction that was more than the dance, more even than the physical magnet of their opposite natures.

"Look at them," someone shouted, and she and Royce Campbell danced forward, then away from each other, in the coy and leaping steps of the dance, enslaved by the incessant music. She felt the blood pumping from her heart, her lungs ached for air, but it was glorious. Her hair was flying, her body, too, and her very soul screamed for joy. Seventeen years old, and chosen by Royce Campbell for this dance, this dance which everyone was watching. They would become two in the minds of many people, and sometimes that was all it took. . . .

Sean Bloodwell, watching somewhere out along the fringes of the dance, was all but forgotten in that moment, and the past forgotten, too. Even the future did not matter—it would take care of itself now, would it not?—because all that mattered in the world right now was Royce Campbell and this dance.

He danced wonderfully, too, with never a wasted motion, all economy and grace and style. And all about him, like an aura, was the glitter of his legend, the timeless, moody penumbra of his Highlands ancestry, of the Campbells themselves, the dark ones who were ready in the day, ready in the night, always ready for love or gold or glory. And if they couldn't have just one, well, they would gladly settle for all three.

The music pounded on and finally dancers began to drop out from exhaustion, but she and Royce kept on, the audience shouting encouragement, clapping time. Her lungs were shrieking now, and every muscle in her legs begged for mercy. But if he could go on, so could she. *That's it,* she thought. *We are both thoroughbreds. We are the best.* Yet, as she whirled and turned, she did not understand— nor did she take the time to think about—the concerned expression on her father's face, as he stood watching them, close by Sean Bloodwell, at the edge of the crowd. It was a look that she had seen before, once or twice in her life, at dark times while she'd been growing up, but . . .

No time to think about that now. They danced on and on, and when she could not have gone on another instant, when she thought she would surely collapse right there on the dance floor, Royce Campbell threw up his hand and put an end to it. The orchestra played on for a few more triumphant bars, having outlasted the dancers, and then ceased. The entire hall was a bedlam of shouting and applause, a general commotion as people once again retreated to chairs, drinks, conversation. Selena's head was spinning and she was trying to subdue the centrifugal impulse when a strong arm gripped her at the waist and quickly, very quickly, she was drawn through the French doors at the side of the ballroom, and out onto a dark balcony there. The doors eased shut behind her, and her eyes began to adjust to the darkness. She gulped in great drafts of air that came in cold off the North Sea. Sharp cliffs dropped away beneath the ancient castle of forgotten kings, down to the pounding waters. Stone battlements reared darkly into the moonless sky.

"Thank you for the dance," Royce Campbell said, his voice easy and casual, giving no hint that for over half an hour he'd been dancing like a dervish. His effortless control irritated her.

"I . . . could have . . . gone on," she gasped.

His laugh was natural. "I know," he said, standing there, cool and smiling. She saw the glint of his teeth, the outline of his strong body in the darkness. Already she was thinking of the many women he must have known, wondering if there had been any he loved, or loved now, with more than his body. The stories of that mysterious beauty who was rumored to be his mistress came back to her, but she pushed them away. He was here now, on this balcony, with her.

But that impassive, almost disapproving look on Sean Bloodwell's face? That concerned, enigmatic expression on Father's?

Later, Selena. This is now.

Her breathing was almost back to normal. She felt him in the darkness, no more than a foot away. She racked her brain for the right attitude, the right tone, the right words.

He spared her the effort. "You're a beauty, Selena," he said, and as if it were the most natural thing in the world, as if all further words were unnecessary, his arms went around her. She felt, for just an instant, surprise, but as he pressed close against her, Selena was aware of another kind of knowledge.

"Royce . . ." she started, but he touched her chin and tilted her face up to his, and she found his lips. There was one fleeting moment of disbelief, as if he might be playing with her, taking her for a schoolgirl on a holiday fling, but one second into the kiss and she knew it was as real as anything had ever been. Nerved by this wisdom, thinking nothing, she pressed herself against him, and felt against her body that which she and her girlfriends and the maids at Coldstream had often dwelt upon, and which seemed, at this moment, to be as naturally hers as the night and this kiss. Her body was burning, too, with an excitement that was more than she, at seventeen, had ever dreamed. And then she felt one of his embracing arms fall away and drop to her side, and his hand slide in between their bodies, down in front of her, where the burning had begun. She swayed in his arms and moved slightly, to help him find the cleft, suddenly dizzy as he touched her *there,* and she felt a weakness in her knees that was different and far greater than the one left by the exertions of the dance. His mouth found hers again and they kissed hard while she clung to him and he massaged her—quite expertly, she was sure, for all the darkness and sudden surprise of this meeting—and she felt something start up inside her that was frightening in its power. She did not want to face it, not yet, not here, and her brain clouded as a subtle, tingling glow nested in her body, burning and growing like savage power beneath his touch.

Suddenly, he released her and stepped away.

"What . . . ?" she cried, in a voice like a sob. The hunger throbbed.

His voice was easy, surprisingly controlled, but gentle.

"A shadow passed beside the door. We must think of your reputation."

There seemed to be no irony this time.

"Oh," she said, and came to him again, "then let's . . ."

"Go somewhere?"

She nodded against his shoulder, so that he could feel her acquiescence. Her entire body, poised upon the edge of carnal sensation, screamed for release. *It's going to happen,* she was thinking. *Tonight it's finally going to happen.*

He didn't answer right away, as if considering something.

"Aren't you to be promised to Sean Bloodwell?" he asked then. "I've heard talk of it."

She drew away. "I'm promised to no one," she said. "Why are you asking? Don't you want . . . ?"

Royce quieted her with another kiss. "Of course I wanted you, Selena, and right now. Tonight. But you must know what it is you are doing, and the consequences."

"I *know!*" she whispered urgently, guiding his hand. A part of her appreciated his concern, but the greater part wanted all obstacles, all bonds, instantly removed, want both of them in a warm, safe haven where love and sensation would never end. She was beginning to sense in him someone different from the raw and unprincipled adventurer about whom she had heard, but her passion was overwhelming there on the balcony that night, and she pushed the thought away.

"My chamber is in the west wing," he was saying. "You're scarce but a girl in a woman's body, and you must understand—"

"I *understand,*" she said vehemently, just as the French doors flew open.

Brian regarded them suspiciously.

Selena spoke first. "Sir Royce, you've met my brother?"

"By reputation, of course," Royce replied pleasantly. "The scourge of rebel peasants." He was referring to an incident in Brian's youth, when he'd first tasted blood in an uprising. "Your sister and I are recovering from our dance, MacPherson. Would you care to join us?"

Brian was skeptical. Thank God he could not see the way her gown must be disarranged here in the darkness.

"No, thanks anyway, Campbell. I've come to fetch her. The family is retiring for the night."

Oh, God, she thought. *No!*

"Come along, Selena."

"Thank you for the dance, my lady," was all Royce Campbell said.

Inside the ballroom again, before they returned to the table at which her father and Sean were speaking, Brian told her what he thought.

"Don't you be hanging about with a scoundrel like that," he ordered, "or I'll be telling Father an' Sean."

"Tell whomsoever you wish," she snapped. "Mind your own business."

"I am," he retorted. "I'm minding the business of the MacPherson family. 'The scourge of rebel peasants!' " he added, mimicking Royce's tone.

"You did kill that man."

"An' 'e 'ad it comin'," her brother growled, lapsing into the idiom he always used when angry or upset. "An' you be watchin' yourself, or ye'll be the ruin o' Father's plans."

That meant Sean Bloodwell, obviously. She said nothing. Last week, or even yesterday, the prospect of marriage to Sean would have been wonderful and exciting. But tonight everything had changed. Everything was altered. She tried hard to smile, and sat down next to Sean.

"I trust you enjoyed the dance," he said, with an amused smile.

She was about to reply, when Royce Campbell crossed the ballroom and climbed the great stairs to the upper rooms of the castle. It was all Selena could do to keep her eyes from him.

She was never again alone with Royce during that holiday week. Brian made himself her guardian, with her father's tacit approval, and she spent the remaining social affairs of Christmas and the New Year in the company of Sean Bloodwell. He was tender and amusing and endearing all the while. Selena even began to feel as if the moments of madness on the balcony *had* been unreal, but then she would catch a glimpse of Royce Campbell dancing, or riding on a black stallion outside the castle walls, and her heart would ache to be with him again.

Finally, it appeared that he had conceived a plan to bring them together. The MacPhersons were finishing breakfast in their chambers when a servant entered, bearing a sealed envelope on a silver tray. Brian took it and tore it open straightaway. "Campbell," he grinned, looking at Selena. Then, reading, "No, it's for you, Father."

He handed the note to her father, who read it, frowning.

"I wonder why he wants to see me."

"Refuse to see him, Father," Brian advised.

"Now, son, that's neither politic nor wise. He's no enemy, even if I don't care for his kind."

What if he's asking for me? Selena thought, and even believed it for the shred of a second.

Royce Campbell was admitted then. He greeted her courteously, but distantly, and she and Brian were dismissed while Campbell talked to Lord MacPherson. Desperate to see him, Selena waited until Brian grew bored and wandered off, then stationed herself in an alcove down the corridor, which Royce would have to pass when he made his exit. Finally, it happened, and as he walked toward her hiding place, she stepped into his path. He was preoccupied, and when he saw her it seemed to take a moment for him to recognize her. Her heart went cold, dropped toward an icy abyss. Then he smiled, and saved her life.

"Selena!"

She grabbed the sleeve of his velvet riding cloak, and pulled him into the alcove.

"Selena, what . . . ?"

"Brian's gone. Shhhhh! He's been watching us all week."

"What?"

She had him in the alcove now, behind a scarlet drapery with golden pheasants embroidered thereon. It was very dark, except where a little light penetrated the gold, and the draperies muffled any sounds.

"We can talk now," she whispered, clinging to him, waiting for the pressure of his embrace. It didn't come.

"What's the matter?" she asked, looking up at him.

He was smiling tolerantly. "That's what I'd like to know."

"But . . . but that night at the dance . . ."

She watched him remember. "Ah, yes, the night of the dance." He smiled and drew her to him. "Unfortunately, our plans went awry. Unfortunately for me. But fortunately for you."

He kissed her. On the forehead! As he might kiss a sister! *What was wrong?*

"But I meant it. I wanted . . . I wanted *you.*"

He held her at arm's length. "How old are you, Selena?"

She drew herself up to full height and pushed out her breasts.

"Seventeen."

He shook his head. "Well, I daresay you look more than seventeen, but seventeen it is, and seventeen's no good for the likes of me."

She bit her lip, and he could not help but see the hurt in her eyes. And the utter seriousness behind the hurt.

"I love you," she blurted.

"Ah, Selena!" And this time he took her into his arms in a way that broke her heart even as it made her love him more. His strong body pressed against hers, and he was quite gentle, but in his voice was another tone, deeper and serious, which she had not heard before.

"Come now, Selena," he said. "You don't know what you love. I'm sure there are plans for your future, for your life. You've a wise, kind father, and I expect when you're eighteen or thereabouts you'll have a wedding, perhaps to Bloodwell, and I know you'll be happy."

"I'll never be happy. I'll never be happy without—"

"Without me? No, don't be a fool, Selena. You've too much fire and spirit to waste your days pining about happiness and such."

He was setting her aside! He was smiling and sympathetic and gorgeous, but he was setting her aside! She struggled to reason, to speak. Still, she knew a fiery woman was exciting to a man, and she knew she had excited him on the balcony. So what was wrong?

"Selena, you don't even *know* me," he was saying. Oh,

rubbish. What did that matter, anyway? She broke away from him, at last, and tried to control herself.

"Are you attempting to tell me that I should be older, before you—"

"No, that's not it at all."

"Will you promise me something, then?" Her tone was cold, as if with finality. Royce responded to it with relief.

"If I can."

"Will you see me here at the ball? Next year?"

"If I'm in Scotland then. Of course, I'll see you."

During the course of the year, Selena had replayed the scene, the conversation, a hundred times and more. Just as the night on the balcony had sealed in her very being a physical need for Royce Campbell, so did the painful moments in the alcove hold the promise of something more than mere happiness. Later, when she returned to the chamber, her father was deep in thought; he barely noticed her return. And he never spoke of his conversation with Sir Royce. To Selena, whatever they had discussed was inconsequential. It meant nothing. Obviously, Royce had not asked for her hand; nothing else could be of significance.

WARNINGS

So now the long year of waiting and planning and dreaming had ended, and she was going back to Edinburgh at last. *I ought to be happy*, she thought; this time, she herself would go to Royce Campbell's chambers. But everything seemed awry. She was dreaming of how it would be, how, with their bodies locked together in love, everything would be clear and true for both of them, when the driver leaned back and shouted into the window of the coach.

"Seems t' be some sort o' roadblock ahead, y' lordship."

Abruptly, Selena broke away from her romantic reverie. These were rough regions through which they passed, and many things could happen. Brian shot upright out of his nap, knocking off his hat in the process to reveal the curly, red thatch of hair that accentuated the volatility of his temperament. His hand went for the dagger at his belt. Lord MacPherson restrained him.

"Easy, lad. Let's first see what the business is."

Quickly, he rolled up the isinglass curtain that gave them some protection from the weather. The wind had shifted since dawn, and now it came at them from the Highlands, icy blasts that promised snow. Selena shivered and buried herself more deeply in the furs and blankets, while her father looked out.

"Highwaymen?" Brian asked happily. He was always looking for a fight, particularly one in which the odds were against him.

"I don't think so," her father explained. "I see a glimpse of purple."

He and Brian exchanged a glance, which Selena could not read. She knew, of course, that purple was the color of the cloaks of His Majesty George III's gendarmerie, but whatever would they be doing way out here on the road to Lauder? Perhaps there *were* highwaymen about.

"They be wavin' fer me t' stop, y' lordship," the driver called.

"Do as they say."

In a moment, the carriage ground to a halt. The horses pawed and snorted in the icy air, their hooves stamping the frozen road. One of the King's men left his small group of companions and their horses at the side of the road, approached the MacPherson coach, accompanied by a cheerless gust of wind and a flurry of snow. Selena saw the bars of an officer on his purple collar, the gold threat of rank on the purple, tricornered hat. The man reached out and pulled open the door of the coach, as if he meant to have hard business within.

"Yes, Lieutenant?" asked Lord MacPherson, his voice pleasant, but with just a touch of reserve to indicate his displeasure at being delayed.

Normally this reserve, this natural assumption of superiority, would have been enough to bring forth at least a *pro forma* apology, even from an officer, because the coach doors carried the MacPherson crest as well as Lord Seamus's parliamentary insignia. But not this time. The officer's arrogance and officiousness were barely contained.

"Security, your lordship. Orders of the Secret Offices. You don't mind if we check your coach, I presume?"

"By my mother's blood—" Brian vowed, almost shouting.

"Quiet," his father snapped. "May I inquire as to the meaning of this, Lieutenant?"

The officer motioned several of his men forward. He looked at Brian, and a challenging smile crossed his mouth. He wouldn't have minded a bit of resistance; he had the men to back him up. Then he glanced toward Selena, huddled in the furs.

"Please unwrap yourself, my lady," he ordered, his tone intimate and insinuating.

"What?"

"The furs, madame. I must search."

She looked at her father, who nodded coldly. "Go ahead, it must be a very special case."

The officer smirked, and Selena did as she was told and removed the travel wraps. The officer poked at them idly with his fist, even as he tried to meet her eyes, to provoke a glance in return.

"Where are you bound?" he demanded.

"You British bastard," Brian flared, " 'tis none o' yer bloody businesss. Do ye na ken who 'tis ye're—"

Lord Seamus put a hand on his shoulder, and he subsided. "To Edinburgh," he replied evenly, "to the Christmas gala, as we do every year."

The coach swayed as two of the soldiers climbed on top to inspect the luggage there, and Selena thought anxiously of her gowns, upon which she was depending for no little effect when she met Royce Campbell again. Gowns fashioned by half a dozen seamstresses from Coldstream village. Gowns of silk and satin and velvet, of muslin and taffeta, with shawls and wraps of ermine and rich Highlands wool. Gowns with high necks, jeweled and glittering collars, that pulled her breasts up, and gowns with daringly low bodices—"eye traps," one of the seamstresses had called them—of white and silver and gold, of red, of a blue so pale it shone unearthily in firelight, and against which her dark violet eyes, her tumbling blond hair, seemed like two dark diamonds in a bed of golden floss.

"Nothing up here but some finery," yelled one of the soldiers, clambering down with his mate.

"I'm waiting for an explanation," Lord Seamus demanded now, with a steel in his manner that brooked no trifling.

The officer, pleased with the authority he had exercised over a nobleman, now saw fit to yield a bit. "Yes, your lordship," he said. "His Grace, Lord North, will be attending the festivities this year, and we are on orders to ascertain that no one enters Edinburgh who might disrupt his visit."

Father's face remained impassive, and this time even Brian revealed no emotion in word or manner. It was clear to Selena that they were no longer outraged, as she had expected, but instead cautious.

"It's those bloody devils, the Rob Roys," the officer finished. "We cannot allow them to surface, not with the prime minister of England as a guest of state."

"Quite right," Lord Seamus agreed. "I wish you had told us in the first place. One has the devil's own time traversing these hills as it is, without more delays. Well, Lieutenant . . ."

He reached out and pulled the coach door shut. In a moment, the horses started off again, and they swayed and rocked down the road to Lauder, leaving the roadblock behind.

Brian looked back nervously, almost as if he were afraid they might be followed. What was going on, anyway?

"Father, I think it's some kind of a trick," Brian said softly. He leaned forward in the carriage, his blue eyes hard with conviction, accepting the possibility of a danger Selena did not understand.

"I know we're invited to the Edinburgh affair every Chirstmas, but I don't like the feel of things this year."

Lord Seamus nodded slowly, his face very serious. Selena thought he looked every inch the nobleman he was. Although not tall, he was solidly built, with a grave mien and a slow, deliberate manner of speaking. He had a sunny smile, but he seemed to keep it for those he loved most, Brian and Selena. And for their mother, before she died. These past few years, he had been more serious than usual, and Selena, who sought to cheer him but who succeeded only intermittently, put it down to mourning, excessive mourning, perhaps, but then his love for his wife had likewise been greater than that which normally exists between a long-married couple. When the pneumonia of that winter had carried her away, Father had been inconsolable. Now, however, she was beginning to understand that his gravity over the past months may have been caused by something far different. Quickly, her mind flashed back over the preceding weeks, seeking an answer. True, people still journeyed to Coldstream to seek his advice, but many of them seemed unduly hurried, almost furtive in their need to speak with him and depart. No longer were there the long after-dinner conversations over French cognac and bowls of fragrant tobacco from Virginia, in the colonies. No, the mood at Coldstream had slowly but relentlessly grown serious, even grim, and as that knowledge came to her, she read a confirmation in the lines on her father's face.

One incident, in particular, had upset him immensely. It

was that day, about a fortnight past, when a wild young
man, half drunk, no doubt, or worse, had come galloping
up to Coldstream, waving his hat and yelling at the top of
his lungs about Scotland, something about "long live Scotland." She had been with the seamstresses in the sewing
room high up in the castle, but when she got to the window
to look out at the cause of the racket, Father had already
reached the youth and calmed him down. Later, at dinner,
when she had asked who it had been, he had just said
"some vagabond, and none too sober, either."

Now her father was considering possibilities that were
beyond Selena's ken.

"Brian, you may be right," he said slowly. "But we have
to look at it from every perspective, and make no rash mistakes. Particularly, we have to see the thing from Lord
North's perspective. It is no accident that he plans to attend the reception in Edinburgh. A prime minister of the
King does *nothing* by accident, much less come to Scotland
at this time, when the American colonists are kicking up
enough of a fuss to keep him busy."

"How much do you think he really knows?"

Knows? Selena thought. *Knows about what?*

Lord Seamus shook his head in discouragement. "Well,
we know for certain that, until recently, they might only
have suspected the nature of the organization. They might
even have thought of it as a kind of fraternity. But . . ."
Here he lowered his voice and glanced around, almost as if
fearful of being overheard, even in the family coach ". . .
for the past two weeks no one has heard a word of MacTavish. We don't know where he is."

"And Darius McGrover is said to have been in Edinburgh again, nosing around."

"McGrover!" Selena exclaimed, remembering the sinister man in black, at last year's ball. "I know him. He looks
like . . ."

"He looks like the devil's bastard, once removed," Brian
snarled.

"If I'd had even a thought when we organized the party
ten years ago," Lord Seamus mused, "if I'd had even the
shred of a thought that things would turn out this way, I
might not have gone forward. But now the Rob Roys are in
too deep."

Selena knew from her history tutor that Rob Roy was the name given Robert the Bruce, the Scottish King of long ago who had cast off the yoke of British rule. But now, with the Act of Union, this Rob Roy talk made no sense to her.

"What is all this about Rob Roy?" she wanted to know.

Brian and his father glanced doubtfully at each other. "It would be better if she didn't know," Brian said.

Lord Seamus nodded tentatively. "Yes, but we've been careless. She already knows a little, which is dangerous. And if the time should ever come, God forbid, when she's tortured by the likes of McGrover . . ."

Torture? What dark night is this—?

". . . well, it's best that she have something to confess . . ."

"Confess?" cried Selena.

". . . because he's merciless. I've heard that he's tortured many an innocent person to death simply because he cannot believe that there *is* such a thing as innocence."

He let his voice trail off, looking out into the distance at the thatched roofs of the village of Lauder. And on his face was that familiar look of concern she had seen sometimes in her younger years. She was trying to remember when she'd seen it, and what it meant.

He spoke again.

"The Rob Roys, Selena," he said, his voice not much more than a whisper, "are a political party that seeks to negate the Act of Union. To make Scotland entirely independent again. We didn't originally intend it this way. It all began, more or less, as high-spirited talk. *Scottish* talk. We felt the Union wasn't working out fairly for Scotland. It seemed to us—and it still seems—that we are getting the dregs, and the British the wine. You see, they have the navy, the army, the great corporations. So, except for private operators like Royce Campbell—and one cannot trust them anyway—the wealth that is coming back from lands across the sea is going to England, not Scotland. London is the center of everything, not Edinburgh or Glasgow. We have gotten a raw deal out of union, and they send against us men like McGrover and his uniformed hoodlums to ensure that we shall remain docile and powerless little provincials. Well, out of the original talk, the meetings, there grew circulations of letters, then a newspaper. Next, some speakers were arrested, and Alan MacTavish's father was taken right off the floor of the Scottish House of Commons. That's why he's such a violent lad. Hanged the man, too, they did, after but a semblance of a trial. It was pathetic. But, in an odd way, there's nothing that allows a political movement to thrive like a bit of persecution. Few tyrants have learned that simple but complex lesson, and reckoning by their enlightened manner of dealing with the Americans, George the Third and Lord North are not going to be among them."

It was beginning to sound quite serious to Selena. Treasonable activity, even treasonable *intent*, were punishable by death. Everybody knew that.

"But what has this all to do with you, Father? And with Brian?"

She looked from one to the other. Brian's eyes widened. Lord Seamus smiled in rueful amusement.

"Because I'm the leader of the Rob Roys," he said quietly. "Brian is a captain."

The implications flocked to her mind like threatening blackbirds, and took up watchful perches along the outposts of her brain. McGrover. The mysterious visitors at Coldstream. The arrogant officer at the roadblock. Treason. The biggest and the blackest bird of all.

"But how . . . ? What could you . . . plan to *do?* I don't understand!"

Time and space parted, turned back upon themselves, and she was on Coldstream tower again, early this morning, while upon her heart descended that mysterious and disquieting premonition. It had been powerful then; now it seemed inordinately menacing.

They were entering Lauder now: the huts, the livery, the mead shop and inn. A fresh team of horses in full harness waited outside the livery; villagers and a few people from the inn came out into the street to see Lord MacPherson pass.

"I can't speak now," he said. "I'll explain as soon as we leave town. There might be a chance to save us—ourselves and the Rob Roys, I mean. But it will require a great effort from all of us."

"I'm ready," Selena said immediately. "I'll do anything that you say. Anything," she repeated.

Brian smiled.

"I wonder," her father said.

She had no time to be angry about their obvious doubt. As soon as the carriage halted, the proprietor of the inn rushed up, bowing and begging Lord Seamus to do him the honor of a "short visit."

"Anythin' ye wish, m' lord. Anythin' a' tall. Whiskey. Tea 'n' rum. Hot mead, hot wine. Sausage and bread."

Selena watched him. She did not like him. A coarse and brutal man, with little pig's eyes, hard and glittering. And something false and insinuating in his bow, his voice, as if he were acting a part that would not be required of him for long.

Lord Seamus declined, and went to see to the hitching of the new team.

"I'll take you up on that whiskey, man," said Brian. " 'Tis damn cold in that coach. Come on, Selena."

Was it her imagination, or did the innkeeper's eyes follow her with a strange, anticipatory fascination? They entered the place, a low, dingy tavern, much like any other provincial public house, and the man, with excessive ceremony, seated them at a rickety table across from the fireplace.

"Woman!" he yowled. "Make haste, will ye?" And from behind the curtained doorway his wife appeared, in a rough one-piece garment of brown wool, across which she had tied an incongruously cheerful yellow apron. Her body was heavy now, but might once have been very alluring, and it was still sensual in a rude peasant way. But her face was another matter. One eye was blackened, and a bruise on her left cheekbone was as deep and livid as a birthmark. She held one of her arms oddly, as if it might have been twisted, or broken and badly healed, and as she came toward the table, her shawl shifted a little, and Selena noticed the welts of whiplash along her shoulder and upper arm.

"You poor thing!" Selena cried. "What's happened to you?"

The woman glanced around quickly at the innkeeper, who glowered impersonally.

"Nothin', nothin', m' lass, an' nivir y' mind." Her voice

was blank and in her eyes was a sullen knowledge that Selena could not decipher.

"But you've been beaten—" Selena started to say.

"Hush," Brian interrupted. "Barmaid, a whiskey for me, and a mug of hot tea. You have sugar? All right, sugar, too. Selena?"

Selena wanted hot wine and bread.

The woman fairly raced to get it for them.

"You shouldn't have done that," Brian admonished.

"Done what?"

"Asked after her like that."

"Why not? Can't you see she's been woefully thrashed?"

"It's not our affair. These peasants don't share our standards anyway. We're too different. They live like animals. If her husband gave her a good beating, she probably had it coming."

"Brian!" she cried, shocked. "People hurt in the same way, whatever their class."

"Look, we've got other things to worry about besides the well-being of serving wenches," he replied, with some heat. "You're just a young girl. What do you know?"

"More than you think," she retorted, flushing with anger. Just because he was her older brother . . .

He grinned teasingly.

"I trust you're expecting to fashion some tryst with Royce Campbell during the holiday, are you not?"

She looked at him quickly, looked away, then met his eyes again.

"I may see Sir Royce, if it's convenient, yes."

"*I may see Sir Royce, if it's convenient*," he mocked, still grinning. "He took liberties with you on that balcony last year, isn't that so?"

"He took no liberties," she said evenly. Which was true. He'd taken nothing that was not freely proffered, and only a little of that which was.

Brian allowed himself an exaggerated, disbelieving sigh. "Ah, little girl, a man like Campbell would take any woman that walks, with no scruple nor thought of tomorrow."

That's not true, she thought, remembering the time in the alcove, when he'd put her off so gently. *He's not what they say*. Instantly, she felt mortified. If Sir Royce took every woman who came along, then what was the matter with *her*? *No, he really cares for me, and that's why he was tender.* Even on the balcony, he had mentioned her reputation. *It was because I was too young last year. That's what it was.*

"An' what d' ye think'll be Sean Bloodwell's state of heart, when 'e finds 'e's gettin' damaged goods, eh?" Brian leaned forward, prodding her.

"Don't you bother me with Sean Bloodwell, you blackguard."

Brian was grinning. "An' I suppose I'll 'ave t' duel Campbell f' violatin' yer 'onor, too."

"Ye'd best not think on that," she replied. "Sir Royce would slap your bottom like a baby's and send you back home weein'."

That wounded him. "You . . . you liar. No man's alive I canna' be takin'. No man a'tall. I'll—"

"Aye. And one day, my little lord hothead, you and your trusty dagger shall not suffice, and it'll be myself puttin' the lilies in your 'ands."

Brian threw back his head and gave a good counterfeit of a hearty laugh.

"You silly little dreamer. You'd best enjoy this ball, an' flirt your silly little head off, because the time's comin' fer you to be a MacPherson."

"I am a MacPherson. What do you mean?"

"You do your part as a MacPherson by doing your part," he said enigmatically. But his sardonic smile said more clearly than words: *I know something you don't know.*

Then the servingwoman brought over their drinks and bread. Tea and spiced wine steamed in pewter mugs. Brian tossed back his whiskey. The woman was looking at Selena's, but not with the gratitude she might have shown at Selena's compassion for her beating; instead Selena read pity and warning in the woman's eyes. Outside, their father called to them, and Brian gulped his tea, rose, and went out. Selena wrapped up her piece of hot buttered bread, finished the wine, and stood up. The barmaid came forward hastily to help her with the chair.

"That's kind of you."

The woman's face was wary, fearful, yet determined. Another quick glance showed her that the innkeeper, her husband, was still outside.

"Ye be of heed," she muttered.

"What?"

"I say ye watch out fer yourself, milady."

"Wh . . . ?"

For a moment, Selena thought the woman was daft.

"Nay. Keep yer tongue an' 'ear me. Ye be watchin' out fer a man called McGrover. 'E 'as 'im the evil eye, an' 'tis restin' on ye."

Then she rushed away and disappeared behind the curtain, carrying the empty mugs. Selena stood there for a moment, stunned. The circumstances were ludicrous. The woman must be mad! Yet she had mentioned McGrover, and so had Father and Brian in the carriage, and now . . .

"Let's go, Selena," her father said, putting his head inside the heavy oak-and-nail door. "We've got the Lammermuir Hills ahead of us."

Selena went out to the carriage and climbed in, puzzled and a little frightened. She herself did not feel threatened yet. That came when her father took out his pipe, lit it, settled back, and began to explain to her the gravity of the present situation.

And what that situation required of her.

It was then that she recalled the meaning of his profoundly concerned expression: there was a call for family duty, MacPherson responsibility, and she would be required to do her part. There must be no reservations, no excuses, and no questions.

She saw all her life, her dreams, fall away into nothingness as he spoke.

"Now, Selena," Lord Seamus said gently, "you're young and there are things you don't know."

"I'm eighteen," she said, "and a MacPherson."

"Aye." He smiled gently, his eyes distant, remembering her as a little girl. "Aye, that ye be. And it's your future of which I'm thinking, so you can get much older and give pride to the MacPherson name. Which you will.

"Now," he went on, spreading his hands in a manner she'd seen him use, setting out a situation or a problem with his political friends. "Now, I know you've been seeing Sean

Bloodwell for almost two years. He is a good man, don't you agree?"

Selena knew what was coming, but she nodded. Yes, Sean was a good man, one of the best, but . . .

"You could use a man like that, if you'll forgive my saying so. He'd keep a rein on you—"

"Oh!" Selena flared. "You're—"

"Wait! Hear me out. I'm your father, and I'm not blind. Now, I know, too, that you, like almost every wild young girl in Scotland, has turned an eye when Royce Campbell's walked by. But, Selena, forget him. He'll only waste the time you spend thinking of him, and anything else you invest would be an even greater loss. The man has no beliefs, no values—"

"He has so!" she retorted.

Her father's eyebrows went up. "Oh? You know him that well, do you? Name one, then. Something he believes in."

Lord Seamus waited and Brian smirked. Selena tried to think. "Scotland," she said finally. "He believes in Scotland."

Her father's laugh was rueful. "You've got a lot to learn, I'm afraid," he said sadly, "and I hope you'll never have to learn all of it."

What was he talking about? Of course, Royce Campbell was an adventurer. And maybe, as some said, a pirate, too. But he plundered against the enemies of the Empire, and that was splendid, that was even patriotic. Certainly, he had a reckless, rebellious nature, but she was certain there was something else, certain there was more to him. And now Father was suggesting a sinister possibility. No, it couldn't be, and she would ask him this very week. . . .

"It may take some getting used to," her father was saying briskly, the way he did when he believed a problem had been solved, a knot unraveled, "but, Selena, I know you'll do your duty, and you'll come to know, when you're a little older, that it was the right thing."

Duty. She had done it before. Both of them had, she and Brian. Ten years ago, when Brian had been fourteen, Father was away on business in London. It was winter then, a deep, bitter winter, with snow drifting to the eaves of the peasants' huts, and blizzard after blizzard screaming out of the Highlands, down on Berwick Province. Food was always scarce during this time of year, and to make matters worse, the previous summer's harvest had been one of the poorest in sixty years. Granaries were bare, root cellars, too, and the dried fruit was gone. The peasants were beginning to starve. Then, one cold, clear day, stirred by need and a confusion as to how to proceed, and under the influence of a sullen, clever, snaggle-toothed stablehand named Bob McEdgar, who had often been flogged for insolence and incompetence, the peasants marched en masse to Coldstream Castle, bent upon seizing the contents of its granaries, which they claimed belonged to them, since they were required by law to turn over half of their crop for the privilege of using the land. McEdgar had convinced them such a split was unjust, and, goaded by hunger, they agreed to the possible truth of his assertion.

The day was bleak and windy, in spite of the sun. Selena and Brian watched from a second-story window as the ragged crowd fought its way across the drifted snow, brandishing pitchforks, cudgels, clubs, and axes. The overseer, who stopped them at the main entrance, was not able to dissuade them. McEdgar shoved him aside, spouting gibberish about hunger making need and need making right. Nor was Lord Seamus's secretary able to appease the crowd, and when McEdgar and the mob learned that his lordship was absent, their mood turned even uglier. They wanted justice. They wanted to see someone who would give it to them. And only a MacPherson would do. If Lord Seamus was away, well, that was too bad. They would appropriate the granaries and raze Coldstream to the ground, and all the tyranny it represented.

"This will not be," Brian had said. Selena remembered it distinctly. Brian's voice had been changing then, one note high, one low. But he had gone out into the courtyard, looked up fearlessly into McEdgar's angry, bloodshot eyes, seen the gaunt face, the bitter, twisted mouth, the head bound in rags against the wind, the knife in his hand.

"So. The MacPherson puppy," the man laughed, reaching out a scornful hand to pat Brian's head. Selena watched. Brian did not move. She saw his fists clenched tightly at his sides, his legs trembling, although possibly from the cold, his slim boy's body a rod of pure intensity.

"God damn yer greedy soul," the mob's leader shouted

into Brian's face, his gap-toothed mouth black and hollow and full of hate. He turned to his followers waiting behind him.

"Let's take what's ours, mates," he yelled, "on to the gran . . ."

He meant to say *granaries*, but he never did. With a speed born of necessity and decision, Brian leaped forward, seized the man's knife-wielding hand, and with the forward momentum of his own body drove the weapon between McEdgar's ribs, deeply into the chest of the peasant rebel.

Selena still saw him in her mind, the image as vivid as any in her life. Yanking the knife from the crumpled body, his boots in the bloody pool that flowed upon the snow, Brian raised it above his head. Blood dripped from the sullied blade; some of it dripped down upon his fiery head.

"Here be the food of rebel bastards!" he shouted at the mob, his voice strong now, no longer wavering. "Here be your milk and your soup!"

The tattered, freezing crowd, fueled until now by red passion, by a raw but ill-considered courage, quieted, full of hatred still, but leaderless.

Then Brian acted. "To each man among ye who drops his weapon in the snow, half a bushel of rye and safe passage home, an' we'll say no more o' this."

There were a few seconds' delayed reaction, as the knowledge penetrated the roiling mind of the mob, then, with a single shout, they obeyed, and the uprising was over. Selena still thrilled to the memory, but there was another aspect of it, too, that lingered: Brian had tasted blood, tasted it too young, too dramatically. She thought it had made him reckless, but that conclusion she kept to herself.

Her own challenge had been much different, but no less harrowing. She'd been only nine, on vacation that summer at the MacPherson lodge on Mount Foinaven, deep in the Highlands of north Scotland. Grandma was alive then, a burly, cantankerous, indomitable woman, and when it came time to return to Coldstream, Grandma had refused to go. "I shall remain until October," she declared, "and Selena will remain with me." Grandma was Grandma, and she did whatever she desired, right up until the time of her death, which occurred three days after the rest of the family had gone south. Three servants had remained with them at the lodge, all of them local Highlanders hired for the summer: a dotty cook, a shy, lisping maid, and a drooling, half-witted coachman who had no more to recommend him than his talent with horses; he was nearly as big and as strong as they were.

Selena, who slept in the room next to her grandmother's, was awakened that morning by the maid's febrile shrieking. Half-conscious, she raced toward the sound. The maid crouched, gibbering now, in a corner of Lady MacPherson's room. And Selena's grandmother, her eyes open, lay dead upon the canopied bed.

Neither maid nor cook lasted more than an hour. Simple and superstitious, and not bound to the MacPhersons as Coldstream peasants were, they fled the lodge, returning to the shelter of their kinfolk in the lost Highlands hamlets. Only the coachman stayed with her, and it occurred to Selena later that he might have done so only because he did not grasp the fact that Lady MacPherson was actually dead. Selena had sent a message south immediately, but it was over a day later before the reply arrived.

Father sent a message:

> Order the village carpenter to fashion a coffin. Hire a coach to bring Grandmother home. You are alone, but you must do it. You shall. Make haste and be strong. Father.

Selena did not like to recall the long days and nights, rocking in the hired coach, with the ghostly burden strapped onto the luggage platform above her head. And there were still nights when, in her dreams, she heard the hollow thunder of ghostly hooves upon the rocky roads of Scotland. Somewhere in the darkness of the past, the drooling, maniacal coachman Selena had hired cracked his whip and the journey had begun. Selena never forgot the sense of duty, nor the frightened stares of the people in the lost hill towns when they spied the shape and nature of her cargo, and stepped back quickly from its path. "'Tis the daughter o' a nobleman fra' the south," they muttered, as the wet, blown horses were unhitched and replaced by fresh beasts, "an' no more than a child, yet she be mad an' driven as a loon." No, they did not understand what it was like when you did what you must, and the long journey burned itself into her brain. Alone, at nine, with a babbling coachman and the body of a loved one, she traversed all Scotland. In a strange, yet real sense, the country had become hers; a bond had been formed, even more powerful than one of blood alone. And on those nights when the dream came to her, she did not so much recall the terror and haste of the trip, but instead the golden stubble on fields of harvested wheat, the stark, relentless beauty of the moors, and the flickering candles in the windows in the houses in the high hills of Scotland.

And she brought Grandma home. Home to the good earth of Coldstream. That was half her life ago. She had done her duty as a MacPherson, and done it alone.

And now she was a woman, in yet another coach, and Father looked at her in that way he had and spoke again of duty. The inference was clear: you are a MacPherson, and there will be times when you will be called upon to act as one.

This was one of those times.

"Selena, you must marry Sean Bloodwell at once. Directly after the New Year. It has all been arranged."

Selena was stunned. She felt pressed back against the cushions by a force against which she was helpless. She'd known for some time, of course, that her father was angling for just such a union, that Sean meant to speak to him about it, but she truly thought they would give it more time, and even take her own feelings into consideration, although, in these modern times, such solicitousness was discouraged.

"I've been in communication with Sean," Lord Seamus was saying. "We shall make the announcement on the night of the ball."

The night of the ball! The night she had planned to capture Royce Campbell!

This cannot be happening, she thought. *It must be the wine I drank at the inn. It must be . . .*

"Upset?" Brian asked, smirking. "You didn't even guess, did you? That's what you get with your mind on that scoundrel Campbell all the time."

His father silenced him with a glance and proceeded to explain as best he could. He sensed what she was going through, but, after all, she was young, she would get over her infatuation with Campbell. And, as her father, he knew best.

"It is an extremely good match, an excellent match," he said. He was not trying to convince her; he was merely stating the facts, as he saw them. "Certainly, Sean is not of the nobility, but that is a small matter. I daresay, with the world going as it is, his chances of elevation to the peerage are quite good, possibly within five or ten years, maybe sooner, if he contrives to swell the coffers of the Empire as he has so astutely swelled his own. And, as a husband, you could not have better."

I could have Royce Campbell, she thought.

"I won't claim you'll have no difficulties. Every marriage does. Nor even that, once in a while, he won't yield to certain temptations. But he has assured me of his desire to cherish you as a wife. Moreover, he is an intelligent, understanding man, and he will treat you well."

Brian was listening to their father, nodding vigorously. Bloody Brian!

Yet, even as she listened, Selena knew the truth of her father's words, and other memories came back to trouble her. She remembered the picnic on the banks of the Teviot. She'd just turned sixteen, and had just recently met Sean. A practiced flirt with an eye for challenges, Selena lured Sean away from the Coldstream group, and they lost themselves in a thicket of lilac at the bend in the river where the willows hung heavy and lush. His kisses then had been like new fire, and she let him undo her bodice, thinking, *Now it's going to happen.* And she would have let it, because that summer Sean Bloodwell was better than anything she could have imagined, and she would have married him right then if her father agreed. But, in the distance, members of the family and servants were calling them to some stupid game. Later, there had been times just as intimate, yet somehow not as exciting, but when he escorted her to the races in Dundee, or to the great country hunts, she always felt proud of his fine appearance, his bearing, his dignity. In fact, she thought, Sean would be perfect. If only she had not met Royce Campbell.

That meeting had changed everything. The price of the

future would be high, she realized, and she had only begun
to pay.

". . . Selena, I mentioned politics before, the Rob Roys.
According to our plans, and based upon intelligence information we have received, the Americans are on the verge
of declaring their independence from England. Some of us
wish to help them, so that later they might reciprocate, and
help us to throw off our own burden. I say this knowing
full well the risk we face should McGrover discover the
nature and extent of our enterprises. I say it also out of
self-interest. As you know, our lives are being altered. We
are neither as wealthy nor as powerful as once we were. I
must look out for the Rob Roys as well as for us. So I must
provide for your future, and in that way look out for you,
too."

He paused, to see how Selena was taking all this.

He saw her stubborn expression, sighed, but went on anyway. "Selena, I am sure I appear to be arbitrary in this
affair, and, God forbid, unromantic, but you will understand in time that it is necessary and right."

He stopped talking. She looked at him. Her father,
whom she had loved and respected forever. And obeyed,
too, at least most of the time, and always in the important
things. How could he be doing this to *her?*

The tightening in her throat was genuine, and so was the
trembling of her lips. She could have held the tears back,
but they were there, and, anyway, it was time for desperate
measures.

"Why, Selena, what's wrong?"

It all came tumbling out. She did not love Sean. She
loved Royce Campbell. They had been . . . alone last
year, and they would meet again at this season's holiday.

"I knew it!" Brian cried cheerfully. "When I see that
rogue I'll slap his face for him. I've been waiting——"

"You'll do nothing," Lord Seamus told him. He left his
seat in the coach, slid over to Selena's side, and put his arm
around her, as he had so often when she was a little girl.

"There, there," he said, as she wept softly in his arms,
"there, there." He went on soothingly, as Selena went on
crying, but she watched carefully through her tears to see if
the crying was having an effect. It wasn't, so she cried still
harder.

"You're just eighteen," her father was telling her again. As if that were relevant to anything at all! "Let me tell you something, too. Sir Royce is bound for trouble. He's much too rash, much too taken with himself. Look at the facts. You cannot help but have heard about his women. Unlike Sean, who would be faithful and loving and always at your side when you needed him, Royce Campbell would be all over the world, aboard strange ships, with strange women, doing God knows what in either case. Would you want to be married to a man like that?"

"Y . . . y . . . yessss," Selena sobbed.

Her father pretended not to hear, and pressed her head down on his shoulder, to stroke her hair. Brian feigned indifference to the proceedings.

"And, more than that, Campbell's life will be filled with danger. I would not be surprised if it was rather short. He is too reckless, too rebellious. The nobility does not trust him. Even his own clan looks askance at his adventures. The search for glory and recognition is a fine thing, to be sure, and the world has advanced because of men who sought those things, but there must be a reason for it. There must be a cause in which the adventurer believes. Royce Campbell believes in nothing and no one, with the possible exception of himself."

"*I* don't think so," she cried. "How can you say that?"

Father seemed about to reveal something, then thought better of it. "Let us just say that I've been audience to propositions of his, and let it go at that."

Last year, she thought. *That time he came to our quarters.* Had something occurred between Royce and her father to make him so unresponsive to her in the alcove? Oh, no, if that was it, if something like that *had* occurred . . . maybe her father had already warned him away! And he wouldn't have thought of her at all during the entire year. She had to know.

"Father . . ."

"Yes, child."

"Did you . . . did you ever speak to Sir Royce about . . . about me?"

Lord Seamus laughed. "No," he said. "No, I didn't, and I don't intend to, either. I—"

"But I must see him, at least once, in Edinburgh. If he's there."

Oh, be there. Please be there.

"And why is that, might I ask?"

"Because I promised him I would."

"You promised *him*?"

"And I suppose *he* loves *you?*" Brian interjected, with no little amusement. "A man that's bedded the love artists of Egypt and India, in love with a sweet, provincial Scottish lass—"

"Stop it," Lord Seamus commanded.

"It was my word of honor," Selena said. "It is all quite respectable, and I shall disgrace no one." *Except possibly myself.*

Her father thought it over for a long time, not bothering to conceal his skepticism. She tried to look as mournful, and as innocent, as she could. Selena felt entirely justified. If her father would marry her away so abruptly, did she not have the right, at least, to speak to Royce Campbell? To see if she *had* been mistaken about him?

"All right," Lord Seamus said. "But you must do so within bounds of the strictest propriety. None of this balcony business, do you understand? I know Campbell and his kind."

Meekly, she agreed, trying to devise a plan. Everything depended on its success, but she hadn't quite decided what would happen, even if she was right about Royce Campbell. Her father's last words showed her just how desperate the situation was:

"And you are going to marry Sean Bloodwell. Our discussion of the matter is ended."

The MacPhersons reached Edinburgh shortly before midnight. Wind-driven snow slanted down like angry spears in the lantern-dotted darkness, stinging their faces as they went into the castle and were shown to the chambers reserved for them. Selena had barely been able to feel her fingertips and toes for hours, because of the cold, and now her skin began to burn and throb. But there was hot wine and, even better, a hot perfumed bath with rose petals strewn atop the steaming water. And there were breads,

cheeses, and a thick, spicy lamb stew to eat. Later, Selena
went to bed beneath a canopy of heavy silk, with golden
tassels hanging down, resting her head upon pillows stuffed
to bursting with goosedown, her young, lovely body caressed by coverlets of satin. Servants had taken her bright
gowns from the traveling trunk, and they hung in a glorious row, ready for service in her conquest, shimmering in
the light of the guttering tapers on the walls. They were for
tomorrow, for Royce Campbell, for the future. If there was
one. Tomorrow, of course, she would see Sean Bloodwell
too, and all the rest of it, but just now that made no difference. It was something that would never happen.

And she did not know, this glittering princess of old
Scotland who was locked inside the body of a clever, lusty
girl, that destiny has few gold rings. But many mazes.

So, still a princess, she dropped down and down into the
blue pool of sleep, her thoughts jumbled together at first,
impressions coming one upon another. Father's seriousness
in the coach. Brian's unsettling remark about "a man that's
bedded the love artists of Egypt and India." She touched
her breasts and body, trying to hold back the thought: *Could
it be that I'm unready for him in that way?* Then the slow
flashing of patterns of light as sleep came, and the blue
pool shimmered. Years ago, and Brian with the bloody
knife, standing above the dead McEdgar, and the hoofbeats once again, in the Highlands, nine long years
ago, sounds and images all mysterious now as the veil fell
upon her. The face of Royce Campbell smiling through
time, the purple-cloaked lieutenant on the road this morning. Except now, as she fell and fell onward toward the
dreamless blue, the lieutenant's face turned dark and narrow, beaklike, and a soaring hawk appeared in her mind.
The towers of Coldstream Castle crumbled in strange silence. Sadness passed within her heart as tall stone towers
fell in dust, but then she heard from far away a rhythm
that was deeper than her heartbeat, yet which arose therefrom, a rhythm older than the sea, older than time, more
compelling even than blood, and it called *duty duty duty*
as she fell the final measure and slipped into the pool.

Her own blood softened then, and her heart leveled out,
beating fine and very slow.

THE NIGHT OF THE HAWK

"I know you'll do the right thing."

Lord Seamus smiled encouragingly, just before it was time for Sean Bloodwell's appearance. Selena lifted her breasts, squared her shoulders, and put on a smile, wondering: What *is* the right thing? What I am told to do? Or what I believe I ought to do? Her own sense of propriety, and her knowledge of the worth of a good marital alliance, told her that her father was correct. And he must be obeyed, too, must he not? Yet her heart throbbed dully, a voiceless murmur that was, this morning, neither private protest nor outright rebellion, as if now it said, all right then, duty, by all means, duty.

But not yet!

Sean Bloodwell entered the room, smiling, and, as always, he seemed to take charge of it merely by his presence. He shook hands with Lord Seamus, bowed to Selena, a well-built man of good height, good cheer, with an open, direct look that almost concealed the hint of steel. He wore a blue velvet dress coat, with knee breeches, and a white silk shirt ruffled at cuff and collar. He glanced at Lord Seamus: *Has Selena been told*? his eyes asked.

Her father nodded. Selena said nothing, and her uncharacteristic silence was immediately noticed by both Sean and her father. Lord Seamus did not look worried, not precisely.

"Perhaps my presence is needlessly . . . ah . . . complicating matters. I'm sure you two young people will excuse me." With that, he went out, leaving her alone. Selena didn't know if she liked that or not. She might speak a bit more frankly, true, but then it occurred to her that everything had been settled and there was really nothing to say.

Sean surprised her.

"I can see by your dour expression that you've been informed of the good news."

He spoke lightly, but there was the faintest undertone of pain in his voice.

They stood there looking at each other. Finally, she sat down in the corner of a long divan, covered with a sleek fabric of burnished gold. *You are in our thoughts each moment. Make haste and be strong,* her father had said.

"It's not that I'm unhappy," she began, fumbling. "It is . . . it is more the suddenness of it . . ."

"Is that *really* it?" he asked, and she remembered he was not a man so easily misled. He came over and sat down beside her, touched her face gently, and let his hand fall. "You know what you mean to me," he said; "at least I hope you do. So, be honest. Perhaps, in my affection, I did not properly judge your feelings before I spoke to your father. If so, I apologize. Are you certain that your surprise is due to the haste of the matter?"

He leaned forward and looked at her closely, his mind, his life, waiting behind those shrewd green eyes.

Selena nodded. Sean considered the situation. He seemed to come to a decision.

"May I speak frankly?"

She nodded again.

He took a breath. What he was about to say was clearly not the speech he had planned for this day. "Selena, I love you. But before I marry you, I must know that *you* are sure."

She looked up at him, disbelieving. This kind of thing did not happen, once a marriage was arranged. Immediately, she began to worry about her father's reactions, the failure of his many-faceted plan.

"Because if you're *not* sure, neither of us will have happiness or peace, and without those things what is the worth of marriage anyway?"

Selena said nothing, trying to put this unexpected response into perspective.

"Do you agree with me?"

"Yes," she heard herself saying in a small voice. Now

that it appeared she *did* have a choice, she was torn between emotions. Sean put his hand on hers. His touch was tender, yet assertive and even proprietary. After all, his hands had known almost as much of her body as Royce Campbell's had known. . . .

That thought jarred her back into alertness. Royce Campbell was as good as in the room with them. But, if Sean sensed it, he was not disturbed. This was between the two of them, and he wanted to have it out so there would be no misunderstandings later.

"I admire you, too," he was telling her. "Your spirit and your strength. And I would give a large part of my life—the rest of it, in fact—to help guide you to the power that can be yours."

"What are you talking about?" she interrupted.

He smiled. "You really don't know who you are yet, Selena. Or what you might be capable of doing. When you do learn these things, and you will if life is kind to you, there will be very little of which you won't be capable. You must discipline your instincts, Selena, and put them to work for something you want . . ."

Royce Campbell, she was thinking.

". . . and I am ready to help you, and to share life with you. Selena, you and I together could be capable of anything, of attaining every goal we set for ourselves."

He broke off. His smile was rueful and he looked more than a little perplexed. "If you don't listen, there's very little use in my speaking."

"Oh, I wasn't . . . I'm sorry."

"Does the title bother you?" he asked abruptly. His one weakness, that lack of a peerage.

"No . . . ah . . ." Then, desperate and confused as she was, Selena thought she had a solution, a way out. "Yes," she said, as if changing her mind. "Yes, I'm . . . I'm afraid it does."

"But your father assured me . . ." He stopped.

She said nothing.

"I see," he said. "All right. If such is your wish, I will so inform your father. I am the suitor, and there are rituals to cover this situation. I will ask you to consider my proposal for a fortnight. If you, *you* alone, do not wish to wed, I shall accept that decision. Do you agree to this?"

A fortnight was far in the future. A thousand things could happen in that time. She agreed.

Tea was called for and served, as they talked around a hundred different topics. Lord Seamus came back in. His glance was shrewd and measuring. He was not a politician by accident. And he did not seem at all pleased with his perceptions. At length, Sean left, with a promise to join them for the banquet, at which Lord North was to speak.

"So. I gather that it might be inadvisable to announce the banns just yet?"

"Oh, Father," she cried, and came into his embrace, "I know how much it meant to you."

He looked away from her gaze, but not quickly enough to conceal a shaft of worry that flashed behind his eyes. She told him what had happened, about the fortnight's wait.

"That may well be too late," he murmured, barely conscious of her presence. Then, abruptly: "This may change everything. You rest this afternoon, child. And think. I have . . . Brian and I must see a number of gentlemen."

He went out, leaving her alone again. And she felt, not relieved at concluding a difficult scene, but instead restless and disconsolate, wondering how many kinds of love there were in life, and which of them might be best for her. Already, with everything most women would regard as happiness right within her grasp, *handed* to her, she had succeeded in disappointing Sean, hurting Father, and God only knew what else. And she had done it all because of a man she barely knew, but whose being possessed for her a strange excitement, almost like the expectation of destiny. It was dangerous and unreadable, as if she, her very life, were mounted upon a great engine over which she had no control. And, what was worse, over which she wanted none.

For a long time she either sat there, staring moodily at the fireplace, listening to the crackling of the burning logs, or paced back and forth across the chamber, looking down into the courtyard below, where hundreds of people, servants and guests both, scurried about in a holiday mood. She watched them, too dispirited even to envy their good cheer. She did not even inspect her gowns, which hung in a long row in the adjacent dressing chamber. Finally, after hours crawled by, there was a change in the nature of the sound outside, an alteration in the easy rhythm of the crowd. Selena did not notice it at first, at least not consciously, but after a time she felt something in her senses quicken, and once more she walked to the window and looked out.

The crowd below seemed greatly excited, and they were gathered around the main gate. She wrestled a moment with the heavy casement window, then threw the window open. It was late in the afternoon, to her surprise, and the sun, pale now and moving fast, dropped to the western horizon. The air was frigid. The commotion rose on the air, the barking of dogs, the shouts of servants and horsemen, the clatter of horses' hooves on the ancient cobblestones. It was the usual courtyard scene, at a great fete, which precedes the arrival of a dignitary or a high official. *It must be Lord North,* she thought, remembering that her father had spoken of the prime minister's expected attendance. And no sooner had the thought crossed her mind than the trumpeters at the main gate blasted out in welcoming fanfare, and a small, elegant black hansom rolled on polished wheels into the courtyard, drawn by two of the whitest stallions Selena had ever seen. A cheer went up, and from the castle, grooms and footmen scurried out to serve the newcomers.

Selena leaned forward a little more, hoping to see. Even if Lord North was British, his arrival was an occasion, and in the excitement she forgot her own problems for a moment. The small buggy, driven by a liveried coachman, pulled directly through the crowd and stopped before the main steps. People were trying to peer inside the hansom, others were applauding, although, since most of them were Scottish, she could not quite understand their enthusiasm. And then, as she watched, her face assumed an expression that would have been one of utter pain and loss had her mind not been numbed by what she saw. From the carriage, as the shouting and applause increased, emerged the long, graceful body of Sir Royce Campbell, attired in the plaids of his clan. But more! He turned and reached into the cab and when he brought his arm out again it was to help out the most beautiful woman Selena MacPherson— and maybe God—had ever seen.

Her heart plummeted, and all dreams fell away. Below, to the accompaniment of cheers and shouted greetings, Royce and the woman had entered the castle. What to do? Was that raven-haired beauty his wife? No, that couldn't be, could it? Might not it be his sister? Yes, yes, it must be! That same dark hair! Certainly, then, she must be his sister!

But Selena had to know. Donning her traveling cape against the chill of the cold stone corridors, and pulling the hood forward so that it would be difficult for anyone to recognize her, she left her chamber and made her way down into the main hall. Young women of her own age were there, gossiping with one another, flirting with the eager sons of lords—exactly as she had done every year until now. This year was different.

Making her way through the crowd, she could not help but overhear the talk.

"Aye, an' did ye see the wench wi' Sir Royce?" asked a red-coated butler, with the kind of leer that reminded Selena of the peasants at home in Berwick Province. "She's the kind be born to make a good night fer any man."

"Aye," agreed his fellow worshiper. "'Tis it his wife, d' ye ken?"

"Nay, I do na. They're a'sayin' he brung the frail wi' 'im when 'e come back from the sea. All I ken is that they're lodgin' in the prince's chambers o'erlookin' Edinburgh 'arbor."

Selena had found out what she had to know. If Royce was in that suite, he would be at the opposite end of the castle, and on the top story. Wrapping her cloak tightly around her, she started the long trek through the dim corridors of the ancient fortress. Torches burned in holders on the stone walls, giving off small light and no heat. Now and then another heavily clothed person approached her out of the gloom, nodded or spoke softly in greeting. Then she climbed several flights of stairs and reached a section of the castle that was being used to house guests during these holidays. Blazes flared and exploded in great hearths, and servants flashed everywhere, bearing food, hot wine, and crystal decanters of smoky whiskey. She shook off her hood and let her lovingly-cared-for tresses spill out. She lifted her chin. It was easy to see she belonged with these people, even if the MacPherson quarters were a little way down the wing.

"The Campbell suite, please?" she demanded of an attendant, scarcely slowing her pace.

"It's right there, milady, next the balcony doors . . ." *Balcony,* she thought, remembering.

". . . but 'e's just arrived an's left no word of callers."

Whatever else he said didn't matter. Selena's brain was working furiously. She would enter, she would say—very coolly— "Sir Royce, I saw you arrive and I . . ." And I what, Selena? "And I . . ." Ah! Yes! "And I bring my father's greetings." That was what he had spoken of last year at the ball! Her father! Perhaps it had been his own ruse to meet her without formal introduction. And now she would use it herself, to see him. ". . . I bring you my father's greetings and his invitation to our chamber for wine before the banquet. I do hope you will find it possible to attend." Then there was the matter of the black-haired beauty. Would she be there in the room with him? Selena walked on toward the door of Campbell's suite, thinking. Yes, she would be there. So Selena would then look at her, quite pleasantly, and add: "And of course the lady is invited, too."

And to her questioning look, Royce Campbell would explain. "Please, allow me to introduce my sister. Selena, what a delight to see you again!"

. . . *what a delight to see you again what a delight to see you again* . . .

Her hand was on the door handle and she heard the click of the mechanism as she depressed it, and she felt the door move as she pushed it, her eyes adjusting to the odd dimness in the room, *Sir Royce, I saw you arrive and,* but that was because the heavy draperies were drawn. Why? *I saw you arrive and . . .*

"Yes? What is it?" snapped a harsh male voice.

Selena, startled, spun around, her eyes adjusting to the gloom now. There, in the canopied bed next to the fireplace, was Royce Campbell. He was sitting upright, the bedclothes had slipped away, and above the powerful chest and shoulders was his dark, chiseled face, out of which his eyes blazed at her. Then the eyes softened, almost with amusement, as he recognized her. He laughed.

Selena stood, incapable of movement, not looking at him now but at the woman in bed with him. She lay on her side next to Royce, black hair fanned out on the satin pillow cover, her soft white shoulder and upper arm exposed, but her arm beneath the bedclothes obviously caressing her partner.

"Selena!" Royce said, not at all discomfited, even enjoying the situation. "What brings you here?"

But Selena did not look at him, only heard him. She saw in the other woman's eyes a sudden, haughty, totally feminine knowledge. And contempt. *So you came for this man, you silly little girl,* said the woman wordlessly. *But, as you see, he's mine.*

You fool, the woman added, with just the suggestion of a smile, moving her head a trifle closer to Sir Royce.

You fool, Selena echoed. Who could deny it?

"Really, Selena, I'm quite glad to see you, but don't you think we might meet a bit later?" Royce suggested, quite pleasantly.

Then she had turned and she was running for the door, and then she was out in the cold corridor once again, with the sound of the door slamming behind her, and the laughter behind her, too: Royce Campbell's, deep and good-humored, and the woman's, mocking and victorious.

Selena barely remembered walking back to her own room, and when she got there much more trouble awaited.

"I think we're being set up for some kind of mass arrest," Brian was saying in his blunt way as she entered. "Oh, Selena . . ."

Lord Seamus was seated at a table, uncharacteristically slouched, head in hands. He looked up.

"Selena! Where've you been? We were worried."

"I . . . I took some air." Quickly, she changed the subject. "What's this about arrest?"

The conversation in the coach returned to her. The face of Darius McGrover. These threatening thoughts muted for a moment the savage pain of Royce Campbell's rejection and the greater pain of her own stupidity and humiliation. Never again. It would have never happened if she'd remained true to her duty.

"Alan McTavish died on the wheel in Dundee Castle," Father said quietly, his eyes slitted with worry. "I learned it

from Will Teviot, the Rob Roys' captain in Ross and Cromarty Province. Now we must reckon with the worst. If he
died too late, poor devil, and if he was made to talk, we
may have been invited here for the last time. 'Tis no coincidence that Lord North himself is here. Perhaps he's come
to see the capture."

Brian cursed, and spat into the fireplace. Selena stifled a
gasp. Of all the horrors to survive the Middle Ages, the
wheel was one of the worst, the most odious. It was an
instrument that would permit an interrogator like Darius
McGrover to break, slowly and deliberately, every bone in
a person's body, one by one. Positioned in tight wooden
grooves, the bones would be crushed by heavy metal
wheels crashing from above.

"All right," Brian said. "Now it's time, is it not? If they
try anything while we're in Edinburgh, I say let's strike!
Strike fast and strike hard! That's the only way."

"Yes," Lord Seamus said without enthusiasm, "and kill
ourselves straightaway in the bargain. I choose not to. In
the first place, we *must* wait. The British hold all the cards.
We do not know *if* McTavish talked. If we act without
such knowledge, we may rashly and needlessly reveal ourselves."

"But if we do not act—" Brian interrupted.

"Let's just go home!" Selena declared. "Enough of this.
We'll go home where it's safe, and . . ."

*And I won't have to face Royce Campbell and that
woman at the ball!*

"We can't do that either," her father said sadly. "We
must attend the banquet tonight and give no sign that anything's amiss."

"But what if they do indeed try to take us?"

He shrugged. Selena had never seen her father so dispirited or tired. She went over to him and put her arms
around him, as he had done to her, so many times, in moments of trial or disappointment. She recognized that she
herself was in danger, but somehow that did not seem as
immediate or as important as his grimness.

Lord Seamus was silent for a long time, then he spoke:
"There are certain plans we might try," he said. "They will
be difficult and there is no guarantee that they will succeed.

And I will have to deal with the devil if we are to attempt them at all."

There was a long silence in the room. Finally, he put his hand on Selena's arm and gently freed himself from her embrace. "I must go now, child, and see to some things."

"No, stay. There's no need. Let's be off from here."

He shook his head gravely and tried to smile.

"No, we all have things to do, now. Brian, go and take care of yours."

Brian threw on his cape and left. Lord Seamus made ready to follow.

"What about me?" cried Selena. "I want to help, too. Tell me what to do."

He turned at the door and looked at her. "I thought you already knew. Sean Bloodwell will be by shortly. And," he added, with an implication that Selena did not then understand, "if we can save you for him, the MacPhersons might not all be lost."

All be lost? she asked, after he'd disappeared. *The MacPhersons? Never!* The long history of the clan swept out of the past then, and bathed her in its solace. Other women had felt as she did now, felt torn between duty and love, felt loss and pain, yet beyond all these griefs, they had remained members of a family, instruments of a cause, in spite of their personal desires, or the apparent tryanny of fate. You could choose neither your ancestors nor your past, and your future was less than flexible because of both. Yet, Selena knew, other women had borne their burdens, and they reached out to her now from legend and story, spoke to her now even from the marble vaults below the wall at Coldstream Castle. They had endured. They had kept the faith, for better or worse. The past belonged to them, but served as a guide to her. The present was hers, and the future, too, if she were but wise.

But treason? Escape? Arrest?

And escape to where? Leave Scotland? Scotland was all Selena knew, and she loved it as she loved Coldstream. She loved not a little her position as a MacPherson, and she loved, too, the rolling moors, sere and dour in fall, bursting with flowers and heather in spring. Farther north, she loved the deep, mysterious lochs, Lomond and Rannoch and Ness, which they saw in summer on the way to the hunting lodge at Mount Foinaven. Dear to her heart as well, brooding there, were the strange, magnificent mounds of the Highlands, the rustle of kilt and caftan, the high and mournful music of the pipes. But dearest of all was Coldstream, with its old stone walls, its mazed and ivied gardens, its twenty-two fireplaces ablaze on a winter's eve.

Leave all that? Leave Scotland? Never! She would do what had to be done. She would marry Sean Bloodwell right away. *I'll tell Father at dinner.* She dressed numbly, thinking of nothing, and then Sean arrived to escort her to the banquet.

According to protocol, the order of entrance to the banquet hall and the seating positions at the long rows of candlelit tables were determined by rank. Thus, most of the tables were already filled, the lower-ranking guests positioned, when the trumpeteers sounded the arrival of the MacPhersons and Sean Bloodwell (whose imminent betrothal to one of the nobility accorded him this honor) entered the hall. Selena was on her father's arm, Brian and Sean trailing, as they were shown to their table. Around them the vast hall was a blazing blur of red-coated waiters, fine-gowned women, and vigorous men, and from the high stone walls fell the draped white, red, and blue of the Union Jack, symbol at once of Empire and Act of Union. Here and there around the hall, as Lord Seamus MacPherson entered, there was applause, but he remained sober and weary-looking. They were seated, and the clapping faded.

"So I expect there's to be no trouble then?" whispered Brian, his red hair flashing and blue eyes gay, as if a burden had been lifted.

"Ne'er fool yourself with the cheers of the crowd. Did you not see McGrover gloating over near the door?"

They looked, but the spot was vacant now. Then the next guests approached the trumpeters, and Selena steeled herself for the worst.

"Lord Royce Campbell," came the cry. "And Lady Veronica Blakemore."

Not married! Well, it made no difference now. She stayed composed, and surreptitious glances at Sean, Brian, and her father, showed that none of them knew of her idiotic afternoon foray. *Idiotic,* she told herself. Yet, mockingly, a part of herself rejoiced that this Blakemore was only a lover. . . .

"The Blakemores are from Jamaica, in the West Indies," Sean was explaining. "I've bought cotton from their plantations, much less difficult to produce than wool."

Selena watched Royce and Veronica. The rugged man, back from the far reaches of earth, a rider of the high seas. Rider of fine women, too. Her face was white and as icy cold as her eyes. Black hair, like raven's wings, fell upon her soft shoulders, and her rouged, swelling breasts were bare to the tiniest rose crescent of nipple at the bodice of her gown. Now she glanced over toward Selena, and she smiled, a horizontal tightening of lips that mocked. Then, as if to accentuate her conquest, she reached out and touched Royce Campbell's arm. He immediately leaned toward her, and she said something in his ear. She laughed. He smiled. She looked once again at Selena, who could not help but feel the rush of blood into her face, remembering this afternoon, remembering the balcony last Christmas, imagining how many times and in what delicious embraces Royce had taken his pleasure with this haughty Blakemore. She summoned a last effort of will and stared directly at Royce, her head high, and his cold ironic eyes came over to her. But, no! Not to her. He looked at her father, and then nodded, and his glance drifted elsewhere.

Finally, last to be announced, Lord North himself entered to the call of trumpets.

Selena had never seen him before, and had not known what to expect. A prime minister of England, certainly, would be a man of great dignity and presence. But she was surprised to see a tired, dyspeptic-looking man shamble to the dais, his little eyes tough and shrewd under the powdered wig. There was considerable applause and, looking around, Selena saw one man clapping harder than most. She shuddered with recognition and a terrible foreboding. The thin, cruel mouth and hooked nose, the gloomy, saturnine, unyielding expression . . . Darius McGrover.

Her father was speaking to Brian and Sean. The applause was dying, and she caught a phrase. ". . . after the banquet, when the women retire . . ."

Brian looked stunned, Sean tense.

"What's going on after . . . ?" she started, but felt her

father's hand on her arm, saw the warning glance, and she felt a shrinking inside her body. Agreeing to marry Sean would solve nothing anymore.

"Come now," her father said, "we must eat." And there was something almost premonitory in his concern. "And," he cautioned Brian, who had been known to empty many a bottle of wine, "when the stomach is drunk, so is the head."

Selena knew it then, for certain. Something was going to happen, but whatever it was, she could not know it yet. She ate. There was no lack of food.

First, there was a rich lamb soup, spiced with Spanish pepper and served with white bread, fluffy as clouds and on which wedges of golden butter melted. Then fillet of salmon, basted in sauce, and surrounded by parsley, watercress, and slices of lemon brought from the Mediterranean during the summer and stored in special icehouses. Next, upon a bed of brown rice, there were hundreds of tiny birds, each one of them stuffed with raisins and sugar, glistening with sweet gravy. Finally, tender lamb, marbled beef, succulent pork, and rivers of wine.

The atmosphere was merry, even ribald, when Lord North rose to speak. He spoke well, but Selena did not like the self-satisfied manner with which he said "um, um," at the end of every couple of sentences, as if congratulating himself. After speaking of the glory that had come to Scotland since the Act of Union, glory which would never have been attained without the masterly guidance of London, he seemed to reach his main point: "The situation in the Empire is, by and large, peaceful and prosperous. We are having, as you may have heard, a little trouble from bands of the rabble in the American colonies, but a whiff of grapeshot or a taste of the lash ought to cure that soon enough. Um, um. We shall resolve to tax them in accordance with their natural wealth, treat them as grown members of the Empire rather than seditious children. Um, um. But have no fear, for they will do their duty in the end." Here he paused and brought his hand down heavily upon the table. "Rebellion and treason will never be tolerated anywhere in the Empire. Wherever treason raises its ugly head, we shall sever that head from the vile body upon which it feeds, that both head and body succumb to law, to order, to the grace of our beloved King."

Once again, the crowd rose to its feet, applauding, but the sound seemed empty to Selena, lusterless, bereft of happy emotion.

When the speech ended, with the guests and dignitaries rising, her father tensed. "Go directly to the ladies' after-dinner chamber," he told her harshly. "Don't wait to be shown there. Forget about protocol. When you reach it, you will find, just to the left, behind the tapestries, a door. Inside there will be a small parlor. Go inside and do exactly, *exactly*, as you are told. Do you understand?"

There was no questioning his tone. She started toward the door, then glanced back at Sean and Brian. They were both gone. She stole one last look, too, at the head table. Royce Campbell was out of sight in the crowd, but she saw Veronica Blakemore listening to, and displaying her charms for, Lord North. The contrast was galling: Selena was in danger, on the run, and that cold Jamaican beauty let her tongue run over her lips, laughed, and bent forward to give the lecherous old Briton just a little peek.

No time for thinking about that now. *Someday I'll wipe that smirk off her face,* Selena thought angrily, then she was out in the corridors of Edinburgh Castle again.

A few maids, busy with trays and tea, looked up as Selena entered, then returned to their work. Quickly, just as she'd been instructed, Selena hurried across the room and opened the small door next to the tapestry that portrayed the battles of Robert the Bruce. Inside, two candles flickered on a polished table. She saw nothing else. Then a strong arm seized her from behind, a hard hand closed over her mouth. Too surprised even to try a scream, she tried to struggle.

"Easy, Selena," a voice said, holding her firmly without hurting her. She could not believe it. The voice was Royce Campbell's.

"Quiet now. I'm going to take my hand away. You'll be calm?"

She nodded, and he released her. She turned and saw him there, the candles outlining the planes of his face. Her mind whirled, overcome by too many impulses and impressions.

"Here. Out on this balcony," he commanded, and for just the shred of an ecstatic second she thought they were going to relive last year, that she would have another chance, but then the part of herself that reasoned logically, and that she counted on to keep her from doing yet another foolish thing, said, *No, Father told you to come here.* Royce Campbell took her by the hand and swung aside the doors. Out on the balcony it was very dark. They were in the wing of the castle set back, away from the city. It would ensure privacy, but was very cold. From his pocket, Royce took a cloth of white silk, waved it several times over the side of the balcony, then waited a moment. Horses' hooves glinted on the stones below, and in a moment the knotted edge of a stout rope snaked over the railing. He grabbed it and secured it to a stone pillar, his hands flashing deftly with his seaman's skill.

"Get behind me," he ordered quietly. "Put your arms around my neck."

"What for? Why are we . . . ?" Now she was no longer certain that Royce Campbell meant her well. Perhaps her father had been tricked in some way, or . . .

"Do as I say. It's your neck if you don't."

Numbly, she obeyed, and he climbed over the railing and then the two of them were out over emptiness. Selena clung to him desperately. Royce slid down the rope and came to rest on the cobblestones. Two black horses stamped there, tossing their heads skittishly. A rider sat upon one of the horses, in black cape and hood.

"All's well, Sir Royce?" A man's voice.

"'Tis wi' the wench, here. I do na ken aboot t'others."

She had not heard him speak with the common accent before, and it surprised her.

"Why are we doing this?" she asked. Too loudly, because Royce immediately grabbed her and clapped a hand over her mouth.

"Easy," he said. "Nothing's happening except that I'm giving McGrover a bit of a run tonight. There now," he said, releasing her. "Mind you, beware."

"Royce, we'd best be off," urged the horseman.

"Aye, Gil," he said to the rider, then, very quickly, he embraced Selena, a true embrace that put her protectively inside his arms, his great strength. Just as suddenly, he released her.

"Ye may understand someday," he said, with a kind of

wry tenderness. "Now, get aboard." With that, he boosted
her up and onto the saddle of the second horse.

"When . . . when will we meet again?" she managed to
whisper.

"Soon, if all goes well."

"Until that time."

"Sir Royce!" the man urged.

"Aye, you go." Then, to Selena, "You mayn't like it
much when I see you next, as it will be beyond your ken.
Prepare for that."

She reached out and tried to find his hand in the darkness, but failed.

"Ye're a good man, Gil. Now do yer best an' we'll see ye
at t' ship, if we've the luck."

"My vow," Gil responded, and already his hand was on
the bridle of Selena's horse, turning it down a long stone
ramp that led away from Edinburgh Castle.

"An' you, milady. Do na call back a farewell. Nary a
word out o' ye, do ya ken?"

It was too dark to see her nod in dull acquiescence, but
he took the silence for assent. The horses were moving
slowly, picking their way carefully over the rough stones.
Dazed, Selena turned to look back at the castle. Royce
Campbell was climbing back up to the balcony. She saw
the flash of his white shirt cuffs as he went hand over hand
up the rope. The door swung open for an instant. She saw
the warm flicker of candlelight for an instant, like the last
warm spark of a lost hearth. Then the door closed.

"Where are you taking me?" she asked, after they had
ridden awhile.

"Sut yer mouth," came the coarse reply. So she did.
They rode steadily through the darkness and Gil handed
her a heavy horse blanket against the cold. The smell was
overpowering—liniment, leather, and sweat—and the harsh
fabric scraped her skin as the horse moved, but she was
glad of the protection. After a time they left the sleeping
city behind and she sensed Gil relax a little. Now, with the
sense of urgency somewhat dispelled, with the heavy blanket around her and the powerful warmth of the horse between her thighs, she tried again.

"Please, could you tell me . . . ?"

He grunted, cutting her off. Then after a minute: "We've 'ad a bit o' luck. I 'ope 'tis the same wi' t'others."

"What others?"

He drew his horse next to hers, and snorted in surprise. "The Rob Roys, milady. I thought ye knew."

"Are you one of them?"

"Ye're damn right, pardonin' my speech. An' by dawn it may be that I'll be one o' t' few. McGrover, the bloody skull, was set t' get the lot o' us. Ye're t' be thankin' God an' yer father fer gettin' ye out lak they did."

"But wasn't that Royce Campbell who got me out?"

Gil snorted and said yes.

"But . . . but McGrover can't do this. Lord North can't do this. We're MacPhersons! My father . . ."

She could not go on. Tears welled up in her eyes, and her throat was dry and burning. She slumped a little in the saddle, and Gil, gentle for the first time, took her reins and led the horses into a slightly protected grove beneath gray, stripped trees.

"Now, girl," he tried, "ye've got t' face it. Ye're father's as fine a man as Scotland e'er knew, but they've branded 'im a traitor now, an' 'tis the daughter of a traitor that ye be. Ye've just begun t' run now, an' the way lies long ahead o' ye. There's no man got out o' the castle this eve who knows where 'e's t' wind up, but there's no man who got out who'd druther be in the dungeon wi' the likes o' Darius McGrover a'beatin' on his manhood wi' a wooden club. . . ."

For the first time, she thought of Sean Bloodwell. Tonight their engagement was to have been announced, her future sealed, her life determined. Fate had prevented it, true, but as an alternative fate had left her adrift, with no perceptible anchor to reach for.

"Do you know if Sean Bloodwell was a Rob Roy?"

Gil shook his head. "But won't be doin' 'im much good, lest he convinces McGrover. 'E was too close to you Mac . . ." Gil changed his mind and said instead: ". . . . too close to some o' the Rob Roys."

Selena was silent.

"Let's go," Gil said at last. "'Tis many a mile to Portobello."

Portobello? she wondered. That was east of Edinburgh,

along the coast. Wouldn't it be better to flee north, into the Highlands?

Hours later Gil reined in along the side of the roadway, passed down a steep, icy ditch, and called to her to follow. They rode slowly down a long, rocky inclination, and in the distance she heard the booming of the surf. She guessed that it was about three or four o'clock in the morning. Nothing was visible save the great irregular shapes of rocks along the coastline, outlined in the eerie light of roiling water. Wind burned along the shore, biting deeply into horses and riders, so that even the blanket offered little protection now. Then there was a break in the rocks, and through it a small cove. She saw a wooden boathouse, light shining through chinks in the rough planking. And on the lee side of the building stood several winded horses, heads down, sides heaving. Gil helped her from the horse and she staggered on stiff, unsteady legs to the boathouse door. The door slammed open in the wind. There they were, her father and Brian huddled around a small fire.

"Selena! Thank God!" cried her father, embracing her. Brian's face was contorted, half smiling, half crying. Danger had drained it of rage. Gil drew the door shut and made for the fire. "Thank God," her father said again, holding her close.

Her body, her very spirit, sagged, begged for rest now, after the ordeal of the midnight ride. The knowledge that they had come safely this far, but that they must go much farther, with no end in sight, crashed down upon her like a wave of pure sorrow, but she realized that to accept defeat would be defeat. Then the thought came to her: *There is no defeat unless you believe it.*

"I won't believe it," she whispered fiercely.

"What?" her father asked. His face was haggard. She'd never seen him so discouraged. Even Brian looked different, as if robbed of a portion of his manhood.

"I said we're not finished," Selena declared. "I said we're not beaten. We're the MacPhersons, after all."

The ratty boathouse, the cold swirling outside, the fatigue of being hunted: these things contradicted her. Yet she spoke with a fire, a spirit, that made them all feel a little better.

"That ye be, darlin'," Gil said. "Ye're a MacPherson, all right." They all sat down around the fire, and drank some whiskey and ate some black bread and cheese that Gil produced from a knapsack.

"It was a good stroke, anyway," Lord Seamus said. "This coming here to Portobello. He'd heard that McGrover expected those of us who got away to flee immediately to the north. Not go east of Edinburgh, as we have. Otherwise, we'd have been trapped on the outskirts of the city. Now, if the boat can only get in close enough to shore in this heavy sea, he'll be able to take us across the Firth."

"He?" Selena asked, barely daring to believe.

"Royce Campbell," Brian muttered, his face expressionless.

"See! You were wrong about him, weren't you?" Selena exclaimed, triumphant. Royce had said that, next time they met, she might not understand things, but this rescue was simple enough to accept.

"Selena, there have been—" her father began, but from far away out over the water came the sound of a hollow booming, just as the first dull light of dawn passed through the chinks in the planking of the shack.

"That'll be the signal cannon aboard the *Highlander*," Gil said, leaping to his feet. He raced out the door and clambered up on the rocks at the edge of the water. Then he yanked his hat off and waved it vigorously.

" 'E's 'ere," he cried, his voice exuberant in spite of the frigid night. "'Tis Campbell. An' 'e made it, just lak 'e said."

How could there have been any doubt? Selena thought, and she felt a chill rush through her body that had nothing whatever to do with the cold.

" 'Tis the *Highlander*, all right," Gil affirmed, coming down from the rocks.

"I'll say one thing about that damn Campbell," Brian groused, "when you buy him he's as good as his word."

"Anybody else could na 'ave brung the ship in 'ere in seas lak this!" Gil declared admiringly. "Why, 'ere's na a man else 'o'd a done it."

He needed to say no more. They all peered into the early morning mist and there, out over the breakers, the mighty

ship came into view. Only a few of its countless sails were
unfurled, just enough for a shrewd sailor to bring the vessel
in close to the shore. The *Highlander* looked black and
enormous out there on the empty sea, powerful and premonitory, like the strange, portentous vehicles that appear
sometimes in dreams. Slowly, it swung to starboard, and
they were faced with three long rows of black cannon, tiers
of weaponry unmatched by any king's navy in the world.
Dimly, Selena thought she was beginning to understand
Royce Campbell and his ways. To have such power might
make a man different, even if he were not a Campbell to
begin with.

Now they could see a small dinghy being lowered into
the sea from the *Highlander*'s main deck. The small craft
bobbed helplessly for a moment, then began to move toward the shore, and in a few more minutes they saw
cowled sailors bending to the oars. The boat rose on the
high riders, then dropped between troughs, and rose again,
the bent men working feverishly. In close now, oars were
feathered and the craft skimmed in on the rock-strewn
shore, making an angry, grating sound.

"Lord MacPherson?" asked a man who seemed to be in
charge. He had a dark, brindly beard, and the savage, intimidating look of a brawler.

Lord Seamus nodded.

"Lieutenant Fligh, sir. Lord Campbell's second in command. 'Tis a privilege to meet you, sir. Long live Scotland."

"Let us hope," Lord Seamus said, and they climbed into
the small boat.

"Gil," he ordered, turning, "you make your way back to
Edinburgh and contact Sean Bloodwell, if you can. Tell
him where we'll be."

"Bend to it, men," shouted Lieutenant Fligh, above the
sound of the surf, and he pushed the boat off as the men
dipped oars against the swell. The boat escaped the pounding ribbon of water along the shore, then skimmed out into
a gentler area of rolling swells. Selena watched the *Highlander,* which seemed farther away now, and tried to see if
she could spot Royce on the deck. Many men were there,
waiting for the dinghy's return, but try as she might, she
was unable to pick him out. Then she felt uncomfortable,

glanced quickly around, and saw Fligh's hard eyes on her.
The horse blanket, which she still had wrapped around her,
was little help against the cold of the wind and sea, but she
pulled it tighter to shut out his eyes. He saw her do so, and
his gaze moved lazily from her breasts up to her eyes. He
smiled, utterly without warmth, and looked her over slowly
once more before he got back to business. She was grateful
for the blanket, at least. Beneath it was only the gown she
had worn for the ball on the night now ended, low-cut, pale
ivory in color, with a silver sash that ran beneath her
breasts. The gown was already ruined from the night's ride,
and now she realized that, except for the horse blanket, it
was all she had for clothes. She felt terribly sad for a moment—all those beautiful gowns, made especially for the
holidays—but then the dinghy came up next to the *Highlander,* and Royce Campbell, elegant and unperturbed in
his captain's greatcoat, stood above them on deck, his feet
braced against the ocean's roll.

His eyes were on her.

Ropes were lowered and fastened to bow and stern of the
dinghy, and davits creaked as it was lifted, with its passengers, into the man-of-war. It seemed to Selena a stupendous
ship, a floating world.

On deck, he spoke to her father first. "I'll take you
across the Firth to Pittenweem, as agreed," he said. "With
luck, if you move fast, you can outflank McGrover's police
and make it north into the Highlands. And I'll have a ship
to America waiting for you at Liverpool in the spring,
when a crossing is possible."

Lord Seamus nodded sadly, and Royce ordered sailors to
take them below immediately for dry clothes and hot food.
"If you don't mind, sir," he added deferentially, "your
daughter may use my cabin. It is the only place aboard
ship that provides a measure of privacy."

Brian roused himself to a look that was part bile and
part amused skepticism. Like many an older brother, he
was solicitous of his sister's honor. But Lord Seamus paid
no mind, and Royce ordered a steward to show her the
way.

Sir Royce's cabin was high in the stern, a small, comfortable, but extremely well-organized room. The rafters of the
ship formed beams along the ceiling, and from these

Royce's hammock was suspended, draped casually with blankets of leopard skin. The cabin was well-insulated, and the small iron stove gave off considerable heat. On a chair beside a map desk, she found laid out for her the rough woolen uniform and rope-soled shoes of a common sailor. Scorning these, she tore off the soaked and sullied gown, dried herself with a large Turkish towel that had been left with the uniform, wrapped the towel around her, and then brushed her hair until it glowed in the smoky glass of the porthole chamber.

Beneath her, she felt the ship turn, moving diagonally to the wind and across the Firth, which was the bay that led into Edinburgh harbor. Then they would be put ashore, and . . .

It would be a parting, again, soon, and they had never yet been together. At the same moment, her mind and body realized why she was here, in this cabin. The feeling she had then was one of utterly physical excitement, in spite of the circumstances.

There was a knock at the cabin's oak-beamed door. "Selena, are you ready?"

It was Royce.

"Yes," she cried, and turned toward the door.

He opened the door and saw her there. A momentary expression of surprise appeared on his face. He looked at her appraisingly, and met her eyes.

"Royce," she whispered.

His face tightened with passion, and he swung the cabin door shut. The iron latch clanged to. She saw the raw desire in his gaze, but for just the shred of a second he seemed somehow to hesitate, too. *Blakemore*, she thought, fighting off a flicker of desperation, and then her arms were around him and her lips were seeking his. Veronica Blakemore did not matter now, and after this meeting she could never matter again, never! Selena pressed close against him and pulled his head down to her own. She found his mouth and felt his passion rise.

"Selena," he said, as if he were about to tell her something, but she cut off his voice with her kiss. The advice of many women throbbed in her mind: *You will know what to do when the time comes*, and all the women of Egypt, of India, and all the Veronica Blakemores spun away into a world of contemptible illusion as she felt Royce's strong arms encircle her, and felt the unmistakable proof of his desire against her body. *Now let him try to set me aside like a schoolgirl,* she thought, feeling her own excitement. Once again, for just an instant, she sensed a hint of restraint in him, as if he were trying to resist, but then the moment passed and they were climbing together the ladder of sensual enchantment.

Driven by need, he tightened his embrace, fairly lifting her to him, and his hands sought the tingling places of her body. Her towel fell away, and so did his greatcoat and breeches, and Selena reached eagerly to stroke and pleasure him. They moved across the cabin toward the hammock, as if joined in a dance that was composed not of steps and twirls but rather kisses and embraces, touches of endearment, and words that could not quite be spoken. A sound, almost like a groan, came from his throat as he lifted her into his hammock and then came down upon her. He tried to be gentle when he entered her, but his need was urgent. Selena felt riven for a moment, but it did not matter, and then she embraced him with her body, and together they were climbing the ladder to a sacred place, faster and faster. She felt him lancing into her, driven by the passion she had set afire, and her own tumultuous passion bathed her body in its glory. It was as natural as a dream or destiny, and the sacred place waited there above them, in which their melded bodies would flow. It seemed as if they had all the time in the world to reach that place, but need made them hurry. A feeling of inexpressible magnificence seemed to be waiting for them there, possession of which would give them wings to soar above the tawdry, spinning earth. Possession of the gift would be like dying and going to glory, going to glory for the space of an instant, a shred of time so small that, in comparison, the length of one human breath is eternity. Royce reached that place, and clung to her, and brought her along with him. They were no longer of the world, but had put the world behind them.

Afterward, she drifted for a time, loving the feel of his warmth. But in time, the glimpse of eternity faded from her mind and, in her body, the blood slowed down. Suddenly, she was aware that he had not spoken, and that he lay tense beside her. She opened her eyes, to see him watching her. She could not interpret his emotions, which he had concealed with his icy eyes, but the look on his face was not so much cynical as mildly perplexed.

"This time I was fortunate and you were not," he said enigmatically.

"I love you," she said, moving close for a kiss.

He gave her the kiss, but said nothing. An entire world fell away from her then, and her heart with it. She kissed him again, to hide the hurt. She hoped he could not hear the beating of her heart. Now she recalled Brian's attitude toward Royce, and her father's warnings about his nature. Abruptly, he broke away from her kiss.

"What's the matter?" he wanted to know.

Selena tried to smile. "Why . . . why nothing. Why on earth should anything be the matter?"

Royce narrowed his eyes and studied her. She watched him. He seemed much taken by her. She knew, because she had seen the same look in the eyes of Sean and the others. But, with Royce, something was different, as if he were slightly puzzled, even a bit wary.

"You are on the run from McGrover, with a long road to travel, no certainty of safety, and you imply that everything is fine?"

"I shall be with you again in Liverpool, in the spring," she said, caressing him where, again, his manhood stirred. And again, he could not resist, or did not want to. He came to her with a moan of pleasure, and they feasted upon sensation, sensation all the keener because their bodies had so recently tasted raw delight. But when they had finished, Selena knew him no better than before.

A noisy knock sounded at the door. "Pittenweem's off starboard, sir," Lieutenant Fligh called. Fligh! Had he been outside all along? At this moment, Selena didn't care.

"All right," Royce told his second in command. "I'll be right up on deck."

Selena watched with admiration and unquenched desire as Royce pulled clothes onto his powerful body. "Here," he said, almost curtly, and tossed her a pair of pants and a shirt from a peg on the wall. "It'll be a good disguise for you." Then he was gone.

Selena got out of the hammock, half-joyful, half-distressed. She had held him; he had been hers. His essence was even now seeping from her. But he had acted—oh, she knew it now—strangely, and then he had left so abruptly. She looked at the clothing he'd given her. The rough uniform of a common seaman. She glumly put it on; it hung from her body, loose and baggy, and she noted with great disappointment the manner in which the heavy folds of the shirt all but concealed the slimness of her waist, the swell of her breasts and hips.

- She left the cabin and was just about to take the passageway up on deck when she saw Brian and her father approaching. They were dressed in uniforms just like hers, which seemed to rob them of their identities. Lord Seamus looked utterly defeated, but in her present mood of reverie mixed with rue, Selena barely noticed.

"A sailor said we might find Lord Campbell down here," said her father.

"He . . . he was here, but he went back up on deck."

"What did he want?" Brian snapped.

"To know how we were managing," she answered, more angrily than necessary.

"*He* asked you how *we* were managing?" Brian repeated, with a look of disgust.

"Yes. And I thanked him for all that he's done."

Brian and Lord Seamus looked at each other. There was a pause, into which Selena read the emotions of each.

"Selena," her father began, "do you remember in the coach to Edinburgh that I informed you of Sir Royce's visit to me last year? And of a scheme he advanced which I considered to be highly insulting?"

Selena remembered. It had seemed insignificant at the time, nothing that would ever affect her.

"I have never doubted Sir Royce's shrewdness," her father said. "He knew we were in danger as early as last year, and he offered to take us all to safety in America. I told him we did not require his services, and that we never would. But he estimated the political situation better than I. This year I had to go to him, hat in hand." He shook his head sadly. "I had to deal with the devil."

Selena's brain was spinning, as if the timbers she stood upon had suddenly dissolved beneath her feet. Father reduced to begging. . . .

"But what is so terrible about being taken to safety?" she asked.

Lord Seamus gave her a direct look. "We had to pay him, Selena. He is doing nothing for us out of the goodness of his heart. I can assure you of that."

Selena sought an explanation. "But it's dangerous for him," she began. "And after all, he is a sailor for hire. . . ."

"Sean was the one who had to pay him," Brian said.

There was a silence in the great ship, broken only by the occasional sound of orders being shouted on deck, and the creaking of the timbers.

"All we have is gone, Selena," her father said, trying to be gentle, trying to make her understand the extent of their distress. "Position. Money. Coldstream. It's all gone. We had to call upon Sean Bloodwell for money to buy our way to safety, if we're fortunate enough to reach safety. And Royce Campbell took that money. Spare yourself further illusions about him.

"Sean's also paid our way to America. We are to meet up with Royce in Liverpool in spring, when passage across the Atlantic is possible. *If* Campbell even makes the rendezvous," he added bitterly.

Selena tried desperately to fit it all together, to assemble the various impressions in a way that would leave her feelings of love for Royce intact. Now, for the first time, she realized fully the extent of Sean Bloodwell's love for her, and also her father's knowledge of that love. He had counted on it as a rock for her to cling to after he himself was gone. Then her heart convulsed in a sudden, painful rage against Royce Campbell, the mercenary cynic upon whom they now depended. This was the man in whose arms she had lain only moments before! Now she knew, too, how they had become beneficiaries of Campbell's power and largess, which she had mistaken for comradeship and love. Money—blood money—had changed hands. (And yet she remembered how it felt in his embrace.) Worse, it had been Sean Bloodwell's gold which was giving them this small measure of safety. And had she herself been part of the payment for this passage? Was that the reason for Royce's momentary restraint just before he had taken her? Selena did not know. In spite of her anger and pain, her body betrayed her, recalling nothing but the sweet madness of his embrace. Finally, with a supreme effort of will, she forced herself to realize what had taken place, and she stormed off down the passageway.

"Where are you going?" Brian called.

"To see Royce Campbell. I have a few things to say to him."

"It will be of no use," Lord Seamus warned.

"On the contrary, I believe that I shall feel much better," Selena replied.

She found Royce on the bridge of the *Highlander*. He greeted her with his customary expression of wry amusement. Lieutenant Fligh, standing beside Royce, eyed her closely. They both saw how angry she was.

"What is it?" Royce asked.

She saw with a sickening sensation how adept he was at giving the appearance of sympathy and concern. *She* had been deceived by certain other of his dramatic techniques.

"I think you are *despicable! Thoroughly* despicable! My father is one of the greatest men in Scotland, and yet you take money, Sean Bloodwell's money . . ."

"Oh, that," Royce said. "His money means something to you now, does it?"

"You . . . you *bastard*."

Royce laughed grimly. "No, young lady. My antecedents have been unsullied for thirty generations, perhaps more. But let me explain something. I *am* taking your father to safety. And your brother, the young hothead. And you. There is no one else who, in this weather and under threat of being charged with treason, would dare have done it."

"But for *money!* When it's Scotland and the Rob Roys at stake!"

Royce looked angry now, and although he controlled it, the feeling was genuine. "I have my principles," he said, "and you have yours. And one of mine is not to invest emotion in lost causes."

"That's not true," she cried. "It is well known that you are a rebel at heart, capable of anything. I know that now. . . ."

"Hold your tongue, young lady. There are things you do not know, among them the measure of a man. Aye! They call me rebel, and I do take risks, but in the end it's my life, and I am the one who must make my choices and live with myself."

"If you are able to do that," she told him, with revulsion in her voice, "you would be able to live unnoticed in a den of wolves . . ."

A strange look came over his face then. She took little notice of it.

". . . but to make a profit from Scotland, from the misfortune of my father and his followers . . ."

She could not go on. Fligh grinned, enjoying the exchange. But when Royce spoke, his voice was softer, as if there were things he truly wished her to understand.

"Selena, many things have occurred which are beyond your understanding now. But you will understand in time. You may not believe that, and I am sure you think that I care nothing for you. I hope we do meet one day. You are going to be a splendid woman, and . . ."

Going to be?

". . . and you have the fire to endure the life upon which you are about to embark, and the intelligence to learn from it. . . ."

He *seemed* sincere. Selena hesitated, not knowing whether to believe him or not. The outrage of his mercenary actions had colored his image black in her mind.

"It is unnecessary for you to go on so. It is quite clear to me that you will make anyone the fool if it suits you."

"That is untrue."

"To a man like you, neither patriotism nor love are sacred."

Now his eyes glittered with a strange, secret feeling. "You are the kind of woman I do not need," he said. "Patriotism is just as private as love, and as unpredictable. Don't begin to judge others until you've learned a few things on your own."

"I can judge others, and I shall! You have taken me, with neither honesty nor love, just as you would take anything that promised to give you pleasure without consequences. . . ."

"If that's what you think." Royce said, looking away.

Fligh was laughing.

"Lieutenant, remember your position," Royce told him. Fligh stopped laughing, but continued to regard Selena with a kind of contemptuous amusement. Obviously, he did not care for her.

"You speak of understanding," Selena was saying. "Well, I understand *you* well enough."

Royce decided something. The cold, ironic smile appeared on his mouth. "All right, Selena," he said, with no feeling at all. "You may think yourself right about everything. I'd best admit my faults. A piece is just a piece to me, whether it be gold or womanflesh. There. I have confessed. How do you like it?"

But Selena had already turned away from him, and was racing down the passageways of the *Highlander*, past surprised sailors, to the security of the cabin. She was trembling, and her heart thundered, but she felt a savage satisfaction. Royce Campbell had been exorcised from her heart, burned from her brain. Now she would turn to duty, to saving the family, to the struggle for the future.

"Well, did you speak to him, Selena?" Brian asked grimly, coming up the passageway with a bag of gear in a sack across his shoulder. Lord Seamus slumped along behind him, bowed and disconsolate.

"I did," she said. "We are finished with him forever."

"I hope not, Selena," Father cautioned. "We must still rely on him for passage to America in the spring."

Liverpool! In her anger, she had forgotten about the proposed rendezvous.

"Well, I am finished with him, even so!" she declared.

She believed it, at that moment. But her body did not.

The *Highlander* dropped anchor off the town of Pittenweem, on the north coast of the Firth of Forth, and the davits strained as the small boat was lowered into the sea. Selena did not look back. She heard the wind in the rigging, the taut smack and slap of the sails, and felt beside her, rolling easily in the swells, the heavy power of the great Campbell ship. She did not look up, nor look back, but in her mind's eye she saw Royce Campbell there on the bridge. *You can't be right*, she argued with him in her mind. *If you are cynical enough to believe that life and love are things that can be bought and sold, you are already defeated, already lost.*

Aren't you?

The other side of the agrument came crashing down.

Sean was the one who had loved, and where was he now? Father was a patriot, and so were she and Brian. And they were fugitives. But there aboard the *Highlander* stood Royce Campbell, money in his pocket, with neither man nor God to strike him down, neither love nor patriotism nor mercy to weaken him.

"I hope I never become like that," she said aloud.

None of them heard her, with the wind and the creaking of the oars, and the sailors struggled to bring the boat in close to shore. The boat rose and fell. Surf beat against the rocks along the coast. Sailors cursed and raged. Finally, just once, she turned and looked back at the *Highlander*. The distance was too great for her to discern Royce Campbell, even if he stayed on deck to watch the Mac-Phersons put ashore. Probably he had not, she thought. There in the tossing dinghy, Selena was poised between two worlds, as clear a division of past and future as there was likely ever to be. She steeled herself against the future, and made a private vow to survive, to endure, to do whatever must be done. The past was almost too painful to confront, but she inflicted upon herself one moment of raw, searing truth. Back there, safe upon his great ship, was the man who had lived within her mind and heart for an entire year. Father and Brian would call it infatuation, silly dreaming, the mooning of a girl, but Selena knew it had been more than that. Far more. Because that man, Royce Campbell, had evoked in her a passion greater than any feeling she had known. What would become of that passion she did not know, and the flurry of movement about her forced it from her mind. But it was there, and, like underground fires that smolder on and on, its future was as unpredictable as it was certain.

The worried sailors were in a rush to get them out of the boat as soon as possible, and carelessly tossed their few pathetic bundles of luggage down on the wet, windy shore, almost manhandling Selena over the gunwales. One of them slipped, and she spun sideways, regaining her balance, but not before plunging knee-deep into the icy surf, and she cried out as if she had been struck. Royce Campbell might stand for all that was heinous and deceitful, or all that was passionate and tender, and the future might lie before her like a parchment on which to write her will, but, oh, it would be lovely to be safe and warm.

"Good luck," called Lieutenant Fligh, who leaped back into the dinghy and pushed off. Merchandise delivered; assignment complete. The small boat moved with great difficulty back toward the shelter of the mother ship.

"Well," Lord Seamus said, picking up a ragged bundle, "let's get going. We'll freeze to death if we stay here. Worse, McGrover's bound to have deduced by now that we're not taking the west road out of Edinburgh."

He hoisted the bundle over his shoulder, bent beneath the weight. There was a look of doom about him, the vanquished refugee, a plight the more bitter for his having been a lord.

"Let's go," he said. "It's a long way to the Highlands."

It was a vastly different Scotland upon which Selena set foot, and she was different, too. Something had begun to change in her, which she did not fully understand, and over which she had little control. But she did have two things: life and time. These are of the greatest value, because of all things known, they cannot be replaced. But it is difficult to appreciate them fully, after the rest of your world has been destroyed.

ON THE RUN

Two weeks later they huddled in a cave in the Sidlaw Hills, northwest of Dundee, still several hundred miles from safety. Lord Seamus lay shivering, wrapped in his wet cloak near a feeble fire that Brian was trying to rouse.

"We've come but forty miles in a fortnight," Brian worried. "The whole of Scotland is alive with McGrover's fiends, I vow."

God, get me through this, Selena prayed. *Let me never be hunted again.*

Hunted. And on the run.

Lord Seamus was seized by a coughing spell. He shook convulsively, and tried to stop. The noise was as dangerous as the fire, beacons to the searching ears and eyes out there in the dark hills, coming for them.

"You'd best leave me," their father gasped, recovering from the spasm. Selena bent to pull the cloak more tightly about him, and he seized her forearm. The grip was weak, shuddery, and his eyes were distorted by fever. "Just let me keep the pistol," he insisted. "I do na wish t' fall beneath the tender mercies of the Secret Offices. Gi' me the pistol, and you and Brian flee."

Outside the cave, far away, there came a faint, steady sound, like fine rain on glass.

"Hoofbeats," Brian said, like a curse. He stood up and kicked dirt and ashes over the puny blaze. "I guess we have to forget about this. We can't risk the light, and being cold is better than being dead. Aye, maybe! God almighty, I was sure we were at least a day ahead of McGrover this time."

Without speaking, Selena gently pried her father's fingers

from her arm, and walked quietly to the mouth of the cave. Twilight was dying, red on the icy hills. To the south, a file of horsemen rounded the bend in the river, slowed, and came to a halt. She saw the white, frozen breath of the panting horses against dark trunks of trees, the horses themselves dark shapes against the snow. She watched intently as the minutes passed and the horses did not move, until the sun dropped down behind the hills and the horses and riders, too, became part of the darkness.

"What are they doing?" Brian asked, stepping up behind her.

Lord Seamus broke into another spasm of a horrible, clattering coughing.

"Listening," Selena said.

The coughing echoed and reechoed across the valley.

"All they must do is guess where it came from."

"Oh, leave me," Lord Seamus groaned, trying to sit up. "What's the use of all three of us dying?"

"What are we going to do?" Selena asked. "We're ended, sure as dawn, when morning comes."

"There's a village aboot two miles from here. Cargill. For all the good that'll do us." Brian worked in the darkness, trying to load the pistol. "One shot at a time, we have, and they out there have muskets. MacPhersons were not born to be rabbits under the gun."

"That's right!" exclaimed Selena. "And we're not going to be trapped in a hole like rabbits, either."

"Now, ye didna 'ear me say I wouldna be listenin' to other ideas," Brian said, after a moment, "an' as for you, Father, forget this business aboot the pistol. We've but enou' rounds for the Britishers."

"What are you thinking, Selena?" Lord Seamus rasped.

"That if we can't see them, they can't see us either. And by tomorrow morning, they won't be any farther away than they are now. Father, can you walk at all?"

Her boldness had served to raise his spirits slightly.

"Aye, that I can. Aboot ten feet, as the crow flies. Don't be a fool. Leave me the pistol and the two of you . . ."

"No," Brian said. He took Selena's hand and they crouched beside their father on the cold floor of the cave. "Selena is right. We shall make one last attempt. Perhaps there is someone in Cargill who will help us. Father?"

"I do na think so, son. The Rob Roys, most of us, were of the upper orders of society, or of the cities. In a town so small, I doubt we've many friends, or even people who've heard of us. Peasants who sense nobility on the run will waste no time in smelling the reward money."

"It's our only chance."

"Father, can't you walk at all?" Selena pleaded.

"It's no matter. I'll carry him," Brian decided. "And we should separate. Selena, you wait here for a while after we leave, and . . ."

"No. I can move faster. If I'm seen at all, they will follow me. You would stand a better chance of evading them."

"All right." Brian stood up.

"Have you the pistol?" Lord Seamus asked.

"Yes. And loaded."

"Then give your sister the knife."

"Why?"

"Come down to me, both of you," Lord Seamus said. They complied, and he reached for their hands. "Now you join hands, also," he told them. They did, the three of them a circle now. "What I must tell you now is the hardest thing I've ever done, but it is necessary. It comes from love. You have heard of the things that happen when a fugitive is captured, and what is done to one. That must not happen to either of you, or to me. Even dead, I would weep should such suffering come to either of you. So you must make me a promise now. Are you ready?"

Brian nodded.

"Selena?"

"Yes, I'm ready."

"First, let us remember the good things," their father said quietly. "Remember your mother, and how sweet she was, and how it was with all of us when you were young. Pick out a special day, one that warmed you so much and in a manner so fine, the heat of it can reach across the years and touch you now in our misfortune. . . ."

Selena thought back over eighteen years that now seemed to have passed with terrible swiftness. She was about four or five, playing in the summer garden at Coldstream, building out of vines and sticks, grass and flowers, her own miniature castle, to be peopled by phantoms now long forgotten. For hours she worked away at that castle, the tiny girl she had once been, and then—she couldn't remember exactly—something had happened. The wonderful structure was destroyed, torn down, or perhaps fallen in upon itself. In response to her tears and cries, Father came out into the garden, viewed the disaster, and pronounced it less than the ultimate tragedy it seemed. And, for the rest of that lost, golden afternoon, he sat beside her in the warm grass, with the perfume of flowers in the air, and together they built a castle, of love as well as grass, that reached up to where he said the sky began. "Right here, Selena," she remembered him saying, as he touched the castle top. "Can you touch it? This is where the sky begins."

"Do you have that memory?" he asked now, rasping in that lost cave in the hills.

"Yes," she answered, squeezing his hand in her own. "Yes," said Brian hoarsely.

"Then, one more thing. Remember Coldstream. Think of it now. Not as it looks when you ride down toward it out of the Lammermuir Hills, but the way it looks when you come up to it from the sea, with the clouds moving in the sky beyond, and Coldstream riding against the sky like a great ship. Carried us for centuries, it has, across . . ." His voice broke, and he coughed again, to hide his emotion. When he spoke again, he was in control. "Remember it that way, and the way it will always be to us, no matter what happens."

"Yes," they said together.

"But that is not the promise," he said. "Brian, have you given Selena the knife?"

"No."

"Do it."

In a moment, Selena felt the cold steel against her flesh, and took it.

"This you must promise," their father commanded. "If you are to be taken by the police, or officers of the Crown, fall upon that knife. Put it to your breast and fall upon it, before their arms are on you. Do you promise that?"

She said nothing.

"Selena, the pain of the blade will be nothing compared to the pain they will inflict upon you, and even that will be nothing to the humiliation of a MacPherson in chains. . . ."

"I promise," she said, and with her finger she felt the sharp blade of the knife.

"Brian, you and I will be together. You must promise to obey me, as you always have. Will you do this?"

"Yes," Brian said, and Selena imagined the two of them encircled and helpless, and what would have to happen then. . . .

She shut it out.

"All right," Lord Seamus said. "I love you both, as I always have. Long live Scotland."

Without another word, Selena made her way to the mouth of the cave, and slipped out into the snow.

The night was colder than it had been; the sky was clearing. Across the valley, patches of fast-moving, wind-driven clouds alternately shrouded and revealed a cold wafer of moon. Pressed up close against the rocky hill, she looked down to the bend in the river where the horses had been and saw, in a flash of moonlight, a circle of the animals and what appeared to be the figure of a man standing nearby, possibly on watch. She waited until clouds welled up again, and slipped away in the momentary darkness.

Dismal as the sailor's uniform was in appearance, it did offer protection against the icy air, and the rope-soled shoes seldom betrayed her by slipping on the snow. Quickly, taking advantage of the cloud cover, she ran about a hundred yards beyond the cave, and then began to climb over the hills, beyond which lay the village of Cargill.

Climbing carefully and fast, Selena felt exhilarated in spite of the circumstances, felt a keenness from the clear air, the decision to run, the activity itself, an intensity mitigated only by the knife she had wrapped in a length of tarpaulin and tied to her belt.

Near the top of the hill, she rested, turning to look down. Far below was the jutting rock where the cave was, and the ribbon of river winding through the valley, and the dark patch of horses and men down at the bend in the river. She saw it all in a pattern of darkness and light, chiaroscuro fashioned by the cloud-veiled moon. Then a wind rose, high and sudden, out of the Highlands. The last of the clouds shot away into the sky, bathing the valley in light. She saw it all in a terrible, frozen moment. Brian at the mouth of the cave, carrying Lord MacPherson on his back.

The heads of the horses jerking upward, as the man on watch cried out, and she herself outlined dark against the gleaming white crest of the hill. The last thing she saw before turning to run again was Brian trying to run for cover. Then she heard the blast of the first musket, and the dull echo of the report rolling through the valley.

She was halfway down the opposite side of the hill—in the distance she could already see the few flickering lights of what must be Cargill—when she heard the thin crack of the pistol. She stopped and waited, not breathing, not daring to think, for at least a minute. Men were shouting, and horses neighed.

But the second pistol shot was as clear as the first.

Then she was running again, not remembering—trying not to remember—the day in the garden long ago. Her eyes blurred with tears which ran down on her cheeks and froze there, to be melted and refrozen as more tears ran down. The knife banged against her as she ran. Someone in the village would help her! There must be someone who would!

Breathless and panting, Selena came to the bottom of the hill. A small stream, lined with brush and thin willows and old, gnarled tree trunks, ran along this side of the village, and a wooden bridge crossed it. Making toward the bridge, she looked back to see, at the top of the hill over which she'd fled, the figure of a man on horseback, scanning the valley below. Deciding instantly, she forgot about the bridge, and dived, sliding on the embankment, down onto the frozen ice. The ice burned her hands, clung to the wool of the uniform. And, crouching there, she saw the horseman start down after her.

The bridge would have led directly into the town, a tiny hamlet of steepled church and low huts, which seemed to huddle together in the cold. Candles flickered in a few of them, the light slanting in evanescent planes through chinks in the planking. The horse was picking its way down the slope now, and more horsemen had appeared at the top of the hill, dark messengers of her demise. But not yet! Not yet! Everything was forgotten now except the possibility of deliverance, the desire for a few more moments of this night, this life, however bad it was. Feeling the knife against her body, she pulled her way out of the bed of the stream, and raced through a stripped thicket, approaching the village from the back.

The first hut she reached was dark, and so was the next. But the third, which faced on the road that ran through the town, showed the wavering light of a fire in the one small window. If someone would let her in . . .

Cautiously, she made her way through a putrid alley between two of the huts, and paused at the corner. And knew she was lost. Because to enter the hut, she would have to go out in front of it, onto the road. And, from one side of the village, she heard the sound of hoofbeats battering across the bridge even before she saw the rider, cape flaring behind him. While, from the other side, another half-dozen horsemen galloped toward her, the moon stark and ghostly on their faces.

Hoofbeats on the roads of Scotland, nine long years ago. There had been death then, too. But perhaps there was another moment to be savored, even in fear, even in flight. No longer caring if they saw her—with luck, they might not—she slid along the rude planking of the hut, pressed tight beside the door, reached for the latch, prayed, and felt the door give way. She leaped inside, slammed the door. Hoofbeats came up the street from the direction of the bridge, and slowed in front of the hut. The other horses drew nearer. Knife in hand, she turned to face the desperate, frightened eyes of a woman huddled beneath a blanket on a pallet next to the waning fire, and the startled, then puzzled look of the man under the blanket with her. The three of them looked at one another for no more than an instant—there was no time for words—and then the door crashed open again, and a huge, raw, black-bearded man stood against the moon, his riding cape draped down to his spurs. Outside, the rest of the horses drew up, halted. Men were shouting.

"Selena," the man said gruffly, and lifted a huge hand toward her. Two of the fingers were missing, a bloody bandage wrapped about the stumps.

She did not speak, but backed into a corner of the stinking hut—*I should have done it in the cold hills. I should not have to end it here*—and turned the blade of the knife upon herself.

The man leaped for her, but before he did so, she had

the time. She had the time to ram the blade into her heart, right up to the hilt, or to fall upon it, or to push against the wall, and feel the steel go into her. The promise flowered in her mind, and all that capture might mean, and everything that would be done to her. She knew what she must do, and she had the time to do it. But she did not do it. In that one mutable instant, she did not want to die. Not yet.

Then the man was upon her, yanking the knife from her hand.

"Dammit," he muttered, "shut up and do as I say."

Outside, men were running for the hut. "Who's in there? I saw a man go in. Is it MacPherson?"

Selena, in a grip of steel, felt herself half flung and half dragged toward the pallet on which the terrified peasant couple lay quivering. Her captor's beard was harsh against her face when he jerked her close and snarled:

"You don't move, and don't say a word."

With that, he yanked aside the bedclothes on the pallet and shoved her down between the naked man and woman, throwing the blankets on top of the three of them. "And you," she heard him snarl at the other two, "one word an' 'tis yer lives."

Beneath the reeking blankets, Selena smelled their peasant fear, and all the rest of them there was to smell. Then the door crashed open again.

"Don't ye move, laddie!" came a voice at the door.

And then the bearded man, contemptuously: "An' what be the meanin' o' this, you scum? I be o' McGrover."

"McGrover? We serve McGrover in this sector. What's yer business in this hut?" The voice held a note of doubt.

A third voice, at the door, told the others outside, "'Tis all right. 'E says 'e's wi' us."

"I be huntin' MacPhersons, what else?" came the bearded man's scornful growl. "We were riding in the Sidlaw Hills. Mayhap I lost myself and rode off course. . . ."

But even Selena, choking in the body-reeking pallet, heard the false note in his voice, and there was sudden movement in the room, a wordless oath, and the blankets were yanked away.

She looked up into the haughty face of the purple-coated lieutenant who had stopped them on the road to Edinburgh. He had *his* instant, this time. He spent it open-

ing his mouth in surprise, beginning a smile of cruel pleasure. It was a bad choice. He should have turned to face
the bearded man, who brought down Selena's knife at a
point just above the nape of the neck—the place on a man
that is like the place sought by the bullfighter on the neck
of his beast—and blood leaped from the lieutenant like a red
torrent as he dropped to the floor.

The hut went wild for a frenzied moment. The bearded
man pulled the knife from his first victim, sidestepped the
rush of the second soldier, tripped him, and sent him flying
headfirst into the fire. His screams came instantly. Selena
leaped out of the pallet, seized a poker, and brought it
down over the man's head. The noise stopped, but too late.
Already they heard the village waking. Two soldiers rushed
into the hut, but the bearded savior pulled twin pistols from
beneath his cape. Explosions flashed blue all around them.
Two more dead.

"Come," he ordered Selena, jamming the pistols back
into his belt. A fifth soldier burst in through the door at
that moment, to be met in the face with a huge fist.

"Ye left me one good one, an' ye've 'ad it, now," the
bearded man said, actually laughing, showing Selena a ragged line of broken white teeth.

He grabbed her hand.

"Let's go," he said, looking out into the street.

Everything had happened so fast that Selena did not yet
trust her impressions. Obviously this man was a friend, and
just as obviously he knew who she was, but . . .

"That's all of them," he said, looking out into the village.
In the doorways of many of the other huts, people stood in
nightshirts, watching, looking on in the doleful, patient
peasant way, afraid to act and not to act, afraid to live or
to die.

"Gutless bastards," the man growled.

"Who are you?"

He looked at her. "I'm Will Teviot," he said. "I'm one of
your father's captains. An' will ye look at this!" With a
sweeping gesture of his arm, he indicated the surrounding
peasantry. "Do ye know what? McGrover 'imself was 'ere
in this village today, an' on the morrow all these good people were t' be huntin' for ye in the 'ills." He turned toward
the man and woman, whose hut had, in an instant, become

the setting for frenzied violence. The woman was wrapped in a blanket now; the man had managed to get into a pair of breeches. He stood there, barechested, barefooted, doing a jittery dance in the lieutenant's purple blood.

"Tell Lady MacPherson what yer stinkin' plans were, pig.

The woman buried her head. The man never stopped his absurd dance as he denied.

"Aw, naw, yer 'ighness, yer lordship, t'warn't t' be lak 'at a'tall. Aw naw yer 'ighness. . . ."

"See this!" Will Teviot raised his mutilated hand. "The scum you serve like low dogs cut these fingers off me in Edinburgh, because I want Scotland free. And see these?" He smiled brutally, showing his shattered teeth. "Darius McGrover did this for me with an iron bar. But I escaped. I got away, an' no luck to you."

He took Selena's knife, made one step forward. His arm made an arc in the air, too fast to follow, and there was a sound not unlike the *scritch* of a scissor snip.

Blood was everywhere, and Will Teviot held a man's head in his huge hand. "Pig," he said. "We're not done yet. Here 'e is, sweets," he said, and tossed the severed head onto the pallet, where the now-screaming woman swayed in terror. Selena herself felt faint, unreal, as if she were drowning in nightmare waters, but something kept her going, something that was more than Will Teviot's steel. It would be some time before she realized it was her own steely will, growing inside her.

"Ye want 'er tongue, do ye?" Will was asking.

Selena shook her head. "Let's go."

They went outside and Will picked the best of the military horses for her, as well as blankets and a soldier's greatcoat. Checking saddlebags, he found food and whiskey, and strapped them onto his horse, then mounted himself.

"Ye've a dead neighbor, my friends," he called to the silent, watching peasants. "Just remember' that Darius McGrover did it to 'im, as 'e'll do it t' you."

Then they were on the horses and galloping from the village, flying toward the Highlands, under moonlight.

Much later, they stopped, dismounted, and Will Teviot unbuckled the saddlebag of supplies. Directly, he uncorked the whiskey and took long gulps of it.

"Do na mind m' manners, Selena," he grinned. "These are rough times 'at we're livin' in. But I swear some nights I do lak 'em fine."

He handed her the bottle, and, after a moment's hesitation, she wiped the mouth with the palm of her hand, hoisted it, and drank. Ravenously, they ate smoked meat and fresh bread. "Them Britishers know 'ow t' travel," Will begrudged, and he told her what had happened.

He himself had been arrested at the castle on the night of the ball, and imprisoned in the dungeons beneath. As a Rob Roy captain, his torture had been observed by McGrover himself, who watched as first one finger and then another were cut off. "The pain was terrible, but I kept cursin' McGrover an' King George," Will said. "O' course, the pain would've been much greater, but McGrover lost 'is temper an' 'it me in the mouth. I passed out. Very unprofessional. When I come to, I was alone, and they hadn't bothered puttin' me in chains. 'Twas very noisy, too, with all the screamin', an' I got away."

Later, he had learned from Gil that the MacPhersons had been landed at Pittenweem, then headed for the Highlands. Will Teviot organized a mission of his own, and set out to find them.

"An' we did, too, sure enough. Yer father an' Brian'll be 'eadin' north wi' the rest o' my men. I'm Rob Roy captain of all Ross and Cromarty Province. We can cross that country with ease and in safety."

"Cross it? What's our destination?"

"A tiny village. Kinlochbervie. Way out on the northwest coast. Ye'll stay there until spring. No one'll get ye there, not even McGrover. The land's too rough, and the Rob Roys'll protect you in the Highlands."

If they could get there, safety seemed possible. Selena knew that country from her summers in Mount Foinaven, at the hunting lodge. She allowed herself to think of the future, and even of Royce Campbell, who, bought and paid for, would be at Liverpool in the spring. But the thought of Royce made her feel betrayed again, and guilty and confused, all at the same time.

"Tell me," she asked Will, "that night at the castle. Did you see or hear anything of Sean Bloodwell?"

"Nay, I didna see 'im, but I'm sure they were lookin' for 'im."

"He wasn't a Rob Roy, though?"

"Nay. Nay, but 'e gi'e us money. I doubt if McGrover'd be makin' great distinctions on a point like 'at."

Soon they remounted and rode on through the night. Dawn came finally, and Will said they were in safe country. But Selena thought the sun was a liar. Daybreak promised nothing more than the beginning of long darkness.

BITTER SANCTUARY

"But I *heard* two pistol shots," Selena said, half-laughing, half-crying.

"Brian did no better than you," Lord Seamus replied, holding her close. "When the time came to do as I'd told him, he tried to take out two Rob Roys instead. Had they been the King's men I do wish his aim had been better."

"That I guarantee," Brian promised. "My marksmanship needs some work. But I will guarantee too that if the Britishers want me dead, they must do it themselves. I'll not give them help, nor even think upon it anymore."

Their father had no such bravado. "Someday it may be necessary again."

Then, exhausted from the trip through the Highlands, he slumped to the pile of blankets on the floor of the stone house, and looked around. "Well, it's solid, anyway," he said.

"Aye, that it is," Will Teviot agreed. "They'll be no Britishers can get ye 'ere."

Will and Selena had arrived in Kinlochbervie, a tiny, rock-rimmed fishing village, two days previously. They knew Brian and Lord Seamus would be along at any time, and the problem was to find lodging for them to spend the rest of the winter. Kinlochbervie had been chosen by the Rob Roys as a hiding place *in extremis*—an exile, truly—but what it offered in remoteness it lacked in accommodations. The inhabitants numbered no more than a hundred souls, almost all of them fishermen, and if the arrival of strangers in the middle of winter stirred their curiosity, it also nudged the acquisitive instinct. Will Teviot towered over them, asking for "a sturdy house for a few fortnights," and jingling gold pieces in his leather purse. They looked up at him, awed at his height but suspicious nonetheless, and they looked at Selena beside him, her gender unconcealed by the cloak and the uniform beneath it. There was a long moment of doubt, until Will explained that he was the girl's guardian and that her father and brother would be arriving shortly. They would be staying awhile because of the father's health, Will explained, smiling at them as warmly as possible with his jagged line of broken teeth.

He jingled the money again.

So one old fisherman and his wife and his rickety son moved out of their stone hut, and made arrangements to quarter in the cellar of the village church—after promising the dubious pastor a "worthy measure" of their golden windfall. The hut was at the edge of the village, on the high, rocky cliff that overlooked the wild winter waters of the North Minch. It had but one room—there would be no privacy—and one fireplace with an iron grill suspended in it, on which to cook. There were no beds, and only a few stools and a block of wood that resembled a table and stank of fish. Fishnets and fishing equipment hung from the walls, and long poles rested in curved hooks that were screwed into the ceiling, which was itself so low that Will Teviot had to crouch over every time he entered.

"'Twill be terrible crowded, and no lie," he muttered to Selena, as they inspected the place for the first time, "but there's no choice we 'ave, as you can see it."

She agreed. At that point, shelter—any shelter—meant rest. She did not reckon with the fact of their bodies confined in that tiny space, not until her father and Brian rode into the village two afternoons later. Lord Seamus, clearly exhausted and genuinely sick, embraced her with great love, and collapsed on the floor. Selena put the kettle over the fire for tea, and cast a worried glance at Brian. His answering look confirmed her worst fears. Their father was very ill.

"So this is be our refuge," said Brian, looking around. "'Tis hardly Coldstream, is it?"

"Do not speak of Coldstream," she said hotly, and stared into the fire. Since arriving here in Kinlochbervie, Selena had resolved not to think of the past, nor of the future beyond April, when they would board ship for America. This was limbo, in the language of the ancient church, and when you were in limbo you were neither here nor there, although you still existed. That was how it would be, she had resolved. She would live, but she would not feel, and she would think of nothing painful.

Like most resolutions, it was easy enough to make, far more difficult to follow.

Nothing in her life had prepared her for what she had to face. At Coldstream, there were servants to tend to every conceivable task, servants to light the fires in the morning and to bring tea upon awakening. Servants to lay out one's clothes, to bathe one, to fetch one's food, or book, or horse. Servants to dim the candles in the eventime and close the canopied bed curtains on love or slumber. Here, in Kinlochbervie, there was their father, and Brian, and Will, and Selena. Mostly Selena.

The problems were obvious: Lord Seamus was sick, food was scarce, the stone house was crowded, winter was harsh. And they could never let down their guard. In spite of the remoteness of the village, and the Rob Roys on watch in the Highland passes, anything might happen, and they would have to be ready to fight or run when—and if—it did. But immediately after the almost euphoric joy of their reunion, tensions began to grow.

It was inevitable, given the circumstances. Lord Seamus needed constant care. Within hours of his arrival, he was deep in fever, tossing about on the floor, and alternately throwing off his blankets, his face pouring sweat, or gathering them about him, shivering like a hanged man at the end of a rope. He gave speeches of portentous gibberish, waving his arms, eyes wide and wild on a vast but unseen audience. He thundered doom and justice upon invisible malefactors. Then he collapsed again. Finally the fever passed, but he was so weak they had to lift his head to spoon hot tea into his mouth.

In the meantime, Selena had to cook, an unfamiliar task made more difficult by the fact that little existed with which to do it. Brian's task was to gather wood for the fire—no easy job in winter on the seacoast—or to buy peat with the dwindling supply of money which also must be used to purchase food. Will Teviot made that his business, and went off daily to the houses in the village, but all he brought back—all there *was* in the village—were tiny bags of beans, grudgingly sold and dearly bought, which must be boiled for half a day in order to be edible. Or slabs of half-dried, half-rotten fish, or once, with great heartiness at his success, the frozen carcass of a hare killed in the Highlands by a boy with a slingshot. Selena had no idea what to do with it, and when her discomfiture became obvious, Will roared with laughter, shoved a sword through the animal, and devised a barbecue above the fire. They drank the last of his good whiskey that night, and had a feast, too, but it was the end of the line for them. In the days thereafter, everything deteriorated.

Will and Brian were high-spirited, strong-willed men, and Lord Seamus was too ill to exert his usual influence over them. They had planned to divide tasks evenly, and to alternate their watches through the night. But very soon the monotony of confinement, the crowded conditions in the hut, put the lie to their stated intentions. His whiskey gone, Will began to frequent the mead shop in the village, where he spent money needed for food on great quantities of potent but harsh brandy, and malt Scotch so thick you could float an egg on top of it. Then he would return to the hut to sleep and sweat in front of the fire, his drunken snores rattling all night long. Brian laughed at first, then cursed, swearing he could stand no more of it.

Selena slept in the corner opposite the fireplace. It was the coldest place in the hut, but she had ensured herself a measure of privacy by draping a large blanket over the two stools, then sleeping behind the barrier. The men did all they could to accommodate her, but the stone house was simply too small. It was not long before she felt Will's dark eyes on her constantly, and at night, when she lay awake listening to the fire and violating her resolution not to think about the past, the demands of her own nature, fully awakened by Royce Campbell, came to tempt and taunt her. They were complicated things, love and desire, and she tried at first not to think about them. But she could not abandon the puzzle. *I have now known passion,* she thought, and the memory of the feeling was almost as keen as the feeling itself had been, the memory of desire evoking greater desire. But Royce Campbell was the complication, because not only were love and desire intermingled, there was also the matter of his cynical, deceitful nature, which she could neither match nor interpret. The sadness came then, when she let herself think about Royce, because that led her to think of Sean Bloodwell. And then the guilt would rise, and she would remember—tears flowing now, sobs stifled—all the plans their father had made. They were gone now, as lost as the summer day when Sean Bloodwell had undone her bodice and told her for the first time that he loved her.

Royce Campbell had said nothing of love, but had taken her and used her and cast her off.

But he could awaken in her feelings and emotions which seemed to her, there in the corner behind her blankets, quite incapable of dying, ever.

Sean Bloodwell was never mentioned in the stone hut, nor was Royce Campbell, but both of them were there.

The winter ground on, day by day. Lord Seamus seemed to be growing stronger, rallying some days, then lapsing into fitful sleep. Brian, like a tethered horse, became impatient, bossy, and Will was alternately morose or ebullient, depending on how much liquor he had drunk. One night late in February, the tensions all came to a head.

Will had gotten very drunk the night before, but managed to struggle out of the hut late in the afternoon. He brought back a few handfuls of dried beans, and that was all. It was too late to soak them properly, so Selena boiled them hard, and when the men began asking for supper, she spooned them onto the usual cracked stone plates and served them with a piece of black bread and cups of weak tea. There was no salt anymore; there had never been sugar. And goat's milk was no longer purchased, in order to save a tiny cache of gold in case someone needed to be bribed at Liverpool.

The men sat in a semicircle before the fire. She handed them the plates. Father hunched over and ate hurriedly, like an animal. His hands shook so, he seemed bent upon eating everything before he dropped the plate. Will took his plate, and grunted, looking down at the hard, ruddy beans. Brian took a spoonful, chewed for a moment, stopped, and looked up at her.

"What is this *merde* you feed us?" he snarled.

"The same your warrior friend buys, drunk, and brings home," she shot back, pouring a cup of tea.

Will Teviot looked up, rage building behind bleary eyes. "Ye didna seem t' 'ave such spite fer me when I saved ye in the hills, now did ye, *bitch!*"

Selena bit her lip, but it was too late. Brian hurled his plate against the stone wall, and jumped to his feet. "Mind yer mouth, ye jagged-toothed freak," he cried, and swung at Will, who leaned away, rolled on the floor, and jumped to his feet, ready for battle. Selena screamed. Lord Seamus was too weak to intervene, and watched them hopelessly. Brian and Will faced each other, fists ready. Then the spirit left their faces, and their arms went down. Will flung himself out of the hut, and Brian told Selena he was going for a walk along the sea to clear his head. When they were gone, she brought her father his tea, and sat with him.

"It won't be much longer now, Selena," he said, making an effort to smile.

She fought back tears. "It's still February. There is over a month yet to pass, and already we are like animals at each other's throats."

"We must bear it. I feel myself getting stronger. We will make it yet. The thing to remember is that anger during times of misfortune is forgotten quickly when luck returns."

"Do you think that's true?"

"Yes. And luck will return. When we reach America . . ."

The prospect was one of the things she had been holding in abeyance, not thinking about, as if to think of it at all might abnegate the very possibility. "Father, what will we do there? What are your plans for us?"

He looked away into the fire for a time, deciding how much to reveal. "I hope to continue the fight against Great Britain," he said then, slowly. "Now, more than ever. Whether in the long run it will lead to a free Scotland, I do not know. But the Empire and all that lies behind it is like a rock in my belly. I hope I live long enough."

"But the trip to Liverpool. Will it be safe? What if McGrover knows we're going there? What if his men are waiting?"

He sighed, and seemed to flag visibly.

"It is our one chance, and we must take it. Would you help me to my blankets now, Selena? I must rest."

She did so, and then added a few pieces of precious drift-wood to the fire, knowing that Brian would yell at her for it, because her indulgence meant more work for him. At the same time, though, he would yell if the hut became too cold. After a time, she crept to her place behind the blanket barrier and dropped off to sleep.

She was awakened by the clatter of the two protective stools being pushed aside. The fire was almost out, and a big form crouched beside her. She smelled the liquor hot on Will's breath, as he bent over her, his hands rough and searching.

"Will!" she cried, in a hoarse whisper. A quick look about the hut showed her Brian had not returned. Then the thought struck her: maybe Will and Brian *had* fought, and her brother was even now lying unconscious somewhere in the snow. If so, she was defenseless, and Will was as determined as he was drunk.

Because of the constant cold, Selena slept in the uniform, but this proved no obstacle, and with one mighty rip, Will tore it down the front. She felt the cold air on her breasts, and then his hands, and then his mouth. A rough hand slipped, fumbling, beneath the breeches and between her thighs.

"Will, stop it! Get away!" she told him as calmly as she could, putting both hands on his shoulder and trying to push him away. It didn't work. Her resistance seemed to excite him more, and he took her nipple between his teeth and bit. She cried out in pain. He seemed startled and raised his head, grinning doubtfully, running his tongue over the savaged teeth.

"I don't mean nothin', Selena, 'tis just that I must . . ." and with that he lay down beside her, pinning her there with one huge arm, and slobbering a drunken kiss on the side of her face. She could feel his manhood, already exposed, throbbing hot against her thigh. Her first instinct was to scream and struggle, but she knew struggling would be of no avail against a man as big as Will Teviot, and she did not want her father to know. So she forced herself to stay calm, to buy time. If he wanted her, he would take her, and no doubt of it, but if she could refrain from enraging him, his drunken state and his passion might be used against him.

"Please, Selena," he was muttering, slobbering, forcing her legs apart with his huge hand, and she started as the hand touched tender flesh. A short, involuntary cry escaped her.

"Lak it, do ye?" Will asked, and shifted his weight to mount her.

"No, no," she whispered, softly now, trying to pull him back down next to her. "Not yet."

He stopped, on his knees beside her, puzzled.

"I said not yet," she whispered, trying for the right tone. With one arm around his neck, she pulled his head down to hers, and with the other hand she sought that part of him in which his brain was temporarily buried.

"Go slowly," she whispered, stroking him. "It will be of greater pleasure if we take the time."

For one amazed moment, he hesitated, and then she could feel him decide, acquiesce. She took a deep breath and kissed him on the mouth, easing slightly out of his grasp as she did so, and thinking incongruously of how it had been with Royce Campbell, how there had been a certain look about him, at one moment, when he had been entirely and utterly in her power. It was a moment that any man could be brought to, and if she could do it now . . .

Selena broke off the kiss and slid a little to the side.

"Lie back," she whispered, and continued to stroke him gently, but a little faster now.

What offered her ploy the chance of success was her knowledge that, for all his strength and ready fury, Will Teviot was a good man. She eased him, befuddled by drink and amazed at his luck, down next to her until he was lying on his back. Slowly, still caressing him, she rose into a half-seated position, braced on one arm. Then she felt his big arm slip proprietarily around her waist. But his breath was coming fast now. Watching for the time to break and run, she lengthened and accelerated her stroke, and he gasped, breath whistling between his teeth. On the other side of the room, next to the fire, Father was sleeping. Only five feet away was the door, but outside it was freezing, and she was half-naked, her breasts exposed. If she could leap up and somehow grab a blanket, what then? Would he pursue her out into the snow and take her there, enraged? Or would he come to his senses? She decided.

"All right now," she said, shifting her weight slowly, to be ready, and continuing to pleasure him at a steady pace. Will panted now, his body bucking beneath her hand.

Then she whipped back her hand, leaped up, and reached the door, yanking it open even as she sought to draw the edges of the ripped uniform back across her bosom.

Brian was walking toward her, only paces away. His eyes widened in surprise, then alarm.

Behind her, in the hut, Will's moan of abandonment and need changed to a growl of anger.

Brian rushed into the hut. The two men confronted each other. Will sought to cover himself, but too late. Brian saw the torn uniform, the fear on Selena's face, and then Will's own downcast aspect of shame and sorrow and disgust. There was no more to be said. It was all over for them.

Will left the next morning. He had pleaded with Selena not to tell her father what had happened—"Yer Father's one o' the bravest an' most decent men I ever knew, an' once 'e let me save ye, 'cause 'e trusted me, so, please, I'm askin' ye, don't . . ."—and she told him she would not now, and never would.

"It was not Will Teviot did that, last night," she told him. "It did not happen. God grant someday I have the chance to pay you back for helping all of us."

So, when he told Lord Seamus in the morning that he was leaving, he explained his decision in another light.

"Sir, 'tis clear we 'aven't the food fer four, an' after all this time, I think ye'll be safe 'til April. I figure on goin' t' Iceland first, an' then mayhap t' Nova Scotia, t' see some o' that New World we've been hearin' about, an' . . ."

If Lord Seamus suspected anything at all, he said nothing. Will's arguments about food and safety were plausible enough, and when he left the village on horseback, turning to wave at them one last time from the top of the rocky cliffs, Lord Seamus waved back, and said it was for the best.

"Godspeed, Will Teviot," he murmured to the empty air, waving across the distance to the horseman on the hill. "Godspeed, and if things come out even in this life, the MacPhersons owe ye a lot before the ledger's closed."

Back in the hut, it was quiet for almost the entire day, but in late afternoon, with the sun dropping down into the diamond-glinting sea, Selena looked up from the sewing of her clothes. The sound was unmistakable. Hoofbeats, coming down from the cliffs. Had something happened? Had Will Teviot been forced to turn back? Or were they under attack?

Hastily, she wrapped a blanket around her shoulders and went to the door. The horseman rode fast, with confidence and flair, yet with a hint of anxiety. The horse was white, and the rider, who wore a heavy winter cloak of blue trimmed with gold, saw her at the hut, and guided his mount toward her, never slackening the pace. He knew it was she. And she knew immediately, felt immediately—the solid, commanding figure in the saddle, the vigorous blond looks—that it was Sean Bloodwell, come for her.

A second chance.

I won't fail anyone this time, she vowed to herself. *I will do what I should have in the first place, before I went mad with Royce Campbell.*

And she believed it. And it was true.

If Sean Bloodwell was surprised at receiving such a passionate, loving kiss from the young woman in the sailor's breeches and the blanket—in the full sight of almost a hundred villagers' eyes—he certainly did not show it.

He hugged her, and kissed her with an abandon equal to hers.

"Selena! Thank God you're safe. I met Will Teviot in the hills. He said your father's none too good. . . ."

Excited and grateful, Selena drew back from Sean a little. He looked tired, and a little older than when she'd last seen him. But it had been a long trip; fatigue was to be expected.

"I'm so glad you've come," she said. "Did Will tell you? We're having a hard time of it here. I don't know if we can endure until spring. . . ."

Sean glanced at the crude stone sanctuary and nodded grimly.

"Better than execution or other things I might name," he said, putting his arm around her and leading her toward the hut. "I must see your father before I . . ."

He stopped as Selena opened the door for him. He saw

Lord Seamus against the wall, an old man wrapped in blankets. The acrid smoke of the fire stung his eyes. He grimaced. Selena read his expression. He understood how far the MacPhersons had fallen. Just a few months ago, Selena had been a princess of nobility, taking for granted all the privileges which were accorded her, taking for granted, too, the attentions of Sean, for whom, as a wife, she would be a precious and glittering prize. But all that was gone. Now she was the daughter of a traitor. She lived in a hut like a hunted animal, and looked to the whims of blackguards like Royce Campbell for transport to safety, having already been his captive and possession in the flesh. She had nothing.

Thank God Sean was the kind of man he was. Thank God, even more, that he was wealthy.

She took him into the house, making no excuses. Lord Seamus struggled to his feet—he had a dignity that only death would ultimately eradicate—and the two men shook hands.

"Please, your lordship," said Sean, motioning the older man back to his blankets. "I met Will Teviot in the Highlands. He said you . . . had been ill."

Her father's eyes were bright. He saw deliverance in Sean Bloodwell's unexpected visit. "Yes, I fell ill on the run, eluding McGrover. But I'm getting better now." Slowly, watchful of his bones, he settled down again next to the fire. "Selena, bring some tea."

"We've no more tea," she said, before she thought, "Brian went to the mead shop to see if he might borrow . . ."

She stopped. Sean Bloodwell was looking at her closely. She tried to smile. ". . . might buy a better kind. That last supply was really quite inferior. . . ."

She didn't bother to continue. He understood.

"Even warm water would be fine," he said quietly, and she hoped that the expression in his eyes was not pity. "Anything warm, in fact, after a ride like I've had."

"Are my men still in the Highlands?" Lord Seamus inquired, in a painfully transparent attempt to change the subject and to spare Selena further humiliation.

Sean's face darkened. He had been familiar with the plan of security: to shield Lord MacPherson in the coastal stronghold, behind the ring of rough country, guarded by hundreds of seasoned fighters.

"There are some men up there," he allowed.

Lord Seamus was not one to cherish illusions in the place of facts, when facts were needed. "Some?"

Sean was equally direct. "Sir, speaking the truth, as I know you want me to do, the Rob Roys are no more."

Selena, busy at the fire, and worrying about what she might possibly put together—or even obtain—for supper, was startled.

"No more? But there must be . . ." All this time they had savored visions of a small army guarding the Highland passes, protecting them. Her father silenced her with a gesture.

"And here above us, in the hills?" he asked Sean.

The young man shook his head. "Four or five stalwarts, and that's all. I was stopped only once. Even the last of them are preparing to melt away into the hills. . . ."

"I cannot say that I blame them," Lord Seamus said, after a pause, "but that means . . ."

He didn't have to say it. That meant a vulnerability more dangerous than before.

"And those taken in Edinburgh, the night of the ball?"

"Dead mostly, by now. The Rob Roys are gone, root and branch, with only here and there a bud saved, mostly by accident. McGrover and the Secret Offices handled it very well. The general public is not even aware that anything untoward has occurred. Torture uncovered the names of the Rob Roys, and executions took place in secret. The bodies of many a fine man now rot in the muck of the lowest dungeons, or feed the fishes on the bottom of the North Sea."

"What about Gil?" asked Selena. "The man who took me out to the coast that night? He was to go back and tell you where to find us. If McGrover found him—"

"McGrover found him," Sean said.

In the stillness, the fire crackled. Boiling water began whistling in the teapot.

"Dead," Sean said. "He came back into the city on the morning you went aboard the . . ." he seemed to have trouble uttering the word ". . . the *Highlander*, and found me in the castle. He told me where you would be, and for how long. He was captured only an hour after he left me."

"Then that means he must have told the police where we're hiding," cried Selena.

"No, thank the Lord. He didn't. I saw it happen. Gil was in the courtyard, and of course it was all pell-mell that day, with the arrests and the interrogations. He had to get out the main gate, but didn't want to be obvious about it, so he spent some time brushing his horse, talking to the grooms, waiting for the right chance. Finally, McGrover himself came riding in, and all the lackeys made for him, to lick his boots. It was Gil's moment. He mounted his horse slowly, and began to amble her toward the gate. There were still a few guards present, of course, and he rode up to them, easy as you please. They stopped him, and I saw one of the guards talk to him for a moment, and then the guard waved him through. I thought it was over then; I thought he was safe. Then the other guard seemed to have a second thought, and looked after Gil, as if he'd seen him before. He must have called out, although I was too distant to hear, because Gil suddenly spurred his horse, and the beast leaped forward into a run, but the sign of flight was damning enough. A sentry on the watchtower brought him down with a thrown lance."

The kettle was screaming now, and Selena set it off the fire.

"What have I done?" Lord Seamus grieved. "Devastation all about, and good men dead. Sean, I am going to make it up. We're going to America to begin again."

"Think of it all as over, sir," Sean managed. "We will all of us survive, and recoup what's lost."

Selena, pouring hot water into a pewter mug, felt a giddy elation at his words, which meant to her that nothing was changed, that they would go on as her father had planned. America, or wherever—he would get her out of here. There would not be Coldstream, not just now, but . . .

Brian entered then, bleak and empty-handed. She watched his face brighten with surprise and relief, and knew he was thinking, just as she had, that Sean Bloodwell meant deliverance. But Brian was less reticent than she had been about the difficulties of their circumstances.

". . . an' we've but three gold guineas saved for oiling the wheels in Liverpool, should such be necessary, and as

for the rest, only a ha'pence here an' a ha'pence there to get
us food. Just now, at the mead shop, they told me they'd
have to see gold, an' I've come back for one o' the
guineas. . . ."

Sean seemed concerned, but he did not hesitate. "I shall
ride over there now. My horse needs stabling for the night,
and I expect they've a place. They do? Good. I shall return
shortly with enough for all of us. Is there . . ." he glanced
around at the hut, ". . . a room in the town where I
might . . ."

"You're welcome to stay here," Selena said, with an ea-
gerness that lacked conviction.

"This town has no inn," Brian explained, giving her a
sharp look as he remembered Will Teviot. "No one ever
comes here."

"We shall decide later," Sean said. "Let me go now,
and . . ."

"I'll accompany you," Brian offered. "We could stand a
measure of Scotland's best . . ."

"No. We need firewood," Selena told him.

"Again? Selena, what do you do? Burn it all at once?
Just this morning, I . . ."

Sean laughed. "Brian, never fear. I shall bring back
plenty for all of us."

Brian went out with him, and Selena waited impatiently
for his return. They had much to discuss. When Brian
came back, alone, he said, "What luck! Just when I had
begun to think all was lost, we're saved."

But Lord Seamus was worried. "I do not know," he said
slowly. "We must talk more. It is too soon to believe we
have found sudden redemption. We are not even safe, and
Sean's presence here means he is not safe either. . . ."

It came to Selena immediately.

Either McGrover or his men might have followed Sean
Bloodwell here to the northwest coast.

Or . . . or, how had Sean himself fled Edinburgh Castle, when everyone knew that he was a favorite of Lord
MacPherson, and all but engaged to Selena?

Brian was too excited to be logical. "This time, sister,"
he ordered her, before going out to find wood for the fireplace, "this time don't be a silly, romantic little fool. Only
saints get a second chance as good as the first, and I don't

know what you are, but you're certainly no saint. So use your head, and when he asks you to marry . . ."

"Brian," Father said, "none of that."

"What shall I do?" Selena asked her father, when they were alone. "It isn't as Brian believes; it isn't as simple as that. I do love Sean. I should have loved him all along. But he knows—we all do—what a fool I made of myself over Sir Royce. Perhaps my chance with Sean is lost, and with it all your plans, and our family's future."

The burden was heavy on her, and her father motioned her to sit down next to him. He put his arm around her shoulders.

"Selena," he said gently, with a hint of the amused warmth that had always been in his eyes when he comforted her as a child, "Selena, God forbid, but this may be one of the last lessons I am favored to give you in this life—"

"Father, no! Don't say—"

"Hush. Who knows what is true? But here is your lesson: when you are free, truly free to choose your own desire, that will be the time when you discover what it is you are, and what it is you believe. Yes, I made plans for you to marry Sean. I made them for your happiness, but I also had the well-being of our family in mind. However, that future is no more. . . ."

"Yes, it is!" How could he say that? Coldstream would always be!

"Selena, face the facts. You must. That future which I had planned simply does not exist any longer. But it also means that you are, in a sense, *free to choose!* Don't you see? It is rather like a new world, and you do not even have to cross an ocean to possess it. . . ."

Yes, she was thinking. *That is all very well, but if I do not accept Sean this time, we will go on as we are. . . .*

"Do you love Sean Bloodwell now?" he was asking. "You are also free to answer that with your heart. Did you ever love him?"

The shards of many emotions splintered and scattered there, in the cold hut on the rocky, wild coast, the emotions almost as broken as her life. It was not as easy as her father believed. Yet she could say, in absolute truth, *I did love Sean.*

"And I do love him now," she decided, apart from the fact that he had come to help rescue them. Brian's words came back to her, too, with a special meaning and poignancy: *Only saints get a second chance.* A second chance. With Sean. With love. To have a future. To do the right thing. After she had failed in her first chance by giving in to her baser instincts, and all but ruining herself with Royce Campbell. Father felt the tension of her body, as she stiffened in his embrace.

"Is something the matter?"

"No," she lied. But something might be. How would Sean himself react when he discovered—as the Coldstream crones had assured her all men inevitably did—that she had been ruined? No, she could not think about that now. It would have to be dealt with at the proper time, in some way. The important thing was that she be honest this time, and responsible this time, and . . . and *mature* this time. The important thing was to make her vows to Sean, to be faithful to them and to him, to be worthy of the second chance.

And where was Royce Campbell now? Somewhere in Scotland, or the world? Where, tonight, would he lie down, and with whom?

Put that aside. You have had your lesson, the hard one from Royce and the gentle one from Father. You are not too thick to learn them both, and well.

Sean Bloodwell returned from the village, bringing with him a bottle of whiskey, one freshly caught fish, a loaf of hard bread, and a dozen potatoes, which, although withered, were not rotten. But he also brought back, without meaning to, an air of tension. Lord Seamus said little, and Brian was almost surly, as the two of them shared the whiskey with Sean. Selena cooked the meal as best she could, but gave up trying to cheer them when she realized what was happening. So many unspoken hopes were pinned upon Sean Bloodwell that none of them dared speak, lest all those hopes be dashed.

And Sean himself was unusually silent, too, as if considering a vast care he did not wish to share with the rest of them. Finally, the eating was finished, and they sat uncomfortably before the fire.

"Brian," his father asked, "how is it out tonight?"

"Cold, Father. Cold and clear. The wind has died."

"I think," he said too brightly, "that I could use a little air. Here, help me up and we'll go out for a moment."

So this was how it would be. She felt Sean's eyes touch her, then move away, and there was a hint of conspiracy in the room, which obscured her embarrassment.

"I have something to say to you," Sean began, when the other men were gone. He was standing, and she got up, too, and stood before him. They were both very serious, and spoke quietly. "And it is not going to be easy."

"Do not say it if you find it is too hard."

"Nay, I must."

"May I ask a question first? It is something I must know."

"Of course."

"How did you avoid being arrested? How were you allowed to leave Edinburgh Castle and come here to us?"

"You know that I was not a Rob Roy?"

"Yes, but you gave them funds, help."

"I did that because of your father, whom I respect. And . . ." he lowered his eyes ". . . and because of you. It was reckless of me, one of the few wild things I've done. I don't mean to say you caused me to participate, to give the money. I did that of my own free will, albeit with you in mind. Nevertheless, the fact that I was not of the Rob Roy party spared me arrest and interrogation. But . . ."

Once again she respected his ability to maneuver, a skill more subtle but not unlike Royce Campbell's bolder strokes. Sean had managed to save himself, and he loved her enough to come back for her, in spite of the fact that he had been in danger because of his association with the MacPhersons.

". . . but I must tell you this, Selena, so that you know. I am a child of the Empire. I am loyal to the Crown, and always will be. Do you know how much I have always wanted a title?"

She knew, and smiled involuntarily.

"Do not mock me. A title is an easy thing to wear, if you have it. But I want one and I shall have it someday. You see, although my father died a wealthy man, it was not always so. In the beginning, when he was building his fortune, the nobility treated him worse than they would have treated the oldest, mangiest, most flea-bitten hound in their kennels. When, in the beginning, he had to deal with them, to slowly buy from them the land under which our coal mines were later developed, he was made to go on his knees before the lords . . ."

Sean's face was hard now, in a way she had never seen, and beneath his words she heard the gall of shame and resolve.

". . . and other things were done of which I do not care to speak. But you must know, even after what has happened to you and your family, and in large part because of it, since I have learned my lesson as His Majesty's subject, there will be no hatred of England in my blood."

She looked at him. *So*, she thought, *such is his condition. And my condition is that I have been known by another man. We are neither of us pure.*

"I understand," she told him, and came closer. His eyes were troubled, and in his face there was great tenderness for her, and pain, and high regard. She understood now, even more clearly, what her father had told her: in free choice one must define oneself. Sean had made his decision, and offered it to her. She, in turn, must now accept what he was, what he believed, or reject him. He was waiting. Never had she loved or admired him more.

"If you will but take me as I am," she said, "then I am yours."

With that, Selena slipped out of the uniform top, and went to him, presenting herself and her nakedness. She had given herself to Royce Campbell, in lust; now she would give Sean the same, in love. In love and wisdom.

His arms went around her and she felt the leap of his desire, but something was wrong, something was terribly wrong.

"I can't," he said, his voice strained with anguish, his face torn between desire and . . . something else.

What could he mean? *I can't?* Of course, he could.

"It's all right," she told him. "I'm sorry if I caused you pain before. . . ."

"Selena, you didn't . . ."

"But I want this now. I want this to be our betrothal and our wedding and our pledge."

"Selena!" Gently, but firmly, he moved her away from his body.

"It can't be now," he said, his voice like a plea.

Then she understood. Not here, in this terrible stone room, with the smell of fried fish hanging in the air like defeat.

"Then you will take this as a promise," she said, taking the uniform jacket from the floor and pressing it to her breasts, "a promise that is true and changeless, even if . . ."

"Selena, listen to me! It's not that. I love you. You are all I've ever wanted. But not now."

"Not now? Why not? I don't understand . . ."

"Because," he said, with the pain of admission, "there is nothing I can offer you now. I cannot even *ask* for your hand, much less take you away to safety. I've already paid Campbell for *that*. I cannot even support you."

He saw her look of stunned disbelief, and lowered his voice, trying to explain as gently as he could.

"Everything's been taken from me, Selena, by act of royal divestiture. I've nothing left, except my life. It was a bargain to which I was forced to agree, and one offered me only because I was *not* a Rob Roy. I came here to tell you that I still love you, but I've come to say good-bye. I will be sailing for India in a fortnight, to seek a position in the Colonial Service there. A second chance, you might say. If I succeed, and fashion a new reputation, I may return to Scotland someday. And if I fail, I will have the peace of doing so far from the mocking eyes of Darius Mc-Grover. . . ."

There was no more to say. Brian had already explained it earlier. Only saints got second chances.

THE WILL IS A BLADE

Sean Bloodwell bought a space on the floor of the mead shop that night, and shared a measure of waning fire at the hearth in return for part of the last of his once-great fortune. In the morning, the MacPhersons joined him there for breakfast, he gave them a few pounds, saddled his horse, and departed. Selena would never see him again, nor he her, and after the conversation in the hut on the previous evening, a certain numbness had overcome the two of them. *This life is gone,* they said to each other wordlessly, with wounded eyes, *this age is done. Ride fast. Ride far. Farewell.*

Then he was gone, whom she loved, into the Highlands, that she loved, and gone, too, riding, into the heart of Scotland, which she loved, soon to be adrift upon the wild earth, as free as she herself was chained to one stone hut. Lethargy and torpor seized her, in the days that followed, and for the first time in her young life, she felt, without caring, the flagging of the fire inside her, on which she had always been able to rely. There was no anger now, not exactly, and nothing like sorrow either, exactly, and not even pain. She felt as if she would not shrink from death, should it come, yet neither did she seek it. She did not know the nature of the gift she had been given: time. And time was healing her, working upon her soul and spirit the trackless magic of its lambent touch.

Three days after Sean Bloodwell's departure, in the early days of the month of March, a blizzard howled down at them out of the Arctic, and for three days she slept, oblivious to everything. Awakening on the morning of the fourth day, she sensed immediately the silence that the wind had filled. And she sensed, in her own being, that the clouds had lifted and were gone.

Outside, the sky was shining and the air turned solid and crystal at the touch of her breath, her life. She had it still, and it was marvelous on a morning as fine as this. She cried out suddenly, gloriously, to the wide-eyed wonder of some village women passing, but then these women smiled, too, and understood. If it was not resurrection, it was at least rebirth.

Selena faced the future, and took stock. First, neither she nor their father nor Brian knew what might happen when they left the shelter of the Highlands. But they would have to leave for Liverpool, so there was no sense worrying about it. What would happen was inevitable anyway, and only prayer or luck could keep them safe. And if they *did* reach Liverpool, and *if* the *Highlander* was there in the harbor, so would Royce Campbell be. That knowledge led to her second conclusion. She could no longer pretend to be a girl anymore. Circumstances, as well as her own passion, had combined to make her a woman. So, in the future, she would behave as one. *I'll be mature,* she thought. *No more giving in to wild impulse, no impractical dreaming.* Behaving as a silly young girl had already cost her the love of a good man, and her chasing after a man without honor had cost her . . . well, admit it, Selena, it cost you your own honor, did it not? But surviving the future would require something of the past to cling to, something she might carry with her always, wherever she went in the new world. Sean Bloodwell had told her, not so long ago either, to make herself an instrument of her own desires, to steel herself, and in that way attain her goals. And her father's advice, now that the MacPhersons had nothing, *were* nothing but their physical beings and their dreams, could not have been more apt: a person truly free to choose what is of value can define himself by that choice.

What was of value? What did she love most, that she might cling to? Was there some goal to keep before her, like a grail?

The peace that came down with the storm, and the need to think, to plan, to fit things together, kept Selena's mind off the tedious circuit of the days. The time for departure was fast approaching, which also cheered Brian and Lord

Seamus—Brian planned to leave for Durness, to obtain horses for their journey—and they left her to her thoughts. Lying alone at night, Royce Campbell would come to her behind the blanket barricade, and stir her body to willing fire, with memory alone, and Selena learned that the memory of pleasure would last as long as pleasure was desired, or longer still. And in her dreams appeared Sean Bloodwell, always looking directly into her eyes, as if waiting for her to speak, waiting for her to decide something of vast importance to their mutual happiness. But she never knew what it was, or never faced his unspoken query, and in the dream she would turn away with a complicated feeling that was a mixture of love and guilt, remorse and loss. Gradually, over the days and nights, only one thing stood out clearly, one place both embraced and surmounted all the rest. Each person of whom she thought, every emotion she felt, every glimmer of a dream or a plan that was hers or had ever been hers revolved somehow on the place dearest of all to her: Coldstream.

Free now to choose anything at all, she wandered the bitter, rocky coast of Kinlochbervie, and chose her ancestral home to hold against her heart, a memory to take with her anywhere. Her heart ached with sweetness, then with incredible loss, as she bent into the wind, alone with her thoughts in the roar of the surf, and yet at the same time in the garden with her father long ago, or at the window on the bitter day that Brian slew McEdgar and became a man, or on the towers of the battlements in December, with the hunting hawk poised and soaring far above the fields of Scotland.

Someday, she promised herself, not knowing how or how long, *someday it will be ours again, and I will walk the halls and sleep in the fragrant gardens and bar the gates to all but us.*

Nerved by her choice, she stopped on the beach, turning first to the sea, then inland toward the dark smoky mounds of the Highlands, making her vow to Scotland and the world, pledging the troth of her will to the living sea, to all the blood that earth had known.

"Someday!" she cried into the wind, and the tears that came were of conviction rather than sadness. "Someday Coldstream shall be mine again!"

Lord Seamus seemed almost fully recovered by the end
of March, and he was in good spirits as he and Selena
shared a bowl of good stew prepared with an accommodat-
ing young rabbit Brian had shot in the hills. Most of the
snow was gone now and the rabbit, slower than the season,
had shown itself white and vulnerable against the brown
rocks. Brian had been two days gone to Durness; they expected him to return with the horses in the morning.

"How long will it take to reach Liverpool from here?"
she wanted to know.

He soaked a crust of bread in the rich gravy of the stew,
and considered the distance. "Fifteen to twenty days of
hard travel. We cannot afford to arrive later than the twen-
tieth. Our ship . . ." he never spoke Royce Campbell's
name or that of his ship ". . . will depart no later than the
twenty-fifth. The crossing itself may take as long as two
months."

He saw her thinking of the long journey, smiled, and
reassured her. "Don't worry. You're young. You'll survive."

"Have we enough money?"

"If we're not robbed. And if Brian is able to get good
horses to trade along the way. We can sell the last mounts
in Liverpool, and buy our way onto the docks. Once
aboard the . . . the ship, there'll be none to touch us."

But the thought of such safety, purchased from a man
like Campbell, caused him to fall silent. They ate the rest of
the supper, not speaking, as darkness fell outside. Yet it
was not so cold tonight; winter was gone, and it almost
seemed as if hope itself had been reborn, too, perennial as
the grass. As Selena was cleaning up the dishes and Lord
Seamus was preparing to retire, it seemed to her that he,
too, began to feel the change. Nothing had happened to
explain it, but the dour, resigned, almost bitter mood of the
past months fell away. He was tender and gay, hopeful,
already far away from this place. It started with something
rueful that he had to get off his mind.

"Selena, I'm sorry about Sean Bloodwell. Both for him
and for you. But there will be other men for you. I meant
no ill in it, neither to destroy him, nor to make you unhappy. Never."

She looked toward him, wondering. He was sitting there against the wall, wrapped in his blankets. His face was extraordinarily benign. His eyes were shining oddly, and they began to glow fondly as he recalled things from the past.

"Do you remember the time we were at Foinaven, when your mother refused to eat the grouse I shot, because of the grapeshot in them?"

"Do you remember the time Brian went out on the North Sea in his new sailboat, and I had to go out and rescue him?"

"I remember how you looked on your first communion day, in your white dress, with the lilies. I thought you were so beautiful that day."

". . . and we were so proud of you, when you brought Grandma home that fall . . ."

He spoke gently, reminiscing, not even looking at her. His eyes were burning now, as if they looked far away, upon a lost horizon. Even though she was standing with her back to the fire, a strange chill prickled her spine, a foreshadowing of something indefinite and inexplicable that was somehow with them in the hut. Then she listened as he remembered the past.

"Do you know, Selena, that I remember my own great-grandfather? Seamus. I was named for him. I remember, as a boy, he used to take me down to the castle wall, holding my hand, and show me the vaults in which our ancestors were buried. 'Here's mine,' he'd say, laughing, pointing at a big empty one, 'and I'd hate to be the man who tries to shove me in it.' Lord, how I must have loved him, but I didn't know it then. . . ."

"Father!" she cried, alarmed.

He looked up, startled.

"You frightened me," she explained.

He looked genuinely confused. "I was just sitting here and thinking about the future," he said. "I didn't mean to disturb you."

Thinking? About the *future*?

"You'd best lie down now. We'll all of us need our strength."

He complied, but there was one more question, for which he apologized even before he asked it.

"Selena. That time on the . . . the ship. Did you feel it necessary to offer . . . to offer payment of your own?"

He did not look at her.

"No," she answered. Truthfully. No payment had been involved. The transaction had been of an entirely different nature.

He seized her arm with an urgency so unsettling that it made her afraid. "Good, Selena. Good. You have never brought me anything but pride. It is I who've failed the rest of you."

He seemed to be fighting back sobs. She pretended not to notice, pulling the blankets close around him, telling him good night. Then he subsided, and soon passed over into sleep. She sat before the fire, still content with her thoughts of the future, but feeling, now, vaguely disconsolate, too. She wished Brian were here. Father started muttering in his sleep not too long afterward, just before she was ready to go to bed herself, and she crept close to see if he was all right. He seemed to be—his breathing was steady and light—but the words, as clearly as she could understand them, chilled her with their anonymous, disembodied portent, as if Time itself were speaking through the dream-tossed visions of his sleeping brain. "Ian MacPherson," he was saying, tongue thick with sleep, "sixteen fifteen, sixteen eighty-four. Seamus MacPherson, sixteen forty-four, seventeen thirty-three. Randall MacPherson, sixteen seventy, seventeen thirty-one. Gloucester MacPherson, seventeen two, seventeen sixty-four. Seamus MacPherson," he was saying, and, too late, she pushed her hands against unwilling ears to shut the nightmare out, "Seamus MacPherson, seventeen twenty-three, seventeen seventy-five . . ."

That was himself.

Outside, the dark sky crouched, studded with stars, a vault of eternity, waiting. The lone stone hut was monument enough. Selena wanted to scream, fought off the impulse. Father's lips were moving still, but she held her ears between her hands and did not hear him, and she closed her eyes and took herself away.

There was a movement of air in the hut. Stars, for an instant, parted in a hush. The fire in the hearth rose, flaming, and in another instant subsided, burning on. She opened her eyes again. Father was sleeping quietly. She took her hands away.

"Hello, Selena," said the voice behind her.

She whirled to face the man who etched the dates on countless tombstones with the chisel of his life.

It was Darius McGrover.

He had entered stealthily and closed the door behind him, and he stood now, implacable and predatory, bent slightly forward, almost as if bowing. His look, as he regarded the horrified Selena, was that of a man who has, against considerable odds, finally reached his destination. He wore high black riding boots, a short riding cape, a dark suit that looked wine-colored—or blood-colored—in the firelight, and a tricornered hat, once fashionable, now battered out of shape by wind and weather. At his belt hung two pistols, a dagger in a leather sheath, and a riding whip. In one hand he held a short curved sword, like a scimitar but not as broad, and in the other a burlap bag. Something was inside the bag, which trailed on the floor, but Selena did not have a chance to study it.

"I've been looking forward to this, very dearly," McGrover said quietly. He tightened his mouth into a thin line, the parody of a smile. "Aren't you going to greet me?"

He made one step forward, just one step, but it seemed that his hawklike face suddenly intruded upon her very soul, filled her entire field of vision. She opened her mouth to scream.

"I wouldn't do that," he said softly. "In the first place, I don't think the villagers would cozen to a traitor. In the second, I'll kill you if you scream."

Her brain worked slowly, buried in a sludge of fear. Did he mean he was *not* going to kill her? Was it Lord Seamus he wanted?

She backed away from him, but saw that there was no chance to reach the door. He looked around the hut, and saw Lord Seamus sleeping among his blankets down on one side of the fireplace.

"So, the rebel leader at rest, eh?" His laugh was cold and mirthless. "We shan't wake him, shall we? And . . ." he gestured indolently with a slow twist of his hand ". . .

and your choice of lodgings leaves much to be desired. 'Tis hardly Coldstream, now, is it?"

"What do you want?" she managed.

"A number of things," he said. "But I'm in no rush. Where is your peasant-murdering scum of a brother?"

His eyes were on hers, galvanic, riveting. Selena realized that the interrogation had begun, wondered how many hapless people before herself had sensed that tone and silently called on God for help that never came. Darius McGrover, agent of the Crown, believed in his heart that he could do no wrong, that all his enemies were evil, that his mission alone was divine. He was efficient, and calm, and utterly ruthless. No sign of human weakness, or error, or confusion moved his heart to pity, and nothing could mitigate a violation of what he believed to be right, loyalty, duty. He was as beyond remorse as he was beyond pity. When those slitted eyes opened slightly, and when a slow, baleful light glowed therein, it was a sign that he knew all he needed to know, and his suffering victim could at last know peace. The peace was always death.

"I said, where is your brother?" he asked again, taking one more step toward her.

Selena did not know what to say. She swallowed, trying to think, and said nothing.

"And where is Will Teviot?" McGrover wanted to know, his voice slightly colder now, but still soft. He glanced again at Selena's father, to determine that he was still asleep.

"Well," he said, again with that tight, horizontal grimace, "I had heard that you noble Scottish lasses were eager conversationalists. I had hoped so. You will understand my disappointment . . ."

He spoke slowly, even politely, and Selena began to relax just a bit, began again to measure the distance to the door. So she was off guard, which had been McGrover's intent, and unprepared for his sudden, slippery lunge at her. Dropping the burlap sack, he leaped forward in one smooth, liquid motion, grabbed her around the waist, twisted her aside, and came up behind her, holding the edge of the cold blade against her throat.

"I prefer close conversations," he said. "Where is your brother?"

"I don't know."

"Now, now." The blade bit into her skin, just a touch. She felt the stinging, keen heat of the first cut. Motionless, her insides roiling, she remembered what Father had said in the coach on the way to Edinburgh. *It's best that she have something to confess.*

"Brian went to Durness," she gasped, trying to bend her head back from the blade. She felt McGrover relax a little.

"That's right," he said soothingly. "When do you expect him to return?"

"I don't know. Tomorrow morning, I think."

"Tomorrow morning. Isn't that nice? And what about Teviot, the bearded bastard who killed so many of my good men in Cargill?"

"He . . . he left."

"With your brother?"

"No. He just . . . left. He was going to try and leave Scotland."

McGrover paused for a moment, putting the pieces together.

"I don't believe you," he said, "but no matter now. We will have a long night to converse about one thing or another. Now . . ."

And with a brutal shove, he slammed her against the stone wall. Her skull struck it a glancing blow, and her head rang, spinning. Before she knew what was happening, he was upon her, pulling her arms together and twisting a thin cord wickedly into the flesh of her wrists. This done, he quickly tied her ankles together as well, and stood over her, surveying his handiwork. Then, showing teeth, he tied the ends of the cords at her wrists and ankles to one of the stools, so that her arms and legs were bent behind her. Now she could not move, or even roll around on the dirt floor.

"Father," she moaned, her head clearing. It was a mistake *not* to have screamed before. Together, the two of them might have had at least a chance.

"Too late for that," McGrover said. Her father stirred at her call, and McGrover stepped over and nudged the man with his foot, drawing a pistol as he did so, and training it on Lord Seamus's head.

"Don't move, ye traitorous bastard," he hissed. "'Tis I,

and in the name of George the Third, by the grace of God King of England, I come to settle accounts with ye."

Lord Seamus braced himself on one elbow and saw what had happened.

"I'm sorry," Selena said, beginning to cry.

"Don't, Selena," her father said.

"Don't, Selena," McGrover mocked. "Sit up. There, that's it. Now put your hands on your head."

Slowly, he did so. He was not afraid, as if he already knew what must happen now. "May I ask you one favor as a gentleman?"

"You're no gentleman," McGrover said, watching the other man's movements.

"Take that as given, then. I am asking a favor of *you,* as the gentleman involved."

"What is not asked cannot be granted. So ask."

"There is no need to harm my daughter."

McGrover laughed.

"Only a savage would injure a child."

"She's no child. She's a woman, and a fine, ripe one at that. But man, woman, child—I care not. To me there's but those who are loyal and those who are not. And you two are not."

"Then you will not promise that you won't harm her?"

"You are a perceptive man," McGrover said sarcastically.

"God help us," Lord Seamus prayed.

"He won't either," said McGrover. "I've heard that plea often enough in my years with the Secret Offices. All you bloody traitors plot to overthrow your King, turn against your country like the heinous jackals that ye be, and when your just deserts are visited upon ye, aye, then ye'll be a-screamin' an' a-pleadin' to God, who listens less than McGrover. Ah!" he cried in digust, and kicked Lord Seamus hard in the stomach. He doubled up, gasping in pain. Selena cried out.

"Shut up, wench, or you'll get it, too."

While Lord Seamus was helpless and out of breath, McGrover bound his hands behind his back and tied his hands to his ankles in such a manner that all he could do was kneel.

"I had to come through the Highlands alone,"

McGrover explained, relaxing now. He left for a moment and came back in with a saddlebag, from which he took a bottle of whiskey. The cork made a wet, popping sound as he jerked it out with his teeth, lifted the bottle first to her, then to her father, and drank. "Aye. I thought ye were well guarded by the last of the Rob Roys, but they had no staying power, did they, when the cause was lost?"

He laughed, drank again, and set the bottle down. Lord Seamus, on his knees, watched him as a man watches a poisonous snake. Selena was almost too terrified to breathe. All she could do was try to control her fear of McGrover.

"Would you like to see the last of your faithful men?" he asked insinuatingly.

But McGrover laughed when they looked toward the door.

"Ah, no," he said. "I didna mean *that*. I meant that, in your final moments . . ." He let the words linger in the room. ". . . that in your final moments you might wish to gaze upon the rapt, loyal faces of your lieutenants."

And he bent to the burlap bag.

Oh, God, no. Not Will Teviot, please, Selena said to herself, and luck was with her, at least in that particular. McGrover did not pull Will Teviot's head from the bloody sack, but rather the severed heads of three other men, rough men, whom it would not have been easy work to subdue. Their faces were frozen in the peculiar, twisted rictus of agony that is the companion of a terrible death, and their wide-open eyes were set on far horizons of despair. McGrover laughed, and set them in a neat row on the floor, about five feet in front of Lord Seamus.

"It is the law that every execution must have witnesses," he explained, "but nowhere does it say anything about the witnesses being *alive.*"

Lord Seamus met his eyes at the word execution, but showed no emotion. Perhaps, earlier that evening, he had been given some kind of an insight, some private vision that even he did not fully understand. Now, in acceptance of his own death, he raised his head.

"By whose authority?" he asked.

"By the wish of my King," McGrover answered ringingly.

"You have authorization?"

"In my heart," McGrover said.

"That will not suffice," Lord Seamus argued calmly, with quiet assurance in the face of disaster. "There must be a document. It is the law of the Scottish Parliament."

"I serve the English King. I take no orders from what you call your Parliament. Moreover, the rights of traitors are self-abridged when they embark upon the course of treason."

"I have committed no crime," Lord Seamus went on. "Unless free speech be a crime . . ."

"Silence! Enough!" McGrover shouted, and his words bounced off the stone walls of the hut and reverberated around them. Outside, his startled horse whinnied and stamped.

"I cannot take but one o' ye back wi' me," he said, mocking the Scottish tongue, "an' I wouldna risk ye're gettin' away, yer lordship, or rather yer ex-lordship, so by powers invested in me, we'll have the execution now."

"No!" Selena cried, and burst into tears.

Her father's voice was almost harsh. "Selena, stop. Remember, as I told you once before. Think of the good things. There were many of them. If you live, through some stroke of fortune or the grace of God, take vengeance for this act which is about to occur. If not, it is as things must be, and we must accept that. And at least we are together at the end."

"A mystic," spat McGrover, taking a long, thin cord from his saddlebag. Selena suppressed her sobs, but went on crying quietly. She could not stop.

McGrover stepped over to her father. The eyes of the two men were locked upon each other. "The law says hanging," McGrover pointed out, "but there are no beams here. So this will have to do. . . ."

Faster than Selena could follow movement, he had the cord around her father's neck and twisted it violently in the manner of the garrote. Selena saw her father's face darken immediately as the blood was cut off and the pressure mounted. Mercifully, it would be quick. She sought words, found none, but then, with the last strength of ultimate desperation, Lord Seamus jerked free of his bonds, raised an arm halfway into the air, met her eyes one last time, and, before the cord bit into his windpipe, told her, chokingly:

"Sel . . . ena . . . the . . . sky begins . . . *here.* . . ."

McGrover twisted the final measure then, and the spinal cord snapped, a thin, sharp crack in the room. Her father went limp, shuddered reflexively, and then lay still. McGrover pushed the body aside, and tossed a blanket on top of it.

"Good riddance," he said. "England is avenged." He stood over Selena. "What did he mean, that business about the sky?"

Selena was howling with grief; she could not speak. Minutes went by, and when she did not subside, McGrover got tired of it. Uncorking the whiskey, he yanked her hair back and poured a healthy dose of spirits into her mouth. She choked on it, coughed, gasped, swallowed some. Oddly, it helped. Her own situation came back to her, and she did not want to die, no more than she had in the village of Cargill, when Will Teviot had seized the knife at her breast.

"I can't enjoy ye when ye're sniveling like a calf lost in a hailstorm, now, can I, lass?"

Enjoy her? "What? What are you going to do?"

"I expect to take you back with me," he said. "Tomorrow. If your brother *is* coming back, as you say."

Selena said nothing.

"He *is* coming back, is he not?"

"I told you that."

"I know you did. But what of Teviot?"

"I told you that, too. He's left for America."

"Ah. And what were your plans?"

"We . . . we had none. We expected to stay here."

"Here?" McGrover looked around the hut and laughed. "Here? You deserve it, I vow. We've prisons in London better than this, and you'll be able to judge that, too, believe me. But, look, meaning no disrespect, your *ladyship*, I don't believe you are telling me the truth."

He sat down next to her and moved his hawk's face close down next to hers. "Have you heard of my opera house?" he asked, his voice gentle.

Her answering look was a question.

"Oh, no, not your usual opera house," he laughed. "My own special one. Deep in the earth beneath London. The music I create there is not for the ears of the citizens who walk peacefully upon the streets. The music I create is of quite another kind. And I have many instruments to do it with. The rack. Thumbscrews. The boot. Strappado produces a fine kind of sound; the victim can barely breathe but must scream with pain, too. A very rare sound, that."

Suddenly, he lowered his hard face down to hers, kissed her brutally on the mouth. His voice was hard, too, when he spoke. "If I had you in my opera, performing, you would sing in minutes. Women such as you are made for pleasure, not for pain." Abruptly, he stood up. "Is Will Teviot with your brother? Are the two of them together?"

"No," she cried. "I told you . . ."

"And I don't believe you," McGrover said. Very slowly, with grave theatricality, he took the riding whip from his belt, flexed it, and gave it a few brisk, whistling cuts in the air.

Oh, God, no. It's coming now. Help, she thought.

"It was . . . I did tell you the truth," she said again, as evenly as she could.

"That's what you say. But, you see, you do not understand about the truth. It must not merely be *stated,* it must also be proven. My work is not merely the simple matter of taking from people the stories they had much rather keep hidden inside. No. It is more than that. It is to determine the truth of what they have already told me. And that is what we shall do here. But first, we do not wish to disturb the sleep of the good citizens of Kinlochbervie, do we?"

Having thus warned her, he grabbed the burlap bag in which the heads had been wrapped, and tied it across her face, stuffing an end of it in her mouth. The fabric was harsh against her tongue, and she tried to breathe evenly, not to choke.

"I will prepare you for a time," he said, making the whip whistle again, "and when I remove your gag, I believe we will more readily be able to determine what is true and what is not. Then, after we have done so, my plans for the rest of the evening are more conventional. I daresay you may even enjoy them. If this exercise does not become excessively prolonged . . ."

Then she heard the whip cut, hissing through the air, and felt a pain deeper than fire must be, more terrible than a brand, burning its way across the backs of her thighs. Even the heavy gag could not stop her scream, and her heart leaped against her bones, seeking escape from the pain of the blow. Unable to speak, her brain was already bargaining with McGrover. *Tell me what it is you want to know. I'll tell you that. Just tell me what it is you want to know. . . .*

Then he struck her again.

She twisted around as far as she could and saw his face, expression intent, lips thin and tight, concentrating on his work. He met her eyes and shook his head. "No, not yet. You may think you will tell me the truth now, but it is much too early. We will proceed." Again he raised the riding whip, and she was about to close her eyes, to try and wriggle away, somehow, from the blow, when she saw the door of the hut fly open. McGrover, his arm back to strike, his eyes seeking a new target for pain—her shoulders, perhaps? or the sensitive lower back?—saw her eyes, too, but he was off balance, he was distracted, and had no time to turn or ready himself. Brian, face livid, lips drawn back in pure hatred, grabbed his wrist, twisted the whip from his hand, and in one smooth motion, yanked his entire body backward, spinning him in the air. There was a popping sound as McGrover's shoulder left its joint, and he came down full-length, stunned and howling, on the dirt floor.

Brian jumped, hung for an instant in midair, and came down, both knees landing on McGrover's angled, beaklike face. Bones shattered like sticks, and McGrover did not move.

Brian got up, started to cry. "He's not dead yet," he sobbed, looking at the unconscious McGrover, "but he's bloody well going to wish he were."

Then he came to free her.

"Are you all right? How bad was it?"

She sat up, rubbed her wrists and ankles, and, more gingerly, the tracks of the whip.

"Bad enough, but the worst part was . . . when he . . . Father . . ." but she could say no more for a time, nor could he, as they both wept, now holding each other, now pacing back and forth across the floor of the hut, bereft of all but life itself. McGrover lay unconscious on the floor, too—though Brian tied him securely—and his face swelled black and huge from the broken bones. Beneath his blanket, their father lay dead.

"His horse is still outside," Brian finally observed. "Did he come alone?"

"I think so. Like an assassin. He wanted to reserve the pleasure for himself."

"All right. But he wouldn't have ridden out here without telling others where he was bound. So we can't wait. It's only fortunate that I decided to push on from Durness, or else . . ." He left that thought unfinished. What had happened was bad enough; words of good fortune were misplaced.

"We'll leave tonight," he said. "McGrover's police would not expect him to get back for at least a day. If we can pass through these outer hills by darkness, we'll be a step ahead of them. . . ."

"If only we were already in Liverpool."

"We will be," he said. "We will be. Don't think. There are simply things that we must do. So don't think. Think later, when there's time and everything's done."

"But what will we do with . . ." Selena motioned to McGrover, their father's body, the three severed heads, which formed a curious triangle in the dirt.

"The poor lads," Brian said, and gently placed them back in McGrover's sack. "We'll even the score fer ye," he murmured, almost tenderly.

On the floor, McGrover stirred, and a long, low moan came from the blackened, blood-encrusted lips. He shifted his body slightly, felt his bonds, and lay still. Selena and Brian knelt down next to him.

"You filthy swine!" Brian hissed. "You are going to pay a hundredfold for what you've done."

Selena could hardly bear to look at McGrover's broken, hideous face, could scarcely stand to remain in the presence of this evil.

McGrover made a strange gurgling sound in response to Brian's words. It was a moment before they realized he was laughing.

"I'll make you laugh . . ." Brian cried, seizing the curved sword. Selena restrained him.

"We have to know about the Highlands," she whispered. "If he has men there."

Brian asked the question. McGrover made the gurgling

noise again. Brian grabbed the man's jaw and shook it. McGrover moaned, and then passed out.

"The bloody fiend. Well, let's be going. We haven't much time."

They could not take their father's body with them, and outside the hut, in the darkness, the earth was still frozen from the winter. "Couldna be dug more than a foot, before the frost line stopped me," Brian told her. So he did the only thing he could do: Lord Seamus was buried, along with the heads of his faithful followers, right inside the stone hut. Working fast, Brian dug down into the dirt floor of the house, which, because of the fireplace and the enclosure, had remained unfrozen during winter, while Selena readied their clothing, saddlebags, and blankets for the trip. She watered the horses, and calmed them, so that the villagers should not be disturbed, and cut lengths of rope to tie McGrover to his mount. They would take him into the Highlands and . . .

She could not think any further than that. In spite of what he had done to them, to their father, she did not want to face what it was that Brian would do to him. She was not ready to confront that yet, in spite of the devastation of the past months, nor did she want to face her own suspicion that the McGrovers of the world had an inherent advantage over the MacPhersons because they did not shrink from violence and bloodshed. To Selena, an admission of that kind seemed very much like defeat.

Then the grave was complete, a long, surprisingly narrow trench in the earth. Carefully, weeping softly, Selena and Brian eased their father's body over to the edge of the slit—his face, several hours after death, was in repose—and lowered him to his rest. Selena arranged over him the blanket in which he had slept during their stay here in the hut; it had become a garment, a flag, a shroud. And her brother placed the burlap sack at his feet, a symbolic gesture to the place that the dead had held in life. They stood beside the excavation, beside the mounds of earth on the floor of the hut, and said good-bye to the ominous, silent emptiness which held the body of the man who had been a part of their passage into life. And they knew, both of them, that they were on their own now. Mother and father were both dead, and all of their ancestors; they were adrift, alone, in time. But her hand sought his and he grasped it, and she understood, too, that they would never be separated from the past, nor even from Father, or what he had been, what he believed. It was a part of them both, like the blood in their veins, and they would carry it with them always.

Selena tried to remember the good things, as her father would have wanted her to, and she was once again a little girl in the garden with him, as Brian muttered an ineffectual prayer. He broke it off, realizing the impotence of empty formulas.

"We'll see your dreams bear fruit in our lifetimes," Brian vowed, telling their father good-bye.

"Yes," Selena affirmed, and a phrase kept running through her mind: *We are such stuff as dreams are made on, and our little life is rounded with a sleep.*

Brian cast down upon his father the first of the spadefuls of earth.

On the floor, McGrover laughed suddenly, that same harsh, sarcastic sound, and words came from his broken mouth. "Pity. Such a nice hole. I thought that you'd dug it for me."

Brian made as if to send their tormentor to unconsciousness again, but Selena restrained him. McGrover would have to ride.

Ride they did, just before dawn. There were four horses and three figures astride. If anyone in the village was awake at the early hour, he would have seen Brian in the lead, then a figure heavily cloaked and bent in the saddle, and Selena in the rear, with the fourth horse trailing by a harness strap attached to her saddle. And, looking from the small window of a fishing shack in the eerie, predawn light, the watcher would have thought, *Aye, the MacPhersons be leavin', strange as they appeared. An' had 'em enou' money fer a fourth 'orse, too, they did. I ought t' 'ave charged 'em more fer t' bread.*

After a little over an hour, the sun was up, and they were into the first of the high ring of hills overlooking Kinlochbervie, where the Highlands began. Selena felt the familiar, wild brace of the air, felt the wind against her face, and saw the sunlight soften the gloomy, mysterious penumbra of the hills. Below lay the village, and she could see the stone hut. Father's grave and tombstone. He did not have the place below the wall at Coldstream, but she knew where he lay. Born at one end of Scotland, he had died at the other, and, in a sense, it was fitting.

McGrover was in great pain, and Brian enjoyed it, now and then urging the horses into a gallop. McGrover cried out then, never for mercy, simply from pain, and it soon became obvious that he could not travel much farther without holding them back. Once, as they rested along the side of the trail, drinking cold tea that Selena had poured into a metal canteen, she asked Brian what he meant to do.

"When he can't take pain anymore, I'll kill him."

She did not know what to say. She had seen death already, many times, and she had seen Brian kill, but what it did to the living, what it had done even to Brian as a boy, was not something good. It was almost as bad for the living as for their victims.

"Ye've some doots, 'ave ye?" he said, in the broad accent. "Then ye think on Father."

"Brian, I'm not sure that's . . ."

"Necessary? Are ye daft, little sister? I'd o' believed ye'd be beggin' me t' wield the blade yerself. 'Tis a fact. I'd thought it, after what McGrover's done to us, an' the Rob Roys. An' ye."

Bent over the saddle horn to which he was tied, McGrover raised his head and smirked at them. The hard riding had opened his wounds again, and blood trickled down here and there from cuts on his ruined face. But he was unvanquished.

"You haven't the guts to kill me, traitor bastards," he sneered.

"Because I don't want to be like you," Selena replied, not sure of herself.

"You think on it," Brian whispered, so that McGrover could not hear. "We've a long way to Liverpool, an' we can't take the scum wi' us. If he lives, we're in double danger."

"Where are we going now?"

"To our lodge at Mount Foinaven. 'Tis deserted this time o' year, an' we can spend a night in peace."

Selena told him of her fears that some of McGrover's men might be waiting for them at the family hunting lodge. He doubted it, and even McGrover laughed. "There's nothing for you at Foinaven," he said scornfully. "A little surprise at Liverpool, possibly. But other than that . . ."

He broke into a maddening crackle of laughter, and they dismissed him with disgust. But they knew, soon enough, why he had said nothing awaited them at Foinaven. Because, as they rode down the well-remembered drive, covered by a tunnel of thick trees, and then out onto the flat, green meadow, at the end of which the lodge was situated, McGrover burst into his horrible, contemptuous laughter. Brian and Selena, crestfallen, saw the charred framework of rafters and beams, the burnt, charcoal-reeking debris.

"Aye! We burnt it fer ye, scum," he said. "T' rid all Britain of the sign o' ye!"

Brian leaned over in his saddle, and knocked McGrover on the side of the face with a big fist. The torturer managed to bend away, and caught but a glancing blow.

"And Coldstream?" Selena asked, steeling herself against the answer.

"I was saving Coldstream for myself," McGrover drawled. "His Majesty has promised it to me as a reward."

"Ye'll get yer reward, all right," Brian said. Grabbing the halter of McGrover's horse, he led them at a gallop across the meadow to the ruin of the hunting lodge. Selena could not think clearly, because of the hostile emotions swooping at her. Their enemies had left them nothing, would leave them nothing. Not even life, if their luck was bad. Brian was right. They should kill McGrover. But . . .

Brian pulled his horse to a halt where the wide porch had once been, cool in the summer, and from which you could look out over the Highlands at night and dream of life and all that was to be. Leaping down from the saddle, he unbound McGrover and yanked him onto the ground.

"Say yer prayers, Britisher bastard."

McGrover gave as good as he got. "Ye're not the lad fer this, ye Scottish puppy. Ye kill hungry peasants mayhap, but not a soldier o' King George."

"Yer a soldier o' nithin' but death, ye piece o' breathin' offal, an' I dona need t' kill ye t' show my contempt fer ye.

My sister'll do the killin' well enough. Won't ye, Selena?"

Selena sat on her horse in the sun of spring, before their savaged home. Father. Coldstream. Scotland. Sean Bloodwell, far away. Her life uprooted. She nodded shakily. Brian was right. It had to be, both for vengence and safety.

McGrover moaned as Brian kicked and shoved him into the rubble of the lodge, and found one stout, upright beam. He tied McGrover to it, and stepped back.

"So long, ye bastard, an' gi'e Satan my best regards."

Darius laughed, but there was a little less spirit in it this time. For the first time since he had come into the hut, the man seemed to feel fear.

"What I've a mind t' do," Brian told him, "is give ye some o' the medicine ye've dispensed fer so many long years, t' draw some blood t' slake the thirst of those ye've wrung dry yerself, screamin' in yer dungeons. But I've naught the time. Selena," he called, "'ow shall it be? The pistol or the knife or the sword?"

Selena got down from her horse and tried to walk resolutely over to the place where McGrover was tied. She saw him watching her approach through the slits of his swollen, blackened eyes, like a serpent trapped and cornered, bitter and scornful and unrepentant, waiting for the blow of the club.

Brian handed her the curved sword and stepped back. She took it, lifted it tentatively, and faced McGrover. He was not laughing now, and she thought that she must at least look determined enough to kill, although her heart was beating in her ears and blood throbbed like a bad wound throughout her body.

"Go on. Do it," Brian said.

I can't, she thought, with a fading sensation somewhere below her breasts. *I know I should, and even God could not think it wrong, but . . .*

"Would it be better if I left you alone?"

She nodded, and her lips felt dry as chalk against her tongue.

Leaving her horse tethered, Brian mounted and took the other two horses and rode down to the end of the meadow. She saw him there, in the sunlight, like a gentleman holding horses for his companions in the morning hunt.

McGrover still watched her, unspeaking. It gave her a small measure of courage, his belief that death was coming at her hands.

"Do . . . do you wish to beg forgiveness?" she asked, giving him the chance for that, at least.

He snorted derisively. "I'll not beg."

"I didn't mean of me, of us. I meant of God."

McGrover laughed in disbelief. "A fool who'd believe such cannot kill me," he said. "The only thing is *will*. Those who lack it believe in things like God. Now, little girl, use that sword to cut my bonds. Ye may be imprisoned, but I give my word ye'll not die if ye set me free."

For an instant, she wavered. It was not because she believed him, and never would she have cut him loose. But she wavered because *he* no longer believed her capable of execution. Was she, in fact, capable?

The morning sun beat down, warm on the sweetness of the new grass, the trees, and all the living plants. Today, amidst that sweetness, the life of Darius McGrover would end. And she would be the agent of its ending.

"How do you wish it?" she heard herself ask in a voice surprisingly strong. *Think of Father*, she thought.

McGrover stiffened. He had not expected this. Down at the end of the meadow, Brian called out, and his words drifted over: "Get it done an' let's be off."

"In the neck, the . . . the throat," McGrover said, lifting his chin, his eyes on her, like those of a snake who grasps a last chance in its mesmerizing power.

"As you wish," Selena cried. She wanted to call back the blade as soon as her arms pushed it, arcing, through the whistling air. *This is not me. I cannot do this*, cried one part of herself, but her arms said *you must!* and the ugly, hooked sword hissed through the air. The edge of the blade was homing toward the side of McGrover's neck; his glittering eyes were on the blade. Selena did not know why—she would not know why until long after—but as the blade moved, level for his neck, something turned in her mind, and her wrists turned too. The blade curved upward. McGrover shrieked in sudden pain and jerked against his stake. Blood was everywhere, scattering like a cloud of raindrops, red in the air. She stood there, gasping. He jerked convulsively, eyes wide with wonder. And reprieve. On the ground, between them, was one of his ears, severed by the blow. Blood bubbled like a spring in the circle where his ear had been.

For a long moment, with Brian's voice drifting again over the meadow, Selena and McGrover looked at each other. Then his head dropped down, his chin rested on his chest, and he was still. The blood poured down upon his shoulder.

She threw the sullied blade down upon the charred wood of Foinaven Lodge and ran for her horse, not looking back.

A STAR TO STEER HER BY

The waterfront tavern stank of bad air, sweat, wine, vomit, and harsh spices used for cooking to hide the taste of bad meat. Brian and Selena entered together, trying to appear like a sailor and his girl. Selena hid her blond hair beneath a ratty shawl, and Brian tried to slouch, to look smaller, in case there were soldiers on the waterfront looking for them. It was Selena who had insisted on the disguises.

"I don't understand why you're so jittery. No one has bothered us all during the trip down from Foinaven, and McGrover's as dead as Henry the Eighth. Isn't he?"

"Yes."

He had taken her word for it. The cut of the sword. The spray of blood, red like pearls on the blades of grass where once the floor of the lodge had been. And McGrover collapsing, after looking at her one last time.

"That's the end o' the bastard, then," Brian swore, riding, throwing out his chest, squaring his shoulders against the future. And it had to be true, didn't it? Even if, somehow, McGrover had not been dead against that beam? Because who might have found him at that time of year? No one used the lodge then, and the local villagers never came to the place unless the family was there, ready to dispense money for services rendered.

But if, somehow, he *had* survived? After all, he knew they were going to Liverpool to meet a ship. And if he had survived, and somehow his men were looking for them . . . It meant that she had failed in a terrible way. It meant that she had jeopardized their future as surely as the Rob Roys' lack of precautions had jeopardized the past.

"McGrover is finished," she told Brian, more vehemently than was necessary, and he seemed proud of her, but in a doubtful way, as if he did not entirely believe her.

So she had insisted on a semblance of disguises. And he had complied.

"Hey, we'll ha'e us two pints o' ale," Brian called heartily, feigning mild drunkenness, as he half guided, half pushed Selena toward a table in a dark corner of the tavern. Yards away from the table, there was a window that looked out toward the harbor. The window was as close to the quay as they had been yet, for they had not wanted to seek the *Highlander* until they were assured of its presence there. And assured of the fact that no British officers awaited them.

That was another question, too, which Selena did not want to face: would the *Highlander* be there at all? Many things had happened since the night of the Christmas Ball, and she had begun to realize that any man who made a deal with a traitor might have second thoughts. Just as anyone who made a deal with Royce Campbell might have second thoughts, watching the cynical smile on his lips, the glitter in his eyes.

But they did not bother with the window at all. A good bit of laughter, swaying, exaggerated stumbling got them to the table.

"What o' me ale?" Brian called again.

"Show me yer coin, matey, an' ye kin 'ave the whole place," answered the barmaid. She was a thick, coarse woman, with good cheer heavy in her voice, but a sullen, dangerous tightness around the eyes. The other customers in the place, about a dozen hard-drinking sailors off boats in port, and four prostitutes, turned to stare hard at Brian and Selena.

We're not succeeding, she thought. *We don't look right.*

In a moment, Selena understood why. A trapdoor opened on the ceiling at the other end of the bar, and a man swung down, hung there for a moment, and then dropped heavily to the floor. Then the men and women at the bar burst into a lewd, hearty round of cheers. A pair of red leather pumps appeared in the trapdoor, kicking prettily, rustling petticoats beneath a bright red dress. It was a saucy young woman. She climbed down a row of pegs that had been driven into the wall. She had lustrous, coffee-colored hair, a luscious figure, and a look about her pretty face that managed to be vulnerable and hard at the same time.

"Eh, Slyde, 'ow'd it go? 'Ow'd it go up there?"

"Gimme a big whiskey," called the man who had preceded the girl, grinning, satisfied, rubbing his groin.

"An' 'ow was 'e, Belle? Is it true the bloke's all talk an' no action?"

"It's a professional secret twixt me an' Slyde," the girl said, provoking another burst of crude laughter. Brian and Selena looked at each other. The tavern was more interesting than they had anticipated, and potentially more dangerous. Not only would any information they might require be for sale, though dearly, but also for sale, at a later time, to anyone who wanted to know, would be the fact that they had been there seeking information. About the *Highlander*. And passage to America.

The barmaid poured Slyde his whiskey, then drew two big mugs of ale and slid them across the bar to Belle, who also did duty as a waitress. She brought them over to the table, first giving Selena an appraising look—measuring the competition—then staring boldly at Brian. Who stared back. Selena remembered that he had been a long time in the Highlands, and that he had always been a lusty boy, but he had best watch himself carefully now.

"Tuppence each," Belle demanded, putting the ale on the table before them. "Pay now."

Brian took a coin out of his pocket and handed it to her. She reached for it and took his hand, held it. Her smile was a challenge.

"Care to 'ave a go at it, hon?" she asked him. "Come on, an' I'll bet the tuppence I'll gi'e ye a ride lak this one 'ere couldna learn in ten years tryin'."

At the bar, the laughter was cruel, and too loud. Brian and Selena were strangers, having wandered into an alien setting and one in which they were unwelcome. They were about to be made sport of, although it was clear from Belle's voice, and the manner in which she stood at their table, pert breasts thrust forward invitingly, chin and bottom held high, that she was more than ready to fulfill her part of the proposition. Brian swallowed and wet his lips, unable to keep from giving her the eye. Selena kicked him under the table, a gesture which was seen by everybody watching eagerly from the bar.

"Hey, did ye see it? The lady's in a fit, she is."

Selena heard something in the way they pronounced *lady*, the way big Slyde, drinking his whiskey, snorted and chortled, that told her the shawl and cheap smock she wore did not conceal her origins. They would have to, if they were to elude McGrover's men, and get aboard the ship to safety. This tavern was the last place a young woman of noble birth would choose to be. Indeed, so was the whole of Liverpool.

It was a foul and predatory city, a port city, both beacon and pit of Empire, with a black heart beating deep within, sounding out the rhythms of lust and avarice and petty crime. From all over Great Britain, the poor and the dispossessed flocked to it, owning naught but tatters and hopes already dead, seeking by whatever means at hand to hoard another crumb of bread, to scratch from the face of God's iron sky one more day of bitter life. The new factories were growing, grimy and stained along the dismal skyline, and in these from dawn to dusk and far into the evening worked the poor and the children of the poor, driven by whips, chained to the machines, sometimes falling asleep at the lathes and wheels, to be maimed or killed thereby. And out of these factories and into the teeming swarm of the city staggered those who survived, hearts black with hate and despair. Better to cut a man's throat in a back alley, an alley awash with feces, urine, all manner of deteriorating garbage, than to bear one more day in the plants, or in the mines of the countryside. Better kill a rich man, if your luck held good, and even the score a little. You could sing with satisfaction, even on the gallows, if you killed a rich man once.

And then there was the waterfront, drawing to it by choice or accident of itinerary the dregs of mankind, wanderers from across the savage earth. Dark-skinned men with gold rings in their ears, whose eyes glittered with strange secrets, wild dreams. Men who had killed, fought, robbed, whored, and who would do far worse should someone invent new evils of excess to surpass the old. Here on the docks with the salt smell in the air, and the smell of strange cargoes loading and unloading, walked men and women in search of momentary escape from lives that were already unsuccessful escapes. They could no more flee desires which had already perverted them than those same perverted desires could fill the emptiness inside their hearts, or the emptiness and cold desolation of Liverpool, at any time of the year. Even spring.

"Oh, I'll wager I could make her do some delicious jumps," Slyde grimaced, winking at Selena.

She looked at him directly for the first time, and saw a roughneck bigger than Brian, with a sailor's wool cap on his head, wool sweater and canvas pants, and a bandanna, frayed and stained, knotted around his thick dirty neck.

"If you can't get 'im," taunted one of the whores at the bar, "better step aside an' let somebody 'o knows how." And Belle, thus goaded, snapped, "I can outdo you lyin' down, on the best day you ever 'ad," which brought more merriment. She leaned down and gave Brian a full kiss on the mouth, pushing her breasts and body into him. Selena saw him look at her, wide-eyed, out of the corners of his eyes, like a drowning man shooting one final desperate look at the safe shore before going down for the last time. Selena did not know what to do. Brian was falling, anyway. Maybe it was best to go along with this, and if worst came to worst, she could run outside and flee down the street to . . . to what? They had to proceed calmly; they had to know where they were going, what they were doing.

They had to find out where the *Highlander* was, of all the ships in this great port, and waste no time getting to it. Watching Brian lose himself in the whore's kiss, Selena resolved to tough it out, somehow, as best she could.

"Looks lak ye got 'im goin', Belle," the barmaid smirked. "I do believe e's *up* t' it, now."

" 'Course, wouldna surprise me if 'e was a mite *hungry*," Slyde put in, signaling for another whiskey. "What wi' that bloodless piece of goods 'e keeps fer company."

In spite of the situation, Selena flared at Slyde's persistent implications about her lack of attractiveness and fire, but she restrained herself. She dared not show anger, which a man like Slyde would take almost as an invitation. She drank some of the ale, and tried to edge a bit closer to the window. Belle let her hands rove slowly over Brian's body until she found what she was looking for. She broke off her kiss, and grinned with cold triumph.

"Ready, luv?"

Brian made the decision which promised him pleasure, and perhaps respite from the hostility of the group. It seemed to be the right thing to do, because they cheered, the ratty crowd around the bar, as he allowed Belle to lead him over to the peg ladder. It was a cheer that proffered begrudging acceptance.

"This won't take long," Brian managed to tell Selena, amid the racuous outcry. And then he was climbing after Belle, up through the trapdoor to the loft where business was done.

Selena edged closer to the window on the harbor, and bent again to her mug of ale. The trapdoor fell shut with a resounding thud, met by another small cheer and scattered cries of good luck.

"Don't ye cry now, sweets, wi' yer boyfriend castin' ye off lak that."

Selena looked up. It was Slyde, of course, just as she had feared. He sat down with a bottle of whiskey and a glass. "'Ere, 'ave some on me," and he sloshed a dollop of the strong liquor into her glass of ale. "Looks lak ye could stand somethin' t' put blood in yer cheeks, eh?" He thought highly of his wit, and chortled darkly. "I've a mind t' stir yer blood a bit myself." He spoke more quietly now, and at the bar, the others returned to their various concerns. Slyde had picked her out, and that was that. Only Brian could save her now, and he was compromised, to say the least.

"Well, say somethin', will ye?" the sailor demanded.

Selena did say something. She said: "And what, precisely, would you have me say?" She was unsettled, threatened, and she forgot herself. The words, the accent, betrayed her position and breeding. She had given herself away as clearly as if the word "nobility" were etched in the flesh of her forehead.

Slyde sat there, greasy-necked, muscled. He heard the tone and accent and knew that Selena was alien to him. Fear passed over his coarse features. A sword scar on his right jaw whitened as blood came to his face, and his eyes narrowed as he tried to puzzle out the situation. He did not have to be exceptionally smart to do so, and he was not dumb. A noblewoman on the waterfront, in a place like this. In disguise. That could mean only two things: Either she was looking for a good time, which he was more than willing to provide. Or something was wrong, which opened to him whole new vistas of opportunity and possible profit. Those in trouble were unswervingly ready to pay.

First things first. "Ye want a hard ridin' from a 'orse that knows the way, eh?" He leaned forward, and she saw in his eyes that frank, knowing, proprietary look she had seen on Will Teviot's face in the firelight. She had even seen it, for a fleeting moment, behind Royce Campbell's eyes. And, yes, had it not been Sean Bloodwell's look, too, that time in the grove by the river, when for the first time he kissed her breasts and she had promised him all else with her eyes alone? That was a man's look. A man's look when he believed he was about to enjoy himself a woman, however false that assurance might be.

Instinct spoke. *Use this, Selena. It may be your only weapon.*

"What d' ye say, eh? Ye got the itch that only a stallion can cure?"

She had not responded, and he was increasingly sure of himself.

"That be the problem, eh?"

Not looking at him, eyes modestly downward, Selena nodded.

Slyde leaned back in his chair. "Well," he said heartily, "ye've come upon the right saddle jockey, ye certainly 'ave!"

What? now? she thought.

"As soon as the loft is free," Slyde was saying, "you an' me'll 'ave ourselves a time. An' you won't find none better'n me, I swear. Yer man there, up with Belle, I'm goin' t' put 'im t' shame. Ye'll see. Hey, drink up now. Get a bit in ye. I don't want ye t' be a'layin' there lak a log."

Again, his rasping chortle, with an intimate touch to it now. Would she be forced to go through with this? *Could* she? Selena didn't know, and as she admitted to herself that she didn't know, didn't fully trust herself to do what was necessary to save herself, she admitted, too, that she had already failed. She had *not* killed McGrover. She had been a coward, had not done her duty at the moment when everything counted. At the moment of truth.

That's not only being a coward, she thought. *That's not even being a MacPherson. You'll be destroyed if you keep acting like this.*

But you would have had to kill a man.

Men have been killed before, and this was necessary.

And is Slyde?

Maybe.

Unconsciously, she hitched her chair closer to the window once again.

"Ye be wantin' some air? 'Tis a bit foul in 'ere."

"No," she told him, attempting a flattering tone. "I just wanted to see the ships. Is yours out there?"

His chest swelled. "I'll say 'tis, lady. An' ye want t' see 'er, do ye? Hey, come wi' me 'ere."

He grabbed her arm and all but jerked her upright, dragged her over to the window, which gave her the first good, long look at the harbor she had been able to get. Her heart fell as soon as she saw it. Finding the *Highlander* would not be an easy task.

There were at least four or five dozen ships in the harbor, ships of all sizes, all types, from all the nations of Europe. Some of the bigger ones were freighters, close in to the docks now. She could hear the shouts and curses of the workmen. The smell of tobacco was in the air, from Virginia far away, and sweet lumber from the endless forests of America, and tea and spices from India, where Sean Bloodwell had gone to seek a second destiny. Farther out were other freighters, waiting to load and unload, and numerous small boats, and then, way out at the edge of her visibility, several men-of-war, big and dark and threatening, any one of which might be . . .

"That's mine, there," Slyde was saying. "The M.S. *Meridian.* An' yer a good man t' ship on 'er, as I'll show ye in a few minutes. Got 'er a cap'n, Randolph's 'is name, 'o'd keelhaul ye fer spittin' on the deck."

Selena looked at the ship, which Slyde explained was being loaded with finished textile products from factories such as Sean Bloodwell had once owned.

"Sailin' fer Boston on the morrow," Slyde said proudly. "Hell of a place. We get liberty there, an' we go into town an' beat on the rebel colonials. Oh, it is a time, we 'ave, I tell you. . . ."

She took another long look. If the *Highlander* was out there, she could not tell. But Slyde might know. The problem was to find out without arousing suspicions.

"An' I could tell ye stories . . ."

She sat down at the table, smiling at him, and he became as endearing as a gruff puppy dog. About to know a noble lady in the best of ways, put her through her paces, an' 'ere she was, takin' 'im as a natural man, wi' none o' them 'aughty ways. . . .

"I bet you've . . . I'm sure you've fought . . . pirates, even," she said, feigning wonder and awe, and watching the trapdoor surreptiously.

"Pirates! Why, pirates, privateers, now I'll tell ye aboot that, indeed. The *Meridian* fights off at least one privateer each time across."

Her intention was to work around to Royce Campbell, who had been rumored a privateer, but Slyde, growing more and more expansive, as he grew more and more drunk, rambled on, from story to story. At one point, he moved over next to her, and now held her with one arm and drank with the other. The hand around her waist roamed freely, fondling her breasts, diving down across her stomach and between her legs. Then Slyde got a little impatient, just about at twilight, and stalked over to throw one of his boots at the trapdoor.

"Hold yer horses," Belle yelled in response. "I got one up 'ere seems not t' 'ave 'ad it fer a year."

Selena flushed at the gleeful howls that followed, but Slyde was treating her like his own woman now.

"All ye bastards be shuttin' yer traps now," he threatened, "or ye'll be bleedin' in the alleys o' Liverpool. This 'ere is a 'igh-class lady, I want ye t' know. . . ."

Selena was almost grateful to him. Indeed, he was not a bad sort, even if at any moment he wanted to take her body for sport. And, she had decided, if that was what it would take to get them safely away from Scotland, she would just have to . . .

But she refused to think past that point. *Out of Scotland*. That would be an ending, truly.

With full darkness came the end of the workday on the

docks, and soon the tavern was filled with jesting and profanity. Many of the men did not wait for their turn at the loft—Slyde was first on the list—and simply took the women out into the alley and had them standing up against the wooden planking of the walls.

Selena decided to risk it. "Is there a ship, the *Highlander,* out there in the harbor now?"

A look of curiosity and recognition brightened Slyde's bleary eyes. He was just about to speak when the trapdoor flew open and Brian, tired but happy, dropped to the floor. Belle followed, looking a bit worn.

"I earned me money's worth that time," she said, leaning against the bar. Half of the sailors were drunk already, and there was an instant clamor for the loft.

"Mr. Slyde's up next," the barmaid declared.

"An' I'll be wantin' it all night, too," Slyde crowed. "I'll be sailin' on the morrow, an' there's a fine wench 'ere's got t' be broken in right afore I go. . . ."

Shouting and yelling ensued, and complaints about his summary appropriation of the loft.

"Nay!" yelled the barmaid. "First come, first served, if ye've the money. Come on, now. 'Ave a drink. There's merchandise aplenty, an' the alley's free besides."

Slyde got up and grabbed Selena's hand, pulling her toward the peg ladder in the wall. Now was the time. At least there were no King's men here. They were safe, and if this was what had to be done . . .

They passed Brian as he came walking back toward the table.

Brian stopped in Slyde's path.

"Out o' me way, matey. It's my turn, an' I've got a fine piece t' service here, as ye can see. I'll see she's worth yer while when I get through."

Brian blinked, disbelieving. Selena saw, with instant trepidation, the little vein throb on the left temple, as it always did when he got angry. As it had on the day he'd knifed McEdgar. But they could not risk this now, not a fight, and she tried to signal him, to tell him that it was all right. . . .

"It's dark now," she said pointedly. "Why don't you be seeking out the *ship* . . ."

"I don't believe you'll be climbing up there with this woman," he was telling Slyde.

"Huh?" the sailor wondered.

". . . I didn't find out too much about the *ship,*" Selena tried again. "Just go out on the dock, and walk carefully . . ."

But it was not to be. Brian saw nothing at all amiss in being serviced by a whore for half the afternoon, but in the name of honor would jeopardize their very lives here in a dive in which anyone would have slit their noble throats for the price of a drink.

"Brian!" she cried.

But it was too late.

Brian let himself be overwhelmed by his nature and by a situation he did not take the time to understand. And Slyde had no idea that Brian was the brother of this young woman whose body he wanted to use as vessel for his urgent passion. He was not about to be dissuaded from that pursuit either. Rough and seawise, he sensed rather than saw the tightening of the muscles in Brian's arms, the way he braced his legs, and when the punch came, the big sailor dropped into a crouch and shot a tremendous uppercut at Brian's face. It struck a glancing blow along the left jaw. Brian spun slightly to the side, snarling, and Slyde backed up against the bar, then pushed abruptly away from it, his body a projectile. Brian did not move fast enough, and the two of them crashed down on the floor, which stank of wet sawdust, tobacco juice, and the usual result of too much cheap liquor.

"No!" Selena cried.

"Hey! Fight! Fight!" came the excited cries of men and whores at the bar. "I'll put m' money on the big guy wi' the bandanna."

"Nay. Ye're daft, ye are. The redhead'll kill 'im. 'E's a born fighter, 'e is."

The barmaid was not so pleased with the action. "Goddamn ye two bastards to hell!" she shrieked at Brian and Slyde, who grappled now in the filth. "Ye take it outside, ye hear. The magistrate'll be a-comin' down on me again, an' I 'ave t' pay 'em enough bribes already."

From beneath the bar, she grabbed a huge, black blunderbuss of a weapon, and waved it at the ceiling. Even drunks headed for the door at the sight of it—anybody could get hurt now—and they poured out into the waterfront street, shouting and pushing.

". . . bloody officers be a-comin' now, sure," the barmaid cursed, and came out in front of the bar, aiming the big jackhammer of a pistol at the two men.

Slyde managed to pull away from Brian's grip, and leaped to his feet, falling back against the wall.

"Brian! Let's get out of here."

But her brother was too far gone now, convinced of victory, and he approached Slyde, feinted, and rammed a fist into his gut. The sailor doubled up, panic in his eyes, and spun away along the wall, over toward the bar.

"I mean it, I'm a-tellin' ye, stop it and get out," called the barmaid, holding the gun on Brian. He paid her no mind, but went after Slyde again. She cocked the hammer back. He didn't hear it. Desperately, Selena threw herself against the barmaid, and the gun exploded, blue and white and tremendous in the dim, smoky bar. Brian stopped, stunned by the sound. It seemed as if he was about to come to his senses when, in one smooth motion, Slyde cracked a bottle of whiskey against the side of the bar and, holding the neck of the bottle, drove it with all his considerable strength deep into Brian's stomach. The sharp, jagged glass cut right through his leather belt, driving even the belt buckle deeply into him. It happened so fast that Selena did not actually see him fall—never remembered his actual falling—but then he was down, clutching at his stomach, trying to pull free the bottle, which protruded from him, and trying to hold in the flood of blood and tissue that poured forth. He howled in pure agony, but mercifully passed over into shock. A dreamy look came into his eyes, as they moved irregularly around the barroom.

"*Now ye've done it*!" the barmaid screamed. "'E's dyin'. Slyde, you goddamn scum. The bloody bastard's a-goin' t' die."

"Don't you call my brother that," Selena said mechanically, and the barmaid stepped back at her tone and accent, surprised, unnerved, just as Slyde had been earlier.

"Oh, Jesus, yer *brother*?" Slyde groaned.

Brian, writhing on the floor, dropping from consciousness, seemed to motion Selena with a bloody hand, and she knelt down beside him.

"God, lady, I didna ken 'e was yer brother. What's . . . why . . . ? and the sailor knelt, too. A few customers still in the bar, who had gone deathly quiet when the blood flowed, now edged to the door and were gone.

"A goddamn nobleman, or something," the barmaid cried, as if this were the last straw, the final indignity *she* had to suffer. She tucked the smoking gun under her skirts and headed for the door, too. "Ye can explain it to the law yerselves," she said. "I ain't be goin' t' no gallows fer bein' in on the killin' o' a young lord."

If you only knew, Selena thought. *You could get a reward . . .*

Brian's lips were moving, and she bent down, her ear next to his.

"It's too bad . . ." he gasped.

"What's he sayin'?" Slyde wanted to know. His eyes went nervously from Selena to the door. In the distance, over the shouting in the street, a whistle blew and hoofbeats sounded. "Lady, I'm sorry, I didna mean t' . . ."

"Shhhh. Quiet. Brian!"

The blood poured out. It was clear there was no hope. Even now Brian's face had grown pale, ethereal, like a painting of a doomed crusader.

". . . too bad . . . about the lilies . . ." Brian hissed between his teeth. A froth of blood was on his tongue, and a bubble of blood swelled and diminished in one nostril as he sucked for breath. Selena understood, and smiled through her tears. Once, long ago, she had told him that his brawling ways would kill him in the end, that she would one day have to place the lilies in his hands.

"Look, lady. I . . . I got t' be . . ." moaned Slyde, listening to the approaching horses.

"Wait," she told him, putting her hand on his sleeve. She did not know consciously, at that moment, why she restrained him. It may have been simply because he was the only one who had stayed behind with her. Or because he was truly shaken at what had happened, even though Brian's death had, in no small way, been his own fault. But she touched him, and he hesitated, waiting beside her.

"Good luck," Brian said, ". . . I . . . hope . . . you make it. . . ."

His eyelids flickered He was gone. No, he was still here with her. *There must be something . . .* she thought.

Something to comfort him. Then she remembered. Father.

"Brian! Can you still hear me?"

Something like a nod. Outside, people were running in the street, trying to get away from the scene of the crime before the police rode up.

"Oh, God, hurry!" Slyde pleaded.

"Brian! Think of the best thing," she cried, taking his bloody hand in her own. "Think of the best thing ever!"

Into his dull, fading eyes came a last warm light, something, a memory, locked in the lost days of his youth. When he smiled, his teeth were dark with blood, but it was a smile of delight.

"That . . . that time . . . with my sailboat . . ." he managed to gasp, "when Father . . ."

And Selena knew what he meant. Brian was seven or eight, and had been given a small sailboat of his own. The family was on holiday down along the shore of the North Sea, at Eyemouth, and the boy had taken his craft out on the water. Too far. Brian's maritime skills were not up to the task of getting back to shore, and a wind rose in the afternoon, dark clouds piled high against the sun. Father had gone after him, to bring him back.

". . . was . . ." Brian whispered, choking, his eyes on her, his hand clinging desperately now, ". . . was . . . the best time. . . ."

Then his head jerked sideways, and his body seemed to collapse, to fall away from her even as she held him. The blood flowed on.

"Lady, we got t' get out o' here," Slyde said. But it was too late. The horses of the waterfront patrol were just outside the door. Selena could hear one of the officers shouting questions at a lingering drunk. "What happened, man? What's going on here?" and the sickening sound of a wooden club on bone, on soft flesh, as the man was beaten. *"In the tavern,"* he screamed between blows, and pretty soon the officer would get the idea and come inside.

"We got only one chance," Slyde said, and pushed her toward the peg ladder. He practically propelled her upward through the trapdoor, and then leaped up after her, slamming down the door just an instant before the sound of heavy boots entered the tavern below. The loft was pitch-dark, and smelled worse than the barroom itself, heavy with the odor of passion and sweat and spilled love. "Get yer clothes off, lady," Slyde pleaded in a hoarse whisper, pawing at her, clawing at himself. "Get 'em off an' get down on the straw." She understood, and then she was naked against bug-ridden straw, Slyde's big, bristly body half covering her. Through a crack in the floor, she saw Brian dead beneath, his eyes open and looking right up at her, as if he saw her there. But it was over. Young Lord Brian MacPherson, born in Coldstream Castle, scion of a great family with all of life before him, Brian MacPherson, after a short life, dead on a bed of sawdust in a Liverpool dive, all things lost. She wanted to cry, but she was too scared. All things lost, and no hope, now . . .

A man came into her narrow sliver of view now, and stood over Brian's body, bending over him so that she could no longer see her brother's eyes. She saw his epaulets—an officer of the Liverpool constabularly.

"It's the MacPherson lad," she heard him say.

And then the head of another man came into view, and stood beside the first. A black, tricornered hat, set slightly askew. But she saw clearly the now-familiar black cape, and the white wrapping, like a bandage, protruding from one side of his head, beneath the rim of the hat.

"Search everywhere," said Darius McGrover. "The bitch cannot be far away. The MacPhersons stick together."

Selena was afraid that Slyde had heard, but if he did, he made no connection. After all, she thought, he must be terrified, too. He had killed a man, and even had he known that she was a MacPherson, hunted by the Empire, he would have had to think a long time before risking a visit to the authorities. He shifted slightly, on top of her now, and she felt his body trembling against her, impotent with tension. She felt like retching, what with the close air and the stink, but held the nausea back.

A banging on the trapdoor then. "Hey! Anybody there? Come down from there."

"Don't make a sound," Slyde hissed. "We've been drunk. We're asleep."

She did as he said. In a moment, the trapdoor crashed open and a candle was thrust up into the loft. Slyde did not move, nor did she.

"Hey! You, there, with your arse in the air!"

Slyde did not move.

Through lidded eyes, she saw the officer hold out the burning candle. She wanted to warn Slyde. He must have felt the heat coming, but he gritted his teeth and waited. When it touched the flesh of his backside, he roared and leaped up, clutching himself and bellowing in pain and outrage. The officer was laughing heartily.

"I did nithin' t' ye, sar," Slyde cried, all hurt and innocence, and Selena, in spite of lying there naked on the floor, forcing herself not to move, trying to burrow her blond hair a little into the straw, felt a sudden respect for the man. He lived in a hard world, and he had to survive.

"What ye be doing up here, mate?"

The officer raised the candle and brought it higher. Flickering light exposed Selena. "Say now, there's a fine piece." He watched her for a moment. Selena did not move.

"What's the matter? She dead?"

"Nay. We was . . . ah . . . we had ourselves a little too much t' drink, an' we been sleepin' . . ."

"You a sailor?"

"Aye, sar."

"What ship?"

"The *Meridian*. Leavin' fer America on the morrow. I was jest . . . jest sayin' good-bye t' my . . . wife . . ."

The officer let out a howl of laughter, which caused McGrover, down below, to ask what was the matter.

"Nothing, sir. 'Tis a lime-eating jackass an' a bought wench. She be drunk to stone, an' he looks 'im a sight with charcoal on 'is arse. Ye wish me t' bring 'em down?"

"Ask them of the guest down here."

"Aye. Hey, matey. What do you know of the man on the floor beneath."

Slyde was up to it.

"What man?"

"Get over here."

Slyde shuffled naked to the trapdoor and peered down, then feigned terrible shock. "Aiiii-Gott," he cried, "who'd be he? Oh, sar, sar, I swear, I been drunk an' screwin' an' sleepin' since midday an' I nivir lay me eyes on the poor bloke. . . ."

"Doesn't matter anyway," McGrover called. "I don't mind 'im dead, or who did it. Ask him if there was a woman with the bastard."

Selena's blood ran cold at his words. But Slyde swore that he knew nothing, saw no one. He even asked where all the customers had gone, which caused the officer to break into another hearty guffaw. He asked McGrover, once again, if he wanted to see the wench.

"Nay, nay," he growled. "The MacPherson bitch wouldna be caught dead fucking with a sailor. Tell the bloke to get dressed and get the wench out of here. And himself back upon his ship. You get the body out of here. I must see to the waterfront search."

Brian disappeared from her view, dragged away, his arms outstretched. The sawdust parted as they dragged him, and it was as if he had left a wake. Beside her, Slyde was pulling on his clothes and boots.

"That bastard gone now?" he whispered.

"Yes," she said. But then, try as she might, she could no longer hold back the tears. Slyde himself appeared profoundly shaken, and the knowledge that it was her brother he had killed came back to him. Clumsily, he put an arm around her bare shoulders. "Lady, I'm so sorry, but 'e would 'ave *killed* me. 'E would 'ave, an' that's a fact. 'E would have, truly, an' I've seen that look in the eyes o' many a man. . . ."

Selena agreed silently, and sobbed on.

"There. There, now," Slyde tried. "Come on, now. 'Ere. Put yer clothes on. I mean no 'arm t' ye. 'Twas just I didna understand." He seemed to think of something.

"Say, lady. Yer ladyship, or whatever . . ."

"Selena," she told him, before she had a chance to think.

"Selena. Look, Selena. Yer in trouble, ain'tcha?"

What to tell him? She fought her way back to self-possession. Something close to the truth. Slyde was not a bad sort, and she needed him. She had to fight now to stay alive. That came first. She had to make it out to the *Highlander* somehow, and this burly sailor, trying to soothe her now in his rough but not untender way, might be able to help.

"I *was* of the nobility," she told him. Past tense. That one word, *was*, seemed as difficult a word as she had ever spoken. "My parents are dead. We've lost everything. . . ."

"An' 'ow was that?" he interrupted.

"I don't know," she temporized. "Politics, or some such."

Slyde nodded sagely.

". . . and that man who was below. He killed my father, and he tried to . . . to . . . kill me."

"Why the mother befoulin' piece of . . ." Slyde snarled. "I ought've jumped down there, barearse an' all, an' wrung 'is neck. Say, what're ye doin' 'ere in Liverpool?"

Selena took a deep breath, and told him. She told him about the *Highlander*, and how they were to meet the ship here, for safe passage.

"Aye," he said, remembering. "Ye asked me that afore the . . . afore the fight. Aye."

"Is it here? The *Highlander*? In Liverpool?"

Into the momentary pause, Selena read more disaster. And it came.

"Nay, yer lady . . . ah . . . Selena. Nay, 'tis not 'ere, an' won't be, neither. See, Sir Royce Campbell's been declared an outlaw by the Crown. 'E set t' preyin' on British shippin' in the West Indies, an' seems t' 'ave tied in wi' them American rebels. 'E's not t' be allowed port at no English dock in all the world. . . ."

And that seemed to be the end of it, there in the foul-smelling loft, wrapped in straw, with only an unlettered seaman for a friend. But he was one friend, and, in spite of everything, he was better than none at all. And, too, hovering just beyond the borders of perception, was a phantom of relief. Royce Campbell would not be saving her, true. But, also, she would not have to face Royce Campbell. And then, immediately, she knew how foolish she was being.

"I've got to get away," she said.

"To where?"

"I can't stay in England. I'll be dead should they take me. Is there no other ship to America? *Your* ship is going to America . . ."

"But . . . Selena, we're a freightin' ship, we can't . . ."

"Oh, but I'll pay, I still have . . ."

She thought of the last few coins in the fold on the inside

of her riding boots. Brian had kept their last pound notes. She could not reach them now.

"But ye couldna do it. Cap'n Randolph, e's a merchant-man, an' don't take passengers. Particularly women. 'E 'ates women, as once 'e 'ad a wife what run out on 'im. An' I wouldna want t' risk it. 'E's a mean one. 'E takes a half-dozen extra crew on every sailin', 'cause some always dies fra' punishment."

"But if you talked to him . . ."

"Nay, I couldna do that."

But the ship was to leave in the morning, and with McGrover searching the waterfront, Selena had mere hours to find shelter, or to escape.

"There must be some place on a great ship like yours," she said to Slyde, hardening herself for what she was about to do. His clothes were still loose about him, his body hard and warm, his mind confused and, soon, quite willing.

"Aye, there is a place in the hold," he said, his breath coming fast. "Near the bow, but in rough weather 'twill be torture. But . . ."

But there *was* a place.

The agreement was unspoken, the contract written only in flesh. *Now I can do anything*, she thought, and believed it was true. Slyde was an elemental man, ruled by basic, simple urges, with a rude kind of honor all his own. He took what was given and accepted the price demanded. When he entered her, Selena felt nothing but a physical rending, permitted herself to feel nothing but that, thinking not of Slyde, not of Royce Campbell, not of Sean or of Brian, nor Father, but rather of Darius McGrover. Slyde was almost gentle, awed, dazed, but she let him work away at her in the loneliness of his mind, his own hungry fantasies. Her vision was of McGrover, and then she was high and cold and untouched on the battlements of Cold-stream . . .

Slyde was moaning into her hair.

. . . and far out on the morning mist soared the hawk . . .

Slyde was panting, belly on belly, now.

. . . and from the cold ice of her mind, the frigid fury of her wounded blood, she fashioned a terrible arrow . . .

Slyde was keening into her ear, calling for her to move, jerking into the cradle she had given him.

. . . and the arrow shot far and true into the pale sky . . .
Slyde was calling.

. . . and impaled the hawk in midflight, wings outstretched, motionless in wonder and surprise . . .

Slyde shot hot and trembling inside her, and only that
brought her back to life and time.

. . . and the black hawk fell dead upon the earth of
Scotland, where her beating heart fell hard about it with a
cry.

On the waterfront, it was dark. On the ships near the
docks, sailors on watch could be seen pacing the decks, but
the lights on the ships that lay at anchor out in the harbor
seemed to move independently of human cause, like insects
of the night, passing to and fro according to some demand
of their own nature. The M.S. *Meridian* was a hundred
yards away, no more.

Selena and Slyde stole out of the darkened tavern and
onto the street. She saw the tall masts of the ships outlined
against the lighter darkness of the sky, thought of the *Highlander*, and of what the sailor had told her about Royce
Campbell joining the American rebels. That was something
she did not believe. *He may be sailing with them*, she
thought, with an inner grimace of wisdom, *but only for
reward, and only for his own perverted pleasure. The
Americans would learn in due time, just as she had.*

"Are ye ready, now?" Slyde asked.

She nodded, and he unfolded his ship's bag.

"This ain't goin' t' be very comfortable, Selena, but I'll
do my part lak I promised ye, if ye do yers as well."

The ship's bag was large, of heavy cloth, with a binding
rope that ran around the top. Selena climbed in and tried
to curl into a ball.

"No. Put yer hands on yer ankles and bend forward.
There. Duck yer head. That's it. I'll sling ye over my shoulder. Don't move, nor say nothin', all right?"

She promised, and then he pulled the rope tight and she
felt herself swung out into air, before coming to rest against
his back. He started down the docks for the *Meridian*. Only
the darkness would make this plan succeed, she thought.
Her body in the ship's bag, curled up though it was, could
hardly appear like a sailor's gear.

Slyde was puffing a little now, and walking fast. He stopped even before she heard the command.

"Halt! By order of the Secret Offices."

McGrover's voice.

She was dropped to the ground, hard on her shoulder, and she almost cried out. Then Slyde pushed her up against what must have been a partition or wall of some kind, and *leaned against her!*

"Aye! Glad ye stopped me, mate," she heard him say in a slurred, drunken voice. "Could use a little breather. Long walk on these docks."

McGrover's voice was suspicious. "On your feet, deck rat. You could do with a little respect, do you know that?"

Abruptly, Slyde's weight was off her.

"Oh, aye, sar. Aye, sar. Don't know that, though, but . . ." the tone changed, half whining, half cajoling ". . . but it's just I was frightful tired, and . . ."

"Shut up. What's your ship?"

"M.S. *Meridian*, sar."

Selena waited for McGrover to make the connection between Slyde here on the dock and Slyde of the *Meridian* up in the tavern loft with the whore. *Me*, she thought ruefully, her legs beginning to cramp.

"What's in that bag, sailor?"

Slyde didn't miss a beat. "M' gear, sar. Would ye care t' see?"

McGrover's harsh laugh. "I've better things to do than stick my nose in your muck. Have you seen a blond wench about this evening? Highborn. Ye couldna miss her."

Slyde denied it, and offered his help in a search.

McGrover was unimpressed. "You drunken bastard. You're lucky if you make it up the gangplank of your ship. Get along with you now, or I'll put in a word for you with Captain Randolph. He'll improve your manners for you, I daresay."

Her muscles tightened. Selena bit her lip to keep from crying out.

"Oh, yes, sar. Yes, sar," Slyde was groveling. "That he will, sar, an' best o' the evenin' t' ye, sar."

The footsteps on the dock diminished. *Thank God.* Again she was hoisted into the air, a little later swaying up the gangplank.

"Who goes?"

"Slyde, comin' aboard."

"Where the hell've ye been, mate? Ye barely made it. We sail at dawn. Captain Randolph was puttin' a few more knots in his cat-o'-nine fer ye specific."

Slyde grunted.

"Want some 'elp wi' yer gear, there?"

"Nay, nay. I'll manage."

Their progress through the ship seemed to take forever, down gangways, ladders, passageways. All Selena knew was that they were going down deep into the ship. She judged their progress only by smell. On deck there was the salt and seaweed odor, pleasant in the cool April night. Then, below decks, sweat and old timber. Tea and some kind of fried meat, near the galley. Then the holds, with their oddly stale, sour smell. Slyde told her the odor rose from the bales of textile products being shipped to market in America. And below that, Slyde puffing, cursing occasionally, the smell of wetness on wood, dank air . . . and something else.

Slyde set her down. Immediately the wetness penetrated his ship's bag and spread onto her clothes. She jumped up when he pulled open the rope. They were in a small space that was neither room nor compartment, and she could tell by the manner in which the beams came together that they were all the way forward in the ship, where keel met bow. And below water level.

"No one e'er comes down 'ere," he told her. "But I'll bring ye food whene'er I get the chance. . . ."

Selena remembered what Father had told her. America could be two months away, and if they struck heavy weather, the plunging bow would drive her smashing again and again against these timbers.

He noticed her chagrin.

"I can get ye back onshore, if ye like, but that'll be all."

No. There was nothing left for her onshore. The whole of her world and life had been reduced to this tiny, triangular chamber in the bottom of a ship, but from this must come whatever the future held. *You are only defeated if you believe it*, she thought, recalling her brave naiveté only months ago.

"No. If you leave the bag for me, I can wrap myself in it overnight."

Slyde brightened, and she saw that he had been afraid. He didn't want her to leave. "Oh, in the morn, I'll bring ye blankets, an' such," he promised, all protector again. "If I do it right, there might be room e'en for a makeshift hammock fer ye in 'ere, what ye say t' that?"

She said it would be wonderful, smiling for him, and he stood there thinking it over. The ship was quiet, except for an odd scratching. It was not, at the moment, threatening, except for that strange, unidentifiable odor. He stepped close and took her into his arms in his direct, demanding way.

"An' there's room in 'ere fer us, too," he whispered gruffly, his lips seeking hers.

Oh, God, I can't face this now.

"You'd better go," she said.

"Why? We're safe 'ere, we are."

He fumbled for her, his hands harsh. He wanted her now, and he was strong. Physically, she had no chance against him.

"*Come on*," he pleaded, forcing her back, pushing her legs apart with a huge fist.

"You'll ruin it," she pleaded.

He suspended his attack. "What d'ye mean by that?"

Selena seized the slight advantage, and spoke to him softly, as if conspiring with a lover. "You've done so well to get me aboard," she said, her lips close to his ear. "You were so brave in the face of danger. But let's not spoil our luck. Don't make anyone suspicious now. Go back to your quarters, right now, before we're discovered, and we'll have the whole voyage to ourselves."

She forced herself to press close to him, promising her body.

"You can have me all the way across the sea," she said, as Slyde blinked, thinking it over. "All the way. *If* we're smart enough not to be discovered now. We must give no sign . . ."

Possessed of the shrewdness and wisdom she had conferred upon him, Slyde reluctantly agreed.

"Then I'll be back later," he grunted. "An' I'll bring ye some food if I can."

He left her, then, but something must have happened to him, or he was being watched closely, for he did not return. The only light came from a hurricane lamp farther down a passageway along the keel, and Selena tried to arrange the ship's bag in such a way that she could sit comfortably on it without getting wet from the dripping timbers of the ship. And without being seen, should anyone come down here. It was impossible, that night. She was cold and terrified. Water was running somewhere in a steady, ominous trickle, reminding her of the wall of water all around her, just beyond these boards. She was by turns hopeful, despondent, terrified, and then hysterical. *You'll get through this*, she told herself. *You'll get through this, and you'll come back again*, although there was precious little evidence to support such a resolution.

Then she was simply cold and tremendously tired. But since it was impossible to sleep—she was afraid to sleep, anyway—Selena put her mind to work, trying to solve the mystery of the faint, disagreeable odor, the periodic scuffling noise she heard. Something in the hold? Men working at night? Or activity in the galley, getting ready for the morning meal?

None of these.

The answer came to her all by itself. It hung from one of the big beams along the starboard hull, slick and wet and gray, with a thin, malevolent face, predatory teeth, and tiny, red, fearless eyes. The rat's long, thin tail twitched like a whip.

Selena realized then that Darius McGrover did not necessarily resemble a hawk.

THE DARK BELOW

Trapped in the darkness in the ship, Selena knew the world now only by imagination, and by what Slyde told her on his hasty, surreptitious visits. The burly, solicitous sailor had managed to get her a section of discarded rigging, which, covered with old blankets, served as a hammock, in which she spent most of her days and nights. And he gave her a knife. For the rats. "Don't ye nivir use it on a sailor, if y're found down 'ere. It'll be bad enough fer ye as 'tis, without harmin' one o' the crew."

Slyde did not suggest—and Selena did not ask—if the knife might possibly be for herself, in such circumstance as the discovery of a stowaway. That was no good. She could not do it, just as she had been unable to do it on the night Will Teviot captured her in Cargill.

All days were similar, once they reached the high seas. The dank timbers, along which crawled the watching rats. The cold. The constant roll of the ship, or a plunging rise and fall when the *Meridian* took the breakers at its bow. The hurricane lamp swinging from its hook far down the passageway. And, now and then, sometimes twice a day— Slyde told her what a day was; she could not measure time—leftover food from the galley. After two weeks at sea, Selena began to fear for her sanity, if not her health.

It began on the morning the *Meridian* sailed. Selena was conscious of movement, slow and heavy, as the laden ship moved out of Liverpool harbor and onto the roads of the North Atlantic, and then, later, the heavy roll and swell of the high seas. Thus, by sense of motion alone, she realized the loss of her homeland, her life. No longer a refugee in the Highlands, with Father and Brian, she was now at the mercy of the ocean. And Slyde. When he'd returned to enjoy his prize, Selena said she had "the curse." Slyde played the gentleman, but he wouldn't do so much longer.

Timeless hours she spent in the hammock, drifting from memory to memory, from desire to desire, until her recollections seemed as warped and distorted as her dreams did. Faces and events blurred, just as time did, in the watery cavern of the ship, and words from the past came down upon her, took on strange meaning. Half crying, half dozing, she would remember the ride down from the Highlands, Grandma's body strapped upon the baggage rack above her head, but Father would be with her, saying, *Selena, the sky begins here,* and it would not be Grandma but Father in the coffin, now carried by faceless, black-coated men into the grove of trees on the banks of the Teviot River—or was it onto the sweet meadow at Foinaven Lodge?—where Sean Bloodwell bent to kiss her breasts, with Royce Campbell striding across the ballroom in Edinburgh, his eyes upon her for the first time, and then swinging out onto the rope with him, out over the balcony . . . no, that was swinging in the ship's bag on Slyde's broad back. No, either. No, too. The only memory on which her pulse beat, on which it could rely, was the memory of the beat of Royce Campbell's pulse, where she touched his neck with her hand, he above her, around her, within her, the place toward which the blade of her sword was homing. McGrover again, twitching a mean, thin tail from the ship beams, and mocking her with red eyes. Blood leaping. Bodies burning. And then a dark shape would rise up against the hurricane lantern, and it would be Slyde sometimes, bringing her the rind of a lime, already gnawed by something or someone, or a piece of dried beef, black bread, a precious half-cup of water.

Slyde kept demanding his due.

The first days, it was easy. The sailor understood—or thought he understood—that it was her time, and he was even excited, on edge, with his secret adventure. But then the ship was out on the vast loneliness of the sea, and the men on board changed, faced now not with the whoring and drinking of a transitory week in port, but rather with the elemental mystery of the sea, which unnerves more learned and steadier men than Slyde. It is the nature of the

sea, just as it is the nature of the black, star-studded abyss,
to reach into the mind and heart of human beings, and to
wrench out of them, in a moment of crisis, all that is there.

Selena, drifting in time, her future unreadable, pored
over faces and memories, and, when she had gone too far,
when everything she knew intermingled and became trackless miasma, pulled herself together with a vision of returning to Coldstream. Some day. Some year. Some century.
And everything would be as it had been.

On the bridge, according to Slyde, Captain Randoph
was reverting to form. One sailor, clumsy at his ropes, had
been hanging now two days, by his thumbs, from the yardarm. His wrists, elbows, and shoulders were already dislo-
cated, and soon the weight of his body would stretch him
out longer than the rack.

And Slyde kept asking for delight.

"I still can't," she told him, the seventh day at sea.

"Hey, Selena, I mayn't be noble born, but I'm no fool.
'Tis not the way it happens, fer seven days! Look at the
risk I'm takin' by bringin' down yer grub. Come on, now.
Blood or no blood, I don't care no more."

"Please. I wish you wouldn't."

"What? Ye wish I *what?* Now, who're ye, anyways, my
sweet? Ye ken what would 'appen if I was t' go up on deck
an' tell the captain I found a stowaway? An' a woman, too?
Ye want t' guess on it?"

"I'm very grateful, and when we reach America, you'll
be suitably rewarded . . ."

"Ah! Don't ye 'old the carrot t' me eyes lak that, ye
bitch. Ye told me already 'ow ye've got nithin', an' it must
be true, 'cause if ye did, ye wouldna be 'ere. Now, afore I
must be rough wi' ye, move aside yer dress so's I can 'ave
ye."

Selena had known it would come to this, and she already
regretted the necessity of what she had had to do in the
tavern loft. But, she realized, if he could threaten her with
Captain Randolph's wrath, she held over him the very fact
that he had brought her aboard. *And,* she thought, *I can
still count on my accent and my name. Ship's officers are
gentlemen, even when they are barbarians.*

She was lying on the hammock as Slyde lifted a leg and
prepared to swing on top of her. The knife was in her

hand, beneath her skirts. She turned her wrist, and the blade of the knife slanted at his groin. He stepped back, hatred and wonder in his eyes, and the ship rolled beneath them.

"Ye've gone mad," he told her, studying the knife.

Selena almost agreed with him.

"What of yer food?" Slyde asked. "Yer water?"

Selena had no answer.

"I'm not an evil man," he said, easing closer.

Selena cast about for a ploy, some trick to hold him off.

"There's lots worse," Slyde said, wet-lipped in the anticipation of pleasure.

Yet there must be a way. The knife still poised, but with Slyde edging closer, ready to pounce, Selena decided on her course.

"*Father!*" she screamed at him, there in the dark hold.

He leaped back, more surprised than anything else.

"*Father, you've come!*" she cried, sitting up, tossing the knife away—but not too far away—and spreading her arms to him, as if for an embrace.

"Quiet, my God," he said, looking around and putting a finger to his mouth. He was a little alarmed now.

"Here! Come to me," she cried, swinging out of the hammock, following Slyde as he backed away, beginning to believe she had already gone mad.

"Ye'll be wantin' food an' water," he suggested, glancing over his shoulder. "An' who'll bring it to ye, lest it's Slyde? So come on now an' be a good girl fer me. . . ."

True. She might scare him off this time. But what about next time? What if Slyde did not bring down her crumbs of black bread, her pathetic half a cup of water? And she had been meaning to ask for a towel, some soap, and a brush.

She stopped.

Slyde stopped, too, no longer backing away. He looked skeptical, and kept an eye on her face. Selena didn't have the courage to continue the charade any longer; the repercussions were too formidable to consider. At the moment an image of herself stalking the rat came to mind, she crazy with hunger, abandoned by Slyde to the incessant loneliness of the hold. She knew it was no use. She might go crazy later, but she wasn't crazy yet. She sagged to her knees on the wet boards, as if to say, "Go ahead. Have at me. Do what you will."

"Now, that's a nice lassie," Slyde said, coming forward. In one motion, he lifted her, swung her over the side of the hammock, and laid her down.

"That's a good girl," he was crooning, his voice already hoarse and breathy. Impassioned by her acquiescence—utterly passive though it was—he lifted her skirts and fumbled at his own clothing, opening his breeches. She saw it all as if in the slowness of dream motion, as the doomed convict must witness his last minutes on the chopping block. Slyde's slow, concupiscent leer, and the way his hands moved, fumbling with his clothes. Far down the passageway, the steady arc of the hurricane lantern as the ship rolled on the mighty deep. Her own distress, too, tossing on the rigged hammock, above three miles of black ocean. And now Slyde's body moving over the side of the hammock, and his hand reaching for her. *Try to do as you did in the tavern. Don't think.*

But her mind was feverish, even if her body was passive to a point far beyond submission. No point in resistance anymore. Not to Slyde or anyone else.

"I don't mean ye no 'arm, Selena," Slyde was crooning. His breath stank of garlic and fish. "It's just that . . ."

And she felt him fumbling and exploring, about to enter.

"Well, now, Mr. Slyde," came the voice, cold and amused.

In spite of her own surprise and alarm, Selena was aware that she had never seen a human being move as fast as Slyde did. He was off her in less than a second, and in scarcely more time than that he had himself buttoned up, standing to stiff attention against the hull of the ship.

The figure stood directly in the path of the lantern, and Selena could not make out his face, but she had little doubt of his identity. Based upon Slyde's frequent allusions to the man's ruthlessness and brutality, she had expected a larger figure. But the silhouette was almost slim, slightly stooped, indolently self-assured.

"So you brought a passenger aboard, did you, Slyde?" That same chilling tone, utterly confident, even bored.

"Aye, Cap'n Randolph, sar, I . . ."

"Save it, Slyde. We'll discuss it shortly. In truth, I've

known since the evening you came aboard. And your frequent visits to galley and hold were noted regularly by my spies among the crew. But I decided to let you get away with it for a while. In the first place, it will be much more humiliating for you to know, not only that you have failed, but that I knew all along of your failure and your . . . stupidity. That's being charitable, and you will soon agree. And, in the second place, wondering what and whom you had down here was amusing to me. It gave me something to think about."

Selena did not move. Captain Randolph was angry, very angry, but it was not the kind of anger which most people manifest, the hot rage against which a calm person can contend. No, he was angry in a far more disconcerting way. He was angry because he enjoyed it, because it left him free to devise and carry out monstrous reprisals against those who had offended him. Slyde, for example, and . . .

"What is your name, woman?" he asked her now, his silhouette straightening imperceptibly against the lantern light.

Selena collected herself. "I am Selena MacPherson, of Coldstream, in Scotland. This is most unfortunate, but it was necessary, and I assure you that when we reach America, you will be more than rewarded for your . . ."

Randolph laughed. "Did you hear that, Slyde? She says she is . . ."

"Aye, aye, sar."

"Shut up, Slyde. I'm speaking. That will be another hunk of flesh out of your carcass. As I was saying, she speaks of rewards. No, Miss MacPherson. Do not attempt to mislead me. You are a fugitive, and you have nothing. Not a pence. The Secret Offices were on every ship in Liverpool, with news to be on watch for you. Pity they missed you, isn't it? No, there will be a reward, all right. But it will be mine, when I turn you over to the governor-general in Massachusetts. I daresay you'll make the voyage back in a hole as bad as this . . ." He looked around at this pitiful place in the bow. ". . . so the least we can do is bring you up on deck now. I am certain better accommodations can be found for you."

He spoke so softly, with such excessive politeness, that Selena's apprehension flared beyond fear.

"Come now. Slyde, would you proceed us up on deck, please?

"Aye, aye, sar."

"Shut up, Slyde. You had best keep your mouth shut. They tell me that water is apt to get into it, when a man is keelhauled. . . ."

The hapless sailor began immediately to plead, but his distress only amused the captain, who laughed.

"Oh, sar, please, please, *sar*, not that, anything but that . . ."

"Anything? Really, Slyde."

Screeching pathetically, Slyde made a break for it, and ran up a short ladder, disappearing somewhere in the cargo hold.

Randolph laughed again, and motioned Selena to follow him. They went up on deck, and the danger of the circumstances notwithstanding, Selena exulted in the fresh, cool air, and the strong wind bending, cracking, in the sails. Blinded for a moment by the sun, she gradually saw the circle of rough men standing around her, their expressions puzzled, or fearful. From the crow's nest, atop the mainmast, came a doleful wail.

"Woman aboard! Woman aboard ship! God help us now!"

At her side, Captain Randolph chuckled mirthlessly.

"Sailors are quite superstitious about women aboard a ship, my dear. They have been known to . . . how shall we put it? . . . *jettison* the offending element. . . ."

She looked at him closely for the first time. He was a highly attractive man, with a regularity of features that was almost too perfect, with all the outward characteristics of human appearance, but lacking heart and soul, blood and torment, which are the heritage of living men.

"But do not be alarmed, just yet. See them? These sailors of mine have been reduced to the primal motives, fear and need. They will do exactly as I say, when I say, no more and no less. They fear me because I have bred it into them, and because, upon this ship, I alone can satisfy their needs."

He stopped, quite pleased with his situation. And his

control over these men was no inconsiderable accomplishment either, Selena realized. The men swinging down from the rigging, to gather about her on the deck of the *Meridian,* and the men climbing up out of the hold to see her, were a sullen, murderous lot. Their eyes threatened her, and she remembered how she must look, the clothes Brian had bought her in Liverpool soiled and wrinkled, her once beautiful hair damp and matted.

"Do not worry," Randolph said, as if having read her thoughts. "You will be allowed to bathe and change in due course. Your only punishment for now will be to remain as you are and observe our dealings with Mr. Slyde."

Curtly, he gave the orders. Slyde was to be found in the cargo hold, and brought on deck. It was done, in minutes. Several evil-looking men—the officer of the day, the bosun's mate, and his second in command, Randolph explained, as if courteously—then stretched the screaming, pleading Slyde out on the deck and tied him hand and foot.

"What are you going to do to him?" Selena asked, trembling.

"Nothing he has not already done to himself, by his actions," the captain smiled.

"But he just did it to help me. I . . ."

"Would you prefer to be in his place?"

Selena started. No, she would not be pleased with that. Never.

"You see," Randolph said, a teacher outlining a lesson for a callow student, "you see what I mean about fear. It is the level at which men are most easily managed. Make them fear you enough, and you are a great leader. As I am. See?" he went on. "Watch the faces of the men tying Slyde. Watch the faces of the others. There. Can you not read their minds? First, there is relief. Because they have escaped punishment. Second, however, you will see something far more subtle. It is like delight mingled with pride. They will *enjoy* watching Slyde get cast overboard, because in their minds they will believe themselves to be my soulmates. They worship power and they will congratulate themselves on being shrewd enough to side with me. Cowing men is easy to do, and there is only one precaution that a leader must take. Make sure the group has a continuous supply of lone victims. Are you ready?" he called to his second in command, a rangy, rawboned officer with a pendulous nose which looked as if its cartilage had been removed, and the flesh of the nose sewn back together.

"Aye, aye, sar. Ye ready, Mr. Slyde?"

Slyde whimpered and cried, struggling hopelessly at his bonds.

"All right, let's do it, then," the captain said.

A thick rope was strung beneath the keel of the ship. Slyde, moaning piteously, was bound hand and foot to one end of the rope. Several strong sailors grasped the other end. The hapless seaman would be thrown overboard and "hauled" beneath the keel.

"He might drown!" Selena cried, seeing what it was they were about to do. "He can't move either his legs or his arms."

"That's the exact idea," Captain Randolph exclaimed, pleased with her percipience.

She averted her eyes as they dragged the babbling Slyde to the rail. Then she felt Randolph's hand on the back of her neck—it was like a steel vise, for he was deceptively strong—and he twisted her face back to the pleading sailor.

"You are not merely an observer, my dear. A part of your punishment for stowing away on my ship is to witness what happens to those who break the rules."

Smiling, he let linger unspoken whatever might befall her later.

Slyde went over the side, and struck the water, flopping in desperation.

"Don't pull him in too fast, men," called the captain to the sailors at the other end of the rope. "Mister Slyde thinks he's a big fish, and we wouldn't want to break the line."

He laughed.

To Selena, it seemed as if they would never pull the rope. Out of sight beneath the ship, the helpless Slyde would be in torment, fighting to hold his breath. After a couple of minutes, Randolph gave a lazy gesture, and the men started hauling rope. Now Slyde would be drawn directly beneath the *Meridian,* his body cut and scraped by the barnacles attached to the ship. It was an evil penalty.

"I seldom use it on a man I'd rather see alive," the captain told her, as they watched the sailors yank the rope.

"But sometimes they survive. It provides suspense, don't you think? Goodness," he added, studying her hair, "I believe we can get you back to humanity. I have clothes in my cabin that might suit you. And I could use . . ." he said it with an unreadable, faintly ironic touch ". . . a little extra beauty on my ship."

Then Slyde had been hauled under the keel. He came up dripping, motionless.

"Cap'n, I think 'e's dead."

"Oh, too bad. Let's have a look."

Slyde lay spread out on deck like a dead fish. Captain Randolph strode over and kicked him hard in the stomach. A second passed, then a thin trickle of water flowed from his mouth and nostrils, followed by a moan.

"Good man, indeed," Randolph observed. "I didn't think he'd make it. Now," he ordered, turning to the bosun, "when he comes 'round, strip him and flog him until he drops, douse him with salt water, and then flog him again. I'll take another look at him then."

Already, men were working on Slyde, bringing him to. The poor wretch was choking and vomiting. Selena, knowing what was in store for him, almost wished that he had died beneath the ship.

But what was in store for her?

"Come along now, my dear," Captain Randolph said, smiling. Gallantly, he offered his arm. Automatically, she took it, with a strange sensation that the arm under the fine cloth of his tailored uniform jacket was neither encased by warm human flesh nor filled with human blood and bone.

"I do hope you'll like my quarters," he told her, and from the tone it was clear that he did not care if she liked his cabin at all.

It was in the stern, high above the rudder, and both in its position and organization reminded her of Royce Campbell's quarters aboard the *Highlander*. She did not have time to dwell upon the comparison, though, because as soon as Captain Randolph guided her inside and swung the door shut behind them, a strikingly beautiful woman stepped from behind a delicately woven Chinese screen.

"Why, darling," she smiled, "you've brought me company!"

A sound like that of a distant rifle shot echoed down

from the deck and into the cabin, and then a howl of sheer agony.

"Oh, my dear, you're using the cat again. Upon whom this time, may I ask?"

"Slyde," the captain said. "He brought aboard our pretty little stowaway here."

The woman's gaze was piercing, disconcerting. She reached out and touched Selena's face, and her eyes sparkled, worshipfully.

"Oh, darling," she said, "you're so cruel and perverse. He doesn't deserve the cat for that. But give him death instead, now, and end his misery."

Again, the sharp explosion of sound, the knotted leather lashes biting into Slyde's back. And, again, his trapped, despairing cry.

"You're much too soft, Roberta," Captain Randolph chided, in a curious singsong, a kind of parody of tenderness. "And, besides, it's the principle of the thing. Selena must learn."

"Indeed," Roberta agreed, "she has many things to learn."

With an understanding that was welcome, and a gentleness that was almost eager, Roberta saw to it that hot water was brought for Selena's bath, and fragrant soaps, thick towels. But whenever one or another of the sailors came to the cabin door with what she had ordered, Roberta herself slid behind the Chinese screen. So, if any of the officers or crew knew of her presence on the *Meridian*, it must be the secret of a very few. Yet, it was puzzling. Randolph, as a captain, could scarcely have been a sterner disciplinarian, even judging by the harsh standards of the maritime profession. And yet, on his own ship, with a measure of discretion but certainly no great secrecy—all that fragrant soap? all that hot water?—he kept a mistress. Or was she his wife?

On deck, Slyde screamed for a long time, then fell silent, even as the lashes cut his flesh. Then, after a time, he started screaming again, and finally stopped.

Selena had been left to bathe in the tub, which Roberta pushed behind the screen for her privacy, and Captain Randolph spoke so quietly with the other woman that Selena could not hear. At length, when the flogging ceased, Randolph said he had to go up on deck and see what to do about the sailor.

"Don't be long, darling," Roberta said, and the two of them kissed briefly on the lips, like an affectionate, long-married couple. The captain left, and Selena, in a lovely turquoise robe Roberta had given her, stepped out from behind the shield, before Roberta's admiring gaze.

"Oh, honey, let's do have a look at you," she said. "If you'd only announced yourself directly, you'd never have had to spend all that time down in the foul hold. We can't have that, now, can we?"

Selena received a sweep of impressions, most of them perplexing, and not a little strange. This woman, quite obviously, was more than hospitable. But not only was her very presence here on the ship disconcerting, it was a contradiction of what Slyde had told her: "The cap'n hates all women. He had a wife run out on 'im once." Selena's expression must have revealed her thoughts, because Roberta was quick to put her at ease.

"Here, now, I know you're wondering about all this, what's going to happen to you. But just you don't worry about it. The captain gives a threatening impression sometimes, doesn't he?" She smiled, and guided Selena to a cushioned chair. "Don't worry about that either, not even his talk of turning you in for a reward when we reach Boston. He won't do that."

Roberta sounded very certain, but in Selena's mind was the further question: then what *will* he do?

"We'll maneuver around him, just the two of us," the other woman said. "Now let me ring and get you something from the galley. You must be famished, and you're so beautiful. You must keep working on your looks, and they will be put to fine use one day."

Saying that, she touched Selena's face—it was difficult not to draw back—and stroked her gently, as one would a lover. Roberta sensed her alarm, but did not seem offended.

"I'm sorry," she said, moving away, gazing at Selena with eyes that were . . . what? "I'm sorry. I didn't mean to unnerve you, it's just that . . ."

Whatever it was, she left the explanation unspoken, and

yanked a pull rope near the door, which sounded a signal bell. In moments, a sailor stood outside the door, and Roberta passed him a message for food: bread, grilled lamb, red cabbage, and a bottle of port.

"Yes, lamb," she smiled, at Selena's questioning look. "Captain Randolph brings live sheep onto his ship, and slaughters them as the need arises. He is not one to give up his pleasures merely because he has chosen a lonely vocation."

There was no denial of the fact, Selena thought, watching Roberta, beautifully coiffed, expensively gowned, perfumed. She was a part of the pleasure. The sailor soon brought up a tray of food, the lamb juicy, hot from the galley spit, and the wine sweet and strong. Selena began to eat and drink ravenously, then remembered the unfortunate Slyde.

"What's happened to him? Will he be allowed to eat? Is he alive?"

Roberta's face darkened. "Child, let me tell you how things are on this ship, and how to have a pleasant time here, in spite of the situation. The first rule is: Ask no questions. Never. When Captain Randolph tells you something, ask no questions, even if you do not understand what he is talking about. And the second rule is: Obey him. He may wish . . . ah . . . certain things that seem odd to you, and you must acquiesce. But I will tell you, too, that if you do not question him, those demands will seem—after a time, anyway—to be perfectly reasonable."

"But the poor man was horribly maltreated, and here I am . . ."

Roberta lifted a finger and pressed it to her lips, smiling and shaking her head gently.

"No questions. No questions. Eat well, and then you may rest. Tonight, after we have dined, the captain and I will discuss plans for you. . . ."

Plans? There was an ominous sound to the word, even though Roberta made it sound natural as the dawn.

". . . and I am sure you have nothing to fear, a smart lass like you. Tell me," she added, "is it true that you were really of the nobility?"

There seemed no point in denying it. Selena nodded.

"Ah! That is fine, indeed. And because of it, you may be

sure Captain Randolph will give you every opportunity."

Opportunity for what? Selena asked herself, but she adhered to Roberta's earlier instructions, and did not give voice to her apprehension. Roberta was staring at her now, in a manner not unfriendly but not entirely amiable either, and those eyes were . . . were *out of place!* That was it! Roberta's eyes were out of place in her face. Too old, or . . . or something . . .

But the food and, most of all, the wine did their work, and in spite of resolutions to stay awake and alert, Selena began to feel the toll of the past week in the hold, at sea.

"That's right," Roberta soothed, and walked her to the large hammock on which she and the captain slept. "That's right, you sleep now. There is nothing to worry about, and when you awaken, all your questions shall be answered. Now you just . . ."

And she helped Selena into the hammock, adjusting a pillow for her, drawing up rich blankets of patterned plaid, Highlands' wool. Roberta's hands were very gentle, Selena thought, drowsy and falling, gentle as they passed up and down her body, adjusting the blankets. *Too gentle,* she realized, but it was too late for more. The warmth of the blankets, the swaying hammock, the slow, steady roll and pitch of the *Meridian:* all conspired against consciousness. Outside the portholes, the sea was blue and white toward all infinity, and the air was brilliant, the sky decorated with wind-driven clouds. Wind slanted steadily into the massive white sails of the ship, and drove her into the horizon, silently onward to the New World, like a knife slashing through water.

Strange, Selena thought, *strange,* but not knowing why, and then, bereft even of wonder, sleep took her like a lover on the high, lonely lanes of the North Atlantic.

You are not defeated until . . .

At first, darkness. Suppressing an instinctive fear, Selena then sensed movement, the now familiar sea roll, and remembered that she was on the ship, in the hammock, but . . .

She was not in a hammock now! She was sitting upright, somewhere in darkness. Wait, be careful. Raise your hand and reach out. Touch. Her arms did not move. Lean for-

ward, slowly. Some kind of bond stretched around her
waist. Just as she was about to cry out, she heard the
sounds. Something much like a moan, and an answer that
was . . . that was a giggle!

The *Meridian* moved in steady rhythm.

Gradually, Selena's eyes adjusted to the darkness of the
cabin, and her situation became clear, if inexplicable. She
had slept far longer than anticipated, even into the night;
Roberta and the captain had moved her from the hammock, put her in the cushioned chair, and tied her into it.
With relief, she noted that her gown was still on; she could
feel it beneath the blanket spread over her. Thus assured,
she did not know whether to make her presence known or
not.

On the hammock, the two bodies were entwined, deep in
lovemaking. Iridescent in the dim sheen of sea light, Captain Randolph clung to Roberta on the hammock, deep in
a kiss. Selena saw Randolph's body clearly; Roberta's was
obscured. The captain had a long back, and angular, almost perfect shoulders, but the legs and arms suggested an
unsettling delicacy, in spite of the musculature. Then, quite
naturally, the two of them turned on the hammock, seeking
a position, still clinging, still touching and giving forth the
tender, moaning cries of physical love, which are almost
the sounds of pain. Delicious in sweet agony, they moved,
and Selena could not tear her eyes away, although she
tried. Then she could not even try, as the enormity of the
vision struck her with the force of a blow, like the cutting
sting of McGrover's riding whip. Captain Randolph turned
Roberta in the hammock, and came up behind her. And
Roberta offered herself in that fashion. Which was also necessary, because it was the only fashion of which Roberta
was capable.

Because Roberta was a man.

"Oh, my God!" cried Selena, before she could stop herself.

There was a deathly stillness in the cabin. The wash of
the sea along the hull whispered to them from far away.

"I *told* you we oughtn't have," Roberta whispered then.

"Set me free!" Selena ordered tentatively, her voice
quaking.

Another silence.

"Well, she would have known sooner or later." It was Captain Randolph, his voice cynical and matter-of-fact. "Care to join us for a romp, Selena?"

"Don't you ruin her, darling," Roberta interrupted. "Of what good will she be then?"

The two bodies, motionless, naked, gleamed before her, faces white against the night sheen.

"She has two choices, anyway," Captain Randolph told Roberta, as if Selena were not even there. "Either she does as we say when we reach America, or, after what she's now seen, we must have a special wedding for her, right here on board the ship."

"Oh, a wedding would be exciting," Roberta giggled, "but we must think of the future."

"Later. Let us think of now." And, there before Selena's troubled, disgusted eyes, each of them fulfilled his desires upon the other. The shock of it was almost strong enough to keep her from thinking about what they had said. A wedding? What on earth did that mean? But this was not the time to ask, even if she had not remembered Roberta's instructions.

After the spectacle was over, the two men got up and threw on robes. Captain Randolph lit a sea lantern, and hung it from an iron hook imbedded in an overhead support beam.

"Well, Selena, so you know. But do not expect that such information will do you any good. You are in no position now, and I will see to it that you will never be in a position, to let yourself be well served by such tidings."

"I don't care what filth you do," she spat.

"Oh, ho," cried the captain, delighted at her fire.

"Shall I set her free?" asked Roberta.

"Of course. It was only to keep you safe, Selena. We meant you no harm, but we had other uses for the hammock, as you observed."

"You're disgusting. I've never met such a . . ."

"Spare me," the captain chuckled, as Roberta loosened her. "Wine? Or are you hungry?"

"Nothing. I want . . ."

"Ah! What is it you want?"

"I want to get away from here."

Both men laughed.

"That could be arranged," Randolph said pleasantly, pouring a mug of wine for himself from a silver decanter. He held it toward Selena, but she shook her head. "However, I recognize a potential profit when I see it, and, since you're awake, let me put the proposition to you now."

Proposition? Immediately, Selena was wary.

"And there will be great profit in it for you, too, my dear," Roberta put in. "Several years of hard work, and you may well have enough money to set yourself up as an American princess."

"I don't want to be an American princess, or an American anything," Selena cried. "I just want to be . . ."

"Scottish nobility again, eh? Forget it. You're alone now. We'll teach you the ropes, though, and you'll do as you're told. We could turn you in and have you hanged, you know."

"Or we could have that wedding," snickered Roberta.

Captain Randolph raised his hand for silence. "I want you to work for me, Selena," he said. "In fact, you will work for me. You haven't any choice."

"Work? For you?" *On this ship?* she was thinking. *Doing what?*

He saw her puzzled look. "Oh, I am much more than a merchant captain. I have many enterprises, and there is one in which your services would be most advantageous."

"You would be marvelous," Roberta agreed.

"Selena," said the Captain, moving closer and looking down at her, "I don't know what you've heard about America. Probably a lot of talk about the democratic rebels there, trying to get up the nerve to declare their independence."

She nodded. "And I hope they do. England is . . ."

"Forget politics. Who cares? It is never going to happen anyway. Even so, America is a lie. People are coming overseas, seeking freedom there, and a good life in the New World. But what do they find? I'll tell you what they find. Poverty. Corruption. Hunger. And the involuntary servitude of indenture. Even the so-called Massachusetts rebels, for all their fire, will permit only property owners to vote."

"But what does this have to do with . . . ?"

"With you? A great deal. As it does with me. You see, many a fine young girl arrives in the New World only to

learn, suddenly and sadly, that the streets are not paved
with gold . . ." Randolph seemed quite pleased with his
observation, and Selena learned why.

". . . so they are scared and disillusioned and vulnerable . . ."

"Just like yourself," Roberta explained.

". . . and I put them to work. Pretty young women, especially. Do you see what I mean?"

"I am never going to be . . ." she began, but Roberta's
insinuating laugh stopped her.

"Oh, not you, darling, except perhaps once in a while,
for a special customer. You see, we want you for your fine
appearance and your ability to inspire trust."

"You will take in unfortunate young women," Randolph
continued. "They will be distressed, needing food and shelter. You will provide them with it. They will learn to trust
you. In due course, they will be put to work."

"That's white slavery!" Selena exclaimed, sickened.
"That's . . ."

"Oh, come now. Let's don't be childish. Do you think I
wish to spend my life hauling cargoes of cloth around the
world? That is merely my cover. In Boston, with your help,
we will assemble a cargo of finer stuff, blond like yourself,
and sail for Asia, where such looks bring high prices."

"After proper training," Roberta put in.

Captain Randolph nodded.

"You'll have a fine house, and everything you need. As
long as you bring me . . . ah . . . subjects. Otherwise . . ."

He did not have to finish. Otherwise he would turn her
over to the British.

"Never!" she vowed.

The other two were silent for a cold moment, then Captain Randolph's viselike grip clamped down on her throat.
Choking for breath, Selena tried to think of something, anything, to dissuade him, short of promising to do his will.
The necessity of giving herself to Slyde in the tavern had
triggered something inside her being, and she had learned
the hard way that yielding in will was as bad—indeed, was
often worse—than yielding in body alone. To have your
will compromised by circumstance or actual cowardice was
worse than a beating, which could only make your body

cry out. But it was hard to think bravely with your breath cut off.

"I think she's trying to say something," Roberta observed, his man's eyes peering out from behind the sooty lashes. Randolph snorted, and released his grip. Selena gulped the air.

"I have a . . . powerful friend . . . in America," she stammered. "You had best not threaten me."

The captain's eyebrows went up, and he looked at Roberta, feigning fear. " 'A powerful friend!' the lady says. My goodness. I'm all atremble. Are you all atremble, too?"

"I certainly am," oozed Roberta. "My goodness. I *quiver*."

"Who is it?" Randolph demanded.

"Royce Campbell."

It did not work.

"You're mad, my dear," Roberta explained, after he recovered from his fit of hilarity. "Royce Campbell cares for nothing and no one, and I don't believe you are traveling with the kind of money necessary to put the glint in his eye. Now, wait," he added, thinking of something else, "are you another of those little lassies from bonnie Scotland who have been blessed by the great pirate's favors?"

Selena was glad for the comparative darkness of the lamplit cabin. The blood rushed hot to her face.

"He's no pirate, and what's more he's now fighting with . . ."

"The American rebels? Don't be daft. Campbell cares for nothing and no one, certainly not for you. He's to marry some woman from Jamaica. That was the news when last I was in America . . ."

Veronica Blakemore! Selena's heart fell. That was the end of it. There was nothing left now. Except herself, and what little she had been able to make of her MacPherson honor, her Scottish fire.

"Kill me, then," she spat at Randolph. "Kill me, because I'll never serve you, and I'll not be a whore . . ."

"Save for Royce Campbell, I expect," Roberta smiled, and Selena squirmed at the man's sure knowledge of the truth of her own body's willful troth. Even now, learning that Royce Campbell was going to marry another, the pang was hot and sharp, the need still throbbing. Well, that was her own fault, too. But they were not going to hear of it. To be hunted was terrible; to be vulnerable, obscene.

Randolph snarled, and seized her throat again. "All right, my sweet, if it's death you want . . ."

"No, wait," Roberta soothed, removing his hands. "Let's give her the wedding instead." His eyes sparkled, delighted, malevolent.

Selena decided there was no longer any advantage in refraining from questions.

"What do you mean, 'wedding'?" she asked. "And where is poor Slyde?"

"Ah!" exclaimed Randolph, as if he had thought of something delicious.

Selena had never dealt with people like the captain and Roberta before, had scarcely been aware of their existence. Even Darius McGrover, whom she hated and feared, was direct and predictable. His malice was badge, capote, and cockade: all he was. And one could count on it. She ought to have killed him when she had the chance, ought to have overcome that snake-charmer's spell he seemed capable of exerting upon her. But she had not. Now, with these two men aboard the *Meridian*, her own sorry situation in the hold, combined with their shifting moods toward her, had kept her off guard. She did not have a chance to decipher the threatening possibilities arrayed against her, and thus the advantage had rested even more completely with the other two. If she meant to survive, she would have to do much better. She would have to perceive new conditions and people as they were, and analyze them correctly. *If* there was to be a future at all.

Still angry, but somewhat mollified by Roberta's suggestion of the mysterious "wedding," Captain Randolph left her bound in the chair throughout the night. It was a long one. Afraid of the unspoken fate that awaited her, and distressed by the exaggerated moans and sighs of Randolph and Roberta as they worked their will upon each other in the hammock, Selena tried to force herself asleep. On the sea, the wind was rising, but the heavily laden *Meridian* rode the swells, bearing Selena across history and time. She thought of rescue, safety, some kind of escape, and forced her bonds, but they would not give.

Come now, cajoled a part of herself she did not like. *Come now, don't be a silly fool. All they want you to do is take hungry girls off the streets. Certainly, later, these girls will be made to do for men, but would they not do so anyway, in their own time? What you will be doing, working for Captain Randolph, is not so bad. The girls will at least have food and shelter. It is better than being a scullery maid or an indentured servant, is it not?*

And all she would have to do, right now, right here in the cabin, was to call out, to say, "All right, I'll do your bidding. I'll do it."

And later, in America, she might be able to escape, to maneuver her way out of Randolph's clutches.

That's the way to survive, spoke the dark voice, insistently, persuasively. *You've got to live, too, just like those faceless girls. You've done nothing to harm them yet. Now, be intelligent. Tell the captain you'll give in to him.*

And then a sound from the creaking hammock, Roberta gasping, "Oh, darling! More, darling, more," and Selena's tempter slunk away into the night. These were people with whom one must not reach accords. The truth of words spoken into air, written in ink on paper, or on flesh in blood meant nothing to them.

"No," Selena murmured to herself, "I will not give in. No matter what!"

And if they keelhaul you, like Slyde? The tiny, peeping voice again.

Well . . .

And if they tie you to the mast and cut you to ribbons with the whip?

Now . . .

And what of this strange wedding?

Selena shook her head to clear it and to drive away the doubts, and then she knew what to do. Her mind left the ship, and she was back in Scotland again, standing down along the shore of the North Sea. And far above her, inland where the land rose and the moors began, she saw the walls and towers of Coldstream Castle riding against the sky. "Like a great ship that has carried us through the centuries," Father had said. But this night, this one night, was the only ocean she needed to travel now, and Coldstream was the ship to do it with. Growing calm, she fell toward sleep, and generations of MacPhersons gathered on the hills of Coldstream to guide her into peace. *Believe,* they called to her. *Believe. Do not give in.* And, at their backs, she saw the strong stone walls, just as, in their faces, she felt the hundreds of years of struggle that had made them what they were. *We are with you, so do not give in,* they spoke. *Even death is not irrevocable, when we are with you.*

She slept, content with that knowledge.

But in the morning, after being dragged up on deck by Captain Randolph, she was certainly afraid. Roberta, newly gowned that morning in a dress of white satin, with sequined bodice and hem, expressed great dismay that, because of his "position" aboard ship, he could not attend the "wedding."

"Twenty-eight bridegrooms," he hissed silkily. "My, how you are going to enjoy all that."

Selena knew then, and on deck her worst fears were confirmed. Several bales of blankets and coats, a part of the textile cargo in the hold, had been placed end to end on the *Meridian's* main deck, and around this improvised bed the crew was gathered. A sacrifice: her flesh to their rapacity. A few of them crowded close and tried to grab her, but Captain Randolph held them back with a curt order.

"In due time, in due time," he drawled. "Pleasure increases in direct proportion to the time it is prolonged. As long as one knows that the ultimate pleasure is a certainty. Isn't that right, my dear? Does your friend, Royce Campbell, share my theory?"

Selena lifted her chin and said nothing. Then, steeling herself, she stared directly at each man in the crew, one by one. Some were transfixed. Some leered. Not a few were slavering openly at the windfall treasure of lust that was about to be theirs. But she could find no pity on the faces of any of them, and lust, already tumescent in their bodies, hung like hot fog around the mast.

Captain Randolph enjoyed the scene immensely, and spent much time tormenting the men by slowly drawing up a list of who was to have her first, who last, how long. And then, laboriously, pretending to reconsider, and change the order again and again. Selena forced herself not to look at any of them now. She would not cry out for as long as she could; her body might be ravaged but her mind would not give in. Instead, she looked out across the ocean and the sky. The sea was high today, and the wind strong, and high waves came in serried, white-flecked ranks. The ship was moving very fast. There was nothing on the horizon, neither sign nor symbol of any other existence in the world except this ship and those on it. She tried to imagine a ship out there, passing by the random chance of fate, and once or twice she almost thought that it was true. But then the *Meridian* would plunge and rise again, and the horizon was a blue-green haze.

"Fine day for our sport, eh?" Randolph bantered. "You won't even have to do much work. Unless, of course, the men demand it. I would advise you, then, to adhere to their wishes. They can be very nasty when displeased."

Selena looked right in his eyes. And spat in his face.

The crew of sailors let out a collective gasp, and Captain Randolph struggled to stay in control, wiping his face with a silk handkerchief. He nodded to his second in command, who came forward and grabbed Selena. She saw the mica-flecked glint in his eyes, and then he flung her down onto the bales.

"Now . . ." Randolph said. "Are we all here?"

No one said anything. Selena could hear them breathing.

"That being the case," said the captain theatrically, "if anyone here assembled has cause as to why this woman . . ." he indicated Selena with a lazy gesture ". . . and these men shall not today be united under the sight of heaven and the North Atlantic, speak now and then forever hold your peace, because it doesn't matter in the least."

Some laughter from the crew, but not much. They were too far gone with passion. And they knew the captain's jests could turn to cruel taunts against them.

"So? No one to speak? Then, there being no objection . . ."

Selena forced her nerve and spoke: "Where is Mr. Slyde?"

There was a stunned silence, as the crewmen shuffled and looked at one another. Captain Randolph, however, seemed pleased at her question.

"Slyde, of course," he said. "I knew there was someone missing. And, since he was doubtless your first husband among the crew of the *Meridian*, we ought to defer to him, don't you think?"

The sullen crew said nothing. It would mean further delay. But they understood that the captain's animosity toward Slyde postponed, for a while, the inevitable moment when he would turn on one of them.

"That is, if Slyde is up to it."

A coarse cackle of male spite.

Selena realized she had made another mistake, which would cause poor Slyde even more pain and misfortune. She had merely wanted to know if Slyde had survived the savage punishment Randolph had inflicted. Now, apparently, there would be more of it.

"I know," exclaimed the captain, "let us have the bride *escort* her first groom to the wedding bed!"

Selena was yanked to her feet, and in moments the captain and a few of his officers were shoving her along passageways below decks. She still wore, incongruously, the lascivious, scarlet gown Roberta had given her in mocking humor. The hem caught on a nail, which ripped it to the knee.

"No matter," Randolph said. "You won't need it anyway." At which comment the others laughed.

Slyde was tied spread-eagled in the bow of the ship, exactly where he had tried to hide Selena. But he had been denied such amenities as a hammock or a ship's bag to keep away the wetness of the timbers. His entire body was a mass of ugly welts and open wounds. They had apparently given him a body flogging, not restricted to the back and shoulders, and where the skin had not been slashed away, it was black and deteriorating. He was more dead than alive, but his head, slumped down on his chest, moved a bit sideways when he heard them coming, and he moaned.

"No more," he grunted then, "no . . . more . . ."

"I've a surprise for you, this time . . ." Randolph began in a hearty, familiar voice.

But he broke off, and stopped. And Selena stopped, too, and the other officers.

Because in the dimness of the hold they were now close enough to Slyde to see, clinging to his shoulders and the back of his neck, and eating of the tattered flesh therefrom, a huge, insolent rat, flicking its tail petulantly at this interruption of his meal.

"My God," Captain Randolph cried, truly alarmed for the first time since he had come upon Selena and Slyde in the bow. "Rat bit. If the damn thing has rabies . . .".

For the next minutes, they all but forgot about Selena. A detail of frightened sailors went down and dragged the moaning, semiconscious Slyde up on deck.

"What'll we do with 'im, sar? Toss 'im over?"

"Yes, yes," the captain agreed abruptly. But just as the men were hoisting Slyde over the rail, he changed his mind.

"No, wait. He spent time with the wench. Something might have passed between them, even before. We can't take a chance. I'm sorry, but I'm afraid I'm going to have to deprive you men of the consummation you were so eagerly anticipating. . . ."

The crewmen, shrinking from Slyde, fearful of disease, fearful of themselves running half-mad about the ship, frothing at the mouth and attacking one another with their teeth, no longer seemed so desirous of Selena. She suppressed an impulse to bare her teeth and snarl at them, but she would have had she not been so scared.

"We'll unite them another way," Randolph decided. "Put them in a dinghy and lower it over the side."

Gingerly, several sailors did as they were told, and placed the battered body of Slyde, dressed only in canvas breeches, into the small boat.

Captain Randolph approached Selena, hand on the butt of a pistol at his belt.

"I'd suggest you accompany your friend."

"You are putting the both of us to sea, with no water? No food?"

"That is the general idea, my dear."

"Even though you are scum, you are also the master of a ship. No man who knows the danger of the sea would do such a thing."

"You have a lot to learn," Randolph replied. "Mr. Slyde may be a sick man. You have been in consort with him, if I may use such an elegant word. And I have a ship and crew to think about."

"And money."

"Yes. That, too."

She stared at him for a long, bitter moment.

"I will take my revenge against you, Randolph. One day. Sometime. And it will be complete."

The force of her words briefly unnerved him, but he covered his reaction with his usual icy humor.

"Selena, I shall look forward to such a stirring consummation. Now get in the dinghy before I have you tied into it. And if you row hard, you might be able to attack the *Meridian*."

Defeated, she climbed into the small craft, and in moments they were out over the side, sliding down the hull. The waves, which had appeared to be of considerable size from the deck of the ship, now seemed huge. Immediately, she and poor Slyde were borne away from the merchant ship, tossed high on rolling swells, then dropped as suddenly into troughs. Walls of water spun around them, fifteen to twenty feet high. Slyde was groaning; already the *Meridian* was gliding away, her white sails billowing. And then there was another, smaller flash of white. It came from the porthole in the stern. Captain Randolph's cabin.

It was Roberta, in his lovely gown. Waving good-bye.

The ship moved away, driven by the steady wind. Slyde passed into unconsciousness, his body curled on the floor of the dinghy. Selena clung to the gunwales, and howled to whatever God there was.

SUMMER SOLSTICE

Wave upon wave crested, driven by the powerful northeast wind, and carried the dinghy again and again to the white and foaming summits of roiling water. At the moment of each crest, Selena possessed two thoughts: Would the craft overturn this time, as the ocean dropped it down between the waves, with an empty, plummeting, heart-stopping roar? And was she spinning, somehow, or why did the M.S. *Meridian* appear to be turning on the face of the deep?

She tried to hold onto the perception as once again the swell began. The wall of water came in at them from the side, tilting the boat. Slyde, jammed between two seats, lying on his back, was washed along the length of his body by the seawater that poured over the gunwales. Still unconscious, he coughed involuntarily as the life-force in him fought against oblivion. Then the wave gathered force, came beneath the dinghy, and lifted it, raised it, threw it like a piece of tinder straight into the sky. And Selena, clinging desperately, once again saw the *Meridian*.

And it *was* turning.

Her heart leaped, then, seizing any possibility, no matter how implausible. Captain Randolph had changed his mind. Roberta's heart had softened. After all, the two of them were erratic, and had passed through several moods and attitudes even during her short time on the ship. Or had the crew taken control? Seamen themselves, they would be conscious of the unwritten law of those who go down to the sea in ships: disaster requires all ships in the area to come to the rescue. This chance of salvation, frail as it was, gave her strength as the ocean withdrew its support. Then it was as if the pillars upon which the earth is founded suddenly fell away, and Selena called out in alien cry as the dinghy dropped to the floor of the sea. Curtains of water curved above, shutting out the sky; shimmering spindrift laced and dazzled in the very air.

Waves lifted them again, as upon a whale's back, and again she sought the ship. Now the turn was definite, and she saw sailors working frenetically in the rigging, adjusting the sails to the new direction of the wind. But the *Meridian* was not moving toward her! Rather, Captain Randolph had executed a turn of roughly one hundred and twenty degrees, commencing a wide sweep around the place in which she and Slyde had been cast adrift. Did Randolph, in his sadistic way, wish to see her flounder there, and drown? Did he want to make certain that she was gone?

Selena didn't know, but almost simultaneously, as wind and water carried her back up into the sight of the sky, a form shaped itself in her brain and an image mirrored in her eyes. *Mirage,* she told herself. *Phantasm. Ghost ship of spindrift and wind.* But then she remembered her own wavering perception aboard the *Meridian,* her suspicion of another ship on the horizon, which she had dismissed as a hallucination born of terror. And she almost dismissed the perception again.

And then she knew. The *Meridian* was turning. It was turning to flee. Selena remembered that Slyde had told her of pirate attacks on these sea-lanes.

Even the drop into the trough of the sea did not punch the breath from her, after such knowledge, and when the great whale came to play with her life again, he lifted not only Selena and Slyde and the dinghy, he lifted a heart so full of hope that it might have been newly born. The ship at the edge of the horizon offered nothing more than hope, however. Selena had to attract the attention of someone aboard the vessel, and that was no simple matter.

Once more, the bottom dropped out of the sea, and Selena fumbled frantically in her mind for a plan. The second ship was bent upon the *Meridian;* it was not moving in her own direction. And, with each passing moment, her chances of being seen at all were grievously diminished. Sailors, hungry for battle and plunder and blood, would have their eyes on the ship they were pursuing, not on a tiny splinter of a boat tossing far away.

She had to think of something that might catch the eye of even one man.

The waves swept her up to their crest once again, and she saw the strange ship closely now, full-sailed, dark, knifing powerfully through the deep. Massed clouds of an approaching storm towered behind her sails. Selena saw it in an instant: pure white of sails, darkness of storm clouds, and the swirling colors of the wild sea.

Color was the answer!

Her timing would have to be perfect, and her balance as well, or she would be lost for certain. The sea, for all its power, moved ponderously, with all of time at its command. Riding the crest, Selena tried as best she could to judge direction and distance, as the second ship homed in on the fleeing *Meridian*. Several times, the dinghy rose and fell. There might be a chance. As nearly as she could judge, with the roar of the water breaking on the shore of her brain, with the angry froth of the sea in her face, the pursuing ship would pass her at no more than hundred to a hundred and fifty yards. So she had one chance, but it had to be right.

Down again the dinghy went—now the approaching ship was big and black and fast—and when it rose Selena was ready. The dinghy tilted as always when the ocean took her, and then, for a timeless moment at the top of the crest, it was perfectly balanced, as it might have been lying at buoy in calm water. And Selena was balanced perfectly, too, on the seat in the stern, standing only in a chemise, lilac colored, so fine that it was no more than a veil. She waved the scarlet gown toward the second ship, one second, no more, until the floor of the sea beckoned her again.

Halfway down and dropping—her stomach in her throat, her hands grabbing at the gunwales—her mind framed the situation and placed the elements together. Randolph, in flight, had turned back in her direction only to bring the other ship near by. Not necessarily to save her life, but only to slow down the progress of the pursuit. Which, if the second ship stopped, was what would happen.

But would she stop?

Because, as the howling, concave sheets of water enshrouded Selena again, her mind recreated the ship and made its interpretation: It had risen, black of hull and white of sail, against the purple thunderclouds, mighty and magnificent against the sky. And on the mast not even a flag, not even a Jolly Roger. Nothing but a rich, bright swath of Campbell plaid.

That was enough. It was the *Highlander*, slicing through the ocean, seeking prey.

Selena knew it, but she had no time to think, and when the ocean threw her into the sky, she stood near naked, clutching the torn, scarlet robe.

She could hear the orders being shouted on deck before she fell again. She had been seen, and the great ship would stop for her. Its three tiers of black cannon swept the sky, and the strong black timbers of the masts slanted into the clouds as the bow plunged and rose. The wind beat the plaid flag; it stiffened.

She would be saved, but what would happen now?

Or would she be saved? She fell again into the angry sea, which did not take lightly to the unexpected salvation of its captives. On the bridge, Selena could see Royce Campbell gesturing, giving orders, attempting to get the *Highlander* as close to her as possible, and next to him the dour, unpleasant Lieutenant Fligh, whom she remembered with distaste. But anybody would do now, even the devil would do—and Father had referred to Royce once as the devil!—as still again the waters parted and she swooped down and out of sight.

The wind continued rising, and it became certain that if a rescue was not attempted in minutes, there would be no chance for one at all. Putting a boat down from the *Highlander* and sending it out to Selena's dinghy was already impossible, and on board the ship Sir Royce had decided upon the only other practicable alternative. Lines with grappling hooks were cast into the water, floated with buoys to prevent them from sinking. He had done all he could; now it was up to Selena.

Forgetting her situation, unconscious even of her appearance in the wet chemise—the gown was now a reddish rag on the floor of the dinghy, out of which the dye was seeping—Selena felt the survival instinct take over. Once, twice, three times the lines were cast toward her, and as many

times she leaned out over the gunwale of the tossing craft
and stabbed her hand toward them, only to be caught again
by the mocking sea. Life beckoned her on the crests of the
waves, but death sought her in the roiling troughs.

"*Now,* Selena," Royce called from the deck of the *Highlander*, and she saw him there with a harpoon gun jammed
into his shoulder, and a lifeline attached to the spear. Only
one line. Of course, the men on the ship could not see
Slyde! She did not know if he was dead or alive, and as
Royce fired the harpoon and the line lanced out toward
her, a curving trajectory bent by the wind, Selena thought:
He's dead! He's got to be dead! But when the spear crashed
against the hull of the little boat, the arrowlike iron embed-
ding itself in the wood, Selena knew she could not let the
man go.

The sea was crashing all around, and it was all but impossible to hear what Royce and the sailors were trying to
tell her. Something like, "Get out! Get out of the boat!"
They expected her to tie the line around her body and leap
from the dinghy; she could not tell them of Slyde, and so
grasped the line and called for them to pull her in. Finally,
they did, and the dinghy drew up close to the *Highlander,*
rising and falling with it. Royce ordered ropes dropped—he
saw Slyde now—and the scowling Fligh passed on the orders. Working frantically, at the edge of endurance, Selena
roped Slyde around the waist, and they hauled him up. He
looked dead. It might have been all right had she let him
go. . . .

No. And then it was all right because she was being
lifted up, up, not even feeling the rope as it cut into her
bare skin, not even caring about the sailors' eyes, or anything else. Except safety. And Royce Campbell, whose
well-remembered eyes had no ice in them, none at all, as
he took her into his arms, called for blankets, and bore her
down into the shelter of the mighty ship. Selena knew then
that everything was going to be all right. She felt herself
slipping, fading, sliding into the darkness all around, but
that was all right, too, that was fine, and it was warm as
love or home had ever been.

Selena knew, upon awakening, that she was in Royce's
cabin. The ship rolled gently, Sun came through the port-

holes. The hammock creaked slightly as it swayed. She moved the leopard skin covering slightly, and turned her head.

"So you're awake," said Lieutenant Fligh. "It's better than being dead, but a lot more trouble."

The tone of his words was neutral, and his face as well, but instinct told her to be wary of him.

"Where is . . ."?

"The captain? On bridge. But you needn't be concerned. He's been with you almost every moment for the past two days."

"Two days?"

Fligh nodded. "And I'll say this for you. You're a tough one. I've seen strong men die of exposure from the same kind of thing you've gone through."

Selena decided he was not entirely pleased with her endurance.

"And the captain has had someone here with you, at all times. I'd best go up on deck and tell him you've come around."

He started toward the door.

"Wait," she cried, thinking of her appearance. "Can you . . . can I . . . have a few minutes to make myself presentable?"

Beneath the covers, she felt herself in a rough gown of some coarse fabric, and beneath that nothing. Fligh grinned sourly. "You'll find a standard uniform hanging on a peg behind that door. It's the only clothes aboard, and it will have to do. I believe you've worn a similar outfit before."

"But . . ." Surely there was something else. For Royce, if not for herself.

"This is a ship, madame," Fligh snapped, "not a seago-ing bordello. And right now we've an unnecessary battle coming up. In which good men might die."

His voice turned bitter for the first time. "Die," he repeated, for Selena's benefit. "And all because of you. Now, get dressed and I'll notify the captain."

Abruptly, he was gone, leaving her there to steep in his anger, which she did not understand. Battle? Because of *her?* It made no sense, but she got out of the hammock, dashed cold water on her face, neck, and wrists, steeled herself for the mirror and found, to her considerable surprise, that she looked rested and reasonably fit, except for her tousled, sea-bleached hair. Quickly, she pulled on the uniform, just in time for the knock at the door.

She had no time to plan how it would be, or even to imagine what it would be like. Seeing him again. So when he entered and pulled shut the door, they stood looking at each other for a long time. His dark, strong face showed nothing, but his eyes were lit from deeply within, with a pale fire.

"Thank you" was all she could think of to say.

He smiled. Not the cynical smile she remembered, with which he faced the world, but a smile almost of relief, from a hidden wellspring of warmth.

"You're welcome," he said, "if you'll accept that sentiment from a despicable bastard like myself."

Violently, she recalled the words she had screamed at him on the *Highlander* that terrible morning last December. She had not understand certain things he had said, then, nor had she understood him. Even now, she was no wiser, had no clearer intimations of what made him as he was. But none of that mattered, not at all, as they came to each other in an embrace, tender, passionate, full of all things unspoken, and things for which there are no words. At first it was more tender than carnal, and he held her so gently, yet so close, that it seemed he almost doubted her very presence, feared her leaving. Their kiss was reverent and joyous, and then it was flaming. Yet she felt in him that maddening hint of something held back. He broke away and looked into her eyes.

"What's the matter?" she asked, the hollow feeling growing again, the hovering sense of an unwanted surprise.

"There is no time, that's what's the matter. We're chasing and closing on the ship that cast you adrift, and I've no idea in the world how you got there. Your battered friend is in sick bay, and close to death. We can't read his symptoms. And you must be . . ."

"I was never better," she said, and snuggled close to him.

"Ship off the port bow," came the cry from the bridge, drifting down to them. "Target ship off the port bow."

"All right," Royce said, ending their embrace, grim and businesslike now. "Tell me what happened on that ship."

Selena tried not to feel any of it, merely to tell it, as if in that way Father's murder and Brian's death and the torment aboard the *Meridian* could not hurt her anymore. But when she reached the part about the mock wedding on Captain Randolph's deck, with the leering men ready to take her, she broke down.

"It's all right," he soothed, holding her again. "I don't need to know anymore right now, but . . ."

"Captain, sir," called an excited sailor, banging on the door. "We're getting into cannon range now. Should we prepare to fire?"

Royce looked iron-hard now. Hearing her story, he had felt vengeance come alive in his heart.

"Aye," he vowed, "by all means. The law of the sea has been broken, and the tempest follows him who does not mend it. Aye, ready the cannon, and ready the boarding parties. We've many a score to settle before the night."

Fascinated, and a little afraid, Selena watched him ready the ship for battle. From a sheltered position on the main deck, she saw the *Meridian* out ahead of them, every sail unfurled, and bobbing in her wake were strange, waterlogged hulks. "'Tis the bastards' cargo," sneered a sailor. "Thrown overboard t' lighten the ship and build 'er speed. But nivir fear, ain't nothin' on the seven seas the *Highlander* can't catch."

Lieutenant Fligh carried out his orders coldly, effectively, but he was of a different mind. "Outrageous," she heard him mutter, "waste of time. No profit in this, and a pile of needless trouble."

But Royce did not seem to mind. If anything, he was exhilarated by the prospect of the battle, quickened as much by the impending fray as by the hot spirit of revenge which had provoked it. She gauged that part of him with a measure of caution and doubt; it was the reckless, instinctively rebellious element of his nature which she could understand—far better now, after what had happened to her—but which seemed disturbingly beyond the control of logic or reason.

The *Highlander* tracked the merchantman off her starboard stern, constantly gaining, edging closer all the while, and turning degree by degree as the *Meridian* sought to angle away from the pursuit. Royce was on the bridge, full of the flight, rapt, lost in it as a man can be lost in the act of love, and that part of him frightened Selena most. Or was it envy she felt?

"Topsail out!" he called, and Fligh repeated the command, "Topsail out!" and then the cry came from the sailors at work in the rigging, as one more white triangle of cloth caught the wind. Selena felt the ship lift and buck beneath her, and the expanse of blue between the ships narrowed still more. She could see the crewmen of the *Meridian* scrambling up the masts, trying everything to milk a fraction of a knot more speed out of their craft. But it was useless.

"Load the port cannons!" Royce called, and again the cry was repeated. Well-drilled crewmen with long-handled rams packed powder in the muzzles of the big guns, and drove the heavy balls down the greased, black tubes, then stood aside with fired torches ready for the fuse.

"Cannons loaded," came the cry, with a quiver in the voices, a passion for blood and plunder that was almost sexual. And Selena realized for the first time since she'd come aboard that this was indeed a pirate ship, as dangerous in its own way as the *Meridian* had been.

"Where is Selena?" Royce called. "Bring her here." To Fligh's immense displeasure, she was brought to the bridge.

"Any cannon aboard her?" he demanded. She might have been a subaltern, summoned for hasty debriefing.

"I saw some. Half a dozen, maybe. I didn't have time to . . ."

He cut her off with a gesture of dismissal. Disappointment.

"Too bad," he said. "It won't be much of a fight."

"Nor much of a profit, either," Fligh muttered, giving her a significant look.

"First tier of cannon, stand by for firing," Royce ordered.

Far above, on top of the mainmast, the Campbell plaid snapped and rippled in the wind.

"To the Highlands," Royce cried then, an exclamation of joy and exultation so intense that it startled Selena. *"To the Highlands, FIRE!"*

Simultaneously, the sky was blotted out, filled with fire

and smoke and roaring sound, a cataclysmic firestorm. The *Meridian* was lost in it, and even the *Highlander* rocked backward in the waves, stung by the cannons' recoil.

"Tier two. FIRE!"

And again the roar.

"Tier three. FIRE!"

The sound rang in her ears. Her eyes were stung by the dust and smoke. The very air seemed to be burning, hung with veils of umbra, orange, and blue, dull yellow, and chartreuse. But mostly Selena was frightened, sensing something indefinable in Royce that made him pace the deck of the bridge like a captured leopard, peering through the smoke.

"Is she sinking yet?" he demanded of Fligh, who could see no better. "Have we got the bastards where we want 'em?"

Directly behind her, Selena felt rather than heard a sickening, crashing explosion. Her entire body shook with tremors, and suddenly she was down on the deck. Royce lay on top of her, and Fligh was getting to his feet, wiping blood from a deep gash in his forehead. Part of a mast bent over the railing of the bridge, snapped like a toothpick.

"We've been hit," Royce explained, with no apparent concern. "They'll pay for it, but at least they're fighting. Ready the cannon," he cried.

The sea wind moved the smoke away, and the two ships stood out clearly, the crews of each taking measure of the other. The *Meridian*'s main mast was still up, but the fore- and aft masts, sheered by cannonballs, had fallen across the decks. Huge sails fluttered like wounded swans. Crewmen were fighting their way from beneath. Several jagged holes showed black and ominous in the hull. The *Meridian* was taking a lot of water. The list became apparent as they watched, and two cannon crews were working fast.

"Seems they want another exchange, sir," Fligh said.

But, to Royce's disappointment, a white flag—more like a towel or small blanket—fluttered up the mast.

"I see our Captain Randolph is not much of a fighter when the advantage is not one hundred percent his," he said scornfully. "Get the boarding parties prepared, and close the gap. We'll tie onto the *Meridian* and . . ."

He stopped. There would be no need of further preparations. Cannon fusillades from the *Highlander* had apparently caused severe damage below water level, because the merchantman listed steeply and dropped visibly into the water, right before their eyes.

"Sail near, forward," Royce told Fligh, who passed on the commands, and Selena saw Captain Randolph, in his elegant attire, come up on deck and make his way to the railing. Roberta was with him, in another of his bright gowns, and it looked as if they might be taking a stroll before dinner. If so, it was their last aboard the *Meridian*. Waves lapped over the main deck now, washing the bodies of dead crewmen overboard. Survivors were wrestling with the dinghy-sized lifeboats, and gulls circled the teetering mast. From far away, Selena heard a faint, menacing hum, an eerie sound that thrilled her spine, tingled the skin at the back of her neck. She was about to ask Royce what it was, when she noticed hundreds of small black objects bobbing in the waves.

"What are . . .?"

But Royce had already seen them. "Rats!" he cried, alarmed. "Tell the men to use rifles, clubs, anything. We can't let them on board!"

His agitation sparked something in her mind, something important that she had to tell him, but there was no time, because Captain Randolph called across the water.

"I'm sending my ambassadors, Campbell!" He laughed bitterly, defiantly. "They have your breeding, knowing every scum hold from Jamaica to Mombasa and points between." Then, to Selena, "Well, my dear, I won't be so presumptuous as to ask for an invitation aboard, but it is a pleasure to see you once again."

Roberta said nothing, dancing in seawater now. He pulled Randolph back to the mast, and the two of them began to climb slowly, as the *Meridian* sank, as the water rose.

"You have what you deserve," Royce called into the face of the sea. Beyond them, sourceless, was that sound, a dull, distant roaring now, implausible and premonitory.

"Will you take aboard my crewmen?" Randolph asked, and pointed to a couple of lifeboats, in which maybe a dozen snarling sailors battled the rats, screaming from the bites. On the *Highlander*, too, sailors were shooting and clubbing, and the air was filled with the frantic squealing of the beasts.

"I'll promise them water and bread, that's all," Royce told him. "No sane man takes vipers aboard. We're at thirty-one degrees west, forty-two north. If they go directly to the south, they'll reach the Azores. It's more chance than you gave Selena."

"As if you cared," Randolph called, quite in good humor. "You only sought a provocation to gun down an all-but-helpless freighter."

Royce's jaw tightened, and the blood went to his face. She could see it there, a sign of his rage, even beneath his deeply tanned skin.

Rats had overrun the lifeboats now, and they scrambled up the wooden hull of the *Highlander*, screaming like enraged birds. "Close all portholes and hatches," Fligh ordered. "Don't let them get below decks!"

The roaring sound came out of the background then, and turned into steady, growing thunder. A great ripple of white water formed, turning slowly, slowly, around the *Meridian*. Randolph and Roberta climbed faster and faster to the top of the wavering mast, but it was sinking now almost as fast as they climbed, pursued by a black and glistening pack of rats, so thick they looked like black bees swarming on the branch of a tree. The circle of water spun faster now, a dance of colors on the sea, flashing dancers around a Maypole on a village green. But at the center of the circle was the mast, and great thunder filled the heavens, obscuring now even the pealing of the frenzied rats. It was the whirlpool, sent by nature herself to fetch the *Meridian* to the floor of the sea.

"Let's get out of here," Fligh cried to the sailors in the rigging, and the men scrambled to turn the ship. He was shouting more orders, but now it was impossible to hear him at all, with the roar of the vortex all about. She held her ears against the sound, watching with a kind of fascinated horror, a trembling wonder, while the waters parted in a deep and whirling funnel, black, green, at the center of which turned the *Meridian*. Randolph and Roberta were clinging to each other now, at the top of the mast. They were afraid, and no longer attempted to conceal it, but they did not expect quarter, nor did they ask it.

Selena noticed that Royce was studying them with a satisfaction she found much too grim, in spite of what they had done to her, and would have done. She put a hand on his arm. He looked down at her, eyes glittering.

"Let's throw them a line?" she asked tentatively. She had to shout.

His surprise showed clearly. Cupping his hands, he yelled: "This is for you!" into the howling maw. "I'm doing this for *you*."

"It's all right. It's all right. We can't do this . . ." and, seeing a coil rope near the railing, she ran for it, stepping over the bodies of dead rats, the flopping, writhing bodies of dying rats. It was hopeless, of course, there was no way she could have thrown the rope into the center of the whirlpool, nor even propelled it that far with the harpoon gun Royce had used to rescue her. But she tried to do it, anyway, and from the whirling mast, Captain Randolph's face showed wonder and something that was almost like respect.

"No, Selena," Royce was shouting, holding her back. "You must rid yourself of enemies. . . ."

"But they'll do me no harm now. . . ."

"An enemy is always dangerous, and remember that. The knowledge may save you one day."

He took the rope, loose in her hands, and dropped it to the deck. Confused, her mind whirling with thoughts of survival, remorse, love, regret, need, and desire, she let herself relax. His arms encircled her, and she leaned upon his strength as they watched the mast spin wildly, so fast that rats were cast off by centrifugal force, and Randolph seemed one with Roberta. The immense storm of sound came to crescendo then, as the black whirlpool seized its sacrifice. With a sudden, crashing thunderclap, the waters came together, closing about the *Meridian*, and great waves slammed together, filling the emptiness in the heart of the deep. Then, almost mysteriously, all of it was green again, and gently rolling, a timeless, hungry beast, appeased, returned to sleep. All was vast and silent. White sails fluttered above. Gulls and cormorants were circling.

Selena felt his hand on her heart, and felt her heart beat strong and steady against his hand.

* * *

It was high May, and the night still and star-filled, the *Highlander* riding the gentle waters slowly southward. "All's clear to starboard," called the sailor on watch in the crow's nest. "All's clear to port." And all was well in the captain's cabin, too, the door secured, and one candle burning. Royce and Selena, alone after a fine dinner of broiled swordfish and Bordeaux, were silent. It was almost a conspiracy of silence, as if, before speech was permitted, with all its nuances, explanations, and misinterpretations, another communication had to occur. His glance was a wish, her embrace, an answer. She lost herself in his kiss, remembering his hands as they touched her again in all the places no longer secret to him. Her body throbbed, already flowing with desire, and he smiled at the rude gracelessness of the sailor's blouse, lingering over each of the button catches, then kissing her breasts as the cloth fell away. Her body arched with tension, need, and she in turn knelt before him, an act not of surrender but acquiescence to their mutual desire, and freed his body in order to possess it for her own. Then she rose and he knelt in his turn, to draw down from the swell of her hips, down across golden thighs, the sailor's breeches. A long kiss of promise and wonder, and his shirt fell to the floor, a gleaming swath of white under the candle. Selena held her breath, still silent, aching with need, as he lifted her into the hammock.

There was no more waiting; neither of them could wait. He was gentle, at first, and each approach, each stroke, was almost like a question. Their mouths were as ravenous for each other as their bodies were, but in the fire of their unceasing kiss the memory of shared pleasure enhanced the sensation of this moment, and all the time lost since December was nothing. Selena fitted herself beneath him, moving with him, proudly feeling his urgency throb within her, proud at her ability to make his strong, gleaming body tremble in her arms. Then he drew up her long legs around him, crossed behind his back, riding higher, faster on her now, and her fading mind listened as she gasped and moaned, felt her body open and plunge, only to open and clutch and plunge again, maddened in joy and agony, wanting them both, wanting both now and forever.

There were many things in her mind, many questions of her own. She thought they could safely wait. She thought this union could mitigate whatever might still be dark in their relationship, whatever lay in wait for them. Questions, words, can always be saved. Sometimes they go away and speak most eloquently in silence. Other times it is best not to speak at all, and this was one.

Selena felt the pressure building, but she no longer possessed enough of her conscious mind to hold on to reality. The candle flickered, and from far away she felt her body moving faster and faster and close to her, so close to her, was the sweet, hot body of her beloved, so little-known, so well-loved, and it was moving into her with strokes so powerful they made her gasp, as if in pain, but left her wanting another and another. And it came, too, and again and once more and then she cried out, clinging to him, and all of the world, all sensation, lived for an instant in an evanescent pinpoint of her body. He *was* her body then, and she his, in soul, in flesh.

For a long time afterward, they were silent. Clinging together, still they were apart. It was as if the piercing pleasure of intimacy had intensified an issue that had yet to be resolved. "This time it was fortunate for you, too," Royce said at last, leaving her slowly, and easing beside her.

Selena's breath, still ragged, shrouded the true doubt in her question: "What do you mean?" she asked, remembering his enigmatic response to their first lovemaking. "What does that mean? Fortunate or misfortunate?"

"I'll tell you, but you might not believe me."

"Why wouldn't I believe you?"

"Because I think you know, without wanting to admit it, that love is more complicated than it seems. We are really not right for each other, in many things, which is why . . ."

Not right for each other? After the glories their united bodies, even souls, had just attained? What was he talking about?

"That was why, when we first . . . became close, I had to tell you there were some things you would not understand."

"It doesn't matter," she said softly, pushing as close to him as she could, feeling his essence already running from her body. A symbol of his leaving her again? No, it could not be. She would not *let* it be! "None of that matters now."

"I hope not. I really do." He nuzzled into her neck, where it met the shoulder, and caressed her breasts with his fingertips.

Yet, reluctant as she was to let it, her mind came to the fore. "But why did you take me? On the ship? When you knew we would have to part? And why did you take money from Sean Bloodwell?"

She moved away from him, just a little.

"That's what I mean," he said. "All I can do is tell you. Truth lies more in the belief of the listener than in the words of the speaker, but now, if you accept what I have to say, both will be equally true."

"No matter what," she told him in a voice that she recognized as frightened, "I believe you love me. I'll always believe that."

I have to, she said to herself. *I've come back from the dead to know this love. I cannot lose it now.*

But, she remembered, too, that he had once said: *A piece is just a piece* in what was a very impressive counterfeit of conviction, if it was counterfeit at all.

"There was something *special*, something different about you," he was saying, "and it bothered me."

"Bothered you? I should hope so. But in what way?"

"My desire for you was never in question, not from the first time I saw you at the ball. But I sensed something in you that made me wary. Because you were different, I knew that we could not simply make love to each other and then go our separate ways. Or, rather, I knew that I could not go away that easily. . . ."

"As you have been used to doing!"

He smiled. "You must not believe every story you hear. And, obviously, I was right. You are not the kind of woman to relinquish the things you want. So I was wary. It is difficult to leave a woman like you . . ."

"Good," she sighed, snuggling close to him.

". . . and it is impossible to forget one . . ."

"Better."

". . . and our lives were complicated enough . . ."

"As long as we're together," she said fervently, "there is nothing we cannot confront. Didn't you know that?"

". . . Selena, I'm an adventurer, and now I'm an outlaw. I did not want to unsettle your life, as I knew would happen, because I knew how much I longed to have you, and I felt the same thing from you . . ."

Oh, yes!

". . . and when we finally did have each other that last morning on the Firth of Forth, it was not something I had intended. It was just that I could no longer hold myself aloof from you . . ."

Selena felt a warmth flow through her body, into every tiny nerve and cell, that was as keen and piercing as his possession of her had been.

". . . so that is why I spoke of fortune and misfortune. The pleasure you gave me, *give* me, is quite extraordinary, because there is meaning, feeling within it, not like some of the others . . ."

The love artists of Eygpt and India, she thought, jealous.

". . . and that was fortunate. But I was afraid that knowing me would lead to your misfortune. Can you understand that?"

Oh, yes. Now she understood everything! He had been in love with her the whole time, just as she had dreamed. And there was something in him, some force, some power of concern and understanding that was hidden behind the violent, daring, venturesome part of his nature. This glimmer of knowledge, glimpse into the shadow of his soul, made her love him all the more, and enflamed her body again, so that it felt as if she had not yet enjoyed and been enjoyed by him, and she turned to him with a cry that begged.

Reverent as it had been with them the first time, now it was wild. Nothing mattered now but the pleasure, the need, which would unite her to the dark side of his nature just as, before, she had been joined by tender love to the sweet part of him. A formless, savage moan escaped her. She came upon him this time, seeking the expiation of her blossoming need, which was also his, came down upon his body and took it unto herself. His hands were hungry against her flesh, and he pulled her mouth down to his. But it was too wild. She could not keep still for his kiss, not even for his kiss, and her head tossed from side to side, whipping him with her long hair, and her body cast back through aeons of buried secrets, dark knowledge, calling up the art of rampant flesh, the tender, soaring, violent art, and she rode only for that art to give him give him give him . . .

. . . all there was.

"Oh, God," he sighed, as, again, they lay closely beside each other.

Selena, still trembling and quivering, could not speak for a moment. And then sudden, peremptory pounding on the door.

"Damn," Royce muttered. "I gave instructions. Yes? Who is it?"

"Fligh, sir. I've got to see you right away."

"Dammit, Fligh, I told you . . . What is it?"

"Sir, I can't say."

"Can't say? What do you mean by this, man? You know I was to be left alone, and that order included you."

The silence was sullen.

"Well? Do you understand?"

"Yes, sir, but . . ."

"No excuses, Fligh. We're in warm and easy waters, and if there was an enemy ship on the horizon you'd tell me. So . . ."

"But, sir . . ."

Royce's voice was uncharacteristically harsh. Selena thought that harshness was probably necessary in dealing with the tenacious, humorless Fligh.

"Go away," he ordered. "Right now. I'll be on the bridge in a couple of hours."

Silence. They sensed Fligh standing just beyond the door.

"*Now,*" Royce ordered, and in a moment they heard the footsteps reluctantly retreating down the passageway.

"Damn him!" Royce said, not without affection. "He's the best first officer I've ever found, but a stickler on every little point. I keep getting interrupted . . ."

He laughed.

"What is it?"

"I just remembered that time at Edinburgh Castle. When you came crashing into the room where Veronica and I were . . ."

Veronica! She had forgotten about Veronica, all those rumors and stories.

"What about her? What about Veronica?"

"We're to be married," Royce said casually. "On June twenty-second. The summer solstice. In Jamaica."

Selena's heart turned to stone. Nothing had happened between them, here or ever. It had all been a mockery. Nothing made sense. And, with mounting horror, she remembered how rich the Blakemores were supposed to be, how recklessly acquisitive Royce Campbell was, even though he wanted for nothing. And, she remembered, this Scottish girl named Selena MacPherson who was naked in the hammock beside him had not a pence to her name, not even her own clothes for him to remove. And she was just as much an outlaw as he.

She thought of these things in the space of a heartbeat. A tiny abyss, like a whirlpool of the soul, opened within her, spinning to draw her down.

"But that's over now," Royce said, his voice soft and assured. "It seems my plans have changed."

And then it was as if fifty thousand distant stars exploded in a symphony of heaven.

"We'll sail down to the Canary Islands," he was saying. "I know a marina there where I can get the mast repaired. Then we'll go to America. I have a plantation in Virginia. We can live there. If you like."

Live? He had said "live there," but he had not said . . .

"Do you think that sort of . . . of settling down will . . ."

"Who said anything about settling down? We'll spend some time there each year, and . . ."

"And what am I supposed to do?"

He leaned up on an elbow and regarded her closely. "Why, come with me, of course. Isn't that what you want?"

Yes, it was, but . . .

". . . and you've nothing to lose now," he was saying. "You are free. Your old life is gone. You can do anything you want, now. . . ."

A person defines himself by choices that are free, Father had said. Everything was moving too fast. Selena was not entirely sure of his meaning, though, now that she found herself in such a situation. Did it mean that she had to choose among alternatives? If so, what were the alternatives? Royce had said nothing but "Come with me."

"But why were you going to marry Veronica?" she asked in a small, hesitant voice. "When, so easily, you are . . ."

"Dropping the idea?" He laughed. "I believed we would have suited each other, she and I. Before I met you. Then, when it seemed that, one way or another, you and I were not destined to meet again—well, I thought, all right. Why not? It would have been as much an alliance as a marriage, because that is how Veronica is. She is like—and she appeals to—what some have called the cynical part of me . . ."

And I to the other part, which I've just seen? Selena wondered. *Or to both parts? If I want to hold him, must I appeal to both?*

She hoped not. Was it her father's lingering influence? But no, that colder part of Royce's nature seemed reprehensible to her. All the more so because Veronica Blakemore found it desirable. She probably enhanced it, too, the haughty bitch. . . .

Selena smiled sweetly.

". . . and it is simplest to live that way, really. Very direct. Seek what you want and take it. Complications are eliminated. Shadings don't exist. The game is in the taking, and if you think only of the pursuit, the rest doesn't matter."

Selena thought of her father, and his long years in politics, and Sean, who had struggled for a peerage against great odds, and had almost attained it. Had that goal not been taken from him, he would, like her father, have tried to serve a long and worthwhile life for his country.

"There's more to life than just . . . than just chasing money and glory," she said, trying not to lecture too much.

"Is there?" He kissed her gently on the cheek. "Well, I could almost believe that, from you."

"You certainly don't need the money."

"Money means nothing."

"Until you haven't any," she said, thinking of her plight. Then she remembered something. "Tell me, the first time we saw each other, at the ball. Did you wink at me?"

"Did I?" he grinned. "I don't recall."

"Yes, you do. Come now and tell me. What did you mean?"

"I just thought we might be sharing a little joke," he said. "A joke about the ball itself, and the excessive pageantry, and the pretenses of the nobility. But you really shared those beliefs, didn't you?"

It was true, she had. Perhaps she still did. But she had changed, and Royce knew it.

"As I have said," he told her, his voice low and intimate, "I knew that you were a woman I would not be able to forget, once we had been together. And now, after what you have endured, you are far stronger, and even more beautiful. . . ."

His kiss was a promise that he would never go away again, but a kiss cannot go on forever.

"Tell me," he asked a bit later, "what did they do to Bloodwell?"

Sean appeared within her mind, strong and direct as he had always been. His association with the MacPhersons had cost him everything.

"They took away his money and lands. He went into the Colonial Service."

"Royally ordered divestiture?" Royce exclaimed, surprised at the severity of the punishment. "They've taken my lands, but I'm an outright rebel. Sean wasn't even a Rob Roy. Those stupid British. The King giveth and the King taketh away. Arrogant fools! They'll be getting all that's coming to them, one of these years, and I intend to give them my piece of the gift."

The prospect of Royce visiting his wrath upon the British was exciting to Selena.

"I believe in anything and everything that will play hell with Britain and King George. . . ."

Royce laughed.

"What's so funny?"

"Your transformation from princess to rebel did not require much time, did it? Or perhaps the one is the best training for the other that we could find in this world."

"The last four months have been my training," Selena said with passion.

"Veronica was a little afraid of you," Royce said. "Ah, she would never admit it outright, she's not one to do that, but she was wary, all right . . ."

Selena was grimly pleased, and then she softened. Royce's sharing of this confidence with her seemed to mean that it was definitely the two of them together, and icy Blakemore on the outside. Where she ought to be!

". . . because she knows what she wants, too. People

who are like that have extremely sensitive antennae. It is they first thing they perceive in their brothers and sisters of the soul. But I don't think she would have survived what you have gone through."

He waited a beat, while she glowed with the implicit admiration, and then added, without malice, "But then she would never in her life have maneuvered herself into such a predicament."

There was admiration in his voice that time, as well. She had to face it.

"And why is that?" Selena demanded.

"Because she doesn't believe in anything enough to jeopardize herself," Royce observed. "She attains whatever she wants, and plays it safe at the same time."

"Everything she wants except you," Selena amended.

His laugh was low and conspiratorial, and he moved her hand to caress him. "It seems that way," he said.

His words bothered her, though.

"In Liverpool, it was said that you are now fighting with the American rebels, and that's why you've been made an outlaw."

"Don't believe a word of it. I'm an outlaw because Fligh and I have plundered every British freighter we could find. In fact, Fligh thinks I'm shirking. As for this American thing, I ran some guns for them, but it was strictly for cash. . . ."

Like taking Sean's money to carry us across the Firth of Forth, she thought. It was maddening. Somewhere behind his exotic, mesmerizing eyes, locked in whatever part of his beautiful body held such things, was a man capable of showing the world a range and depth of feeling such as he had shown her when their bodies were locked together. But when she sought that part of him in words, it always seemed to slip away.

"Do the Americans have any chance? Of humbling Great Britain?"

"Not a prayer," he concluded. "They protest a lot and shout in the streets, and there are many hotheads with proclamations, but it will be a cold day in hell if they ever pull together. They are much too fractious."

"But if they would have a chance to succeed, would you support their cause in your heart?"

"But they won't succeed. I told you once before, I do not shrink from risk, but it is for the risk alone. I do not cherish lost causes."

She realized that he did not mention the Rob Roys by name, to spare her further hurt, and she was appreciative of that even as his words disturbed her.

"But in the end you must believe in *something*," she cried, frustrated.

"I do. Danger. The sea. Adventure. Pleasure . . ."

"No. Something more. An idea. A cause."

"And you? Having lost everything—something I would not permit to happen to me—what do you retain to believe in?"

"Coldstream," she said, without hesitation.

"Ah, Selena, Selena," he said sadly, after a moment of silence, "don't you see that such an idea will only torture you, like a self-inflicted obsession? You'll never go back. You can't go back, not anymore, not ever. . . ."

"Don't you dare say that!" she cried, taking her hand away, sitting up rigidly. The candle flickered in the cabin, fell upon the strong planes of his face, and was reflected in his eyes. He seemed to want to comfort her. Finally, he spoke: "I do love you, Selena, and that is one thing in which you must never fear to believe. And if you wish to believe in the other, in Coldstream, then do so. I am capable of respecting that which I cannot understand. Perhaps those are the kinds of things we ought to respect the most, even if we do not ourselves believe in them."

He drew her back down to him, and she simmered, hurt, remembering inconsistencies in his words, his actions. Wondering whether he ought truly to be trusted, after all.

"So why did you say, that time, 'a piece is just a piece'?" she demanded brusquely. "Because if that's all I am . . ."

"Yes," he said, remembering. "I believe I was under attack by your tongue at the time, and it seemed to be what you wished to think of me, wished to hear me say. So I obliged you."

"You're ever so obliging, aren't you?" Selena pouted. "Did you learn such manners in your Highlands?"

Royce smiled. "I learned things of which you cannot dream. In our region, the measure of a man is the amount of trouble he can stir up and then resolve. Obviously, there

is still more than a bit of that impulse in my nature. When
such an impulse is encouraged—even demanded—in one's
youth, the effects are permanent. You, growing up in the
south, were exposed to more refinements, I daresay. That is
why your manners are genteel. But I suspect your nature
has been strong enough to resist such superficial training."

There was a glint of mockery in his eyes.

Selena was angry. "What you say is unfair. I've changed
because I had to, yet I am still who I was, and Coldstream
is still there . . ."

Royce feigned no amusement this time.

"You had castles and balls and gentility," he snapped.
"Do you want to know how I was molded? Do you want to
know what I was made to do at six years of age? What I
wanted then to do with all my heart, and begged to do, and
am prouder of than anything?"

His turn to be accusatory, this time. Mutely, she nodded.

"It happens in the spring," he began, "as it will as long
as there are memories of Campbells. In the spring, too, it
came to me in my turn, as it has to every Campbell man-
child since first our plaid was fashioned and lifted on a
pole. There is a vow appertaining to this thing as well,
which stipulates that never shall a Campbell reveal to an
outlander what it is that we do there near Loch Nan Clar
when the ice breaks and the wind rises and the rivers start
to flow . . ."

"But I'm a Scot! I'm no outlander!"

Royce smiled, teeth glittering in the candlelight.

"That's not what I meant. Everyone *not* a Campbell is
an outlander, but you are with me now, and we have been
one. Perhaps that will be sufficient to appease whatever
gods watch over the keeping of vows."

Selena felt a tremor of hovering dread. There were, she
believed, consequences to promises and oaths. They were
not lightly made, and must be faithfully kept. Currents of
dark power moved by night, if one's word went unkept, if
blessing or curse remained unconsummated.

"If it would be best that you not tell me . . ."

"I thought you wanted to know."

"I do. I want to know everything about you, but . . ."

"Surely you're not superstitious!"

"It's . . . it's not that. But there are things . . ."

"You even believe in God, don't you?"

"Sometimes," Selena said, after a moment, thinking of the devastation wreaked upon the MacPhersons during the last months.

"Well, you can do that," Royce told her, with a lazy, indulgent kiss. "That's allowed. Because I met Him, and there are no longer any obligations attending a vow in His name."

"What do you mean? You met . . ."

"God," Royce said simply, and nodded. "It was my time, in the spring. The sun was falling that day, and I was readied in the usual manner. First, I was stripped naked and my skin was greased from crown to sole with bear oil, for symbolic strength and to protect me from the cold. It was in our hunting lodge near Loch Nan Clar, and the torches were already lit. I will remember forever the way my shadow loomed against the stone walls, and when I saw the shadow, the way the light had thrown my image upon the stone, I knew there would never be need of fear again. Selena, it was an exultation I cannot describe. I knew, at that very instant, that nothing could touch me. Not then, that night, nor ever. . . ."

Please, God, Selena hoped, barely breathing.

". . . Then, after the oiling, they girded me in the tanned hides of wolves, strong with the scent of the wolf, with boots and gloves and hat of fur, against the night and other things. . . ."

"Who dressed you?"

"My father. Two older brothers, who had already met the challenge. Several uncles. It was all very sober, and quite impressive. The mere practice of ritual contains its own power. It was as if I were a knight of some kind, which I was, in truth. Third, we knelt, all of us, before the fire. We formed the shape of the letter C. And we touched."

"Holding hands?" she asked, thinking of Father and Brian and herself in the cave in the Sidlaw Hills.

"Nay!" he laughed. "That is what the women do when a hailstorm is coming. Nay, we touched the tips of daggers. You see, I was going out into the Highlands for my rendezvous. I was on the attack. It was my time. God could only wait."

"I don't understand."

"Let me tell it. After we rose from the fire, I sheathed my dagger, and was given a leather pouch. Inside was a little whiskey for the cold, but no food. I also had rope and some wire, but that was all. The great door was opened. I went out into the darkness. The door was closed. I was alone."

"Were you afraid then?"

"No. Excited. Overjoyed would be an even better word. Because, you see, this was my *time*. I could be a man in one night. I set out for the Highlands above the loch. It was a night with no moon, which is a traditional part of the ritual. If one is meant to succeed, it will be with the help of a vision greater than eyes can provide. Midnight came and fled, and I skirted the northern shore of the loch and began to climb toward the caves of Ben Kilbreck Mountain. I stopped for a time, and had a bit of the whiskey, and then I had to hurry because the time was running. If I did not choose my cave before dawn, it would be too late."

He noted her still-mystified expression, and continued.

"At that time of the year, you see, the wolves of Sutherland Province have their pups . . ."

"You were hunting wolves? A six-year-old boy?"

He smiled wryly. "Not quite. Listen. Wolves, like man and woman, mate and live together, quite as a family even in the larger body of the pack. The male hunts food and carries it back to the den during the period that the mother is nursing the pups. He leaves the den at dawn, to prey upon smaller animals, and returns when he has made his kill. I waited for that moment."

"You killed the father?"

"No. I entered the cave, the den, after he had gone, dressed in the skin of wolf, smelling like a wolf. My first task was to suckle from the she-wolf herself, then to kill her, then to skin her and remove the dugs themselves, to take them home as proof of my suckling."

Selena gasped, and almost cried out. A boy with a dagger, crawling upon hands and knees into the reeking stink of the den. That boy had become the man beside her, whose naked skin was warm against her own. Together they exuded an essence of their own commingled bodies, the den smell of a man and a woman, love or lust or heat.

"I did this," he was saying. "My smell was foreign to the she-wolf, and she came at me. It was quite simple, and it might have been worse . . ."

"You might have been killed."

"No. I knew that would not be. I knew it from the time I saw my giant's shadow wavering against the stone. No, I braced for her rush, and caught her beneath the jaw, deep in the throat. I drank her bitter milk while the blood poured from her, while the litter of pups squealed and yelped. Their cries of loss and terror would summon the father, of course, as was expected, and in moments I could hear him scrambling on the rocks outside the cave. But I was ready when I saw him, a dark, howling shape in the mouth of the cave, illuminated by a crescent of rising sun. The puppies, emboldened by his presence, were yapping and nipping at me now. I threw them off as the father charged. There is nothing to match the rage of an animal whose young are threatened, and nothing as dangerous as the wolf in such an instance. . . ."

"But *why* did you have to do this? Why did they make you do it?"

"No one *made* me. I *wanted* to. It is the way things are, because we Campbells believe that the only thing one must fear is God . . ."

". . . and you said that you met . . ."

". . . and that God exists only at the instant when man is poised upon the thin line between life and death. So . . ."

". . . God, and He was . . ."

". . . for me, that father wolf, charging, fangs bared, out of the sun, with his whelps gnawing at my fur. I dropped him with a dagger to the heart. He died with his teeth at my throat. Then I cut his throat where the skin is soft, and bent my mouth to it. And on that dawn I drank the blood of God."

Selena, who had been unconsciously holding her breath, now let it out, an exhalation of wonder, terror. All Scotland knew that the Campbells were a different breed, and now she thought they might even belong to a different race, half-man and half-animal. Or perhaps they were simply closer to what man had once been, still in touch with the raw power of impulse, the heartbeat of a feral universe. Hesitantly, she reached out to touch his body, as if afraid that some alien force would be transmitted from his body to her own. A conduit of trembling fingertips to touch a vessel of throbbing power.

"I skinned the wolves," he was saying, "and killed the pups, save one. I carried the hides home with me, and the one living child. The other one had died that night."

"What other one?"

"Myself. I was a child no more."

"And when you reached the lodge? There must have been a great celebration."

"No, there was nothing."

"Nothing? Not even . . . ?"

"No. You see, why should there have been? My return was expected, as it had been expected that I would succeed in the task. We don't applaud a river simply because it flows to the sea, or a wind because it howls in the trees. . . ."

And then she understood completely. Royce had been raised to be like a natural force. He was meant not only to survive but to prevail. Softness—which included an affection for lost causes, poetic idealism—had been bred out of him. It was dangerous to cherish illusion in a hard world, and yet he was so very tender with her. . . . That was not artifice, she decided. It was a natural part of love, as elemental to him as ruthlessness was, as revenge was, as savage exultation was.

And yet, she thought, too, where had this led? This Campbell rapacity and headstrong valor? Already he was a pirate, an outlaw. And what next? A man of incomparable bravery, many gifts, great strength: the world had already cast him outside the pale, and she was there with him.

"I must go back up to the bridge soon," he was telling her. "Fligh has been nervous and troubled lately. I'd best have a talk with him. But now . . ."

"Whatever happened to that puppy? The one you brought back?"

"Ah, yes. The final part, the omen. The wolf cannot be domesticated, of course, but it is also true that a puppy of a few weeks, suddenly robbed of its parents, will form an attachment or bond with a human, if that human takes him, cares for him, nurses him. And this I did. For one year after the time of my proving, I cared for that wolf until he became large and strong enough to go back into the Highlands on his own. And on the day of the omen reading, I opened the gate of his kennel and stood aside."

"But don't they all run away? Isn't it in the blood?"

"So men say, but it is not always true. Many times the animal cowers in terror of freedom, just as men do, and that is the evil omen. A bad death will come to the boy who has captured such an animal."

"And yours?" Again, she felt the presence of dread.

But Royce smiled. "My wolf left," he said. "He looked for a moment at the open gate, then at me, and then at the Highlands beyond. There was something in his eyes, almost like human language. Not gratitude, not at all, nor even surprise. It was a thing much like respect, like a nod between two honest men who understand each other's natures. Unyielding but not vicious. Then he left, not looking back. As those same men might part. It was like the closing of a contract, whose terms have been met. Our responsibilities to each other were concluded."

He fell silent, eyes half-closed, thinking. Selena wondered if there existed between Royce and herself some kind of unspoken contract. Was the bond of the flesh enough to imply the presence of a deeper union? And what of marriage?

"Sometimes when I return to Kincardine and ride out into the hills, I think he is still there. Watching me. It's absurd, after all these years. But not impossible. But the feeling is so . . ."

"But now that you're an . . . outlaw, doesn't it hurt not to be able to return?"

"No," Royce Campbell said. "Because he is there with me. He is there *for* me, in spirit if not in flesh. Drinking blood, I became God, and roam the universe. He is my son, upon the earth of Scotland, and our hearts beat as one."

They made love one last time, made love as Selena had vaguely heard, uncertainly imagined it could be made, and which was called forbidden on all the fearful pulpits of Europe. Or perhaps the priests wished to keep it as a treasure, shored up for themselves, this sweet, lingering speech of the flesh in which Royce Campbell gave her long, aching instruction. For it was more than a treasure, it was transcendence. It was transport to a strange new world, and

unimaginably soft ripples washed again and again and forever upon the walls of her soul, until blood as well as flesh
found tongue. Tender waves spread upon the horizons of
her lidded eyes, driven gently by her cry, and proudly they
rocked the easy boats that lay embanked in touchless time.

The salt taste of him was as welcome as the world.

Part Two

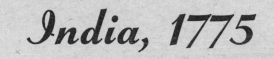

India, 1775

NADIR

Royce pulled on his greatcoat, against the chill of the deck at night, and bent to kiss her.

"Sleep well, my darling," he whispered, "because when I return we'll . . ."

A sudden, tremendous sound rattled the ship, the painful crash of rended wood. Selena barely had time to pull the leopard skin about her, when the battering ram knocked the savaged cabin door from its iron hinges. Fligh leaped in, brandishing a blunderbuss. Six grim-looking crewmen dropped the ram and flicked swords in the air.

"I'm afraid you'll have to delay your plans," Fligh told Royce. He was nervous and obviously unhappy, but quite determined. "You've delayed ours, with the wench here." He indicated Selena with the barrel of his huge pistol. "And I see she's resplendent in her usual attire."

"What's the meaning of this?" Royce demanded, taking a step toward his lieutenant. "You can't . . ."

Fligh's arm went up. The gun barrel was dead level. His body stiffened.

"Too many things are going wrong," he said. "We didn't contract for a pleasure cruise, or to shepherd you and the MacPherson bitch on a lay ride all over the hemisphere."

"Shut up, or you'll . . ."

"I'll do nothin' o' the kind, whatever it is. Nay, sorry, Captain. Ye're a good man when ye're mind's on business, but when it's on this piece of woman, ye're quite another thing."

The other men nodded grimly. Some of them gulped and swallowed and looked away. But they stood firm.

Royce measured the situation. Mutiny. But why?

"Now, Fligh, you and I have always been able to bargain before."

But Fligh was beyond bargaining this time, and when Selena took a good long look at him, saw him lick his lips over and over, she saw that he was scared of a great deal more than Royce Campbell. Royce noted it, too.

"You and the crew know the fate of mutineers, do you not?" He was unafraid, but not imprudent enough to charge a blunderbuss and six naked cutlasses.

"I'd hardly call it mutiny," Fligh shot back, "to try an' save yer neck when the captain's mistress brings a sick man on the ship. An' when he permits it."

"A sick man? You mean that sailor down in sick bay who was flogged aboard the *Meridian?*"

Slyde, Selena thought, shuddering. *The ratbite. Rabies.*

Royce came to the same conclusion as soon as she blurted out what had happened to the man in the hold, with the big rat chewing tatters of his flesh.

"That's no problem, Fligh. Don't you know anything about medicine? Certainly, if he's got rabies, well, the man's doomed, and there's nothing we can do. Just keep him locked up and . . ."

"Aye, but I doot 'tis the rabies," muttered one of the men, looking over his shoulder in fear.

"Then what the hell . . ." Royce growled, taking one more step toward Fligh.

The lieutenant dropped back half a pace. "Captain, I'm warning you. I don't want to kill you." All the same, there was a click as he cocked the hammer back.

Royce thought the better of it. "All right, let's have it."

"That man down in sick bay is howlin' an' frothin' somethin' terrible, sir . . ."

"Of *course,*" Royce said, exasperated. "I told you to keep him locked away from anyone else, and nothing can harm . . ."

"But, sar, it ain't that," groaned one of the sailors.

"Then what is it, man? Speak up, for God's sake. You'd better, or you'll be kissing a whip from here to Cape Horn."

"Well, sar . . ."

"*Tell* me!"

Fligh cleared his throat. "Slyde has a big bulbous chancre in the area of the groin, sir. You let him on board, and also we ha'en't been makin' our share o' gold this trip, so we got to protect ourselves, an' . . ."

He went on talking for another couple of seconds, but Selena did not hear him, nor did Royce. The bite of many an infected animal might spread rabies, but the malevolent swelling in the groin meant only one thing: the plague.

And Mr. Slyde, Selena's erstwhile savior, was afflicted with it.

Selena had been with Slyde a long time, of course. And she had also had acquaintance with the rats in the hold.

Even Royce's dark skin paled visibly as he registered the news and turned toward her.

"The Black Death!" he said, between his teeth. "It killed half of Europe, not all that long ago, and now if it's back . . ."

"It's back," Fligh said, resigned. "It's right here aboard this death ship ye're runnin'. An' that's the point. The lot of us is too scared t' trust yer judgment anymore."

"Come on, Fligh, Jesus . . ."

"So we're takin' over till we can get to Spain or Portugal an' put ashore. No false honeymoon cruises on this jaunt, I vow." He shot Selena an accusatory glance. She met his eyes, unashamed. Fligh took that as a challenge. "At least Blakemore didn't cause so much trouble when she was aboard," he added.

Royce flushed in anger. This time Selena felt pain. It seemed to satisfy the dour lieutenant.

"All right, Captain. We won't be killin' ye unless 'tis necessary. Just hold out yer hands fer the irons."

Three sailors stepped warily toward him, bearing the ugly cuffs and chains.

"And perhaps the lady would like to step into some clothes for a change," Fligh said.

Selena tossed away the leopard skin. The men turned instinctively to see her naked body. Royce leaped forward. Fligh saw the blow coming, but, distracted by Selena, could not duck in time. Royce's fist caught him square on the side of the jaw. He dropped like a poleaxed bull, and Royce twisted the heavy pistol from his hand. Immediately, he swung its muzzle toward the rebellious sailors, but it was too late. One of them—the mean-looking one with an odd scar across his throat, as if he'd been slashed or gar-roted—yanked Selena from the hammock and held her in front of him. His burly arm circled her waist. She caught his stench of salt and sweat and fear. His other arm crossed her, too, at the neck. It held a sword.

"'Tis five days sailin' t' Tenerife, Cap'n," the man grit-ted. "All's we want is t' get off this ship. Now, lookit the situation here, an' the lady, an' all, an' put that gun away."

Fligh picked himself up off the deck. The other sailors, swords at the ready, tensed for his orders. Royce shifted the weapon tentatively from one to another of them. He met Selena's eyes, and she saw that he had already measured the odds and found them formidable. The sailor who held her moved his hand up and cupped her breast.

"All's we want is off this ship at first port. This 'ere's no regular mutiny. We got our health to think about, with the Black Death. But . . ." and here he slowly caressed Selena and then squeezed, to make her whimper ". . . there's worse can happen, if ye get m' drift . . ."

"You son of a bitch," Royce told him. "I'll tear out your manhood with my fingernails . . ."

Fligh shook his head to clear it. "Nay. Nay, Cap'n. Ye're a good man but ye won't be doin' that. So let's discuss this logical and smart. This is what we 'ave. Slyde in sick bay, still alive. 'E should be 'eaved o'erboard, but no man jack o' us'll touch 'im. So we 'ave t' let 'im die there. You an' the woman will be prisoners 'ere in the cabin. We'll bring ye food an' all." He smiled bitterly, rubbing his jaw. "I daresay ye'll not find it unpleasant." He made a motion to the scar-necked sailor, who released Selena. She wrapped herself in the leopard skin. Royce was listening, intensely alert. "An' when we reach port at Tenerife, ye say nithin', see? Nary a word. Because if they's t' find out that we came from a plague ship, we'll all be killed. Nay, we'll go in by night, on the dinghy. Ye can explain whatever it is ye must. But we'll take no lives here. That is, unless ye try t' thwart us. Is that clear?"

Royce inclined his head, not speaking. It was very clear.

"Cap'n, ye know me. I'm as good as m' word, an' so are ye. There'll be a guard on ye. At the door. It won't be a pleasant bunch of sailin' days, with all of us waitin' an' prayin' not t' get the plague. An' if we do git it . . ."

He did not finish. He did not have to. Panic. Mayhem. "So now let's be, eh?"

Situation clarified, agreement reached, Fligh and his mutineers retreated, setting the battered door in place as best they could, bracing it with beams. Selena could hear the guards muttering outside. She turned to Royce with a questioning look, then saw how crestfallen he was, and went to him.

"Darling, it's my fault. If I had let Slyde go, if I had let the waves carry him away . . ."

He smiled sadly. "But that wouldn't have been you, don't you see? Although I must admit that, if you had, there would be no plague to panic my men. I suppose I can understand how they feel," he added, after a moment.

Simultaneously, they examined all the elements of the situation and came to the same conclusion. Trying to be frank and controlled, each saw his own fear reflected in the eyes of the other.

"How long were you with Slyde?" he managed to ask.

She told him.

"The only chance is that, somehow, you were not yourself infected. Otherwise . . ."

"How does it spread? The Black Death?"

"Oh, God, but it's a fearsome thing. It spreads like lightning, like an evil lie. And none to stop it. Out of the sewage and slime of Calcutta or Venice or Constantinople crawls the gray rat of doom, old and hoary, satiated by one last feast of excrement. He coughs and dies, the bastard, and his fleas leave their host with as much haste and loyalty as he himself has left many a sinking ship in his time. The fleas carry the germ of the Black Death. They must find other hosts to survive, and they most assuredly do. Other rats, animals, human beings . . ."

"Does everyone . . . ?"

"No, never everyone. Always, some are immune. But the plague killed half the population of Europe. *Killed* half. Most of the rest were ill. From time to time there is an outbreak. One hears of it, in passing, as if a storm had hit some place far away. Fire has been used as the answer. Towns are quarantined and burned. Fire kills the rats and the fleas. But not all of them. And now we have the infection on the *Highlander*. . . ."

Selena realized his ship's fate touched him deeply. "I think I'm all right, though," she said, stepping away from him. "At least I feel all right. How does one know?"

He saw her move away, and smiled, reaching for her. "Anyway, we're together," he said. "Let's not think about it. Our plans have changed, that's all. We'll think of something. By summer solstice, in high June, I had expected to be showing you my tidewater plantation in Virginia, but now . . ."

God knows where we'll be, she thought. But at least they would be together.

"But how does it start?" she asked again. "How does it begin?" If she knew the facts of the plague, perhaps its danger would be reduced.

"You'll know it when it comes," he muttered, turning away from her, stepping to the porthole. The Milky Way swept across the sky, remote and phosphorescent. Beautiful as diamonds, cold as ice. And just as neutral to their plight. "The weakness and the fever strike as suddenly as a hammer blow, and just as powerfully. You cannot move, or eat, or lift a hand to drink a cup of water. Sweat pours out of you, and with it, life. Then a hard, deadly carbuncle forms in the groin. Oh, 'tis hard indeed. And in it lies the poison of the disease. If it can be lanced at the right time, there may be hope, but even then . . ."

He threw up his hands in a gesture of hopelessness, turned away from the stars.

"And there may be frenzy, as well, both among the infected and among the observers. Bodies turn black, and death is near. It is a disturbing sight. Those near such death are apt to run amok. Perhaps it is excusable. Even natural . . ."

Selena shivered in the leopard skin, and did she feel—or was it merely imagination?—a foul heat spreading across her skin? Down between her thighs, gooseflesh formed, and she shuddered, not able to help herself. Such pleasure the flesh could give, to make one die, but terrible anguish too. *No!* It would not happen to either of them. Somehow, they would conspire to . . . to what? You could not wall yourself away from that which was invisible. A sound escaped her throat, much like a sob. Royce came to her, held her close.

"What is it?"

"I'm all right," she said, but she was thinking of the vow he had broken, when he told her about the strange Campbell ritual of the wolf. A vow was engraved in the black granite that lay at the edge of the universe, in which the stars, too, were embedded. Sorrow came to those who broke a vow. There would be retribution.

Bright dawn bathed their bodies in light. Selena stirred, and felt him there beside her, and permitted herself moments of quiet rapture, forbidding herself to think of anything but this. He slept deeply, one strong arm thrown over the side of the hammock, his back toward her. A strange and complicated man, beautiful to her, but with a past as wild and trackless as was the unquenchable thirst for adventure which shaped his life, all this future as far as he could see. That was what he wanted, the far-flung, boundless mystery of it, unfettered by sentiment or political belief or national loyalty. That was what he wanted, and that was what made him happy. That and Selena beneath him in the night, to give him love, to milk his lust with the skill of her clutching flesh. But still . . .

The *Highlander* was moving very fast; wind cracked in the rigging, swelled the sails. Oceans bucked beneath them. Sun fell across his eyes, there beside her. Immediately upon awakening, his mind was on the problem.

"We may have a chance . . ." he began, but she pressed her finger across his lips, indicating the guards beyond the door with a tilt of her head. He obeyed, and groaned softly as she reached to pleasure him in the way he had taught her.

They were startled to icy fright by the scream. At first the words were indistinct, somewhere in another part of the ship, but then the cry came again, closer this time.

"'Tis Slyde! 'E's on the loose!"

And then a series of answering screams and cries of fright, as the alarm was passed throughout the ship.

Selena looked at Royce, who in a flash was out of the hammock, pulling on his breeches and boots. Then he was pounding on the door, yelling at the guards.

"Let me out! Maybe I can help. This is still my ship!"

"Maybe if I can just dump the poor wretch over," he said to Selena.

"Ye jest stay put, Cap'n," the guard retorted doubtfully. "I'll reckon Master Fligh'll be able to 'andle it . . ."

"Jesus Christ," Royce stormed, as more screams reverberated in the ship, and then there was a great commotion outside the door, and their guards yelled in horror. "'Ere 'e comes, Lord God. We got to . . ."

"Let's get out of here . . ."

They fled, and then Selena heard another sound, like an animal panting in an agony too great to understand. A rattle was in the sound, too, like broken breath, or blood, or death. . . .

"Where's m' Selena? Where's m' . . . lovin' beauty?" Slyde.

Selena hugged herself, and felt a terrible fear. With her eyes, she begged Royce to do something. Slyde battered feebly on the barrier, and one of the beams fell away. All the sailors had fled. The infected man was coming amongst them, driven by delirium, or frenzy, or the death throes themselves.

Royce glanced around the room in desperation. All weapons had been taken from him. Another beam fell heavily out in the passageway, and the cracked, rended door began to sway.

"We can't let him in here," Royce said, and seized a straight-back chair, advancing on the withering door.

"Mr. Slyde," he called, "go up on deck. Hear me, up on deck."

Panting and gasping were the only answers, and a muttered, "Selena!"

She got out of the hammock, hastily put on the uniform, and stood behind Royce. Somehow, Slyde had managed to shove away the last of the bracing beams. The door fell in, and there he stood.

Selena screamed in a horror so pure that it startled even Slyde, far gone as he was.

It was incredible that he could still be alive, or able to move. He was naked, but for a ripped fragment of hospital gown that hung from his neck like a tattered cape. His body had been salved, to help heal the whip cuts, and he gleamed as if putrescent, but beneath the slime his flesh was black and getting blacker. Beside his genitals, high upon his inner thigh, was the tumor, black and malevolent, with a crust that was hard even to the eye. Blood leaked from his maddened eyes, and dripped from his mouth and nose, from his ears. Incongruously, Selena thought of McGrover. He was like the Black Death, which could travel anywhere, appearing with sudden, deadly surprise.

"Help me, somebody," Royce called. "Fligh. Bring a gun. Shoot this poor . . ."

But, although the ship was filled with cries of alarm and consternation, no one came, and Royce did not expect help. Brandishing the chair at Slyde, he pushed him, animal-like, back into the passageway. Selena followed, a few yards behind him. Slyde's great burst of manic energy was waning before their eyes, and although he tried to speak, no words were intelligible.

"Go, go backward, slowly now," Royce soothed, pushing the chair at the diseased man, and then, with a final lunge, they were out on deck in the open air. Crewman backed away, silent now.

"All right, that's it, Mr. Slyde . . ." Royce said, talking softly, moving Slyde toward the rail. The diseased man crumpled once to his knees, staggered back to his feet, mesmerized by the chair, by Royce's soothing tones. And then they were six feet away from the rail, with Slyde's blood tracking the deck. Then four feet away—how bright and blue the sky was, how clean the wind. And then Royce lunged forward, just as Slyde began to fall again, ramming the legs of the chair beneath his arms, and with a mighty groan of effort, shoved the poor seaman up and over the rail. He spun headfirst over the railing, but made no cry, and dropped straight to the embracing ocean. The chair fell after him, and bobbed there in the waves, marker on a watery grave. Slyde. It seemed years since Selena had met him in Liverpool.

Involuntarily, Royce made washing motions with his hands, as if to cleanse himself, and retched abruptly.

"There, that's it, you fainthearts," he said, turning to face the crew.

He found himself encircled by naked swords and daggers and big-muzzled pistols with the hammers cocked back. Calmly, he reached out an arm, and Selena came to him.

She felt enveloped by his strength, but she also felt the faintest tremor of tension pass through his body and into hers.

"What's this, now?" Royce asked the crew. His voice was calm and strong, but she could sense the effort required.

There was no answer for a long minute. The men squinted against the sun, wet their lips. They were scared to death. Finally, Fligh spoke.

"Better get back t' yer cabin, Cap'n. An' the wench, too."

"Why? Slyde's gone, and I'm the one who . . ."

"We thank ye fer that, we surely do, but . . ."

"But what? Out with it, man."

"But we're afraid ye're contaminated. The plan's the same. All of us'll drop off at Tenerife, then ye can do what ye will."

Royce regarded them steadily for a long time. "Agreed," he said then. "I require only a keg of fresh water from the hold. From the hold, not the galley, do you understand? And I will fetch it myself. And also I want fishing line, and hooks of various sizes. A piece of green wood, perhaps three feet long. That's all."

He waited, and the men looked at one another, puzzled. At length, there appearing to be no threat of any kind, it was agreed.

"What have you thought of?" Selena asked, when, back in the cabin with the water and supplies, Royce barricaded the cabin from the inside.

"Simple," he explained. "There are bound to be a number of others infected, merely by chance. Slyde's food came from the galley, and his dirty tray was returned there . . ."

"But so were ours. Our food also came from . . ."

"No, there's a small hope. My food is prepared separately. Now, I have water untouched since we left Virginia, and . . ."

And now all they had to do, for four more days, was to catch fish from the afterdeck in the stern, or perhaps shoot a gull with the bow and arrow he fashioned of green wood and fish line.

The first day passed slowly, and carried with it a quality of waiting. Waiting for a fish to take hook, for a gull to land on the coiled anchor rope near the stern porthole.

And waiting—the shipboard silence was more than ominous—for the invisible enemy Slyde had left with them. Royce was tense all day, shamed by having lost control of his ship, by not being able to protect her better than he had, and by the many complications that awaited at Tenerife. Near twilight, a small eel took the hook. Royce cooked it on the cabin's small, well-protected iron stove. Sickened, initially, by its appearence, Selena was surprised to find that it did not taste bad at all, but hunger may have helped her in that judgment.

They slept, though poorly, until the first of the screams. Then they did not sleep.

"It's here," Royce said simply, and she clung to him.

Compared to that night aboard the *Highlander*, the trek through Scotland with her Grandmother's body seemed like the stroll of lovers in a summer meadow. After the first scream of terror—some sailor felt the weakness hit him, felt the ugly tumor swelling in his flesh, like a form of lust for which there was no satisfaction—there were many more. Then there were gunshots, and cries of rage as men fought, some to stay aboard, others to cast them over. As if that would have helped. In the cabin, Royce tried to doze, watching the door.

"They don't know yet," he told her, "but one or the other of them is bound to remember that I took fresh water in here with us. It can't help them now—it may not even help us—but they won't be thinking logically. They'll blame us, and try to save themselves by killing us."

Selena believed him. Death bred death, as terror bred terror. Man's grasp on reality, fragile enough on land, unsettled by the relentless power and majesty of the sea, became completely unhinged in the face of terrible death.

"It's the principle of sacrifice," Royce explained, with his old, cynical smile. She was glad to see it. Things seemed more normal, less frightening, when viewed with his cynicism. Perhaps that was its purpose after all. "Men have always believed that killing someone else, whether for politics, or religion, or law, or just for the plain dark malice of it, would somehow help to save themselves. I don't believe in the madness of those forms because I see all the horror they do."

This time, Selena had no answer for him. It was hard to

believe in anything redemptive, with the crewmen going mad all over the ship, with uncertain salvation still days away. Nevertheless, she tried to pray in moments when he wasn't watching.

They made it through the second day with an exotic, purple-and-orange-feathered seabird. Royce killed it with an arrow, to which he had tied a fish line, and dragged it back up to the cabin, to clean and cook it there. Its flesh was tender and crumbly, and gave off a natural juice that tasted like sugared water. Their hunger satisfied, they found even the screams on deck less terrible.

On the third day, there was nothing. Water ran low, and the heat increased. The ship was silent, yet still it shot southward, driven by the wind. How many men were left to tend the sails? Who was in command? They must be only one day from port, if they were on course.

"I've got to go up on deck," Royce told her.

"I'll come with you."

"No, I want you to stay here where it's comparatively safe."

"But I can't. If something happened and you didn't return, I'd have to come anyway. I couldn't stand not knowing."

"I'm thinking of the Black Death."

"It's all over the ship," she said, "and we haven't gotten it. Maybe we won't."

"You don't want to take a chance like that."

"I have to. I'll be careful."

In the end, he relented, and removed the barricade. Slowly, they made their way down the empty passageway, hand in hand. On the gangway leading to the main deck, they saw the first dead crewman. His skin was black, distended lips a brilliant red. In his death agony, he had literally clawed through his canvas breeches, trying to tear the tumor from his flesh. He had failed.

Then they came out onto the main deck and into the sun.

"My God, my ship," Royce cried. Selena realized, from the tremor in his voice, just how much he relied upon the mighty *Highlander*. And what they saw was ghastly, the composite of a life of nightmares. They did not know how many crewmen had gone overboard, or how many were sick or dead below decks. But it was not difficult to count the corpses sprawled on top, or captured by death in strange postures, as if attempting to run for the railing. In the rigging of the ship, high up in the sails, dead men were tied. They had tied themselves into their positions in order to tend the sails, so that the ship might reach the Canary Islands. So they might reach what they considered was safety and surcease. Even now, stricken men moaned, dying, high in the masts, their eyes on the far horizon. Hoping. Hoping until the last breath had left them.

"Worse than I thought," Royce muttered. "There's no way we can sail her without a crew. It's impossible . . ."

There was a drawn-out moan from the bridge, something like a call for help. But no one was visible there.

"Come on," Royce told her. He took a pistol from the belt of one of the dead men, and motioned her to follow him. She was thinking that he ought not have touched the weapon—it might be contaminated—but it was too late, and they climbed quickly to the bridge.

It was Lieutenant Fligh, on his back, conscious but failing fast.

"Fligh!" Royce exclaimed, keeping his distance. "When did it hit you?"

"Two days ago, sir. I'm sorry. It just . . . came down on me like a load of stone dropped from a crane. I . . ."

"Here, I'll get you some water . . ."

"No, no . . . too late . . . too late for that, just . . ."

"How many are left alive?"

"Don't . . don't know. At least eighteen overboard, some ill, some dead from . . . fighting. I . . . I came up here . . . alone . . . thought it would . . ." he tried to laugh, but it was a hoarse cackle, mixed with blood and spittle ". . . would save me. Not more than twelve left . . . I think, probably all sick or . . . dead . . ."

Before their eyes, he faded. His head lolled, and his limbs jumped spasmodically. Selena, sickened, put her hand to her mouth.

"Fligh. Wait, what's our course? What's our course, man?" Royce asked.

The lieutenant's eyes opened slightly, as his failing brain registered the question. He smiled slightly; it looked like a leer.

"I did my duty, Cap'n," he wheezed. "We're straight for the Canaries. Steady as she goes."

One hand went up, an abortive parody of a last salute, and then he went into a last frenzy, and was dead, and there was nothing but the steady rise and fall of the *Highlander*, and the driving wind.

"Oh, God, my poor ship," Royce murmured once again, looking up into the masts where dead sailors stared openeyed forever toward a horizon they had already crossed. "Let's go below. The weather's holding, and the wheel's locked in place. I'll do a sextant reading to make sure Fligh was right. We should reach the Canaries in about twenty hours. That would be dawn tomorrow."

"What about these men?"

"What about them?"

"Aren't you going to . . . do something?"

"I don't want to touch them. It's bad enough that they carried the germ. Now that they're dead, the bugs will abandon them and seek new . . ."

He dropped the pistol with a grimace of disgust, and wiped his hand on his uniform. "Jesus!"

"What about the ship?"

"I'll set a fuse to the powder kegs, and blow her to kingdom come."

"But . . ."

"There's no other way. Even if she were safe, I'd never be able to man a crew for her again."

Royce remained confident. In spite of the fact that the two of them could no longer maneuver the ship, it was possible to steer it with the rudder. Royce would do that, and carry them past the eastern tip of the Canaries. He would rig the fuse and light it. They would drop off and row to shore in the dinghy, and make their way to Tenerife, to pick up a ship for America. And the noble *Highlander*, sailing into the South Atlantic, would blow sky-high, with her cargo of death aboard.

They were three in the hammock that night: Royce, and Selena, and fear.

There was a fourth in the morning.

Her body knew it before her mind did, knew it before her mind was fully awake. It was very hot, and wet. Yet, next to her, Royce was shivering, trying to pull the leopard-skin coverlet over every inch of his hunched, shaking body. She leaped from the hammock.

"Oh, no!"

His perspiration had soaked through the hammock, leaving a dark, wet mark all along it underside, and even the leopard skin was dripping.

Her cry shook him from the merciful sleep to which he had clung.

He knew immediately.

"Sorry," he said, trying to smile. "I believe there's been a change in plans." Instantly, he was shaken, a spasm of shivering from which he could not escape. Selena was reminded of her father, sick in the winter cave. Almost everything since that time had been disastrous, until she'd met Royce again. And now . . .

"Is there something I can do?" she asked, going to him, putting her hand on his dripping, fever-hot forehead. "Something . . ."

He pulled himself out of the convulsion by an effort of the will.

"No, no . . ." pushing her hand away ". . . you mustn't touch. No! It's dawn now. Listen. Listen, Selena. Go up on deck. Hurry. The islands should be out ahead of us. Remember, we must pass them by, but closely. You have to go on the bridge, and adjust the ship's wheel. Point her toward the edge of an island, but not too close to shore. We can't afford to run her aground. The islanders would know of the plague then, and kill you when you go ashore. . . ."

You? That meant herself. Alone. And that meant he . . .

Royce saw it in her eyes.

"I can't," he said. "Now go on deck, and do as I told you."

In a daze, she went down the passageway, past the dead crewmen, whose bodies were swelling now, horribly bloated and discolored. *Somehow*, she was thinking, *I'll find a way to take him with me*. Her concentration helped her block out the odor of decay that hovered about the ship, and far ahead the low green sweep of the Canary Islands was like a cool paradise, a promised land. They would reach them somehow, together.

As best she could, Selena judged the course of the *Highlander*, and it seemed to her that they were drifting too much seaward. Holding her breath, she climbed the ladder to the bridge—Fligh was stone-still, watching her with dead eyes—and struggled with the knots he had used to fix the ship's wheel in position. Above, the dead sailors waited to see how she would do. *You have the wind,* they told her. *You have the wind of God, and we've given you full sail. Now all you have to do . . .*

All she had to do was turn the wheel. But which way and how much? Gingerly, she experimented. She turned it one notch to the left, which, she thought, would bring the *Highlander* closer in to the land, but after several minutes, she saw that, if anything, the ship was heading westward, farther out to sea. She remembered something Brian had said a long time ago, about the rudder controls on his sailboat. Opposite. You turn left when you wish to go right. She overcompensated the first time, but after ten or fifteen minutes she was confident that they would pass no farther than a quarter mile from the edge of the nearest large island.

Now the problem was to save Royce, somehow. She raced down from the bridge, back toward the gangway, devising plans for getting him into a dinghy. But he met her, half-dressed, staggering out on deck into the sun. He was leaning on a sword, but immediately knelt down on the deck. He took a measure of their course.

"You did well, Selena," he said, with effort. "There are many places we might have sailed . . ."

"Stop it! Now, here, let me help you. Get up. We're going to the lifeboat . . ."

Royce raised his hand in demurral.

"You are," he managed.

They looked at each other.

"Look around you," he said. "Do you see what happens? That is my fate. I have two responsibilities remaining. One, to see you to safety. Two, to take my ship to an appropriate . . ." he was seized by a terrific spasm of pain, hugged himself until it passed ". . . an appropriate end. And I can hang on that long. Now get me over to that boat, so I can work the block and tackle for you." He tried to smile.

"I hope you're a strong oarsman, but the tide's going in, and it shouldn't be . . . too hard for you . . ."

She swallowed and held back the tears.

"I'm staying."

He looked up at her.

"I knew you'd say that," he said, "but no, you're not."

"I am."

"Selena, Selena. Be hard, this once. Be like steel. What good is it to us if we both die? There won't even be a memory of our time together, short as it was. . . ."

"I don't want a memory. I don't *care* about memory. I want . . ."

"A memory is better than nothing, because it means something lived in the world, if only for a moment. Stay alive, for that at least."

"I don't care . . ."

"Yes, you do. You must. Besides, it's not in you *not to care*. You were *born* to care. Perhaps this is for the best. In a way, I was unready for you. I was unready for all you have to give. Now, get me over to that lifeboat."

Selena hesitated still, but she wavered. Royce Campbell saw it, and, intent upon saving her, pressed his advantage.

"You and I," he said, "Selena, you and I will be like me and the wolf puppy of my childhood. Where you go, I will always be . . ."

"But not if you *die*," she protested.

He nodded, and managed a smile. "Yes," he said, meeting her eyes, "yes, even then. You have the memory and thus carry me with you. As long as you are alive, we are both alive, don't you see?"

Soundlessly, she began to weep.

"I have my duty," he said, "even in the face of death. I must see to the fate of my ship."

She sobbed, and tried to hold back his words.

"I am dying, Selena. Face it. You are strong enough. But I do not die utterly, so long as you live. Now, give me that chance for life. As for my death, it is ordained, and I must do it at once, long ago, I went into the Highlands to speak with God. I have lived my life upon the sea, and here it is that I am meant to die. You can see that, can't you? Now, get into that boat, and go for both of us."

There before them, the lush green trees of the soft islands spread off to port, and in the distance she saw what seemed to be a fishing village.

"Now," he urged softly, "now, or it will be too late. You did well, navigating. Very well, and I'm proud of you. That's Tenerife, just yonder. Take the dinghy ashore. Go to Tenerife. Tell them you escaped a pirate ship. And tell them you're a rebel against England. Also your lineage. The Canaries are in the hands of Spain. Such information—such status—cannot but serve you in good stead."

And, just as he had when first they'd met at the Edinburgh ball, he winked.

"I've always been greatly taken by Scottish princesses," he said.

Selena tried to smile, couldn't, and pressed her hands to her temples. The Islands slid along beside them, close and gentle and safe. But it seemed that all her life, however short, was here on this ship in the afflicted, suffering body of this man. . . .

But even if his body was sick, his will was strong and his intelligence intact.

"Selena," he said, using his last, most powerful argument, his psychological trump, "Selena, Coldstream. Do it for Coldstream. Just get into that boat!"

The word cleared her mind, hit her like a jolt of adrenalin. Coldstream!

"You'll never see it again," he said, "if you let yourself die."

Selena stood there. The islands were going by, the surf gliding gently to the shores of white sand, breaking indolent and warm.

She managed to raise the dinghy and swing it over the side. She climbed into the boat. He stood by the block and tackle, barely able to stand.

"Brace yourself. I'll hold as hard as I can, but I don't have much strength left, and I still have to fire the powder. You'll have a quick drop."

In the little boat, she felt coming a last, sharp change of heart.

"Don't," she cried, "I'm staying."

"No," he said, and jerked the rope. She dropped down to the water, almost tumbling into the waves as the boat struck the surface. But it set down all right, and directly the tide carried her off toward shore. The day was exquisite, beautiful, all the colors as clean as the wind. Perfumed fragrance of plants and thick trees drifted out from the shore. But Royce was on the *Highlander,* dying, leaving her.

"Good-bye," she cried, her voice thin over the water, tears pouring down her cheeks. "Good-bye. I love you," she called.

He lifted his arm in a feeble wave, but his voice was strong.

"Not good-bye," came his answering call. "I go with you, so not good-bye. And I send my wolf-God with you, too."

The ship was moving very fast, still at full sail, and she barely heard his last words:

"When we are born again," he cried, thin over the face of the deep, "my wolf will lead us back together."

Distance made words impossible after that, but she watched him at the rail of the ship until she could no longer see him, only the ship. The tide pushed her onto the shore, and she watched the ship until she could no longer see it either. She waited for the sound of the explosion, but it didn't come and didn't come, and then she realized that he would spare her that. He would take it far off to sea, take his *Highlander* and his waning life and all his dreams far out to a lonely place where he could look up into the naked sky and make communion with the strange compelling forces out of which he had emerged, and present himself to them, and tell them he was ready. Ready to go home. Ready to return.

STRANGE PASSAGE

Against her wishes, Selena had been tutored in Spanish for a little less than one year. A drab room on the third floor of Coldstream Castle had been set aside for educational purposes, and in this prison she and Brian endured the often less-than-patient ministrations of a strong-willed but shapeless female from London, who was said to speak six languages, of which Spanish was rumored—rumored by Selena and Brian, that is—to be one. It did not matter anyway. They could barely understand the woman's London English, and when an epidemic of measles swept through Berwick Province, the cultured lady quickly fled the drawling hinterlands, seeking safety from disease, and, once more, the refined, nasal honking of London salons.

Good for her, Selena thought. Of what earthly use would Spanish and its oily insinuations ever be to Selena MacPherson?

Now, standing alone on a beach in the Canary Islands, which Royce had told her were controlled by Spain, Selena saw as clearly as if it were yesterday the big horses that drew the coach to the castle gate, the British governess waiting there with her black, bulging luggage. Then Edward, the chief steward, helping the lady into the coach, before it drove off. She had cheered to herself. She would have cheered out loud, except that Edward, who knew about the time she and Brian had burned the lady's copy of *Don Quixote*, saw her watching from her sickroom window and shook his finger in stern disapproval.

Oh, please forgive me, Selena thought, thinking of the lost lady and her own childish stupidity. *Please.*

The ocean was empty now, toward the horizon Royce

had chosen. But out of the north sailed a small one-master, presumably toward the port of Tenerife. Selena didn't care. What did it matter? Strong within her was the natural tide of grief, and strong, too, the impulse to crawl down among the sweet trees of these islands, to sleep her way into oblivion and join Royce there, but . . .

Wherever you are, I will be. You must live for both of us.

And she remembered that he had put her ashore to live, and that took courage. The small boat was perceptibly nearer now. It reminded her that life was going on, as usual. Interested in spite of herself, she tried to make out the flag on the mast, but the craft was still too far away. Here on the shore, she could no longer see Tenerife, but remembered having spotted three or four vessels at anchor in the harbor there. She decided to follow the shoreline around the bend, and approach the town on its seaward side.

The waves washed in, one upon another. She walked barefoot in the cool surf, soothed by it. The ocean's timeless rhythm, and her own exhaustion, eased her grief, dulled her mind. Far away, she imagined—or did she actually hear?—a great, deep booming, like the cracking of ice on the lochs on brittle January nights. Ended. Over. Strange, long-necked birds watched her come toward them, then took wing in long, gliding flight, tucking fantastic stalks of leg beneath them. Lizards and giant turtles basked on the warm sand, barely noticing her passage. Small animals and tiny birds darted for cover in the forest that ran right down to the sand.

How exotic it all was, how unbelievable! Never before had she seen trees like this, with great, wide leaves, big as the crosscut saw blades that were used to lumber forests. And it was so warm! Already she could see the town, and it, too, was different from any hamlet or village she had ever seen. Except for what must be the church, with its squat, white stucco steeple, not a building was over one or two stories, and the port and marina of which Royce had spoken were little larger than a medium-sized fishing village on the coast of Scotland. And from this tiny patch of the whole earth, she must make passage. To safety. Wherever that was.

A group of slim, dark figures far ahead were playing or performing some kind of exercise at the water's edge, using long poles or sticks, and when Selena drew nearer, she saw that they were raking for clams. Young boys, brown and bare to the waist, and she did not intend to frighten them, but that was what happened. One of them looked up from his rake, and froze right there in the sand. His mouth seemed to be opening and closing, but no sound came out of it. His response alarmed Selena momentarily, until she remembered her appearance. The old sailor's uniform, with a young woman in it. A very blond young woman, with uncut, tousled hair down to her breasts. In this area of dark-skinned, black-haired people, and walking toward them barefoot on the white beach, she must indeed seem an apparition.

"Por favor!" she tried, raising a hand.

The boy broke out of his immobility, found his tongue. "Yiii!" he cried, falling to his knees, *"Madre de Dios! Madre de Dios!"* and pressed his hands together in supplication. His companions were less susceptible, but no less stunned. They stopped working, and took her in. One of them shifted his weight, as if preparing to run.

"Tenerife?" she asked, and pointed to the village beyond.

"Sancta Maria, Madre de Dios," the supplicant was praying, crossing himself with wild abandon, and then: *"Mea culpa, mea culpa, mea maxima culpa,"* with his eyes shut tight.

His fear alarmed the others, though not enough to induce them to join him on their knees, and suddenly they were running away down the beach—all but the prayerful one. They broke into a run as animals do, without signal or warning, and all at the same time. One instant they were still as stone, and the next they were in motion, running without fear now, when they saw that she was not pursuing. But they did not stop, or even slow down, and soon they were gone far up toward the docks at Tenerife. Spreading the news.

Selena came to the kneeling boy, and stopped. The words of his prayers were run together now, a mixture of Spanish and Latin that made no sense. Conscious of her standing right before him, the sound ceased, too. His lips moved furiously, however, and he bowed his head, as if waiting for an ax to fall.

"Hello," Selena said tentatively, and smiled.

The quivering boy lifted his head and opened his eyes, saw her standing there in her wild blond beauty, framed by the sun. It was too much for him. He shuddered once, all through his body, and slumped sideways to the sand, his head resting in a pile of clams. A tiny martyr among the stones by which he had been brought low.

It amused Selena for a moment. She would have to tell Royce about this as soon as . . . She was no longer amused. The boy stirred. On the horizon, the one-master drew nearer to port. She could see the flag. The Union Jack. Bad. And coming toward her now, from the direction of the village, were a number of men, trailed by the skipping, dancing boys who had given the warning. She was afraid, but walked to meet them.

About ten paces apart, by unspoken agreement, she halted, as did the men. One of the boys babbled something in Spanish that Selena could not decipher, and the tallest of the men, who stood at the center of the little group, replied to him curtly. The boy spoke no more. The man looked like a peasant, but unlike his companions, who had on rough-looking garments, he wore a loose white shirt that was almost like a blouse. His eyes did not seem intelligent, but he had the bearing of one who is used to a measure of obeisance.

"*Yo . . .*" she said, pointing to herself, trying to remember words, "*Yo . . .* Selena."

The man frowned. "*Inglés?*" he asked, and pointed at her hair.

"No, no. Scottish."

It did not register. They all looked perplexed.

"Scotland," she told him, as if that would help.

Shrugs all around, and some discussion of her uniform. They seemed to relax a little and so did she, and commenced to speak quietly and very fast among themselves. The boy who had been overcome by religious ardor skirted her widely. His companions ragged him hilariously, and one of them threw a stick and let out a good-natured curse. "*Madre de Dios!*" he cried, in mock anguish, and the others howled. The man in the white blouse shut them up again, and turned to her.

"Se-le-na," he pronounced carefully, pointing.

She nodded.

He smiled. Not a kind smile, nor one with any special meaning in it. Simply a smile to indicate that a little progress had been made. He jerked a thumb at his chest, which swelled a bit.

"Rafael," he said.

"Rafael," she repeated. "Sí."

"Sí!" the men said, turning to one another. "Sí!" They were very pleased.

Unfortunately, their immediate chatter in her direction elicited no similar communication. Finally, trying to be friendly, babbling about someone called "Señora Celeste," they led her, almost gallantly, in the direction of the town. Selena walked as quickly as she could, smiling almost continuously at the men. It was not that she felt any special desire to please them—things could turn dangerous at a moment's notice—but rather that she wanted to reach the town before the British ship landed. It was a peaceful freighter of some sort—she could see no cannon aboard— but ever since the night of Lord North's speech in Edinburgh, the sight of the Union Jack flying from flagpole or mast invariably nerved her to wariness. Staying one jump ahead might mean the difference between life or death.

They did not lead her onto the docks, but rather up a long stone stairway to the street of the town. It was dusty and rutted and filled with horse droppings—and pigs eating therefrom—but the men pointed down to the sails in the harbor below, quite pleased to show her the view. She kept on smiling, and nodded vigorously whenever it seemed to be in order.

The buildings were mostly alike, made of a very light type of wood that was unfamiliar to her. Some of them had walls of woven grass that reminded her of the thatched roofs of peasant huts in Scotland. The men led her to the largest building in town, and stopped.

"Señora Celeste," they explained helpfully.

Selena smiled and nodded again. Señora Celeste must be a person of considerable consequence.

And not only that. Considerable bulk as well. After an

interval of at least ten minutes—down on the docks Selena could hear the cries welcoming the British ship—a heavy, but stylishly dressed woman made her way to the door, and regarded the men with intelligent interest, her eyes sharpening just a little when she saw Selena there among them.

"*Scot-tish,*" Rafael pronounced, carefully. "Se-le-na." And then burst into rapid Spanish for the rest of the story of her appearance on the beach.

Señora Celeste nodded, then raised a hand to quiet him. Thanked him—*Gracias! Gracias!*—profusely, and beckoned Selena. Her voice was very friendly, and her smile most kind. Selena almost sighed with relief.

"Come in, my dear," the woman welcomed her. "Come in. I'm sure you have a long and interesting story, and I'm in need of one, stuck out here as I am at the edge of the world. And I wouldn't be surprised if you could use a bath and a good meal, as well. Now, come in, come in."

Her touch was gentle, and she was obviously happy to see Selena.

"A glass of wine for all of you," Celeste called to Rafael and his group. As she went inside, Selena could hear the men congratulating one another. They had done a good thing. She was not displeased with their effort either.

Señora Celeste's building was something on the order of a hotel, but it also seemed to be a rather elegant private residence. Some of the furniture was constructed of bound lengths of fine wood, like wicker, but much of it was European, sturdy, highly polished. Mirrors hung on the walls. Green and flowering plants were everywhere. Wild birds of startling colors jumped and called from perches in finely wrought cages. A number of well-dressed men were playing cards in a screened veranda overlooking the harbor, and servants moved about on various errands.

"Please excuse my appearance," Selena begged. "You've no idea what I've been through."

"Oh?" Was there a sharpness of tone in the query?

"Let me tell you right away," Selena decided, glancing uneasily toward the quay. Even now, the British ship was easing up to the pier. Sailors in the rigging rolled and furled the sails.

She told Señora Celeste the story of the pirate ship that

Royce had suggested. The thought of Royce made her sadness genuine, and she almost believed the story herself.

Madame Celeste had one major reservation.

"But a young girl as beautiful as you? One would think you'd have been guarded day and night. For the . . . services you were able to provide. How did you manage to get free?"

"I had help," she said. "One of the sailors was less an animal than the rest."

Celeste laughed loudly, her fat cheeks rippling. "All men are animals, my dear, when it comes to that. Don't you know?" Subsiding, she wanted to know whose ship it was.

There seemed no point in lying about the rest of it.

"It belonged to a man named Royce Campbell," she said, dropping her eyes. "It was called the *Highlander*."

Pause, then: "Well, well, my dear, is that so?" There was respect in the tone.

Selena nodded. Celeste patted her hand, and Selena was certain that she could trust the fat woman.

"You've been had by a rogue, all right, my dear, but you've been had by the best of rogues, I daresay." She clucked her tongue. "Well, we'll take care of you here until you decide what you want to do. . . ."

Once again, Selena glanced reflexively at the British ship outside.

"Is something wrong?"

Selena wasn't up to the entire explanation. Instead, she relied on Celeste's apparent perspicacity. "I'm Scottish," she said simply. "I can't say I'm too fond of the English these times."

"Ah! I knew you were nervous about something. But never you mind. Let's get you upstairs to a hot tub, and out of sight. Some of those sailors are bound to be up here soon, wanting their rum . . ."

She let her voice die away, as if there was something else those men might want. Selena looked up. Celeste was smiling.

"But you already know about that, don't you? No, no. Never you mind. Don't worry. I don't run that kind of place. Not at all."

The bath was incomparable, baking the dirt out of her pores, the tension from her muscles, even the fear and fatigue from her very bones. It did everything, in fact, but wash away the memories of Royce, which kept welling up, and the shattered dreams of all that might have been. Two men, two splendid men, she had already lost in her life, and had it not been for the friend she had found in Señora Celeste, Selena might have been tempted to consider the knife Father had once asked her to use. But the bath was a balm, and while she bathed, servants entered and left. The rich, warm smell meant food, and it was there in the room, hot on a silver serving platter, when she toweled off, brushed her hair, and slipped on a loose dress of lavender silk that had been laid out for her. It was noon now, and the sun was hot and high, but the windows of the room had awnings and were shuttered against the heat. She ate a meat that tasted like roast pork, with a fine gravy, buttered bread with a tender, brown crust, and a fresh green salad. There was chilled white wine, almost sweet, and the two glasses she drank soon did their work.

Selena barely remembered Señora Celeste entering, and helping her to bed, and the invitation to "dine with some good friends of mine this evening" seemed like a summons to something as remote as Judgment Day.

She awoke late in the afternoon, warm but very refreshed. Another of the servants had left her a pot of tea, still hot, and a plate of biscuits and muffins.

Selena heard footsteps in the hall. Doubtless the servant. She walked quickly to the door, to express her thanks.

The door was locked.

She blamed herself, this time. Completely. She did not even feel betrayed. On the *Meridian,* she had promised herself to be more careful, to master her judgment of people. There was only one person to blame when one's own counsel was ignored. In cold anger she drank the tea and ate, not knowing when she would have food again, not knowing what to expect. When the knock came at her door, Selena felt defiant.

It was Señora Celeste. "And how are you feeling, my dear? Were you able to rest comfortably here?"

"My door was locked from outside," Selena snapped, and let her eyes convey all the fury she could muster.

Celeste's fleshy face fell in a look of deep personal affront.

"Why . . . my dear . . . certainly you don't think that . . . oh, no, you don't understand. There are many sailors in a port such as this, and while I attempt to remind them of their manners, one cannot be too careful. Some of them are fond of another variety of establishment, of which you may have heard, where things go on upstairs. I secured the door for your own protection, just to be sure. . . ."

Selena listened. Was it possible? The protests of the fat woman seemed genuine enough.

"I have given many girls my counsel and aid," Celeste was saying. "There are two fine young women here right now, and you may talk to them at any time and ask them if I have not proved myself to be a woman of honest and charitable character. Come now, I'm sorry for having given you fright. . . ."

In the face of Celeste's aggrieved protestations, Selena wavered.

"Come along, please, and join me and some of my guests for dinner. An American freighter, the *Massachusetts,* is in port now, bound for the Orient. Her captain is a born Scot, too, and very charming. Perhaps you'll be able to learn something of aid in making your own plans."

Celeste smiled and opened her arms as if to embrace Selena, as if to forgive the young woman for her cruel mistrust.

But Selena was still suspicious. Something seemed ever so slightly amiss. She went to the window and found it unlocked. If she had had to escape, she could have done so. And, down on the waterfront, just as Celeste had said, was the American freighter.

"I'm sorry," Selena apologized then. "Forgive my suspicion. It was ill-mannered of me."

Her big-bosomed, big-hearted hostess waved the words aside. "Let us forget the entire matter, dear," she said. "We'll not mention it again."

Something about the captain of the *Massachusetts* troubled Selena, but she could not decide what it was. His manners were impeccable, his bearing above reproach. He did make bold to flirt, but so totally within the bounds of propriety that Selena felt it was merely part of his social manner, something he felt he ought to do for the entertainment of the young ladies present.

There were three: Selena, Roxanne, and Marinda. A striking girl with lustrous, roan-red hair, Marinda was Spanish and had come to the Canaries from Andalusia. Her father had brought along the entire family and had sought to establish a cotton plantation in the interior. Her mother had died of fever shortly after their arrival. Two older brothers had returned to Spain in disgust. And, finally, the natives had killed her father. Out of the goodness of her kind heart, Señora Celeste had taken Marinda in until a ship bound for Spain should dock in Tenerife.

Roxanne was French. Her hair was almost as blond as Selena's, and she was not quite as cultivated as Marinda appeared to be. Roxanne seemed the most experienced of the three, and they soon learned of her adventures, which she related with rueful, world-weary good humor. Two years previously, she had run away with her lover, a French naval officer, of whom her burgher parents had not approved. Hers had been an experience of bad luck and bad love. The naval officer had been deficient in honor, just as Roxanne's mama had divined. He had jilted her finally in the Azores, after telling her he was leaving for the Canary Islands and she could do as she wished for the rest of her life. Roxanne had promptly spent the last of her money on a dagger and a ticket to Tenerife, only to find that the naval officer had lied about that, too.

So Celeste had taken Roxanne in as well, until she could book passage on a ship back to Marseilles.

"You certainly are among the most fortunate of young women," said the master of the *Massachusetts,* whom Celeste introduced as "Captain Jack," "and adventurous ones as well."

He seemed sympathetic. *What is it about him that bothers me?* Selena asked herself. There was something vaguely familiar about him, but .. . .

"They're young. They'll survive," harumphed a stuffy British captain who was also at table with them. He paid them only the bare minimum of social attention, however, being himself clearly outclassed by Captain Jack. Rafael, whom Selena had met on the beach, was also there with his wife, a young lady with the sturdy good health of a peasant. She seemed to feel Rafael had done a great thing, although she was not quite certain exactly what it had been.

They ate in Celeste's private dining room. She had been truthful when she said that hers was not a typical waterfront establishment, nor even an actual inn. She did have a public room adjacent to the dining area, but insisted that order was maintained. Some sailors were drinking at the bar. Selena could see them as she ate.

"Blimey, et war the oddest thing," wheezed the British officer, his mouth full of roast veal and sweet potato. "We picked the poor bloke out of the drink nigh on three days ago. 'E said 'e'd been driftin' fer o'er a day, e'en then. Sounded like a mutineer t' me, 'e did, so I 'ad 'im flogged while I asked 'im some questions."

"A castaway?" Jack asked, with interest. "Naval or merchantman?"

The British officer laughed. "Neither," he grunted, gulping down a good half-pint of port. "Privateer. Said he was impressed on with Royce Campbell, but couldn't take it no more, so jumped ship . . ."

Royce Campbell! Selena froze. It was all she could do to keep from looking at Celeste. She weakened, failed. But the fat woman went on eating, quite serene, and gave no sign. *I can trust her,* Selena thought, with immense relief.

". . . said drowning was preferable to serving a bastard . . . ah, oh, pardon me, ladies . . . like Campbell, and . . ."

"Where is he now?" Jack inquired "I could use an extra crewman or two. I'm shorthanded this voyage."

The British jerked his thumb. "'E's right in there, like any bloody seaman, a-swillin' down the sauce. 'E's the one careful not t' lean back on anything," he added, chortling. "Oh, me, when I order the cat laid on, I don't spare my bosun's arm."

Gleefully, he wiped his eyes with a napkin, shaking with mirth.

Selena looked in the direction of the taproom, and spotted the sailor. It wasn't difficult. He was looking right at her, an expression of fear and horror on his face. She understood at once. He had been on Royce's ship. She re-

membered him, working on one of the cannon crews, when
Royce had shelled the *Meridian*. He had not dared mention
the plague—not if he wanted a job again, not if he wanted
to *live*—and she understood, too, that he would not betray
her. She felt the touch of a warm, once-familiar emotion
way down deep. It took a moment before she recognized it
as the sense of safety.

"And what are your plans, Miss . . . ah . . . ?" Captain Jack was asking.

"Selena," said Celeste, avoiding the last name.

"I . . . my plans were to make my way to America."

"America, eh? Fine place for a lovely young lady like
yourself. My brother does a measure of sea running between England and Boston, as do I. He's remained attached to Liverpool as his permanent base, however,
whereas I myself chose Boston. We sometimes contrive to
meet one another on the high seas, and we were supposed
to have done so this time. But he must have been delayed.
The rendezvous did not occur. Tell me," he asked the British captain, "have you seen his ship, the M.S. *Meridian*?"

Selena did not hear whatever the British officer replied.
Now she knew why Captain Jack had disturbed her: a certain slope of his forehead, the telltale delicacy of feature,
and a kind of perverse intelligence around the eyes. Captain Jack *Randolph!* And he would make no more rendezvous with his brother on this side of hell.

Selena, who had been feeling rather secure, even content,
felt the sense of well-being slip away in the darkness, leaving no trace.

"Will you have sherbet or mousse?" Celeste was asking,
her fat finger circling the air for a waiter.

Selena's luck held, and her secrets still seemed safe a
little later when a small orchestra began to play dance music. Even the sailor had departed. Celeste winked and got
heavily to her feet, leaning on the back of a chair. "I had
best attend to a few details," she said to the small group.
"Please, all of you. Remain here. Enjoy your evening."

"We shall certainly make every attempt, my lady," said
the British captain, who was slightly drunk now. He ogled
Roxanne with a mixture of lust and belligerence.

Captain Jack asked Selena to dance and held her close. She could feel his sex swelling against her, and he grinned when she looked up.

"You've a room upstairs, I suppose?"

She gave him her most winning smile. "Not for you."

He was undaunted. "Come now. I'll be back from the Orient by and by, and if you're still here . . ." he coughed discreetly ". . . I'll run you over to America, for a favor. Just like that."

"Just like that?"

"Well . . ." He glanced meaningfully at the ceiling and the rooms upstairs. *My God*, she thought. *I've no money and Celeste has said nothing about how I'm to get out of here. Is this the way?* Marinda was dancing intimately with the second officer of the *Massachusetts*, and at the table the British captain maneuvered his hand, getting into position for a sortie beneath Roxanne's skirts.

But Celeste said she didn't run a place like that!

"Come now, sweets, I haven't got all night. Must sail in the morning. Now, you just run your delicious little bottom up those stairs, and I'll join you in a bit. And don't worry, I'll give you such a time you'll think you've died and gone to heaven."

He pressed even closer to her, straining. "Feel it?"

There was a hard, no-nonsense glint in his eyes now. What should she do?

"All right," she told him, "you wait here. Come up in a few minutes."

"That's my girl," he gloated.

Her smile was brittle, but she kept it until she got out of the dining room. Celeste was in the front hall, going through some papers or records at a desk. She started when Selena came up behind her.

"Oh, my, what a fright! I wish you'd have announced yourself," she puffed, putting the papers away. "Why, what's the matter?"

Selena told her, and once again the fat woman proved she could be trusted.

"Captain Jack Randolph," she lectured, when the tumescent officer came out of the dining room, walking swiftly— if a bit uncomfortably—toward the stairs. "I warned you to keep your shenanigans on the dance floor. Now, you've insulted this fine young lady, who's my personal guest here, and I think you owe her an apology."

To Selena's considerable surprise, the captain did as he was bidden. Flustered, abashed, he asked Selena's forgiveness for his "temerity," and even promised to take her to America, should she still be in Tenerife on his return voyage.

"Thank you, Jack, that's better," Señora Celeste told him. "But I'm sure another ship will be by before that. Anyway, I don't know if I'd let one of my girls on a vessel with you."

He muttered another apology before leaving the inn and retreating to his ship.

"You've got to know how to handle them," Celeste said calmly, putting her hand on Selena's. "Now, why don't you retire? Perhaps this has been too much for you?"

It sounded like a very good idea, and Selena went upstairs to her room. She had the key this time—Celeste had given it to her—and as soon as she closed the door behind her, she turned the bolt. It slid to with a heavy, reliable click. A small oil lamp burned dimly on the table. She adjusted the wick, and the room brightened. The sailor was sitting on her bed, a knife in his hand.

"Make a sound and ye're dead," he hissed.

Too startled to cry out, she nonetheless registered the fact that he was as scared as she.

"Tha's a girl," he sighed, relaxing. "'Ow did ye get off the ship?"

She told him.

"Any others?"

"I don't think so. Even Roy . . . even the captain was dying . . ."

The thought of her beloved, dead now, and floating somewhere in the black fathoms of the sea, was like an assault. She swayed.

"Here," he said, "are ye sure ye're not ill?" He got up and let her slump to the bed.

"Then we two must be the only ones left o' the *Highlander*, an' what de ye think o' that? I got off right away, when I seen 'ow the men was goin' mad. Now, tomorrow, I'm shippin' fer the Orient aboard the *Massachusetts*, an'

I'll stay out there 'til I die, probably. Ye won't say nithin' aboot 't plague, will ye?"

She shook her head. It would be mad to do so.

"Then neither will I. Ye're a smart girl, an' I'm sorry aboot ye're . . ." He tried to think of a polite word to describe Royce's relationship to her, couldn't, and gave it up. "Sorry about the captain. Ye take care of yerself now, unnerstand?"

With that, he climbed out the window, moving the shutters apart, hung for a moment by his fingertips, and dropped to the ground with a soft, thudding sound. She heard him walking off toward the docks. A haze of moments drifted by, and she was almost asleep when another set of soft footsteps sounded in the hall. And stopped outside her door. There was no sound for a minute, and quietly she crept over to the door.

"Who's there?"

The voices were a relief. Roxanne and Marinda. She threw open the door.

"Are you all right?" they wanted to know. "You left the dancing so early."

"I'm all right. I was just tired."

Roxanne smiled. "We know how it is. The men also tried to make love to us, but Señora Celeste told them '*basta* is *basta*,' and made them go back to the boat. She is a fine lady, don't you think?"

Yes, she was indeed, a fact repeated and confirmed when a servant brought up warm milk for them to drink.

"Sleep well," the servant said courteously, solicitously. Almost as if they would be doing him a great favor by complying.

In the morning, Selena was disoriented, coming out of sleep. At first, fighting to open her sleep-shrouded eyes, she thought she was still with Royce in his cabin aboard the *Highlander*. But there was no easy motion of the hammock, nor his sweet body beside her. Then the smell of seaweed, salt, and wind seemed all about, but that could not be either, because she was in a bed at Celeste's inn. A hard bed. Hard? Her arms would not move. Dreaming? Captain Randolph's ship again? Startled, she opened her eyes.

She was on the wooden floor of a small bare ship's cabin. At sea. It was well after dawn. She was tied hand and foot, and so were Marinda and Roxanne. Roxanne stirred then, too, and opened her eyes.

"Oh, no!" she wailed, and burst into tears. "We have been deceived. Oh, how did it happen?"

"Because you little girls were too trusting," Captain Jack smiled, stepping in from the passageway. "My, my. I guess we can untie you now. You won't be going far, way out here at sea, now will you?"

He was in good spirits, and he quickly untied the three of them. Marinda seemed stunned.

"I guess Señora Celeste put too much powder in your milk, eh, Marinda?"

"Celeste?" they cried.

"Certainly," he grinned. "Do you think she takes in runaway girls with no money for her health? Oh, no. She's a shrewd businesswoman, and what an actress, too. Don't you agree? She charged me a pretty penny for you three, but don't worry. I'll turn a nice profit when I pass you on. They'll pay fine gold for young ladies like yourselves, exotic foreigners. Provided you're well-trained."

The three women rubbed their wrists and ankles, shook the stiffness from their bodies.

"Who will pay?" Selena managed to ask.

"Whoever has the money," Captain Jack responded, with that mocking grin. "I'm in business, you know. I believe those who disapprove of my vocation call it 'white slaving.' But, like all merchants, I merely provide a desirable commodity for those who can afford it."

"Where are we going? Where are you taking us?"

"Bombay, my fine ladies. You might say you're on the way to adventure in the Orient. Now, get up and get down to the galley. I want to get some food in you. Must be presentable at market, you know. Later, we'll begin your training. Rotation system, I should think. One of you every third night." Then he dropped his easy manner, and his eyes hardened. "But don't think of trying anything funny," he snapped. "It'll go very hard with the one who does." He looked directly at Selena as he spoke. "I've got good money invested in you, but don't become overconfident. Some of the buyers like to see the marks of a little discipline on the skin of the commodity. It denotes spirit. But it certainly stings when it's being administered, I can assure you of that."

The sailors, apparently, had been warned to leave them alone. After eating a breakfast she could neither taste nor remember, Selena went up on deck alone, and looked out at sea. The ship was pushing south, and off to port Africa glided by, a phantasm green as jade. She felt too dispirited even to be afraid. She felt stupid and worthless. She felt utter chagrin. The tiny voice began to mock her again: *So you risked death aboard the* Meridian *because you would not serve Randolph and Roberta as a procuress, and yet you allowed yourself to be tricked into becoming the procured, you silly fool of a victim. You were too moral to participate in white slavery, so now you have become a white slave yourself!*

There is no escape this time.

But it's a long way to India. We have to round the Cape of Good Hope, then up across the Indian Ocean . . .

Plenty of time to be well-trained, though.

"No, I'll not be," she said aloud. "I'll think of something," and to underscore her resolve she struck the ship's rail with her clenched fist, startling a one-eared sailor who was mopping the deck a short distance away. He scowled, ducked his head, and quickly turned aside.

The three women were installed in the tiny cabin, and hammocks were provided. A trunk of old but suitable clothing had been shipped with them, apparently out of the goodness of Señora Celeste's heart. (She prided herself on taking good care of her "girls.") Trying the dresses on for size filled the time, and kept the three women from thinking. Finally, Marinda could stand the situation no longer. She burst into tears.

"I can't bear it. I can't. The captain told me he wants me tonight. Why did *Papá* ever take us away from Spain? Oh, why . . ." and she was lost in her sobs.

"Come now, it won't be so bad," Roxanne said, trying to soothe her. "If it's got to happen, pretend he's your lover, or someone else, and not Jack."

"But that's just it," Marinda sobbed. "I've never had a . . ."

"There must be something we can do," Roxanne said.

"But what?" Selena doubted. "Even if we find a way to avoid Jack here on the ship, when we reach India . . ."

Marinda wept, distraught.

Selena tried to think. "Still, anything can happen." She thought of all that had occurred since last December, all the strange, unexpected experiences, both good and bad. "Sometimes if you can just provide a bit of room in which to maneuver, or if you can find a way to postpone whatever is going to happen, why, sometimes that's enough. The entire situation can change!"

She adjusted her dress and headed for the door and the passageway leading up to the main deck.

"Where are you going?" asked Roxanne.

"To see the captain," Selena replied, her mouth set firmly. "You try to comfort Marinda."

"It won't be so bad. It won't be so bad," Roxanne was saying as Selena went up on deck.

One of the officers took her to the bow, where Captain Jack was bent over a tablet, painstakingly mapping the African coast. He looked up in some surprise when he saw her, and grinned expectantly.

"I'm glad you came up on deck to join me," he began. "I've observed your beauty and spirit, and I must say I find it . . ."

"How you find it is no concern of mine," she interrupted. While she understood that little could be done to alter the situation aboard the *Massachusetts*, she had no intention of submitting willingly to degradation. "I am here to ask that you take me tonight, rather than Marinda."

"What?" He gave her a slightly astonished, patronizing smile. "I'm so sorry, my dear, but my plans have already been made. Marinda looks a juicy girl, but she will require tutoring. She is too retiring, at present. But I shall change that. I do believe, in all modesty, that I have the skill to stir the beast in her nature. . . ."

Selena gave him a contemptuous stare. The arrogance of the man! "You flatter yourself, Captain. Have you not learned that a woman responds but little to your type of man?"

Captain Jack reddened perceptibly, but contained his anger. "Ah, my dear. You shall respond to me. And I am saving you for last. The best for last, as the saying goes, eh?"

Selena laughed derisively, facing him squarely. She was aware of the risk she was taking by speaking to him in this manner, but she considered the risk worthwhile if Marinda might be helped thereby. She wondered whether she ought to tell Jack about his brother's death. Judging by what he'd said at Señora Celeste's, Jack had been close to Randolph. On the one hand, the news might distract Captain Jack enough to cause him to leave the three of them alone. On the other hand, it might stir him to vengeful rage. . . .

She was staring at him, debating the question in her mind, when she caught a sudden flash of color out of the corner of her eye. Immediately, there was a flurry of consternation amidships, and moments later a sailor yelled: "Man overboard! Man overboard, off the starboard bow!"

Captain Jack gave the necessary orders, but it takes a considerable amount of time to slow and turn a ship at sea when the ship is running full sail to the wind. Selena saw— or thought she saw—a last momentary flash of white arm, a roan-red fan of hair floating on the sea. Marinda had made her decision.

"I didn't know she was going to do it," Roxanne wept. "She told me she was just going up on deck and . . ."

"It's all right," said Selena, trying to comfort the French girl. "It's not your fault. It's *his*," she added, looking hard at Captain Jack, who stood disgustedly at the ship's rail, calculating the amount of money he had probably lost when Marinda went over the side.

"What did you say?" he asked.

"I believe you heard me clearly enough."

"That I did," he gritted, "that I did. And you had best be prepared for me tonight."

Not long after twilight, Captain Jack summoned Selena to his quarters. She had steeled herself for what must come, and she felt cold, hard, and calm. The captain's cabin unnerved her somewhat because it reminded her of Royce's quarters aboard the *Highlander,* but that, too, she shut out of her mind.

"Well, my dear," Jack said, taking her hand and drawing her into the cabin, closing the door behind him. "Would you care for a glass of wine first?"

He was making an effort to be charming and solicitous, perhaps recalling her accusation that he did not know how to make a woman respond.

"Nothing," she told him coldly. "Do your will."

Jack hesitated for just a second. "I didn't mean it to be that way, my dear, I . . ."

"I mean it to be that way," she said. She did not even look at him as she removed her dress and flung it to the floor. She did not look at him as she walked to the hammock, swung into it. She lay there, not moving, staring at the timbers on the ceiling. She said nothing.

"Aha! I know what you're up to!" Jack growled, pleased at his sagacity and knowledge of women. "A challenge, eh? You want me to stir you, isn't that right."

Selena said nothing. She did not move.

Nor did she move when Jack joined her in the hammock, after frenetically divesting himself of breeches, boots, and shirt. And she did not move, either, after he had entered her.

Captain Jack tried hard to arouse her, but Selena lay cold as stone beneath him. He kissed her on the mouth, on the neck. He kneaded her breasts with his hands and caressed her nipples softly. He pumped her deep and hard, then very gently. Selena did not move, or respond in any way.

"Dammit," Jack groaned finally.

"Are you through?" Selena asked.

He was not, of course, but the question, contemptuous as it was, goaded him. Grunting, he made another furious assault upon her body, taking his pleasure.

"Are you through now?" Selena asked, as he lay sprawled upon her, panting.

"No, you little bitch," he hissed. "No, not by a long shot, as you'll be learning on many a night. Now get out of here. You've done the thing for which a woman's made."

Selena put on her dress and left the cabin. She said nothing. She did not look at him.

And he did not send for her again.

Days went by. Weeks. Sailing the Cape of Good Hope was terrible, the roiling sea far wilder than the fray from which Royce had rescued Selena. Every wave seemed to hold death like a giant sledgehammer just over the tip of the bending mast. By contrast, the Indian Ocean was calm, the wind warm and unceasing. Early one morning in August, Selena and Roxanne were standing on deck, savoring the cool of dawn. Far ahead of them rose the gigantic red ball of the sun. But this morning it did not rise out of the timeless sea. Instead, it appeared above a vast, yellow, shimmering expanse of land.

Ancient India. Patient. Waiting. They trembled and did not look at each other.

THE CREATOR

I won't let this defeat me either, Selena tried to convince herself. *I'll talk to the first European I see. Even if he's British. Maybe . . .* her heart balked at the absurdity of it *. . . someone will have heard of Sean Bloodwell.*

Captain Jack paid them a farewell visit in their cabin, and quickly disabused her of that illusion. He was in good spirits again, now that the difficult voyage was over.

"You didn't think I'd be so clever as to land in the port of Bombay itself, did you now?" he sneered sarcastically. "Oh, it could have been done safely, I suppose. The British East India Company is none too strong in the state of Maharashtra. Most of those clerks and fortune hunters are over in Bengal, in East India. You won't find any red-blooded saviors over on this side."

He laughed, happy to deflate a last hope.

"Then where are we putting ashore?"

"Daman," he said. "North of Bombay, at the mouth of the River Narbada. I've delivered some lovely cargoes here previously, and the bids always run high. Very clean deals, too, and I've never heard a word of complaint later. Neither from client nor commodity. So I assume they found one another mutually compatible, or some agreement decidedly more terminal was reached. . . ." He laughed again, deliberately contemptuous, and motioned them to follow him up on deck. Roxanne, as was her nature, seemed calmer than Selena, if not resigned. "It's death or life," she told Selena as they had dressed earlier that morning. "Life is much sweeter, as long as you can bear it." Now, climbing the gangway one last time, the wild, ripe smell of India already flooding around them, she whispered, "Do not worry, Selena. Do not think of it. There is a scale of justice in the world, and Captain Jack will have his head crushed by it."

Selena started to laugh, broke it off in time when Jack turned to give her a suspicious glance.

"Listen well, my dears," he told them magisterially when they were on deck. "There are two things about India that you ought to know. One, it can eat you alive . . ." he snickered, pleased with his little entendre ". . . and, two, nothing is ever what it appears to be. I learned those things on fifteen voyages here and, moreover, I know exactly how to treat the natives. Dominance and respect are what matter. That's why the British will eventually triumph over the Dutch and the Portuguese and the rest. We know how to colonize. We know how to treat the Wogs."

Selena barely heard him, stunned to speechlessness by the alien scene. She had anticipated a seaport much like those in England and Scotland, a bustling, orderly port, different only in that it would be filled with brown-skinned people. It took only moments for her to see that this land to which she had been carried against her will was more remote and incomprehensible than she could ever have imagined. A wide brown river, its brown banks packed with animals and filth and humanity, emptied slowly into the muddy harbor, itself packed with ships and sails and smaller craft. Men worked on water-rotted, sagging docks, unloading or loading ships, babbling, unmindful of the chaos. The din of voices was persistent and vaguely frightening. And beyond this waterfront confusion was nothing that Selena would have called a city. Instead, as far as the eye could see, there were shacks and hovels and shelters of stick and tattered cloth, over which waves of heat shimmered. Thousands of people were pouring into the filthy river, chanting and gesticulating, scooping water into their cupped hands, letting it fall upon them, then retreating to the reeking shore, where another flood of humanity waited to enter the water. The blasting heat of the sun was wet with tropical humidity; the very air stank of beasts and human sweat, and a hundred kinds of offal. The land, yellow and sickly green, looked flat and sad.

"There she lies," Jack told them, with a proprietary sweep of his arm. "India. Just as I told you. Nothing is what it appears to be. You take those stupid Wogs, jump-

ing up and down in the river over there. What are they
doing? They are bathing. Ah, but the water is filthy, you
say. Of course it is. They are not bathing to become
clean—they have never been clean in their lives, don't even
know what it is—but to *purify* themselves. The Hindu bastards. It has something to do with religion. Purification is
merely symbolic, so they can do it with water that would
kill a good sturdy Yorkshire hog in the space of five seconds." He laughed, pleased with himself. "With brains like
that, they might even qualify for Christianity."

The *Massachusetts* was being unloaded now. Large
crates were craned out of the hold, swung onto the docks
by diminutive, chattering men. Roxanne expressed a
thought that had also crossed Selena's mind.

"We know that you are a superb merchant, but who in
this pitiful town can buy us?"

"Don't worry. The rich don't live in hellholes like this.
You will be taken to a place out in the country, to be observed. I have no doubt *someone* will find you suitable.
Being French may stand you in good stead. Even way out
here at the edge of the earth there is many a lusty rajah
who craves the French method . . ."

"You filthy . . ." Roxanne spat, and raised an arm
against him. He caught it easily, twisted it behind her. She
cried out in pain.

"Leave her alone!" Selena shouted.

"All right," Jack gritted, releasing her. "All right. But let
me give a word to the wise. That uppity European stuff
doesn't work out here. If you want to live, you'll do as
you're told. Had you tried that splenetic little stunt on a
maharajah—and I hope to sell you to a maharajah, they
pay well—he'd have had you stuffed full of hot peppers,
pressed into a wall of spikes, and flailed to death with bamboo."

Roxanne rubbed her injured arm and said nothing. The
view of Daman, the propinquity of an unknown fate,
worked away at her spirit, minute by minute.

"I can understand why Marinda jumped overboard," she
said quietly.

"Hey-o!" Captain Jack cried. "Here comes Haruppa.
We're in business now."

A wizened man in a filthy loincloth trotted up the docks,

and spotted the *Massachusetts*. His thin, reedy voice humbly besought permission to board. It was granted.

"Haruppa's a contact agent. He represents the principals. Sold a girl named Gayle through his offices last trip. Spirited girl, too. Probably a lot tamer by now, though."

Selena hated Haruppa on sight. A slimy, scraping, ingratiating little man, he grinned like a monkey and let his eyes roam her body like a dirty hand.

"Haruppa, you stupid, filthy Wog," Captain Jack said, demonstrating for them his commanding manner with the natives, "I've got two for sale this trip. Had three, but one wasn't quite up to it. What do you think? Any interest?"

As if the words were an invitation, Haruppa stepped over to Selena and Roxanne, and reached out as if to touch Selena's hair. She stepped back in instant revulsion. Just as quickly, his thin, surprisingly hard hand cracked across her face. She cried out in pain, her head spinning. Haruppa was grinning.

"I told you," said Captain Jack, "the rules are different here."

Slowly, the vile little man inspected the women, squeezing, pinching, taking his time.

"Goddamn it, Haruppa," Jack complained, after a time, "if you didn't have purchasers waiting, you wouldn't even be here. Now, you've had your entertainment with these girls, and you know as well as I that they're meant for better than you."

Haruppa bowed in apology, all but sweeping the deck with his tongue.

"Thankee, thankee, great sir," he oozed. "Yes, yes, bring ladies like last time to Damanhaya, house outside city . . ."

He actually called these acres of hovels a city!

". . . and there wait many buyers, even Ku-Fel."

"Ku-Fel?" Jack exclaimed, in recognition and surprise. "Isn't she the one who bought Gayle last trip? For her maharajah? What happened? I hope Gayle gave no cause for displeasure."

Bow. Scrape. Grin. "No, no. Gayle do fine, great sir, just like you. All look forward see you again, and lovely ladies here."

With that, he trotted away, and Jack turned to them.

"So, girls. Let's get you into the crate."

"What?"

"That's right, my dears. You don't think I'd sink so low as to display your charms to the swill-eating residents of this great metropolis, do you?"

In truth, Jack was more concerned that the legal authorities not become aware of his secondary business: traffic in womanflesh. His main cargo, also packed in great wooden crates, was made up of fine New England harness, bridles, saddles, racing gear, refined accouterments with polished spangles, just the thing for a maharajah's midnight ride. So the crate in which Selena and Roxanne were ensconced was carried out over the water by crane, along with the rest of the cargo, and deposited on a long, flat wagon. Through cracks in the wood, they could breathe, partake of the stink of Daman, and watch the swaying rear ends of the water buffalo that pulled the wagon. It was terribly hot, and the smell of the city and its people all but overwhelming. Selena would have sobbed, except she was too busy gasping for breath. Then the noise diminished and the smell, too, as they left the city behind. It became a little cooler. Selena caught a glimpse of Captain Jack, arrogantly riding a spirited Arabian stallion. It was hard to decide if the horse or Jack showed more disdain for the world. The horse she admired; she hated Captain Jack with all her heart.

Finally, the buffalo halted, voices babbled, and the crate was crowbarred open.

"Had a nice trip, I trust," Captain Jack laughed. "Fix yourselves up, now. I'll be showing you soon."

And there was Haruppa again, rubbing his hands, licking his lips like the crewmen aboard the *Meridian*. Part of the male language that was the same all over the world.

Steeled against humiliation, Selena and Roxanne were surprised but still suspicious at the relative decorum of the proceedings. There was no auction block; they were not made public spectacles. Instead, it seemed as though some kind of family party were going on at this house called Damanhaya, a cool, white, amazingly beautiful palace, more than stunning after the horror of the city. From time to time an older woman would come into the room in which they had been told to wait, a wide, bright room of muted colors, with odd, decorative columns all about. The women were usually middle-aged, well-dressed in shining,

spotless saris, gaudy headdress, many rings and jewels.
Some spoke English, and asked Selena and Roxanne to
stand, turn, or smile. The first two or three of them asked if
they had known men. Selena just nodded; Roxanne said
"yes," in a quiet, matter-of-fact voice. After that, the word
must have been passed, because the question was no longer
put to them. Later, though, a dark, mannish woman, with
slitty, sinister eyes and two gold teeth, asked them to expose their breasts and show their legs. When they balked,
she said something, a word like a growl deep in her throat,
and two men appeared instantly from an adjacent chamber.
They wore togalike uniforms and carried nasty swords.
Again, the growl. The soldiers disappeared. And the girls
did as they had been instructed.

Then, for a long time, no one came. Refreshments were
brought: fruit drinks of an unfamiliar but very pleasant, if
pulpy, delicacy, and a sweet, very thin, waferlike bread.
The two women tried to relax on the unaccustomed, low
lounges, and wondered what was happening.

"Those women!" Roxanne exclaimed. "They give me
shivers. And the one with gold teeth!"

"Yes. I expected men. I don't understand. I wonder how
we're doing? Haruppa seemed very pleased with the girl
called Gayle that Jack sold last year."

"I think in this country it is more than necessary to
please the men."

"Do you know what all these people remind me of? In a
strange way? It's like a gathering of the clans in Scotland,
once every year or so. A huge festivity, where there is entertainment, business deals are made, trades and such matters . . ."

"Hey-o, my lovelies," exuded Captain Jack, bursting into
the room. He had been drinking, his face was flushed, but
he was in fine spirits. "The offers are being prepared now. I
believe you've done well, indeed. I'm proud of both of
you."

The sarcastic tone was still there, but not as cutting as it
had been. Clearly, he felt his business was successful and
all but concluded. When he left, Selena realized, she and
Roxanne would probably be separated. She would truly be
alone then, having lost her last contact with the West. And

she knew so little about what was happening, what would happen!

"Yes, I do believe the stupid Wogs are ready to cross my palm, as the saying goes. . . ."

"Why did the women come in to see us?" Selena had to know.

"You mean why not the men? Simple. The women you saw were harem mistresses. In charge of the wives and concubines of their maharajahs. You see, they were shopping. It is their business to provide constant delights for their rulers—you will learn more of that very soon, I daresay—and, in the harems, their rule is as unflinching and beyond question as is their masters' in the political realm."

"How hideous!" said Roxanne, shivering.

"*Au contraire*," Captain Jack demurred. "It's a very orderly system, once you get the hang of it." He laughed. "India has many cultures, most of them overlapping, all of them ancient. Women are highly prized. Older women, that is. The mother is revered. Younger women, like yourselves, have your purposes, too, though. You must please the other object of sacred reverence among the Indians. Surely you have noted the statuary in this room?"

But they had not. They had been too upset and preoccupied to notice such distractions. But now Selena and Roxanne took a long look at what they had casually dismissed earlier. White, marblelike ornaments, on shelves and pedestals, larger ones standing in the corners of the room, two of them just outside the window, overlooking the gardens, upon which ivy climbed. All of them, every one, a representation in stone of the phallus.

"Look at it this way," Jack chortled, "I have brought you here to be of service to the gods. Certainly, there are more than one."

"How did you get involved in this filthy business anyway?"

"Come now, what's so bad about it? You'll have a good, easy life. Do as you're told, and you'll want for nothing."

"But it's like . . . like exile, or jail."

"What isn't, my dear?" he asked, cynical now.

"Where will we . . . be sent?"

He shrugged. "Don't know, for certain. If Ku-Fel takes you, it would be somewhere in the interior. You can say good-bye to civilization then. You'll never get back out."

"Ku-Fel?"

"The ugly one with the two gold teeth. Meanest woman I've ever met. Tricky. The soul of India, that one. She tells me Gayle did please her maharajah, though." He laughed.

"What's so funny?"

"Nothing. It's just that when Ku-Fel bought Gayle, she didn't know the bargain she was getting."

Noting their puzzled expressions, Jack explained. "They got two for the price of one, so to speak. You see, Gayle was . . . what is the delicate expression? . . . in the family way."

Selena's heart went out to that unknown girl, bearing a child in this primitive, far-off land.

"Yes," Jack was chortling, "if you run into a little European kid somewhere out in the wilds, tell him Daddy Jack says hello."

"You haven't a decent impulse in your . . ."

"That's right," he agreed cheerfully.

Somewhere outside their chamber, a brass gong sounded, then sounded again. Turbaned servants came for them, bowed solemnly, and led them into a great hall, the opulence of which Selena had never seen, not even in the greatest, richest castles of Scotland. Gigantic, multicolored Oriental rugs covered the lustrous floors, and delicate tapestries hung from the walls. A long table, covered with white and glistening cloth, was laden with exotic food and drink, and guests sat cross-legged before it. One side of the room was open to the garden, where cooks tended the fires. There, too, was a statue of a Brahman cow, made of gold. An Indian, with the peremptory manner of royalty, rose from his place at the head of the table.

"Captain Randolph," he said, in a clipped, artificial, but not unpleasant manner. "Will you and the ladies please be seated beside me?"

Selena stifled an impulse to seize Roxanne's hand as they crossed the great room under the gaze of hundreds of black eyes. She caught sight of Ku-Fel, watching her through narrowed lids, like a snake. Seated just behind the sinister woman, so black and so motionless that Selena gasped, was a young boy, motionless as a piece of onyx, with the largest, most tragic eyes she had ever seen.

Captain Jack, relishing the attention, led them to their places, and helped them to their seats with a display of gallant aplomb.

"Now, to begin," the man said. "Business first, and then we dine and pleasure ourselves. Is that not right?"

Jack agreed, leaning toward Selena and whispering, "He's the Nawab of Maharashtra. He's been giving the British a lot of trouble, but he appreciates my skills."

The nawab smiled thinly. His eyes were extraordinarily forceful. He did not look like the kind of man who would be greatly impressed by Captain Jack.

"All these stupid Wogs are alike," Jack hissed, "except some of them wrap a sheet around their arses instead of just a kitchen rag."

"The decisions have been made," pronounced the nawab.

"Here's the good news for you two girls," Jack gloated.

"Ku-Fel, representing the Maharajah of Jabalpur, will purchase from you the young lady called Se-le-na, to take her for concubinage straightaway, and to instruct her in such arts as will bring delight to their mutual master."

"Jabalpur," Jack hissed. "That's in Central India. Goodbye, Selena. I'll remember you."

"Ku-Fel acknowledges Captain Randolph's previous sale, the girl Gayle."

Jack took it as a compliment, a tribute to his sagacity, but Selena caught something dangerous in Ku-Fel's gaze when she nodded to the captain.

"And the girl Roxanne," the nawab was saying, "has been selected to join my own court in Bombay."

Beneath the white cloth, Selena felt Roxanne's hand grasp her arm. The look on her face was one of relief. She knew! She knew where she was going and with whom she would be. The waiting was over. Selena, by contrast, had yet to meet the man who would be master of her fate. Whoever he was, he had to be better than Ku-Fel.

"And he's not at all the worst-looking of men," Roxanne whispered, then dropped her eyes and bowed her head to the nawab, a perfect response. Selena was about to congratulate her friend—her future seemed at least bearable—when she caught some mysterious signal in the eyes of the black boy seated behind Ku-Fel.

Be silent, he seemed to say. *Don't speak. Wait.*

"Now, where's my gold?" Jack cried. "Pay me, and let's get on with the feasting."

Again, the nawab's thin, disconcerting smile. "There is your gold," he said, and pointed to the statue of the cow.

Jack was amazed, and so, too, were the guests. In spite of the difference in cultures, Selena could gauge their surprise and gasps and hisses and sudden, questioning glances. *All that gold for two women?* Inexplicably, she felt drawn again to the black boy, and, although she fought the impulse as hard as she could, her effort failed. She glanced at him, and saw it there in his suffering eyes.

This was a place of great evil! Something terrible was about to happen.

"Good lord!" Jack cried, on his feet now. "I guess you Wogs know quality when you see it. But how on earth will I transport all that to my ship . . . ?"

The nawab rose now, too. "Do not worry. We shall melt it down for you. Would you like to inspect your reward?"

Selena knew that she would remember as long as she lived the ominous, humming stillness in the great hall, the calling of birds and chittering insects in the gardens outside. Cooks at the fires stood at attention, and guests watched in silence, as the nawab led swaggering Jack across the gorgeous carpets. The golden cow stood there, jeweled eyes sparkling. It glittered in Jack's eyes: the immensity and weight of it, a fortune even to a king. And all his! He stroked the awesome smoothness, silenced for the first time in his life in the presence of wealth beyond his imagination.

"And it opens, too," the nawab said, very quietly.

He touched a tiny protuberance near the cow's golden udder, and hidden springs responded. The body of the cow parted, revealing the hollowness within.

Jack had time only to comprehend the emptiness when the "cooks" leaped forward in a body, grabbed him roughly, and jammed him inside the hollow space. The twin sides of the idol were pushed together. A locking mechanism clicked into place. And the statue was set upon the fire.

"We will melt it down for him," the nawab explained casually to his guests.

Roxanne fainted.

In moments, Jack was screaming, calling for mercy, for help, calling on every god. Selena, in spite of her loathing for the man, was ready to cry out, but again she received that alien yet entirely authoritative impression.

Be silent, the black boy told her with his eyes. *Be silent, there is nothing you can do.*

The nawab returned to his seat, and bade the feast begin. People ate and laughed, barely noticing the melting cow, or Jack's pitiful howling and insane babbling. Selena sat transfixed, putting a cool cloth on Roxanne's forehead. No one paid any attention to them, just as no one gave notice to Jack's agony. It was as natural as night, or life, or death. A punishment to fit the crime. What crime?

"I wish that you should understand," Ku-Fel whispered in her ear, having crept mysteriously to her place at the table. "The man named Jack sold my maharajah a girl, Gayle. She was with child, and was of no use to my master. This nawab is a friend of my . . . or *our* master. The British have taught us one thing: it is of extreme importance to settle all accounts."

Jack cried out one last time, but it was as if a horse were dying, or a great bear, its leg severed in the jaws of an iron trap. The cow was dripping down into the fire. The smell of burnt flesh was all about the room. Servants were showering perfume, spreading incense, to lessen the smell.

"The account has been settled," Ku-Fel said. "Let it be a lesson to you. No one wishes you harm, but you must do as you are bidden. I will make you what you must be. I will create out of the flesh and soul of you the woman you must be to please a god."

Selena must have been conscious enough to register some slight surprise. Ku-Fel smiled, showing her golden teeth.

"The Maharajah of Jabalpur is your god," she repeated. "Forever from this day."

The black boy closed his eyes and fixed her with his mind.

Say: I understand.

"I understand," Selena said.

"That is good," Ku-Fel praised. "That is very good. We

cannot be friends, but we need not be enemies. I will teach you what you will need to know."

Selena could not eat, but tried to stay in control. Eventually, Roxanne came back to consciousness, and was led away, dazed and confused. There was no time to say goodbye.

And when Selena turned to seek out the dark boy again, he was not there. His space was as empty as if he had never existed at all. Ku-Fel was there and watched her, though, and her golden teeth glinted on the flesh of tender fowl.

On the smoldering grates, warped gold hardened around the charred bones of Jack Randolph.

Still alive, trapped but undefeated, Selena had not enough passion for anger, or tears. For the first time in her life, she was confronted with too many things that she could not understand. She slept that night, a former princess of the nobility of Scotland, in a beautiful room in the nawab's white palace. It was far larger, and far more luxurious, than her room in Coldstream Castle had been, and instead of the sconces and smoky tapers on the wall, there were golden candelabra, silver-framed mirrors, and all the easy touches of vast and casual wealth. She slept alone and unmolested, in a fine bed. It was the bed of a princess, a queen.

And Selena was a slave.

Haruppa stood that night in the great court, salved by the sweet whisper of the mango trees, running through his fingers, over and over, the coins he had been given for luring the Englishman back to Damanhaya for revenge. The smooth touch of the metal was pleasant, and also his last. He stiffened abruptly, and sank to the hard yellow stones. A dirk was yanked from his body, and Davi, the dark one, feet muffled in horsehide and wearing about his neck on a chain, for luck, the severed tip of an elephant's tusk, vanished into darkness. "That is for Gayle," he said.

THE FIELDS OF EDEN

So who is God, can you tell me? The mythical wolf of a Scottish knight, stalking the Highlands forever? Or a rajah of timeless India, as yet unknown, unseen, but who already possessed such power over Selena that he might as well have held in his dark-skinned, indolent hand her beating heart?

The Maharajah of Jabalpur. Master of millions. Master of Selena. Remote in the Indian interior, he ruled as of old, by a combination of cruelty and whim, intelligence and caprice. So said Ku-Fel, drawing out the word *caaa-preeece*, as Roxanne might have done. There, in the Pradesh heartland, in the land of his ancestors, the Great One had not yet been assaulted by the persistent, unremitting mercantile sorties of the gold-and-silver-and-spice-loving Westerners. That was all coming to him. Meanwhile, he loved to have a woman with gold in her hair.

The great barge bore him one, Selena, drawn day after day by drudge elephants up the sluggish Narbada River, toward Jabalpur. The snub-nosed barge was easily as long as the *Highlander* had been, and a permanent shelter, like a fine-sized house, rested on the flat expanse of its massive deck. Within this shelter, Selena had been assigned a small chamber, all of bamboo. Bamboo comprised the walls, the ceiling, the floor. A curtain of delicate bamboo reeds slid across the door, to offer privacy. The pallet on which she slept by night, waited by day, was likewise of the same wood, and covered by the finest blankets Selena had ever seen, the silkworm's masterpiece.

She did not like the low, yellow country along the coast, and the heat kept her inside, but after several days—many people were aboard, including Ku-Fel and the black boy, but no one troubled her—Selena left her tiny chamber, made her way out onto the barge. To her surprise, the low-lying, tropical delta had been left behind, and she saw a luxuriant, hilly country of raw beauty. Along the shore of the river, six elephants plodded forward, eyes in the dust, attached to the barge by a complicated harness of leather, chains, and rope. Cursing drivers rode the great beasts, striking them ineffectually with short wands, which she later learned were used to guide them, and on the barge, sweating, loinclothed men with long poles kept the barge from going too close to shore. The sun was high, the weather warm and pleasant here in the hills. She removed the diaphanous rose-red shawl Ku-Fel had given her, with a gold-toothed grimace, when they set out from Daman. "It is the first of many beautiful things for you," she had said. "If you were born to please."

"I am pleased to see you on deck this morning." A low, formal voice spoke just behind her, interrupting her memory. She whirled in surprise, and found the black boy standing there.

"I am sorry for startling you," he said in perfectly modulated English. He smiled, to express further apology, but the tragic light never left his beautiful eyes.

"It's all right. I didn't hear you approaching," she said, and looked at him closely for the first time. The previous glimpses she had had of him left her with the impression that he was Negro, probably, and about ten or eleven years old. Now she saw that her original judgments were mistaken. His skin was as smooth and black as obsidian, true, which lent an appearance of youth, an appearance seemingly underscored by his small stature, but his features were more like those of the Indians she had seen. And, although he stood no more than five feet in height, his slight, wiry body was solid and sinewy, not that of a boy. She guessed that he might be twenty, perhaps, but otherwise he was a mystery to her. She tried, but could not feel with her mind the signals he had sent her on the day of the nawab's feast. Or maybe she had imagined them, frightened and overwrought as she had been.

"I am Davi," he said, bowing slightly. "I shall serve you in all that you wish."

"Thank you. I'm not sure . . ." she began, momentarily nonplussed by the depth of his eyes, which never left her, which seemed to bore into her brain. She turned to the shore, the countryside.

"When will we get there?" she asked.

"Many weeks, many weeks," he said, his voice still soft. "In our land one soon learns patience. The journey is of over five hundred of what you in your lands call 'miles,' and all the way it is by barge and elephant. But we will reach the palace in due course, as we always have, and there is much for you to learn."

He seemed sadder, saying that, but grave and, in an odd way, very wise and gentle for one so young.

"This is the Satpura Range," he told her, gesturing toward the hills. "The Narbada runs through it, all the way to Central India. When we reach the plateau of Chota Nagpur, you will see the lands of our master. Very rich lands, and very remote."

Again, she had the sense of extraordinary sadness when he spoke the word "remote," as if somehow it bespoke a personal isolation that he could neither express nor abnegate.

Silence came upon them. On the banks of the river, the drivers were cursing the beasts. Thousands of people were at work in the rich fields that stretched out as far as the eye could see, a quilted patchwork of colors and crops among the verdant hills. Far away, a group was chanting, perhaps a song to ease the labor, perhaps a prayer.

Selena could not stop herself. Davi seemed to want to help her, and, anyway, he was the first person in whom she had sensed sympathy since Roxanne had been taken away. She had to find out some things.

"What will it be like?" she asked. "Jabalpur? What is the maharajah like?"

At that moment, almost as if summoned to intervene, Ku-Fel charged out of the shelter.

"Davi! Davi!" she cried angrily, seeing him with Selena. "There you are, you worthless thing. Where is my herb tea? Why haven't you brewed my morning tea?"

Selena saw the sudden fright in Davi's eyes, but also the quiet resolve. He had borne much suffering in his time, she decided.

"Believe nothing!" he told her, quickly, quietly. "Even the obvious may be deceptive. And trust no one until you speak to me. I will help you. This is a land far more dangerous and arbitrary than . . ."

Whatever it was, he didn't get a chance to tell her. Ku-Fel, approaching almost at a run, struck out with one of her big, mannish hands, a chopping motion strange to Selena, at the side of Davi's neck. He cried out in pain, and seemed to be stunned, or paralyzed.

"Leave the concubine alone," Ku-Fel warned. "You can't do anything about it anyway. And I want my tea when I awaken, or you'll be hanging by your thumbs until sundown. Do you understand?"

Davi slunk away, leaning to one side, rubbing his wounded neck. Selena was acutely conscious of Ku-Fel's anger and her strength.

"What was he saying?" the woman asked, slitting her eyes.

"I . . . I simply asked how far we had to . . . travel."

The ugly harem mistress did not entirely believe her, but decided to let it pass. "There is no use asking such questions," she said, in a near snarl. "Time does not exist in India, not as you have known it. I see that you're curious about Davi," she added in the same breath.

The sudden question, the slitted, suspicious eyes, unnerved Selena, and she nodded, even though afraid that her admission might bring grief down upon the black boy.

"Then I'll tell you all you need to know," Ku-Fel offered, showing her teeth to signal that truth would be forthcoming. "You see, Davi is a Dravidian. Four thousand years ago, the Dravidians, small and dark like him, had India all to themselves. Then the Aryans came, howling down from the north. They were warriors, rapacious and fearless, and, although the process took centuries to complete, they had little trouble displacing Davi's race. There are still some of them left, mostly in the south, or in the large cities, where they do work not allowed to those of the higher castes. Such as myself."

Selena recalled Captain Jack's brief digressions regarding Hinduism, some long-buried fragments of her tutelage about castes.

"Will I have a caste?" she asked.

Ku-Fel burst into deep, roaring laughter. She was thoroughly, genuinely amused. "Well, you won't be an Untouchable, I will grant you that, emptying slop jars and the like. And you won't be a servant like Davi, although, in a sense, you will be a servant. No, you have no caste. You are a concubine, fit to amuse the maharajah, and no more. Leave it at that, and ask no further questions. There is always the chance that you will please him greatly, and enjoy a measure of power thereby, but you may never bear his legitimate children. After all, you can never be a Brahman. You are not even Indian."

She paused, and her eyes glinted cruelly. "You are only a pretty whore with golden hair," she snarled. "We've taken care of your like before."

Gayle, thought Selena.

Then Ku-Fel was smiling again, as if the scorn and the anger had not been there at all. "One more thing," she said, "you'd best be wary of Davi. Some of these Dravidians claim to have special powers, from their prehistory. Old secrets of knowledge and communication. But don't believe it."

"Why . . . why not?"

"Because. Look at what's happened to them. They were defeated. They have nothing. India is Aryan now, and Hindu. The gods have given *us* the rules of life, the keys to Nirvana."

Selena said nothing.

"You will come to my chamber after the midday meal," Ku-Fel ordered. "I believe it is time to begin your instruction."

She waddled off, ungainly but powerful beneath her sari, swinging those huge, hard-edged, chopping hands. Selena stood there on the barge, fighting the feelings of loneliness and distress that were blooming in her heart like evil flowers. The lack of certainty troubled her most, the lack of anyone to trust, to rely upon, to ask for help in time of need. Everything changed, shifted. Everyone to whom she spoke seemed—with the possible exception of Davi—to treat her with an amusement that was not even contemptuous. And all of them told her to beware. Of India. Of themselves. Of everything! Davi told her to beware of Ku-

Fel. Ku-Fel told her to beware of Davi, hinting of preternatural powers.

Was that what I felt with my mind? His power?

But if he had such powers, why was he nothing but a servant, despised, humiliated, often beaten? No, there would be little help from him, in spite of his assurances. His own condition belied his words, belied even the mysterious tragedy in his eyes.

Selena looked out across the great plains of Asia. Scotland, half a world away, came to her when she summoned it, and she set it, like a beautiful jewel, between her violet eyes and the hills of alien Sutpura. From the hard little village of Kinlochbervie, where Father lay buried beneath a hut of stone, to Mount Foinaven, weed-ridden where the lodge had been, to the dark, smoky lochs in the Highlands, where waited the wolf that was the mate of Royce Campbell's soul, to the honey-drenched moors, to mighty Edinburgh, and finally south to Coldstream, she saw it all, embraced it, held it, loved it as you love for the first time, pure and forever and never to be tarnished. She was lost now. She had not seen a European, not one, and they told her the interior was too remote even to attract her countrymen. Plenty of money for them along the coasts, and in Bengal, especially. Sean Bloodwell might be there, if he was still alive. (Europeans die like flies here, they had told her.) And even if, somehow, he should learn of her presence in this vast land, what could he do? What could one man, a clerk with the government, or maybe the East India Company, do to free her from a great maharajah?

So she was lost now.

But still she carried Scotland in her soul, when the days beat down her spirit. When the nights were dark.

"Pray, let us begin," Ku-Fel said, motioning Selena to a low pallet. Her chamber was larger than Selena's but otherwise identical. Selena sat, crossing her legs. The barge moved slowly, water washing easily against its hull. Ku-Fel studied Selena for a long time.

"Disrobe," she ordered curtly.

Selena must have displayed her fear, because the harem mistress was slightly more gentle in her explanation.

"It's for your own good," she said, "and for mine, as

well. If you please our master, so do I. And if you please him, you please me. And," she added obscurely, "we keep Rupal from our throats."

Rupal? Was Rupal another of the maharajah's mistresses, or the maharajah himself?

"Hurry, now," Ku-Fel prodded.

Self-consciously, barely containing a flash of anger, Selena slipped out of the sari of lavender silk, and stood naked in the bamboo chamber. In spite of the situation, she was proud of her body, and instinctively drew in her stomach and lifted her breasts.

"Ah, yes," breathed Ku-Fel. "Ah, yes, indeed. You will be most pleasing to his eyes. Perhaps if you ate a bit more heartily until we reach Jabalpur, however. Your breasts are splendid. How old are you?"

"Eighteen," Selena said.

"Well, no wonder. But your backside could use a few pounds. You will be most pleasing to his eyes," she said again.

Selena bent for the sari.

"Yes, go on. Dress. Now our real work begins. We must make you exquisitely pleasing to his body, as well. How many lovers have you . . . had?"

Selena balked, as perhaps Ku-Fel had guessed she would. Without heat, quite calmly, the big woman pulled aside a piece of the bamboo floor mat and took out a long, thin piece of metal. There was a wooden handle on one end. At the other, Selena saw a tiny letter or symbol fashioned of iron, like a lopsided letter Z.

"You will not, of course, endure this today, child, since your instruction is just beginning. And I would, with all my heart, prefer that you never face it. But there is sometimes need for discipline, and I urge you to understand most hastily my position as your superior. Outright disobedience to the harem mistress in the maharajah's court will earn you this letter. In a tender place upon your flesh. The instrument, of course, will have been heated white-hot in a fire. Do you grasp my meaning?"

Selena nodded, speechless.

"It is merciful, I assure you. Girls who displease our master often . . ." She said no more.

"I've had . . . one lover," Selena confessed, hating herself for revealing it.

"And other men?"

"I have loved another man, but we did not. And once I was taken against my will." (Or, of necessity, to get aboard the *Meridian?*) "And by Captain Jack."

Ku-Fel frowned. "That is not many. Your lover, did you please him?"

"I think so. He said so."

"How? In what ways?"

"As . . . as it is done."

"Child, I know how it is done. I must know the ways. With your body?"

"Yes."

"Hands? Mouth?"

"*Yes!*"

"Well, thank God you have had *some* experience. Was it pleasurable to you?"

Selena nodded and dropped her eyes. Blood rushed to her face.

"Good." Ku-Fel smiled. "I guessed as much when I first saw you. That is why I chose you, do you know? Your friend, the French girl, was obviously more experienced in technique, but she would be too studied, too mechanical, I'm afraid. I did not tell this to the nawab. Perhaps that is what he wishes. But you! No, you will feel passion in a good man's arms, and you will show it, and that will please him as much as any technique.

"Of course, we will now proceed to learn those," she added.

Selena was forced to listen, feeling cheap and tawdry. Yet, as she realized that concubinage was not just a dim possibility for her but an unalterable fate, she also knew that her very survival might be premised upon her success. *I have to survive,* she thought, *even if, right now, there seems little to survive for.* Having seen Marinda, forlorn and desolate, drop beneath the all-erasing sea, Selena knew that a death such as that would have no meaning for her. It would, in fact, be more obscene than mere vulnerability was. It would be giving in to vulnerability.

She would not do that.

She would survive by whatever means were at hand.

"There are certain tubes or veins in the man's sac," Ku-Fel was lecturing, "which, when pressed persistently but gently during the spasms of his transport, will enhance his delight."

She described where they were, and how to apply the touch of the fingers.

"And it is also most important, if one is to be called for again and again and again, to be able to prolong and extend the period of his pleasure. . . ."

She described such bodily grasps and squeezes, and how to train oneself to perform them. That afternoon, and on many subsequent days, as the great barge was dragged step by plodding, elephantine step up the waters of the endless river, Ku-Fel summoned Selena to her chamber, to instruct her in the sixty-four legendary positions of the *Ananga Ranga,* apotheosized in the *Kama Sutra* of Indian knowledge. She learned the *avidarita,* demonstrating for Ku-Fel's edification that she had the agility to lift her legs high enough; she learned the *venuvidarita,* and opened herself so wide; and she learned the *vinarditasana,* which meant that the man, if sufficiently strong, would lift her to himself, and, holding her the while, move her gently and forever from side to side, until . . .

She looked up to find Ku-Fel giving her a knowing, gold-toothed smile.

"Yes?" Selena asked.

"I think you will do well indeed."

"I was just thinking . . ."

"Good, good," said Ku-Fel. "We need not fear Rupal, then."

"Who is Rupal?"

"You will learn what you require at the proper time."

"But I need to know now. You implied that I should be afraid of this Rupal."

"Did I? No, child, I did not intend to."

There was little point in going on. Ku-Fel's evasions were merely extensions of previous evasions, her words were as reliable and permanent as shifting sand. And yet, Selena thought, Ku-Fel was, if not afraid, at least cautious of this unidentified Rupal, and was that not unusual if Ku-Fel was the all-powerful harem mistress?

"Go now and bathe yourself," said Ku-Fel one afternoon, after her instruction. "We have passed Narsinghpur, and tomorrow we shall disembark. You will not see the maharajah immediately upon our arrival, but you must be, from the start, as lovely a concubine as you can. Because it will not be easy for you, in the harem."

"What do you mean?" ask Selena, who had been almost lulled by the long, tedious, mesmerizing journey. "What do you mean, not easy?"

"Jealousies, child. Jealousies. Gayle was as good a student as you, but in the end . . ."

In the end . . . As always, Ku-Fel hinted, teased, warned, but did not explain. On her pallet that night, the air almost chilly, and the night starry on this High Central-Indian plateau—all the stars were different here! That unfamiliarity was as terrible as anything else—Selena could not sleep. Perhaps it was the lack of motion. Usually, the trudging pachyderms pulled them through the night, but now Ku-Fel had ordered a halt, in order to decorate the barge suitably for Selena's arrival, and they anchored along the shore of the river. She had grown used to the midnight chattering of the drivers, the gentle sound of water.

Once, dropping off, letting sleep gather her up, Selena felt a movement, the passage of an inexplicable curtain of air, right there in her chamber. She was awake again, and tried to ease herself back to the gentle precipice, beyond which everything was peace and forgetfulness. She would not think about the maharajah, or the mysteries of which Ku-Fel and Davi had hinted. She wouldn't permit into her mind the memory of Captain Jack's terrible screams, or the bloodless manner in which the nawab and his friends had let the captain suffer and die. This new world was difficult enough to comprehend—let along confront—in the day. At night it was a thing she did not wish to contemplate.

Again, the passage of something in the darkness, and a muted, muffled sound, oddly familiar, that struck a familiar emotion deep within memory.

Ku-Fel had been adamant that Selena not go out of her chamber during the night. The hills were believed to shelter bandits, and, as Ku-Fel put it: "The maharajah has already traded gold for your golden skin, your hair, and he would be disturbed should he have to ransom it before it was even possessed." And, too, Ku-Fel had ordered that no one but herself enter Selena's chamber. Even Davi, the puzzling dark one, was made to stand outside her door when he brought food or drink, and wait until she took them from him. Always he would look at her with those huge eyes, in which the full weight of human wretchedness stood out so clearly, and with so little apparent reason.

Selena heard the sound again. There was no doubt about it now. Something was in the room with her. The buried senses, formed in her ancestors half a million years ago, sprang to life. Tiny hairs came to life on the back of her neck. She had the impression of a small animal, pathetic and lost.

"Who's there?" she whispered, her voice quivery.

Then the sound came, clear and unmistakable. Someone sobbing, trying to conceal it. Selena reached out into the darkness beside her pallet, felt the small, shaking body lying there. In the darkness, it was impossible to see. But her touch was sure.

"Davi? Davi, what's the matter? You could be punished for being here. Don't you know?"

She felt him nod. He sobbed hard for a moment, keeping the sound as muted as he could, and then brought himself under control.

"I had to come," he said, his voice husky in the stillness.

"But why?"

"I must tell you something. It is heavy on my heart."

Against the instinct of her intuition, Selena was somewhat suspicious. Davi *was* crying, and certainly he had seemed as sad a person as she had ever known, but too many strange things were building, and everyone warned her to beware.

"If you wish," she said, a trifle coldly.

He sensed her reserve. "Oh, please, please," he begged. "You are the only one in whom I have felt compassion for seven years. That," he added, in a softer voice, "is when it was done to me."

"*What* was done to you? Davi, speak. I cannot bear these hints anymore, this feeling that something sinister lies in wait for me just beyond the next door, in the next room . . ."

"That is India," he said. "You must live with that. But you are right. Forgive me. Let me tell it all. As I said, you are the only one in whom I have felt compassion, and I cherish it. But I must be honest with you, and tell you now, lest, later, you feel I have not been truthful, and thus come to hate me . . ."

"Hate you? Why . . . ?"

"You see, I cannot love," he said.

"You cannot . . . love?" It did not sound right. If anyone Selena had met in India could begin to love at all, surely it was Davi. "Is that why you were crying?"

She sensed his movement of affirmation in the darkness.

"I cannot contain it sometimes," he told her. "It is too much for my heart to bear."

"But everyone can love, if he will just let himself."

"No, no," he disagreed. "All that is lost to me now. I am a dead man, and even the power . . ."

He changed his mind, and said no more about the power, but before Selena could interrupt, he carried her to a time ten years before when, he said, "my heart was young and full of hope.

"I am a Dravidian, as you doubtless know by now. The peaceful, defeated peoples who must now, forever, bow down and lick the feet of masters, both foreign and domestic. Masters who are stronger in all the ways that do not count, and who have taken from me the only thing of importance. The ability to love. You see, as a child I lived in Bombay. We were of the lowest caste, but there were many of us together in a community. This offered protection, being by ourselves, and the life was not unpleasant. About ten years ago—I was eleven then—my heart was full indeed. Sul-vey had been picked, for me, as beautiful a girl child as India ever bore, and on my fourteenth birthday, we were to be joined."

"Married?"

"No, more than that. Joined. For all time. According to the ancient ways. And our twin . . ." he seemed about to use one word, but abruptly passed over it, changed his mind ". . . our twin *loves* would unite to form . . ." Again, he seemed to have some difficulty choosing the word or words with which to explain himself to her. She remembered his earlier hesitation.

"Power?" Selena guessed.

He was silent for a moment, and she knew she had been right, but she didn't know why, or what it meant.

"Yes," he said, very softly, "but I cannot speak of that yet. You would not grasp it, or you would not believe it. Let me just say that Sul-vey and I were to become one. But that was the year the black crows came." He spat the words "black crows" with deep, uncharacteristic bitterness.

"Black crows?" Some sort of plague, like locusts, which had descended and destroyed Davi's livelihood?

"The Portuguese missionaries," he explained, the revulsion evident in his expression. "They came to Bombay that year. Strange men and women in black cloaks, who never smiled, and had no light in their hearts. And they came to the town where we Dravidians lived. At first, we were like children. We were stupid for them, and performed, and did the ancient songs and dances of our people. No, no, they said, after we had entertained. You must not do these things which you have been doing for thousands of years. You must not do them because they are idolatry, profanity, they will destroy you. We did not understand. We did not understand any of the things they told us, which had to do with a onegod person, and this onegod person loved us all so much that he killed someone called begottenson. It was hard to understand, you see. If onegod killed begottenson because of such great love, then what would he do to *us?* We were afraid, because the black crows had great ships, but some of our fathers thought they saw in the black crows a chance to elevate ourselves. The older men would meet and discuss what the Portuguese told us about school, about education, and eventually it was decided that, even if onegod did not smile upon Dravidian ways, the education of the black crows might make it possible for us to rise above our caste in an India that was becoming colonial, more open, less restricted. And I was chosen.

"I was chosen, because in those times I had a high, sweet voice, and my songs had been noticed by the black crows when they came to see us perform. 'We will take him,' they told my father. 'We will take him, and in return for the gift of his song, with which he shall praise onegod in our church, we will teach him the speech and the manner and the knowledge of the West. When he returns to you, he will be equipped to deal as a man with the merchants of

Europe, thus reflecting great credit upon Dravidians, and he will also serve onegod by carrying out his will.' Which, they said, was to take wealth from India, where it was ill-used and unappreciated, and carry it to Europe, where one-god had great need of it.

"I did not wish to go, but I obeyed my father. I said farewell to Sul-vey, and said that I would be with her al-ways in my mind, and that our minds would be forever joined. I would be gone from her no more than two years, said the black crow who came to get me. But I could see already in his eyes that he was lying, and that, for some reason, the thought of Sul-vey and I speaking of union horri-fied him. I later learned," he added bitterly, "that the black crows and onegod and all of their ilk conspire to make filthy the things that are of most pleasure and beauty in life.

"But they were quite good to me, and I was learning much that would be of use to me later. Numbers, and of money. Geography, countries. And how men traded and bargained, so that both of them might take profit from their having done business with one another. And I learned their songs and hymns which I sang for them in their ugly church in Bombay, that had a great high tower on it inimi-cal to India and the Indian soul. And they called me '*An-geli, perfecti angeli*,' and touched my face when I sang the hymns to onegod.

"Two years went by, and then almost three, and it was drawing near that I should return and join with Sul-vey. In my mind, I could feel her excitement and desire, and mine was the same. Our time approached, and our souls were wrapped about the same dream. Also, I was becoming in the manly way, with hair on my face, and my voice was beginning to deepen, as it is with a man. This was noticed and frowned upon by the black crows, who were less fre-quent with their cries of '*angeli*,' and I sensed, one night, very late, a great danger to me. The impression was so strong that I left my pallet in the loft of the ugly church, and made my way to a large, dark room where I had seen the black crows gather like birds of death to talk of evil in their strange tongue. I found my way to a place outside the door, and heard them speak. It made no sense to me at first. 'The voice, it is going,' one of them said. 'Soon it will be gone.' Another said—and now I realized it was me of whom they spoke—'We received an allowance of an extra year from his father, and it is almost over. He is due to marry soon. It is the way of the Dravidians.'

"There was, for a time, great silence.

" 'But God has given him great talent,' said the leader of them, an old man, the one who had looked upon Sul-vey with such horror. 'If he returns to his town, we shall lose him, and he will be pagan once more.'

" 'But what shall we do?' the others cried.

" 'There are means of adjusting the voice,' said the man, 'and I believe onegod would wish us to do it.'

"They sat in silence for another long time, and then they nodded, like birds feeding. I believed they would pray, pray that somehow what was natural about my voice growing into that of a man be hindered by onegod, so I would sing like *perfecti angeli* all my life.

"But they did not pray," he said. Once more, he began to weep.

Selena guessed, and her skin grew cold at the horror of it.

Davi was brief. "It was done with a knife," he said. "I was given nothing for the pain, not even poppy, as is sometimes given to those in our land who must suffer surgery. They told me to offer it up to begottenson, and he would smile on me when it came my time to die. And then it was over, and in my mind I felt Sul-vey shrink from me. Of course, I could never return. I felt all of life shrink from me, and even inside myself there was nothing there had been."

There was nothing she could say.

"Nor did my voice remain high and sweet," he concluded, his tone thick with hatred in the bamboo room. "And when it did not, I was told to leave the ugly church. The black crows told me I had failed onegod, that the loss of my sweet voice was a punishment being visited upon me by begottenson himself . . ."

"That's terrible. That's . . . not true. But, then what? You had the education, certain Western knowledge . . . ?"

"Ah, yes," he said in disgust. "But I was still a Dravidian. You people of the West seem, somehow, to dislike greatly those who have skin of a darker hue than your own.

My 'knowledge' was as useless to me, wrapped in my skin, as a woman would be."

"But you can still *love*. I know how hard it must be, after what has been done to you by evil people. Monsters, those black crows and all like them who claim a special closeness to God."

"No," Davi insisted. "Love is not one thing alone, not only spiritual. To love must be of the body as well as the spirit. No, I am only a slave now, with everything lost, and great danger surrounding me always. Because I have lost, along with the capacity to love, the . . ."

He hesitated.

"The power," Selena said. "No, you haven't."

She could feel his intensity, an almost preternatural form of self-concentration. And doubt.

"That is impossible," he said. "One must love to have the power. What do you mean?"

"What is the power, precisely?"

"We know it as the ability to speak in the wind, to meld with one whose mind and heart are warm. But I can no longer do that, after the knife . . ."

Selena reached out and touched him. Then, impulsively, her arms were around him. "Yes, you can! Yes, you can do it! I felt it the day in the nawab's palace, when you were warning me. You were, weren't you? Yes, I knew. So you see . . ."

But Davi was sobbing again, and trying to still himself. The sound of his weeping this time, though, was very different, as if his heart had once again begun to beat, as if after long silence, the memory of song returned to him.

"I will use the power to help you if I can," he promised, when once again he had control of his emotions. "I cannot love fully, but you have helped me to understand a great thing, and I will repay you if I can."

Somewhere on the barge, footsteps sounded.

"But I am afraid," Davi whispered. "I am a cipher, and the punishments are terrible for one such as I."

The sound ceased.

"Tomorrow we will come to Jabal-Mahal," Selena said. "And I must know what to expect. Tell me of Gayle. Tell me of someone called Rupal."

He stiffened in fear. "Of the second," he pleaded, "please,

no. One of my rank is not permitted to speak her name."

Her? So it was a woman!

". . . nor to think of her, nor to fix her image in the mind. But of the girl called Gayle, I shall tell you some, although it grieves my ˙heart. You see, Haruppa, who served as agent for your sale, likewise came to Damanhaya last year with Gayle, who, although not as beautiful as you, had golden hair like yours, and was very much a woman born for the pleasure of a man. And Haruppa has paid for his sin," he added with a victorious tone.

She asked him how, and he told her. She remembered the feel of Haruppa's hard, filthy hand across the cheekbone. "Thank you," she said, feeling harder, more vengeful than she had ever felt before. *I may have need of this feeling,* she thought. "I will pay you back someday, for that favor," she said to Davi.

"It is of no importance. It was my pleasure. For it was he who brought Gayle to Jabalpur, and to all that has happened since. You have heard that she was with child, have you not?"

"Yes," Selena said. Captain Jack Randolph had paid terribly for his stolen moment of sensual ecstasy. But what of Gayle? And the poor child?

"Her country was Scotland, like yours," Davi was saying.

Selena, startled, felt a wave of complicated emotion sweep over her, bathing her heart in warmth, her mind in light and hope and loss. *Scotland!* To hear the word spoken, so far from home, was magical, wonderment. And the proximity of another girl from that beloved land was . . .

"Please!" she cried. "Speak!"

And Davi did, but not with joy.

"What you must first understand about Jabal-Mahal, and all which occurs there, is that everyone exists for the maharajah. We live to please him, first. If there is anything left of ourselves after that, we may live a bit for ourselves. But everything, and everyone, is his . . ."

Like the feudal lords of old Europe, Selena was thinking.

". . . Gayle was adept at many things, but obeisant selflessness was not one of them. And there was the added misfortune of her being with the child of the British sea captain. At first, it did not matter, because no one knew and she did not tell. But, as always, it soon became evident. The maharajah was said to be enraged; Ku-Fel said he was beside himself. Never in my seven years at the palace had I heard of such anger and thirst for revenge. And this other one of whom you asked, she, too, had a hand in it . . ."

"Rupal?"

"Shhhhh! There was much more to it than merely the expected child, and much I myself do not know. This you may learn when you are established in the harem."

"I shall speak to Gayle. She comes from Scotland . . ."

"No, that will be impossible. Gayle is dead."

Selena said nothing until her heart slowed down. The great palace of Jabal-Mahal could be a deadly place.

"So the maharajah ordered her killed?"

"I do not know, but I do know that he did not save her. She could not have been removed without, at least, his tacit acquiesence."

Rupal? Ku-Fel? Someone else with the power to order death? And all over a child. Selena asked what had become of the baby.

"Our maharajah allowed her to have it, on the slight chance that his blood would be apparent in the baby, that his humiliation would be mitigated. But it was not to be. The child was blond as an angel."

"Then what?"

"Then Gayle was put to death."

"What of the child?"

"It is now about four months old. It was to have been drowned at birth. The presence of such a child, in a nursery filled with the maharajah's own children, would only serve to make her life a misery, a constant reminder to the maharajah of Randolph's original perfidy, and a constant source of fuel for his own anger and retribution."

"A little girl? Why . . . why wasn't she . . . destroyed?"

Davi had become very nervous. "The order was never carried out," he said.

"So the little girl is still there?"

"Not exactly," Davi said.

"Then where is she?"

"I do not know exactly," Davi said. "She was taken from her mother at birth, and brought into the countryside and given to a good woman who promised to see to her safety."

"Taken? By whom?"

Davi said it very quickly, as if to say it would remove the weight of a dangerous secret.

"By me," he said. "I did it. I once was weak and alone, and there was no one to save me. I did not wish it to happen to another."

Selena thought of the great risk, the torment which would have befallen this strange, touching man if he had been—if he was ever—discovered. *He will not be revealed by me,* she vowed.

"Do you think . . . can I see her sometime? The child?"

"We shall see. It will not be possible at once. Your movements will be greatly restricted and constantly watched, until you please the maharajah enough to be granted a degree of liberty. I must first go to see the country woman, Shan-da, and ask where the child has been hidden. We shall see, in due time. . . ."

There was no mistaking it now. Somewhere on the barge, someone was walking back and forth, stopping, walking again.

"I must go," Davi whispered.

"One more thing. This Gayle. She was from Scotland. Where? I mean, did she name a province or a city?"

She could see Davi shrug, a quick movement in the darkness, as he rose to leave.

"I do not know of that," he hissed. "But many times she spoke of Greenlaw, as if it were a place rather than something judicial. . . . Sleep well. Let us be safe. In danger, I shall try to reach you with my mind."

He was gone without sound, without Selena seeing him go, but she was thinking . . . Greenlaw. Her body trembled. Greenlaw was a small peasant village in Berwick Province, long under the sovereignty of Coldstream Castle. Many times she had ridden there with Father, to collect the taxes due them, or to watch him serve as judge to matters of local dispute. How Gayle had left Berwick Province and come into the evil grasp of Jack Randolph, Selena did not know. But she did know that a girl she might once have seen, even spoken to, with the natural and self-satisfied condescension of the princess for the peasant, had traveled the path that Selena now followed. And had traveled it unto the end. Death. A Scottish girl, who must also have gazed upon Coldstream Castle, who must also have looked out over the moors when the rains of spring were dark upon them, and thought of life, and love, and the future.

And now Selena had come to Jabalpur, too, as poor as Gayle had come, just as much a captive. And armed only with her wits. And Davi.

Davi would truly be of help against Ku-Fel, and Rupal, and the maharajah. Selena felt a flicker of confidence. Why, in Scotland, this Maharajah of Jabalpur, this Lord of Jabal-Mahal, would not have counted for a sturdy yeoman! That was one thing she knew for certain, and it shored up her perspective, gave her courage.

But she was wrong.

At midmorning of that day in October 1775—bright, vibrant spring in the Southern Hemisphere—Ku-Fel organized her party and bade them disembark the barge. They had come the last miles up the Narbada ostentatiously, with great ceremony. The barge itself had been decorated at Narsinghpur, decorated as befit a bride, and all along the way people came from the countryside to gawk and cheer. Many-colored streamers covered the bamboo shelter, and the barge itself, and trailed in the waters of the river. Servants in coats of gaudy silk banged gongs, sounded cymbals, rang bells; the elephant drivers, similarly attired, hung glittering metal from the harness, draped colored blankets over the monstrous, gray beasts, which curled their prehensile trunks in irritation, and sounded their great blasting calls in response to the high-pitched, eerie whine of the flutes.

Selena was seen by no one, as had been intended from the start. Ensconced in a closed sedan chair, which was a hundred times as comfortable and a thousand times as opulent as the best of the Coldstream coaches, she was borne down a ramp to the shore of the river. She saw the heads and bodies of the people through a veil of gauze that had been stretched over the opening, and she could see the powerful shoulders of the men bearing her, and the sweat glistening on their thick necks.

"May she give our master a dozen heirs!" cried some

fool, who did not know of her origins, nor had guessed that, for Selena, the pleasure she would provide was primary, offspring quite a secondary object. Gayle's example showed blond children as undesirable. Even deadly. If Selena could believe Davi.

Through the gauze, she saw Ku-Fel mounted on a splendid horse, one of literally hundreds waiting at the river, and then the caravan moved off. Prancing horses, shouting people, all, and Selena, still in the sedan chair. The way was not long. Jabal-Mahal, the maharajah's palace, lay just to the south of the city, and along the banks of a beautiful, man-dredged tributary to the Narbada. Selena, who expected a mansion somewhat similar to that of the nawab's in Daman, but probably a bit smaller, was reduced to silent awe as the estate came into view. The road on which they passed turned from packed earth to smooth brown stone, and then to a kind of blue stone, and finally to white stone. And then she saw it, wide and white and glistening before her, shimmering in the sun, dancing in the long, perfectly aligned reflecting pools, as domed and spired as an apparition in a dream of heaven. Jabal-Mahal, her home. In comparison, the bulky stolidity of Coldstream seemed ponderous and dowdy. Here there were no battlements, but low, cool verandas, and no castle wall twelve feet thick, but instead a fence of thin black metal, forged into patterns of petal and flower, a work of art in itself.

And what was that, something white—no, several objects—on the tips of the thin white columns that surrounded the main gate? Another splendid touch, a final work of art, upon which the maharajah's subjects might feast their eyes before returning to their humble work in the fields of Pradesh? Something like that, or perhaps something with religious significance.

She heard the gradual silence of the crowd as people approached the main gate, a silence of fear. And then she understood why. Pressing her eyes against the gauze, she saw the white objects quite closely, and recognized them for what they were: the white dismembered bones of a human body, perched upon the pillars. Arms. Legs. Rib cage. And on the highest of all, a perfect human skull, the fine teeth grinning at her, the dark sockets of the eyes seeking her out in the sedan chair.

Gayle, of Greenlaw, Scotland, welcomed Selena to her new home.

"It was done with horses," Rupal told her that night, touching Selena's hand and smiling conspiratorially. "A horse was tied to both arms, both legs. They stretched her out for many hours, and paused when she lost herself in unconsciousness. I tried as best I could to give her certain drugs on the night before it was to happen, but Ku-Fel prevented me from so doing." She lowered her already soft voice, and Selena had to lean forward, closer to that soft, lovely face, those confiding eyes. "Ku-Fel ordered it, you know. That Gayle be torn apart. I am so glad you have come to us. We just join forces against Ku-Fel at once.

"They severed the head later," she added, in the unsettling way she had of expressing herself. It was hardly noticeable, in the face of such dark beauty, such endearing charm, but now and again she would say something, and it would be like a flash of sudden cold. Selena was reminded of all the mysterious doors in the palace, and of all she did not know that lay behind them.

Ku-Fel had taken Selena into the harem wing of the palace immediately upon their arrival, and whisked her inside. Selena saw nothing but milling, turbaned horsemen, and little Davi, far back in the courtyard, lifting his hand to her in a surreptitious gesture of goodwill. Inside, Selena did not even look at the marvelous fixtures, the art, the indications of a luxury far beyond wealth. Instead, she babbled her fear and trembling outrage about the skull.

Ku-Fel heard her out, and even sought to calm her down, ordering that tea and food be brought posthaste.

"It was none of my doing," she said. "Poor Gayle. I sought to save her. It was Rupal, she did it. She persuaded the maharajah to draw and quarter the girl. Rupal," she muttered, "the only one to avoid my brand . . .

"And, of course, you, child," she added immediately, showing her gold teeth, hiding her eyes behind the fleshy lids.

"Was she angry about the child, too?" Selena wanted to know.

"The child?" asked the harem mistress in some surprise.

"Why, no. Why should she be? After all, the child was born dead."

Selena knew something was very much amiss, and tried not to show surprise. Either Davi had lied to her—*Oh, no, then I haven't even one friend here*—or he was mistaken. Or Ku-Fel was lying. Could there be another child?

"Come now, eat, drink. You must rest. I must introduce you to the wives and concubines."

This occurred late in the afternoon, before all of them were summoned to the maharajah's quarters for the evening meal. It was at this meal that he would select the woman he wished to possess that evening, and all of them were well-prepared and beautifully attired.

"There are thirty-three of you, in all," Ku-Fel explained. "It is a sacred number."

Selena looked around quickly. There seemed no more than two dozen women, all of them dark-eyed, all of them supremely lovely, looking at her closely, yet without seeming to.

Ku-Fel smiled at her consternation. "Some are always with child," she said. "Some are nursing. And some are ... in the punishment cells."

She was introduced to the women in the order of choice, which meant the frequency with which they were selected to share the maharajah's nights. Rupal was number one, although Selena was surprised to learn she was a concubine, not a wife.

"Only seven wives are permitted," Ku-Fel explained. And she introduced Selena to six of them.

"One of them is with child?" Selena asked.

Ku-Fel showed her teeth. "No, no. I am the seventh wife. Indeed, I was the *first*."

Struggling to suppress her amazement, Selena saw the flash of hatred in Rupal's eyes as the number one concubine regarded the harem mistress. So that was it! Or, at least, a part of it! Being wife and harem mistress would explain Ku-Fel's great authority—indeed, the meekest of the women trembled even at her presence—and it would also explain Rupal's anger. She must wish to be a wife in name, too, but if there were already the sacred seven, then someone would have to be ...

"You must help me," Rupal was saying, her tender eyes

locked on Selena's, her hand gentle and sisterly. "You have now seen our master from a distance, and he has seen you. Tomorrow night he will call for you, after the evening meal. And when he does, this is what I want you to do . . ."

On the first night at Jabal-Mahal, Selena, trying with inconsistent success to conceal her excitement, had seen the maharajah for the first time. From her position, far down at the end of the long, low tables, she had seen him, and, if it were possible, she was now more confused than she had been. In her imagination, she had anticipated any number of men: heavy and coarse, with dull, slow, self-indulgence written all over them. Hard, lean men, with thin, cruel mouths, who looked as if they had just bedded a woman or tamed a horse, and who regarded these pursuits as essentially the same. Or soft men, whose lives of ease and luxury had robbed the steel from their bodies, the ambition from their minds.

Instead, she had seen something else.

The display of wealth was so blatant, yet so casual, that it barely seemed to matter. Rugs, tapestries, rich fabrics, jewel-encrusted dinner plates, and drinking goblets of pure gold were as common as a pewter mug in a mead shop in Scotland. At the head of the dining room, where the maharajah was seated before a wall of leopard skin, and on a rug of tiger skin, and beneath a canopy of some thin fabric hemmed with jewels, Davi hovered in attendance, and once Selena thought she saw him glance her way, give her an encouraging look. But perhaps not. She was not sure, and had no time to think about it. Here, in this place, which made the great castles of Scotland seem like poor, bare halls fit for dogs, a slight, watchful, dark young man ruled like the most absolute of emperors.

He was no taller than Selena, with a rare perfection of form, of which he seemed well-aware, and which he accentuated with an unusually colored pair of breeches—dark, but neither blue nor green—and a loose white shirt, open across his brown chest to the navel. On his chest, around his neck, hung a large, glittering stone, majestic and red, which Selena took to be a ruby, and upon his shoulders rested a capelike shroud, which Davi removed when he seated his master. He would not have been considered

handsome, or perhaps even manly, by European standards—he seemed too slight, too *pretty* almost—but she
noted immediately, by his bearing and presence, by his
sharp, dark, watchful eyes, that he would have been reck-
oned with, would have been considered a person of consequence, by Father, and Brian, and . . . even Royce.
There was an animal quality about him, and a trace of
something that was not arrogance, not exactly. Rather, it
was like an unstudied acceptance of superiority. For his
superiority, being a gift of the gods, had to be borne as duty.

She tried during the course of the meal—which consisted
of vegetables, various fruits, and yellow rice with a hot, not
unpleasant spice—to watch him. He did not look her way
at first, and seemed preoccupied, even tired. Now and
again he would motion Davi to come near, and quietly
convey an instruction or desire. To the wives and concubines closest to him, Ku-Fel and Rupal, and two others
Selena knew as Ashina and La-vey, he sometimes smiled or
spoke a few words, and now and again he would smile,
pleasantly and a bit wearily, at one or another of the many
women around the table. These, for their part, showed no
great obsequiousness or fear in his presence, and soon, if
Selena closed her eyes and made concession to the clipped,
exotic speech, the dinner table seemed like any large banquet of friends and relatives. Ku-Fel and Rupal smiled at
each other much too widely, Selena noticed, and watched
each other too carefully. But, she also saw, their inter-
change was not lost upon the maharajah. He watched them
watch each other. He looked vaguely perplexed, and then
wearier still.

This was the man who held the absolute destinies of millions of Indians in his hands, and all the rich interior of
Pradesh.

This was the man who might have ordered the death of
Gayle, who might have ordered, or at least approved, the
killing of Gayle's child. If that death had occurred.

And this was the man who would soon hold Selena close
to his smooth, brown body, which was as straight and hard
as a sapling. And not at all unpleasant to gaze upon. He
met her eyes once, and looked away.

Yet, even at the dinner, which was ordinary enough in
its own alien way, Selena could not help but be disturbed.

Just as she had been told, nothing was definite here, even truth was indeterminate; she had no way to decide whom to trust, or even if anyone could be trusted. Even Davi, who was in the room throughout the meal, and who had promised to be her one true friend here in Jabalpur, did not so much as make a move in her direction, and the one smile she thought she saw might just have been a ripple of the muscles of his dark face.

It came to her with brutal force: until her position was clarified, and possibly even thereafter, she simply could not afford to make mistakes. Of gesture, of judgment, of any other impulse. It was crucial now, even to her life. She would have to study every sign and signal, weigh each of her own actions, and those of everyone she met. She must be wise, or perhaps die.

And, whether to Davi's discredited onegod, or to the God Vishnu, whose eternal dream produced the universe and all in it, or to the old bearded desert god of the Bible, with whom gray ministers had frightened her on the long-ago Sundays of childhood, she would have to pray.

She tried most of the foods on the platter, and found all of them exquisitely prepared, the tastes subtle and complementary. Her body took nourishment, and her mind calmed. The meal did not last very long, and Selena realized it was almost over when she saw many of the women discreetly straightening their gowns, touching their hair now and again in a surreptitious gesture of grooming. It happened very simply. The maharajah whispered again to Davi, and he moved a few paces along the table and whispered something to Rupal. She dropped her eyes and bowed slightly in the maharajah's direction. Her downcast gaze was modest and grateful, but Selena did not miss the characteristic pride and boldness of her expression. Nor the sudden hard flash that darkened Ku-Fel's coarse features like a thundercloud on a bright day.

Why had this young man ever married a woman like Ku-Fel? Selena expected that she would never know. If she guessed one thing correctly, it was that Oriental tyrants, however attractive, did not readily share the vagaries of their motivations with their concubines.

The maharajah rose to leave. Rupal followed, several paces behind. The two disappeared through a curtained passageway. Davi followed momentarily, to see to a last demand, carry out a final charge before the master retired to the pleasure Selena knew Rupal was only too ready to purvey.

The love artists of Egypt and India, she remembered. Soon she would be one with them.

". . . the maharajah," Rupal was saying, "is a man of passion, however remote and contained he may appear. He is one who, if given certain forms of love, which I am sure you have already learned from Ku-Fel, will grant demands that, under the light of reason, he would dismiss with a flick of his hand. And his overbearing passion is to *know*. He wishes to know everything that occurs in his territories, to know where everyone is at all times. Because, with such knowledge, his control is increased and his power enhanced. But his desire for such knowledge has led to many spies, many versions of truth . . ."

Selena certainly understood that!

". . . which requires greater and greater efforts on his part—of which he is wearying—and less knowledge of which he can be sure. Now, I asked you to help me, and I know you can. But I am sure, too, that you are wondering—and wisely—why I should make such an approach to you, so soon after your arrival here, when you do not even know me."

Selena's look was an unspoken affirmation of that premise.

"Two reasons," Rupal said, her voice soft, persuasive, infinitely understanding. "One, I need your help. Two, I do not wish to see you suffer. You have no idea what it is like to incur Ku-Fel's wrath. She is a monster, and nothing will stop her revenge if she feels her position has been threatened. Oh, I have seen it many times. The poor woman who is to be punished is brought naked into the chamber of discipline and hung by her toes from a high rod. Then, in the presence of all the wives and concubines, she is beaten hideously by Ku-Fel with a flat length of elephant hide, which leaves no cuts but produces a terrible suffering. Finally, when the victim is screaming for mercy, Ku-Fel calls for the hot iron, and, on the inside of the thigh, where the flesh is very tender, she makes her mark of shame.

"I wish to spare you this torment," she said, and touched Selena's face.

The question was natural. "But if what you ask me to do incurs Ku-Fel's anger," Selena asked, "am I not certain to find myself, very soon, in a similar predicament?"

"Not if you are clever in dealing with our master. You must remember, as I told you, his love of pleasure from a woman, and his desire to know all. Give him pleasure, and sow doubt in his mind, and you can advance your own position and help me at the same time."

"You have mentioned that I can help you. How, precisely?"

"There is something I need to know," Rupal said, leaning forward. "The child. I must know where the child is!"

Selena thought fast. She had to decide what to say, how much to reveal. And she did not know how best to proceed. Perhaps Rupal already knew what Davi had told her on the barge, and was speaking with her now in order to learn if she could be trusted with a secret. Or was she trying to ascertain if Davi had revealed something he ought not have, in which case an answer on Selena's part would be dangerous to Davi. Was the child dead, or was it alive somewhere in the country with the woman Shan-da, whom Davi had named? And did Rupal already know what the answer was?

"Why do you wish to know about a child?" Selena asked, steeling herself for the rebuke that was sure to follow. "Why am I the one to help you find out? And what child?" she asked, feeling uncomfortable with the deception, but knowing that it was necessary.

Rupal believed that Selena truly did not know about Gayle's blond baby, or at least she was satisfied to give that impression.

"Because you are a new concubine!" she said, with heat. "You will be fresh to the maharajah, and he will not dismiss your interests as quickly as he does ours. He will not believe you have become caught up in the politics of the harem. *And,*" she added, "he will be monstrously enraged if the child is still alive."

"I . . . I do not think I would wish to see him enraged."

"But you don't understand. Ku-Fel was to have killed

the child. If she has not, he will hold it against *her!* And that will help us . . ."

Or *you,* Selena thought, with a sense that skill in this sinister art of deception, while welcome, would also be damning.

". . . that will help us reduce her influence, or have her put aside altogether."

"Why should the maharajah wish to see the child dead?"

Rupal's answer this time was consistent with some of the things Selena had been told earlier: "Because he felt he was cheated," Rupal explained. "Gayle was with child by another man when she came here. He wanted both of them dead."

Yes, but Selena thought of something else.

"But could not Ku-Fel herself have been outraged? It was she who inspected the girl and made the purchase from Captain Randolph?"

Rupal sat back, and for the flash of a second Selena saw that glint of reckoning, that cold intelligence.

"Ah, you are a bright girl, a bright girl, indeed," she said, warmly again. "And you doubtless wish to know why I want to find the child?"

Selena said she did.

"Because I can find a way to have her taken to Calcutta," Rupal said. "It is not good that she grow up far from her people, where no one looks as she does . . ."

"I look as she does," Selena said, too quickly.

"How do you know?" The suspicion was hard and sharp as the blade of a scimitar.

"I . . . I just meant the . . . the blondness," Selena said hastily.

There were traps everywhere. Pitfalls. And all the contradicting stories and explanations. It would get worse. She thought of the seven lies required by the injudicious one.

"So will you help me?" Rupal demanded.

"I . . . I am nervous," Selena confessed truthfully. The evening meal would begin in minutes, and then . . . "I . . . I shall try . . ."

Then Ku-Fel's signal bell rang for them, in another part of the harem.

"You go first," Rupal said, "so she'll not know we've been speaking."

"So you've been speaking to Rupal," was the first thing Ku-Fel said when she inspected Selena's appearance, her skin, her sari. The rest of the women were there for her inspection, as always, but she paid little attention to them. All knew it was Selena's night to be called.

Selena smiled and said that, yes, she had. There seemed nothing else to do. But she did not understand how Ku-Fel had known. There must indeed be spies everywhere.

"She has a good imagination, I'll say that for her," Ku-Fel hissed. "Did you know that she is desperate to escape here and go to Calcutta? No, of course you didn't," she continued, still smiling, as Selena tried to fit together Rupal's desire to find the child—*if* the child were alive—and the desire to take it to . . . Calcutta!

"Ah, she wants the excitement of Bengal, that is all. But do not worry. No one has ever escaped this harem, and no one will. I will corroborate one thing, though," she offered, drawing Selena aside so that the two of them might enter the dining room together and sit near the master, "what she told you about the elephant whip is entirely true."

The brass gong sounded, and they entered the opulent, sweet-smelling room and went toward their seats. Davi stood, ready for the maharajah's entrance. His eyes met hers for the shred of a second, and it was as if her mind were suddenly washed by ominous light:

Beware! he told her with his power. *Beware! And speak not of Shan-da!*

The Maharajah of Jabalpur bade her enter his scented bedchamber, and nodded to his servants. The curtains were drawn. They were alone. But the High Lord barely looked at her. He yawned and settled into a low, couchlike bed, and idly pushed several soft cushions to the floor. He yawned again.

"Do you dance?" he asked, as if he did not care. His eyes were weary, almost without expectation. "Do you have any talents which might amuse me?"

It was going to be vastly different than any experience she had known, Selena realized. Here in India, at least in Jabal-Mahal, it was she who was expected to arouse and please and win the man! *Well, you did that already with*

Royce, spoke the tiny voice of her conscience. No, do not think of Royce, or you will fail here for certain. And this may be the only chance to establish for yourself a rapport with the maharajah, hence a measure of safety.

Selena had been prepared, by Ku-Fel and the others, to be subservient, obeisant, and obedient to this man's every whim. He regarded her with that aspect of languorous impassivity which she had observed in the dining room, but which she guessed was only one part of his nature, and perhaps not even the most significant part. But then he said something which caused her own nature to rise, in spite of Ku-Fel's instructions.

"Ah, you are a blonde, too. Ku-Fel knows how I admire them." His face darkened slightly, as he thought of another woman. "Gayle was a blonde."

The manner in which he spoke the name gave Selena a sudden insight—indefinite but instinctive—into the mystery of Jabal-Mahal. She permitted her nature to speak then, rather then submit to the caution she had been warned to practice.

"I'm *not* Gayle," she told the maharajah. "You can see what is left of Gayle at the gateway to this . . . to this zoo!"

That's the end, she thought. *Maybe the MacPherson blood was fashioned for self-destruction from the very beginning. Certainly the MacPherson tongue was.*

The reaction to her impertinence—a foreshadowing of her likely fate—shone in the maharajah's eyes. The lower lids closed up, and she sensed that he was a man capable of great, precipitate cruelty. But she met his eyes and faced him unflinchingly.

"Proud prince," she said. The rest of her control melted away as anger came boiling up. *If you are going to speak, speak now!* "Proud prince, who kills his lover with horses. *I,*" she said, "would have had the courage to do it myself."

Immediately, his mood seemed to change.

"You would have?" he asked, in his clipped, precise way. "You have great certainty."

Then she interpreted his tone. Curiosity. Pure curiosity, fascinated now by what she had said and the manner in which she had spoken. Rupal may have been correct: the maharajah wanted to know about everything. She sensed that the man would prod and explore and inquire, but only to a certain point. Obviously, he had sought inadequately the reasons for his lover's death, and the persons responsible. Perhaps he shrank from examining the nature of his court, just as a sinner might be loathe to scrutinize his own soul.

"I did not order her killed," the maharajah said, waving the matter away, as if he had relieved himself of any connection with the skull and the shattered skeleton at the entrance to his palace.

The full measure of Selena's courage returned to her then, like a drink of Highland whiskey on a frosty night, like the thrill of the Gathering of the Clans, with the plaids and pennants of ancient Scotland stiff and crackling in the wind, and with something that must have been like the taste of the blood of a wolf.

"You know nothing," she snapped at him. "And knowing nothing is your greatest desire!"

He stared at her, too surprised even to form anger.

"And that will destroy you in the end," she said. She spoke it as a truth. Knowing nothing—or very little—had contributed to the hubris of her youth, from which, only now, she was recovering.

A long, long silence passed between them. She stood straight, as a princess ought to stand, especially a princess in the land of barbarians. Her posture was strange to one used to the bent knee, the deep bow, even the groveling of supplicants. Rage was there, even an instinct to murder. She could see it. But the curiosity won.

"What is it about you that is not like Gayle? You look as she did. You have the hair of floss. But it is not the same. What is it?"

"Because," she said, "I am Selena MacPherson, daughter of Lord Seamus MacPherson, of Coldstream Castle. And in my land one like you would peddle rugs. I am a . . ." *Why not*? she thought ". . . I am a queen!"

Silence. Then he smiled.

"I see the difference," he said. "I understand that part of it now. But, tell me, how do you put it . . . majesty? Have you not contrived an excessively devious plan to visit me?"

He laughed, and she was once again a slave.

"I shall explain it when you tell me why you killed her," she snapped, hoping to regain that moment of pride, of grandeur.

"I did not," he said flatly. "In fact, I loved her very much."

The disbelief must have been more than evident in her eyes.

"That is the truth," he said again. "I wept when I learned that she was dead. I loved her. She was killed and the child, too. Ku-Fel has told me. Beyond that, nothing I have been able to learn makes sense to me. There are too many stories."

"I can understand that," Selena said truthfully. She knew the endlessly unfolding schemes of courts, the compulsive necessity of courtiers alternately to seek the blessing of, and then deceive, their sovereign. "I can understand that, but you were here! You *must* have known."

It was as if he looked right into her. "I was not," he said. "It happened in my absence. I was in Kanpur, to the north, discussing what we must do when the British traders come into our regions. It took place in my absence. And I do not . . ."

She understood. Again, Rupal had been right. "You do not wish to admit you did not *know* of it? That is correct, is it not? And the bones are on the wall because to remove them would be to admit you did not sanction the killings from the start."

He waited, then nodded. She saw his eyes narrow again, but this time she saw the respect. Her life, anyway, was safe for a little. It was her turn to wait, but again only for a moment.

"I think the child is alive," she said.

Electricity fairly danced from him, and he became incandescent with pure intensity.

"Oh, great lord Vishnu," he breathed, raising his eyes to the silken canopy that covered his chamber, "pray that it be so." It seemed as if he meant it.

From a place of soft shelter, very near, she felt the light dance again in her mind.

I praise you, I respect you, Davi said.

"We will become one now," the maharajah said abruptly, motioning her toward his couch. "We are close al-

ready, and then we shall be closer still. You are right about
me, in a sense. I know my own world, but very little of the
world outside. There is a mystery which we can solve.
And," he added, looking frankly, directly and—she
thought—honestly into her eyes, ". . . and I have great
need of you."

Saying that, he took her, and brought her down with
him.

It is all right, Davi told her with his mind. *It is what you
must do.*

"Pleasure me," the maharajah ordered.

He was a man like any other, and as good a one as
Selena had yet known. True, his ways were foreign to
her—his initial passivity in lovemaking more curious than
disconcerting—but then, he was used to being served. He
demanded service. Selena did not choose to disappoint him,
knowing that she had no other choice but this, and knowing, too, that any hope to better her position here in Jabal-
Mahal rested with him and with no other. (Or with Ku-
Fel?)

And was it true, too—or did she simply imagine it?—
that, on her first night with the maharajah, speaking up to
him, making her mark with him, she was already dreaming
of escape? Had she not already seen the possibility of someday fleeing this passionate, appealing, quicksilver man,
whose emotions glinted now and again above the surface of
his apparent passivity, like the tips of icebergs jagged above
the sea?

Davi was with her for a time, but then she felt him slide
away; she would be all right. The maharajah bade her strip
naked for the pleasure of his eyes, and then, slowly, to fold
away his garments, too, revealing his body's readiness. In
her mind, she locked away the times she had been with
Royce—those had been sacred—and, realizing that the human being makes love in the same ways, whatever the
emotion behind it, she bent to please him. Soft and teasing,
she traced again and again, with tender fingers, the throbbing length of him, the hard gourd of his lust. He was
keening, writhing, when she ceased, just before the ultimate. He understood, and held and kissed her deeply,
while she waited for his fire to subside. Then, once again,
she began, and then again, and after that another time, and

always, between times, they kissed and embraced, until she, too, felt genuine passion take her up the first low foothills of sensation. Before he asked her for another kind of pleasure, she gave it to him, this time kissing him until she felt the quivering rigidity that precedes release, and then again she stopped, now to take his caresses and dark kisses in her turn, she herself now well up into the high ranges where air is scarce, and rare.

Afterward, he was drowsy, slightly self-satisfied. But the curiosity in him, and what she realized was a certain insecurity—or, at least, a willingness to admit doubt—kept him from sending her away. Ku-Fel had told her to expect that, and not to be concerned about it.

"You have pleased me greatly," he said, his hand tracing the soft curves of her body, lingering where she had grown scarlet with passion fulfilled, gathering place of the blood. "No one has pleased me so since . . ."

He did not finish. Selena guessed it might be Gayle; it could also have been Rupal, who was called most often to his bed.

"I am here to serve you," she said in a neutral tone.

"Are you really?" He smiled. "It did not seem so before, judging from your hard words."

"They were not hard. It was what I felt."

"That is good. You are much like the . . . the other one."

"Gayle?" she prompted.

He nodded, but said nothing. There was bitterness in his expression, and pain.

"I swear to you, if I knew who had done it, I would act against them. But I do not know how to find out. One lie is as plausible as another. But I am as much a prisoner here as I am a master. The two go together. But we will find the child."

She had the impression that, for him, the child's existence was some form of heavenly gift, a living symbol of an affection for the dead girl that had been genuine, if magisterial.

"But how do you know it is alive? Who told you?" he said.

"I cannot say now."

"There must be no secrets from me in this palace." He

laughed immediately at the ridiculousness of the statement.

"I do not know for certain. I must find out, and I will tell you when I do. But you must promise that the little girl will come to no harm, and, if it seems best, that she be given over to Europeans in Calcutta, to be raised with her kind."

She watched him as she spoke, and realized, from his attention and from his smile, that she was able to captivate him now because she herself was different, exotic. He had never—with the possible exception of Gayle—been with a woman who spoke to him as Selena did, who asked questions, stated conditions, made demands.

But what would happen when he tired of this novelty? When he wished again for a woman who would tremble at his touch, entertain him with a combination of debauchery and debasement?

He did not tire of her that night, however, nor for many more. Returning to the harem in the morning, Ku-Fel would be waiting, with a question behind her slitted eyes. Selena would say, "He was pleased," and then again in the evening after dinner, the maharajah would whisper a few words to Davi, who would in turn summon Selena for the evening's tryst of pleasure.

And love?

Possibly, for him, if he could feel love in the manner she had learned of it, the European emotion.

For her? She was attracted to him, took delight in pleasing him, and enjoyed the ministrations of delight he freely gave to her. But her life was not here, could not be here. At first, even after it was obvious that she had become his favorite, Selena was restricted. She could not speak with Davi, nor ask him of the child; she no longer felt his mind. It was as if their fragile union had been broken. Ku-Fel seemed to delight in Rupal's jealous misery, but Ku-Fel, too, began to ask: "Of what do you speak when you are with him? Do you speak of me? Does he continue to brood over the other blond woman?" Gayle, who continued to preside over the main gate to the palace, grinning forever onto the plains of Pradesh, where she had last seen the light of day.

"He speaks of little," she always told Ku-Fel. "He does not confide in me."

In a sense, this was true, because the master always preserved a certain reserve, a distance from Selena even when they were together, ascending the slopes of passion. He kept asking her of the child, but all she could say was that she had learned nothing more, and did not wish to jeopardize another life until she was certain that searching for the girl and bringing her back to the palace would be safe. He accepted that, for a time, and they spoke of other things before and after he enjoyed her.

Sometimes it was of Europe and the world, of which he believed he possessed great knowledge. "I do not understand," he said once, "how it is possible for you Westerners to claim superiority. I know of Europe, and even of your precious Scotland. A rocky land roamed by goats, in which everyone lives in a tiny room filled with smoke, eating gristle during the winter and grass when the sun is warm."

Selena explained that Gayle's experience in Scotland was not one shared by all, that, although no palace as beautiful as Jabal-Mahal rested on the moors, nonetheless great buildings, beautiful in a different way, attested to the culture of Europe. "And we have laws," she said, "courts, and judges, which treat fairly the unfortunate brought before them. We do not have one man, locked inside a . . ." she almost said "harem," ". . . system, ruling by wile and guess, ignor . . ."

She had gone too far that time.

"Ignorant, you say," he snapped, with steely hostility. "Your laws! Fairness!"

On and on he went, oblivious to the female prisoners in his own harem. But, as he spoke, she realized the partial truth of what he believed. She had only to look at her own situation, to see what had happened to her. Once more, her old passion flared, the desire to be what she had been, the desire to stand upon the battlements of Coldstream Castle and feel the ancient stones cold beneath her hand.

He sent her away early that night, and Rupal looked pleased.

"The master is tiring of his new toy," she said, smirking, and passed on to her chamber. There was no more talk of Selena helping her in the constant war with Ku-Fel. But the next night, with Rupal dressed in her best sari, and ready for passion, the maharajah called on Selena again. Hatred gleamed, malevolent and palpable, in the sultry depths of Rupal's eyes. Selena knew she had an enemy who would give no quarter, and, what was worse, an enemy whose plans were too obscure to her to decipher. Rupal smoldered, waiting.

The business of the child was very much on everyone's mind, but seemed to be held in abeyance. Ku-Fel cannily said no more, and Selena still did not know just to what extent the harem mistress had actually participated in the execution. Nor did she know if Davi had told her the truth.

She made up her mind that she would have to see him.

The following night, in the master's bedchamber, she decided to be blunt.

"Pleasure me now," he ordered, reclining and moving his garments aside.

She ignored his request. "Why did you marry Ku-Fel?" she asked.

He sat up, looking as if he could not comprehend her temerity. Then he nodded. "It is a good question, is it not? I'm surprised you did not ask it sooner."

Saying nothing, he led her into a part of the palace she had never seen before. They entered one of these chambers, which was quite dark. Here and there, she saw light glint on metal, but it told her nothing. The maharajah drew aside what appeared to be heavy curtains, which obscured the night light of moon and stars. And what she saw then was breathtaking. It was a room of gold and silver, an entire chamber of costly metal and stone, and at its center rested a chest of mahogany, which he approached almost with reverence. He drew Selena with him, and forced her gently to her knees before the chest. And opened it. The breath caught in her throat, and she made a sound that was like a sob. The chest was filled with a colossal assortment of jewels: diamonds, rubies, sapphires, jade, opal, onyx, gold and silver necklaces and bracelets, spangled with intricate arrangements of more jewels.

"That is why," he said. "Ku-Fel is the daughter of a powerful caliph in Rajasthan. This chest is her dowry. My father arranged everything, when I was not yet ten. We were married shortly afterward." His voice was matter-of-fact. "The caliph needed to marry off his daughter, and my father wished Jabalpur to be richer than it was."

Selena could not tear her eyes from the fortune in that mahogany vessel. It might mean the fulfillment of every dream to kings of great nations in Europe, but here it reposed, something to look at, something to admire.

"Jabalpur is," the maharajah concluded. "Come now, let us return. Tonight I wish to taste your essence as you taste mine."

She could not put the cache of stones out of her mind during the lovemaking. Not even the delicious touch of perversity in the pleasure he proffered could banish the glitter of indescribable wealth. And Selena realized, even as she drew from him the grateful sobs of his ecstasy, that the Indians, for all their subtlety and mastery of nuance, would fall before the commercial onslaughts of the Europeans, like sheep before the slaughter. They loved wealth and luxury as they enjoyed flesh—as now the maharajah enjoyed her own—but they had not yet seen, had never had to see, that wealth meant freedom, and power, of another, wilder kind.

In a flash, she understood Royce Campbell more fully than she ever had.

In an instant, she grasped what it was that Sean Bloodwell had sought.

And, in a heartbeat, she realized all that Selena MacPherson no longer possessed.

There upon the tender, velvet couch, the sensations of love crying out around them, candelabra gleaming, firelight dancing on their glistening bodies, Selena decided to be free. Somehow, sometime, but not here.

She would have to escape this place to be free, but she would do it.

There upon the couch, deep in his embrace, listening to the slowing beat of his heart, the calming of his breath, and smelling the smell, tasting the taste of spilled love, she knew it was time to begin. Giving him sexual pleasure of every conceivable variety had not won him to her; he took that as his due, would have had her punished for not offering it. No, in order to establish a hold over him that would advance her escape, she would have to discover something about which he felt uncommon passion. Therein lay vulnerability, the uses of which she already knew. The uses of which had laid her low, and left Father in a stone hut, and Brian dead on the sawdust floor of a bar.

"If you ask Ku-Fel to loosen my restrictions," she pleaded tenderly, stroking his chest, "I am ready to find Gayle's child for you."

His glance was sleepy but suspicious. "You wish to travel about the countryside?"

"No, merely to walk the grounds of Jabal-Mahal freely."

"Why will this gain you information you have not been able to acquire in the two weeks since your arrival here?"

"I believe it will. That's all I can say."

Selena was correct in her judgment. The maharajah's remorse about the death of someone for whom he had felt an uncommon attachment, and his desire to see the child of her body, led him to order Ku-Fel to release Selena from constant attendance in the harem wing of the palace. But, once released, Selena had more misgivings.

What if it *was* true that the master hated Gayle and actually *had* killed her? (*Nothing is as it appears.*) And now wished to kill the child as well! He was quite capable of it. On the previous week, a band of seven thieves had been brought to the castle, accused of poaching wild game in the forests to the north, the maharajah's private hunting preserve. They admitted their crime, hoping to avoid the rigors of interrogation and to provoke a speedy execution. They were unsuccessful: He had ordered them roasted slowly over banked fires, and for a long day they turned on spits of agony over the coals, until they burst, swelling, juices running from them as from a piece of grilled meat.

So Selena must be cautious, and deliberate. She wanted freedom, but not the freedom of death. Moreover, if the child did exist, and she was able to bring her back to Jabal-Mahal, many things would become clear. She would be able to judge the reactions of Ku-Fel and Rupal and the maharajah himself toward the child, and then she might know exactly what was happening here. And exactly what had happened.

Maybe.

But could she protect the child? And get her to Europeans in Calcutta?

She delayed another day, undecided. The responsibility

for the child was a burden greater than she had anticipated, and she shrank from bearing it.

Davi came to her, instead, late that night. Danger made him tremble.

"We must act," he said. "The girl is ill." She sensed his anxiety.

Selena sat up on her pallet.

"The girl-child is failing," he whispered. "We must do something, or she may die."

"What is the matter?"

"Shan-da does not know, but it seems her soul is sick from strangeness. There are none like her in India, and even young as she is, the child must sense it. Have you discussed this with our master?"

"He says he loved the mother. He says he wishes to protect the child, to carry her to Calcutta and people like herself."

Davi was silent for a time. "Do you believe the master?" he asked. "That is not what Ku-Fel told me. She spoke of his rage."

It was Selena's turn to consider, but she had already determined her answer. "More than Rupal and Ku-Fel," she said, "do I trust the lord."

He actually laughed, this sad, black little man, for the first time since she had seen him. "You are doing very well," he said, "for one whose skin has no color. All right, act. Ask for horses. Say nothing of me. Simply explain that you have an intimation of the child's presence. In India, such feelings are signs of divine intervention, and you will be indulged. I will arrange to be with the party that leaves here in search of the child, and I shall lead you to Shan-da."

It was done, and two days later, Selena passed through the white columns of Jabal-Mahal, where the black sockets of Gayle's eyes held her in their gaze. She rode a black Arabian stallion, sidesaddle, and with her were half a dozen armed soldiers to protect them, and the maharajah, and Davi, who was to ride near Selena's horse, and gentle it, if necessary. And who would lead them to the child. She felt in him the need to hurry, and guessed that whatever plagued the little girl had increased in intensity, and danger.

About the maharajah, however, she was satisfied. His excitement, his concern, seemed akin to that of a new father. He was indeed a man of many facets, and Gayle must have somehow awakened in him—or gifted to him outright—a strain of romantic love, to which his own culture was, if not immune, at least unaccustomed. She sensed no pretense in him now, only genuine desire to see and save all that remained of someone he had once loved, and who had been taken from him. Perhaps he even believed, as Selena did, that the secrets behind Gayle's terrible death rested with a child who, as yet, possessed no tongue.

Selena hoped it would all go well, too. In her renewed desire to steel herself for escape, to be once again someday all that she had been, she realized that, if the child were found and protected, it could not but stand her in good stead with the master. If, on the other hand, the child had already died . . .

Too late to think of that. One thing at a time. And Davi had been right. Her confession of "intimations" had caused much uproar, even awe. Rupal paled slightly at mention of the child, and then retreated into a cold, watchful reserve. Ku-Fel said, "*It cannot be! The child was born dead!*" just as she had originally told Selena, and, almost hysterical, pulled Selena into a tiny wing of the palace, entered through a false doorway. Here were the punishment cells, where lovely young women—like Selena, but dark—who had been excessively willful, or disrespectful, or maladroit in pleasing the maharajah or Ku-Fel, previously whipped and branded, now hung for days, slowly twisting, bound at the wrists.

"These are in Nirvana, compared to what you'll receive if you prove me wrong!"

Selena had quailed momentarily, then decided she could no longer retreat.

"And if I'm right," she said, in a tone of righteousness and defiance that stopped the moaning of the suffering girls, "you will be here yourself, and I guarantee it."

And she sensed—strong and raw and sweet to preceive—Ku-Fel's genuine fear.

"You do not know our ways, golden head," the harem

mistress grunted, recovering well. "You do not know our ways, and you have much to learn. I would put my brand upon you now, but for . . ."

But for the well-known fact that Selena had already won the master's support for her quest. This, it seemed, disturbed Rupal more than the maharajah's constant choice of Selena as his partner during the nights. And disturbed Ku-Fel beyond all apparent reason. Selena sensed the proximity of answers, an end to mystery. But the fear of her rivals held a dark promise of violence, with herself as victim.

Too late to change course now, she thought. *Neither Sean nor Royce would think of it, and both of them would be proud of me.*

They set out to find the child. Jouncing along on the horse, Selena remembered that the end of the year was approaching. Almost a year ago, she and Father and Brian had set out for Edinburgh, and toward a future none of them could have imagined, not even in nightmare. Even the things that had not changed outright were subtly altered. Blossoms no longer sprang from roses, but from simple grass. And even the thorns of the roses were hidden within, and deadly when you touched them. The world, as always, was beautiful, but rock was flower and blossom itself became rock.

Paradox did not elude Selena. In the preservation of his personal honor, her father had lost everything. Equally, in the willing loss of what she had long regarded as sexual honor—the withholding of her physical self—Selena had gained not the violation and debasement threatened by brimstone priests, but the love of Royce Campbell. Just as—she understood now—the gift of her self to Sean Bloodwell would have produced passionate love as well. And now, in India, where all the rules were indeterminate, wildly different, sexual honor did not even exist, at least, not for the maharajah's concubines. Sexuality had become, for her, an instrument to be used in order to win back the personal honor, the family honor, the *real* honor. All that mattered. All that had been lost.

She did not yet know how it would be done, but that it would be done she did not doubt.

She understood something of politics now, however distasteful she might once have thought it. The mere fact that the maharajah was riding out with her, here on the high plains of Pradesh, proved something. It proved he was not plotting with Ku-Fel. It proved he was not in bed, enjoying the pleasures of Rupal. It proved that she had measured something in his emotions, in his needs, upon which she could build.

That was what she had learned, and she would start with that.

Now she knew India, and she knew Scotland.

Make yourself the instrument of your own desire, Sean Bloodwell had told her once. *You can have anything you want.*

FREEDOM! cried her heart. She rode out onto the flowering summer fields of Pradesh, in November.

Trailed by six Sherpa warriors who would kill on command, with a grin.

Once, along the road to Shan-da, one of them cried out in what seemed to be fear, and pointed to a strange cloud formation in the northern sky.

"What is the matter?" Selena asked, unsettled by his nervous babbling.

"Look," the maharajah told her. "The clouds! It is the head of a wolf! In our land, that is an evil omen."

But not to Selena.

THE TRIAL

Alone among the people of the village, the woman held her ground. The others, watching the maharajah approach with his guard of murderous Sherpas, slid or ducked or ran for hiding, inside or behind or beneath the square brown earthen huts of Katni.

They rode into the village, the maharajah in the lead now. He looked upon the scene with mild, instinctive disdain. He was neither secure enough, in spite of his vast power, to disregard such fear as normal, nor corrupted enough by power to desire it. The woman standing in the road, however, stirred his curiosity.

The Sherpas grimaced threateningly—one of them howled—and made their horses dance. These particular men had originally come to Jabal-Mahal from Rajasthan, when Ku-Fel had married the master. They were, if anything, more vicious than the local warriors. But they ceased their threatening gestures when he raised his hand to them.

Through it all, the woman stood her ground, merely looking at them all, not disrespectfully, nor fearfully either. Just looked at them for a time, and then met Davi's eyes.

She was old, thin, but no longer lithe, with gray, straggly hair and skin just a shade darker than that of the rest of the villagers. Her black, luminous eyes were fixed on Davi, and glowed with knowledge. Selena understood at once. This was Shan-da, to whom the child had been given for protection. And she possessed the power.

"Well, Selena," prompted the maharajah, in a bored tone of voice, "is this the stable to which you have led us? What do your voices tell you now?"

"The child is here," Davi interrupted, getting in return an angry glance for his presumption.

Shan-da said nothing, and gave no sign.

"Alive?" Selena managed.

Again, she heard nothing, saw no gesture. But, with her mind, she received the unmistakable impression of imminent tragedy.

"Yes," Davi said. "Barely."

"How do you know?" the maharajah asked suspiciously. "What do you know about it?" He motioned to one of the Sherpas, who helped him dismount. The warrior grinned horribly at Davi beneath the dangling ends of his black mustaches, greased to a sheen. He sensed an opportunity to spill blood.

"It is a sense I have," Davi answered truthfully. But the master snorted derisively. "People in your position, Davi," he admonished, "know nothing until they are told something. Don't be presumptuous, or it will go hard with you when we return to the palace."

Davi dropped his eyes, but Selena could see, by the way he gripped the reins of his horse, that he was determined to act as necessary.

"Let us see about this 'sensation' of a child's presence," the Maharajah said, and started up the road toward the center of the village. "I am becoming impatient, and if the girl dies because of this delay . . ."

He did not finish, but instead halted after several paces. Shan-da stood before him. She had not moved, and he could easily have passed around her, yet she seemed to block his path. For the first time, the master truly looked at her. He did not know what he felt, but he did feel something. It irritated him.

"Selena," he snapped, "is the child here in this village, or not?"

She felt the words in her mind, Davi and his growing power. She could tell he was afraid. *Yes,* he told her, *but accede to Shan-da.*

"The woman knows," Selena told her lord.

His glance was sharp, skeptical, as if he sensed some play of forces in which he did not believe but which he could not entirely dismiss.

"Here? In these hovels? Let us get her out and take her . . ."

Shan-da spoke for the first time, in a low, resonant, disturbing voice. It was particularly disturbing because she presumed authority over them all, the maharajah included.

"I must have assurance that no-name will not be killed as her mother was. My karma must not be blemished, nor hers, before she is ready to die in her own time."

Even the Sherpas were stunned by her temerity, as they might have been in the presence of a guru, or wise teacher.

"The death of the mother, Gayle," she told the maharajah, "has sullied your karma incomparably. In the next life, you shall be as a dog with running wounds."

"I did not kill . . ." the master began, real fear in his voice. This woman might be mad, in which case he was confronted with evil forces. Or she might truly be a wise one, matriarch of the spirit of India. Then he recovered himself. He need give explanations to no one. "You have heard incorrectly," he said.

She did not yield. "Then why have you not sought out and punished those who are guilty?"

"The things I do, I do in my own good time," he snarled, but he was uncomfortable. Selena remembered the time in his bedchamber, when he had confessed to an inability to discern the truth about Gayle's death. Now Selena suspected, too, that he might not want to know who had been responsible, because that would require him to act, and such action might only give rise to more chaos. Again, she thought of the vast difference between Eastern and Western traditions.

"Now," he said, addressing them all, "what is the meaning of this? Selena? Davi? Let's go to the child. This . . . no-name. You haven't even given her a . . ."

Shan-da frowned. "I am but a temporary protector. The name is given by a child's permanent guardian. Now, your promise of safety for the unfortunate baby?"

The maharajah gave it.

Good as her word, Shan-da turned and led them up the dusty road and into the center of the grouping of huts. Neither turning, nor stopping, she entered one of the huts. Several women wearing heavy shawls about their heads, dark marks in the center of their foreheads, dropped immediately to their knees, looked at the floor. There was no sign of a baby, nor any baby things.

"If you've gone back on your word . . ."

"I have not," Shan-da said. Going over to the corner, she pressed a wooden rod half-buried in the mortarwork, and a panel of bricks slid aside, revealing a tiny chamber. Inside was a makeshift cradle, and in the cradle a dark child, wrapped in strips of cloth from head to foot.

"What is this?" the maharajah cried. "That child is as Indian as any I've . . ."

But Shan-da, undisturbed, lifted the child gently, wet her finger on her tongue, and drew it down across the child's tiny face. A white mark appeared in the wake of her finger.

"Soot," she explained. "The child is thus hidden whenever strangers approach Katni." One of the other women handed her a damp cloth, and she sponged the baby's face, removing the camouflage. Then she unwrapped the strips of dark cloth from the child's head, and wispy, golden hair appeared. The baby let out a tiny cry, weak and spiritless.

"Oh, you poor, poor thing," Selena cried, and without thinking, stepped up to Shan-da and took the child as if it were her own. The child was very pale and thin. She had been asleep, but now stirred and mewled again. And opened her eyes to see Selena holding her. What appeared in those eyes was something like surprise, and the eyes were very beautiful, large, and of darkest blue. Selena could see no part of Jack Randolph in this child; her mother's blood must beat within her veins. Thank God for that. "We've come for you, little darling," she cooed, and rocked the child gently in her arms. The majarajah, watching, now drew near, visibly affected.

"What's the matter with her? Why is she so weak?" he demanded of Shan-da.

"I believe it is an illness of the spirit. She has been well-fed, with rich goat's milk, and cereals of grain beaten soft. But we are all animals, master, and we crave those like ourselves."

"But she is alive . . ." he said, no longer interested in the woman's explanations.

Selena saw the moods reflected in his face. First, tenderness as he watched the child. Then sadness as he remembered its mother, along with that flash of unresolved anger.

The mystery of who had killed his lover. His concern returned to the immediate situation.

"Woman," he told Shan-da, "we shall leave you now and take the child with us. She will have the best of care. In the morning, I will send a messenger with a gift for you. It will be of great value, and . . ."

"I need no gift," Shan-da said. "What I have humbly done will be reflected upon my karma, and I shall be rewarded in the next life."

Almost chastened by this object lesson in purity, and perhaps reflecting upon its divergence from the scheming and machinations of his court at Jabal-Mahal, the maharajah promised instead to send food for the people of Katni, and prime seed to yield them larger crops. This Shan-da would accept, and they prepared to leave. Selena carried the golden-haired girl-child out into the sun, and the Sherpas rolled up their eyes as they would have done in the presence of magic. One of them kept pointing from Selena to the child and back again, as if Selena had conjured her up.

"What is he saying?" she asked Davi.

"I do not know for certain. It is a tongue of the mountains. But he is afraid of something. *'Soul of the dead one,'* he seems to say."

The maharajah was walking down toward the other end of the village with Shan-da, inspecting it as its rightful lord, and Selena was comparatively alone with Davi.

"Davi," she asked, "I know you saved the child and brought it here. But where were you on the day Gayle was executed?"

"With the master," he said immediately. "He was in a neighboring region, as you know, discussing what response he might make to the British merchants. . . ."

"I know. But the execution itself. We do not know who ordered it, but who carried it out?" A plan was forming in her mind. "It must have been warriors like these, ordered to do the job. Perhaps these very same Sherpas from Rajasthan."

"Of course," he said.

"But then why does the master not simply ask them, or," she added, angrily, "put them to the torture. In that way, he will learn who gave the order. . . ."

Davi was shaking his head. "I do not believe the master wishes to know," he said. "And besides, some of these soldiers belong to his father-in-law, in Rajasthan. It would not do to . . ."

Now Selena was almost certain, but much remained to be done before she could move the maharajah to action. The strategy she would use was provided—although at first it hardly seemed so—by Davi himself. As the maharajah remounted and prepared to depart, taking care that Selena was safe and comfortable with the child aboard her own mount, Davi and Shan-da stood for a short time, saying nothing, merely gazing at each other. Then the little man turned away, a smile on his usually somber face, and swung up on his own horse. The maharajah noticed not only the smile but the long glance as well, but refrained from asking about it at the time.

The ride back to Jabalpur took forever. Once, the child woke up crying, and they had to stop in order to allow Selena to feed it from a flask of goat's milk Shan-da had given her. She used a tiny spoon made of the smoothest wood, and the child ate hungrily, her large curious eyes never leaving Selena's. "Soon you shall have your own name, little one," the maharajah promised, bending down and making playful faces. He was tender but proprietary, accepting the child as his own. Something flashed quickly in Selena's mind, like a faint warning, dimly perceived. But there was a long way yet to travel. The horse's gait soon soothed the little girl. It was almost dark when they rode up the white stone road into Jabal-Mahal.

Gayle's skull regarded them.

"Have these taken down and properly buried in the Western way," the maharajah ordered Davi, gesturing toward the bones, but not looking at them. Selena believed, then, that the master had decided to proceed against Gayle's killers, but the next afternoon, when Davi called for her and led her out beyond the palace wall, on the eastern side where one could look out toward the high mountains of Chota Nagpur, no decision had been made. Nothing had transpired; she had not been sent for.

The cross stood there, small and delicate and white above the green grass.

"Did I do well?" Davi asked her.

Selena looked at the tiny black letters printed on the crossarm:

GAYLE
Scotland-India
"Long Live the King"

"What? Who told you to put that?"

"The master. Why, is something wrong?"

"But 'Long live the King!' " The mere expression once again stirred up bitter memories of what had happened to her, to the MacPhersons.

"He said it was a prayer of your people," Davi explained, looking worried. "Have I done something wrong?"

Oh, let it go, she thought. *Gayle was Gayle, not you.* She knelt down then and made her promise. She made it directly to the girl who, from this quiet spot, had seen the rugged mountains to the east, whose heart might have been haunted by loneliness, whose memories cast back to the softer hills of home. It was the tie between the two of them, something sacred which they shared, and it was that as well as Selena's concern for the little girl that made her say to the hills, and the grass, and the sweet flowers and the ibis and the wind, all Indian, and in each of whom God dwelled:

"I will protect your child as if she were mine, and love her as best I can, and raise her in our traditions if I can. And . . ." *one thing more,* she thought, ". . . I will send her home, with honor, to Scotland, should the chance ever come."

I will send her home for both of us, she thought.

"You pray far differently than it was taught by the black crows," Davi observed.

Selena stood up, brushed a few wisps of grass from her sari.

"I hope so," she said. "Do the gods of India answer the prayers of foreigners?"

"It is strange, but I do not think I have ever heard the question before," he mused. "Yes," he said, after considering it, "if you pray where they are, they must hear you, for the soul of India beats even now in the earth beneath us, and the sky above us, and the river down there among the hills. So, if a prayer is made in India, and if it is genuine, they will answer it. I do not think they care who makes it."

"It is genuine," Selena said quietly, turning, leaving Gayle of Greenlaw in that high, quiet place, where the wind rippled the grass, where the words of her prayer began the flight to heaven.

In the palace, Selena had been lodged by herself in a suite of rooms, which she shared with the baby and a staff of nurses and maids. The maharajah was sparing no effort to ensure the child's health, and, when not devoting himself to choosing the perfect name for her—something to combine her maternal heritage and her future as his daughter-in-fact, the living symbol of his dead beloved—he watched her in the cradle, eating, being bathed, playing with her toes. Selena, to him, was now a substitute mother, and, although he gave her everything she needed in her task, he no longer sent for her in the evenings to share his bed and pleasure his flesh.

They talked now and then, of course. One day he was ready to move against those shadowy figures who had destroyed Gayle. But the following day he had decided he could not do it. Too much might come unloosed that had been successfully bound up already. Why take a chance? Better the devil you know than the devil you don't. He knew, because she had told him, that Davi himself had kept the child from death, but he did not ask who had given the order, and when she told him one afternoon in the nursery, "I can tell you who I think it was, but Davi can tell you *who* it was," he took quick refuge in the prejudice of his caste.

"In the first place, Dravidians are all liars," he declared. "And, in the second, they are too incompetent to plan anything. If he *did* save the child, it was purely by accident. He forgot what he was supposed to be doing."

She told him about the power.

"There is no such thing," he pronounced. "After a time, those of the higher castes, if wise and disciplined enough, may be given certain wisdom that is withheld from lesser men. But a Dravidian? Never. No, Selena. Davi is no use to us . . . to me . . . when we seek information."

"But you're not seeking information at all. You don't want to know the truth."

This angered him, because he prided himself greatly on his knowledge and administrative skill.

"Well, what about Shan-da? I think she had the power."

No, he remembered Davi's silent exchange with the Shan-da, unnerving, but: "A shrewd village mystic with plenty of nerve and that is all," he said. "Now, stop your imaginings and tend to the child. See, she is trying to sit up! Did you see it?"

He was also preoccupied with a British commercial party that was rumored to have been in Jamshedpur, after having come out from the Bengal region. He was concerned about what they would want, about how to deal with them.

"Many of my fellows have been deceived by these connivers," he worried, "but those who have ignored them, or tried to hinder them, have lost, too, by not sharing in the wealth they can bring."

"As I told you," she explained respectfully, "Western ways of business could benefit you, and ease this worry in your mind. Davi knows some things which might be of help, and I myself know some . . ."

He scoffed at this. Women knowing of business!

". . . and our way of law would readily rid your mind of the doubt about Gayle's death . . ."

"Silence! If I wish to know I will order everyone tortured!"

"Yes, and everyone will confess. You will have them all executed, is that right? Everyone in your palace? Yes, and then the guilty one will have been punished, true, but no one will remain for you."

He stormed out of the nursery that time and did not return all day. Eventually, the little girl drew him back, but he discussed no more of his current problems with Selena.

For her own part, Selena had fallen in love with the child. After much explanation, and several sketches by Davi, workmen at the palace were able to construct a serviceable rocking chair, and in this she fed and talked to the little girl, and rocked her to sleep sometimes in the night. Shan-da may have been right in her diagnosis of loneliness and spiritual torpor, because the child's physical health was not especially deficient. And, after a few weeks at the palace, with Selena's constant care, she became as bright and cheerful as any happy baby. Indeed, Selena watched over her with a passion. Thinking of her own future, she had begun to wonder if she herself would ever have a child. Previously, the thought had always been remote: something that would happen in due course. If the maharajah began calling for her again, regularly, she supposed that it would happen, as it did to the rest of the women in the harem. But this child, still unnamed, with her blond hair and blue eyes, reminded her of herself, of her own happy childhood. A child of Royce's might not have been this blond, but if it had been by Sean Bloodwell, well, the likelihood was very great . . .

Women of the harem, wives as well as concubines, came by to see the child, and the famous "chair that moves but does not move," of which they had heard. Selena could tell that most of them were jealous of her arrangement, as they were automatically, reflexively, and quite harmlessly jealous of any small favor or perquisite granted any of their number. Ku-Fel herself never appeared. Indeed, because Selena took her meals in the nursery, the two had not met since Selena's return from the visit to Shan-da. Once or twice, in the night, Selena awoke with the distinct feeling that Ku-Fel was present just outside the locked nursery doors, but she knew Davi had made it a point to sleep concealed close to the entrance, and she knew he could come to her aid should any threat arise.

Rupal did not come either, until one afternoon in mid-January, when the child was about a half-year old. Then she appeared in all her soft, splendid beauty, her eyes and voice as tender and vicious as that of a velvet serpent.

"You ought to have paid heed to me when first I asked you," she said enigmatically. "Now, again each night, I give our master the pleasure that God placed between my legs."

Selena's response was a hard, but cautious, admonition. "I would beware of plots, if I were you."

Rupal laughed, like ice tinkling in a pewter mug.

"No, it is you who should beware."

If her intention was to upset Selena, she succeeded. But she also put Selena on guard.

"Davi," she confided to him later that evening, "I am afraid something is going to happen. What do you think? Is the child in danger?"

He bowed his head sadly. "A true master of the power would be able to tell you," he said. "But I am incapable of full love, and thus cannot sense all that is important. Only with those who do possess love can I speak, and even then only a little . . ."

"But, Davi, you can love. Fully. And you will. That other thing is nothing . . ."

". . . but I do sense much tumult, hostile colors," he said. "When the aura about the palace is dull and red, wavering like fire, then I know hate is at its zenith."

She told him of Rupal's warning.

"Do not worry," he said. "If something occurs to you or the child, I will rally the Sherpas to your aid immediately. They live to impale trespassers on their spears."

"And if Ku-Fel trespasses?"

His eyes darkened. "Then I shall do what I can."

He was resolute enough, in spite of his perpetual fear, so she asked him again, as she had once before, to tell the maharajah it was Ku-Fel who had demanded, over and over, assurances that the child had been born dead. To Selena, such an obsession was evidence of culpability, or, at least, of complicity.

"He would not believe me," Davi said, and Selena knew that, for the present anyway, he was right.

She fought sleep that night, Rupal's face before her, Rupal's words: *No, it is you who should beware,* ringing in her brain. Davi was outside, as usual, and he said he would remain with her, but she could not sense him. Probably because of her own turmoil and fear for the child. The word had passed that tonight, once again, Rupal the concubine would share the maharajah's bed, and there was something oppressive and disconcerting about the fact. For all his power and headstrong ways, Selena already knew how impressionable the master could be. And, although she had grown more confident in her own persuasive skills, she suspected that Rupal could do better. Rupal was no foreigner, either, attached to a baby's cradle by virtue of hair color.

Were Rupal and Ku-Fel acting together now? In spite of their long-standing animosity?

Selena could only guess. *Which,* she thought bitterly, *was more than the master allowed himself.*

She checked the little girl, who slept peacefully, her mouth slightly open, her large eyes closed against all that was to be, open on a world of dreams. *Which is just as well.* Selena touched the child's face in a gentle goodnight, and went to her own pallet, resting there uneasily for a time, seeking Davi. She had an impulse to open the doors and check for him at his hiding place, but thought the better of it. He was probably asleep.

Now, at last, she drifted off, came back, drifted off again, down the long blue corridor, and at its end the beckoning door to peace. She crossed the threshold, and the palace was gone from her, and the earth, too: all but her slow-beating heart and the solace of forgetfulness. But the palace itself was far from slumber. In the maharajah's chamber, Rupal smiled wickedly to herself, arched her body and writhed, and the master moaned in ecstasy, lost in his own kind of forgetfulness, oblivious to all but the sensations she was giving him, one upon the other. In the harem, the wives and concubines were settling in for the night, pleased in an impersonal and almost unconscious way that Ku-Fel was not with them, to supervise and berate and order them around. In the barracks, some of the Sherpas were nervous, discussing the "soul of the dead one," or Gayle's child, and other warriors laughed and mocked their fear.

And in the discipline chamber, where the punishment cells had been vacated on her order, Ku-Fel slitted her eyes against the heat of the fire, and thrust into it the iron rod with its ancient symbol which meant "damned." In the wild parts of Rajasthan, her home region, it was believed that such a mark upon the flesh of a living person could prevent rebirth, cease the endless cycle of karmas, and end an existence once and for all. She did not entirely believe this herself, but it was a good story, and the threat of it was often more bitter to the victim than the pain of the brand itself.

Selena awoke to darkness and the guttural hiss of the Sherpas. Almost instantly, a rough, foul-smelling hand was over her mouth, and she was seized and lifted by a warrior of savage strength. Twisting her head from side to side, she saw another right behind the one who held her, and a third bending over the cradle where the baby slept. *No*, she tried to scream, and her heart thundered almost loudly enough to be heard where Davi slept.

Two of the brutes yanked her toward the doorway, their teeth glittering in the darkness, and one of them grunted an order or command. Selena did not understand what it was, but just as they rushed her down the corridor, she heard the child cry out, and keep on crying, the sound following her all the way down to the concealed entrance to the punishment cells.

Ku-Fel's gold teeth greeted her, and the long elephant-hide whip dangled from her hand. She nodded to the Sherpas. With one smooth motion, powerful arms turned her upside down, and ropes bit into her ankles as they tied her to the bar. Her sleeping gown fell away, down over her face, and she could see only a dimly lit circle of floor.

"Cut away the garment," Ku-Fel growled. "I want her to see the blows coming."

It was roughly done, and the tip of the knife cut her skin at the back of her neck.

She could no longer hear the child.

The smell of the fire that heated the branding iron filled the room.

Selena looked up and fixed her eyes on Ku-Fel, resolving not to show fear. At least not yet.

"You had Gayle killed, didn't you?"

"You'll never know, you pretty little whore."

"And you ordered the child killed, too, didn't you? But as long as you knew it was still alive, you couldn't make a move. Not against Davi, nor against Rupal. Either of whom might use it against you."

"You Westerners are the questioning kind. *Too questioning*," she barked, and laced the big whip viciously through the air. The blow caught Selena across the abdomen, a combination of incredible, cracking, stinging pain and heavy force. The air went out of her, and she almost lost consciousness, retching, coughing, too winded to cry out.

"You were the one who killed the child," Ku-Fel was explaining, as Selena tried to concentrate in the roaring world of pain. Standing around, the Sherpas were chortling and discussing—she assumed—her physical attributes. And what alterations four strong horses might make in them. "I learned of your perfidy and decided to take appropriate action before notifying the master."

Selena tried to clear her head.

"You were jealous of the child," Ku-Fel was saying, rehearsing the story she would tell the maharajah, "you were so tired of caring for the poor little thing that you did away with . . ."

"No!" Selena cried, and then she thought she understood what had happened, and how she had played a part in the larger conflict at court. The Sherpas who waited now to see her suffer were loyal to Ku-Fel. She had brought them with her from Rajasthan on the occasion of her marriage, and she had used them ever since. She had used them against Gayle, whom she had hated, during the maharajah's absence. And now they were helping her against Selena, because Selena had not been the instrument that Ku-Fel had intended her to be. Chosen to delight the master and to take his mind off the memory of Gayle, Selena had not only been unpredictable in the constant struggle with Rupal, she had found out about—and then sought out—the child. So Ku-Fel was taking one last desperate gamble to reestablish her unchallenged supremacy. She would kill the child and, in the morning, present a whipped, tortured Selena to the master, half out of her mind with pain, and willing to confess anything.

The maharajah would be made to see everything clearly, at last.

The second blow struck Selena high on the backs of her legs. She screamed at the top of her lungs and her body quivered on the bar. Her cry echoed in the tiny room, and then died out. It was very quiet. With her eyes closed, Selena waited for the sound of the whip cutting through the air. But it did not come. She opened her eyes.

The master stood in the doorway, holding the child. On his face was a look of horror and sudden understanding. Davi stood next to him. And behind them were more Sherpas than Selena could count.

"It was the child who saved you," Davi explained later. "The child and the superstitions of a dull mind. You see, this must have been one of the Sherpas who was terrified when he first saw the child, because he saw in her the spirit of her mother. So he must have been guilty of participating in Gayle's death, or at least he must have known it had taken place. When the child awoke and began to cry, he could not kill it as he had been instructed to do. The crying was so loud and so persistent that the maharajah came running to see what was the matter, and Rupal, flying after him, pleading for him to come back to her. It was something to be seen."

"How did you see it?" she asked, remembering that she had not felt his presence.

"From the floor," he said. "They tied me and gagged me when I was found there."

"Why didn't they kill you?"

"Ku-Fel told them not to. She said she wished to deal with me personally, later. That there were certain questions she wished to put to me. Probably about my taking the child, and who knew of it. But now there will be questions for all of us."

Selena had explained to the maharajah, three times, the procedures of a Western court. He had modified a few of them, preferring himself as judge, jury, and prosecutor. Seated upon a throne of gold in his official room, and surrounded by servants and guards, he summoned the witnesses before him. Ku-Fel, haughty and unabashed. Rupal, self-contained, with now and then a bitter smile. Selena, who did not understand why she was a member of the group. And Davi, who was afraid.

"It will be me who is accused of all," he mourned to Selena. "Ku-Fel and Rupal will see to that. And I am afraid for you, as well."

She had learned to trust Davi's premonitions. The master had understood a little of the *form* of a trial, but almost nothing of its substance.

"Did you order Gayle's death?" he asked Rupal.

"No, master," she said.

"And did you?" he asked Ku-Fel.

"No."

He looked at Selena in disgust and lifted his hands, palms upward. *So now what?*

"If I may speak," Selena said.

The master nodded.

"The point of this exercise," she told him, "is to establish what did happen. May I ask certain questions?"

He nodded.

"Davi, do not be afraid. Answer truthfully and completely. Who told you to save the child?"

"No one. I did it by myself."

"How did you know it needed to be saved?"

"I believed that it would be killed."

"You had certain information?" the maharajah prompted.

"No, master. I sensed it."

Selena saw Ku-Fel grin, and Rupal relaxed noticeably. The maharajah himself, recalling Davi's silent uncanny rapport with Shan-da, nonetheless looked amused and disbelieving. Selena snapped him back to attention with a question to Ku-Fel.

"Why did you have your Sherpas abduct me and try to kill the child?"

"The child is not dead," the big woman shot back. "I never had any intention of harming it. And you were to be punished. Such is my right as harem mistress."

True. The maharajah was *nodding!*

"Punished for what?" she demanded.

"Insolence of many forms. It is my right."

Rupal was trying hard to suppress a smile of triumph. And Selena understood that, in the master's mind, the apparent satisfaction of rituals and protocols could be used against her, *even though* she was trying to discover the truth about the death of a woman he had loved, mother to a child he loved—if anything—even more.

Her next question was ill-conceived and delivered in mild panic.

"Did you," she asked Rupal, "order or conspire in the killing of Gayle? Or in the attempt to kill the child?"

"No," the sultry beauty answered coolly, "and you were not even here at the time it happened. What right has she . . ." addressing the master now ". . . to put us to shame like this? I have pleased you well, and Ku-Fel has served you loyally through many years . . ."

Selena grasped it. They were acting together again. Their

shifting needs had drawn them into yet another tenuous alliance. It might not last long after they had disposed of this Scottish upstart, but that would be long enough. Selena was losing, and she knew it. Her questions were being evaded; they knew more tricks than she. Davi would not be taken seriously in anything he said, but what if . . .

What if the power could be put to work?

It was her only chance.

"Master," she asked, "may I speak to Davi?"

He looked curious, as if about to witness a new twist, some form of entertainment. He nodded.

Davi looked at her, but instead of returning his glance, she closed her eyes and concentrated. *Open your mind*, she pleaded, *open your mind or it is lost for both of us.*

A long moment passed, and then she heard, or sensed: *It is already lost.*

No! You must help me.

I cannot.

Yes. Yes, you can. I love you, and you, me. Together we are one, and one is enough. Now listen to what I say, and open your mind to all when I so bid you.

No more did she speak as a nervous interrogator, paling before deceit and evasion. No, she stood straight now, alone in her mind upon the Coldstream battlements again, and pronounced her words as a Scottish princess should.

"You," she declared, addressing Rupal, "and you," pointing to Ku-Fel, "did conspire to kill Gayle, and succeeded in so doing." Not giving them a chance to answer, she went on. "And, Ku-Fel, when you knew that the child had not been killed, as you had ordered, you became fearful, lest Rupal had succeeded in taking her. The child, alive, would win the master's favor. Nor was Rupal certain—were you?—what had become of the baby. So your conspiracy broke down, and once again lapsed into the perpetual hostility of the court. But if you could kill me and kill Davi, too, and make it look as if we had been responsible for most of the trouble, truth could be forever shrouded.

"And the master," she added challengingly, sarcastically, "is one who loves the truth, who wishes to know *everything*."

"I do!" he flared.

"Then if you do, Davi will give us the truth."

He looked puzzled.

"Now, Davi, are you prepared to listen to the answers Ku-Fel and Rupal are about to give and judge their veracity?"

He looked doubtful.

I will be with you, she told him. *Love.*

He was fighting his fear, trying to understand. "Yes," he said, quavering.

Selena asked the questions: Did you, Rupal, conspire with Ku-Fel to kill Gayle, and use your Sherpas to do it? Did you, Ku-Fel, order the child destroyed? And did both of you, last night, plan to kill the baby and blame me?

After each question, both of the women answered resoundingly. *No!*

Davi's eyes were closed. Beads of sweat poured from his black face, a shower of tiny pearls. He was taut with effort. When she finished her queries, he opened his eyes.

"What is the truth?" she asked him.

They will kill me.

"Then we will still be together," she answered him aloud. He saw that she meant it.

"Master, these women are lying," he told the maharajah, meeting his eyes. "They are lying in all things. It is as Selena has described."

Ku-Fel let out a roar of vengeance. Rupal was more restrained, but no less uncertain. "I am not about to be called a liar by a Dravidian poseur," she huffed.

The maharajah himself was smiling. "Really, Selena. You expect me to believe one of the lowest caste? It is not how things are done."

"You said you wished to know the truth."

"I do, but some possess it, and some do not. Davi does not."

"He does." She explained about the power, in which previously, he had expressed disbelief.

"You have told me that before. I'm sorry, Selena, but . . ."

"Wait. He can also see into your mind . . ."

No, no, Davi was saying. *I am not strong enough.*

You must.

". . . and that will prove he has seen inside the souls of

these . . ." she pointed, and enjoyed saying the word ". . . these killers."

The master debated with himself for a moment. If he tried this trick, he might be a dupe. On the other hand, it was amusing.

"All right," he said, "I shall hold a word in my mind." *I cannot*, Davi was pleading. *He is the master.*

"I will be with you," she said aloud, as the maharajah thought of a word and concentrated. "Go ahead."

Davi reached out for her, and Selena took his hand, an act which repulsed Rupal and Ku-Fel.

"I am holding a word in my mind," the master said, "that no one could possibly guess. It is . . ." and here his voice deepened with sincerity and conviction ". . . very personal to me."

Silence came over the room. The maharajah looked directly at Davi, who met his eyes. His hand was trembling in Selena's grasp. After a time the master spoke.

"Well, what is the word, Dravidian? You've had your chance."

Davi looked at Selena and she saw tears in his eyes, felt the pressure of his hand. It was going to be . . . *all right!*

"*Greenlaw*," David said.

Selena pleaded for merciful executions, but the maharajah demurred violently. Not only had his pride been stung to the quick, he knew now, finally, the extent to which the struggle between Rupal and Ku-Fel, with all its bizarre twists and incredible turnings, had visited disaster upon his palace. "No, they shall not have death for what they have done," he raved. "I shall torment them to the edge of endurance, and then give them something by which to remember me for the rest of their lives." First he had Rupal subjected to the water torture, until she howled maniacally and called upon demons. She was stretched out between two pillars, tied by her ankles and wrists, with her head lower than her feet. Then the end of a long strip of rough cloth was jammed into her mouth. A gleeful Sherpa pinched her nose closed, while quart after quart of water was poured into her mouth. Gasping for air, Rupal found nothing but water. It was like drowning, over and over and over again. Just before the hapless woman would lapse into

unconsciousness, the Sherpa would release his grip on her
nose, permitting her to breathe. Slowly, the cloth which she
had swallowed would be pulled out of her throat, with the
blood and the mucus of her insides thick upon it. When
Rupal had all but lost her sanity due to anguish and despair, the maharajah had her cast into a leper colony far
out in the countryside, from which she could never return.

Ku-Fel suffered much, as well. She was first hung up by
her thumbs in the lowest dungeon, where insects bit her
naked flesh and the rats of Pradesh climbed upon her body,
trailing slime. Then her tongue was pulled out with hot
pincers, and the master sent her back to Rajasthan. He sent
a guard along with her: the Sherpas who had conspired
with her during the time she was at court in Jabal-Mahal.
But the Sherpas were killed first and tied into place on
their horses. If Ku-Fel managed to reach her homeland
alive, she would be surrounded by a guard of putrefying
corpses.

The maharjah was mad, wild for revenge. He did not
even seem to care if war with Rajasthan should be the result of his vindictiveness. His honor was the only thing that
mattered, and he saw to it that his honor was avenged.

It was the savagery that alarmed Selena most, and which
cast a deep pall over her relationship with the master.

And then there was the child.

IN QUEST OF STEEL

She grew gloriously toward her first year, bright, playful, exuberant. Soon she would be walking, speaking, and Selena thought it was high time that she be taken to a European settlement in Calcutta, from which, if fate was kind, she might eventually return to her maternal homeland, and to her kinfolks, thus fulfilling Selena's promise. Selena herself was resigned to concubinage here at Jabal-Mahal for as long as she could envision, but if they waited too long to move the child, the transference might have a terrible effect upon her spirit. At least, before her first year, a sound adjustment was quite possible. She loved the little girl deeply, dearly, but it would not be good to keep her here.

The maharajah bridled whenever she mentioned the subject, however, and his eyes narrowed, showing a fiery glint. He said nothing, but his meaning was plain: the little girl is mine; she stays with me. It would not do to mention that he had promised—or at least implied—otherwise.

Then there was the matter of the name.

"It should be a Christian name," Selena once ventured to say.

"The child was born here in Jabal-Mahal, and this is India," he told her. "Moreover, this is Jabalpur, in Pradesh, where I rule. The child shall be given an Indian name."

"When?" Selena wanted to know. Privately, she called her Gayle; in public, simple endearments like "darling" or "love."

"When I have the appropriate impulse" was all he

would say. "I wish to find something perfect. It can be none other."

For a time after Rupal and Ku-Fel were removed, Selena once again enjoyed the unremitting favors of her master. But it was different now. Not that it was no longer good. Rather, something had shifted in their relationship, and, more especially, in the maharajah himself. The trial and its result had been more than disconcerting to him.

One night he loved her hard, with no gentleness. His body pounded down upon hers, and his stalk of flesh rammed deeply inside her, again and again. She thought at first that he was approaching the frenzy of imminent, tantalizing release, which she understood from the responses of her own body during love, but it was something else. It was a need to dominate her, to master her, to make her cry out in pain.

She did.

He ceased, and grinned above her in the darkness. "You do not like it? I had been informed that Western men do it so."

How? Who had told him that? "It's not true," she said. "You're hurting me."

"No, that is the way. Gayle told me, many times, about Captain Randolph. So I decided to attempt it. Perhaps it is because I am growing tired of you."

If he waited for an expression of anguish, it did not come.

"So," he said, sliding off her, as if an issue of great import had just been resolved, "you may return to your quarters."

After that, it was almost impossible to speak with him about the child or to plead with him about making arrangements regarding Calcutta.

"Little no-name," she murmured to herself one afternoon, playing alone with the girl in her special nursery, "what's to become of us? What's to become of you?"

It was March now, early fall of 1776. Upon the hills of Pradesh the colors were changing, just as they did far away in Europe. But here it was winter that approached, and even if it was to be a gentle winter, she did not look forward to it. Nor did she look forward to much of anything now, except an occasional conversation with Davi, who sensed her disconsolation.

He entered that day, bearing as usual a tray of refreshments for the afternoon: juices and sherbets and sweetbreads thinly sliced. The child loved to see him come, and tried first to totter over toward him. But that took too long, and she dropped to her hands and knees, crawling fast, saying something like *A-vee, A-vee,* and reaching up for a treat. She responded to his gentleness as well, and Selena often thought that the two of them, she and the Dravidian, were the only ones in the whole place—including the maharajah—who responded to the child as anything but a thing. Certainly, the master was solicitous, but to him the girl was a symbol, not a human being. A symbol for whom an appropriate name had to be fashioned, which took as much time—if not more—as devising the perfect epitaph. Then she understood. If this baby stayed here, she would be as dead all her life as, even now, her mother was dead beneath the white cross.

"You are worried?" Davi asked, setting the tray on a low table so the child could reach it. But he did not so much ask it as say it. Nor did she have to answer.

"Much is happening," he went on, "and none of it calming. This morning a messenger arrived from Rajasthan, demanding the return of Ku-Fel's dowry, upon threat of war. The master is most distressed. In the first place, Ku-Fel is alive. Somehow she made it through the mountains. Perhaps the dead Sherpas were guard enough and scared away brigands. Or even suitors," he joked. "Ku-Fel without a tongue is not so bad. Then, too, if he were to return the dowry, a great part of his wealth would be gone, and he would be forced to deal with the approaching British merchants from a position of weakness."

"They are close? The British?" She was still a MacPherson, all right, and felt a shiver of distaste course through her, like bad blood. But they would be European and, as such, brothers in a lost land.

"Yes. Three days ago they bargained with the Nawab of Allahabad, for purchase rights to his crops of grain and wheat. They also suspect the presence of certain metals beneath the earth, of which I do not know, a vein which is said to extend through Pradesh, and which is controlled by our master. But about which he knows nothing either. So, if he must bargain from weakness and ignorance, he is lost. He needs the dowry, and he might even decide war is preferable to losing it."

Selena remembered the time the master had led her into the vast room of wealth, and she had seen the chest of matchless jewels.

"So you have seen it?" Davi asked, reading her thoughts.

She smiled. "It is incomparable. With a handful of any of the stones in that case, I could live like a queen for the rest of my life. . . . If I were out of here," she added.

"About that, Ku-Fel was correct, I am afraid. The discipline cells may be gone, but once one is here, one remains. One of your appearance fleeing through the countryside would stand out like a rabbit in a school of fish."

She tried to laugh at his joke, but it was difficult.

"But you could flee if you planned it," she suggested.

He shook his head. "I am Dravidian. I go where I am kicked."

They sat there in the nursery for a time, wrapped in their mutual sadness, until Selena felt the little girl's chubby hand pulling at her sari. She looked at the tiny face with its tentative smile. *Is everything all right?* the baby wanted to know. *Let's play.* And that snapped them out of it for the time being.

Just as Davi was about to leave, taking the trays and glasses with him, and just as Selena was putting the child down for her nap, a great commotion broke out somewhere in the front courtyard of Jabal-Mahal.

"War? Already?" Selena wondered.

"No," Davi said, rushing to the windows and looking out. "A group of men is coming up the road. They must be . . . yes, they are the trading party. Your people," he cried, happy for her. "You may not be permitted to speak to any of them, but you might at least look."

Not speak to them! She would find a way! One of them might have heard of Sean Bloodwell, even get a message to him. She rushed to the window and saw them. The distance was great—several hundred yards—but they were Europeans, all right. She could tell by the way they sat their horses, erect, confident, with just the slightest trace of arrogance, which seemed to be a British trait. There were six altogether, speaking to the gate guards as their horses stamped. It was too far away to see any of them clearly. She was straining to see when one of the maharajah's attendants came to the door.

"The master wishes your presence at once," he said to Selena, impudently neglecting the ritual bow of courtesy.

"I shall be there in a moment."

"*At once*," the attendant repeated, with a hard edge to his voice.

"Go," Davi said. "I shall see to the child."

Wondering about the reason for this sudden call after so many weeks of coldness, Selena followed the attendant out of the nursery, down the gleaming white marble halls of the palace, and into the wing in which the maharajah performed his public, judicial, and administrative functions. It, too, contained a raised platform with a golden, thronelike chair upon it, and a long carpet stretched out in front so that supplicants and subjects might approach their temporal deity on their knees. She had never seen one who did not do so. Yet, she had never heard of an Englishmen who had done so to a foreign ruler.

At least it would be interesting.

The attendant stood aside at the entrance to the master's private office and waved her inside with a leer and a casual gesture. She found the maharajah greatly vexed, although he tried not to let it show.

"Those British traders are at the gates," he said. "I have given the order to let them enter. I shall grant them an audience immediately."

He said nothing, and neither did she. It was not her place. But it seemed to her as if he actually wanted her to speak. The silence went on. He paced a bit, not looking at her.

"I was summoned here," she said tentatively.

"Hmmmmm?" He looked up. "Yes." He spoke quickly, in his clipped tones. "This is difficult for me. I wish you had never set foot inside Jabal-Mahal. Yet, I have appreciated you, in my way, and even—as you say—I may love you . . . but . . ."

He let the thought lapse. She waited.

"I did not mean to offend you," he started again, "with my words about your setting foot here. It is simply that . . .

that since you have come I now realize I have certain . . ." he gritted it out ". . . certain *weaknesses*, I lack certain information, and such deficiencies will not be of use to me. In dealing with these British."

He paced a little more now, and then glanced out into the courtyard to note the progress of the trading party. Servants were bringing them toward the palace; Selena could hear the hooves of the horses ringing on the white stones, a sound that called back memories for her.

"My ruler friends in other parts of India have done badly in their dealings with the traders, with the East India Company. We cannot understand it. *We* own the land. *We* have the power. *We* possess the wealth. But suddenly much of it is gone, and the British are swarming about our provinces, and even our people begin to obey them. I sadly fear that a time may come when India shall cease to be what she is, and become instead some terrible bastardization of East and West . . ."

He stopped pacing and looked at her.

"These are your people," he said. There was a note of pleading in his voice. "You understand them. I want you to be present with me when I begin the audience. You will listen but must not speak unless I grant you leave. The sight of one of their women here may cow them."

She did not want to tell him that such a sight, a Christian woman obviously subject in all ways to a pagan ruler, would be guaranteed to elicit just the opposite effect. Perhaps that might nerve one of them to help her! *Dream on, Selena.* If anything, knowing how men were, it would only make them contemptuous of her, and perhaps jealous of the maharajah.

"I understand the British," she said coldly, "and I hate them."

He smiled. "So you are perfect as my adviser. Come, let us go to the throne. You stand to my left . . ."

"Davi has had training in business matters," she said.

An odd, unpleasant, yet satisfied expression appeared on his intent, dark face. "You must know this anyway," he said, "so you may as well know it now. I am having your little black friend arrested right now. And executed in due course."

She could not believe it. It could not be true! "Why?"

But it was. His sudden cry rang in her mind: *Selena! Help!*

"Even now it is being done," he told her. "I cannot stand to have in my palace a piece of lower-caste scum who has seen me in weakness and error."

"We are human," she cried. "We all possess weakness. We all err. It is . . ."

Selena! They are putting me in chains!

". . . it is natural."

This knowledge did not move him. She had not the slightest idea what to do. Other than to defy him. But, in a strange way, she and Davi were one, and the maharajah could not act against either of them, this minute, with the visitors at the gates. But she had done other dangerous things, too, she told herself. And she could do this one.

"Release Davi this instant," she demanded, looking at him coldly, their eyes level at each other. "Release him and bring him here, that I may know he is safe. Or I will not help you with the British."

Selena! Davi pleaded.

The maharajah stared at her, incredulous. But he was doing his own calculating, too, and she saw him accede to her demand before he spoke. But, she saw as well, he also knew that *later* would arrive, when he might do as he wished.

"Free him now," she said again.

He did not speak to her, but instead turned away and gave the necessary orders.

Davi, it is all right, she spoke with her mind, but in a little while, after he had been brought to the throne room and placed on a low chair, present to watch the British, both of them knew it was not all right. The maharajah was a young man and not an untalented one, but the pressures upon him of late—the trial, an impending war, the British foray—caused him to dismiss logic, to act upon impulse. And his impulses were the willful, arbitrary reflexes of the one born to power, and luxury, and the righteousness of caprice.

He mounted to his throne, drew about him a robe of silk, took in his hand a silver staff with the silver head of a tiger at one end, silver talon of an eagle at the other, and bade the doors be opened, the visitors approach.

Selena looked up with mild excitement as the great golden doors parted, revealing the small group of men standing there. They had not been allowed the time to change from their riding gear, and Selena knew this had been done intentionally, that they should appear with the sweat and dust of the road before the impeccable ruler of Jabalpur. She saw them shuffle there a moment, and then begin a slow approach toward the end of the carpet that led to the throne.

First confrontation, she thought, and then her heart went cold and her mouth dry as dust.

The man who stepped forward, into the lead, with his broad shoulders, erect carriage, thick hair of reddish-blond, and bold yet friendly eyes . . .

. . . was *Sean Bloodwell.*

He was not looking at her, and this gave Selena time to curb her wild, contradictory emotions. She had not realized, as a silly young girl in Scotland, how truly powerful and competent he looked, and how assured. The sun of the Southern Hemisphere had tanned him well, setting off the shrewd intelligence in his eyes. She watched him as, walking slowly, formally, he first glanced at the maharajah, to measure the latter—his degree of *hauteur,* his probable character—and then glance down at the beginning of the ritual carpet. He knew immediately what it was there for, and stopped just at its edge. He looked up at the maharajah, bowed slightly. The master lifted his chin, and waited.

"I am a citizen of Great Britain, and a subject of King George," he said straightforwardly. "I am aware of your customs, sir, but I am admonished not to bend knee to another ruler, even one so great as yourself."

Selena saw the maharajah deduce the principle that was concealed in the flattery, and frown.

"Nor would you wish a subject of yours to bow down before the ruler of another land."

Selena saw the maharajah accept the principle.

"I and my colleagues come as representatives of the East India Company, to establish trade with . . ."

And then, confident that he had made his point about not approaching the maharajah on his knees, Sean let his eyes wander just a bit, take in the throne, and the canopy, and *the woman standing beside the Indian* . . .

Their eyes met. For the space of a second, he stopped speaking. World and time passed between them in a glance, and the currents of loss and memory, the stunning electricity of surprise, came down about them. Sean Bloodwell, to whom she had been promised. Who would have been the first to have her, the day of the picnic on the banks of the river, had not family come hunting to tease them. Who had lost his fortune because of the MacPhersons. But in whose eyes—yes, it was there—love still shone, fierce and true as instant fire.

And, she knew—she felt it in her heart—the love for him that had never died.

". . . establish trade with your rich and wealthy province, so that we may both profit thereby."

He was looking at the master again, still in command, the only sign that something had occurred a certain paleness high on his cheekbones. And Selena could gauge its meaning.

The maharajah considered it, but he had already decided.

"On those terms and under such conditions," he said, "you may approach and state your business in greater detail."

The men came forward then and took up standing positions before the throne. Sean did not look at her. She saw that he wanted to—her eyes did not leave him for one instant—but that he wished to maintain full composure. To do what he had come to do as best he could. And save the greater problem for later, when there would be time to consider it. He was passionate still, but more in control of it than he had been. Selena could understand that very well. The last time he had given in to the impulsive side of his nature, by granting money to the Rob Roys, it had earned him divestiture and exile. And caused him the loss of the love that had originally inspired his gift.

He looked fairly prosperous. He wore high riding boots, silver spurs, a tan riding suit, brown coat, and about his neck a yellow scarf, now streaked with dust from his trip. He held in his left hand a broad-brimmed hat, useful against sun and wind. With his right hand, he gestured easily as he put his proposition to the maharajah, who listened as if he understood.

"What we propose, sir," Sean said, combining at the same time a degree of respect with a courteous assumption of equality between the two of them, "is a threefold plan. One, we will purchase from you, at fair prices to be mutually determined, a quantity of your grain crops, for shipment to England and America, particularly England, which has a rising population and a fixed area of arable land. Second, we of the East India Company effect with you an exclusive contract, to be shared in no particular by any other country or company, which would allow us to market in your region any and all products of your desire that we may supply. . . ."

Selena saw the maharajah nodding. He understood. The matter did not sound too disadvantageous, if the terms could be worked out right. . . .

"Why do you think I have need of you?" he asked suddenly, in his most bored, most self-assured tone. "I possess wealth in forms and proportions of which you have not dreamed."

The chest of jewels, Selena thought. *He thinks his bragging will impress them.*

It did, but not in the way he had anticipated. Instead of inducing in Sean and the other merchants the kind of meek respect sought by the maharajah, it merely whetted their appetites.

"Frankly, we are interested in that, too," Sean said. "And, if you deal with us, your wealth might even be increased. Is the wherewithal of which you speak in liquid form?"

For a moment the maharajah sat there on his fantastic throne, with nothing but a blank look on his face. Then he motioned for Selena.

"What is this liquid of which he speaks?" he whispered to her.

"It is not that," she said, catching Sean's eyes as she bent her head to the master's. "He means do you have items of value that can be directly exchanged and maintain their same value. The jewels."

The maharajah nodded, feigning shrewdness.

"Yes, I have liquid," he said.

Selena saw the momentary look of bafflement from Sean, and then a glint of amusement in his eyes. *He thinks I rule this man,* she thought, greatly alarmed. *He thinks I rule him and that I am just as carefree and willful as I used to be.*

Nothing is as it appears to be! That was practically the first piece of advice she had received upon arriving in India, and nothing had occurred since then to prove it incorrect.

Now, watching Sean, she saw that his original shock, which had mixed love and concern and even anguish, fell away. And in its place she saw something terribly distressing: a look of amused congratulations! As if he were saying to her: "Well, you've made your mark again, and if it's what you want, more power to you."

Oh, God, he was slipping away already, and she hadn't even spoken to him.

"Our third proposal," Sean was saying, "is long-term in nature."

"In nature?" the maharajah interjected, thinking perhaps of grass and flowers.

". . . and is to occur over a period of years," Sean amended. "Beneath the ground there are often valuable materials, other than gold and silver, and so on, which are of use to us in the West. We wish to buy rights to these materials . . ."

"You want to buy my land?" the maharajah yelled. "What is this? I will not tolerate such . . ."

"They wish to pay money for metals beneath the earth," Selena spoke up. "The land will still be yours."

Distressed by Sean's reaction, she no longer cared about the protocol. Her voice was flat and even and dead. She caught Sean's look of bewilderment. Admiration for her authority and knowledge, but a reappraisal of her role in this palace. He was in doubt again, and that at least was good. He would not leave without trying to learn the full nature of her situation. Or predicament.

"The land will be mine, even after the money. So." The maharajah nodded agreeably. "Gentlemen," he continued, "I like what you say. Let me now provide you with rest and food, drink and shelter, and in the coming hours we shall discuss these things of which you speak. Perhaps you shall dine with me tonight? Yes, of course. And afterward, women. A gift to speed you into sleep. I have many."

His voice had hardened so imperceptibly that only Selena could have noticed. He pointed to her now, showing off a prize.

"But you may not have this one," he smiled. "She is mine. I do what I please with her, and she pleases me as well."

Had he seen her interest in Sean Bloodwell? The looks that had passed between them?

"So, we shall dine and talk further in the evening," he told them. "Now, go, and make known to my servants whatever it is you desire. I have everything."

Sean and his colleagues retreated, and were led out. The doors closed.

"So, my darling," the master said, "you served me well, and I will have further need of your mind. And your body," he added. "From now on, each night, it is you I wish to have with me."

Because of Sean Bloodwell? she wondered.

Yes, Davi answered her.

Without thinking, she looked at him. The maharajah caught the glance and scowled. Selena saw that he had guessed. Davi could read his mind, *and* speak with Selena. His lower lids squinted up and death was the sentence that flashed in his eyes. In time, that sentence would be carried out.

The master was twice jealous now.

Alone, before the evening banquet, Selena looked at herself. At her face and her body, reflected back at her from the polished wall of glass in the maharajah's bedchamber. Not so many minutes ago, that same revealing glass had shown her beneath the master himself, performing with art and cunning the exercises he had demanded of her. She had not been wrong about his reactions to the Europeans, and to Sean especially. He lost no time in asserting his ownership of her, his dominance over her. The lovemaking was quick and savage: its purpose had had nothing to do with love. Before leaving to dress for the banquet, he had bitten off a final order: "I want you to make sure those foreigners do not cheat me in these negotiations, especially regarding that strange lease of the underground. You will employ yourself this evening with their spokesman. I believe he is susceptible to you. But you will be with me tonight, of course. And every night for some time."

But his object was not love!

Then, standing before the mirror, she looked more deeply at herself. She looked into herself, and touched her soul, with the hopes and dreams dormant but still alive within. No one had ever escaped the harem, but then no one had enjoyed the possibility of receiving the aid of someone as resourceful as Sean Bloodwell. But would he help her? Certainly, he would. *If* he knew that she was being held here against her will. At this moment, though, he probably had the impression that she was here of her own volition. Hence his smile before the maharajah's throne. But no true Scot would leave a compatriot, much less the woman he loved, in bondage, if there was anything at all that could be done to set her free.

I will get out of here, she thought, her mind working furiously on a variety of plans.

It was the best of times to escape, with Sean and his colleagues there. But, on the other hand, rumors of war had led the master to increase the palace guard. Still, the Hindu night could hide a thousand things, and it might just be possible to flee. . . .

But she always kept coming back to one inescapable fact: she would be, each night, with the maharajah himself. And he did not wish to let her go. Then, too, what about the child? She could not leave her here.

Perhaps Sean would have an answer. Or Davi.

She proceeded to dress with extraordinary care, selecting a sari of pale blue. The color reminded her of Royce Campbell's eyes, and she felt hurt and guilty. Pulling her hair back, she bound it high with diamond-studded combs, in Rupal's style, and then touched rose water to her neck and shoulders, to the place between her breasts. In the mirror, she looked stunning, but she felt anxious and afraid, and not a little contrite. The sudden turns of life no longer appeared to be tangential, sending one off on a new course to uncharted territory. No, they now seemed curved, vastly curved in time. You would begin a journey to a far land, strange mountains, new people, but once you arrived there everything began to look familiar again, and you realized that leaving one's own heart was an impossibility. In

Scotland, she had not treated Sean with the respect and devotion he had clearly merited, not only as an outstanding and resilient man, but as her intended. That was her failure, and she accepted the culpability for it. Her passion for Royce had been as true as anything in her life, but now she saw—not too late, she hoped, for the lesson to do some good—what he had meant in telling her: "The plans that have been made for you and Sean will give you a life of meaning, rich with accomplishment. I held back from you because I did not wish to spoil that life." Royce, as wise as he was wild. *My problem,* Selena decided, *is that I lacked the will to shape my life even when I had the chance to do it. Now I must fight just to be free for a day. Well, so be it. I shall fight. And if heaven gives me a chance to undo the harm I have already done to Sean, I swear by all the stars in heaven I shan't let him down again.*

There was, too, a quiet moment of reflection, and a tear formed in the corners of her eyes as she thought—a thought strangely like a prayer—of Royce Campbell. But that had been, and it was ended. Perhaps, in the great plan of time, she had been given to him only for a moment, to become wiser, more mature, so that later she would possess gifts of truth and trust and character, gifts to bring to a good man and become one with him.

Davi appeared at the door. She could tell he was excited.

"The master is calling for you now," he said. "The guests are seated."

Selena took a deep breath and a last look into the mirror. She saw a beautiful young woman, whose eyes and face reflected fear and resolve, defiance and decision. And hope.

The maharajah had spared nothing in order to give the appearance of opulence and luxury. Guests reclined on soft, intricately embroidered cushions, placed before low tables laden with fruit juices, wines, breads, cheeses, vegetables, fish, and the prime delicacy from the kitchens of Jabal-Mahal: tiny birds stuffed with sweet berries and basted in brown-sugar sauce. These were eaten whole, by holding the tiny talons, and severing the legs with one's teeth. The six guests, dressed in robes provided by the maharajah, looked up as Selena entered with the master. She saw immediately how the evening had been arranged. There were seven of the low tables in the room, and a European alone at six of them. Harem concubines, attired in their best, stood about the room, waiting to serve as companions, should it be the master's will. Those not selected for this task, would dance, make music, carry trays of dishes and food. And, along the walls, behind the six tables, were closed, tentlike canopies, to which the honored guests might retire at will with a woman. She guessed that the men were naked beneath their silk robes.

The seventh table, slightly elevated, was for the maharajah. And for Selena.

Davi guided them to it and seated them. The maharajah clapped his hands, and six of the concubines moved forward and seated themselves next to the guests. Selena saw their expressions, which ranged from surprise to amusement to outright delight. Sean Bloodwell, however, looked as if he had expected it, and she began to wonder—with a proprietary twinge of jealousy—how often this sort of thing had happened to him in his business dealings. His concubine was Ashina, who was sly and willowy and who knew how to captivate a man.

"This is how I have arranged it," the master told her quietly. "I myself will not deign to cavil and debate with them regarding mundane affairs. But, after the dinner is well begun, you will circulate, speak to each of them, and bring me news of their specific offers. Take your time. Do not appear anxious. And be cautious and detailed with the big fellow over there. I have given him Ashina, but he looks a man who would keep his head, even with the best of women."

She saved Sean for last. The music had already begun, and the visitors were heavy with food and drink when Selena approached Sean's table. The five Englishmen had been eager to speak with her, to ask her questions—many of them highly personal—about her role in the palace, but she had turned them aside, making it appear to them that she was only a hostess asking after their pleasure. Thus, she had contrived to spend little time with them, in order to have as much time as possible with Sean.

She caught Ashina's pouty glance as the other woman moved off. Selena sat down across the table from Sean

Bloodwell. Their eyes met for a long time, and her heart stuck in her throat. She could not think of a word to say. Initially reserved, amused, he saw her blinking back the tears. And, at that instant, she saw that he had understood her situation. He did not yet know how she had gotten there, and he did not need to know. That would come later. All that mattered now was that she was there against her will, and hated it, and had to escape.

"I didn't think it was in the Scottish blood to carry on so at the sight of an old acquaintance," he said, with a slight smile, as if to say *cheer up* and *hold on*. Then he lapsed into the idiom to distract her while she got her emotions under control: "'O'd e'er a thought a future member o' t' 'Ouse o' Lairds 'd be a sittin' east o' nowhere, naked as a jaybird in a body kilt an' chewin' off the heads o' little birds . . ."

"Oh, Sean!"

"Careful, Selena. That rajah of yours is giving us the evil eye. I've known my share of them, and when the chips are down they're all deadly as cobras. Almost like England, wouldn't you say?" he added. Then, loudly, abruptly: "A lease is a lease, young lady. You drive too hard a bargain!"

She was surprised for a moment, more at the sound of his voice than anything else. Then she grasped his ploy.

"My master must retain control!" she said, loudly, too, and slightly angry, then looked around, as if embarrassed, and lowered her voice.

"I must speak to you of . . . of personal things. But I need answers about the business things to take back to . . . him."

She inclined her head slightly and indicated the maharajah, who had called Ashina to his side, and was listening to music and stroking her hair, and whose attention, subtly concealed, was on his golden-haired mistress.

"We must speak quickly," she told him. "This may be our only chance."

"Do you want to get out of here?" was the first thing he asked, meanwhile bringing his fist down upon the table as if making an intractable merchant's demand.

"Oh, God," she said.

He smiled. "Well. I was just starting to make a bit of

money, and I run into you again. Maybe I didn't do so well in my last karma, as the natives say . . ."

But he saw her face fall, and returned to the situation. He spoke fast. "All right, Selena. Jabalpur is only Jabalpur. There are other territories, as the drummer says. This is my situation. I can remain here for tonight, then two more days and nights. I might be able to return next year . . ."

Next year!

". . . if I've made some real money by then, and try to buy your way out. But your best chance, if you can make it, is to get away now. My partners and I work for the East India Company. We're adventurers, and doing quite well at it, though by no means as well as I did in Scotland . . ."

His face darkened for a moment at the memory, but he shrugged it off.

". . . but that is my problem. If you can get outside the walls tonight or on the next two nights, we'll leave right away. For Bombay. You see, Robert Clive, the former head of the company, blew his head off last year. The glory days of making a quick fortune are gone. Warren Hastings, the new head, is a splendid man, but too cautious, too political. The grand times are over in East India. My partners and I thought we'd just head down the Narbada River and see what we could open up in West India, and, you never know, I'd like to take the money I have and make a break for America. Once those rebels are brought under control and the situation is stabilized, well, *there's* a continent that has a penny or two for a good man to make. . . ."

He read her expression.

"Yes, Selena. I'm loyal to the Crown." The steel was in his voice. "I'll have that title yet. I'll have it, and I'll go back to Scotland and claim all that was taken from me!"

Their desires were identical. They wanted restoration, honor, position. But they had different perspectives, different emotions. It hardly mattered. They shared one overriding impulse.

The hardness left his face, his voice. "Selena, I've thought of you a thousand times. And I've never stopped loving you. What horror befell you, to bring you here?"

Nor had she ever loved him more, either. "I was stupid," she said. "But I won't be again. If you can help me to escape from here, may I . . . may I go with you?"

Just a tiny skeptical flash in his eyes just then. He knew her.

"*Be* with you," she said. "Yours. Not only to make it up to you," she added. "But now I am able to bring with me something that we both need, and something that was taken from you in the past."

"You?" he asked doubtfully. "That is more than sufficient, but . . ."

"Money," she said. "And I earned it."

This time the steel was in her tone, and he appreciated the quality of it, the hard, flinty self-knowledge and courage revealed in it. But he did not seem to think there was much to her promise. In fact, it didn't matter. For Sean, she was enough.

"For the second time in my life," he told her, "and, God, how I wish I could stretch my arms across this table, and . . . For the second time in my life, I will take a risk for you. *If* you can get away from here on one of the next three nights. I haven't the men to . . ."

"I understand." Selena thought fast. The little girl. "There's also a baby," she said.

"*Still not enough*!" he cried, for the master's benefit. "A child?" he asked.

"Not mine, although I sometimes wish she were. I can't explain it now. But she will have to come, too."

"All right. I've made my decision. I will do what I can. But . . ." and in his eyes appeared the slightly analytical remove that told Selena he remembered what she had been, how she had acted in Scotland, ". . . but, when I bring you from here, we are equals. I have never deceived you, and you must never . . ."

Her welling tears, as genuine as love, stopped him.

"How will I meet you?"

"*Ah, now we are reaching agreements*," he said, expansively.

The maharajah looked over and smiled tightly. He pushed Ashina gently away from him. She would have to be ready to reward this fine European entrepreneur for yielding to the perquisites of Indian deities.

"I have one friend. A black man called Davi. You see him there behind the master . . ."

"I forbid you to call him that. To a Scot . . ."

"I know. We are one in that belief. My slavemaster. If, tonight, I cannot be at a place by the palace wall where you will find a white cross with the name Gayle on it, then come back tomorrow night. And, if not that night, the third. I will send Davi in my stead . . ."

"But after three nights, I cannot promise . . ."

"I understand."

"But next year . . ."

"*There will be no next year,*" she said, each word a chiseled letter in a piece of stone. "I am going to live again, I am going to be free, and I am going to make my life what it was meant to be.

"*Without hurting you anymore,*" she added. "*No deceptions.*"

It seemed to her that the voices in the room, the laughter, even the persistent flutes, grew still when she spoke. But it was only the effect of the blood rushing to her head, dulling her ears, as she said what she truly believed.

"Selena," he said, "you are instinctive. You are a natural force. You would not willfully hurt someone any more than a typhoon would. Now we must get you out of here, and have the life and position we were meant to have. I shall be at the place of the cross, three nights running. Name a time."

"Two in the morning," Selena said.

"I will speak to my colleagues and we shall be there, ready to flee. I shall seize the sky for my father and yours, mark my words! And I shall have you, too." He paused. "And you shall have me. In total honesty. Fair and square."

"Fair and square," Selena said.

The truth of his promise was in his eyes. When one bargained with Sean Bloodwell, one knew that he would keep his word and never falter, until the terms of the agreement were violated by one of the partners to it. But he would not be the partner guilty of the transgression.

The plans for escape were settled now, but all the risks were yet ahead. "Tell your slavemaster," Sean said, "that we need time to think matters over. Tell him it may take as much as three days. And," he added, knowing the politics of the region, "bring to bear all the pressure you can. Tell him we might even be able to make a better bargain with

Rajasthan. We need not be hasty. It might serve us well to wait. Rajasthan will possess his territory if they make war against him and triumph. Tell him he had best bargain with us quickly if he wishes the support of British troops."

"British troops? Can you bring some here?"

"No," he said, "but the maharajah doesn't know that. In the meantime, it will keep him confused. Now, tell him."

"Take those messages to your master!" he thundered, making it appear as if he had made his final offer.

"At the cross at two," he whispered. "Three nights running."

Then she returned to the maharajah's table, passing the smiling Ashina, who planned to enjoy Sean as much as he enjoyed her. Selena made her face into a mask as she watched the concubine lead her own man, so long lost, into the canopy provided for the purpose. Servants drew the curtains closed.

Davi was watching. He knew. Selena had risked her life now, irrevocably. And his, too.

Sean was already coupled with the lithe, supple body of the concubine, Ashina. Near to Selena, but far away. She would see him no more, until they met at Gayle's cross on the hill, by night. If they did not meet there, through some mischance or tragedy, they might never meet again. She could not bear to think of it, with freedom so close, with love once again beating inside her. Upon command, she retreated to the master's bedchamber, imaged in the mirrors, purveying such delights as he savored, spectator to the whore's art. When she did *this,* he sighed. When she did that, he *moaned.* And when she did the cunning things, he died the little death. She hated it. There was no emotion in it at all.

All right, I've had to survive, she thought, *but when I leave here I shall be only for Sean. We are apart, but already together.*

She worried most about revealing—by a gesture, a look, a quiver in her voice—that she had a plan to escape. Already, she was certain the maharajah regarded her more suspiciously than usual, even now, when he was satiated, lying beside her. She fought to stay calm.

"So the big fellow gave me three days to think it over,

did he?" the master asked lazily. "And what was your estimate of him?"

"I thought he was hard to deal with," she said.

"I didn't mean quite that," he returned, reaching over and kneading her breast possessively. "I wondered if you were as taken with him as you seemed."

Had it been that obvious?

"You know that I am yours," she told him, cringing inside, giving him a sensual caress. "My rapt attention was designed to lull his suspicions. And I did learn of the possibility that he might be able to supply you with troops, should Rajasthan attack . . ."

He let out some sort of Hindu oath and moved away from her. Mention of the war reminded him of all his troubles.

"Yes," he snapped, "and now you see! Had it not been for you and Davi, and that so-called trial of yours, none of this would have happened, and everything would have gone on as before. Perhaps I was right all along. Certain things should not be known. Knowledge causes more problems than existed previously."

"You could have gone on not knowing who killed Gayle?"

"I think so. I have the child to remind me of the happy times. And when she grows up . . ."

He did not finish. He did not have to. And, with a growing sense of horror and incredulity, Selena grasped what he had in mind for tiny no-name: a horrible form of sexual reincarnation. Now she could not fail to take the child with her. In fact, if the child did not go with her, she would have to remain, to protect her, and try to escape later.

Now, if she angered him—a little, but not too much—he might send her away, and she could start the plan . . .

"Knowledge is never a problem. It is what you do with it. And it was you who insisted on pulling out Ku-Fel's tongue and sending her back to her homeland in disgrace. And now such rashness may bring a war. . . ."

"Silence, woman! You know nothing of our ways. There were things I had to do."

"You wish me to leave?"

His eyes turned crafty, and he encircled her waist with his arm. His skin was hot against her naked belly.

368   FLAMES OF DESIRE

"So that you can share your delights with the Britisher?"

"He's not British, he's Scot . . ." she said without thinking.

His eyes were hard with a knowledge she did not like at all. Anger. Jealousy.

"In future, I believe I shall deal directly with the trader," he snapped. "Take from your mind any ideas, my bright one, of seeing that man again. And if you so much as try . . ." His hand was on her throat, tightening menacingly. ". . . I shall have you impaled upon a spear and set in the market of Jabalpur. You may think you writhe well for me here in my bed, but you have no idea how poetically a woman twists and moans when she is lanced by the impaler's spear."

He meant every word of it. She saw that angering him had done no good, but merely made him more suspicious.

"May I check on the child?" she asked.

"She is fine. The nurses are with her. Do you wish to leave me?"

"No, no, of course not. I only . . ." And to distract him, she moved close into an embrace and tried to stir his lust.

"No more tonight," he said, pushing her away. "Let us sleep. My cares are many, and tomorrow will be trying."

But he slept restlessly, and Selena lay rigidly beside him, waiting for an opportunity to slip away. It never came.

At noon of the following day, Selena was brooding in the nursery. True to his word, the master had forbidden her to leave his wing of the palace. The little girl was playing happily with some of the Indian children of the maharajah, when Davi entered.

"Were you able to see him?" she asked excitedly. "What did he say?"

Davi looked grim. "He was disappointed, of course. But there is another matter."

"Yes?"

"Your man's colleagues have refused to support him in abducting you. They refuse to take the risk. He will be alone."

She thought of Sean and herself, alone in Central India, five hundred miles from Bombay and the sea. He would have but one horse, probably, and the baby with them . . .

"But again he will be there tonight. His fellows did agree to stall the master for another two days. Your other problem is Ku-Fel."

"Ku-Fel! What do you mean?"

"The Rajasthan army is approaching. Slowly. But there is no doubt of it now. They are coming in force, and Ku-Fel herself rides at the head of the columns."

The fact struck Selena with the force of a blow. Even if she and Sean were able to escape the palace, they would still have to elude an army that was swarming toward Jabalpur. An army led by someone who would be indisposed to let her go anywhere but to the land of the dead. Slowly, at that.

"I have thought of this matter," Davi was saying. "I have considered the situation—the Sherpas, the security, and the closeness with which you are watched. There is something you must do, if you are to be free."

She looked at him, waited.

"There are times when to do such a thing is necessary," he was saying. "And there are times when it is just. As in the instance of Haruppa . . ."

Murder! He was speaking of murder, but whose?

"To be free, you may have to kill him," Davi said.

Murder the maharajah in his bed. No. She could not do it.

"I will be able to create a diversion of some sort," he was telling her. "You can leave that to me. I shall be able to free the way for you, at least for a short time. But, to get out, you may have to . . ."

"I couldn't. I couldn't! I'll wait until he is asleep, and then . . ."

"I know that you wish it to be done without harm to him, but think of what it is you are going to have to do. First, you must somehow flee the bedchamber itself. Then you must make your way to the nursery, take the child in spite of its nurses, and go to the outer wall . . ."

There was another thing, too, Selena was thinking, not even forming the words in her mind. But Davi was worried enough already. If he thought she had yet another task to perform before she left the palace, he might retreat into the paralyzing fear that he had learned over the years.

". . . and, even there, your problems have only begun. So you must be ready to do what is necessary."

Good advice. Hard advice. She remembered how it had been at Foinaven Lodge, the blade in her hand, Darius McGrover's eyes fixed upon hers. She had failed that time. McGrover must have laughed at her lack of nerve. She had not done what was necessary, and he had come after her. Even now, somewhere, he must walk the earth, forgetting nothing.

She remembered Captain Randolph and Roberta, climbing the mast, pursued by rats, and the *Meridian* sinking, spinning in the vortex of the sea. She would have tried to throw them a line, but Royce Campbell had stopped her.

You must rid yourself of enemies, he had said. *That's why you've come to this.*

An exile. An outcast. A slave who must tremble before the casual mercies of strange masters . . .

"You wish to be free," Davi said. "And you wish to live your dream, returning home one day . . ."

"But I don't know if I can do it."

He said no more, and simply looked at her.

"You must decide. After that, I shall help in whatever way is necessary."

She nodded.

The day passed, and Selena was in turmoil. No, it *must* be possible to escape without doing murder! And if she had to do it, how might it be done? Could she? McGrover had eluded her just by looking into her eyes and daring the blade. By dinner, she was sorely distressed and several of the concubines took note of it.

"Why, Selena," one said spitefully, "is it your time? You look so pale and thin, with all the blood gone."

The others cackled gleefully.

And when it came time for Davi to summon the woman of the master's choice, he passed down along the tables to Ashina's place and whispered to her!

Did the maharajah know what she was planning? How was that possible? Unless Davi . . .

"I do not know," Davi told her later. "He said 'Ashina.' That's all. You are to spend the night in the nursery."

And so the second night was lost, under guard of far

more Sherpas than was necessary to watch one woman and a babe. Selena could not sleep, and instead knelt for a long time by the child's crib, watching her sleep, watching her grasp the blanket with her tiny hands. Watching her sigh quietly in her sleep, blissfully ignorant of all the happiness life had already bestowed upon her, and of all the danger yet to come.

Danger may come but harm shall not, Selena decided then. She would do whatever must be done. Death would be better than to live in slavery.

"Davi," she told him in the morning, "take the master a message. Tell him that tonight I have a new delight for him, that he has never experienced with any lover before. Did you see Sean at the place of the cross last night?"

"Yes, and he grows anxious for your safety, for tomorrow he must leave without you."

"That will not be. We are leaving together. And the child, too. You offered your help, but I must warn you it is dangerous. Will you do it?"

"I will," he said, with just the slightest tremor.

"Then tonight we move," she said. "Together. One. There is no more love than that."

"I only hope that I have love enough," he mourned.

"You do," she said, and embraced him as she would have a child. Then, with total trust, she told him her plan. He listened, his tragic eyes wide, dark upon the risk of it, the dangerous unpredictability.

"So you begged for my attention, did you?" smirked the maharajah that night, lounging on his love couch. "And what can you give me that I have not already experienced?"

"You shall see," Selena smiled, and allowed the wisp of gown to slip down from her shoulders, off her breasts, hips, and to the floor.

"You are beautiful, as always," he admired. "But promises must be kept as well as made." He drew aside his own clothing.

"Come. There is much to do. We may begin the battle with Rajasthan tomorrow, after the executions."

The word startled her, but she managed to control herself.

"Executions?"

"I am killing the Englishmen," he said. "All of them. They made mention of troops, but none are forthcoming, and . . ."

"But if it was a promise, they would keep it," she said hastily. "It is a long way from Bengal, and . . ."

He looked at her and narrowed his eyes. "What do you care?" he asked.

"I . . . why, not at all," she said, and let her hands languorously fall across her breasts, down her stomach and thighs. His eyes followed.

"Yes, and the English will be gone, and I will crush Rajasthan, keep the dowry, and once again the world shall be mine. Now, proceed."

It is going to happen now, she thought. *Davi! Be ready!*

He lay back, amused and expectant. She knelt before him, leaned over him. Then, from a small pouch of beige leather, which she had brought into the bedchamber—she had told him that it contained his "surprise"—Selena withdrew a tiny jar and unscrewed the top. Inside was a pungent cream, a small dab of which she touched to her fingertips.

"You must relax," she soothed. "Lie back and relax. You must enjoy every sensation."

He did, and Selena first touched a small drop of the cream to the smooth red tip of him. He sighed in pleasure and writhed slightly. The cream, she knew, would be tingling his skin, an effect that was hot and cold at the same time. Ku-Fel had given her the cream months ago, for use on a special night.

This night was nothing if not special.

Slowly, listening to his moans, she touched dabs of cream to several places on his parts, and then, even more slowly, she moved from one dab of cream to the next, gently rubbing the sweet salve into his flesh. His breath came faster, a keening, almost a gasp.

You made me your whore for pleasure, she thought, nerving herself for the moment. She glanced at the beige pouch. It was open and waiting. The decision was up to her. *Master!* she thought, with trembling scorn. *I accept no master unless it be for love.*

Now he was covered with the stinging cream, and she

moved her hands in soft, wide, sweeping arcs over his belly and thighs, now and then touching his sex. When she did not touch the parts to which she had applied the cream, they would burn with a delicious fire. And when she did touch them, his skin would turn suddenly cold. Even now, he was on the brink of release, but holding back, not wishing it to end. His eyes were closed, and he writhed in delicious agony upon the couch, sobbing with sensual joy.

Selena took a final breath and reached into the wallet.

She leaned forward slightly, and brought down upon him the deep, startling coldness of her kiss. His body thrust upward to meet her mouth, and deeply she held him with the ice-and-diamond glitter of her teeth.

And she brought down into his heart, into the smooth brown chest, the blade that had to fall if freedom waited.

For one long, exquisite, agonizing moment, he lay still. It seemed there was not even pain, or perhaps a pain so piercing that it transcended experience, an ecstacy such as had been given no man before.

He lifted his head, face distorted with the torture of release, and his essence left him. His manhood thrust upward from his groin, joined to Selena. The dagger thrust upward from his heart, joined to Selena as well. Death and life together, at one perfect instant. And in an instant, twice released.

His eyes fluttered, glazed.

The breath went out of him.

She opened and let him fall away from her, releasing her hand as well. The twin juices of his body fell and flowed.

Davi, it is done! she cried, barely believing. *Be ready!*

My life is yours, Davi told her with his mind.

For a long moment she stood there over the dead man, not courageous enough to tear her eyes away. She was fascinated; she was transfixed. His beautiful body, his almost perfect face turned into stone. It was obscene. Moments ago, this man's blood had throbbed through his veins, hot for her, and his breath had come keening. And now his body was still, eerie and premonitory, and he did not move. She had done that to it. *It.* She had done it not because of the body, but because of the alien force that had occupied his mind, a force, a will, that promised her luxury and pleasure. Humiliation and debasement.

I'm sorry, she said to him. *You had my body because there was no choice. But you never had my spirit, and it was not right for you to try to possess it.*

Sometimes it is necessary, Davi had said.

You must learn to rid yourself of enemies, Royce had said.

Well, she had done that, and he lay dead before her; he could do nothing to stop her now. Yet all around the two of them lay Jabal-Mahal, with its myriad strangenesses and dangers, like a living body outside his dead soul. Waiting to take revenge upon her. Waiting to even the score, as Roxanne had said all scores were evened, in due course.

If you waited long enough.

The Hindu night. The human heart. The dark, curved bowl of the universe. Trackless aeons, nameless stars. All of history and time. In the daytime, when the call comes and the heart yearns to be free, or in the nighttime when the blood leaps toward forever, then, then, striding the earth or sailing high upon the sea or riding on the very wind of God, *then* we shall take the world into our hands and fling it toward the stars.

And then we shall seize the sky!

Make yourself an instrument of your desires. Sean Bloodwell.

A person defines himself by choices that are free. Her father.

There is no defeat unless you believe it.

That was Selena, and she left the dead man where he was, heading for the nursery where the child slept. The child was the second thing. There were four things she had to do.

Davi was as good as his word.

Selena approached the nursery, and he was there, braced straight to his full five feet, conversing with the Sherpas. Or, rather, he was goading them, angering them, distracting them.

"Are your people descended from the gorillas in the Himalayas?" he was asking one of them. "You Sherpas look like gorillas, did you ever notice that?"

The big warriors, dumbfounded, looked at one another, as if they could not believe what they were hearing.

Davi knew what was coming, had to know, but his heart

was set and his mind hard. He did not tremble or show
fear. He saw Selena without seeming to, and she slipped
behind the guards and into the nursery.

"Why, you little black monkey bastard," growled one of
the guards, "you dare say something like that again and
I'll use your face to mop the floor."

"We'll crush you like a fly, birdbrain," snorted another.
Selena closed the door.

"Ten Sherpas equal the brain of a bird," Davi was saying, "so you ought to be very familiar with . . ."

She heard a grunt, and then running.

Go. Now, Davi told her with his mind. *It is all right.*

Quickly, she walked over to the cradle, reached down,
slid her arms under the little girl's sleep-limp body, and
lifted her up. The child stirred, gave a soft cry, but did not
awaken. She slept close to Selena's shoulder. She herself
wore only a plain sari, and the child had on a light gown.
Taking a blanket, she drew it around the girl, and moved
to the door. Paused. Opened it. Far down the corridor, enraged Sherpas were pursuing little Davi. He was taking
them into the front courtyard, which was opposite the wall
at which Sean waited . . .

And then she stopped stock-still. Executions! The maharajah had told her he was ordering the execution of the
English trading party. Did that mean Sean was already in
custody, under arrest, in the hold beneath the palace which
held men and women who displeased the master?

Go! cried Davi's mind, reverberating in her own.

No time to think of it. Thought was useless now. She
opened the door, hurried down into another unfamiliar
wing. She had only seen it once before. From all sides now,
she heard a great commotion, shouting, cries of glee. Outside, bivouacs of soldiers, on the watch for Ku-Fel, set up a
hue and cry. Men were running somewhere ahead of her.
She ducked into an archway, and they pounded past her,
laughing.

"The Dravidian's gone crazy," one of them chortled,
running. "He offended Bo-Huk and called him a gorilla.
They've got Davi out in the courtyard now, I understand.
It should be quite a show."

Selena said a wordless prayer for the tiny black man at
the mercy of these barbarians, then eased out of her hiding

place. The coast was clear. The child cried once, as if dreaming. Selena walked hastily, seeking her goal, but tried to keep from breaking into a run.

Be there, Sean, she thought. *Oh, please be there*!

She went far down into the depths of the wing, and the crying and shouting from the courtyard seemed to diminish. But she knew that was only illusory. Pictured in her mind was little Davi, dashing among the soldiers, giving them their sport, but seeking escape even as he served as a diversion for her own.

She did not want to think of it.

Then she was there. The great doors gleamed in the night, unguarded, and open to all her dreams. She had to hurry; it must be at least two already. She tried them, and the doors parted. Holding the child with one arm, she moved back a section of the heavy curtain that shut out the light on all this glory.

The chest was exactly where it had been, in the center of the room, set on a small, slightly elevated platform, like a sacred object upon an altar. Carefully, she laid the little girl down next to it, and opened the mahogany casket, the breath going out of her once again in the presence of such beauty, such vast wealth. Even in the dimness, the angular facets of diamonds glittered like the eyes of the devil. Bloodred rubies regarded her, hypnotic in their power. Time stopped, and it was all she could do to reach out, touch those cold hard chunks of power, feel the frigid arrogance of them against her fingertips. The girl moved on the floor and coughed. Hurry. She dipped both hands into the casket. The jewels rattled one against another like ice. She brought up a great handful of them, dipped down again, let the stones fall. *Selena, hurry. You must hurry*! But one final time she bent and reached down into the chest, trying to hold them all, trying to *embrace* the very essence of wealth. Up came her arms, fairly hugging the glitter to her breasts. And up with the jewels came something else.

White and rounded, with black holes and glittering teeth. Gayle's skull.

Diamonds struck the marble floor, spun off into the darkness, and Selena leaped up and cried out. The child awoke, afraid, and began to cry.

Now you've done it, idiot. Keep your head.

She had dropped the skull, and it looked up at her balefully, accusingly, from the floor beside the chest. She understood, of course. The maharajah had permitted burial of the skeleton, but, as a memento, secreted this relic with the rest of his prizes.

Far away, the shouting rose, and in her mind she felt Davi trying to reach her, but his message was cut off by his confusion and pain.

"Éna?" sobbed the child. "Éna?"

"It's all right, dearest. In a minute, it will be all right."

Gayle watched then, as Selena bent down to the floor and swept her hands upon the cold smoothness of it, gathering to herself what scattered stones she could. There was neither time nor light to look; she simply swept whatever she could reach into a corner of the blanket, fashioned a pocket, and tied it securely.

"All right," she said, picking up the little girl, drawing the blanket around her. The corner with the stones was heavy; it hung down and bounced against her thighs as she walked.

A horrible lancing shadow of pain came into her mind, and a silent scream. They had begun to inflict on Davi whatever torture had been selected. The yelling warriors would be milling around, not wanting to miss anything.

She knew then that she would make it to the wall.

Davi, she cried, sobbing aloud, *Davi, there is no way to thank you.*

She was running now, out of the wing of the palace and across the smooth lawn, the grass dull and brown in the winter. The little girl, startled by her flight, had stopped crying, and chuckled to herself, as if this were some funny kind of night game.

Once again, Davi's pain split her head. Ahead was the wall, the finely worked metal spires and scrolls set in white stone, with enough space to slip through easily. It was not, as in Europe, a wall to protect the people within, but rather to decorate the palace. A thing of beauty to gaze upon. Selena slipped between the bars, and out onto the high hill that looked toward the east. The white cross was there, eerie, almost luminescent in the night.

It is you . . ." Davi tried, and again she felt the shadow of an incredible surge of pain. Far off, she could see the

FLAMES OF DESIRE

bonfire of the troops, and something seemed to be rising out of their mass, something being lifted.

The baby began to cry again, frightened by the darkness and the haste. Selena looked around. There was no sign of Sean.

It is you who should be . . .

She could hear his screaming, far away in the courtyard. *Oh, God, what are they doing to him? Where is Sean?*

The shadows on the slopes of the hill led only to darkness and the valley below. Selena turned first one way, then another, fighting panic. Reaching the wall was the fourth thing, and the last. He *had* to be here. They had to be free now.

It is you who should be thanked, Davi said at last, and the bonfires in the courtyard illuminated his wriggling black body. He was thrust up over the heads of the raucous Sherpas, impaled on a pole, dying. He had been fortunate. The Sherpas, exuberant, careless, had jammed the pole in too far, or overestimated the length of his small body. The point of the stake had touched his heart, and, bearing his full weight, the sharp point pierced it.

I did love, he called to her, dying. *I did. Against all odds. Because of you. I leave my life in expectation of happy rebirth. Now, go. Fulfill your karma.*

There was no more, and the sudden, angry groan of disappointment from the courtyard told her that Davi had returned to the mind of Vishnu, out of which the world had come.

His body, a husk that had always been too small to contain his power, his spirit, now shivered one last time upon the pole, quiet as his heart.

Selena began to cry again, but stopped, not wanting to upset the child. She heard an odd pounding down along the wall.

The soldiers in the courtyard quieted suddenly. An instant of shame, a vestige of humanity that was still in their hard hearts, forced their eyes upward at the tiny black martyr. Then they forgot about him, and the shouting began again.

The pounding rounded the corner of the palace wall, and appeared in the form of a galloping horse, rider leaning into the wind, giving free rein. Sean. Even in the darkness she saw that he was in rags. He pulled the horse to a skidding stop, and instantly, his strong arm reached down and pulled them, woman and child, up on the horse with him. Just as quickly, as if he had not stopped at all, they were galloping again, Selena holding on to his strong body, holding on to the little girl, who was too stunned by this odd, rhythmic movement to make a sound.

Down the great hill they went, beginning a long circle that would carry them into the west.

"An army is coming in this direction," she tried to tell him.

He nodded but it made no difference. He seemed to have decided something. He was totally his own man now. He was free, and that was what mattered. Then they were heading due west and he slowed the horse a little.

"Where are we going?"

He laughed, delighted, determined.

"Bombay!" he cried. "And that's the first stop. There are two more. America. Then, although it may take a little time, home. And you are coming with me."

He was so exultant, so confident, Selena herself forgot about the five-hundred-mile trek to Bombay, and all the years ahead. It would be. They *would* return to Scotland. It would be because he said it would be. She pressed her cheek into his back, and laughed, delighting the child. It was going to happen! She grasped it now. She was free! "*Aaaaaaiiiiiieeeeeeee!*" Selena cried, and it was a blood call of joy, pure joy and the thrill of wonder, a sound such as she had heard Royce Campbell make when he readied the cannons aboard the *Highlander*. The horse galloped on under the Indian sky, and the sound of its hooves struck the pebbles of the roadway. But Selena did not mark this. She was no longer in the Orient. Whatever years lay ahead in her journey, they were gone now. They had already passed. She and Sean were home now, together, in Scotland. Fog drifted in off the North Sea and hung in the gardens of Coldstream, where once Father had built her a house that reached the sky. Bees hummed above the heather of the moors, and in the smoky Highlands . . .

Finally, Sean reined in the horse, to let it rest. He leaped from the mount, and helped Selena and the little girl down.

"Are you sure she's not yours?" he asked, smiling,

touching the bright yellow hair. The child, quiet, looked up at him and smiled. A bond had been formed between man and child just that quickly, a bond that was to alter all their lives.

"She is ours now," Selena said.

With the baby still in her arms, they embraced and kissed. He saw her looking at his clothes.

"All I could find," he said. "I had no hope of meeting you tonight. I'd been arrested and placed in what passes here for a dungeon."

"How did you get out?"

"Luck of the draw," he said. "Or maybe God. Whatever. A Sherpa rushed in and said the maharajah had been killed. Stabbed in the heart. Chaos overtook the place. Somebody was being killed in the courtyard. Exactly as I would have been tomorrow. The six of us seized the opportunity and broke out. I mounted the first horse I saw. I hope my friends' luck has been as good as mine. I'd also like to thank whoever put the dirk in that maharajah. He confused the guards and gave us our chance."

"She," Selena said.

"What?"

"Thank *her*," Selena said. "A kiss will do."

The little girl laughed.

"Or you can make love to her. When the time comes, a kiss will be extraordinarily insufficient."

He understood. "My God, Selena, I never . . ."

She smiled, at peace for the first time in so long.

". . . you . . . you killed for me . . . ?"

"No, for us. For you and me and the child."

"What's her name?"

"Davina," she answered. "And we're free."

He frowned, just a touch of a wrinkle on his forehead. "What's the matter?"

"Free is all we are. A little cash would speed our trip."

Selena smiled, handed the child to him, and, as he held her, she untied the knot in the corner of the blanket, cradling the contents carefully in her hands. He looked but said nothing. He could not speak. Even Davina was fascinated by the colored stones, in which the light danced and shone.

"I have made it up to you," she said softly, herself trans-fixed, hypnotized, by the jewels. "I have paid you back."

He continued to stare at the glorious stones. The world was there in her hands, in the tattered corner of a baby's blanket. All the world was theirs.

"God, Selena," he sighed at last, "they must be worth a million pounds. How did you get them?"

"I earned them," she said with just a trace of bitterness.

Already, Coldstream Castle was close enough to touch.

Part Three

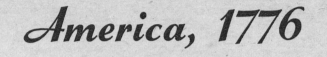

America, 1776

A FAREWELL TO SADNESS

It was Ku-Fel's rapacity and bloodlust that saved the three fugitives. Not yet knowing of the maharajah's death, driven by a fierce desire for revenge, she flogged her army onward, marching them hard even in the night. Sean and Selena could hear the columns advancing on Jabalpur, hear the songs of the soldiers as they slogged along, and the high honking calls of the armored warrior elephants. They had plenty of time to find concealment, and Sean camouflaged for them a shelter in a deep, leafy ravine, not far from the route of march. Trees of night wrapped them within a protective shroud, from which they saw Ku-Fel pass by, astride the thick gray neck of an elephant. She leaned forward, as if to move the beast along faster. Her torchlit face shone tongueless, transcendent, looking neither left nor right.

"The Indian gods have decided to let us pass," Selena whispered. "It seems we have proven ourselves worthy."

She remembered her prayer at Gayle's grave, and how Davi had assured her that the gods always listened to a genuine prayer. So she said another now, of thanksgiving. They slept that night in the sweet-smelling thicket, not far from the Narbada River, and the child lay between them, happy, quiet, and content. In the morning, they rode westward along the riverbank until the horse tired. Then Sean approached the pilot of a river raft and, showing him the tiniest sliver of a diamond, contracted with the man to take them all the way downstream to Daman, whence Selena had first come to Jabalpur. They boarded immediately, and the pilot's zeal in speeding them on their way was exceeded only by the glitter of the diamond in his eyes.

The current was fast and true, and in weeks they reached the yellow coast, three blond Westerners, gazed upon by the small dark natives as if they were indeed children of the sun. Selena almost believed it to be true. A new beginning had come to them, and she wished to be worthy of it. So, after contemplating the matter for a long time, she decided to be truthful with Sean about Royce Campbell. He had not asked about the Highlander, nor even mentioned him, so Selena wisely guessed his rival must be on Sean's mind. When first she'd told him about her transport from Liverpool to the Canary Islands to India, she had said only that a "sea captain" had saved her and then died of plague. Now, as the river craft neared Daman, beyond which lay Bombay and passage west, she decided upon absolute truth. She did not know what Sean's reaction might be, but she wanted everything to be understood between them, nothing to linger from the past.

It was the morning of their arrival in Daman. During the river trip aboard the cluttered raft, there had been no chance for real discussion, much less intimacy. And, in truth, the tension of the journey, and their constant doubts as to safety, made speech difficult. Words had seemed unnecessary, though, for there was an unquestioned bond between them. Now, however, it was time to speak.

She steeled her resolve and approached him just as the pilot guided the craft out of one of the delta channels and into the harbor of Daman. Sean was standing by the ramshackle rail, holding Davina, teasing her with a jeweled trinket that swung from a chain. The sun caught it, light danced. Davina's tiny hand flashed to hold it. The jewel spun away. She chortled and gurgled, delighted with the game.

Sean grinned as Selena approached. "They say if you show diamonds or gold to a girl-child, she has a destiny of wealth. Did anyone ever show you . . . ?"

He stopped abruptly, and his eyes turned shrewd. She knew he had probably anticipated something like this, and she knew, too, that there was little she could hide from him.

"What is it, Selena?"

"I've . . . I've kept something from you," she said.

He studied her for a moment, and she felt in him not

wariness—nothing as forbidding as that—but rather a kind of intelligent understanding, tempered by affection. His nature would change as little as his concern for her, and she understood that his knowledge of her own nature was as complete as was possible in another's mind.

"It's about Royce Campbell," she said.

His eyes darkened imperceptibly. In pain?

"He's dead now," she said.

Stillness. Davina had stopped laughing and regarded her with the deep, total attention of a child, her blue eyes depthless, puzzled. The shouting on the docks seemed to diminish and fall away. Even the slap of the water on wood seemed to cease.

Sean waited.

"But . . ." she struggled, "but . . . there was a time, well . . ."

"It does not matter, Selena," he said. "That is in the past. I love you and I trust you, and we three are together. The past does not matter. Spare yourself . . ."

"No," she shook her head, fighting off the easy way. She had to say it, for now and for the future. "He was the one who saved me," she said in a rush. "He was the sea captain I told you about . . ."

"In which case I am more than grateful to his memory," Sean Bloodwell interrupted.

"And on his ship we were . . . together," she finished.

For a long time Sean said nothing.

"You did not have to tell me this," he said finally, that touch of pain still about his eyes, "but since you have, let me say that the most important thing is not the fact itself, which you might justly have kept in your heart forever. The most important thing is that you have wished me to know the truth. You were always a splendid girl, Selena, but now you are a woman, stronger and braver than I could ever have expected. And I expected a great deal."

He fell silent for a moment.

The little girl looked at him, then at Selena. She smiled tentatively, wanting them to speak again.

"We both did what we wished to do in the past," Sean said then. "That is what free individuals are meant to do. Let us be glad for the happiness that is past, and look to the future. Together. Let us so pledge now and we shall speak no more of what you have told me."

Tears of joy, sadness, love, flooded her eyes. That he could understand so much! That, somehow, the past was not yet dead. That all future promises, all vows, would rise in her heart, and fly, and never come down to tawdry earth.

"Yes," she sobbed.

Davina, startled, stuck out her little lower lip and started to sniffle.

"There, there," Selena said through her tears, reaching for the little girl. She clung, however, to Sean. "There, there. Everything's all right now."

"Everything's all right," Sean repeated soothingly.

And they believed it.

"Sahib, sahib, where you want go?" called the pilot, gesturing toward the crude and crumbling harbor.

"Down the coast to Bombay," Sean told him.

"No, oh, no, no, sahib. Not my boat. My boat, she sink on high sea. You must take other."

"Damn," Sean said. He sounded more worried than angry. "What's wrong?"

"I'm beginning not to like this. I should have guessed it sooner, but better late than never. How far down the coast is Bombay? Fifty miles?"

She tried to recall the trip aboard the *Massachusetts,* but could only remember her growing panic and Captain Jack's mocking leer.

"I don't know," she said. "Maybe the pilot does."

"Exactly the man I wouldn't ask. He's the problem."

The raft was slogging now in the mouth of the river, and the sinewy raftsman ruddered and poled and oared it in toward one of the docks. Daman looked to Selena just as it had the first time: teeming and filthy. She remembered Haruppa and his filthy loincloth, the sting of his hand on her face. *Davi killed him. Good.* One less evil onshore. But why was Sean worried about the pilot? He'd done well, all the way down the Narbada.

"Because he knows we have one diamond," Sean whispered, when she asked. "That satisfied him, as long as we were out on the river. Now, however, he knows we have to get to Bombay. And he's probably guessed we have other jewels. Obviously, we're not traveling in a group, like most Westerners. And, just as obviously, we're running from something."

She looked at the pilot, who quickly looked away. On the docks, a hundred brown hands reached out, some to help pull the raft in to mooring, in hopes of reward, some for alms.

"He's going to make some fast friends from that bunch," Sean deduced, "and I wouldn't doubt that he'll have plenty to tell about the diamond."

Selena felt the quiver of fear that passed through her, and it was all she could do to keep from touching the hard lump of stones that were still tied in the corner of Davina's blanket.

"What do we do now?"

"We act confident," he said, reaching out and grabbing a section of dock, pulling the raft to, and swinging up. "All right, hand up Davina. Then come up yourself. We'll worry the pilot a little, before I pay him. Maybe he does know somebody around here who can take us. . . ."

The pilot already looked worried, as if he were about to be cheated, and tied hasty knots, following Selena and the child onto the docks. At least a hundred people crowded around, curious, suspicious, sullen. Some looked threatening already, though there had been no provocation.

"You like job I do for you, sahib?" the pilot began diplomatically.

Selena looked up and down the length of the godforsaken harbor. It smelled as she had remembered it, just like the clumps of human offal awash on the tide, the dead and dying men and animals along the riverbanks. The hordes of Hindus entering and emerging from the river, washing their sins away in the filthy yellow muck. Eyes were everywhere. Had they really come all this way to meet their end here?

She was certain those dusky eyes could see right through the cloth of the blanket, could see the jewels she had earned in India, in thrall to an Indian prince.

"I do good job, right?" the pilot prodded. "You pay me now, sahib, see?"

He held out a hand. Little Davina, who had been smiling and making noises at the surrounding group of watchers, quieted suddenly. The crowd itself stilled, conscious of conflict, expecting something.

"Of course I'll pay you," Sean said, with his easy, commanding manner. He made it appear perfectly natural. "I require further transportation," he said to the pilot. "Secure that, and you shall have your reward."

The pilot thought it over a moment, looking at first doubtful, then aggrieved. Then he looked angry, and started babbling and waving his arms, telling his countrymen how he had been cheated by the foreign devils.

Sean guessed what was happening. His ploy had failed. Now he sought to make it up.

"Here, then," he said, reaching into his pocket. "If you're so anxious for . . ."

Too late. The words had been spoken; the damage had been done.

The crowd was menacing now. And the pilot was pointing to the corner of Davina's blanket. Moreover, the others saw the tiny jewel of payment pass from Sean to the pilot and, although this quieted the pilot himself, it only whetted the appetite of the others. They moved closer, warily, fearing a trick the foreign devils might possess. In their eyes Selena recognized the lewd greed, the sick desire, the illness that wealth can bring, just as easily as it can proffer joy.

"Sean," she said unsteadily. "*Sean.*"

He turned and faced the group. They stopped, watching him, watching her. Watching the corner of the blanket. Selena saw herself floating, dead, in the yellow water.

"I must go to Bombay immediately," Sean told them, smiling with just a trace of unsteadiness. "Who will get me transportation? He shall be rewarded."

Everything stopped for a long moment.

The pilot, sensing trouble, perhaps sensing danger to himself and his own tiny diamond, leaped back into his raft and cast off. He poled frantically until he was free of pursuit, and then made gestures with his hands, partly of farewell, partly of ablution.

"Well, Selena," Sean said, stepping over to her, putting an arm around her waist. "I believe we'll stroll downtown."

His decision, and the suddenness with which it was carried out, momentarily confused the surrounding men. Sean pushed through them, and they parted slightly, just enough. Selena could smell their greed as readily as their bodies, and imminent violence tingled electrically above them. Sean walked away from the dock area and toward the low buildings of the city. He walked slowly, his head erect, now and then smiling and bowing at the people on the streets, who joined the original group, babbling, learning of wonders and wealth, until over a thousand people followed them.

"If the Rob Roys had had this kind of a mob," Sean said, "your father would be king and I'd be prime minister now."

"Maybe we could find shelter in some building," Selena suggested.

"It's either that or sprout wings. I don't think there's any kind of Western settlement here yet. God, I'd even settle for a Spaniard."

"I'd even settle for an Englishman. Anybody but McGrover." The mood of the crowd became even more menacing, a rising torrent of envious, accusatory shouting.

"They're nerving themselves up for it," Sean interpreted. "All it will take will be one of them tossing a rock, and then the whole mob will be upon us."

Then they reached a kind of rude intersection, a Y, where two small roads melded into a larger one. An official-looking building of white stone, squat, but with the suggestion of a dome, stood in the center of the Y. It looked stronger than the surrounding hovels.

"Here," Sean said, and guided her into the street, "we'll cross over to . . ."

He stepped into the roadway, an act which, for some unfathomable reason, inflamed the crowd. Someone threw a stone. It glanced off Sean's shoulder. He turned to face the mob, and stepped in front of Selena and the baby.

"You are very courageous, aren't you?" he said scornfully. "What do you want of us? Money? You want money, well, all right . . ."

He turned and held out his hand for the blanket. Selena met his eyes. It was all going to be lost now. Every hope was gone again.

"It's the only way," he told her, his voice steady. "They may kill us anyway. But I'll throw the jewels into the street, and while these swine are rooting around for them, killing each other, maybe we can make it over to the stone building.

Life. Seventy feet away, in a stone shelter. She thought of Father, dead in a stone hut. Gray, cold. This was white, smooth, and the sun shone on it. The road was yellow, dusty. The diamonds were heavy in the blanket. The price of life.

She gave him the blanket, as two more stones landed near them, hurled by hotheads far back in the crowd. Sean lifted the blanket above his head. The dark eyes followed it, and the noise of the crowd diminished somewhat.

"Selena," Sean told her quietly, "I'm going to attempt something that might give you a chance to get the baby into that building over there. Judging on the basis of my experience in Bengal, I'd say it's one of the nawab's provincial offices. When I begin speaking, go toward it. Slowly."

Selena held the child closer and anxiously measured the open space she would have to cross. Sean still had the blanket up over his head, moving it slowly from side to side. The movement had a curiously mesmerizing effect on the crowd.

"Yes, I have more diamonds for you," Sean said then. His voice carried over the mob and all around the intersection. Selena turned, as casually as she could, and started walking.

"But shall I distribute to you that which is not even mine?" she heard Sean ask.

The sound of the crowd swooped to a dull, puzzled mutter.

"What is your meaning?" someone asked.

Selena was halfway across the intersection now. The white building rose in front of her. She saw a dark face at one of the windows. A man wearing a turban looked speculatively down at her, and then looked over the crowd.

"This wealth I would give you gladly," Sean was saying, "but I bring it to your nawab. Would you take it from me and risk his wrath?"

Selena reached the steps that led into the building and turned to see Sean standing alone before the muttering mob. Sean had effected a shrewd stroke by mentioning the nawab. The men in the front rank, facing him, seemed to hesitate. A few stragglers at the edge of the crowd melted away down dismal alleys.

"Which of you shall have the honor and reward for escorting me to your nawab's representatives?"

Selena, halfway up the steps now, breathed a sigh of relief. Sean's ploy was going to spare them death at the hands of the mob. She knew that for certain when several of the men in the crowd began to argue fiercely with each other for the honor Sean had suggested. Sean lowered the blanket and started across the intersection, just as a haughty Indian in a glistening white turban appeared in the doorway at the top of the stairs.

The people in the crowd scattered and fled; save for the sound of Sean's boots on the gravel, all was quiet. Davina's eyes brightened at the sight of the turban. Selena waited. One danger was gone, but others lay in wait. The Indian fixed his condescending gaze on Sean, who reached the base of the steps, and bowed. The Indian was amused.

"I call upon the nawab," Sean announced, "for purposes of opening trade with him. I am prepared to make a most generous gift if an audience is granted."

The Indian smiled.

"Who arranges the audience," Sean added, "shall also be generously rewarded." He smiled.

"Allow me to invite you into my office," the Indian said, coldly courteous.

In spite of the imposing quality of the building itself, the room was bare and dirty. Flies hung lazily on the walls and ceilings. Sean and Selena were motioned to cushions on the floor. The Indian sat down, cross-legged, before them, his eyes moving from Selena to Sean and back again. He ignored Davina.

"You are British?" he asked.

"Yes," Sean said.

Now the Indian regarded Selena and the child.

"Where are your men, your guards? Where is your party? We have been dealing with the Portuguese, and always they travel with many persons."

"We have come from the east. A war in the interior caused the unfortunate loss of my party. Only the three of us have survived. But I bear the authority to further trade between your nawab and the East India Company."

The Indian considered it.

"Where is your master?" Sean prodded. "I must see him at once to present myself to him."

"He is in Bombay. At his residence there. And . . ." his eyes narrowed craftily ". . . you spoke of reward?"

"First I must reach Bombay. Then you shall have your prize."

The Indian shook his head. "All I have heard thus far are words. You do not travel impressively. What can you possibly give me?" His face turned hard. "You had best speak the truth, or your deaths will be far worse than those which the beggars in the streets would have visited upon you."

Sean matched him, bluffing coolly. "And you had best mind your tongue, or I'll see that it's torn out. Your nawab expects me, and . . ." he reached into a pocket of his breeches and brought out a small, perfect ruby ". . . in confirmation of my words to you, I shall first give you this stone. You shall receive many more if you arrange our passage to Bombay."

The Indian leaned forward and took the stone, giving it close inspection. When he looked up, his expression told Selena that they were safely to Bombay.

"I will, of course, accompany you," the Indian said.

"Of course," Sean agreed.

The journey was made by horse-drawn coach. Two Indians, armed with long, hooked knives, rode on the backs of the horses. The Indian official and the Europeans rode in the coach. At intervals the party halted for a change of horses, and food, little of which Davina could eat. Finally, Selena broke some of the hard, flat pieces of bread and soaked them in water, giving them to the baby bit by bit. Davina stopped her whining and fretting, and fell into a doze. As they approached Bombay, Sean asked, "Where is your master's residence?"

"Outside the city."

"Close to the waterfront?"

The Indian laughed. "The waterfront is ugly. Foreigners swarm about, and the worst of my race as well."

"But I must go there. Before I see your master."

The Indian was skeptical.

"One of my company's ships should be in port by now," Sean explained, "laden with goods for the nawab. I must establish its arrival."

Once again, he reached into his pocket and brought forth another of the smaller stones he had contrived to keep on his person. The green of jade shone for the Indian, and he nodded, then called new travel orders to the guards on horseback.

The waterfront, far larger than Daman's, was growing quiet when the coach arrived. It was twilight, and the day's work was over. Nevertheless, dozens of ships lay at anchor in the harbor. Others were tied to the docks, some to be unloaded, others to take goods aboard.

"Is your ship here?" the Indian inquired.

"Have your men take us along the docks."

The order was given, and the coach was drawn slowly along the line of the waterfront. Sean kept looking out, shaking his head. Selena watched him, wondering how he would get them out of this situation.

"No, that's not it either," Sean said, shaking his head in disappointment as they rode past yet another ship with a Portuguese flag atop her mast.

"You know," Sean exclaimed abruptly, in the manner of one who wishes to take his companion's mind off unpleasant business, "I've been admiring that turban of yours ever since we met. How are those things held together, anyway? It seems a marvel to me."

The Indian blinked, pleased. He removed his headpiece. "Here," he said, and with a deft flick of his fingers, the impeccably fashioned turban became a simple length of cloth.

"I find that astounding," Sean admired, reaching out to feel the cloth.

Selena watched him, then glanced out of the window of the coach. She saw a ship directly beside them. It flew the Union Jack. She saw the letters of its name on the hull: *Blue Foray*. A merchant ship. A number of sailors were getting ready to raise its gangplank for the night.

Then she heard a sound that, afterward, she was never able to forget. She had heard a similar sound before, in Kinlochbervie, but this time it came more suddenly. She whirled to see Sean bending over the Indian, his face red with blood and concentration. The cloth of the turban was around the Indian's neck. Soon his face was redder than Sean's, and then it was blue.

"Halt," Sean called, and the coach stopped.

"Easy now," he said to Selena, as he alighted and helped her down with the sleeping child. Sailors at the gangplank looked up, and on deck an officer glanced over. The mounted guards were looking around, watching Sean carefully.

"Yes, you come join us, too," Sean called, as if the Indian waited for them inside the coach. He took Selena's arm and guided her toward the ship. She saw that he had the blanket.

The guards were dismounting, suspicious now. The sailors were ready to hoist the gangplank. Time seemed to stop for all of them. Then the muscles of the dead Indian in the coach were caught in a final spasm. His body, which had been slumped half on, half off the cushions, twisted and fell. It fell just a little. There was a sound. The guards reached for their deadly swords.

"We're English," Sean said, in response to the inquiring look of the officer on deck. "We must come on board." He glanced back at the guards, who were gingerly approaching the coach.

"We *must*," he said.

The officer looked at them, then at the coach. A guard pulled open the door. Head and shoulders of the body came into view. The officer nodded. "Stop yer gapin' and haul away!" he ordered the sailors. Sean guided Selena up and onto the deck of the ship. Sailors heaved rope, and the gangplank rose.

"You'll be well paid," Sean told the officer, who proved to be captain of the vessel.

Below them, on the pier, the Indian guards let out a combined wail of outrage and lament, followed by piercing cries for help. Dozens of their countrymen began to appear, as if by magic, from buildings and alleys and nooks along the waterfront.

"It's not what it appears to be," Sean told the captain. "When did you plan on sailing?"

The captain looked at him for a long moment, and then

at the wild, gesticulating men who were gathering on the dock.

"In a couple of days," he said slowly, "but circumstances require that my plans be altered."

NIRVANA DEFERRED

Captain Flanders flew the British flag on the *Blue Foray*, but he was very much his own man.

"I must confess I am in this business for pecuniary reward," he told Sean. "I'll take you anywhere in the world you want to go, and I'll get you there safely. I guarantee to deliver whatever merchandise and personnel are placed in my care. You guarantee to pay me for such delivery. And," he added, with a glance at Sean's disreputable attire, "I assume every man is honest until I learn differently.

"No questions asked," he added.

The two men looked at each other. Then Captain Flanders grinned. He was a bulky man with a too-fierce scowl. He used it, obviously, to obscure his indomitable good spirits, lest someone get the better of him. He ought not to have bothered. His measure of men was as good as Sean's, and they looked each other over now, liking what they observed, as the ship got under sail out of Bombay, heading onto the Indian ocean. Luck was with them; nightfall had delayed or discouraged pursuit by Indian vessels.

"I did what I had to do," Sean told him anyway. "I had to kill in order to save . . ."

He gestured to Selena and the baby, but did not explain who they were. True to his word—"no questions asked"—Captain Flanders said nothing, although his eyes showed considerable curiosity.

"Right now," Sean said, "we need food and clothing."

"That can be arranged, if I do say so. How would you like a beefsteak, thick as your wrist, with red juice running hot out of her."

Selena was astonished. "Here? Aboard ship?"

"Mayn't be wise to reveal my machinations," Flanders said, laughing slyly, "but every time I dock at an Indian port, I have a few good men bring me some of those heifers that wander around in the streets. I don't believe they ought to go to waste, do you?"

"No, sir," Sean said.

He led them down to his cabin, opened a small cabinet, took out a dark green bottle, and popped the cork.

"For our health," he said. "Made up in the Highlands near Loch Nan Clar. Best you can get . . ."

Sean took the bottle, tipped it, and drank thirstily, gratefully. Selena watched, smiling, but her mind reeled at the sudden mention of Royce's sacred loch. Moreover, Davina stirred in her arms, waking up.

"Thanks," Sean said, coughing, handing the bottle back to Flanders. "You're a Scot."

"That I be," Flanders said, with just a touch of reserve, believing them to be English, as Sean had said. "I grew up in Perth. Left it, though, when I got my hunger for the sea."

He took a swig himself and handed the bottle to Selena.

"Actually, I was born in Scotland, too," Sean was saying.

Selena lifted the bottle and drank in the manner of the men. After all, she had done it before, that time on the run with Will Teviot, fleeing through the Highlands. She let the strong, heartening liquor take hold of her. The senses have memories, just as the mind does. Her taste remembered Scotland, and the ritual drink of whiskey on frosty mornings, before riding out onto the moors for the autumn hunts.

"Is she Scottish, too?" Flanders was asking as Selena put the bottle down. Sean smiled. "Sometimes I think she is Scotland," he said.

Davina came fully awake now, and cried out in hunger and discomfort.

"Is there somewhere I can take care of her?" Selena asked, rocking the child in her arms.

"Oh, I think that can be arranged," Captain Flanders said.

* * *

The intended destination of the *Blue Foray* was Virginia's Chesapeake Bay, but, true to his word, Flanders plotted a course for New York. It was April 1776, and he believed they could complete the trek by October, if the trades held up. "'Tis half the world we must traverse," he said, with the quiet excitement of a born sailor, "and nothin' t' do it with but God's own timber and my own sails t' catch His wind. But it'll be a long voyage. Do you have anything to occupy your time?"

"I believe I can think of something," Sean said, his eyes on Selena.

She met his eyes, and saw her own desire reflected in them.

From the first, the two had assumed that they would be together. Not to accede to this second chance that fate had given them seemed almost sinful, and neither of them wished to defy this gift of destiny. To have a plan for their lives, after such a long time adrift, was a joyous thing. As they sailed across the Indian Ocean toward the Cape of Good Hope, they began to discuss what their lives would be like. They were able to do so with considerable confidence. The ship's carpenter had constructed a cradle for little Davina, a tiny bed made of driftwood and bits of spare lumber, and in a hollow space in the driftwood, Sean had hidden the jewels. Likewise, he had plans for the future.

"If you agree," he told her one day, "we will be partners. With the jewels, we possess an incredible capital base, which we can put to good use, building a place for ourselves in American society and trade."

He was speaking quietly in the small cabin Captain Flanders had assigned them, lying on the deck, hands behind his head, and looking out the porthole. The moon was huge, red and warm in these southern latitudes, and the strange arrangement of the stars had grown natural to Selena. She rested on their hammock, and Davina was asleep in her cradle. It was true now. They were free of India, and nothing was going to draw them back. They had begun to relax.

"We *are* partners," she said.

He waited a moment. "There is one thing."

"Yes?"

"The political situation in America. We do not know exactly what is occurring there, and we won't until we arrive. Captain Flanders told me that, when last he was in New York, it seemed that a gang of rebels would actually try to break away from Mother England . . ."

"Good for them!"

"That's what I mean, Selena. I know how you feel, and why. But you must not only curb your passion against the British, you must hide it. You see, our success in America is predicated upon dealing with the British rulers there, the various governors-general, who are representatives of George the Third . . ."

"George the Third," she spat.

"Selena, I mean it! If we are ever to see Scotland again, we must not get ourselves involved in rebel politics. You have already seen what the consequences of such a course of action can be. And I have learned my own lesson all too well. These foolish rebels, whoever they may be, will get no further than the Rob Roys did, and I want no part of them."

He talked on, softly, logically, persuasively. Of course he was right, Selena thought. She had learned the lesson, too. Or, rather, her mind had learned it. Her heart was quite another thing. But she would steel her resolve, and this time, this time for certain, she would be as mature, as controlled, and, if necessary, as cunning as any Britisher sent to ferret out disloyalty.

"I will still be Selena MacPherson," she said. "Perhaps someone will remember, someone will know me?"

"Possibly. But unlikely. It was your father they were after. It was only McGrover who made it a point to hound you and Brian. And now McGrover is in England, most likely, working over some poor bastard in a dungeon. And I am a sworn, loyal subject of the King, and rich besides. And so are you.

"And," he added, looking over at her with tender expectations, "I want you to be Selena Bloodwell before too long. Before we reach America. If that is what you wish."

The thought had been so inevitable that neither of them had mentioned it before. Now that he had, they looked at each other for a long moment. They did not speak. All the past, each day, each year, had brought them to this moment. Together. It was as if their union had been willed from the very beginning. Then time itself seem to blur, and all things were intermingled. Did she say "Yes," giving her promise as he was coming toward her in the cabin, or was she already naked in his arms when she said it? And did he say, "I love you, Selena," before or after he stripped her for loving, and kissed her breasts as once he had on the banks of the Teviot River? And did she answer then, or was it later, as she embraced him with her body, wrapping herself about him, clinging to him, never to leave. The melding came upon them so naturally that Selena had no time to imagine what it would be like, but within moments her body knew it was going to be far better than she could have anticipated. Sean kissed her deeply, again and again, where her body was hungry to be kissed. Lingering over her, he aroused her with kisses and caresses, loved her with a sensual skill that left her light-headed, gasping with a desire for more and more. He bade her body arch like a bow for his love, and then he gave her that love, strongly, deeply, skillfully, taking her to the heights more times than her pleasure-riven mind could number, until at last he shuddered in her arms and called her name.

They lay together for a long time, suffused in the afterglow, and slowly floated back down to the world, where waited the bits and pieces of their lives and cares.

"I want you to know something," she whispered, after a time.

"No. No confessions."

"This is not a confession. Something else. A promise. A vow to which you have a right, knowing how I have . . . knowing things I have done in the past."

"Don't. It doesn't matter anymore."

"Yes, it does. You have a right. Sean, I vow this. I will always be loyal to you, and faithful. There is nothing and no one left in this world that I value, or love, or respect more than you. And I am going to be worthy of so great a gift . . ."

"Selena, I know you will, but you don't have to . . ."

"Yes, I do. Because now I have made it a vow, you see. A sacred promise. When you make a vow it goes beyond yourself, and, I swear, if I ever break it . . ."

"Selena, Selena. Stop this. We are one now, in all ways, and so we shall be. Partners in everything."

He did not explain, just then, all the plans that were on his mind. Another, sweeter kind of desire flared again in their bodies, and they gave way to it joyfully, and, once again, took a just measure of the delights for which the flesh has been created.

Captain Flanders performed the ceremony on deck of the *Blue Foray*, September 5, 1776. It had been Selena's wish to wait until they were north of the equator, in the Northern Hemisphere once again, and at 1 degree north latitude, 32 degrees, 2 minutes west longitude, she and Sean met and embraced and took each other's hands, facing each other beneath the full and open sky. That sky was brilliant, cloudless, swept clean by the trade winds, royal blue to the north, shimmering where the sun was. The waters of the Atlantic were alternately blue as sapphire, green as jade.

She had no wedding gown. The white, billowing sails were her wedding gown. Innocence and truth were in her heart, as they had been when she was a little girl. The crew itself was there, to a man, rough men like all those who go to sea, but men gentled a little by Captain Flanders' unremitting civility and the aura of a ceremony in which man and woman pledge life and love and heart. No one spoke as the two met before Captain Flanders, remembering their own pasts, thinking of their lives and their own young dreams. Wind surged, filling the sails, lifting the ship, and they moved forward into the future, locked together for a moment by a destiny greater than all of them, and just as unknown.

Captain Flanders cleared his throat. "I haven't had much occasion to use this authority," he began, "but I'm glad I can use it today. Would the . . . would the couple face me, please?"

Sean and Selena took their eyes off each other and faced Captain Flanders. Over the rail of the *Blue Foray*, Selena saw the ocean rolling on forever. The same ocean that had taken Royce Campbell had also led her to India, and to Sean: love given and love taken away. But, in love with Sean though she was, convinced as she was of the rightness of this impending union, yet she sensed a delicate imbalance in the course of her life. It was as if something were being kept from her, some element which, when she possessed it, would restore perfect equilibrium.

"Do you, Selena MacPherson, take this man to be your husband?"

Her eyes were blurred with a film of tears, but her voice was clear and strong. "I do," she cried, as if to God and the sky, and to all those she had loved who dwelt now in far regions. She wanted them to hear, and in the absence of chronicles or chisels, the walls of Coldstream Castle must be imprinted with this faraway call of her heart.

Captain Flanders coughed. "And do you, Sean Bloodwell, take this woman to be your wife?"

"I do," he replied, and she felt his hands tighten on her own.

"And do you both swear, before God and these witnesses here assembled, that you make your promise freely, and with no mental reservations of any kind, and that you will live as man and wife until . . ." he had a little trouble with the phrase ". . . until death do you part?"

"We do," they said in unison.

"Then, let's see . . . then, by the authority vested in my office, by the customs of ships at sea, I pronounce you man and wife."

There was a long silence, suddenly broken by Davina, who chirped excitedly and pointed a chubby finger into the sky. Everyone turned, wondering what she had seen.

It was a large bird, traveling alone, high against the royal blue of northern sky. It was beautiful, with its wings outstretched, coasting on the wind.

But, at such a distance, no one on the ship could identify what kind of bird it was.

"A good omen," Captain Flanders decided, and called for a keg of Madeira from his own private stock, his contribution to the wedding party.

The voyage passed swiftly, with great happiness. Selena's anticipation quickened as they sailed nearer and nearer America, until she could barely contain her excitement. Sean spent a great amount of time deciding how to go about contacting business sources in New York, and how discreetly to deduce the nature of the political situation, how best to evade difficulties, negotiate pitfalls and shoals. Finally, on the morning of October 28, 1776, Captain Flanders announced that the *Blue Foray* would sail into New York harbor before sundown.

All afternoon, Selena paced the deck, watching intently for the first faint glimpse of her new home, seeing it rise again and again out of the sea, only to have it fade into a mirage of spume and sun dance. Davina stayed with her for a while, toddling on the deck, carefully watched, but finally she tired and was taken below decks for a nap. Sean said he would stay with her—the two of them got on exceedingly well—and, besides, he had to remove the jewels from their hiding place, and put a few last touches on his plans.

Selena went topside again. Captain Flanders, grinning at her impatience, asked her up on the bridge, where she would better be able to see. She agreed enthusiastically.

"How far to New York?" she asked.

"Here," he said, still grinning, and handed her the spyglass. "I'd say about two hours if the wind holds."

Did he mean it? It was all she could do to keep from trembling as she put the glass to her eye and turned the adjusting screws. Was he teasing? Was it . . . *Yes!* Yes, by God in heaven, there it was, dark and low-lying along the edge of the ocean, and as they sailed closer, driven by wind, it emerged more and more clearly. She saw the mouth of the harbor—my God, it was huge—and almost made out individual buildings. There were many ships.

"British," Flanders said. "Probably guarding the harbor. There may be war by now."

War, she thought, with distaste, but even that could not sully her spirit.

And then, quite accidentally, she swung the spyglass to the side, a bit southward, and saw a man-of-war, a bigger ship than she'd ever seen before, bigger even than the *Highlander* had been. She thought it was British, of course, because of what Captain Flanders had told her, but then why was it going toward the southeast at such speed, rather than guarding the harbor? She adjusted the spyglass for a better view, and the big ship slid past her, black, monstrous, and silent. The letters of the ship's name stretched across her hull, and they passed by, one after the other, as in a dream: S—E—L—E—N—A.

She jerked the spyglass upward to the top of the main mast, and found the flags.

The unmistakable swath of Campbell plaid.

And another flag of a coiled serpent, which she later learned was the flag of the American rebels, that said, DON'T TREAD ON ME!

Her heart thundered; agony made her gasp.

"Is something the matter?" Captain Flanders asked.

"No," she said. "No," she repeated, in a stronger tone. "It's just I'm so excited to finally . . ."

She did not finish.

Captain Flanders laughed, thinking that he could easily supply the rest of the words to her sentence.

Selena resisted the impulse to sag upon the rail of the bridge. She would have done it—would have been forced to—but one emotion saved her. Surprise.

She was surprised that her heart still beat, severed as it was. Severed by surprise itself, and joy, and overwhelming sadness. She had lost him, buried him in the sea! And *he* thought he had lost *her!*

Waves of gulls winged out to them, calling in the sky. Their cries, commingled and muted by distance, seemed like the call of some lonely, forlorn animal, lost and pining in the high hills of home.

THE CRUCIBLE

The city into which Selena disembarked, with her husband and their adopted daughter, was rough, raw, and raucous beyond her most imaginative expectations, just like the country of which it was part. She had never seen a harbor even close to the size of this one, and passage between twin coasts, through something Captain Flanders called "the Narrows," was like moving into the nave of a savage cathedral. And everywhere, it seemed, was wilderness.

Was this a city? How could it be?

She knew immediately that Sean had been right. It would be the height of idiocy to take sides with a band of rebels from this wild land, no matter how much antipathy her heart held for England.

There was the British Empire, and the British Navy, and London. Westminster, Whitehall, St. Paul's. There were the vast estates, the great country houses, wealth and culture and accomplishment. All the might and power and easy tradition of the British Empire.

And then there was this. New York. Selena was surprised that the English would even allow the name "York" to be used for a place like this.

And yet, had not Royce Campbell somehow lived to ally himself with these rebels, and *against* all the might of the old country?

Her heart was in furious tumult, which she fought to keep from Sean, when Captain Flanders received permission to put into port.

"Well, here we are, Selena. What do you think?" Sean exuded, putting his arm around her. He held Davina, to bring her safely down the gangplank. "Isn't this the perfect place to build a dream?"

Dream. What a word. She had dreamed the black ship— black, as for mourning. She had dreamed it, but it had never been there! *It did not exist!*

She had made her vows, and the future lay free for the taking.

Within his embrace, she suppressed a shudder created by the chill of the past, and steeled herself. As she could. As she must. She had made her promises, and they were forever. Her love was for Sean and Davina. The past was over, complete. The future lay before them. Difficult or easy, it must be built of truth and honor, love and will.

These she possessed, and these she had to command. These she would give.

"Yes, it is. It is a place to build dreams," she replied, and put her own arm around Sean's waist.

Captain Flanders, on the bridge, smiled and called down to them: "Deal's a deal, and I got you here safe and more than sound."

She waved back to him, trying to give him the smile he deserved.

"You can get ready to put ashore now," he called. "Got everything you need?"

"Only a fortune in my pockets," Sean whispered to her exuberantly. "This city is mine. And maybe the country, too."

Selena laughed with him, patting one of his jacket pockets, feeling the reassuring hardness inside. Everything that counted, everything that mattered, seemed to be hard. Wealth was hard: diamonds, rubies, even gold. The hearts of the victorious—men or women—seemed always to be hard. (But at what effort, and price in pain, was all of this achieved?) And even a man's love was hard when it was in your body.

Yet would you have it any other way? Could it *be* any other way?

No.

Davi? Still, he had had to be hard, too, in the end.

Well, perhaps not. Yes, he had to, in order to be free. Of life.

With a vague feeling that, in spite of the distance she had

come, in spite of the degree of maturity she had reached, she still did not fully understand what love was, or what life was, Selena MacPherson Bloodwell set foot upon the violent shore.

It was readily apparent that this new land was much like the old: vast differences in wealth lay right before their eyes. Along the banks of the Hudson River, along a place called Bowling Green, were the fine, stately mansions of rich merchants. Sean's eyes were drawn toward them right away, and their elegant perspective pleased Selena, too. Along the dock proper were the offices and warehouses of a busy port; it was easy to see the East India Company's office, and on its clapboard wall the lettering of some rebel said, in faded paint, No Tax on Tea! Yet, within a few minutes walking distance from the waterfront were sections that reminded her of Liverpool, where the groaning riffraff now working on the docks—Negroes blacker than Davi had been, and runty, reddish-hued men she later learned were Irish—retreated when evening came, to try and drink their way out of squalor and misery. Beyond this, farther into the town, she saw the steeples of five or six churches, the two Anglican churches, Trinity and St. Paul's, being the most imposing. Indeed, they were the only truly imposing things in that section of the town. And along the Battery was the small fort, symbol of British Power. Selena stared at it.

"You'll have to go over there and register your arrival in the city," Captain Flanders advised. "They'll come a-lookin' for you if you don't."

Selena felt a twinge of apprehension at this news, but Sean remained calm. "Thank you, but first I shall attempt to see the harbor master. We require information about the city, such as where to find suitable lodging. We shall attend to protocol in due course."

"I shouldn't wait too long," Flanders said uneasily. "Talk is that war's on. You see the men-of-war here in the harbor, and the lack of freighters. And war makes men powerfully suspicious."

Sean thanked him and they walked down the pier to the harbor office. Yet, for a place at war, New York seemed very placid to Selena. True, there were the warships in the harbor, but they were British warships in every port on

earth. And the office of the harbor master was almost som-
nolent. Several young assistant officers leaned back in
chairs, their feet atop desks. Blue smoke rose in the air as
they puffed leisurely at pipes. Faded notices were pinned to
the walls. They all stood to acknowledge the presence of a
lady. Sean asked to see the harbor master, using a tone of
voice that was courteous but commanding. One of the as-
sistants, who introduced himself "Grimsby at your service,
sir," hastened to an office in the rear of the building, while
the other men bent to their desks, attempting to look busy,
all the while casting surreptitious glances at Selena.

"Lord Weddington will see you now," Grimsby said,
coming out of the harbor master's office.

"Everyone in the world is a lord," Sean muttered in disgust as Grimsby led them to the office. And Richard Weddington, harbor master of New York, looked every inch the
young, confident scion of a long line blessed by noble birth.
He appeared to be about thirty years of age. His hair was
yellow as a jonquil. His eyes were green. He was not as tall
as Sean, but when he rose to greet them, Selena saw his
breeches tauten upon the muscles a man would use to ride
a fine horse, and ride it long. His tone was friendly; his
manner was intelligent.

"Dick Weddington at your service," he said, offering his
hand to Sean. "Come in. Please be seated. Here, ma'am,
allow me," he added, coming around to place a chair for
Selena and the child. He motioned Sean to another chair
and returned to his own seat behind the desk.

"Just arrived in New York, eh?" he asked. "What vessel
were you aboard?"

"The *Blue Foray*, out of Bombay," Sean told him.

"Ah! Flanders' ship. Fine man, Flanders. A Scotsman."
Neither Sean nor Selena said a word.

"At least we have a merchant ship in the harbor," Weddington said, with a smile that acknowledged the wartime
situation. "Parliament's Law of Interdiction, you may have
heard. Forbids trade with these rebel colonists. Oh, a great
deal of military shipping comes in, mostly for our military
and for Americans still loyal to the King, but . . ."

With a disappointed look and a toss of his hand, Weddington told them that there was little for a harbor master
to do. Selena, who had been watching him closely, sensed

something in his demeanor that, while not exactly false, seemed somhow inconsistent.

"May I be of help to you?" Weddington was asking. "You've been in India?" he inquired of Sean. "My God, I'd have given an arm and a leg to get out there. But Pater believed that America was safer!"

Selena searched her mind. Weddington? *Lord* Weddington! Not the young man seated here before them, but his elder. One of the few Englishmen Lord Seamus had respected. Weddington had not been a liberal, but Selena's father had always thought him to be a reasonable man. Now, smiling at Weddington's son, Selena hoped that she and Sean would not, with a hint of Scottish brogue, arouse in the harbor master any latent suspicions or memories.

"This war," Sean was asking, "will it hinder a man seeking his start in business?"

"It depends upon the line you're in," Weddington replied. His glance turned just a bit shrewd. "You're not just starting in business, I daresay? And I don't believe Grimsby mentioned your name."

The interview was taking a turn that neither Sean nor Selena had anticipated. Instead of the visit Sean had envisioned, a simple quest for information about New York, they had been led into confrontation with a lord. And now it was becoming an inquisition.

"I am Sean Bloodwell," Selena's husband said.

Had he pronounced his name a bit too defiantly? Selena thought so. But Weddington's expression revealed nothing.

"Ah, Bloodwell. Yes. What line of business *are* you in, Bloodwell?" His tone was perceptibly harder now. Selena could see him making his calculations. Weddington could see before him a fine-looking man, a woman with beauty of form and face, and with more than a hint of aristocratic bearing. The man had come from India and was seeking introduction to business opportunities in New York. Hence, the couple must be rather well provided for.

"What, indeed, are your interests, Bloodwell?" Weddington pressed, leaning forward over his desk.

"I have certain general plans," Sean said frankly, having decided on a bold response. "I will need to learn the situation here in America before I decide upon a definite course. And I will need to learn it from someone upon whom I can rely."

He shot Weddington a hard glance of his own, and an appraising glance as well.

"Trade, real estate, and banking will certainly be among my activities," Sean said. "We came here to your office to seek information as to lodging, but since you seem so interested in my affairs, I think it only fair to ask if you, as harbor master, can recommend to me men of trade on whom I can call."

The two men looked at each other, each trying to interpret the nature of the other. Weddington looked at Selena for just a moment, as if he were about to ask her a question. Then he turned back to Sean. "You are prepared to enter *three* major fields of commerce?"

"I am," Sean said. "*We* are," he amended, glancing at Selena.

Intelligence flickered in Weddington's eyes, and a new measure of respect. "I will do what I can to aid you," he said then, and banged a bell on top of his desk. "You will have to decide yourself whether or not I prove to be reliable."

In answer to the bell, Grimsby appeared in the doorway. "Yes, sir?"

"Grimsby, I am placing you in charge of the office for the rest of the day." He rose from his desk. "You seek accommodations," he said to Sean, "and, I am sure, good food. And a place for the child. And," he added, nodding to Sean, "you may find there are services worthy of reward that I can provide. There are some rebels in New York, but it is still a place where a clever man can turn a pound note to a profit. I do not shrink from becoming one of those men."

Sean smiled in appreciation of Weddington's candid remark, but Selena, taken aback by what he had said, blurted her question before she could hold it back.

"Do you mean some of the Americans are *not* rebellious?" she asked.

"Heavens, no," Weddington exclaimed, as he led them out of the office building and onto the docks. His horse and coach were waiting there. "Why should they be? No point in it, is there?"

Sean shot her a hard look, chagrined at the outrage in her tone. "It's just that I'm surprised . . ." Selena fumbled.

But Weddington seemed not to notice. "Just in the last few months," he said, as they were climbing into the coach, "our military commander, Lord Howe, chased the rebels and their commander, a Virginia farmer called Washington, right off Long Island. The entire uprising might have ended if Washington had not gotten away with his army. Too bad, it is. Business suffers, and what ought to be a busy harbor becomes naught but the berth of gunships. And gunships bring no profit," he added, with a sidelong glance at Sean.

"That I vow," Sean agreed. Selena, observing them, listening to their exchange, could sense a relationship being established between the two men. It seemed a business relationship of some sort, but there was a quality in it that she could not decipher, as if some element in their exchange was not being revealed. Whatever it was, Sean seemed not to notice.

"What must you do as harbor master?" he asked, as the coach set off for a place called Fraunces Tavern, to which Weddington had directed the driver.

"Much more than I had anticipated, for far less reward than I had imagined," Weddington replied. "I must log all ships in and out, ascertain that all persons arriving here in America register with the security officers. I deal with all the major men of trade in New York, and naturally, I give information and aid to those who request it. And, most assuredly, my men and I must be on the watch for contraband."

"Of course," Sean said. "But what do you mean by 'far less reward'?"

"Precisely that. Pater forbade me to join the service in India where great sums can be made. Still, I was pleased when he was able to arrange my current appointment. But we must acknowledge facts. A harbor master thrives when his waterfront is filled with merchant vessels. I receive a share of all docking tolls, you see. But I do not receive such tolls from naval warships."

His tone was rueful. Sean responded to it with a query that demonstrated his merchant's imagination.

"The sailors and soldiers here?" he asked. "How are they

clothed and fed? What is the source of their provisions?"

"Why, most of what they require is sent from the British Isles."

"Would it not be less expensive, and far more effective, to buy foodstuffs and uniforms right here in America? There is an army to be provisioned, and a navy . . ."

"Sir, while many of the Americans are loyalists, about a third of them strongly in support of King George, the others are divided among those who support the rebellion and those who are neutral. In order not to stir the passions of the citizens who are not loyalists, the military has been reluctant to provision itself entirely with American goods. After all, a loyalist farmer looks much like a rebel farmer. The loyalist is often afraid to sell to a military buyer because his rebel neighbor will not be blind to the transaction. Barns burn easily in dark of night, after the soldiers have gone. And the rebels themselves sell very dear, or not at all. This is a different country, very independent in its ways. The farmers in the Hudson Valley, and on Long Island, do not like to see troops marching across their fields."

"It occurs to me," Sean said, "that a civilian merchant might buy supplies in large quantities from all the farmers, whatever their political leanings, and sell them to the British Army and Navy at less than it would cost them to ship provisions from England."

Dick Weddington was silent for a moment. "Sir," he said then, "I believe you are going to have a splendid future here in America. Let us have an ale on that future at Fraunces Tavern."

Sean settled back, clearly pleased with himself, but Selena worried about supplying the British forces. One worry led to another, and she remembered Flanders' advice.

"Don't we have to register at the fort?" she asked.

"Oh, you can do it tomorrow," Weddington said. "Lord Howe's head of security is something of a fanatic, but both of them know Pater, and both of them know me. I'll accompany you to see him in the morning. I believe we can be of use to one another. Now tell me, sir," he said to Sean, "you also mentioned an interest in banking and real estate . . ."

The two men began to talk again. Davina, wiggling and curious, climbed all over them, trying to see out of both sides of the coach at once. Selena looked out at the rude, winding streets through which they were driving, and at the crude, unpainted buildings. Animals roamed freely, and the streets were spotted with their droppings and with other debris. Then they were away from the piers, and into a better area, clean and well-organized, heritage of the Dutch sense of order and propriety. Now she could sense the energy in this new place, but it seemed ridiculous to her that buying real estate here would ever turn much of a profit. There was simply too much room. It would take a thousand years to fill up all the space. About the purchasing business, though, she could sense potential. But Sean would be involved in feeding and clothing an army and navy that were committed to the eradication of a tiny band of men who shared, somehow, a dream—half-patriotic, half-vengeful— that still lived within her.

She was—she and Sean *were*—on the right side this time. There seemed no way they could possibly lose.

Yet why did it feel so wrong?

Selena was delighted, however, with the tavern—it was really a restaurant—and the accompanying hotel. Weddington waited for them in the taproom, and they went upstairs. Selena arranged to have a Dutch girl named Traudl stay with Davina, and ordered for the child a light meal of broth, bread, and warm milk. Then she and Sean went back downstairs to dine.

"Do you think you can trust him? Weddington?" she asked.

"Absolutely. His connections are superb, and he seems a gentleman as well."

"Where are the jewels?"

"On my person. In the morning, I'm going to find out the name and location of the biggest bank in town. I'll trade one for ready capital, and vault the rest. If that's all right with you."

"Yes, but . . ."

"But what?"

"But it can't be this easy."

Sean laughed. "What are you talking about?" he said. "Easy? Nothing's been easy at all. If I were you, I wouldn't get confident just yet."

"You needn't worry about that," she snapped, but then

quickly gave him an apologetic kiss. It was the first trace of a harsh word they had exchanged, and it unnerved her not simply because it was their first night here, but more because—*Face the truth, Selena!*—she wanted not the slightest wedge to come between herself and Sean, lest the memory of the man who rode the bridge of the *Selena* intrude to disrupt her future as he had disrupted her past.

Royce is still what he always was, and always will be. A reckless, instinctive rebel. He was right when he said that trouble follows him. He wants it, needs it. It is too bad. Anyway, you are wiser now.

It had been Royce, of course. Hadn't it?

She began to go soft with memory, confusion. *If he had named the ship for her, he must care so much. . . .*

Weddington, watching for them from the bar in the taproom, came out to join them, and they entered the dining room. It was very modern, with fine wooden furniture, and the latest in weaponry displayed along the walls. It was crowded, too, but immediately—in spite of the laughter and chatter—Selena sensed an undercurrent of uneasiness. It vanished almost as quickly as she had perceived it, and at first she thought it might be her own nerves. But she trusted her intuitions now—as she had certainly been forced to—and they were usually reliable.

"Is something the matter?" she asked Weddington quietly. "Why did everybody seem . . . nervous? Just a moment ago."

"Oh, that." Weddington dismissed it with his easy grin, and waved for a waiter's attention. "Lord Howe has just departed. He'd been dining here in one of the private rooms."

"Howe? Is he particularly fearsome?" The Howe brothers had reputations as fairly reasonable men, at least insofar as military men are reasonable.

Sean accepted a menu and waited for Weddington's response.

"It wasn't Howe so much, I daresay. He had that new security officer with him, however . . ."

Instantly, Selena thought of Darius McGrover. She felt a chill crawling over the skin at the base of her neck.

". . . and the man's a bit on the zealous side."

The menus were handed around. A barmaid came in from the taproom with three huge mugs of ale.

"Thought you'd appreciate these," Weddington said. "I ordered them for us when I was at the bar. . . ."

They raised the mugs, clicked them together, and drank the strong, cold ale.

"Well, Selena. Do you see anything interesting on the menu?" Sean asked. His upper lip was wet with the thick foam of the ale.

"Everything," she answered enthusiastically.

"Let's try the venison," Weddington suggested. "It's perfect right now, in the fall. I say, how about venison steaks all around? They're better here than in the best game preserves in England."

Sean looked up and nodded. Selena could tell he was thinking about something of considerable importance to him. After a few more swallows of ale, he spoke.

"Sir," he said to young Weddington, "do not be offended that I approach this matter at table, but I have reason to make haste with my affairs. As you know, I seek profitable ventures. You have indicated that you have considerable knowledge of New York and the tradespeople here. If, as you have also said, you are interested in profit yourself, I would be pleased to have you as an adviser."

Weddington gave him a long look.

"I can assure you that your aid will be as well rewarded as it is genuinely sought."

Weddington continued to look at Sean, not so much trying to decide upon a response, Selena thought, as attempting to resolve certain unspoken considerations. Then he smiled.

"By all means," he said, and raised his mug. Sean lifted his, too, as did Selena. "I believe I have been seeking just such an opportunity as this," Weddington said.

They drank. Selena could read the satisfaction in Sean's expression. He believed that he had secured the aid of a man who could give him entrance into New York's trading circles, and it seemed that he was right. *Now I am on my way back to the top,* he must be thinking.

And she hoped, with all her heart—for him, for herself, for little Davina—that he was right. Disaster could not oc-

cur all over again, could it? Disaster, and loss, and being
on the run? Lightning never strikes twice.

It doesn't have to.

The dinner was excellent, and enlivened by Sean's air of
adventure and Dick Weddington's good spirits. The young
merchant seemed to know or know of almost everyone dining at Fraunces, and he spoke of personalities throughout
the colonies who, he said, "might have had a chance to
make something of themselves if they hadn't gotten involved with that fool revolution."

Selena had all she could do to hold her tongue, especially when Weddington actually revealed that ". . . now,
in the long run, the principles of freedom *are* immutable,
just as that fellow Jefferson said—big, shambling guy, falls
all over his feet, looks like a farmhand—but the British
Empire is the British Empire . . ."

He seemed a little wistful when he said that. Selena
thought he was thinking of home. It was a feeling she could
understand.

Sean steered the conversation away from politics, wanting to know if Dick knew of any parcels of land immediately available for purchase. He also sought an office for
business, and a suitable residence.

"What were you thinking of?"

"One of those mansions down on Bowling Green."

Dick leaned back slightly, not so much surprised as admiring.

"For a start," Sean added.

"We shall see," he replied. "There *is* a turnover of resi-
dents, particularly older men who've come out from home.
They don't like the place, sometimes, and go right back.
And what were your plans?" he asked Selena.

It suddenly occurred to her that she had not thought of
her plans. Yes, she was free now. She could make plans.

"Well, there's Davina, of course . . ."

"Your daughter?"

She and Sean spoke simultaneously, almost with vehe-
mence. "Yes."

Dick looked startled but said nothing.

"Well, I haven't given it much thought," Selena said.
"Not yet, that is . . ."

But Weddington's words had struck a spark. It was true. Freedom was not an end in itself. She had not considered this before, because her entire effort had been directed to the attainment of freedom. But once freedom was possessed, once a person was secure—and Selena was secure now, wasn't she?—then there were a thousand things one could do.

The thought was as exhilarating as the ale. Nor had she eaten such solid fare in some time, and the combination of the two soon made her drowsy. Lucky that there was no long distance to travel, only to go upstairs after the rich slice of chocolate cake with whipped cream in a frothy mound on top of it. She felt totally relaxed for the first time in so long, and the mood carried through Dick Weddington's leave-taking—he would join them again in the morning to accompany them to the fort—and it was still with her when she settled into bed.

"Sean, what if it's true?" she asked suddenly.

"What? What are you talking about?"

"Dick Weddington mentioned the new director of security. What if he's . . . what if he's Darius McGrover?"

The bed was soft and warm. Sean was beside her. Darkness surrounded them. Davina slept peacefully on a trundle bed. They were all safe, but Selena was frightened.

"What if we go down there tomorrow, and it's Darius McGrover . . ."

"It won't be," Sean said forcefully, as if by the authority of his words he could banish the possibility. "And, even so, we are here legally. We are people of means, as well. Even McGrover can do us no harm if we do not become enmeshed with the rebels."

"But don't you see? With Darius McGrover and myself, the situation is changed. *Different*. It is as if we were trapped in some deadly game. You see, at Foinaven Lodge I had my chance to end the game, and I should have done so. I see that now. I should have killed him. But I didn't, and this time it is his turn, and . . ."

He put his arm around her, and she felt his strength and love.

"I'll take care of you," he said. "Don't worry. I'll take care of you."

She settled in close beside him. He was right. Of course

he was right. McGrover was dangerous, and her impression of his diabolical interest in her was accurate, but there was no point in letting that fact intrude upon them now, when everything was beginning to go so well. Traudl, the girl who had stayed with Davina while they'd dined, would come by again in the morning, to play with the little girl while Selena looked at houses and Sean did his banking. *After* they registered! She was thinking of hiring Traudl permanently, as a companion for the child. She had, already, a still-vague but increasingly strong suspicion that she was going to be very busy.

"Come now," Sean was saying into her hair, "we'll get established here, and I'll make the right connections. Nobody will support Great Britain in this war as arduously as I will, and I *will* be recognized for it. And the time will come when . . ."

The peerage. The return to Scotland. The restoration of his good name, and all that went with it. Trumpets blasting in the high caverns of Westminster. Lord Sean Bloodwell. Sir Sean. Sir Sean Bloodwell. Lord and Lady Bloodwell. Of Edinburgh and Coldstream. Yes, that was what he saw. That was his dream, and she had given her solemn vow to share it. Already he could see it rising up out of the blue sea in greeting, welcoming and praising him: glorious, mighty Britain, the jewel set in the sea.

Too tired to make love, they drifted into sleep. And Selena did sleep, but the room was too warm, or the feather mattress oppressive. Because, although she slept, she dreamed. A constantly shifting series of impressions came down upon her. The dagger was in her hand, poised above the maharajah's heart, except it wasn't the maharajah anymore. It was Darius McGrover, with hollow spaces where his eyes ought to have been. She tried to bring the dagger down, but he laughed—gapingly, silently, like Gayle's skull!—and brushed her hand aside. Captain Jack Randolph was screaming somewhere in a golden cow, and, in the garden at Coldstream, Father showed her where the sky was, his face looming huge and tragic in her warped field of dream vision, and the gray rat, blood clinging thickly to its whiskers, crawled up over the tatters of Slyde's shoulders, winking at her, one ear gnawed off at the root. It had to stop; she tried to make it stop. But, too far from wakefulness, too far into tossing sleep, she failed. Ku-Fel's face was upside down; Sherpas were laughing and pointing; the elephant whip was cutting through the air. Chandeliers spun in a lost land, and the Highland fling rose from the crying of the instruments and pipes. Royce Campbell's dark face, then, which became Sean's, which became Royce's again. Wolf in the Highlands. Eagle against the sky. A coiled serpent. Waiting.

And the great dark ship sliding soundlessly across the all-erasing, all-embracing sea. Poor Marinda in that sea, her bones washed white and lonesome.

"Selena," a voice called, hollow and premonitory in the distance.

"Selena!" the voice called, over the vastness of the deep. To the north, the sky was royal blue. Father's face, smiling in benediction, there.

Grandmother's coffin jounced on the roof of the coach. Horses thundered down the rocky roads. A manic coachman leered and drooled and cracked his whip.

"*Selena!*"

Candles burned around a coffin somewhere. Great sadness. Someone had died, or something was dead. No, not that. No, some*thing* was lost! Something precious had been lost almost before it had been possessed. Candles, coffin, were in memory of that. The great ship slid into the night . . .

"*SELENA!*"

The voice was urgent now, and right beside her. Someone was holding her, she could not get free, she was tied into the chair in the cabin of the *Meridian*, and Roberta was laughing, in a white gown . . .

She came awake, hot and confused. Sean was holding her. Seeing that she had awakened, relief sounded in his voice.

"You must have had a nightmare," he explained.

She nodded in agreement, and said nothing. The strange, distorted impressions of the dream lingered, and it took minutes to shake them off. And yet, even when she thought she had rid herself of those impressions, the tinge of an unpleasant emotion remained, faint but definite, far back in her mind. She knew what it was. The black ship. Royce. *Guilt.*

And she turned to Sean with an ardor that, while genuine and loving, was inordinately sudden, too, as if by quick, hard love she could erase a memory. And she did.

Man and wife now, and used to each other, still they loved with passion. Selena knew now without thought just how long he wanted to wait, after their first deep kiss, before he wanted to be touched. So she made him wait longer. This he understood, and understood, too, that her delay in stroking him was not in the least reluctance, but rather a wish that, when the touch came, it would deliver tenfold ecstasy and tenfold promise of more delight. And Selena knew that his touch was withheld as well, and for the same reason, and she cried out not when it finally came, but rather when she knew he had ceased teasing and would certainly touch her *now*.

They made it last as long as they could, as if each time might be their final one. So it should be the best there was to have, the best there was to have given. Because it was— and would always be—a gift. To take it for granted would be to risk ingratitude, to threaten destiny itself.

Selena had grown to know, even before his body tensed, the exact moment he would turn to move upon her. Sean had learned, by touch and instinct, when she wished possession. Tonight, when that moment came, it was all the sweeter for they were *here*, they were *safe*, and the future seemed as certain as the ecstasies they knew to be in store for them now.

He came upon her and soon they were together, riding the gorgeous rush. Her dream sank away into the backwaters of her mind; there was nothing now but sensation. Then it came suddenly, surprisingly. It was upon her, taking her in a swelling, incredible flood, with her mind dim and unsteady far back in the haze.

"Oh, my God!" she cried, as the pleasure seized her, gripping her body and shaking it in spasms, "Oh, God, oh, R . . ."

She caught herself in the nick of time—she hoped—and turned the sound into a growl of pleasure, and buried her mouth in Sean's neck, biting. She felt him lose himself in her, the hot glow of his essence, again and again.

"Oh, *Sean*," she said.

"Darling," he responded, kissing her wetly, gasping. He

had not heard the name that had trembled on her tongue. Thank God. It would never happen again.

The fort on the battery that served as the administrative center for the fledgling City of New York—and which also served at the moment as headquarters of Lord William Howe, commander of the British Army which had just beaten Washington—was solid but unimposing. The cannons which covered the harbor and guarded the mouth of the Hudson River were authoritative, but not overbearing. The place was a military edifice, no mistake, but the air about it was relaxed, confident, almost urbane: an art carried by the Imperial British to every corner of the earth.

Dick Weddington was waiting outside Fraunces Tavern when they came out into the crisp fall morning. Even the ride by horse-drawn coach into the ring of slums around the harbor did not seem especially distasteful. Or maybe it was because Selena, somewhat anxious about the coming interview with the "security director," did not notice the squalor as closely as she had on the previous evening. She was *sure* now it was going to be McGrover, but she did not mention it, not wanting the men to think that she was upset. Instead, she watched the passing scene beyond the cab's window. Here a group of sweating Irish immigrants were laying an extension of the cobblestone road that led to the ferry slip, supervised by a thick-necked, choleric roughneck that Selena took for Dutch. There, along the street corner, a big Negro was arguing and gesticulating fiercely among a small group of white men. It surprised her. "Isn't that a healthy risk for him to take?"

"No, he's free," Dick said. "There are quite a few free Negroes here in New York. The rule is that if a master brings a slave with him to free territory, the man is still a slave. But if he has papers attesting to his freedom, the law must recognize those papers. Of course, what happens is that a gang of men will corner one of the darkies, and ship him off to Savannah or someplace like that. No paper in the world will do the poor buck much good then."

Selena recalled, all too clearly, her recent experience of bondage, and her sympathy was aroused.

"Yes, but you have to understand the situation," Dick explained. "These blacks take away jobs from the Irish and such. There is much hostility. Every now and then there is a riot, and the last time several Negroes were burned on the docks."

"Burned alive!"

"Certainly."

Selena looked out the cab window again, with a new wariness for the violent potential of this place. Some of her father's friends had spoken of it as a "last great chance" for human government. It might well be that, she concluded, but if they burned people here as they did elsewhere, there was quite a distance to go.

Dick led them into the fort and over to the wing in which the offices stretched down either side of a corridor. He was well-known there, and many officers and soldiers called out a greeting.

"Hey, Dick. You get any business yet?"

"No, dash it! Your friends in the navy have the harbor blocked off. How am I supposed to earn a living?"

They laughed at his plight.

"I hear you've got Washington on the run to the north," Dick offered, in a congratulatory tone.

"Aye! That we 'ave. The farmer's passed through White Plains. We think he's on his way to Boston."

Dick's eyes narrowed oddly when he heard this information, but he responded cheerfully as ever: "That's the way to fight. Return the troops to England by Christmas, right?"

"Right, Dick. Burgoyne is up around Boston waiting to cut the rebel troops to mincemeat."

"Ah, good news indeed."

Then, abruptly, they were in a square, sparse office, standing before an austere, bitter-looking man. He sat behind a desk and looked up at them when they entered. He had piercing eyes and a hard mouth. Trust was not a part of his nature. Selena thought immediately of McGrover, and her heart was pounding. But that was due to relief. The name on the plaque on the desk read Lord Ludford.

"Friends of mine for registry," Dick Weddington said.

Ludford gave both of them a searching look. He did not trifle with anything as formal as introductions. Instead, he took a sheet of parchment from a leather case and dipped a quill pen into a spotty inkwell. He stared at Sean.

"Name?"

Sean told him.

"Birthplace? Father? Father's occupation?"

"Edinburgh. Richard Bloodwell. Merchant."

Ludford's eyebrows lifted slightly at the mention of Scotland, but he gave no other sign.

"Point of origin? Ship? Reason for being in New York?"

"Bombay, India. *Blue Foray*. And I hope to enter business here."

Ludford went on writing, not missing a beat.

"Assets?"

Sean stiffened slightly and looked at Dick. He had not, of course, given any indication, even to his new partner, of the extent of the fortune he and Selena had brought with them. Dick was curious and guarded, too. He waited.

"Assets? Amount thereof?" Ludford asked, more sharply this time, and looked up.

"I would estimate . . ." Sean decided.

"You do not know for sure?"

"Of course not," Sean grinned, brazening it out. "What man does unless he has very little . . . ?"

Ludford's lips pursed, and his voice showed a degree of respect.

"Give me an estimate then. I'm sorry, but this office must know. We are endeavoring to keep track of funds, as much as possible, to deny them to the Continental Congress. That's the rebel government," he added needlessly.

"Ten thousand pounds current," Sean said authoritatively. Dick nodded, seeming to accept it and approve of the sum. Ludford did not seem suspicious. But Selena had to suppress a gasp. The sum was but a sliver of their joint wealth. And, immediately, she perceived a new series of problems: bankers might readily convert a few stones to cash, but would not a seemingly unlimited supply of precious jewels arouse great suspicion? And when the extent of their fortune was discovered, would they not be in considerable danger from many sources? In a place in which ten thousand pounds was impressive, what would be the reaction to a *million* pounds?

Fear or respect or envy or hatred? Or all of them together?

She had the feeling someone was speaking to her.

"Name?" Ludford was saying sharply, as if he had already said it a couple of times.

"Oh, I'm sorry. Selena Bloodwell."

"Maiden name?"

"MacPherson," she said. It was hard to keep the tone neutral. Ludford did not look up. She could almost feel Sean's relief.

"Place of birth? Father's occupation?"

"Coldstream, Scotland. Landowner."

Ludford looked up at her. "Nobility?"

She nodded.

"You ought to have stayed home, ladyship," Ludford said. "The rabble run things here. No place for a woman of breeding."

Selena let that pass.

"Did you bring with you any assets belonging to your own family?"

"Why, no, I . . ."

"All right." Ludford stopped writing. "Let me explain a few things to your friends, Dick. First, as to property. The two of you, man and wife, may make whatever mutual arrangements you wish, as far as your finances are concerned. But a woman cannot hold property in her own name. Remember that."

Selena flared. Why, even at home in Scotland, if Father had not gotten into all that trouble, her own title to Coldstream would have been inviolate, even as a woman! What was this?

". . . yes, those so-called democrats say they'll change it when they get power, but I doubt it. Now you, Mr. Bloodwell. When you own property in our community, you may vote. But not until then. So if you wish to participate in the affairs of the New York colony, I suggest you look to this. . . ."

"I intend to. Immediately."

Ludford stood. Interview concluded. It had gone very well, Selena thought.

"One more thing," Ludford added, in a cautionary voice.

"Yes?"

"These are critical times. We are in search of a master spy, who is apparently working directly from New York harbor. So I must tell you that, in addition to the uniformed soldiers who are serving as police during the military action, I have my own plain-clothed man watching the city and I have sent for the best treason detector in England."

"Yes?" Sean asked again.

"For your own protection," Ludford said. "Until you get settled. One or another of these men will look out for you. You may not be aware of them, but they'll be there."

Sean nodded courteously, but he and Selena understood at once. They would be watched. Now she understood the uneasiness that had pervaded Fraunces Tavern on the previous evening, when Ludford had dined there with Lord Howe.

Riding in the cab back into the business district, Selena fought to keep her anger under control. It would not do for Dick to perceive in her behavior any hint of rebelliousness or ingratitude. He had been watching her closely in Ludford's office, and already she thought he might have developed suspicions about her. But to be spied upon by plain-clothed operatives! And some horrible man from England was arriving to hunt traitors. . . .

"Tell you what," Dick Weddington offered. "Sean, let me drop you at the bank and then take Selena over to the waterfront to look at what the housing market has to offer. We can meet for lunch, and this afternoon you and I can devote ourselves to Bloodwell-Weddington Enterprises. I'll turn the harbor over to my assistant, Grimsby."

"That is very kind of you. And Selena can spend a little time with our daughter. . . ."

"Oh, Sean. Davina is fine. We've just arrived . . ."

"Yes," he said, "but it's a new place and . . ."

"She'll be fine," Selena maintained. "I'd like to participate when the two of you . . ."

"Not this time," Sean said. "You take care of Davina. You'll be a participant in everything. Don't you worry."

She let the issue drop for the time being. It was silly to become overwrought because of the plans for one afternoon, but Ludford, damn him, had managed to upset her with his mention of property and voting, too. Had this information affected Sean in some subtle manner? Those jewels and the wealth they represented were *blood money!* She had risked her life to get them. She accepted the fact, of course, that the MacPhersons bore a responsibility for the loss of Sean's early fortune. But they were partners now. Davina would get on quite nicely with Traudl. Sean was being too solicitous and protective. There was business to be attended to, and the road to Scotland had to be paved.

Weddington dropped Sean at a busy corner near the bank building, which was a stone structure three stories high. In the daytime, the business district was swarming with people on the move.

"Good-bye," he called, and then snapped the reins at the bays. "Your husband is going to make much progress in this country," he said to Selena.

"I think so."

They rode in silence for a while, then Dick asked:

"Something happened, didn't it?"

"What? What are you talking about . . . ?"

"It's all right," he soothed. "You're with a friend. A closer friend than you yet know. You see, if my judgment is any good, I believe we share a considerable number of opinions and attitudes."

What did he mean? Was he trying to trick her into revealing her true feelings? What did he suspect? Was *he* one of the plain-clothed agents Ludford had mentioned?

"No, something happened, didn't it? Why did you leave your country? Did you have to? And how did you get to India?"

"You certainly ask a lot of questions . . ."

With frightening abruptness, Dick sawed the reins, and the horses almost reared as the bits cut into their mouths. Instantly, they were off the main street that led down to the waterfront, and moving at a brisk, rackety pace through something that resembled an alley. Weddington jerked the reins again, and turned onto a side street. Someone leaped at Selena from a space between two buildings and in an instant had jumped into the cab beside her. The thought of abduction flashed through her mind, and she lifted her arms to strike at the intruder. He caught them easily and held her firmly, but without hurting her. Dick laughed.

"You boys should do as well against Howe," he said.

"We shall," smiled the man who had joined them. "We certainly shall."

He was quite young, fair, and very attractive. In spite of his youth, his voice was cultivated, touched by easy assurance. His eyes revealed high intelligence, authority, and great cleverness. He dropped Selena's arms.

"I was just telling Selena that she's among friends."

The young man nodded. "So she is, if you say so. But with her beauty, I'm sure she would be accepted in company far more elegant than ours."

Selena looked at him more closely. It was not only the flattery. He really *was* magnetic. In spite of herself, without wanting to, she felt her body responding to his closeness.

"But perhaps we shall meet at a better time and place," he was saying to her. Then, quickly, to Dick: "What have you?"

"They expect the general to move against Boston. What news from the field?"

"No, he's turning at Peekskill in November, and moving south. I'm leaving New York. I'll join the staff for the duration. Too many people are looking for me here."

"Have you anything we can count on? For morale?"

"I don't know for certain. But there is talk of an attack to the south. In New Jersey. Probably around Christmas."

Weddington was enthusiastic. "What a surprise that would be! A Christmas attack! The British stack arms and drink themselves into a groggy stupor when the end of the year comes around . . ."

Selena could not quite believe what she was hearing. Weddington had said "the British" as if he were not one of them. . . .

"We've a long way to go, from Albany to Trenton, so don't build hopes too high. Anything might happen. The trick, as he explains it, is to avoid a fight until you are certain that it can be won. I suppose we ought to take our own advice."

He laughed then, and she heard in it a touch of Royce Campbell's spirit and confidence, with just a hint of invincibility. They reached the end of the street, and, as suddenly as he had come, the young man leaped out of the cab and was gone down the street.

"Good," Dick said to her. "Howe thinks he's moving

north toward Boston, and already he's planning a maneuver to turn the army south. . . ."

"What are you talking about?" Selena demanded. "Who's 'he'?"

"Washington, of course. And in a week or so he's going to have himself one superb adjutant."

"You mean that . . . that young man who just . . . in an *army?*" She spoke a bit more vehemently than necessary, still disturbed by the physical effect the "young man" had had upon her.

Weddington laughed again. "Alex can do anything he sets his mind to. Last year, and himself just a student at King's College, he literally galvanized the Continental Congress with his theories on government and finance. I see that you were attracted to him."

"I was . . . I was no such thing!"

"Don't be alarmed. It's natural. All women respond to him like that. It makes his friends, myself included, a bit envious, I'm afraid." His voice took on a serious tone. "I wish he would curb his penchant for womanizing, though. I'm quite sure it'll be the cause of Alex's downfall, sooner or later."

"Alex?" she asked, thinking that if a man of only twenty years was to serve as an aide to the rebels' top general, their cause must be tattered indeed.

"Alexander Hamilton," Dick said. "Born in shady circumstances in the West Indies. He means to have as much wealth and power as anyone, and he's a democrat besides." He paused a moment. "I *think* he's a democrat," he added. "What did you think of him?"

"I was just thinking that boys who barely shave cannot possibly hope for victory."

"And how old are you?" he asked with a grin.

She was startled by her own response: twenty, and to remember all she had lost, all she had been through, and all she had endured to reach this place of comparative safety. . . .

"Twenty. Almost, anyway," she said aloud.

"You see?" he said complacently.

The horses drew the cab down on the Bowling Green, and the great houses stood there, watching on the Hudson.

"I doubt these will compare with Coldstream Castle," Weddington said. "But I'm sure you'll adjust."

She turned toward him, her entire body jerking as if pulled by a string of surprise.

"You *knew!*"

He nodded, smiling. "Yes. I put it all together in Ludford's office, when you gave the name MacPherson, and then Coldstream. I remembered what my father had told me about the Rob Roys, and how all that business saddened him. He greatly admired your father, too. And he thinks Lord North's policies will lose the New World for Britain. Aha, I see it in your face again!"

"What?"

"That slight turn of your lips, that almost imperceptible wrinkle at the bridge of your nose whenever something British is mentioned."

She touched her face. "Is it that obvious?"

"Only to a trained observer. But you should beware of revealing such prejudices, especially with a war in progress. This city can be dangerous."

"You are right. But what do you mean? Trained observer?"

"Selena, you're no fool," he said, reining the horses at curbside in front of a row of mansions. He was correct in that assumption, too. Hamilton's sudden appearance, the flurry of information exchanged by the two men, and Dick's attitude: all led to one conclusion. He was the master spy that Lord Ludford was seeking.

"We're one and the same in our partisanship," he said. "Let us cooperate, not least so that our fathers' lives are enhanced. This fine new land requires no king."

"But . . . but Sean's beliefs . . ." she doubted.

Dick waved away her objection. "He's a bright man. He'll be one of us before he knows it. When I understood who you were, and guessed at your ideals, not to mention your wealth, I felt I could rely on both of you."

"I'm not so sure," Selena said. She knew Sean, and his passions, and his dreams.

"Well, wait and see. I brought you along when I picked up Alex so you could see that, even though New York is strongly loyal to the King, there are still people like us here, there is still hope. I'd never think to involve you directly unless . . . unless, of course, you proffered your help."

She did not refuse him, but she could not accept his premise that the rebels had any hope whatever. She and Sean had not come to New York for politics. They had come for safety, and money, to use the city as a way station on the journey back to Scotland. That was the agreement, and they were partners.

"I'll say nothing of this conversation," she told him. "But I don't believe that I'm interested."

"As you wish." He climbed down from the cab and offered his hand. "Besides, we're here to find you a home and a substitute for Coldstream. At least for a time. The other is my affair. And I assure you that, in business, I'll make your husband the most loyal, most accomplished partner he might ever have imagined."

She believed him. He was a smart man and he knew his way about. There was a certain danger, but . . . but because the danger seemed removed, and because he shared her antipathy for England, Selena accepted the situation.

As they walked up to inspect one of the mansions, Selena wondered about the rebels. Did they truly have a chance? Then she had a sudden, piercing thought. She had to know something, and it could wait no longer.

"Did you ever hear of a man named Royce Campbell?" she asked.

INTIMATIONS

The house on Bowling Green was splendidly suited to a
rising young merchant and his wife and child. They moved
into it during mid-November, with the Hudson already
gray, and the air so cold one's breath frosted even at midday. Dark clouds rose in the northeast, and hung so low
over the city that Selena could see the river reflected in
them. Thin, cheerless flurries came every other day until
finally, with December, the skies sent down an avalanche
of snow. It hung upon the black cannons of the Battery
fort, iced the pitching masts of ships in the harbor. Soldiers
paced and stamped, warming themselves at bonfires on the
Green. The fires reminded Selena of Jabal-Mahal, and
Sherpa warriors, and dying Davi impaled on the stake.

She was weeping quietly at the large front window. Davina, now just over one and a half and already a sturdy
walker, came over to inspect. A cheerful little girl, she
seemed to bear no marks of her violent early days. Selena
had made a promise to return the child to Scotland one
day, to seek her kin, but she and Sean had no intention of
giving her up, ever.

"Éna?" the little girl asked doubtfully, seeing the tears.

"Yes, dearest?" she responded, bringing the sobs under
control.

"What's matter? Cry?"

"I feel . . . sad," Selena explained, taking the child into
her arms. "I just feel sad sometimes."

The child put her tiny arms around Selena's neck, hugging her.

"'Ove," she cooed, "'ove," and then leaned back, grinning. "See? Better?"

"Oh, you little darling," Selena cried, and tried to keep from sobbing again. The little girl's attitude was right, too, was it not? Selena should be happy. What *was* there to cry about? Everything was going so well.

Each day, Sean would leave the house in a horse-drawn coach of his own, and his Negro driver, Beauchamp, would wheel him over to Wall Street and his office. The street was only a disreputable alley, in truth, and one could see at a glance that it had little to contribute to the future of he city, yet many offices were centered there. Bloodwell-Weddingon Enterprises was one of them. In his careful, methodical way, taking care not to arouse suspicion, Sean had traveled once to Boston and then to Philadelphia—both of which were larger than New York—in order to convert the maharajah's jewels. Now, with a capital of something over two hundred fifty thousand pounds, he had opened a small commercial loan establishment. He worked long days, meeting and getting to know merchants of the city. Dick Weddington had introduced him to some of the key men at first—Adolph Rinehart, the banker; William L. Duckworth, the brewer and manufacturer; and Gilbertus Penrod, the leading real-estate trader and speculator—and after that Sean made his own way. Sean had been very pleased with young Lord Weddington's help but, as ever, he wished the main effort to be his own. Banking and real estate were Sean's major preoccupations in these early days; he left to Weddington plans for the mercantile operations.

"You know," he said to Selena, one night in mid-December, "I can't help savoring the good fortune that brought Dick to us. He may well be an Englishman, but when it comes to profit and loss, he thinks like a Scot. He's already sectored the Hudson Valley and Long Island into likely purchase areas, and he's drawn up sample purchase contracts, one for farmers and food supplies, one for clothing manufacturers. He's even hired a staff of purchase agents, and a fine, eager lot they are. Benjamin Zeuchner, Jonah Welch, and Nathan Hale are the brightest lads I've seen in many a year. They'll be all over the area very soon, drumming up business . . ."

Sean went on speaking. He could see before him, stretching out toward the future, sweet, rolling vistas of power and accomplishment, position, security, and wealth.

Selena smiled, and tried not to reveal her growing sense of alarm. Those bright young men of Weddington's would buy supplies, for certain, and Sean would sell them to the British military, but she knew that Zeuchner and Welch and Hale, and probably many more, would also be in search of military intelligence for the rebel army to use. They would know the specifications of a sound uniform or a high grade of beef, but they would also know how to discern and report the movement of British troops, or the political mood of the colonists in the outlying regions.

Sean had once again demonstrated the scope of his imagination and the power of his will. But, in his self-absorption, he had a blind spot: politics. So determined was he to keep any political connection at arm's length, he did not read the situation in the colonies as adeptly as he might have. He spoke, for example, of an early end to the war. Dick Weddington told Selena that such an outcome was impossible. "If we falter now," he said, "we shall be hanged for traitors. As Jefferson wrote, 'We pledge our lives, our fortunes, and our sacred honor' to the cause of freedom. No, Selena, we're in this to our necks, in more ways than one. We're prepared to fight until 1780. Perhaps even beyond."

1780! Three more years. Three more years of suspicion and struggle and spies in the street. Three more years with Sean indirectly involved in espionage. And if it should be discovered by the authorities? Selena did not want to think about the possibility. Weddington or no, and hatred of the British notwithstanding, she knew that she ought to have said something to warn Sean as soon as she'd found out what was going on. Had she spoken to him early enough, they might readily have evaded any involvement in the colonial struggle. But it was too late now.

"Don't *worry*, Selena," Dick had assured her. "In your heart, this is what you want. Sean is protected by not knowing. Thus, if discovered, the fault will be mine. And, if he'd let himself consider the matter, he would be on our side as well. We are going to whip the British so dramatically that all history will ring with the shock."

"But how do you *know?* What makes you so sure?"

"Because we have to win," was his answer. "None of us will be able to survive hanging."

Small comfort in that.

Two months in America, Selena was thinking, *and already I'm involved in just as much trouble as I ever was.* She sat there in the fire-warmed parlor, watching Sean pore over plat books and ledgers. She felt empty and sorry and a little afraid.

"You've been a little morose lately, haven't you?" she heard Sean ask.

"What? Oh, no. Not at all." She tried to smile, but the muscles in her face would not obey.

"No, come on now." He got up from his chair and came over to her, knelt down beside her. "Tell me about it. I don't want anything to upset you. We have had enough of such things in the past."

She could see the concern in his eyes and she loved him for it, as ever. He protected her, and cared for her, and thrilled her with his lovemaking. And yet . . .

He was waiting for an answer.

"I don't know how to tell you," she began slowly, trying to find words that would explain her melancholy feelings without hurting him. "It's just that . . . that sometimes I feel hollow inside, as if time were slipping by, and nothing . . ."

"But, darling, New York is just temporary. In a few years we'll be prepared to return to our true home."

She touched his lips.

"Sean, this town may be scarcely civilized, but it *is* bustling. It is exciting, in its own wild way. You do things every day, and I spend my days here in the house, directing the servants, amusing Davina, and then when she's at her nap, I sit here by the fire and listen to the wind howling down the river. . . ." She shook her head and touched his face with her fingertips. "I thought we were going to be partners in everything," she said. "I want to do something, too."

He smiled, and the look of concern left his face. So *this* was the problem! Why, then it was not serious at all! Had he, perhaps, suspected something else?

"Of course we are partners," he said. "What is it that you want to do?"

She began to tell him of something that she had been considering. "Sean, have you seen how the women dress here? It's frightening. Even the prettiest of the girls walk around in gowns that seem fashioned from flour sacks. . . ."

"Probably they are. This is a frontier country. . . ."

"And wouldn't it be fine if someone were able to design and sell really beautiful gowns right here in New York? There are so many gowns and costumes that can be made. Gowns that don't have to be shipped over from Europe. And I've been thinking that the effect of a sari, properly translated, could make an exquisite garment. I don't know how to sew, but seamstresses could be hired, and I remember how the seamstresses at Coldstream made their designs and cut patterns . . ."

Sean understood. "You aren't speaking of opening a shop, are you?" he asked.

Selena nodded. "Yes. Sean, I *want* to do it. I know I could make a success of it. . . ."

Sean shook his head. In the old country, daughters of the nobility did not keep shop. And, here in the new land, as Lord Ludford had illustrated so bluntly, women did not participate in public life or affairs of trade. Women could not even vote!

"But what will people think?" Sean wondered. "After all, we're just getting established here, and . . ."

"I want to be a real partner," she told him. "Just as we agreed when we were on the *Blue Foray*. Just because something is not done here does not mean it is against the law, and there is no *law* against me having a dress shop, is there?"

He had to agree. There was no law against it.

"Oh, Sean, do agree to it. Please agree to it. What I have in mind is not the keeping of a fish cart, but something fine that will appeal to women of my station. . . ."

Sean understood that, as well. When she saw the smile forming on his lips, she knew he had agreed.

"All right," he said. "I'll wager you would have found a way to carry out your plan even without my formal approbation. So this is what I shall do. I'll rent you the best shop in town and have it all fixed up for you . . ."

"No," she replied, shaking her head. "No," she repeated,

a bit more gently. "I'd rather . . . that is, I'm very grateful, but really, I'd like to . . ."

Sean looked a little rueful. "You'd like to do it on your own, is that it?"

She nodded.

"Well, perhaps that's best, too. But watch out for landlords in this town. The men in real estate here are especially crafty."

"I know," she said, "I sleep with one."

They laughed then, and embraced, and were in accord once more. But Selena was troubled by more than inactivity and Dick Weddington's espionage operation, even though he'd told her, time and again, "Selena, it will never involve you, and I've even set it up so that Sean will be in the clear." She was also disconcerted by something else that he had told her about.

Royce Campbell.

"If you'll forgive my impertinence," he had said that day on Bowling Green, "I was wondering when you would ask. Selena is not the most common of names, and I daresay there is but one vessel on the seven seas so christened. Knowing Campbell's beliefs, I also felt that you would share our feelings toward Britain, which is another reason why I approached you so directly and so soon. . . ."

Royce Campbell's beliefs? she had wondered.

The story, as Dick Weddington told it, left no doubt that Royce had somehow survived the plague. But the man about whom he spoke seemed different from the one she had known. There was, in Dick's rendition, no evidence of the lighthearted, casually reckless adventurer Selena had loved. Instead, he seemed a man possessed of inner fire, a driven man.

"He shipped into New York sometime last fall," Dick related. "He was on some half-arsed excuse for a freighter that had picked him out of the drink somewhere on the Atlantic. First minute in port, and he's calling for directions to the nearest shipyard. Nothing would do but that he have a ship, his own ship, no questions asked and money no object. He attracted much attention due to such speed, and also because of his appearance. He was gaunt, burned by the sun, and his eyes were afire with a strange, icy light, as if he'd had a glimpse of heaven somewhere on the edge of the earth and needed the ship to sail back there and seize that vision again. Nor did Campbell remain silent about his political loyalties. It seemed he had a score to settle with the British, something they had done to a person who meant a great deal to him . . ."

At this point, Dick had cast her a sidelong glance, but she said nothing.

". . . and he vowed that the cannons aboard his new ship would be trained on anything and everything that flew the Union Jack.

"Such talk was balm to those of us who had already made up our minds for independence, but the authorities were less enthusiastic. The shipyards in Boston and Providence and New York were closed to him. As harbor master, I did what I could, but I knew no one would build him a warship. Then he went on down to Baltimore. His sea fever must have died down somewhat by that time, because he handled the matter with a touch of discretion. . . ."

"So the *Selena* was built in Baltimore?"

"No. They wouldn't build it for him there, either. But he hired an entire shipbuilding crew in Baltimore, right on the spot, and then hired a ship to take the entire crew down to the West Indies. Apparently, he had some property there, or knew some people . . ."

Selena remembered Veronica Blakemore, who had been from Jamaica. Memory of the cold beauty with the raven-black hair was not pleasant.

". . . and there in the islands the ship was built," Dick went on. "And Campbell is at sea again, and our hopes for victory sail with him. I tell you this, I'd not like to be a British captain facing down the sixty cannon on that mighty craft."

Selena remembered Royce on the bridge of the *Highlander*, and the savage joy with which he had readied his guns for the *Meridian*. Involuntarily, she thrilled to the memory. She trembled. And, at the same time, she realized her excitement must be perceptible to Weddington. Abruptly, she had started away from him, walking up to the house that she and Sean were to purchase shortly thereafter. Her heart was in tumult, and she tried to think logically. The feeling she had experienced upon seeing the *Selena*, and again when Dick had spoken of Royce, was a feeling she could

no longer indulge. It could only lead to false hopes and a
breaking of vows. She had learned. Dreams, no matter how
delicious, led to trouble. She was a woman now, not a
schoolgirl with a pride of beaux and a room full of ball
gowns. She would put away forever thoughts of that which
might have been. It was the best advice that anyone could
have, and she gave it to herself.

Selena waited until the Christmas holiday was over before she bundled into furs and scarves and ordered Beauchamp, their Negro driver, to take her into the business
district of the city. She had previously studied a list of
agents that was published by the town fathers, and she had
selected Gilbertus Penrod as the potential agent to help her
in securing a location. Penrod was one of Sean's competi-
tors in real-estate acquisitions, but the man was well regarded. He and his wife, Samantha, were likewise important figures in the social life of the colonial city.

Selena was a little nervous on the drive downtown, and
her mood was not improved when Beauchamp contrived to
turn down the wrong street, snarling several coaches and
hansoms at an intersection. Disgusted, Selena poked her
head out of the window and inspected the scene.

"My God, Beauchamp," she called out to him, "have
you no brains at all?"

The big black man turned and scowled at her.

"Hit war Binlow and Bowers' fault, ma'am," he claimed,
accusing the horses. "I didn't have nothin' to do wit hit."

But the fault had clearly been Beauchamp's, and the
other drivers were yelling at him, and telling him to get a
move on. A crowd was starting to gather, laughing at the
big driver's ineptitude and, now, his refusal to accept responsibility for it. Selena felt the red flash of anger dart
through her brain.

"Don't lie to me," she told him. "If you'd been a servant
at Coldstream, I'd have you stretched to your toes and
flogged down a peg or two."

She shouldn't have said it, regretted it instantly—
especially because of the fate she herself had endured as a
mere object for the use and pleasure of others—but the
crowd on the street loved it, and called their encouragement. Beauchamp, however, did not react likewise.

"Ma'am," he said, with a good measure of outrage, "I'se a free nigger, an' you got no call to talk to me that way."

So saying, he got down from the cab, tossed the reins on the seat, and stalked away.

Damn, she thought, sitting there. The other drivers were still shouting, and the crowd, having lost Beauchamp as an object of amusement, now turned to her plight, which they found quite entertaining. No gallant strode forth to give her aid.

So be it. She climbed out of the cab, holding her skirts carefully over the muck in the roadway, and climbed to the driver's seat. *To hell with Beauchamp,* she thought. And, with the gathered crowd cheering her on—they were more than a little surprised—she grabbed hold of the reins, sawed the horses to the left, and slashed at their rumps with the leather ends of the reins. Startled, the horses made a tight turn, practically under the very hitches of another team. They reared, neighing in protest. The cab nearly turned over, righted itself. The turn was complete. Shouting, she slashed at the horses again, and Binlow and Bowers, Sean's prized harness team, dashed off in the direction they'd come.

The crowd along the street murmured appreciatively and called their congratulations after her.

"That was some woman, eh?" the men said to one another. "Doesn't take anything from horse or nigger, did ya see? Spirited gal'd give a man a ride, too, I'll wager. An' a looker. Did ya see that golden head o' hair?"

Everyone had seen it, truth to tell. Selena's scarf had fallen free in her climb up to the driver's seat.

Everyone including a thin, hard-looking man, with darting, intelligent eyes and a predatory mouth. And a hat pulled low over one side of his head. It gave him the aspect of a hawk with its head cocked to one side, calmly considering the best strategy of attack upon its prey.

Someone else had seen her, too. Big and rugged-looking in his beard and coarse dockworker's clothing, Will Teviot concealed his surprise. Since leaving Kinlochbervie and fleeing Scotland, he had learned to hide his emotions. It was a skill he had had to learn in order to survive. And it was a skill he would need more than ever now that he had come to New York. While at work on the docks in Yarmouth, Nova Scotia, to which he had fled after leaving Scotland, no one would have partiuclarly cared that he had been a Rob Roy. But it would be different in New York with a war against England in progress, a war that stirred Will's fighting blood again.

My God, the little spitfire made it to safety, Will thought, remembering the shame of his attack upon her in the Kinlochbervie hut, and curbing an impulse to go after her. *That was an expensive team of horses, too.*

He wondered if Selena was still the fiery young girl he had rescued from McGrover's men in that peasant's hovel. He hoped so. But there was no time to think of it now. He was in New York to seek out the man who had helped him escape from Scotland and, by way of repayment, to offer his services. Will Teviot shambled off down the street, a little self-consciously. Passersby always noticed him, and looked up at the big man who was heading their way.

The man with the tilted hat waited on the street corner, too, until Selena was out of sight. He did not follow her, either, but instead turned down toward the Battery, walking swiftly. In moments he was at the Battery fort, and not long after that he was seated in Lord Ludford's dry, chill, Spartan office, speaking hard words, very quietly, deliberate as a judge. The question: whether to move right away, or wait and see how much else might develop that would be of use to His Majesty's forces?

Haste was ruled out; the men decided to wait. His Majesty, this morning, could use as much good information— and good luck—as he could get. The news, even now, was spreading like wildfire throughout the city, received by rebel supporters with a joy that was hard to suppress, and causing many a fence straddler and sunshine patriot to give this whole matter of independence another thought.

Because, on the previous evening, Christmas night, General Washington had lashed out with a craftily fashioned attack, crossing the Delaware River and capturing a thousand of the Hessian mercenaries fighting the British cause in New Jersey. And, even more sanguine to the rebel cause, the Virginian had managed to preserve his own army, once again evading the pursuing British, retreating safely to the easily defensible heights near Morristown. It was as

Dick Weddington had explained to Selena: As long as you have an army in the field, you cannot be considered beaten. Selena understood that feeling very well: *You are not defeated unless you believe it.*

Gilbertus Penrod seemed in high good spirits when Selena entered his real-estate offices that morning. She had hitched her team outside and climbed down from the driver's seat under the appreciative gazes of several fast-walking businessmen. Inside, she opened her fur coat, to show the dress better, and unwrapped the scarf from around her neck.

"I'm Selena Bloodwell," she said.

Penrod looked up with interest and, after a moment, approval. He was a man of average height, with sandy hair and the ruddy complexion and slightly swelling paunch of a man used to roast joints of beef, potato dumplings in gravy, and a healthy jolt of strong porter with his meals. He certainly looked like a man who enjoyed a party, and his well-tailored suit bespoke prosperity. It ought to, Selena thought. Gilbertus Penrod was the biggest landlord in New York, and just lately—people were calling him a fool—he had acquired a three-hundred-acre tract of land on the East River. Sean, however, was not calling Penrod a fool; he had wanted the land as well, but he'd underbid. It was his first real setback since arriving in New York.

Selena stood before the man who had bested her husband, and she saw that his curiosity had been aroused by her appearance. He stood up and motioned her to a chair. His manner was cordial and gracious, as befit a man who was doing well at his work and enjoyed it, too.

"Mrs. Bloodwell. Of course. What can I do for you?" he asked. "Is this a business or a social call?"

"A business call," she answered. Then, thinking of the glittering parties the Penrod's were known to give, she added, "Afterward, if all goes well, who knows?"

Penrod pressed his well-manicured hands together, and smiled in genuine delight, inspecting her closely and with no lack of appreciation.

"Perfect," he said. "Now, as we say in the trade, what can I do for you, Mrs. Bloodwell?"

For the next ten or fifteen minutes, she explained what

she had in mind. A small shop for high-quality women's fashions, with an area, either upstairs or in the back, in which seamstresses might work. "It will have to be well-lighted," she specified, "so they can see what they are doing. It improves the work and increases the amount of work they can do. . . ."

Penrod nodded, impressed by her judgment.

". . . and I'd like it to be a brick building in a good area. That way it will be accessible, not dangerous to go to, and, as for the brick, cool in the summer and easily heated in the winter."

"Well," he said, when she had finished, pressing his hands palms down on his desk, "you are certainly a thorough woman, Mrs. Bloodwell, just as—I have heard—your husband is. But why have you come to me? Surely he . . . ?"

He kept his features blank. Too blank. Was he thinking *trouble in the family?*

"I have my husband's full support," she said, with a reassuring smile. "It is just that I wish to proceed from the very beginning."

"The best possible way," Penrod agreed. Already, he was taking her seriously. "The best possible way, indeed. And, I might as well tell you, I think you're on to a good thing. At home, I seldom hear Mrs. Penrod or any of her friends speak of the local couturiers—if such they may be called—with anything but the most profound sadness."

"That is what I had hoped," said Selena.

And Gilbertus Penrod laughed with delight.

"Mrs. Bloodwell," he said, "I think you and I are going to get along well. Very well, indeed."

Selena sat there for a moment. She said nothing, nor did she show any emotion. But she sensed already that the life she and Sean had thought they wanted here in New York—the life Sean still wanted—was about to end before it had fairly begun. Something *was* missing in her life; something *had* been missing. *Coldstream, of course, but . . .*

"Don't you agree?" Penrod was smiling. Only a second had elapsed, and he was not yet aware that Selena, sitting there before him, was trying to fit things together in her mind.

. . . but we can't have Coldstream yet. No, the house

*on Bowling Green is not enough and . . . and pretending
to be something I am not will* never *be enough. . . .*

Even if it wins you Coldstream? asked that tiny, galling
voice.

Selena stopped short at the thought. It was true: she
could *never* have enough until she possessed Coldstream
Castle once again. She was doing the right thing. The dress
shop would hold at bay those dark feelings with which she
had been oppressed. Her instincts had been correct. She
needed something—temporary, of course—to ward off that
other feeling . . .

"Well, Mrs. Bloodwell? Shall we move forward?" Penrod
was asking.

. . . the feeling that *something was missing!*

This knowledge was accompanied by the usual dollop of
guilt. *Ingrate! Whiner!* taunted the tiny voice. *You were
never as happy in your life as you were with Sean on the*
Blue Foray.

"Mrs. Bloodwell?" There was just the faintest touch of
concern in Penrod's voice now.

Yes, her instincts had been right. This shop would fill
the empty feeling. It was a feeling that ought not to be
there anyway, merely the shadow of anxiety that is always
experienced by those who have survived great dangers. It
was natural, but it meant nothing. *Your problem is that
you have more than enough,* she admonished herself.

"Let's take a look at some locations," she told Gilbertus
Penrod.

SYMBOLS OF SORROW

Winter of 1777. The rebel army was encamped near Morristown, New Jersey, to which Washington had retreated after his successful surprise attack on Trenton. Everyone agreed that there would be at least another year of war. Dick Weddington, who paid Selena periodic visits to her shop—and she needed cheering, with the rush and chaos there—was very pleased at the prospects. "A hundred plans are in the wind on both sides," he told her. "And a hundred rumors for every plan. It's my job to deduce what is true, and pass the word to our forces. By the by, Alex sends his greetings from Morristown."

He would always watch her closely when he mentioned Hamilton, to catch her reaction, as if he suspected more than mere attraction between the two. Selena thought that she had successfully refrained from showing anything but polite interest. After all, what else was there to show? Besides, she was too busy to engage in frivolous conversation. She had enough work to keep her occupied, and in gray, depressing February the work seemed more of a burden than usual. When April came, and she opened her shop— she had named it La Marinda, in memory of the poor Spanish girl who had chosen death before dishonor—the incessant activity would slacken. She would be able to enjoy the fruits of her accomplishment, and no longer feel so harried, her time divided between family and shop.

And, with the summer, everything would be fine again. Wouldn't it?

The light of dull February dawn pushed thin wedges of pale sun through the storm shutters outside the bedroom windows. At long last. For the past hour, Selena had been lying in bed, fully awake, her mind on the coming day and all that had to be done at La Marinda, where six crotchety and often recalcitrant seamstresses were busy fashioning a line of clothing Selena had designed.

Then Sean shuddered into a stretch, turned over in the bed, and came drowsily awake. He had been keeping long hours in his study during the winter evenings; he wanted his pleasure in the morning.

"It feels much keener then, anyway," he said.

Whatever misgivings Selena felt about the demands upon her, she and Sean still shared pleasure happily, cherishing their bond. She watched him come out of sleep, with his needs and desires and dreams. First, his needs. He rolled over and cupped her breasts, pushed up close to her with a drowsy growl. They made love slowly, affectionately, with high delight. Sleep had refreshed their bodies, which responded joyously to every sensation, and the quiet peace of dawn offered an aura of security in which they confirmed their union, rekindled their love. Selena put her concerns somewhere far away, and gave herself to his skill and the wonder it aroused in her body. Soon, too soon, she felt her mind fading, felt the delicious itch glowing in her flesh, and then intolerable pleasure assaulted her in waves. The pleasure held her in its grasp and she belonged to it and to Sean who gave it; the love and the pleasure owned her, shook her to the end of all desire.

But she did not forget.

"You're pensive this morning," Sean said a little later.

"Not really. I was thinking of all I have to do." But she had been thinking, guiltily, of Royce Campbell. Making love to Sean was wonderful, but the memory of Royce intruded sometimes in the afterglow. Selena did not let herself wonder why this should be so. It was not that she would be afraid of the answer, but rather that the answer itself would evoke more questions.

"Are you going directly to Wall Street after breakfast?" she asked, to take her mind off the subject.

"No. Some bankers are calling on me at the house, and I expect to be busy with them here until noon. They wish to appoint me to their board. They also desire some of our capital. Have Otto drive back here to the house after he takes you to the shop."

She agreed, and they both got up and began dressing. Otto Kollor was their new driver, a Hessian mercenary who had been wounded, captured, and then released by Washington's forces after the debacle at Trenton. His wound had left him with a limp. He could no longer be a soldier, and he had not wanted to return to his repressive homeland. Selena thought him dull and overbearing, but even though he *was* very slow, she could not bring herself to admonish him. Not after what had happened to Beauchamp.

"Don't blame yourself for that, Selena," Sean kept telling her.

True, Beauchamp had blundered that morning after Christmas, and Selena had reprimanded him justly. That had been that. It was not her fault that, later, some thugs had apparently gotten hold of him—angry, no doubt, at his public insolence to a white woman—and beaten him to death. His body had been found in the Harlem River. But Beauchamp's death led to certain unsettling implications. Dick Weddington, who made it a point to examine all untoward deaths for evidence of espionage activity, told her: "Selena, don't blame yourself. But from the markings on the man's body, I'd judge that Beauchamp had been tortured. There was a rumor, just after Christmas, that a Negro was being interrogated at the Battery, but I haven't been able to attain corroboration. Anyway, what could Beauchamp possibly have known?"

"Just a terrible coincidence," Sean had said. "Knock on wood."

Nevertheless, the event disconcerted Selena, and the effect was a lingering, distasteful one. Sometimes, when she was especially afflicted with the winter doldrums, when even work could not drive cares from her mind, she would feel that the blood of three people was on her hands: Davi and the maharajah, and now Beauchamp.

Selena ate a hasty breakfast, and barely had time to listen to little Davina, who chattered about the snowman she and Traudl had made yesterday. Selena had returned home in darkness on the previous evening, and had not seen the creation. Now she went to the window, saw it, praised it, but had to rush off so quickly that the little girl seemed vaguely disappointed. Kissing Davina and Sean, she hastened outside, out into the damp cold. The seamstresses would already be waiting in the snow outside the shop, and how they would gripe and complain when she arrived late!

She looked around for the coach, but it wasn't there. Otto, late again! Perhaps they should try to hire yet another driver, but it was difficult to get people to sit out in the cold, urging a team of horses down icy streets. Also, Sean had reasoned that it would serve to bolster their reputations as loyalists to have as their driver a soldier who'd fought Washington. Impatiently, she went around the corner of the house and down the alleyway to the stables. The coach was out front, and just as she approached, Otto led Binlow and Bowers from the stable.

"Otto, could you please hurry?"

His wide, flat face displayed an instant of wisdom.

"You vant go to town *schnell*, eh?" he grinned. Then he painstakingly hitched the big horses to the coach.

"Otto, *please!*" She climbed into the coach.

The driver turned sullen. "I do mein best," he protested. "I do mein best *alle der zeit*."

He gave her a very hard look, and it unnerved Selena. Then he climbed up into the driver's seat, favoring his gimpy leg. They set off, the horses unsteady on the ice. Selena tried to decide why Otto's resentful stare had bothered her. Then she knew. It was the gaze of a subordinate who knows he will soon rise to a better position. But how? And with what assurances? Suddenly, she felt afraid of Otto Kollor.

The seamstresses were waiting outside La Marinda, just as Selena had feared. Six women, their eyes angry and accusing as they warmed their hands over a small charcoal brazier at curbside. Young boys set up these braziers in winter, charging customers a penny to warm their hands over the glowing coals.

The seamstresses immediately demanded that Selena reimburse them for the expense.

"I come in early, Miz Bloodwell, so's t' do that sari effect on the muslin frocks fer summer, just like ye told me, an' then ye wasn't even here yet. My poor, poor hands be freezin' cold. Won't be able t' sew a stitch fer hours. . . ."

That was Callie Fox speaking, a big-bottomed, whining woman, whose lack of delicacy was partially excused by speed of performance.

And Selena remembered that she *had* told the women to come in early. All she could do was open the door, let them in, and hope they got down to work as soon as possible. With the April opening approaching, Gilbertus Penrod kept dropping by to see how things were going. He had a ten percent interest in the shop.

Selena had not needed his ten-percent investment, but she had accepted it for two reasons. First, she was pleased at the interest of one of New York's most important men. Second, she hoped to attract the attention of his wife, Samantha, and, through her, the best clientele in the city.

Now Callie Fox rushed up and broke Selena's train of thought.

"Miz Bloodwell! Miz Bloodwell!" she cried, close to serious apoplexy as usual. "It's Mr. Penrod at the door! It's Mr. Penrod at the door!"

"Well, let him in," Selena said impatiently. He stopped off regularly to inspect progress, so his visit was scarcely surprising. He came in briskly, and bent over her hand. But his manner was different. She could not believe it for a moment, but the self-assured Penrod was actually tense.

"How are you, Selena?" he asked, glancing around. No, not merely glancing, he was *checking*. But for what?

"I'm fine. We're a little behind schedule but . . ."

He didn't even seem to hear her.

"Ah . . . would it be all right if . . . if Mrs. Penrod were to stop by . . . I mean, quite soon, before the clothes are really ready for the opening? To take a look. She has friends and . . ."

"Of *course* it would be fine!"

This was just the kind of thing for which she had been hoping! The interest and potential sponsorship of some woman who had friends who were interested in—and who could afford—good clothes. "Why, I'd be . . ."

Penrod watched Callie Fox until her broad beam disappeared back into the workroom. Then he collected himself and spoke quickly.

"I've got to ask your help," he said. "Late this afternoon, you may have to provide a service. I do not think it will be dangerous, but it is necessary . . ."

"Well, what . . . ?"

He held up his hand to his mouth, looked around the room again.

"Could you hide someone here?"

Selena was startled. Gilbertus Penrod, thoroughly established and formidably reputable, wanted her to *hide* someone!

"I'd have to know why," she said, after a moment.

"It's better if you don't," he replied.

Selena remembered a time, long ago, when Father and Brian had discussed just such a question. They had concluded that it would be best if she had something to confess. Penrod disagreed.

"Best if you know absolutely nothing," he said again.

She felt a surge of apprehension pass through her body. *By now I should be adept at this sort of thing,* she thought. The secrets and maneuvers and desperate machinations of men! They were predictable in only one thing, and that knowledge could not help her now.

"I'd certainly like to be of help . . ." she temporized, smiling at him, trying to read his mood and expression.

Now she regretted even the little she knew about Dick Weddington. His activities held the possibility of dangerous repercussions. And Gilbertus Penrod was surely among the strongest loyalists, an adamant supporter of the King. What else could he be, having reaped the social and financial benefits of colonial New York?

Penrod was growing increasingly nervous, however. He spoke softly, but his smile was nervous and tight.

"You will come to no harm, I assure you. . . ."

"Ah, familiar words," she retorted. If a man of Penrod's power needed help from her, needed help badly enough to expose the vulnerability behind his armor of casual superiority, then she was right to be suspicious.

"The only thing is, I have to know now. It's a small thing, and won't take long. It might not even be necessary. But you have the room, and the crannies . . ."

He indicated the sewing areas, gestured toward the back rooms, lifted his head toward the ceiling.

". . . and it seemed to me you are a woman I could trust . . ."

Selena thought fast. Should she take the gamble?

". . . that I *do* trust, in fact . . ."

Very shrewd of him, she thought. He had already given her the bait: contact with his wife, Samantha.

"All right," she said abruptly. "I'll do what I can. But who is it going to be?"

"You will find out when the time comes." He rose to leave. She was still wondering whether she had made the correct decision. There was no way to be sure.

"*If* the times comes," he added. "And I cannot thank you enough."

"It's all right," she assured him, less than enthusiastically, thinking: *Now I'm involved with a rebel spymaster and a loyalist leader. Is that good or bad?*

No sooner had Penrod hurried out of La Marinda when Callie Fox approached Selena. The seamstress was still blowing her thick fingers, as if to relieve them from chill, but they were pink with warmth.

"What'd 'e want, Miz Bloodwell, eh?"

Selena glanced up sharply.

"Why . . ."

Why did the woman want to know? No. Don't reveal a thing.

"Why, Mrs. Penrod may be in later this morning. To look over our gowns. I hope you're up to schedule on your assignment."

"Miz Penrod!" Callie Fox exclaimed, much impressed and a little afraid. And she hustled back to her work.

For almost an hour after Penrod's departure, Selena went about the shop, getting it in order. Countless bolts of material, all fabrics, all colors, were arranged in bins, on shelves, in stacks along the walls. Many more, unrolled, uncut, were spread out on tables at which the seamstresses worked. The activity served to restore Selena's composure. By the time Samantha Penrod appeared, a little before noon, Selena was calm and confident, the mistress of her domain.

Mrs. Penrod had extraordinary presence. Not a great beauty, she managed by dress, grooming, and a force of character that was immediately evident to Selena to give the impression of strength, warmth, and physical magnetism. She was desirable. But it would take a strong man to hold her interest, to please her, and Selena understood why Samantha Penrod attracted the most illustrious company in New York. In spite of the situation, Selena felt comfortable in the other woman's aura.

"Mrs. Penrod, welcome to my shop. Your husband was here earlier, and mentioned that you might be stopping by."

"Call me Samantha, please." she smiled, removing her gloves, and a lush cloak of beaver and ermine. "Gilbertus has told me so much about you. And your husband. Do you mind if I have a look at what you've done so far?"

"I wish you would. There've not been too many New Yorkers stopping by to make inquiries. . . ." She said it with a wry tone, to which Mrs. Penrod responded:

"If this city has a future, my dear, we're going to have to fashion it ourselves."

They both laughed, and there was a quality in the woman's manner and style that Selena liked very much. Wary as she had had to become, Samantha's warmth and confidence were disarming.

Careful, Selena. There are things you don't understand.

Mrs. Penrod moved to the long row of hangers on which Selena's designs were arrayed, and slowly made her way from one to another. She did not speak, merely took each item in turn and inspected it closely for style, stitching, and accouterments. Silence. The seamstresses, openmouthed at the presence of such a well-known woman in this fledgling shop, gaped and stared. Down toward the end of the row, pausing over an evening gown, stark white, and simple as a sari, but bare at the shoulders and throat, Selena saw the color rise in Mrs. Penrod's face. What was the matter? Was the gown immodest or in bad taste?

"My God, Selena!"

"What?" she cried, hearing the anxiety in her voice. "It's made to be worn with . . . ah . . . a gold necklace, or something . . ."

"These are beautiful! And this gown is . . . exquisite. Do I recall Gilbertus telling me you spent some time in India? Why, what you've done here is extraordinary. . . ."

Selena started to thank her, but Samatha cut her off.

"Not necessary, I assure you. I am the one who should thank you, and there are many other women in New York who'll be doing that soon. You're truly gifted . . ."

The seamstresses, a little stunned by this wealth of praise, looked at one another, excited and proud. Selena took the opportunity to introduce them to Mrs. Penrod.

"These are the women who ought to be thanked. What I know of designing, I learned from them, and from the seamstresses back home in . . . in Scotland."

"Scotland? Is that right? Ah, yes. Gilbertus told me. Your father was in the House of Lords, was he not?"

Selena admitted it, her tone flat and even. Samantha Penrod smiled, seeming to withhold some comment upon the fact. Again, she turned to admire the row of designs. "And what are your plans for showing these?"

"It was my intention, when the weather gets better, to have a demonstration. Right here at the shop. The only problems are that I don't really have any models, and that I'm not quite sure how to pass the word around. Sean knows lots of people, but they're all businessmen, and . . ."

Samantha raised her hand. "I must confess, my dear, that I came here this morning with ulterior motives. Each spring, toward the end of April, Gilbertus and I give a masked ball, and I hope you and your husband will be able to attend."

"We would be delighted," Selena answered. This was exactly what Selena had hoped for.

"I always try to do something to make the event different each year." Again, Mrs. Penrod glanced at the dresses and gowns. "I thought perhaps it would be interesting this year if some of my friends might wear your creations before and during dinner. After dinner, of course, we costume ourselves for the masque . . ."

Selena scarcely believed what she was hearing.

"It might be a way of introducing your shop, you see. . . ."

No. More than an introduction. It was an outright gift.

Mrs. Penrod took Selena's silence for deliberation and pressed on, seeking to persuade her. But Selena had already decided. Of course she would agree. But, she wondered, why were both of the Penrods so interested in her?

Finally, arrangements were made, plans discussed. Mrs.

Penrod invited Selena to lunch, but business was pressing, there was much to do, and Selena had to decline. Samantha extended her hand, smiling, and the two women parted, friends already. Selena decided her wariness had been nothing more than the result of agitation, although she was still puzzled by this sudden stroke of fortune. And the seamstresses were overjoyed.

"Goodness, ma'am! A fine lady lak that. An' she took me hand, too, yes she did. Are we goin' t' be the best shop in New York? What d'ye think?"

"We may already be the best shop in New York," Selena told them, proud of them, pleased with herself. Only Callie Fox sought the cloud around the silver lining.

"You think you're something, don't you now, Miz Bloodwell? T' be a hangin' out with the rich swells . . ."

"What's the matter with you, Callie? No one's forcing you to stay here."

A bitter smile. "Facts, Miz Bloodwell. I need the money, and you need me. I want more money, truth to tell."

Selena smiled, and attempted to cut the woman off. "All right," she said, loud enough for the others to hear, "you've done a fine job, and we're going to do very well. We haven't sold a single gown yet, but we will. So, starting this week, you will each receive an extra half-pound wages.

"A half-pound!" they exclaimed. It was quite a lot of money.

"Only a half-pound?" Callie Fox whined, but went back to her work.

"You're slower than the others today, Callie," Selena responded, in a moment of anger for which she was soon to be sorry.

"I always do my work, no matter how long it takes," Callie replied sullenly.

Selena pondered how she would attempt to deal with Penrod's request, and she was pleased when it began to snow heavily in the early afternoon. Her first plan had been to get the women out of the shop by telling them that she absolutely had to return home early today. But now, as the sky darkened and the wind drove rattling flakes of snow against the shop window, she saw the seamstresses glance at her every few minutes. *Let us get home before the blizzard sets in.*

Several times, Selena went to the window and watched the people hurrying past, bent into the wind, then returned to her desk, murmuring, "so much work, and now a storm," just loudly enough so that they could hear her. Finally, as if submitting to the forces of nature, she said, "All right. It's no use. You'd best get on home. But be here bright and early tomorrow morning."

The women bundled up in their cloaks and scarves and boots, called their good-byes, and went out.

Every one of them, that is, but Callie Fox. The big-bottomed seamstress bent over her work, her lower lip stuck out like that of a belligerent pig.

"Callie, I said you could leave. The storm seems to be getting worse."

Callie Fox did not deign even to look at Selena. "You criticized my work," she said accusingly. "I'm going to finish what I started, just like I always do."

Selena fairly danced with frustration and annoyance. She had everything well-planned, should Penrod's mysterious caller appear. She had even managed to dismiss the seamstresses. But now Callie Fox was kicking up a row.

"Look, Callie, I must close up the shop and get home myself, before we're snowbound here."

"Oh, is that so?" Callie answered, a shrewd peasant glint in her eye. "Where's your driver, Otto Kollor? Did you expect to walk back to Bowling Green?"

Now Selena used her initial stratagem: She had to get home early. Otto would be along any minute.

"But you criticized my work!"

"Callie, I'm sorry. Now, please . . ."

It happened then. The door crashed open and a man rushed in. He was breathing heavily and had obviously been running hard. He wore dark, nondescript clothing, and had a ragged, faintly incongruous beard.

"Where?" was all he said. It was more a command than a question.

Selena had considered the problem all day. There was no celler in the building, and the upstairs did not even have a closet. Anyone seeking a man in La Marinda would first look among the rows of hanging gowns or among the piled bolts of cloth. She had thought of another possibility, and although the hiding place was not inviolable, it was the best she could think of. But she had intended to be seated at the sewing machine herself. Instead, to Callie's speechless outrage, she pressed the man down beneath one of the machines. Callie had been working her slow way across the hem of a gown, a long train of cloth falling to the floor. Selena pulled it up, arranged it, saw the man hunched down next to the footrest, and draped it over him. For a good measure, she tossed the remnant of another bolt of cloth onto the machine, a careless, haphazard sprawl of fabric.

"Back to work," she ordered, just as a British soldier burst into the shop, winded and panting.

"Did ye . . . did ye spy a . . . a man come running . . . minute ago . . ."

He paused, gulping air, looking around. Another solider appeared in the doorway, musket at the ready.

Selena feigned fear, and stepped backward, between the soldiers and the machine under which the man was hiding. Callie Fox, red as the uniform coats the soldiers wore, seemed angry and about to speak.

"What is this?" demanded Selena forcefully, to cut the seamstress off. She was certain now; Callie Fox could not be trusted. But who *could* be trusted?

"Ma'am, begging your pardon, but we're going to 'ave t' search this building."

He wasn't begging anyone's pardon; his voice was harsh.

"No. Where is your authority?"

The first soldier smiled mockingly. "We don't need any authority. What are you? One of them rebels?"

"I'm a loyal British subject."

"That's what they all say," replied the soldier with the gun. "We seen a man run in here, and we're lookin' for 'im."

"You saw no man run in here. This is a simple dress shop. Now, if you don't mind . . ."

She moved forward a little, as if to escort them to the door.

"Halt," said the soldier with the musket, raising it slightly.

"All right," Selena said, thinking that she had resisted enough. "I'm sorry," she said smiling. "it's just that you startled us. I am a loyal subject, as you can confirm. My husband is friend to Lord Ludford . . ."

The soldiers looked at each other, properly impressed and mollified.

"I'm sorry, ma'am. We didn't mean t' bust in 'ere, but we was on the chase, y'know 'ow 'tis. Still, we must 'ave us a look around."

"By all means," Selena agreed. And then, while the seamstress looked on in stupefied and admiring amazement—Callie Fox seemed impressed, for once—Selena took the men upstairs, into the back room, among the hanging garments and bolts. She even lifted aside some of the draped material that hung over the edges of the worktables.

She did not approach the sewing machines. And she did not have to. Her psychology had worked. The two men, hostile at first, then just a little abashed, now felt like guests in her shop, and began to act as such.

"We got t' thank ye, ma'am, an' you can be sure we won't be blastin' in at ye again."

"Next time we'll knock, sure," his companion hastened to added. "Now, we got to be off and find our man."

"Who is he? Perhaps we here at the shop might be on the watch for him and his kind."

"Just some rebel, no more than a lad. We'll get 'im, don't ye worry now."

A lad? The man who'd rushed in and was now sheltered beneath the sewing machine had been bearded.

The soldiers went out, thanking her, apologizing, thanking her again.

The door slammed shut against the wind. Neither Selena nor Callie moved for a minute; neither of them said a word. Then the draped fabric was pushed away from the sewing machine and Selena found herself staring into the bold, measuring eyes of the erstwhile quarry. He could not be seen by Callie Fox, but he removed his beard momentarily for Selena's edification.

It was Hamilton. "Perhaps your assistant ought to leave now," he said.

Selena motioned for Callie to get her wraps. "Do as he says."

"But, Miz Bloodwell," the seamstress protested, putting on her cloak and trying to catch a glimpse of Hamilton, "I can't leave ye, and how're we t' know yer all right . . . ?"

Selena did not know what to say. "It isn't what it seems to be," she started, knowing that sounded not only unconvincing but suspicious as well, when Otto Kollor came driving up in the coach. Sean, having observed the oncoming storm, must have sent him down to take Selena back home.

"See, there's Otto now. He'll take care of me. You just let me handle this, all right?"

Callie Fox shrugged and went outside, pausing to talk to Otto, and pointing almost immediately toward the shop. The big Hessian tried to peer in through the frosted window.

"Well, now," Hamilton said calmly, coming out of his hiding place. "I can't say that was comfortable, but it certainly proved to be welcome."

He yanked the false beard off entirely. His face was smooth-shaven, just as young, bold, and handsome as she remembered. His eyes were even bolder than his face. He stepped close to her.

"I believe we might get along well together." Even his *smile* was proprietary. "If there's *anything* I can do . . ."

"There isn't."

He feigned disappointment in such a way that she was sure it was just another ploy in his approach.

"Perhaps, on the occasion of our next meeting . . ."

"There won't be any . . ."

But, as she spoke, two things occurred. First, she realized that Penrod had asked her to shelter a rebel leader. No, that couldn't be; Hamilton's appearance must have been accidental. Second, she caught a glimpse of Otto Kollor through the shop window. He was leaning forward, bent into the wind and snow, talking with Callie Fox. The seamstress was gesticulating excitedly, and now and then Otto turned to the shop, shaking his head.

"I believe you are safe now," she told Hamilton. "I must take my carriage home."

"If I were you, I'd watch out for that big-bottomed cow. I don't believe she's on our side."

"Don't be presumptuous enough to include me on your side. But how do you come to say that about Callie?"

"Because she kicked me five times while I was under the sewing machine," Hamilton replied. He was serious. "It was only when I put a knife to her underparts that she desisted."

Selena saw it at once. Callie was telling Kollor. That meant . . .

"Look, you've got to leave. Or stay here, and let me leave. I've got nothing to do with this."

His glance was direct. "Come now. I know your past. I know your bloodlines. And I sense your instincts. You are one of us and have been since you left your mother's womb. That's your nature, my lady. The only difference between us is that you were born rich and I was born poor. But that doesn't matter, because we share the same spirit. And we'll both turn out rich anyway."

He had moved very close to her. She met his eyes, all right, but her body was doing those disturbingly familiar things again. Outside, Callie Fox disappeared down the snow-drifting street, and Otto Kollor waited.

"I must be going."

"No, we must wait for Weddington."

"I can't. I don't trust . . ." She inclined her head toward Otto, who was now stomping his feet and beating himself with his hands to exaggerate the chill.

"We can have him eliminated. Don't you do that to your drivers?"

He smiled. He had actually *heard* about Beauchamp?

"That was . . ."

"Do not think of it. Have your husband threaten to dismiss him. Hessians can't get jobs too easily, and he is lame as well. He will be tractable."

"You seem quite confident."

"I am. And in more ways than one. Look, you are one of us, you are like me . . ." He moved closer.

Too close. But he did not touch her. Intimacy came naturally from him, sweet as an invitation to delight. With his bearing and confidence, he was close to irresistible. Against her will, in spite of the circumstances, she felt herself going . . .

They were both startled when Weddington entered. Selena gasped, and Hamilton stepped back, raising his fists in defense, then smiled in relief as he recognized his compatriot beneath the snow-covered hood.

"Dick," Selena cried, turning on him, oblivious of big Otto pressed up against the window, "Dick, you've used me badly. You have, and you know it. I keep getting deeper and deeper into something I don't understand . . ."

"You don't understand fighting the British . . . ?" Hamilton started, trying to make a joke. Weddington raised his hand, and Hamilton ceased.

"First you get me involved just a little," she accused Dick. "Then you say it won't involve Sean. But it does. Of course it does. I should have been true to my vow and gone to Sean right away . . ."

The two men exchanged glances.

". . . and now Penrod is involved, and you've tricked him, too, somehow. The pillar of the business community, and my partner. Do you have no sense of shame? How can you attract followers at all . . . ?"

She stopped when she saw the puzzled, somewhat chagrined expression on Dick's face.

"What is it? *Now* what is it?"

"Selena, didn't you guess? Gilbertus Penrod is the foremost financial contributor to the cause of the Continental Army. We thought you were with us. And I meant what I said. If I had not thought you willing to be with us, to help us hide Alex, I would never in a thousand years have asked you. But what was this about a vow?"

She explained her promise to Sean: no political turmoil, and no giving vent to her anti-British feelings.

Hamilton just shrugged. "It's up to you. But we must meet again, don't you think? Dick, I'd best get out of here. Maybe there'll be some money on my next trip. Is there a back way?"

There was, and, while Otto was out of sight, tromping up and down the street to keep warm, the young rebel made his escape, bearded once again. Selena reached for her own cloak, still angry, somewhat fearful about the broken vow, and puzzled about her reaction to the apparently incorrigible Hamilton.

She started for the door, but Dick restrained her. There was sympathy in his expression.

"Well?" she asked, still governed by the anger. "What else do you want me to do? What other surprise will you have for me, to get me more involved in . . . *treason?*"

The sound of the word on her lips brought on a quiver of nausea, which she suppressed.

"I understand now," Weddington told her. "I have gone too far this time. I ought to have told Penrod to be perfectly forthright about what was to occur, about who . . ."

"And you ought not to have gotten me involved in the first place."

Selena was trembling now. Everything seemed to be coming down upon her: misunderstandings, conspiracies, complications. And, in the back of her mind was the old, sure knowledge: *There is retribution when a vow is broken.* But she did not want to admit, just then, that she had been enthusiastic when she'd first learned of Dick's espionage work.

"All right," Dick concluded. "You'll be involved no more. Unless you wish to be. But Alex was right. You're just like him. You're just like us. Because you have that necessary spark of independence in your soul . . ."

Memory carried her back then to the captain's cabin aboard the *Highlander,* when Royce Campbell held her in his arms and said, *"Selena, you've got the fire . . ."*

Don't think of that.

". . . it's a spark that maybe one person in a thousand possesses. The rest of them go their way, doing exactly what they are told to do, never thinking, never judging. Never *acting!* That's why we need you. You're strong. You *can* act . . ."

"I really must be going."

He smiled a bit apologetically. "I understand. You've made your promise, and I've made mine. But will it be all right if I continue to stop by from time to time?" He raised his hand as if taking an oath. "No politics. I promise."

Selena had to smile. She agreed. After she locked the shop, they parted.

"What were you and Callie Fox talking about?" she couldn't resist asking Otto Kollor as he helped her into the coach.

Either Callie Fox had misread the entire situation, or Otto was not as dull as she had thought. "Ach, it var her *sprechen,* all time talk, talk talk. She did say you had a poor man in there, hiding of the *Soldaten.* Das var a gut t'ing you var going, Frau Bloodswell."

"Bloodwell," Selena corrected.

She saw it in his eyes again, that look of someone who knows important things. His eyes were slyer than she remembered.

"Let's go home," she said, and they drove off into the sightless swirl of the storm. The ice and snow slowed them, and it was very dark when Selena saw the lights of their house on Bowling Green. Davina had already been put to bed for the night, but Sean was waiting for her.

"I was worried," he said. "I thought I might have to saddle up and come searching for you."

Selena shook off the snow and hung her fur and scarf on a peg near the doorway, and pulled off her boots.

"Why don't we get another driver?" she said.

"Because he was late in a storm?" Sean asked. She could tell by his tone that he had no intention of doing any such thing. And she also understood that she had best let the matter drop. If she told him that she thought Otto might be spying on them, he would want to know how on earth she had gotten the idea. He would want to know what she had to hide. She could not mention what had occurred today at La Marinda. Nor could she breath a word of Penrod's request that she hide Hamilton, and certainly she could not say a word about Weddington, Sean's associate.

"I just don't like Otto," she said.

He embraced her, and told her not to worry, and they went in to a fine supper of veal stew and fresh-baked bread and wine. She told him of Samantha Penrod's visit and of the masked ball to which they'd been invited. Sean was very pleased, at first, but then, gradually, his mood seemed to fail, and he appeared to be trying to pretend a cheerfulness he did not feel. She did not respond to his mood at first, but when his morose aspect lingered on toward bedtime, she asked him what the matter was.

"Is it something to do with my shop? Or don't you want my gowns worn on the night of the ball?"

He looked at her for a long time, almost sadly, as if wondering whether to speak at all.

"No, it has nothing to do with your shop," he said. "But

mention of the ball brought my mind back to the Christmas Ball at Edinburgh."

"I don't understand."

"Well, I guess it's not that, exactly. I was thinking of another man we knew then, and that thought recalled something I heard a few days ago from Lord Ludford. I've been trying not to think of it since then."

He was talking about Royce Campbell, obviously, but . . .

"I'm sure you know this already," he said quietly, his eyes not leaving hers. "There is a rebel ship on the sea that bears your name."

He was genuinely hurt; she did not know what to say.

"But . . . but I'm married to *you*," she stammered.

"My name does not begin with an *R*," he told her, holding her gaze.

He *had* heard, that night they were making love. And ever since that night he had been keeping it to himself, suffering, not saying a word.

"I'm sorry," she said, hugging herself suddenly, as if warding off a chill. "It happened that once, but it will never happen again."

He looked at her.

"Not even in my mind," she promised. "I have been faithful to you, and I always will be. Not because I have to be faithful, but because I want to. Oh, Sean. We've been through too much, learned too much about how the world is, to let anything break us apart now. . . ."

The tears in her eyes were born of love and loyalty, and Sean knew it, and took her into his strong embrace.

"You should have said something right away," she told him between kisses. "You should not have had to suffer alone when there was no cause to suffer at all. . . ."

He kissed her hungrily and pressed her body close to his. Enveloped by an inexorable tide of passion, they sought with their flesh to burn out all doubt, to push aside the burden of the past. He lifted her and carried her up the grand staircase, then down the long hallway into their bedroom. The candles had not been lighted, but the storm had ceased. Moonlight reached them from the icy blackness of infinity. It was a cold light, but the moon gleamed upon their naked undulations until, hot as passion, warm as pleasured flesh, it blossomed like a mighty flower. Became, for one moment, a sun. She held him with her body when the moment came. Dazed circles of light exploded behind her closed eyelids, so many that she could not count. Nor count the minutes in which she held him.

Then it was over. Wordlessly, they slept, Sean deeply, Selena peacefully. Royce had not been with them. She had a dream of him, however, shortly after dropping into sleep. He was somewhere on the high seas, standing on deck, braced against the roll of the mighty deep. A black cloak stirred and rippled about his shoulders as the wind took it, and his eyes were on the western horizon. Heading for America. His presence was so real, so very close, that she almost felt him there with her in the dream, and awoke suddenly with a sob to find him gone.

Awake, she felt a pang of disloyalty and kissed Sean as he slept. Then, still nervous, she pulled on her robe and walked to the window. The moon shone cold again and very bright. Icy and watchful, it hung in the black abyss, at once an observer and an omen.

Like the man Selena saw then, as her glance fell to the frigid and snow-scoured street. He stood very close to the house, his cape so black it actually glistened in the snow-shine and the moonlight. She could see him so clearly, so closely, that she put her hand to her mouth, stifling a cry. He stood still as stone, rapt, undeniable, implacable. And he seemed, just as naturally, to sense her presence, as a predator will incline its head to the slightest ripple in the wind, to the slightest turning of a leaf upon a tree. And, like a cobra, his eyes caught her, trapped her there at the window. Selena stood motionless, incapable of movment, as, slowly, slowly, with an extended parody of saturnine grace, the man removed his hat. Lifted his angled hawk's face to her, and turning, ever so gracefully, revealed the ear that ought to have been gone. The ear she had severed at Foinaven Lodge.

It might have been made of rubbery gum, or even wood. But it was attached to his head. McGrover was here. He was the man who had been summoned from England to track the wolf of treason to its lair.

Selena shuddered, and closed her eyes. When she looked again, he was gone.

She crept back into the warmth and safety of the bed.

Sean and Selena Bloodwell were wealthy and powerful now, well-known as loyal to the King. Darius McGrover could be no more than a functionary in Lord Ludford's entourage. Selena would, of course, continue to devote time to her shop as a woman in business. Nor would she spurn—indeed, she would eagerly accept—the Penrod association.

But she knew it was time to be careful. Very careful.

And, falling once again into the embrace of sleep, she realized that, ever since her arrival in America, she had been waiting for this moment. She had been listening in the night for the scurrying, ratlike sounds which meant that luck was running out.

The past is something that can never be denied, or changed, or pushed aside. But it is the business of the living to make the future what they will.

THE MASQUE

"You look absolutely ravishing, my dear," Samantha Penrod said, "and everyone is delighted with your gowns."

She herself was dressed in one of Selena's inspirations, a luxurious creation of silk, satin, and beads, and the two women stood at the entrance to the long, oak-beamed dining room in the Penrods' mansion. Selena, herself the object of many an admiring gaze, had carefully chosen a garment of royal blue satin, with a deep neckline and velvet trim. She watched happily as women and men alike applauded a high-necked, long-sleeved, stark-white creation with just a touch of ruffles at wrist and neck. It was worn by young Isabel Rinehart, the banker's daughter.

Surprisingly, Mrs. Penrod sighed. Selena turned to her.

"Just the guests, my dear. What with the war, I had to be especially careful about whom I invited tonight. But I think everything seems under control, don't you agree?"

Selena agreed. She did not know about Samantha's parties in years past, but of one thing she was certain: problems of the winter had flown. She had kept away from any further connection with politics; Dick Weddington had likewise been as good as his word, and had not involved her in any way after Hamilton's appearance at La Marinda. And, at home, she and Sean had been very happy. Royce Campbell had not been mentioned again. Everything seemed under control, indeed.

"Thank you, Samantha, for all you've done. You know how grateful I am for this chance to show my gowns. Now tell me, how is the evening to proceed?"

"Nothing elaborate. After dinner, all of us will retire to don our costumes, and then descend to the ballroom for the masque. What disguise have you chosen?"

"I shan't tell," Selena replied, thinking of her Scottish peasant girl's costume. Sean already knew how she would appear, having come into the room where Traudl was working on the costume. Sean himself had kept secret his own disguise, wagering that she would not be able to know him even if they were dancing with each other. That was a challenge, and she was eager to prove him wrong. She saw him now, handsome and elegant in formal dress, the white of his shirt collar matching the gleam of his teeth as he laughed at something that had been said. He was standing near the sideboard, holding a glass of spicy wine punch, talking with a mixed group. Several women whom Selena did not know were eyeing Sean quite frankly and appraisingly; Selena felt both proud and jealous. But the pride held sway. Samantha begged to be excused to make a last-minute check on the readiness of the serving staff, and Gilbertus Penrod joined her.

"Well, Selena, tonight we begin to rake in the profits, eh?" He was in an exuberant mood, resplendent in evening dress and a silk cravat. "By tomorrow morning, half the women in New York ought to be knocking on the door of La Marinda."

Selena continued to watch the guests as they arrived, and took a deep breath, trying to subdue, at least a little, the exhilaration that was causing her heart to race. Already her designs had shown every sign of success and acceptance, and that meant she would enter New York society in her own right, not merely as a friend of the Penrods, kind as they had been, important as their support was and would continue to be. *And* she would be the full partner she had told Sean she wanted to be. Her confidence continued to grow as she studied the gowns worn by the women. Except for her own creations, the best seemed to be in the English style of two or three seasons past, with here and there a newer gown—possibly French—that made the English ones look dowdy indeed. Her own designs had scarcely any competition.

Then the orchestra began to play quietly in the background, and guests began to move toward their places at the many tables. Selena let her glance sweep the crowd one final time before going to join Sean and make their way to the head table. Suddenly, incredulously, she froze on the spot. Entering through the main doorway, chin lifted and eyes bright, as casual and arrogant as any man possessed of money and power and a fine woman, was Alexander Hamilton. Selena's eyes were drawn to the woman. She was startlingly beautiful, raven-haired, ineffably self-possessed, with just the hint of a smile at the corners of her tempting mouth, a smile that mixed amusement and boredom, mockery and the promise of delight. Veronica Blakemore. Selena recalled her feelings on that long ago evening at the Christmas Ball in Edinburgh, when she'd seen Royce with Veronica.

She still has the same smile, Selena thought, not liking, either, the fact that Veronica was with Hamilton tonight. She did not have time to dwell on her displeasure, however, because Hamilton's presence led to an entirely new—and dangerous—train of thought. If Hamilton could arrive here openly, with little or no fear of being identified, then this gathering must be . . .

She remembered what Samantha had said about the guest list: Glancing quickly around the room, she saw that Lord Howe was not here, nor his brother, the admiral. Lord Ludford was not here, nor any of the other luminaries she had come to know as the backbone of British presence in the city. And, come to think of it—she shot the group a reconnoitering glance—even the men talking to Sean did not look especially familiar. Except for Dick Weddington, who was studying the crowd, too, with pleasure and satisfaction. She soon discovered why.

"All set?" Gilbertus Penrod asked. "Come, let's go over and have a drink with your husband before we're seated. Isn't this a splendid group? We'll raise a lot of money tonight."

"A lot of money? Certainly, if my gowns . . ."

"Of course. Of course, your gowns will have great success. But I meant the fund raising."

This time she did not even ask a question. He responded instead to the perplexity in her expression.

"Didn't Dick tell you?" he asked. "No, he must have thought that you already knew. This is a fund raiser for the Continental Army. Hamilton is here to take the proceeds back to General Washington. These ninety-day enlistment periods are brutal, and the spring plowing is coming near.

If the general doesn't pay off his troops, he won't have any."

"A fund raiser?" she managed. True, no loyalists appeared to be here, but there *had* to be spies. There were *always* spies. Or stories, and rumors, and reports.

Now Sean was involved, whether he knew it or not. His avoidance of politics had succeeded all too well; both sides regarded him as neutral.

Selena thought her luck could get no worse, but she and Sean were seated at table with Hamilton and Veronica Blakemore. It was as if a tightrope had been stretched the length of the dining room, and Selena was bade to march it with her arms tied behind her back.

Trouble began immediately.

"You seem vaguely familiar," Veronica Blakemore said, yawning delicately and flashing a hand cold with jewels. "Didn't I see you once in the provinces somewhere?"

She smiled—a smile for Selena. Hamilton caught it, however, and sensed what was happening. Female byplay. The prospect amused him.

"Now, Veronica," he said, feigning displeasure, "let's not spoil the evening."

"Far from it." She put her hand on his arm, to display her intimate intentions toward him—which Selena guessed had already been long established—and gave Selena another smile, this time one of cold challenge.

See the man I have? You could never take him from me, not in a million years.

"I don't believe I caught your name," Sean was saying to Hamilton. "You're in trade?"

The look in Selena's eyes must have been one of pure, raw warning. Hamilton saw it, but his own expression betrayed nothing. Whether he had read the situation, she could not tell, but he decided on a prudent course.

"Alexander," he said, extending his hand. "No, not trade, I'm afraid. Not yet. I'm still at my . . . ah . . . formative education. Public administration, you might say. I have, however, every intention of entering lucrative fields when the chance arises."

Sean was pleased. "Mr. Alexander, I wish you all the success in the world. This is just the country for realizing such an aim."

"And it's going to get better," Hamilton said, spooning soup.

"It's very good already," Veronica said in her honeyed voice, eyeing Sean suggestively. Her very manner was an invitation.

Hamilton saw this, too, and could not restrain a laugh.

"I beg your pardon?" Sean asked, looking up.

"Forgive me, sir. I was just thinking of that foolish man, Jefferson. You have mentioned the wealth of the country's future, and I agree with you. But we shall have to stave off the idealists and lunatics represented by Mad Tom."

"Isn't he the one who wrote that declaration?" Selena asked, trying not to look at Blakemore.

Servants came and removed the soup bowls; more servants were bringing the fish course, fresh river trout grilled over charcoal, seasoned with pepper and a white wine sauce.

"The same," Hamilton said. "Skilled with a pen, but crazy as a loon when it comes to providing a blueprint for society."

Sean was interested now, probably believing himself to be in the company of a staunch and clever young loyalist. Selena, in fact, was beginning to wonder just what was going on. Mr. Hamilton did not seem at all a rebel now.

"Must you go on about these things?" Veronica pouted prettily. "I find them so *dread*fully boring."

"We'll have enough time later for your kind of diversion," he told her bluntly. Then, once again to Sean and Selena: "Do you believe that Jefferson truly advocates the right to vote for people who don't own property?"

"The very idea is preposterous!" Sean exclaimed, putting down his knife and fork at the sheer enormity of the concept.

"*And* a nation based on agriculture," Hamilton added. "Ridiculous! We are a nation on the cutting edge of history. All about us the world becomes more industrial. Wealth lies in the hands of business, and those with wealth must run the affairs of the nation. The rabble must not be permitted to share power. After all, they will be sufficiently blessed as their share of the wealth trickles down to them."

Suddenly, rakishly, he winked at Selena.

"Don't you believe what you've just said?" she blurted.

"Of course. Certainly I do," he said. Then he laughed and changed the subject. "Would the two of you care to join us after the dance? I'm having a quiet little party at a place on Long Island." He spoke to both Sean and Selena, but looked directly at Selena.

Selena saw the alarm and anger that Veronica could not hold back. Then she recovered. "Now, dearest. We had *plans* for tonight, if you remember?"

"All plans are subject to change," Hamilton said, looking at Selena still more boldly than before. Even Sean, occupied with analyzing what Hamilton had said, did not miss the intent.

"Success sometimes requires that one's more troublesome appetites be controlled," he said pointedly. "It was you who just spoke of the excesses of the rabble."

Hamilton studied Sean for a moment, and there was a new respect in his voice when he apologized.

"Sir, you are right. I am often quiet senseless in the presence of beauty. I offer my apologies for any offense I might have given either of you."

"No offense was taken," Selena said.

"I quite agree," Sean said quietly.

"Beauty, indeed!" Veronica protested.

Selena felt a twinge of sharp, spiteful satisfaction. The cold, haughty beauty was just the least bit off balance now. Having won Hamilton, now she had to hold him. Hold him under the constant strain of his obvious attraction to beautiful women. Sean, seated beside her, knew what was going on. But he did not take it seriously. She knew him well enough to know what he would be thinking: *This Alexander fellow shows a lot of promise, but he'd better get this wench chasing out of his system or it'll be the ruin of him one day*. He would be thinking that Hamilton was still a boy, really. But, if that was true, why were Selena's juices flowing again? And why were the nerves of her body taut for pleasure and surrender? But she must not let it show, lest Veronica know, and, with such knowledge, regain the upper hand.

At the same time, Selena tried with all her might not simply to forget but not to remember at all the vision that tried to move into her mind, the vision of Veronica seated next to Royce Campbell on that terrible night in Scotland.

She was trying to do precisely that, when Blakemore returned to the attack, this time with a sensitive—might she have known how sensitive?—ploy?

"I know," she exclaimed suddenly. "It was Scotland. I saw you in Scotland!"

Her voice seemed deliberately loud, and people at nearby tables broke off their conversations and turned momentarily toward them.

"That's where it was," Veronica repeated. "Yes, both of you were there, and . . ." She turned to Hamilton. "At the time they were rather in the position you enjoy today, Alex. Indeed, you might take a lesson from . . ."

Hamilton retained his self-possession, but Selena could guess at the effort by the tiny purple vein that was throbbing over his left temple.

"Why, Veronica, you haven't touched your wine," he interrupted.

He reached for the glass and handed it to her. "It delights the palate. It also does wonders for the mouth," he added, with the faintest glimmer of wry admonishment.

It worked, if only because Veronica was so surprised. Most of the time, Selena guessed, Hamilton gave her free rein, for the amusement it would give him. But her question still lingered, and Sean, with his usual cautious discretion, put it to rest.

"Yes," he said, "I remember well. We met in Edinburgh, over the Christmas of 1774. Since then, my wife and I have done rather well in India. We expect to do as well here, and return home at some time. Have you been back to Scotland?"

Veronica merely shook her head, still smarting from the humiliation Hamilton had handed her. And now Hamilton himself had heard something of interest.

"You'd go back to Scotland, when our nation is at the forefront of . . ."

Once again, Selena tried to head him off. She was almost fast enough.

"Of what nation do you speak?" Sean demanded. He was no longer just curious; he was suspicious. Selena saw him glancing around the room. Not having gone to many large New York social gatherings or parties before this one, he might thus far have overlooked the fact that the main loyalists were absent from this dinner-*cum*-masque. But it would not be long before, with his innate shrewdness, he would put two and two together, and turn to her to supply the "four."

"Why . . . the British Empire, of course," Hamilton said.

This time Veronica laughed, and she did not bother to conceal her derision.

"More wine, dear?" Hamilton asked.

The waiters were now taking away the fish course, and bringing on the meat, a succulent dish of duckling stuffed with rice and basted in a port-and-honey sauce. Sean leaned to her and whispered.

"Something's wrong here."

Selena shook her head.

"Alexander seems to know you well enough," he said, giving her a hard glance. She saw all his hurt, all his old suspicion, flowing back. *That damn Dick Weddington.* And yet—she had to admit it—she did not believe Dick to be bad at all, nor even duplicitous. True, he had gotten her into some scrapes. But that was because he had thought she shared his beliefs, his rebel nature.

As she *did!*

That was the terrible part. She had made vows and had tried to keep them. The marital vow, to Sean, she had kept inviolate. But the other promise, to keep to herself the anti-British feeling . . . why, that seemed to go against her very nature. . . .

"Is this man a friend of Gilbertus?" Sean asked sharply. "Perhaps Gilbertus doesn't quite know what kinds of people come to an affair this large. Perhaps, by mistake, Samantha invited a few who are untrustworthy. . . ."

When the waiters left the table, Sean took a glass of red wine, which had been poured for all of them.

"To the British Empire," he called, standing at his place. His voice carried very well. All eyes turned toward him. "To England," he cried, his tone resonant and sincere. "To all she has been. To all she will yet be. And to victory in this war!"

For an immeasurable portion of a minute, it was as if time and life had fled that dining room. Selena saw Hamilton move back slightly in his chair, and saw in his eyes the spark of realization. Something was drastically wrong. A mistake—possibly deadly—had been made. Selena also saw Veronica's smile as she looked up at Sean and put her own two and two together. Danger. And she saw Sean himself, commanding, fervent, and sincere, with the glass of red wine lifted in the air.

The toast was answered with an ardor equaled only by its falseness.

"And to victory in this war!" they proclaimed.

Gilbertus Penrod was white as a sheet.

The chatter as the dinner drew to its conclusion was as bright and animated and frenetic as any Selena had ever heard, and the undercurrent was electric enough to deliver a shock.

Even Hamilton was subdued, and said nothing of consequence. Blakemore looked complacent, not oblivious to, but rather not particularly caring about, the political statement that had just been made. In her eyes, Selena's husband—hence Selena—had looked a fool. And that was enough for her. Almost enough.

"I guess I put this Alexander fellow's nose back in joint," Sean confided to her, as the waiters were bringing the sweet, which was apple pie with cheese, and coffee strong enough to send a cloud of aroma into the air. "He's not saying much now, you'll notice."

And that was true. *But,* Selena thought, *I suspect he's thinking fast.*

The guests' withdrawal to change into their costumes provided an interval necessary to restore equilibrium to the gathering. Selena was delayed on her way to the changing rooms by numerous congratulations on her designs. Samantha Penrod intercepted her before Selena was able to get into her costume.

"Gilbertus has just informed me that Sean doesn't seem to be here," she said. "Do you know if he planned to leave after the dinner?"

"No, of course not." Maybe it had something to do with his disguise.

"Gilbertus was worried about the toast. We did not know that Sean felt so strongly . . ."

Selena herself was more than a little concerned about the ramifications of this party, and she could not see how Sean could help but draw the correct conclusions as to its nature. She was attempting to reassure her hostess, however, when Dick Weddington joined them.

"Do you know where Sean might be?"

"I thought he was changing into his costume."

Weddington shook his head. "That toast . . ."

"I told you many times," she said, "that Sean will not yield on the issue of his support for Great Britain."

"I had hoped that, after a time . . ."

"You must never take Sean Bloodwell for granted," Selena warned him. "He may be immersed in his affairs, and thus he may seem quite above politics. That is, in a sense, true. But he has been badly wounded by politics in the past . . ." *and badly wounded by love, too,* she thought ". . . and he has no intention of suffering again."

"But if he discovers everything," Weddington worried, "my plans for the Long Island and Hudson Valley spy network are ruined."

"There is nothing we can do now," Selena concluded. "Let us get into our costumes."

Sean's apparent absence triggered a tiny warning in her mind, but, donning her peasant outfit, a catlike mask, and a scarf of Highland plaid, Selena hoped that his sudden disappearance had something to do with his mysterious costume. She adjusted the scarf to conceal the telltale gold of her hair, and checked the mirror. The mask covered her face from mid-forehead to mouth. The scarf was effective. And the costume, with its long, full skirt, quite obscured her figure, although the blouse accentuated rather than hid the youthful swell of her breasts. Oh, well, that was all to the good. She was momentarily unnerved by the stark deception that a mask can work upon human identity, but immediately the element of mystery became intoxicating. She realized that it had been years since she'd attended a costume ball. In fact, the last ball she had attended was the one in Edinburgh Castle . . .

She descended to the ballroom, excited my memory and anticipation, and the masque commenced.

The first dance was a reel, introduced to New York during the past several years by the many Virginians who had come north to attend political gatherings and meetings of the Continental Congress. Whirling and spinning to the music, trying to guess the identities of the dancers, Selena's body told her that she was still only twenty years old, hardly more than a girl. She rejoiced with the knowledge, laughing and spinning exuberantly, enchanted by the dance and the feeling of freedom it gave her.

Her first partner was a pirate—not tall enough to be Sean—and then she danced successively with an Indian in war paint, two devils, and a creature inspired by Greek mythology, whose headdress sprouted any number of serpents that were made of wire and cloth. She thought one of the devils might have been Sean, a suspicion enhanced by the fact that he did not speak to her. But the devil did not stand as straight as Sean, and after consideration she dismissed the possibility. The game was interesting, and the dancing exhilarated her. She felt happy and excited.

The evening grew very festive, that moment of tension at dinner now forgotten. Pausing between dances to catch her breath, Selena sipped punch beneath her feline mask, and watched the dancers in their multitude of costumes, trying to decide who they were. Blakemore (the preposterous bitch!) had been too vain to conceal herself well, too spitefully independent to accede even to the spirit of the masque. She wore (what gall!) a tight-fitting, low-cut gown, with just the suggestion of a train, and a bejeweled tiara that also suggested royalty. Her mask was but a little snip of gold cloth, and she held her chin high and haughty as she danced. Her partner, in the costume of a barrister, robed and wigged, danced with debonair grace. Hamilton. The sight of them dancing together—Hamilton, to whom Selena was attracted, and the conceited Blakemore woman—struck yet another chord of emotion in Selena. She remembered not only the wild exuberance of Edinburgh now, but also feelings of jealousy and competitiveness. *Anyway*, she thought, *Veronica did not win Royce either*. She felt a certain satisfaction as she reflected upon that fact, but memory of the Christmas dance was sullied, somehow disturbing.

The music stopped for a time and then began again. Selena did not believe anyone had yet guessed her identity—with the exception of Sean, who knew her costume, but whom she could not spot—but she was wrong. The masked barrister stood before her.

"Dance?" he smiled beneath his purple mask, and she took his arm for a grand promenade.

"You've lost your queen," she said, as they faced each other and bowed.

"I have no queen," he said. "I am a republican. She is amusing, isn't she?" His voice turned hard. "She was born to a great family in Jamaica. I was also born in the islands, though not to such genealogical distinction. At one time, she would not have deigned to spit on me, but she likes excitement, and she senses money and power. An adventuress, in short. She had a man, Royce Campbell by name, but he turned rebel and George the Third, in all his wisdom, saw fit to appropriate Campbell's lands. Have you ever heard of him?"

"I think so," Selena said.

Then Hamilton returned to the mood Selena associated with him, that of the youthful, clever man who is master of all he surveys.

"I shall offer you a lesson in politics, Selena," he said. "Do you mind?"

"No, of course not. What is it?"

"Veronica is the lesson," Hamilton said. "She will tell us—you and I and everyone here—when we have victory in our grasp."

"Veronica will tell us that?"

"Yes." He laughed. "When she cares enough about something to betray us, she will go over to the side of the loyalists. She has an unerring instinct for defeat."

"Do you think so?" His description did not sound at all like the woman Selena thought she knew.

"I know so," Hamilton said. "I have spent most of my life attempting to become accepted by the society into which she was born."

"Why?"

"Because I was not born to it. Besides, she *is* most amusing. But do not forget our lesson. And, more to the point, you are the one I desire. If you could find a place for me in your heart . . ."

She was flattered. His spell was working on her body once again. But she was also angry. He had been too bold, importuning her right before Sean, right at the dinner table.

"Now I understand why your general's army is still entrenched in Morristown," she parried. "You should tend to important affairs, and not the frivolous."

"I'm hurt," he said, his eyes showing no hurt at all. "We are discussing the most important of all affairs. And, as to strategy, we occupy the road to Philadelphia, which mighty Howe will attack this summer. If he gets around to it."

"And you will win?"

"Of course, I always win."

"And General Washington?"

"He has not lost since I joined his staff."

"He has fought one battle since you joined his staff."

"But we were victorious. My strategy never fails."

"*Your* strategy?"

"Of course. Why do you think we won?"

The music was ending; the dance was winding down. They were both aware of the current of excitement that flashed between them.

"But this time your strategy does not succeed."

"What?" he asked, holding her precisely one moment longer than any other man would have.

"No," she said. "The answer to your suggestion is no."

He smiled beneath his mask, not at all daunted. "Well, your husband is a fine-looking man. Perhaps another time. I cannot resist a woman who scorns me . . ."

"I don't *scorn* you . . ." Selena began, and saw by his clever smile that he had maneuvered her into just such a protestation.

"I am sure you would never do so base a thing," snapped the approaching Veronica, her eyes on fire with malice.

The sight of proud Veronica so reduced by jealousy gifted Selena with a measure of sinful pleasure. Blakemore might once have taken Royce away from her, but this moment belonged entirely to Selena, along with every twinge of satisfaction it contained.

"Wares too readily peddled tend to decrease in value," she said very sweetly.

Hamilton laughed with delight, then turned to Veronica for her reply, as if he were watching an exchange of blows at a prizefight.

"That is one of the maxims of your peddler husband, I suppose?" Veronica managed.

"Let's not speak of husbands," Hamilton advised. "They distress me. As do jealous women," he said to Veronica, softly but sharply. She quieted immediately, but the humiliation cut deep. With a quick movement of her hand, she jerked off her mask and glared at Selena. She said nothing, but she did not have to. There was a promise in her angry eyes, a promise of revenge. What galled her most was that Hamilton, to whom she had given herself, seemed to value much more highly a woman who resisted him. It was not the way she had learned the game, and this was not the way it was supposed to work out. Unable to countenance humiliation, she had exploded. And, having done so, she had shown herself to be a piece of goods. Expensive goods, without doubt, but still goods. It was not the way she thought of herself. Restoration of her self-esteem would require the humiliation of Selena, if not her destruction.

That was the promise in her angry eyes.

"Where is your husband, by the by?" Hamilton asked, after Veronica had stormed off.

"I must confess that I don't know for certain. But I think he's the man in the hangman's costume."

She indicated a tall man who stood alone near the sideboard, quietly watching the ball. He wore a soot-colored hood that covered his head and face and fell down to his shoulders. His boots and trousers were black, as was his loose-fitting executioner's shirt.

"I'm not entirely comfortable with the implications of his costume," Hamilton said. "Are you sure?"

"Well," she said, "he wasn't here during the early part of the dance, and Sean did contrive to keep his costume secret . . ."

"How unfortunate," Hamilton said, with feigned sadness. "There is little hope for me with a woman who plays love games with her husband. I believe he is looking at you, too."

It would have been difficult to tell if the hangman was looking at her or not, because of the hood, but Selena suppressed the impulse to return his gaze. Instead, she talked a bit more with Hamilton, seeking to make Sean jealous. She felt comfortable with the young rebel now, and he seemed to have been much impressed by her handling of Veronica Blakemore. And, although he gave no indication that he would cease to solicit Selena's favors, Hamilton's tone and manner indicated an acceptance of her as a person, not merely a woman from whom pleasure might be won. Or by whom it might be given outright.

Better if it must be won; he placed a higher value on it then.

The hangman appeared beside them when the music began again.

"May I have the honor of this dance?" he asked, bowing slightly. His voice was muffled by the hood.

"I must consult my counsel," Selena replied saucily, turning to Hamilton. "What say you, barrister? Shall a young maid dance with death?"

"Better you than I, my dear," Hamilton replied, withdrawing gracefully.

Wordlessly, the hangman led her out onto the floor. He seemed to be studying her intently, as if trying to identify her, as if he were not certain it was she, and suddenly she had a strange feeling that he might not be Sean at all. The sensation was one of deep disquiet, and she looked up with alarm at the opaque material that covered his face.

McGrover!

Her heart pounded hard inside her chest as, very slowly, he reached for her hand, and took it before she had a chance to bolt from the floor.

"Are you enjoying the masque?" he asked. The sound of his voice was familiar, but she could not place it exactly, it was so muffled. It *could* be Sean after all, couldn't it? The grip of his hand on hers was not ungentle. But the costume was upsetting.

The dance was a rollicking one that had originated in the hills of east Virginia. Several members of the orchestra were sawing away on instruments that resembled violins, which made a strange, not unpleasant sound. The music was fast and the dance also, and the dancers linked elbows with their partners, parted, linked arms and whirled again. Selena felt better when they began dancing, and her misgivings spun away. She had decided, once again, that the hangman was Sean. *All right,* she thought, *we shall play our game.* She gave him a smile, waiting for him to give her a clue. When he did not speak, she was utterly convinced he must be Sean, and that he did not wish to reveal his identity by the sound of his voice.

The dance required them to part and exchange partners for a time. Selena saw, with a measure of regret, that the hangman was paired with Veronica Blakemore, whom he seemed to be examining with considerable attention. Veronica sent Selena a spiteful smile of challenge, and it was almost with relief that Selena linked arms with the hangman again.

"Do you know this dance?" the hangman asked suddenly.

"No," she said. "I like it though."

They spun around, approached, linked elbows, whirled. People were clapping on the sidelines, in time to the insistent beat of the tune.

"I grew up with quite another kind of dance."

"As did I," he said after a moment. "But where did you grow up?"

A game. She considered the fabrication of an imaginary past, but the spirit of the music, the laughter and shouts of the dancers, reminded her of the heady dances of the Highlands.

"*Scotland!*" she cried, whirling again. She loved the way it sounded on her tongue, and, in spite of all that had occurred since she'd been driven from her homeland, at this moment, dancing after so long, every memory was good. "*Scotland,*" she said again, proudly.

"*Selena,*" the hangman said, in a tone that is known all over the world by anyone who has ever been in love. It is the tone that is used when you speak the name of a beloved to whom one has come home.

Selena knew at the very instant she heard him call her name. The hangman was Royce Campbell. She wanted to cry out. She wanted to scream with joy. She wanted to go to him and lose herself in the wonder of his embrace, in the glory of his very being. But the music went on and on, and they kept on dancing. After the initial shock, her mind worked furiously. He was a hunted man, and had taken a great risk coming to New York, even if the Penrods' party was not a Tory gathering. Nor could they speak, or hold each other, not even for a moment, here in the middle of the dance floor with the music pounding on. Then, with a shiver of dread, she caught a glimpse of Veronica, who was looking toward them, her eyes glinting with suspicion and malice. She had guessed. She knew! *I can't even speak his name,* she thought.

"Is there a place in the house?" Royce was asking.

She knew at once that he meant to be alone with her, and her heart cried out with longing and despair. The rooms on the ground floor were filled with guests, talking, drinking, laughing, walking from one room to another, admiring the Penrods' elegant home. And anyone would easily be seen ascending the grand staircase that led from the ballroom to the upper floors. There would be a back stairs, for certain, probably in the kitchen, but . . .

"It's . . . it's too dangerous," she said, wanting to burst into tears of helplessness and need. "Veronica."

She saw the hangman look over at his former lover. She saw Veronica's cold smile. They had to whirl and part again, and it seemed an eternity before Royce was back with her.

"Where do you live?" he asked.

No. Oh, no. He could not come to Bowling Green. Never. "On Bowling Green," she said.

The music stopped then, abruptly, the sound of it reverberating all over the room.

"Are you happy, Selena?" she heard the hangman ask.

She had no chance to reply.

"What a touching sentiment from a traitor," hissed a voice just behind them. "Don't move. There are men at the doors."

Selena whirled and saw armed men there, men from Lord Ludford's offices, and she saw a pride of soldiers as well. The sight of two of the men made her gasp in anguish. In the doorway, next to an armed guard, stood Sean. While behind them, with a knife at the hangman's back—she saw the pathetic artificial ear as closely as she might have seen the approach of her own death—was Darius McGrover. *Fool,* she thought, incongruously. *Vain fool.* The rubbery ear was tied on with a string, as an eyepatch might be. And she knew, at the same moment, that he would do far worse than remove an ear from the person who had divested him of his own.

"Don't move, anyone!" McGrover ordered, in his old voice of certainty and command.

Had *Sean* called him here? Selena could not believe it.

"That's good," McGrover cried, as Ludford's men and the soldiers began to close into the room. "Now, we know most of you are loyal." He said it as if he did not believe it. "We are only looking for one or two. Forgive me if I ask you to remove your pretty, little masks."

Too many things happened simultaneously; Selena was unable to register all of them. She saw Hamilton dive through the crowd, and she saw the momentarily stunned look on the faces of the security men nearby, before they, too, leaped forward. Inches away, she was suddenly conscious of movement, and caught the blur of the hangman's arm as it swung past her in a flashing arc, ramming an elbow into McGrover's solar plexus. The ever-present knife leaped from his hand as a cry of agony escaped him, and he jack-knifed forward from the waist. He was not even bent double when the hangman braced himself and, fists together, slammed a double uppercut to McGrover's slack jaw, catching McGrover's tongue between his teeth. A shower of blood pearled about his head, and his artificial ear jumped from its string-tied mooring. In the meantime, whether by plan or accident or simply the human tendency to band together and flee in the face of danger, people crowded toward the doorways, temporarily blocking the entrance of soldiers and security men. Had Hamilton waited even seconds more to make his move, Selena reflected later, everything would have been lost.

McGrover was spinning in midair, in the process of dropping unconscious to the floor. Selena was turning from him to look once again at the hangman. But he removed that identity, pulling the hood from his head, eyes searching for a route to escape. He was not afraid. He was exhilarated. She could read the emotion in his flashing, depthless blue eyes.

"*Who's fortunate this time?*" he managed to ask, and she thought he would have smiled had he had the time.

But he did not. He made his calculations, ran a short distance, and made a flying leap toward the balcony, where the banistered staircase turned, leading to the upper floors. Some of the crowd hunkered at the foot of the stairs. People were shouting. Soldiers were pushing and shoving them now. Curses and threats filled the air. A few of the security men, watching Royce Campbell flee, tried to order the soldiers back outside, but the confusion was now too great.

Selena stood next to the inert form of McGrover, her eyes turned toward the empty staircase, and her heart bursting with tears of holy blood, and joy.

She did not know how much time went by, but she felt the hand on hers and looked up into Sean's slightly worried eyes.

"Are you all right?" he asked.

She nodded numbly.

"Lucky I spotted Hamilton, wasn't it? I'd heard about him, of course, and I notified Ludford's office. This will be a major break for us. There can be no doubt about our loyalties now."

What was he saying?

"Penrod's thanked me up and down for what I've done. He had no idea what kind of scoundrel had infiltrated his party. Just the type of thing Hamilton revels in, I've heard. Well, he got away. And I'll bet he won't be back. Selena, are you all right?"

Again, she nodded, as the fact of it came to her. Sean, arriving back at Penrod's house with the soldiers, and intent upon pointing out Hamilton to them, had not noticed the hangman. Would McGrover tell him? McGrover was, someone said, in the hospital now, his tongue almost severed by his own teeth. Still, he could write, couldn't he? Or had everything happened so fast that even he had not fully registered the implications of Royce Campbell's presence?

What were those implications?

Selena shuddered again, and fought to hold back an inexpressible but almost tangible sweetness that threatened to embrace her. Like a drug. Or a dream of Nirvana.

Thinking her afraid, Sean put a protective arm around her. They left the Penrods', and went home.

Nothing was under control anymore. Nothing in the world.

THE CITY UNSLEEPING

Darius McGrover spoke thickly, words on a blue, swollen tongue. But his malice, clear, cold, and changeless, surrounded him, a penumbra of ice. There was no mistaking malice or intent, in spite of the damage Royce had done to his mouth. Death was on his mind.

He was bolder now, but still circling, like a hawk in the sky, measuring its prey.

He measured Selena as he stood in the doorway of their house on Bowling Green. Traudl had answered the door, but Selena had refused to let the man enter.

"You may believe that you are safe this time," he hissed, moving his painful tongue as little as possible, grinning with cracked teeth. "You may think that, because of your wealthy loyalist husband, you are secure."

Selena lifted her chin and stared right back at him. She said nothing. She was afraid, but it was unlikely that he would make his move now. This was a warning call, to unnerve her further. This was the challenge, the figurative throwing down of the gauntlet. Still, she felt comfort in Traudl's presence, just behind the door. It was another human being with her, near her, as she faced the monster.

"But you are not secure," McGrover continued. "Oh, it may seem so to you now. In spite of my suspicions about each and every one of your friends at Penrod's little affair last week, my superiors will only allow the apprehension of those clearly on the rebel list." He spat in disgust.

"You have foul manners, as well as everything else."

"You are fortunate. I am not spitting blood anymore. Your doorstep is relatively clean." He spat again, mocking her. "You might even say it has now been blessed."

She said nothing.

"Lord Ludford is cautious in political matters," he went on. "It is his belief that we must not harass the influential of this city, even though they may have certain rebel sympathies. He feels that the triumph of our arms on the field of battle will quickly bring them around to our side. So I am restrained, at the moment, from moving against the Penrods and the Weddingtons . . ."

Thank God, she thought, *they are still not certain about Dick.*

". . . and the Bloodwells. At least not against one of the Bloodwells. Oh, I have tried. I have informed my superiors of the young Sean Bloodwell who gave financial aid to the Rob Roys. But he has redeemed himself most shrewdly, I must say. Bringing us the news of Hamilton's presence, and then taking us to the very site of the masque. Yes, very clever indeed."

"My husband is a loyalist, if you must know," Selena said coldly.

"And you, my lovely one?"

"I am a citizen of the British Empire," she told him contemptuously, her scorn greater than her fear.

"And clever, as always, I see. Just like your father. Do you recall what his cleverness earned him, in the end?"

There in the doorway, staring at him, Selena was forced to relive the scene she had almost succeeded in blocking from her conscious memory. Father on his knees. McGrover, sneering, twisting the garrote. And Father, just before his death, jerking free of his bonds, raising his hand, choking out the words which, more than anything, had bound them together in life. *Selena, the sky begins here.*

She vowed it then. Somehow, some way, she would do what she ought to have done at Foinaven Lodge.

"You are a dead man," she told him. Her passion rendered the words almost as indistinct as his own speech.

He seemed to take a step back, almost surprised.

"What?"

"I am speaking to a dead man," she said. "You will leave me alone or I swear to you, on my father's grave and memory, that you will not survive the summer."

Her hatred registered in his expression, but he recovered, mocking her. "That leaves me June, July, and August, doesn't it?"

Behind her, Traudl made a sound. Not quite a sob, it was more a suppressed squeak of terror and fear.

"Will you enlist your husband's aid?"

"I might."

"Well, he is influential, and might slow me down," McGrover admitted, quite frankly. "But you and I have a special relationship, do we not? When I realized you had given me the slip in Liverpool, I thought you were bound for America. At once I made application for a transfer to the colonies. They did not allow me to come, at first. They think me overzealous. All this time, I have been yearning for you, though. That is what a blood bond does to one. It is like a hunger that one cannot slake, a need that must be satiated. You had your chance to kill me, and you failed. I cannot forgive that, and the blood bond will not let me rest. I will not be the coward you were. And to think I had almost given up hope of finding you. I did not know, of course, of your little sojourn in Hinduland. Did you please the potentates? Did you take them unto yourself, so to speak, and please them well?"

He grinned again. Selena did not speak. Traudl was practically whining. It was fortunate that Sean had taken Davina for a ride in the carriage today. Or was it? With Sean here, would McGrover have been bold enough to make his approach? Probably not. Anyway, it was Selena he was after. Anyone else was secondary.

"And now you are here," McGrover said, very softly. "And so am I."

They looked at each other. Selena began to close the door.

"One more thing," McGrover warned, raising his hand. "I would not rely on your glorious husband for unquestioning support."

Still she said nothing, but there must have been a twinge of doubt in her eyes.

"I know who the hangman was," McGrover added enigmatically. "I remembered while I lay in hospital."

"I don't know what you mean," she said unsteadily. Uncertain of his ploy, she hesitated. He sensed her vulnerability, and bored in.

"Your old lover come back, isn't that so?" he asked.

Traudl went very quiet.

"I did not know it was he," Selena said uncertainly. "We were costumed. We were only dancing."

"*This* time," McGrover said. "But what of the past? Indeed, what of the *future?*"

"That is over, and long past. My future is with my husband . . . and child." She said it; it had to be true.

He knew better, a snake with the gift of vision, peering directly into the heart of his enemy.

"And I suppose you would hold to that story if I applied a whip to the soft parts of your body? No, no. I remember the Christmas dances, and I distinctly recall the evening on which you paraded yourself before him." He seemed to smile with a private memory. "Yes, I believe you would have given yourself to him on the floor of that cold balcony, had not your brother intervened so crudely . . ."

He had been there? Hiding in the shadows, while she and Royce clung to each other, the first precious instant of their mutual discovery?

"I told you that it's all over," she said, and closed the door until he was only a thin, sneering figure in a narrow space.

"I will put the two of you together again, mark my words. You have promised me death, and I offer you the same, twofold. I will unite you and your pirate lover, and display you both, for all the world to see. On the yardarm of his own ship, in New York harbor. Hung by your adulterous, traitorous necks . . ."

Traudl broke into sobs. Selena tried to jam the door shut, but McGrover had pushed the edge of his walking stick in the open space.

"And I know where he is hiding," McGrover cried. "Yes, right now! Even this afternoon my men and I will move to take him. You hold that knowledge close to your heart, my dear. And while you are dreaming your juicy dreams of his embrace—ah, don't you think I know?—he will already be descending into the embrace of death which I have prepared for him."

She pushed all her weight against the door, and he suddenly removed his walking stick. The door crashed shut, and Selena crashed against it.

She could hear him laughing as he went down the steps. She did not look after him.

Traudl was sobbing, her innocent, simple mind in turmoil over the sinister man, the obvious danger. And the terrible words: Adultery. Treason.

"Ooohhh, ma'am! Ohhhhh! What's going to become of . . ."

"Traudl, you must control yourself," Selena said, putting her arms around the chubby nursemaid. "This is one time when we'll both have to be brave, whether we feel like it or not. And, for reasons you don't need to know just now, I must ask you to keep this incident between ourselves."

Traudl's eyes widened.

"You mean and not tell Mister . . ."

"That's right. The man you saw at the door is a liar and a poseur. He is dangerous, but I must handle him in my own way. And I can."

Saying it, she was almost convinced. She had to hurry. So she had to maintain her resolve. If Royce was in danger, she had to be prepared, to warn him. Somehow. But if she made the wrong decision, the wrong move, everything might be lost. She recalled Sean's words on the evening of the masque, after they had returned home.

"Selena, this is it," he had declared. "We've discussed it before, God knows, and I think you've done your best to be careful. Perhaps the problem is simply that you haven't been able to sense situations that might lead to trouble. Although, by now, I think you ought at least to be able to do that."

It had hurt, that *at least*. And to say anything, by way of explanation, would just make things more labyrinthine.

"So, you have a business connection with Penrod, and, from what I hear, it might prove lucrative. Well and good. But these are complicated times. God forbid that Howe in the south and Burgoyne in New England should fail to crush the rebels this year. It's very bad for business, as you know. But, above and beyond all that, you must *not* be seen in any house or public place in which your reputation might be held up for inspection."

That was Sean, utterly confident, making his pronouncements. Sean, with a continental spy as a business partner!

Perhaps Sean was right. She should *at least* have learned a few more self-preservatory ruses.

Right now, in the parlor of the Bowling Green residence, trying to stay calm for the benefit of the stunned and panicky Traudl, the only help Selena could think of lay in the person of Dick Weddington himself. He might know what was going on. He might even know where Royce was, now that the colonies' foremost rebel raider was back in port.

"Traudl, have Otto saddle a horse for me."

"But, ma'am, he's out driving the carriage for Davina and Mister Bloodwell."

"So he is. Well, then, I'll do it myself," she decided. But it occurred to her that McGrover or one of his men might be watching the house. If she rushed out now, and rode down to Wall Street, the connection between herself and Dick Weddington would be clear, if, indeed, it was not clear already. (She assumed that McGrover knew Sean was not at the office; thus the pretext of rushing to Wall Street in order to see him could not pass the test of credibility.)

"All right, Traudl. This is what I want you to do. Now, I know this isn't your job, but I can't . . . ah, *rely* on the kitchen staff just now. You take a shopping basket. I'll give you money. As soon as you get a good distance from the house, you flag a cab. Go to Sean's office and see if Lord Weddington is there. If he is, tell him to return with you. Tell him it's of the utmost importance. And have the cab drive into the back alley. I'll be waiting there."

"But what if he's *not* there?"

"Then say good day and leave. Do you understand?"

Traudl nodded slowly, an honest, good-hearted girl suddenly plunged into a welter of thrust and counterthrust she had not the experience to understand. But she got herself under a semblance of control, and, true to her training and character, she had to get a couple of things straight. It was a matter of conscience.

"Excuse me, ma'am, but first I got to know some things, honest and true."

"Honest and true," Selena said.

"That evil man who was at the door, with the funny ear tied on. Are you certain—I mean, I don't *doubt* you, ma'am, you've been good to me as my own mama and papa would have been, had they lived—but you sure you don't want to tell Mister Sean he came here? And what he said?"

"Not just yet. It would upset him. And don't be afraid. That ear of his—I cut it off. Myself."

Traudl's eyes went wide. She couldn't even get out her next question for a moment. But she did.

"An', ma'am, he said about treason and . . . and . . . ah . . . adultery? I was raised not to have no truck with sin, and . . ."

"You should have no worries over your soul on that account, Traudl. I am guilty of neither, whether by omission or commission."

It was true, but the statement—and the matters involved—were quite over Traudl's head. Soon she would make her own interpretations. But now she hastened to carry out the orders, and Selena spent a restless hour waiting for Dick Weddington to arrive. Thinking of Royce Campbell.

Selena was grateful she had at least known he was alive; seeing him for the first time when the hangman ripped off his hood at the masque would have been too much for her to have borne. The very *knowledge* of his existence had been troubling her since first she'd glimpsed the *Selena*. Now, having seen him, *touched* him, she was afraid to let her heart go, lest the emotional tumult prove too disconcerting to endure. But what could be done? And she was married to Sean. *All right,* she decided. *But he saved me once, and if he is in danger from McGrover, I must do all I can to save him.*

Time dragged on forever, and she paced and watched the sun start down over the wild hills of New Jersey, across the great Hudson River. The May afternoon was warm and clear, but Selena had barely noticed it. Many people promenaded along the waterfront; any of them might have been one of McGrover's spies, watching the house. Cabs came and went, the horses trotting by, the harness bells jingling. Finally a cab drew up to the house, and she saw Traudl, fairly blushing with tension and importance, direct the driver to the alley that led behind the house. But something was wrong; she couldn't see Dick Weddington in the cab. It disappeared around the side of the house. Selena raced through the rooms on the main floor, to meet it at the back entrance.

She understood why Traudl had been blushing so much. Dick Weddington unbent himself from his hiding place on the floor of the cab, and untangled the heels of his boots from the poor nursemaid's skirts. Selena shot a glance at the cabdriver to see if he looked the reliable type, and another face from the past sprang into her vision. The big black beard, the strong, good-natured—and now a little abashed—expression. Will Teviot.

She was too glad to see him to remember with any animosity what had happened to them in the stone hut in Kinlochbervie. She would have invited him in, but Dick waved him away.

"Another time, Selena," Will said. "God, but 'tis good to see ye 'ale an' 'earty, that I vow."

Then he was off and she was hurrying Dick Weddington into Sean's quiet study on the second floor. No one could hear them there. She closed the door and told him quickly of McGrover's visit. He listened as his face darkened with concern.

"How long ago did McGrover leave?"

"A little over an hour. So far, Traudl and I are the only ones who know he was here. And who know what he said. Can you trust Will Teviot?"

"Will? I'd trust him with my life. I was the one who helped him flee the British, after he'd left your family in Kinlochbervie. I was sailing from Liverpool at the time, coming out to the colonies. Pater had told me of the Rob Roy business, and, from Will's desperation, I had a suspicion that he was one of them. I took him aboard with me as a valet. He left ship at Nova Scotia. Can you imagine? A valet! I'd rather have Will with me in a back alley, settling scores with McGrover."

Selena smiled. Will Teviot, who had rescued her, was bold and violent and strong, but in his own way he was as innocent and loyal as a little boy. The sort you would want to protect even as he was protecting you.

"What are you going to tell Sean?" Dick was asking.

"I was going to try not telling him at all. He is already upset, after the masque. I don't want to harm the rebel cause, but, here I am, more deeply involved than ever. I just don't know . . ."

"All right. Forget that for the time being. Let us consider first things first. There comes a time when everyone must fight for what he believes, and that time will come to you."

Royce had said something like that once. "*If it is necessary to kill in order to save your dream . . .*"

And right now it was necessary to save Royce Campbell.

"You say McGrover indicated that he knew where Royce was hiding? Well, it is possible. God, how did he find out, though?"

"Where is Royce hiding?"

"Forgive me, but I'd prefer not to say. But it's not far from here. He's in a small, false room in a residential house. We often conceal naval officers there, when they are here for consultations, or to receive orders. John Paul Jones was there last week, in fact. But I thought it was absolutely safe . . ."

His voice trailed off, and his brow furrowed as he calculated.

"Where is the . . . the ship?"

"Don't be modest." He grinned. "The *Selena* is in harbor at Port Washington, on the North Shore of Long Island, being provisioned for the next assignment. Did you know she sank seventeen freighters last year, and once took on five British men-of-war and sent them to the bottom in the space of an afternoon?"

Selena was thrilled and proud, but there was in Dick's tale the parlous whisper of strange violence, the mysterious flicker she had seen in Royce, the call of the wild that echoed down the trackless Highlands, the sign of the wolf. She recalled the wild white cumulus, driven by wind across the diamond skies of India, and how the strange wolf-headed shape of the clouds jittered the Sherpa guards.

But that wild Royce had to be saved, too, along with the gentle one who had loved her. Along with the chief naval defender of the colonies. They all occupied the same body. No way to separate them.

Dick explained that his "purchasing network" was in operation and working beautifully. The *Selena* was being fitted and provisioned with goods and produce his agents had purchased from Long Island farmers. Many other ships had been similarly fitted, and the British had not yet discovered either location or tactic.

"He's supposed to be out there by tomorrow morning. If a British patrol rakes Long Island Sound, it's sure to spot a ship as big as the *Selena*. And, you can bet, if they know Royce is in New York, they know his ship can't be far away. McGrover is acting because he's remembered who the hangman was . . . *is*. The British Admiralty has put a price of fifty thousand pounds on Royce's head, dead or alive. And there's another one hundred thousand pounds waiting for the captain of the ship that sends the *Selena* to the bottom."

"*No one will ever do that!*" she snapped.   "I guess not," Dick laughed. "Not with that kind of spirit as his weapon. Now, here's what I think. *If* McGrover knows where Royce is hiding, then he knows our most secret location. Thus, we can't transfer Royce to another location, those being equally vulnerable. *All* we have to do is to conceal him until a bit after midnight, when he'll leave for Long Island on horseback. What we ought to do—and if I could think of such a stroke I most certainly would—is to make a bold move. To do something even McGrover wouldn't expect. We need a hiding place that is not a hiding place at all, something right under the guns, so to speak."

Selena was thinking hard. There was La Marinda, but . . .

"What about here at your house?" Dick Weddington suggested.

He wasn't jesting.

"Look, I know there was something between you and Royce, and I know you're married. I also know Sean doesn't want you involved in any of these political machinations. But it's more than that now. This may be the matter of a man's life. You've told me about McGrover and his threats. You know only too well what he'd do if he took Royce Campbell into custody."

"But it's still daylight. How can you transfer him now? And here? Where . . . ?"

"I noticed you have a back entrance, other than the one I came in."

"The cellar?"

"Good as any. You won't even have to see him. We'll get to him before McGrover, if we can. . . ."

"What if McGrover's bluffing, and using you now to lead the way to Royce?"

"I've thought of that, but we can't take the chance that he is. We're always aware the other side may know everything we're going to do. The trick is to execute our plans so fast that they haven't time to react. We have passageways and a system of messengers. We can get Royce out, and do a number of feints and ruses in the streets for a couple of hours. The problem is: where can he find shelter until early morning?"

He waited.

"My household must not know," Selena said. "They cannot know."

So he knew that she had already decided.

I won't be able to see him, she thought. *I will have to pretend it isn't happening.*

Can you do that? asked the tiny, nagging voice of her conscience.

She did not answer it. Instead, she told Dick of a danger she could not prevent.

"There are fourteen people on the service staff here. There is nothing I can do to guarantee that no one will see him, and give the alarm."

"In which case you know nothing. Neither how he got there, nor why." He paused a moment. "So it would be best if you did not find an excuse to go into the cellar yourself. Pretend nothing is happening."

Then he was gone, on foot, through a system of alleyways constructed by the Dutch founders of New Amsterdam. Constructed not for passage, however, but for the drainage of refuse and rainwater. Selena felt confident about his route of escape, until she suffered an ugly insight: with the possible exception of a sewer, there was no place on earth in which a piece of breathing offal like McGrover would rather lurk.

"Be careful, Dick," she breathed, praying.

Sean and Davina came home from their ride, happy and laughing, touched by the sun, and the aroma of dinner on the stove—dough balls stuffed with chopped lamb, rice and spices, gravy—drifted in from the kitchen. Outside, the sun was going down. Men walked homeward on the streets;

cabs and horses came and went. *Royce.* Twilight came early, it being May. They played cards for a while in the drawing room; a servant entered unobtrusively, lighting the lamps against the falling sun. *Was that a noise at the back of the house?*

"Where's Traudl?" Sean inquired casually. The nurse-maid usually joined them in a game or conversation as they awaited dinner.

Selena, who had been doing quite a good job of conceal-ing her tension, started unduly. Sean, watching Davina at play with blocks, did not seem to notice.

"Perhaps she's busy," Selena hoped. The last thing she needed was jittery Traudl revealing, by her manner, the events of the day. Properly primed, the Dutch girl could be counted on not to speak of that which was forbidden to her. But expecting her to maintain a pose of equanimity was simply too much to ask.

"Where Traudl?" Davina asked, as they sat down at ta-ble.

Traudl customarily ate with them as well: Sean believed it created more of a family feeling for the little girl, to offset the intimidating size of the house and the impersonality of all the servants.

"I'll get her!" Selena blurted. She had tried to sound ea-ger, but she knew she sounded harassed instead.

"Send someone," Sean said.

"No, that's all right . . ." And before he could protest further, she was on her way out of the dining room.

Traudl's room was not in the big attic, beneath the eaves, with the rest of the staff, but rather, due to her posi-tion, on the second floor. It was a small bedroom in the back of he house, modest but comfortable, and the nurse-maid was as proud of it as a general might be of his first star. The door was ajar. Selena pushed it open a bit more. And peeked in.

Traudl, galvanized, stood at the rear window—the one overlooking the alley—her chubby body stiff as a tree, her hands doing something at her mouth, twisting there as if she were trying to tear a cry from her very throat. Selena did not even have to guess what it was. Later, she could not even remember crossing the room, to stand beside Traudl at the window. Dick Weddington peered from the corner of the neighboring house, hard by one of the drain-age conduits. And, emerging from behind him, leaping across the distance in swift, leopardlike strides, Royce Campbell made his way to the back of the Bloodwell house. Selena herself had made certain the cellar door was unlocked. Barely a sound, and then nothing. Dick Wed-dington was gone. Royce Campbell was inside her own do-main, their hearts beating beneath the same roof.

"Oh, ma'am!" Traudl moaned. "Must be a thief. We must tell Mister Sean at once."

"We'll do nothing of the kind," Selena told her.

Hastily, with as much confidence as she could muster, Selena attempted to explain. The evil man at the door to-day was looking for the man who'd just gone into the cel-lar. No one must know. Traudl had to help Selena. Traudl had to be brave. No harm would come to her.

The nursemaid, almost gasping for breath—she was that upset—did not quite seem to hear. Or, if she did, was not quite sure she ought to believe. Sensing this, Selena made it a command.

"This is an important matter and none of your affair. You saw nothing. We're most pleased with your work, and we want to keep you here, but . . ."

Traudl began to sob. *Now* she understood. Selena thought so, anyway.

"I'll say you've a touch of spring cold, and have a kitchen servant bring up your dinner on a tray."

Nerved by necessity—or was it Royce Campbell's prox-imity?—Selena made it through dinner, chatting quietly, and half-mad with tension. Sean had seen some excellent property on the drive, far to the north on Manhattan Island. He thought it well worth looking into.

Selena agreed to inspect the property, rather too enthusi-astically, but Sean's mind was already on his planned work for the evening and he didn't notice. He kissed both of his girls and retreated to the study. The rest of the evening was uneventful. It was already Davina's bedtime, and, with Traudl "indisposed," Selena wiped errant bits of food from the little girl's face, took her upstairs, gave her a quick bath, and put her into her nightie for bed.

"Traudl sick?" Davina wanted to know.

"Not very. She'll be fine tomorrow. Want to say your prayers now?"

Davina got down on her knees next to her little bed. The soft rag doll and the big pink bunny rabbit waited for her.

"God bless Daddy, God bless 'Ena, God bless Traudl. God bless Coldstream Castle . . ." She didn't know what it was, but she liked the idea of a castle. ". . . and God remember Mommy."

Selena waited, uncertain of her own emotions, for the day Davina would reason that "'Ena" and "Mommy" were somehow not one and the same.

"That's a fine girl." She tucked Davina into the bed and turned down the wick of the lamp. "Good night."

Traudl was in the hall, waiting. She looked positively ill.

"I've got to talk to ye, ma'am."

Something was wrong. "Of course."

They went back into the nursemaid's room.

"I hate to have to say this, ma'am . . ."

"Just calm down, Traudl. Go ahead. Tell me what it is."

"You know, ma'am? What I told you this afternoon? About how I was raised not to have truck with wrongdoing?"

Selena nodded. *Not this again.*

"Ma'am, I mean no offense, but I'm beginning to think I'm amidst somethin' that's not right."

"Traudl, I assured you it was none of your concern."

But the dauntless nursemaid had made up her mind. She had to have it out. It took a lot of courage, and there were tears of trepidation in her eyes, but she shivered and made her proclamation.

"Ma'am, I won't be able to tolerate anything illegal or immoral. I got my soul to think of, an' . . ." She broke into tears. Once more, Selena comforted her.

"I'll do the worrying for both of us, all right? Sometimes there are things . . ." She broke off. What was the use? Traudl's understanding of events was entirely different from her own.

She went to her own study, across the hall from Sean's, and tried to refine some sketches she had in mind for next year. But not even the excitement of her success with La Marinda could drive from her mind the knowledge of Royce, close enough to speak to, close enough to touch. . . .

It had been easier at dinner, when she was forced to think of other things.

Once, at about ten-thirty, Sean stuck his head in the door and asked if she would like to share a measure of port with him. She barely noticed. "I'm going to bed," he said, sometime later. She registered that information, but indistinctly. Eleven-fifteen. At two in the morning, perhaps two-thirty, Royce would be gone, to Long Island, to the *Selena*, bound for the high seas that, more than anyplace else since the Highlands, were his home.

Let it go, she thought. *Don't be a fool.* She had a glass of wine to make her sleepy, and went to bed just before midnight. Sean was already asleep. Traudl peered out of her doorway to see who it was on the stairs, but quickly retreated into darkness. Selena undressed, put on her nightgown, and slid into bed beside her husband.

Sometime during the evening, it had begun to rain lightly. With a steady, gentle rattle, it fell upon the slate shingles of the great house, and down upon the cobbled streets. It ought to have been soothing, but it was not. Rain and night, life waiting in shelters, life held in abeyance. She got up and walked to the window. Bowling Green was dark and flat as the rain fell upon it, and the gray river rippled white where the raindrops fell. *Royce.* All the times in her life that gentle rain had fallen in the spring. Twenty years. *Royce.* Sean was sleeping, and the world; gray skies folded the soft spring earth in the promise of summer and sustenance and warmth. Rain upon the blooming fields of May. Raindrops heavy in the newborn heather. Rain upon the battlements of Coldstream Castle, that reached the sky itself, and in the castle where hearth fires crackled, Selena dreaming into sleep. *Royce.* Time was so short, and life so sweet and dear. Rain forever, soothing and forgetful, upon all the graves of ancient earth, upon the seven seas that held the bones of sailors in the rolling deep. *Oh, Royce!*

Suddenly she was flying down the upstairs hall, possessed of another mind, or possessed of no mind at all. She floated down the stairs as if in a dream, not so much driven by a force as drawn to one. His life was constant danger. She could not bear it, not to have said good-bye. If something should happen . . .

But how could she explain it, being found in the cellar with a man? With Royce?

Her thoughts were disjointed. She would go down. It would all be over quickly. *It doesn't matter! I have to . . .*

Traudl, distraught with anxiety, watched Selena from her slightly open door, watched her mistress's billowing white gown against the darkness as Selena flew down the stairs.

It was one-thirty. Perhaps too late already . . .

Selena went through the downstairs rooms, and into the kitchen, walked to the door that led down to the cellar. Wait. It would be dark. She took a length of candle from a box on the kitchen counter, and lit it on the flickering flame of an oil lamp that was kept burning by night on the iron stove. Then she opened the door and started down into the cellar.

The candle flame wavered, flared, and wavered again in the damp, drafty air of the cellar. Selena thought she heard a movement, but she was not sure. Down the stairs, slowly. Too soon, yet, to call out. Halfway down, she stopped and stretched out the candle. Boxes of supplies. The sturdy pillars on which the house was founded. Discarded furniture. Other junk the servants had cast down here, awaiting the rubbish scavenger. No more sound.

She would speak his name when she reached the bottom of the stairs. By now, he must have seen her.

Selena reached the bottom of the stairs "R . . ."

From behind her, a hand grasped the flame of the candle and extinguished it. Darkness. A rough arm enveloped her.

"Quiet, lady, and you won't get hurt."

Tensing to struggle, the voice struck fever. *Royce!* But his hand was over her mouth now, and, coming at her from beneath the cellar stairs, he had not seen . . .

He did not know who she was! He did not know whose house he was in! Dick Weddington had done what he could to minimize the danger.

Now she felt something hard and sharp at the base of her spine.

"You'll come to no harm," Royce was saying. His voice was gentler now. "Don't scream. I'll take my hand away from your mouth if you don't scream."

She nodded, a difficult task against the pressure of his hand.

Slowly, his grip loosened, and the hand went away. But not too far. He was waiting. His other arm was like a steel band around her rib cage.

"Royce," she gasped.

It was all she could say, and all she could think of saying. They stood in the darkness at the bottom of the cellar stairs, unable to see each other, the candle gone out. But he knew her voice, and she sensed the incredulous astonishment in the muscles of his body.

"Selena?" he asked, although he did not need to.

"This is my house," she said.

There was nothing for a moment, and then, without prelude, without sign, their arms were around each other, and they fumbled into a kiss that was as long as forever, yet over before it started.

"Dick didn't tell me . . ." he started.

She put her fingers against his lips, and they kissed again.

In the few moments that followed, something happened to them. It was something timeless and unreadable. Nothing mattered, except their being together, neither danger, nor disgrace, nor even—at that moment—the possibility of death. Far away, Selena's vows spun within her mind, remonstrating, cautioning. Far away. All things, at that moment, were clear, and she felt as pure and clean and perfect as she ever had or ever hoped to feel. There were many kinds of love in the world, and this was *the* moment in her life, the moment that comes only to the blessed, courageous few, the moment of realizing forever that Royce had always been the one, and would be even if he died, even if he had to live on only in her heart, which now beat against him like a bird in glorious paradise.

Once again, they kissed—this time it seemed to go on for hours—until she remembered and broke away. She had to ask.

"When did you know who I was? At the masque?"

He laughed softly. "Not until you spoke the word Scotland. I doubt anyone on earth could say it with the reverence you do. I asked you to dance because the resemblance disturbed me. I had long since given you up for dead. I lived on memory alone. I named my ship . . ."

"I know."

They kissed again, caught in wonder, having come together against all expectations. But the iridescent moment was already gone, flown like a glorious bird. And they both knew it. The future waited hard by the alley door.

"I had to see Hamilton that night," Royce was telling her. "There was no other way to reach him. I needed funds for provisions, and he was at the Penrods' to receive moneys. But for the risk I took, we might never have learned . . ."

"*I* knew!" she cried. "I saw the ship once. I knew you were alive."

Royce said nothing for a moment, and when he spoke his voice contained both knowledge and sadness.

"And you did not attempt to reach me? You are not free to love me, are you?"

Selena wanted to avoid the pain of the situation. "I do love you," she told him. "Of course I am free to love you."

He was unconvinced. "Shall I return for you then? Will you come with me now? Tonight?"

"I . . . I cannot . . ." She faltered. And then she gathered her strength, against what loss and sorrow she could only guess, and told him of her marriage to Sean Bloodwell.

"Are you happy?" he asked, after a time.

Are you happy? The words reverberated in her mind. It was a simple question, but the emotions it evoked were as complicated as life itself. Yes, of course, she had been happy with Sean, protected and secure, but . . . But how can one answer a question about the mortal realm after one has just been blessed with a vision of heaven?

"Are you?" she asked him, unable to reply to his question.

"It doesn't matter. I have things to do now. What I do at sea, for the country and for what until now was my memory of you, has been enough to fill my life. You gave me that kind of courage, that kind of knowledge. After I thought you lost forever, I decided, in remembrance of you, to believe in something as you always believed, with spirit and passion and total fire, whether a cause be won or lost."

Selena was more touched than she could have expressed, just then. But he had said something that bothered her.

"*That* was my gift to you? That you should believe in, lost causes?"

He laughed. "No. Rather that I should believe enough in a cause, a person, believe enough in *something* to fight for it, no holds barred, no quarter given, win or lose. That is the gift you left me, and there is no way to measure the worth of it. It is invaluable. When I realized what your secret was, what drove you . . ." He stopped, sensing something amiss. Her nervous silence had told him that something was not quite right.

"You and Sean are supporters of the cause of freedom, aren't you? Surely you can't be Tories, after all you've had to endure?"

"Sean is a loyalist," she replied. "I . . . I do what I can. You must understand how difficult it is. I've . . . I've made promises."

It felt as if he'd drawn away from her, although he hadn't moved. A moment dropped into abyss. For the first time in her life, Selena felt false. It was as if she had misrepresented herself to someone whose admiration she sought above all else, and then, given a chance to redeem herself, she had to stand there silently. It was as if she were betraying him or betraying his idea of what she was. But that was not true. It was not that simple.

"How . . . how were you saved?" she asked quietly, still in his embrace.

He sighed. Miraculous salvation for both of them had brought them back together, but only to more difficulty and sadness. "After I put you ashore near the Canary Islands," he said, "I set a fuse to the powder magazines aboard the *Highlander*. Then I passed out. When I regained consciousness, more dead than alive, I found that the wind had extinguished my fuse. So I lit it again and crawled out on deck to see the ocean and the sky one last time. Birds were circling when the magazine exploded. That's all I remember. When I came to my senses again, I was in the water, holding on to a piece of the hull. I crawled upon it, and lay there waiting to die, half awash in the sea. Whether it was God or the sun, salt water or even my wolf, the plague boil burst. Or my body was so depleted that not even sickness could possibly feed on it. In time, I was picked up. I came to America. I survived."

"I'm glad." She clung to him. "I'm so glad."

There might have been a sound somewhere outside. They stopped talking and listened. *He's different,* Selena was thinking. His strength was greater than ever, but the recklessness was gone. He was still wild and driven, but the forces which drove him were subtly different. She hoped it was a part of what she had given him, what he called her gift to him.

"And you?" he asked.

Briefly, she told him what had happened since their parting at sea.

"You survived too."

The darkness of the cellar swirled around them. Outside, over cobblestones, there was a sound. Horses or men? Or both? They could not tell.

"Our time is running out."

She nodded, pressing her head to his chest, trying not to let the tears begin.

"Do you still think of Coldstream?"

"That's why Sean is . . . that's why *we're* trying to stay out of political trouble. He wants a title. My very blood wants to feel those stones again. They belong to me. I *feel* the centuries they hold. But I'm afraid I've already jeopardized everything."

The years had neither diminished his perceptiveness nor reduced his quick intelligence. "Selena, I understand. If I could help you with your burden, I would. You want Coldstream terribly, but you want a rebel victory, too. And, in your position, you can't have both."

He fell silent a moment, not as if he had stopped speaking, but rather to fashion his next words. They came. "Selena, I know how it feels. Because I also want what I cannot have."

She dared not believe.

"You, Selena," he said. "Nothing else will do. I must have you, and somehow, someday, I will."

Oh, you can! You can! her heart cried out. *Please.* But she did not speak. There were men outside now, coming to take him to Long Island, then to the sea. They kissed again. She thought of Sean and her vows. She felt as if she were being untrue to both men.

"I don't want you to leave," she managed.

"Nor do I want to. But I have made my choices, and you have made yours. Some of them, at least. I regret but two things: that I did not appreciate you sooner for what you were, and . . ."

He stopped. Outside, on the street, voices of men could be heard.

"Yes?" Selena asked.

". . . and I regret that I cannot help you now as once you helped me. I regret that, together, we cannot find some resolution for your dilemma. Come away with me," he urged once more. "Or wait for me."

Selena felt like sinking to the floor in sheer exhaustion. It was all so complicated. Now it was Royce whose vision and purpose were pure. She was the one with the reservations, the one who had to make the self-serving qualifications that previously she would have scorned. But he was right. She had made her decisions, and she would have to live with them until she decided that they were no longer valid.

On the street there were voices. Several men speaking low.

Royce prepared to depart. He kissed her softly on the forehead, eyes, mouth. He kissed her on the neck, as he had done long ago when they had possessed each other, bathed in holy fire. Then, before she could do anything about it, before she could even wrap her arms around him one more time, he had stepped away from her, into the darkness.

"Royce!" she cried, much too loudly.

"Quiet. Don't let me jeopardize your life any more than I already have."

He was leaving. No. Not this way. "Can't we . . . can't we be together sometime? At least once? There are things we must talk about, things we must say . . ."

Instantly, he was back with her again, holding her more tightly than she had ever been held, as if to press his very soul into hers, and to meld their souls forever. She felt her mind going, and the thin thread that was connected to reality began to come unraveled . . .

"Oh, dear God, Selena! If we would never have to part again . . ."

Far away, someone was knocking on a door.

She kissed him as she had kissed no one before, so desperately and so hard that she was not sure where her being ended and his began.

"But tell me . . . send word through Dick . . . if you need me. If you wish me to come for you . . ."

Oh, if I did that, she was thinking, *if I did that, it would be forever.*

"The day will come. I know the day will come."

There *was* a knock on the door. Selena heard it, but at first it did not seem to matter. They were lost in an embrace. Her flesh was hungry for him. But her mind refused to die completely. There was Sean to think of, and Davina, and here she was, a married woman, holding the love of her life in her arms, but it could not be . . .

He was gone from her. "That's at the *front* door?" There was alarm in his voice. "They shouldn't . . ."

Something had gone wrong. A trap. The banging continued, and gew louder, at the front of the house. And now, above them, the cellar door slowly eased open. Friend or foe? Foe. The highly polished buttons on the uniform of a British soldier gave him away. He had a musket, held at port arms, across his chest. He was being very cautious; the door inched open.

"McGrover," Royce murmured. "He's come. Selena, kill him, next time you have the chance."

With that, he leaped up the ladder, slammed his head full force into the vulnerable parts of the soldier with the weapon. She could see Royce dark against the lighter darkness of the rain-silver night. There was running, and a shout. More shouts, from down the alley. Weddington's men, she hoped. Moaning, the soldier sat up, and called for help. Sean's voice carried down to her as he opened the front door. He was angry. "What's the meaning of this pounding?" he demanded. "Stop it! Don't you know it's the middle of the night . . ."

His voice ceased. Selena knew he had recognized McGrover. She started up the stairs. Her body shuddered. Her heart pounded, wild for a thousand reasons. McGrover was telling Sean something. Selena could not hear the words, only the oily insinuations thick on his broken tongue. She reached the top of the steps and walked through the kitchen, moving to confront what awaited her

at the door. It seemed the natural thing to do. She did not
have the time, then, to recapitulate her communion with
Royce. But already she had begun to change. She *was*
changed. The realization came to her with a shock of surprise. She felt different, faintly exhilarated, even as she saw
Sean, in his robe, facing her old nemesis, the bloody, implacable monster in his tricornered hat, with his cape and
that absurd ear.

Selena strode to the door, lifted her chin high. Her body
was erect, proud. There was fire in her eyes. After the
doubts, the hesitations, the vague semi-deceptions of so long,
things were beginning to change. The fiber of her soul
thrilled to a secret knowledge. She locked her eyes on
McGrover's. He saw what was in them. So did the gaggle
of security men, standing around him on the front steps.

Sean glanced at her, then looked again. What he saw
took him back to a time in Scotland, a time before these
times of danger and exile. They all saw courage, raw defiance.

Selena MacPherson Bloodwell was no longer afraid.

THE BOLD MUST DECIDE

Selena could read the demon's face. He had come to the house, secure in the knowledge that, this time, at last, he had Selena where he wanted her. And Bloodwell, too, for good measure. What better way to convince Lord Ludford to give him carte blanche where the traitorous rebels were concerned?

But now, seeing her, he was not quite so secure. Still, he pressed on. Pretending to ignore her, he spoke to Sean.

"Sir, we have reason to believe that a rebel sea captain is being harbored here at your residence. As you are well aware, we require no warrant. Stand aside, please."

Sean did not move, more because of surprise than resistance.

"A rebel sea captain?"

"His name is Royce Campbell," McGrover added helpfully, with a smirk in Selena's direction.

Now Sean looked at Selena, recalled that she had not been in bed when he'd awakened to the pounding on the door. He was just about to speak when the soldier who'd been assigned to guard the cellar door came limping around the corner, holding his genitals with one hand and his musket with the other.

"Howard!" McGrover demanded. "What happened?"

"He . . . he got away. Came ramming up at me out of the cellar, and . . ." he winced in pain ". . . got away."

McGrover swore. "Take that soldier into custody," he ordered his men. Immediately three of them sprang at Howard, the hapless incompetent who'd let the quarry get away. "Take him back to the fort. Give him a thousand lashes—don't spare your arms—and if he lives through that, hang him here on Bowling Green as an example to these rich fence-straddlers. They'll learn where their loyalty belongs."

He glared at Sean, who returned him a look of revulsion.

"I don't believe there's anyone such as you describe in my house."

More than anything else, McGrover's obvious cruelty and high-handedness had made an impression on him. Nontheless, he glanced uneasily at Selena.

"There may have been someone," she told McGrover coolly. "Something awakened me, and I went downstairs. I was just about to hold a candle into the cellar when your soldier opened the door. I saw a man leaving our house. He knocked the soldier down. It was not Private Howard's fault."

Sean was looking at her closely. She held her ground. McGrover waved away her explanation. "Howard can writhe and whine and scream just like all the rest, and I need an example. You two might serve very well, also." He made a forward movement, as if to step into the house. Sean stood firm. Selena kept her eyes on McGrover and smiled.

The effect was broken by Traudl. Her short blond hair was half in curlers, and she came blithering down to the front door, worried to distraction by all that was on her simple mind.

"Oh, Mister Sean—ma'am—I don't know if I should tell ye. I've been puzzling it, but I just saw . . ."

She saw McGrover there in the lamplight, and her jaw dropped down to her rounded bosom.

"What did you see?" snapped McGrover.

Traudl looked from Sean to Selena to the floor.

"Nothin'," she said. "It must've been a dream."

Heartened, McGrover gave a nod, and, as a body, he and his men surged into the house. Sean slugged one of them, who dropped to his knees. Three men grabbed Sean. Two held Selena. She bit one of them in the hand. Traudl started to scream. A rough soldier's paw cut her off.

"Do you have any idea whose house it is you invade?" Sean demanded. "In the morning, Lord Ludford will hear of this. I'm a loyal subject, and . . ."

"Aye, that ye be," drawled McGrover, in a broad, mock-

ing imitation of the Scottish brogue. "But this be no par-
tiot's 'ouse, ye know. Rather, t'd seem t' me a viper's nest."

Brusquely, he ordered soldiers upstairs, to pen the rest
of the servants in their rooms.

"The chubby wench knows something," he snapped to
his security men. "Get her in the cellar, and these two as
well." He pointed to Sean and Selena. "They might feel like
telling us a few things, when they see how I make love."

Sean struggled, but he was held too fast. Selena had no
chance, gripped from behind by a strong soldier who had
her arms in a painful grasp. When she moved, he put on
the pressure. Pain. She did not move.

In a minute, they were in the cellar. Men brought down
a couple of lamps. It was quite dark, but the lamps were of
sufficient strength to show McGrover, smiling as he ripped
away Traudl's robe and nightdress, revealing her soft, pale
body.

"Aha! I have a feeling you don't care too much for pain,
my dear."

Poor Traudl, choking with fear, let her wild eyes plead
with McGrover, implore Sean and Selena for help.

"Stop this at once!" Sean ordered, struggling one last
time.

McGrover stepped over and brought the butt of his pistol down on Sean's head. He dropped to the floor, unconscious. Selena screamed.

"Now, what did you see?" McGrover demanded of
Traudl.

She was trying to say what—or who—it had been, but
she was too terrified to shape the words on her tongue.
Grinning, McGrover stepped over her naked body. "Part
her legs," he ordered the men who held her. Then he
crouched down and gripped the long-barreled pistol.

"I'm sure you like it hard," he said softly, "but I don't
think you've ever had it this . . ."

He said no more. Out of cellar shadows sprang at least a
half-dozen men, all of them in black masks. Quickly, brutally, silently, they fell upon McGrover and his men. A
long knife slashed into the guts of one of the British and
drove powerfully upward, gutting him from groin to breast-
bone. The sight of gushing blood and entrails, after everything else, proved too much for Traudl. She succumbed in

a faint. Not one of the hooded men so much as spoke, as the remaining two guards fell to club and knife. Selena felt herself yanked free of her tormentor, and saw the heavy hickory that split his skull in half before her eyes. Then it was McGrover's turn. The pistol had been knocked from his hand at the beginning of the battle, and then he had been grappled to the ground by the biggest of the hooded figures. Royce, she thought. But it couldn't be. No time to think. The hooded figure atop McGrover rammed his forearm across the monster's throat. His dagger cut free McGrover's clothing, exposing his manhood. The other hooded men, jobs done, gathered around, except for the one who bent to tend to Sean.

"Should be all right," he muttered. "Now, hurry."

The man—could it be Royce?—kept his arm on McGrover, whose bulging eyes remained defiant, unyielding, even as his body gulped for air. With his dagger, he gestured to McGrover's private parts, somewhat misshapen and now shrinking fast. A flick of the wrist, tossing the dagger in the air, catching it by the blade. He handed Selena the hilt of it.

She stopped, for a moment still as time. The house roared in silence. There was nothing. Either the servants, far up in the attic, had heard nothing, or they were already dead in their beds. She looked down at Sean, who stirred faintly on the cellar floor, bathed in dim light. *Get it over with. The less he sees, the better. This is my responsibility. Vengeance is a private thing.*

The man watched her. McGrover watched her. She held the dagger, motionless.

One word took the shape on her tongue. "R . . . ?"

The hooded figure cut her off with an abrupt finger to the place on his hood where his mouth would be. *Quiet! No names!* And he pointed at the dagger in her hand. *Time. Time. Hurry.*

Still she waited, transfixed as much by what it was she might do here as by the almost certain knowledge that Royce had returned to save her once again. It was confirmed.

"*Sometimes it is necessary,*" came the words from beneath the mask.

He lifted his head, his veiled eyes on hers. She met his

sightless gaze, and stepped forward. McGrover tried to cry out; now he was afraid. Now he believed it. He knew better than to expect a second chance; he had no doubts about her anymore.

But she did not move toward the target that the hooded man had exposed.

"An eye for an eye," she said. "A throat for a throat." Royce understood. He moved his forearm from McGrover's neck and pinioned the man's shoulders to the floor. McGrover's breath returned; he panted desperately.

"Others will come," he croaked. "You will never escape my web."

"Yes, I will," she told him. And drove the point of the dagger straight down through his throat, cutting off his voice, severing his windpipe. There was some blood, but not as much as Selena had expected. He thrashed pitifully, his body fighting for air. His body wanted desperately to live, and the struggle was ferocious. One minute, two. Three minutes. McGrover's face was blue, almost black. Blood bubbled at the edge of the dagger blade, as his body tried to suck in the air it could no longer hope to have. All the while, McGrover's eyes were on Selena. He never looked away, no matter how his body pitched and tossed. It was a terrible death she had given him, far longer than he had given Father, more agonizing than the maharajah's had been. Selena hated to watch it, but she did not regret it, and the fact must have shown in her eyes. Because, even at the last moment, McGrover jerked his head, a congratulatory nod. *You have won. My regards.*

Then he was dead, and gone to the hell that had spawned him.

Sean was stirring. The men had to move fast. Royce gestured toward the upper floors of the house, where the soldiers were.

"How many?" someone asked.

"Three, I counted."

The work was over quickly, short and brutal. Seven men lay dead in the cellar. And Royce was gone.

"There must, indeed, have been a man here earlier," Selena told Sean. "He returned with reinforcements. You were unconscious and McGrover was beginning to torture Traudl when they came in."

Traudl was in her second-floor bedroom, recovering from the shock. The most trusted servant was caring for her. Sean slumped on the cellar stairs, the bodies and blood before him. He rubbed his head and moaned in pain.

"We'd best get a doctor. Come, and I'll take you . . ."

"Wait." He was thinking. "This is very bad, I don't know . . . God, my head's not clear . . ."

One of the servants was at the head of the cellar stairs. "Someone to see you, Mister Bloodwell."

"Well, that's it. We're finished now. A bunch of security men dead in my house, and . . . well, who is it, dammit?"

"Lord Weddington, sir."

Dick Weddington. A friend. Selena's heart leaped. She helped Sean up the stairs. They met Dick and retreated to the study.

"My God, what happened!" Dick cried. He was in riding clothes. His boots had mud on them, caked in the space between the sole and heel. One did not acquire such mud in a stirrup. Selena knew already, but Sean did not. He was too concerned about the future he believed to be lost. Dispiritedly, he described what had happened, and Selena finished the story, omitting only that she herself had killed Darius McGrover.

She suppressed an impulse to go back down to the cellar, to make sure he was still dead.

"You know, this could be in your favor," Dick suggested shrewdly, glancing at Selena.

Sean raised his head. "And what in hell are you doing out? It couldn't be much after three in the morning."

"Oh, I'm sorry. I guess you didn't get my missive. I'm bound for Long Island and Westchester for a week. To see how my new men are getting along. . . ."

"Oh. Yes. But you were saying . . ."

"This need not involve you, or the firm," Dick said, leaning forward and speaking quickly. Dick had come to know Sean. Knew that his loyalty to the Empire was a willed, fully rational emotion. Knew that he expected reward for what he gave. And, finally, knew that Sean would not change his mind. So he pitched his strategy to that knowledge.

"Did you ever expect Ludford to do anything like this?" Dick demanded, feigning a little more outrage than necessary. "*You* were the man who notified Ludford of Hamilton's presence at the masque. And now they send McGrover in on you, when it's clear from the start that this McGrover was some kind of madman. In fact, I've heard that Ludford was very uncomfortable with the man. His excess of zeal was dangerous to security itself. Now that's been proven. Look, I'll delay my trip. You get some rest. And in the morning we'll go down to the Battery and see Ludford. He can pick up his bodies. If he wants the support of decent, restrained people in this town, he had best remember that dignity denied is dignity defiant. Ludford will be happy to find out about McGrover, don't you worry," Dick added. And he knew what he was talking about.

The ploy worked. Sean was convinced that, by accident, his house had been used for mayhem, and, with all the bodies lying about, McGrover's mention of Royce Campbell seemed a preposterous fabrication. How could that be?

Or did he believe it? Selena was not sure. For his part, Lord Ludford remained cool and canny, as befit the guardian of state security. He handled the situation with caution and dexterity, so much so that his own motives were obscure. In effect, Ludford told Sean that the battle in his house might well have occurred anywhere. Ludford himself had been concerned about McGrover's excessive zeal ever since the man had arrived from London. There had been nothing he could do about it, because McGrover was a favorite of Lord North, having rendered certain services in the past, best left unmentioned. But, of late, McGrover was thought to have been pursuing some personal vendetta, which Ludford did not detail. Whatever the nature of this vendetta, it was the ruthless interrogator's personal passion. Obviously, it had caused him to ignore the fact that, for some months now, rebel groups had had him earmarked for assassination. Ludford himself had warned McGrover of these reports. Selena listened to Ludford speak, and concluded that he was probably glad to be rid of McGrover, but justly skeptical of the monster's bizarre demise.

"So there you have it," Ludford told Sean. A tragic error on McGrover's part. An outrageous attempt by an overzealous investigator to besmirch the house of a Tory. And worse, McGrover had been careless, letting himself be spotted in the streets. Followed to the Bloodwell home, he had been ambushed there. Ludford assured Sean that everyone knew of Sean's loyalty, and the security director immediately wrote his superiors in London, praising Sean's bravery and cooperation in keeping confidential this incendiary situation. He also knew how to serve himself: buried in the same letter was an admission that he had not yet been able to identify, much less capture, the rebel's master spy, who was working impudently somewhere in New York.

But after that night, Sean was not the same. Selena would see it when he glanced up suddenly from his ledgers, his eyes fixed on a faraway scene. Or when he stood at the window watching the security men, who were ever present now "for the protection of the Tories on Bowling Green." Or she would see it when he thoughtfully regarded the now subdued, troubled Traudl. And she would even feel his remoteness when he took her in the warm summer bed, sheets cast off, their bodies naked and gleaming. He would love her as well, as skillfully and tenderly as ever, and she would respond in kind. Just what was the nature of the new quality she perceived in him? Was it disappointment? Or sadness? Was it wariness, or a conviction of danger? Had his estimation of her changed? Was he himself somehow different from the man he had been when they were joined under God on the deck of the *Blue Foray?*

She did not know what to do, and so she did nothing, hoping he would return to himself. It would do no good for her to make great protestations of innocence. Such protestations are invariably self-defeating. Harbingers of grief.

They made love, and kissed, and whispered good night. In the summer of 1777. Changelings, bound together. In sleep, he turned on his side, away from her, and thrust an arm over the edge of the bed. She tossed, neither asleep nor awake, golden hair tangling on the perfumed, lavender pillow. The satin sheet slid from her young, burning body. Neither she nor Sean knew what would be, but sleep took away, for short, sweet hours, the need to care. A confluence of forces and events was about to occur. Finally, the day arrived.

Callie Fox was still at La Marinda, but in Selena's need to talk to Dick, she was incautious when he arrived at the shop.

"You're here," she cried, with a touch of desperation.

Callie Fox glanced up from her work. She was suspicious. Dick began talking of a purchase for the wife of a friend, and Selena forced herself to calm down. After a time, Callie Fox excused herself and left. But not before she took a good long look at what she thought was going on, and not before she let them both know that she had her own opinion, all right.

Selena waited until the seamstress had gone down the street, then turned to face Dick.

"I've got to see Royce," she said.

He gave her a long look, half sad, half resigned, as if he had known that this day would come. Since her arrival in New York, he had been her closest friend. And almost from the first, he had also known of her past involvement with Royce. So now, he did not ask why. He knew why. "Royce is at sea," he said.

"When will he be back?"

"He's due in to our Montauk supply point sometime in late August. He's been trying to disrupt the British blockade of Boston harbor."

Selena calculated. It was late July.

"I could go to Montauk," she said.

He was sympathetic but firm. "Selena, don't be a fool. There is no doubt that Ludford trusts Sean, and my sources tell me he's convinced Sean had no knowledge of that incident at your house in May. But, Selena . . ." He stepped close to her, speaking urgently. ". . . Ludford is not so certain of you."

The information shook her.

"Royce Campbell—although it could not be proven that he was there that night—would be a glittering prize. McGrover remembered your connection with Campbell, and he told his superior about you many times. It's stuck in Ludford's mind. Why do you think those security men hang about Bowling Green? It's not to get a glimpse of your ankles, I can tell you that."

Selena blanched; they considered *her* potentially disloyal. *I'm not,* she thought resolutely, *I'm just loyal to something else, and I'm going to stay that way.*

But it was clear that Dick was trying to dissuade her from seeing Royce.

"In fact," he was saying, "if I were Sean, I'd be more than a little watchful myself."

"I'm afraid he is." She told him about the moodiness and doleful self-absorption.

"You once told me something about your vow . . ."

"Seeing Royce has nothing to do with my vow," she said, too quickly. *Late August in Montauk,* she was thinking. Montauk was a remote village on the Atlantic, at the easternmost tip of Long Island. The Penrods went there annually to summer . . .

"Selena, don't try to fool me. Men are men and women are women. I know you and I know what he feels toward you . . ."

"You do?" Her heart shot into skies of roaring glory. "He *does?*"

Dick Weddington smiled ruefully.

"Just once," she pleaded. "I promise—just once. I have to see him alone, in a quiet place, so we can talk things out and lay it all to rest."

"*That's* what you have in mind?"

"I *swear!* Dick, try to see it as I do. We loved . . ." the past tense was as difficult a thing as she'd ever said ". . . each other. We thought each other dead. We've seen each other for only a couple of minutes. It was worse than never having seen each other at all! I *must* see him, and I'm afraid I'll just go by myself sometime, and ruin everything for you, your work . . ."

Outside, Otto Kollor drew up in the carriage, come to fetch her home to dinner. "Perhaps if Sean would take Davina and me to Montauk . . ."

Dick Weddington succumbed. "All right, Selena," he said, "but I'm warning you. Put that affair with Royce to rest, or you'll have nothing but trouble for the rest of your life. I know what love is. I've been in love, too. But you have a fine husband, a lovely daughter, everything. We'll win the war. Sean won't like it, but he'll adjust . . ."

Maybe, she thought, fingers crossed.

". . . and your future will be as secure as anything can be. Don't blow your hard-won security to kingdom come!"

"I won't. If I see Royce, just once, just the two of us . . ." *Then the old haunting things can be laid to rest.*

"I'll figure something out for you," Dick said. "Some

pretext. I'll send a message around to your house. All right?"

Yes. She agreed. She saw Dick outside, locked La Marinda and climbed up into the carriage. She greeted Otto so gaily that the Hessian driver was startled out of his complacency. He didn't smile, though. Otto was satisfied with himself today for a number of reasons. The master had relied on him, told him to keep his eyes open. He'd halted the horses to get a bit of information from Callie Fox, just up the street. And, through the window, he'd seen the mistress talking earnestly with this Weddington fellow. He didn't like the looks of it. Not one bit. Their heads had been too close together. He also remembered that Weddington had been there last February, with the man who'd fled the soldiers.

It might not mean anything, but it was worth mentioning to Herr Bloodwell.

Summer heat had built up throughout the day, and Selena ordered the dining room draperies drawn aside and the windows thrown open so they could enjoy the river breeze as they dined. "Wouldn't it be nice at the seashore?" she asked brightly.

Davina was in her usual good spirits. Traudl was almost recovered from the terrible affair in the cellar, but it had left her more serious than before, almost grave. Sean came a bit late to table. He had news; she could tell by his face. But he said nothing just then. The meal was light: cold, sliced meat, potatoes, salad, beer. Finally he told her, as if watching to see how she would react.

"Word came from London today. Through Ludford's office."

Selena looked up guardedly. "Oh?"

"You'll recall he commended me by letter to London? Well, they responded. I'm to be decorated."

He didn't seem as cheerful as he ought to be, she thought.

"You do understand what this means?" he asked, still with that uncharacteristic grimness in the face of such good news. "I'm formally recognized again, after all this time. We can go anywhere. The years of exile are over . . ."

"And, after the decoration, you may get your title . . ."

"No," he answered flatly. "That will take more service than I've given the Crown so far. But, after the decoration . . ."

"What award is it?" she asked belatedly, realizing that her delayed inquiry could easily be misconstrued as a lack of enthusiasm.

"Order of the Golden Spur."

Selena was impressed, as anyone would have been. The Order of the Spur was granted only to those who made "personal service to the monarch, in danger and risk of death." True, Ludford had been playing politics, as Sean knew only too well. Ludford was using Sean as an example to the rest of the burghers of New York, telling them none of them would be neglected should they cast their lot with the Tories now.

"Is Daddy a king now?" asked Davina, who had been following the conversation closely.

Even Traudl laughed at that, forgetting, for the moment, her hovering melancholy.

And Sean smiled, too. "You will never know," he teased, "just where a bit of industry might lead, as long as you have a cache of Indian jewels as well."

Nevertheless, his severity did not dissipate. After the meal was over and Traudl took Davina off to bed, she asked him about it.

"I think something's wrong on Long Island," he said. "It has something to do with Dick's factors and representatives out there. One of his men, a young fellow by the name of Nathan Hale, seems to have switched locations. At first, he was working in the Port Washington area. He did fairly well, but he was never too good at keeping his records current. It seems, however, that he purchased more goods from local farmers than found their way back to my warehouses. . . ."

Selena knew why. Those supplies had found their way into the hold of the *Selena*.

"It's probably just an oversight that'll be straightened out when Hale gets a chance to go over his books. But that won't be soon, judging from his latest itinerary."

She looked at him questioningly.

"He's moved from Port Washington out to the eastern

end of Long Island. I had no advance word of it, and Dick is usually most faithful about keeping me posted."

She seized the opportunity to try and make her point.

"Oh, Sean, I was just thinking while driving back here in this heat, wouldn't it be nice if we went out to the ocean for the rest of August? The Penrods are out near Montauk at their cottage, and Samantha told me about a new summer hotel there now, called the Colony. And I thought . . ."

"The Penrods again? Look what almost happened the last time we became involved with them. Let him have his ten percent, but . . ."

"Sean. We wouldn't be going to visit them. They'd be there, but . . ."

"Well, you may be right. It would be. nice. But it is the harvest season, and I'm very busy right now."

"Not even for a week?"

Sean considered it. Selena waited, hoping. It would be dangerous, but she could see Royce one last time. Just to talk. She might have to take with her a message related to the military conflict, but that was incidental to her now.

"All right," Sean agreed, giving her an indulgent smile. "Why not? I don't think I'll be able to come with you, but you take Davina and have a good time. Lord knows winter will be on us before we turn around. It's best you enjoy summer as much as you can."

Selena felt happy and guilty at the same time, and tremendously excited, too.

"Thank you, Sean," she said. Getting up from her chair, she went around to his place at the head of the table and gave him a kiss.

"Don't worry," she told him.

"Now why. should I do that?" he asked, looking up, and she saw the mood of the past weeks come down again over his face.

Later that evening a message came for her. She had stayed in the parlor, sewing, in order to be near the door. Fortunately. The message was from Dick Weddington. *Montauk plans complete,* was all it said.

She put it in the fire in the iron stove in the kitchen.

IN WORDS ALONE

In the summer of 1777, the cause of the American revolutionaries remained unresolved. The vast sweep of America, the extent of which Selena was only beginning to grasp, required that troops move hundreds of debilitating miles through rough, untracked country even before a battle took place. And the reports of such confrontations often did not reach the coastal cities until weeks after the event itself. Waiting for news produced tension. Dick Weddington told Selena that Lord Howe (who had stopped calling Washington "The Farmer," and spoke now of "bagging the Old Fox") was on the move, by sea, toward the general's entrenched positions at Morristown, which blocked Howe's planned attack upon Philadelphia. In the north, "Gentleman Jack" Burgoyne, the sybaritic British general who moved through the wastes of northern New York with his personal service of china, silver, crystal, a wagonload of champagne, and thirty wagonloads of personal baggage, had also found time to take Crown Point, on the Hudson, in June. The Americans, under the command of Horatio Gates and Benedict Arnold, were maneuvering to close with Burgoyne—and might already have done so—but the main event was Howe versus Washington.

"So Sean agreed to let you have a little time on the ocean?"

Dick seemed anxious, almost distressed. His features were prominent, his skin stretched tight, with fatigue.

"I'm going," she said simply. "Davina and I. And I'm taking Traudl and a few servants."

They walked slowly, trying to appear casual, along the

water's edge at Bowling Green. Selena no longer felt safe talking to Dick at La Marinda, with Callie Fox around.

"Selena," Dick said, making sure no one was within earshot, "your trip to Montauk is more important than you think. But I would be remiss if I did not warn you of its danger."

"Royce will be there?" she asked quickly.

"That he will, if he is not delayed by some maneuver at sea. And you already know that I think your seeing him is personally dangerous to you."

"I know. But I must. I think if I were able to talk to him—just to talk to him—"

"Yes, but I am going to have to ask you to see him for a reason that has nothing to do with you."

That was the cause of his grim concern.

"Anything. I'll be happy to . . ."

"You had better hear me out before you volunteer."

"Volunteer? For what?"

"Selena, I've told you that Howe is moving by sea toward the Chesapeake Bay, on the way to Philadelphia. Now, Washington may be able to hold him back. And he may not. Alex is optimistic, but then he's always optimistic. What we are going to try to do, if we can get the message to Royce Campbell, is to attack Howe at sea, while he's in the process of ferrying his army."

"That sounds like a good idea," she said, wondering how this would affect her.

"You have to take him the message, Selena. Along with details of debarkation, orders of battle, intelligence reports. There's no one else I can send."

Selena was stunned for a moment. *Spying? She, a spy?*

"Why, you have an entire network! All your so-called purchasing agents and factors . . ."

He shook his head, disconsolate. "No more. The British just executed Nathan Hale. As far as I know, he didn't give them any information as to the rest of the men in my organization, but I can't take any chances. Made a nice speech, though, Nate did. I regret he 'had but one life,' too. I could have used several more of him, truth to tell."

"Certainly, I'll tell Royce what you want," she said, deciding. The execution of a man she did not even know, rather than frightening or dissuading her, only served to enhance her determination.

"There's more to it than that. First, we don't know if the British coastal watchers know that Royce will be putting in to port for resupply. If so, it's very dangerous, even more so than it's already been. Second, I'm afraid Sean is getting an inclination that there's more here than meets the eye."

She told him about the Golden Spur. "I guess I might have been wrong about Sean," he admitted ruefully.

"I told you that from the beginning. He's always going to be loyal to Great Britain. The fire burned him once before. I told you that, too."

"Aye. You did. I was ebullient, then, and the war was young. Now I know why old men in London direct British intelligence. They are not carried away as easily by high spirits. This is the time of my testing. I shouldn't be involving you at all."

"Don't think about that." Selena did not want him to change his mind; in spite of the danger, she had to see Royce. "Sean did know about Hale, though," she added.

"Anything else?"

She thought a moment, remembered. "Something to do was his switching locations, from Port Washington to . . ."

"Montauk. Bad. Very bad. Both militarily and for me. Sean *has* to know something's very wrong. It's only a question of time . . ."

"Then tell me what it is I have to learn," Selena demanded. "There will be precious little time as it is. If I do find Royce, I have no intention of discussing Lord Howe, to the exclusion of all else."

Dick managed a smile. "Selena, I believe you mean that," he said.

Long Island was one long dusty road, and the August sun hammered down on the roof of the stagecoach. Little Davina fretted in the boiling interior of the vehicle, and Traudl had to gasp for air. Drops of perspiration flowed from her; now and then she almost moaned. Selena braced herself to endure the swirls of dust, kicked up by the hooves of the horses. They were switched at relay points every ten miles, blown and exhausted. It took an entire day to reach Montauk. But when the wild, white, untrammeled beaches came into view, and the clean, rolling sea, Selena felt her heart swell. It was, in a sense, a contradiction. She had come here to see Royce one final time, and to settle things between them in a manner both of them deserved. Then, if they met by chance in the future, there would be no regrets or misplaced hopes. Each would know the other's heart.

But when she saw the Atlantic, with its white surf gently beating on the shore, it did not seem an ending at all. It seemed a beginning.

The Colony, a small new beach hotel—the one about which Samantha had written—was built far out on a peninsula. A wide porch on all four sides of the building gave a constant view of the sea, and Selena dined alone on the east porch, enjoying the twilight and the cool breeze.

"Well, if it isn't the little shopgirl herself."

She knew the voice, and she was terrified. Not by the voice itself, nor even by the person to whom it belonged, but by the fact that the voice and the person were *here*.

Veronica Blakemore.

She put on the sweetest smile she could manage—it would have been sweeter had the journey not tired her—and looked up to face her tormentor.

"What? All alone?" Veronica cried, in a mocking whisper quite loud enough to attract the attention of almost everyone dining on the porch. "But at least you were admitted to a good hotel."

Veronica's eyes were hard, still with the promise of revenge in them. Then Selena became aware of the man standing just behind the black-haired Blakemore. Polished boots, impeccably tailored uniform, gleaming belt buckle, and epaulets. There was a faint look of distaste on Lord Ludford's severe face as he listened to Veronica, or perhaps it was displeasure at having been seen in public with her.

"We're dining here, too, Mrs. Bloodwell," Lord Ludford said, intervening as politely as he could. "Perhaps you'd care to join us?"

Don't you dare, Veronica said with her flashing eyes.

Selena toyed with the idea of accepting the invitation, if only to bedevil Veronica, but, stunned by Ludford's presence, she needed time to sort things out. Declining graciously, she was able to suggest that, just possibly, on another evening, if Lord Ludford would be staying . . .

Ludford looked momentarily discomfited—this ever-suspicious martinet who scrutinized the morals and manners and movements of others—and Selena's original surmise became an active, if less than charitable, suspicion. Ludford and Veronica had not come out here to the end of Long Island simply to dine.

But then . . . ? Smiling, making polite but inane comments before Ludford led Veronica to a distant table, Selena grappled with the situation's complexity. Had not Ludford been a bit distant? No, he had even congratulated her on Sean's Order of the Spur award (to which the adventuress had replied, "Isn't that *nice,* and a *commoner,* too"), and he had, at times, seemed *overly* friendly. That was when she thought she knew for certain that he was here to bed Veronica.

Ludford and Hamilton, she thought. *Both sides of the* . . .

That fact brought her up short.

Was Veronica providing the British with information about the rebels with whom she came in contact? Or was it the other way around? Or was she doing *both?* Then, too, she recalled what Hamilton had said. If Veronica was siding with the loyalists, the rebels would win. The thought gave no comfort just then.

The waiter appeared and asked if she would care for a sweet. But the heat combined with this new problem had ruined what was left of her appetite. She had, moreover, a long night ahead of her. "No, thank you," she told him, half-distracted, and in a moment left the dining area.

Don't lose your head, she advised herself. She had not cared for Blakemore since first laying eyes upon her at Edinburgh Castle, but she must not let her own animosity lead to a false judgment about Veronica's skill. *Look at it logically.* She was a beautiful woman, whose attractiveness to men was more than a matter of record. The main question, then, was whether Veronica was actually what she appeared to be: a haughty creature of whim and pleasure, born to be embraced, admired—or was that merely a pose, behind which she was truly much more? In this case, a spy herself? Or even a double agent?

Selena did not know, but, as Dick had once suggested, it was necessary to assume that the other side knew everything you were going to do. The trick was to do it before they could stop you.

Oh, no, she thought. They would have plenty of time, if things did not go well.

What Selena had agreed to do would have been tricky enough under the best of circumstances. The eastern end of Long Island was split into two long prongs of land, Montauk Point and, to the north, Orient Point. Between them were any number of small bays, inlets, minuscule harbors, and islands. The *Selena* would anchor some miles off Montauk, and Royce could come into shore by small boat. The location to which the boat repaired was changed with each landing. This time it was to be a little more than a mile west of the Colony Hotel, across from Gardiners Island. The problem was that Selena could not be certain exactly which night the rendezvous was to occur. Royce had been—or ought to have been—sailing off the Grand Bank of Newfoundland, attempting to intercept and sink British shipping. That was far away.

There was more than a lone chance that he would not show up at all, but she didn't think of that. Climbing the stairs to the small suite she shared with Traudl and Davina, Selena realized still another unfortunate fact. Even if Ludford were himself here strictly for pleasure, her own movements would be more suspicious with the passage of each day. A single woman might indulge in a midnight walk on the water's edge one night. But every night?

She entered the suite. It was lamplit but dim, cool and pleasant. Nursemaid and ward had eaten in the suite. Davina slept now in a trundle bed, and Traudl was down on her knees beside her own bed, saying her prayers.

"Amen," she said aloud, and stood when Selena came in. "Did you enjoy your dinner, ma'am?"

The question was innocuous enough. Perhaps it was Selena's perspicacity, or perhaps just nerves, but she perceived in the question some inquisitorial intent. If Callie Fox watched everything, and told Otto all she knew, and if Sean had instructed Otto to "keep an eye open," then why not Traudl, too? For a moment, she felt violated, as if a loved one no longer trusted her. Then, sadly, coldly, she faced the facts. What she was about to do would be considered suspect by almost everyone. But she had to see Royce. That came first. While she believed in the rightness of the rebel cause, the message she carried to help that cause was subordinate to one last tender meeting with the man who had both possessed and saved her.

Now, after praising the chef and the dining room and the hotel, she urged Traudl to rest. She had hours to wait. It was not even eleven yet. She turned out all but one lamp, and took it over to a chair near the window. There was a crescent moon tonight, and the sea rocked into the stark shoreline, waves of molten silver, rolling fields of gold. Somewhere out upon that sea, not too far away if God looked down tonight, the mighty ship that bore her name would already have dropped anchor, furled countless sails. A boat would already be moving across the water, bound toward her.

Traudl, tired, fell asleep quickly. In minutes she was snoring lightly. She tossed a little, then quieted. Now. No, wait. Selena would have dearly loved a glass of wine, but it would not do to enter the public room downstairs on her own. Gilbertus Penrod would have made a fine escort—the Penrods' summer cottage was a short distance away, near Montauk village—but it was far too late. She would send a card, or call on them tomorrow.

Finally, it was midnight. It was time. She could hear quiet music coming from one of the porches, where a few couples might be dancing. An evenly spaced row of torches ran beside a boardwalk, down onto the beach, but it was deserted. Selena stepped away from the window, checked Davina, and slipped out of the room. The corridor was empty. She descended the stairs. No one at the main desk; no one in the lobby. Just in case someone might be observing her, she pretended to admire a few of the oil paintings on the wall, all of them more or less faithful renditions of Montauk in various seasons of the year. Then, with what she hoped would appear to be casual impulse, she slipped out onto the porch. Another theatrical pause. *Ah, doesn't the evening air feel good. Wouldn't it be nice to step out onto the beach . . .*

Then she was out on the boardwalk, passing along beneath the row of torches. Another fire glimmered in the lighthouse off the Point; somewhere a buoy tingled, sounded. Then she reached the end of the boardwalk, her shadow great in the light of the last torch. She reached down and took off her shoes. *Now to stroll easily out of the reach of the light, and then . . .*

A sound stopped her, just where the darkness began. Selena halted, letting her eyes adjust to the pale rind of moon, the pallid iridescence of the sand. The sound came again, familiar and low, near a clump of beach brush only a dozen yards from her position. Again, the throaty groan, but Selena did not need it in order to know what was going on nearby. For by now she had seen the two white figures locked together there. Passion had overcome them, but they had preserved a measure of caution, anyway. Veronica had not removed her gown, the skirts of which rode up to her waist, folds of satin crushed into the sand. Her lovely legs were bent, knees drawn high, and her ankles, lightly crossed, rested on Ludford's undulating back. He had not seen fit even to draw his breeches down, but had taken her summarily, with the minimum of exposure. Selena saw the frenzy set in—my God, was *that* what it looked like?—and used the moment to ease away. In a minute, she was running down along the water, the sand wet and alive beneath her bare feet, the air electric. She felt as if she might run forever. She felt as if, at any moment, she might begin to fly.

"It is a natural breakwater," Dick Weddington had told her. "Look for that. A chain of rocks extending out into the bay. That's your landing point on the first night."

Was this it? She peered into the darkness, waiting for the moon to come out from behind the clouds. This had to be it! But there was no sound. There was nothing. The moon disappeared again, and it was very dark. A thousand terrors bloomed then, an unholy cluster of latent disasters. She was being watched, had been watched since her arrival at the Colony. Even now, up behind the dunes, British agents struggled to suppress their gleeful snickering. ("Look, mate, there she be." "Silly fool of a woman." "Aye. Thinks she be pullin' the wool o'er our eyes. Thinks she be meetin' 'er old lover in a secret glade. Let's wait, an' get us an eyeful." "An' 'im, too." "Aye. 'Im and 'er together." "They say she be a reg'lar princess, in the old country. That her father lost everythin' fer dabblin' stupidly in treason." "Aye. Lak father lak daughter, eh, mate?")

Of course. *That* was why Ludford and Veronica were fully dressed, back there on the beach. They were only pretending. For Selena's benefit, as a further ruse, a distraction. Skill and guile and cunning, and she had been victim of all three. What a stupid . . .

An unusual sound in the soft ripple of nighttime surf, an unnatural sound in water. Then again. Again, again, again, steady and growing louder. Muffled oars in water, and the thin hiss of a wooden boat sliding onto the sand. Selena stood up, and peered down the beach. Nothing, but . . .

But there in the darkness, less than a stone's throw away, three dark-clothed men in a boat, with feathered oars. One of the men jumped onto the sand. Her heart knew. It was Royce.

Neither speaking nor crying out, she raced toward him across the sand. His back was turned; he was doing something with the boat.

"Look out," someone grunted. She reached him, arms outstretched.

He whirled and grabbed at her. She flashed through the air, a dreadful, empty, sickening feeling, and slammed heavily down onto the sand, before her brain had a chance even to register his harsh grip upon her. For a moment she had no breath and the scudding clouds seemed to carry legions of bursting stars. Then his face came down over hers.

"Selena!" he whispered. "Good God! What the hell are you doing here?"

"I . . ." she gasped. "I . . . have your message."

He was astounded. "You what? From Weddington?"

She made an affirmative motion, fighting for air.

"My *God!* Are you crazy?"

She made the motion again.

A moment, then the white flash of his teeth. "Well, I guess you couldn't hold out against your own nature anymore," he said. "But warn me next time, all right? I might have killed you. The only thing that saved you was that I noticed my assailant was wearing a dress. That's happened before, of course, but usually not from behind."

She saw an ominous-looking rope knife in his hand. He

put it in his belt. She leaned up on one elbow, her head spinning slowly.

"You really are the courier?"

She nodded.

He stepped to the boat and told the sailors to row out about a hundred yards and hold steady there. "If I'm not back in an hour, leave. Return tomorrow, same time. If I'm not here then, consider me lost, and take the ship to Sandy Hook, south of New York. There will be instructions for you there."

He rushed the boat into the water, and in a moment Selena heard again the dip and ripple of muffled oars. Royce took her hand and led her up the beach to a sheltered place in the dunes, a wild, eerily beautiful stretch of mounded sand, driftwood, and scrub brush that ran for a hundred miles along the Long Island shore. He brought her down to the sand with him. She waited for his kiss, his embrace.

"Now tell me," he said, his voice businesslike and brisk. She said nothing, astonished. He sensed her surprise.

"We'll have a moment later," he said. "The cause comes first. Quickly," he ordered. "The message."

Selena buried her disappointment.

"Lord Howe is at sea with five thousand men," she began the recitation. "Eight hundred mounts, possibly a thousand, and more to come from the Maryland countryside. The loyalists there will speed his road to Philadephia . . ."

"Philadelphia?" Royce said, shrugging in surprise. The night was so dark she could barely see him. If the cells and nerves of her own body had not told her it was he, her companion might have been anyone.

"Yes," she said. "Washington is still dug in at Morristown."

"Still?"

"Yes. But he will try to move toward Elkton, in Maryland, to stop the British."

"No one will stop the British." A third participant had entered the conversation. Royce and Selena whirled around. There was Lord Ludford, squatting in the sand only a few feet away. He gripped a big pistol, the hollow muzzle of which was blacker than the night. He moved the muzzle in a leisurely gesture from Selena to Royce and back again.

"Well, if it isn't the mighty Campbell," he mocked. "Where is your sense of quality? I daresay you've been reduced to rutting traitor girls on the beach."

He moved the muzzle back to Royce. He kept it there.

"Surprised to see me here? Don't be. I did not expect to see you: It was your little friend, Selena, whose movements were of interest to me. . . ."

Selena did not even see the rope knife cutting through the darkness. She sensed movement beside her, a quick, deft, utterly ruthless thrust. Ludford's arm, severed just below the elbow, fell onto the sand before them, hand still clutching the pistol. Ludford's finger had begun to jerk against the trigger before Royce cut off his arm, and now the finger seemed to be trying to press the trigger, a reflexive twitching, but it was too late. Arm, hand, and pistol lay in a pool of blood; great gouts of blood spurted from Ludford's stump, as his heart pumped wildly.

"All right," Royce said, still very calm. He motioned Selena back, away from the blood. He stood up.

"God, *I'll bleed to* . . ." Ludford began to scream, trying to grip his arm with his remaining hand, to stanch the flow of blood.

Royce put the rope knife to Ludford's neck.

"Shut up or you're dead already. First, I want you to apologize to Selena for your language."

"But I'm *dying!*"

"I only care when *quality* dies," Royce said. "Now apologize."

"I'm sorry," Ludford babbled. "I'm sorry . . ." The blood was everywhere. Selena felt sick.

"Sorry? Sorry for what?" Royce was very calm.

"For my language. For . . ."

"For everything?"

"Oh, yes, oh, yes oh . . ."

"Good," Royce said. "That's called by the clergy an act of contrition. Now you're supposed to go straight to heaven . . ."

He shoved the knife directly into Ludford's left eye, right through the socket and into the man's brain. Ludford jerked upward to his full height, left the earth, as if jumping, and came crashing down, the bloody husk of what had once been a man.

"Damn," Royce said now, as they stood looking down at Ludford, and the blood, and the severed arm, and the gun. "That was stupid. I lost control of myself. When I sense a battle, I can't hold myself back."

Hold himself back? He'd been cold as ice throughout! She must summon an equal composure if she was to tell him about Hale, about Dick's fear that his network was collapsing. Taking a deep breath first, she told him the rest of the message with which Dick Weddington had charged her, the plans of Lord Howe.

"I may be too late already," he calculated. "They must have landed along the Chesapeake Bay by now. But I'll have to try and get there . . ."

The two of them stood there on the empty beach. Not much time until the boat, waiting for him, was supposed to go back to the *Selena*. He could not afford the time, and now, with Ludford dead, a twenty-four-hour sojourn here on Montauk was unthinkable. The British would be swarming across the peninsula shortly after dawn.

"Selena, you're at the Colony?"

"Yes. And . . . and Veronica is there, too. She was with Ludford . . ." She did not know exactly why she said it. Was she testing him?

"Then let me take you back there. I have to do something anyway."

So saying, he bent down, wrenched the pistol from the rigor mortis grip of Ludford's dead fingers, and jammed it into his belt. Then he lifted the security director up over his shoulders and started down the beach toward the hotel. Selena followed. She was half afraid of Royce having seen again that sudden flicker of violent, totally inexorable strength and decision. But, more than ever, she felt all the force of her love. Already, she knew that there would be no time to talk, nor to resolve anything. No hope that she could bank the fires and put to rest the passion that still arose when she thought of him. And unless she put those passions to rest, the future would be restless and unpredictable. There are some things in life that must be resolved. If not, life turns into waiting, and it is often a waiting for something which can never come. If that is what was to happen, then it was best to know it from the beginning. She might spare herself the pain, and save herself the heartbreak.

"In the cellar," she said, as he strode along the beach with his burden of death, "you were the one, weren't you?"

He said nothing, walking.

"McGrover," she prodded. "You returned that night."

"Yes," he replied. "We must care for each other, and see that scores are settled. We will be true to each other in our way, even if we cannot have each other now."

Selena felt as she had the time McGrover had come threatening her at the house on Bowling Green. Afraid no more. But this feeling was more powerful. It was transcendent, traveling out in currents toward Royce, to be returned by him. It happened in silence, walking. But they were one, in a mystical sense, in a sense more fateful than they had become one in body, long ago. And still there were miles to go.

Two lights burned in the windows of the Colony. One in the lobby, one in an upstairs suite. The torches along the boardwalk had been extinguished. Royce did not hesitate. He bore Ludford up the boardwalk, and up the entrance stairs. One light was on in the lobby. A clerk, dozing behind the desk, looked up too late to see Selena reach the upper floor, but he did see Royce climbing the stairs. And Royce saw him.

"Fellow had a bit much," he joked to the clerk, who, in the gloom, saw a uniformed gentleman a bit the worse for wear being trotted up to bed by a sympathetic friend. The clerk went back to sleep; no one was expected for the night. No one would bother him.

On the second floor, Selena stood aside. Royce said nothing. He knew. He climbed the stairs to the third floor, where the light had been. Selena followed. Then down the corridor, to a closed door. He knocked.

Royce waited for Veronica to open the door. Selena stood off to one side, out of the light, so that she would not be seen. "Yes?" Veronica called invitingly. Royce did not respond, but in a moment the door swung open. Veronica was smiling. She saw Royce. And Ludford. Royce put Ludford's body gently on the floor, just inside the room.

"Here's your entertainment for the night," Royce said. Ludford stared blankly and forever at the ceiling.

For just a moment, Veronica looked as if she would faint, and then Selena was sure Royce's former mistress would scream. But the woman was as hard as she was haughty. She lifted her chin and faced Royce. Her smile was rather weak, but she *was* smiling.

"Darling," she said, "how very kind of you to think of my happiness after all this time."

"And how very characteristic that your happiness should be the first thing to come to your tongue."

Veronica heard that, but she did not care.

"By the by, your Scottish tart is stopping here. Is that why you've come by?"

"I have no idea whom you're talking about," said Royce, protecting Selena, "but I would advise you to watch your neck. You are in a dangerous game with these British."

Although not loud, the conversation awakened a man in an adjoining room. "What's going on out there?" he called roughly.

"What's happened to you, Royce?" Veronica asked, struggling to keep her eyes off Ludford. "You were once an intelligent man. Any day now, your head will be shaved to the neck by a British cannonball. You no longer know what you are about."

The man in the next room was rumbling and stumbling toward the door, muttering about the disturbance, the late hour . . .

"We shall see," Royce said and slammed the door. Then, taking Selena by the arm, he raced with her down to the end of the corridor, where a double window overlooked the porch. He helped Selena out onto the roof of the porch, and she waited there while he climbed out. She saw Veronica come out of her room; Veronica began to scream. The man in the adjacent room peered out and looked around. Royce was halfway out of the window. Traudl, holding her robe fearfully in front of her breasts, also appeared in a nearby doorway. She saw Royce Campbell only from behind. But she saw Selena clearly, the light of the hallway lamps falling gently on her face. Then Royce edged out to the end of the porch, dropped catlike down onto the sand, and whispered for Selena to follow. He caught her as she dropped down. The only thing that delayed pursuit, and thus allowed them to have a few moments unobserved, was the horrified discovery of Ludford's body by guests of the hotel.

"Selena," Royce told her on the dark beach, "I must leave. Again."

"I know."

They clung to each other for an infinite second.

"Will you be all right?"

"Yes. I'll say I was out for a walk. No, I'll say I was on the porch. I'll say I saw a man running." *Everyone but Traudl will believe that,* she thought. *At least for now.* "Now, you go. I've got to get in. The baby will be disturbed."

"I'm sorry. Now you are more involved than before, and that is dangerous. I cannot even remain to help you."

"Don't think of it. I just wanted . . . I wanted to talk to you. One last time . . . at least . . ."

Royce stiffened when she said *one last time.* She sensed the words hurt him, or surprised him.

"So that is truly your final choice? Nothing comes later?"

A person is defined by choices that are free.

"I'm not free to choose," she said. "At least, I don't think I am. Not now. Not yet."

Be with me! Be mine! she wanted to scream. Upstairs, in the hotel, Davina began to wail.

"No, you're not free," Royce said. His lips were on hers for such a short time that, later, she almost believed the kiss had been imaginary. "Freedom is first belief, then fact."

"Good-bye, Selena. We both have much to do." With that he was gone down the beach, and like a phantom he disappeared into the night.

Selena rushed back into the Colony. Veronica was loudly commanding the attention of everyone.

"It was Royce Campbell!" she cried, over and over. "It was that rebel pirate with a price on his head!"

Selena stayed in the background for a few moments, before hurrying off to her room. In spite of the circumstances, she felt a grim satisfaction when she heard Veronica wail. There was shock in Veronica's cry, that was true, but there was also the faintest note of a woman scorned. But Selena knew a spurned woman could be dangerous, and she suppressed the impulse to savor the fact that it was she Royce loved, not this woman who had once smiled boldly at her from Royce's bed. Selena had other problems, the first of which was Traudl. The nursemaid looked up at her when Selena entered the room, her eyes wide with fear and accusation. She was holding Davina, who had stopped crying. Selena reached out and took the child.

"There, there, it's nothing," she soothed.

She did not look at the Dutch girl. The righteous anger of God was in Traudl's eyes.

Late the next afternoon, Lord Bailey came out from New York. He had been Lord Ludford's aide-de-camp, and was now elevated to his commander's position. He sought information about the terrible assassination, and was pleased at his shrewdness in deducing—aided by Veronica's testimony—that Royce Campbell had been the culprit. Bailey was also greatly taken by the distraught woman, and tried his best to comfort her. And, being a Lord, he naturally refrained from speaking to any servants or to anyone else of an inferior rank. It was fortunate for Selena that his sudden promotion in rank had affected only his bearing, and not his brain.

TIME WILL TURN BACK

If she lived to be a hundred, Selena would never forget the roll of the drums. Stirring, unsettling, premonitory, hypnotic, their sound bounced off the stone walls of the fort, echoed and reechoed on the cobblestones outside the guardhouse, melded in the luminous October air, and rippled along the waterfront of old New York. It was a horrible, telling toll of sound, those drumbeats, fateful and relentless. Up on Bowling Green one could hear, and all along the Battery, and even as far away as Wall Street. People who had not gone down to the fort to watch the spectacle stopped one another on the street, or heard the sound and looked up from their desks, nodding sagely or sadly at their fellows. "Well, hear those drums? Aye, they'll be a-hangin' him very shortly now."

I'm not going to be able to bear this, Selena thought, biting her lip. Then, disgusted with her cowardice, almost physically sick with guilt and impotence: *You'd better bear it. He has to.*

Since returning from Montauk, life had been a nightmare. September and October, the most glorious months of the year, had slipped by, barely noticed. Even the surprising American victory over "Gentleman Jack" Burgoyne at Saratoga, and the subsequent entry of France into the war on the side of the rebels, failed to stir Selena. British Security was in a panic, however; New York was very tense.

If it was true that Selena was no longer afraid, it was also true that she had ceased to care whether she was afraid or not. Almost. But she sought in vain a ray of light, a kind face, a happy word: anything that would offer surcease from the sorrow into which she had been plunged, and her dark, painful knowledge of the reasons for that sorrow.

And all the while that Selena was crushed by sadness, burdened by powerlessness, Lord Bailey's minions performed upon their prize captive the spine-shattering techniques of a trade at which Darius McGrover had excelled. First, they beat the soles of his feet with rods of wood and iron. Then the joints of his fingers were crushed, one after another, in the slow, shrieking pressure of the thumbscrews. Then pincers and metal bands were applied to various parts of his body, and tightened gradually to extract blood as well as information, and to crush bones as well as glands. Each day, day after day, the man was brought into a dark hole at least seventy feet below the surface of the earth, and each day he screamed his way into unconsciousness. Finally, Lord Bailey was told that the man had broken. Even if he possessed any more information, it was of value to no one. He was a babbling lunatic now, driven mad by pain and privation.

"All right," Bailey said. "Let's get the trial over with and hang him high."

The nightmare had begun on the very evening Selena, Davina, and Traudl returned from Montauk. Throughout the trip, Traudl had said nothing, just stared out at the passing landscape, oblivous even to Davina's entreaties for games or endearments. Selena was anxious about the nursemaid, and could only guess at the pressures of the simple girl's conscience. Had she known for certain just how relentless those pressures were, she would have worried more.

It all began at dinner.

"How's my little girl?" Sean exuded, coming into the dining room, grabbing Davina, and tossing her into the air. She giggled and wriggled and shrieked, delighted to see him again.

"I thought you were going to stay out at Montauk at least a week?" he said to Selena.

Traudl nervously wadded her napkin into a ball. Sean noticed and frowned, curious.

"We were," Selena said quickly, "but that stupid war changed our plans, and I thought it best . . ."

She had planned how to handle this matter. She would

describe how the slain Ludford was found in the hotel, and how she had decided to return home, lest something happen to them, too. But she had not counted on Traudl's participation. The poor girl, usually so reticent, had borne more than she was meant by nature to bear. She had also rehearsed her little speech, and once she began there was no stopping her.

"Oh, Mister Sean," Traudl blurted, "there was terrible things a-happenin' out there by the seashore." She was practically in tears; her surge of confession carried with it an overflow of emotion.

"Go ahead, Traudl," Sean said gently.

"Sir, sir I got to . . . got to quit . . ." Traudl stammered.

Sean gave Selena a measuring look. "Why?"

"Because . . . because . . . I'd rather not say. Could you . . . write me a good letter of recommendation, please?"

"Of course, Traudl. But I wish to know your reasons. Now, tell me."

Again, Traudl couldn't quite face it. In tears, she had begun to blubber.

"Would you prefer that this be done in private?"

The girl was about to say yes, but Selena did not care for the idea.

"If Traudl gives a reason, it will be done right here. And right now."

Sean nodded in reluctant agreement. "All right, Traudl. That's the way it will be. Tell us."

Her words were a bit hard to understand, the syllables lost in the sobs, but the essence came through clearly.

"There was a man," Traudl explained. "In Montauk. Mrs. Bloodwell . . ." She met Selena's eyes then, her own wavering a little, but her chin held high in Christian rectitude.

"All right, Traudl, leave the table," Sean ordered. He was very calm. "Have one of the servants fix you a tray. You may leave in the morning. I shall arrange for recompense and have your letter prepared."

Dinner was very bleak. Davina's chattering sounded like a small, silvery bell in the bottom of a coal pit. Later, Sean drew Selena into his study.

"Since you didn't deny the charge, I presume it's accurate."

"I don't lie."

"That's something, anyway. Who was it?"

"Royce Campbell."

Sean nodded. He didn't even seem particularly surprised.

"I was not unfaithful."

"You needn't go into that. It is the least of the problems we face now. And I never believed you would be unfaithful, not in the physical sense. Your own word means too much to you for that."

Slowly, he arose from his chair, and began to pace back and forth across the room, thinking of something.

"What was Royce doing there?"

"I'd rather not say."

"Ludford is dead. Royce did it, didn't he? Were you involved?"

"I saw it."

"Selena, were you . . . have you ever been involved in this rebel business?"

After a moment, she nodded, and began to speak.

"Stop! I don't want to hear it! You have no idea how dangerous things have become. I'm involved, too, although not in the way you might anticipate. And now I have to save you from this mess."

"Save me?"

"Do you understand to what extent you've compromised us? Both of us? Selena, you've broken your word. You've let us down."

He was more sad than angry, and his concern gnawed at her. "It was . . . it was something I . . . had to do."

"I see." Although he didn't see at all.

"Perhaps I cannot be anyone but who I am. Perhaps none of us can. What else can one be true to? It might be wrong even to try to deny our own natures."

"I doubt that," he said, a bit cynically. "Not if it will save one's skin. Which is the issue with us right now. I may have been honored by the King, but that won't protect us forever."

The moments passed, and neither of them spoke, or even looked at each other.

"Selena," he said at length, "I believe I can save you.

You have no idea how far things have gone. I did what I thought I had to do, as you will learn, and things were done over which I had no control. You may not understand, even when you find out, but I had no idea of your involvement . . ."

Save her? What was he talking about?

". . . but I am going to make two conditions, and you will disregard them at your peril." He did not wait to see if she would accept the conditions, and he did not permit her to question them. "First, you must give up your shop and public life. It is not a question of propriety. It is a question of survival. You must play the meek wife, and remain at home. Second, you must never again, under any guise or pretext, see Royce Campbell. I am not even referring to a romantic meeting. Nothing of the sort. Although, to be honest, I could not bear that. No, I am referring to something that concerns the fate of your lovely neck."

"What?" she asked, her voice husky. "Please." Her mind was on the spy network, and the message she had carried. "I have a right to know."

He shook his head. "Selena, I suppose you thought that I might reconsider one day, and come to your way of thinking about this war. I know Dick thought I would. But that is not going to happen. I have charted the course of my life, and I mean to be true to it. Do you understand?"

Selena nodded.

"Had I known what I now know of your involvement with the rebels, I might have acted differently. I might have tried to think of some other way to deal with the situation. But you must understand that I not only felt used and betrayed, I sensed great danger. And who would not have? When I learned of the spy network that had been set up right under my nose, within my very company, I acted. I had to act, or else be vulnerable to the charge that I was a willing accomplice. I went to Lord Howe myself, and to Ludford. Now, because of Ludford's death, Bailey is handling the affair."

Selena might have been able to piece together the implications of his words, but she was too stunned to think clearly.

"Dick Weddington is under arrest, Selena. They are even now interrogating him at the fort. You had best pray—and pray very hard—that he is as true a friend to you as he seemed . . ." His voice faltered, and he walked to the window, shaking his head in helpless dismay. "God, I truly did not know they would apply torture to him. Not here in America. And to think I was the one who turned him in . . ."

Selena went over to him and put her arms around him.

"The mere murmur of your name on his parched lips, Selena, and you will be done for. There will be nothing I can do to protect you then."

"But why . . . why are they treating him in such a beastly manner?"

"It is more than interrogation, Selena. It is vengeance and celebration combined. He was not only the master spy who had eluded them for so long, he was also a member of the nobility. Thus it is as if he betrayed Great Britain doubly, and now they are making him suffer for recompense."

Selena thought of her father, and the Rob Roys. British policy had not changed.

"And he was harbor master and merchant as well," Sean was saying, "respectable positions which they feel he has dishonored . . ."

Selena could only weep. Each long day thereafter was agony for her, agony made greater by knowing that, whatever her own sufferings, they were an immeasurably small fraction of the tortures being inflicted on Dick Weddington. Sometimes she would go out onto the front terrace and look down the Hudson and into the harbor, and she was almost certain that she could hear Dick screaming. During the night, sleep refused to come. The rush of events since her trip to Montauk recapitulated itself in her mind, a sequence of events that seemed to point toward certain disaster: the meeting with Royce, Ludford's death, Traudl seeing Selena on the porch, Traudl's confession to Sean, Sean himself.

He did not ask again about Royce Campbell, but Sean was hurt, and Selena grieved because he suffered. Tossing in her bed at night, Selena tried to put her life, her love, into perspective. *I do love Sean,* she thought, heartsick. *But something is no longer what it was when we set out on our journey* . . .

That tiny, relentless voice came back to question her.

Do you feel as you do simply because Royce has been

gone so long, and is more exciting, whereas you have been married to Sean and know him well? Do you love danger and adventure more than domesticity? Come now, young lady, and face the truth: you love in Royce what you have always indulged in yourself, willfulness and independence. Yes, and rebellion, too. And see what such desires have brought you, once again.

Selena wept. "That's not true, that's not true," she whispered.

Beside her, Sean stirred, but did not awaken. Oh, if she could only decide, and then *choose*! But it was all so intertwined and heartbreaking. On the Montauk beach, joined with Royce in a communion of body and soul, rapture and danger, everything had seemed so clear. Now, when she saw how Sean was trying to protect her—protect her from the consequences of having broken her promise to him—she felt her insides come apart.

And the mission she had undertaken had borne no fruit. The information about Lord Howe's movements, which she had carried to Royce, had been too late to be of any use. Howe had landed along the Chesapeake even as Selena was telling Royce that he would do so. In a desultory but eventually effective manner, Howe occupied Philadelphia, hitherto the wellspring and citadel of rebellion, and Washington's gallant attack at Germantown was a complete failure. Upon hearing the news, Selena's spirit flickered slightly: She wondered where Alexander Hamilton had been during the battle, and how he might remove himself from responsibility for the loss. Thinking of him reminded her of how she had bested Veronica Blakemore, and of the latter's vow of revenge.

Sean could not help but notice her lingering malaise, and he did his best to shore her up. But he had plenty of worries himself. He had provided the information by which Weddington came to be arrested, true enough. But he had not known at the time that his wife might be arrested in her turn. Once, in a moment of doubt, he halfheartedly suggested that they try to leave the city, suspicious though it would look.

"I'll never run again," Selena snapped.

Brave words, or foolish ones?

Certainly they did not seem brave in the cobblestone courtyard in front of the prison guardhouse. Nor did Selena feel at all brave, seated beneath the scaffold of new timber erected for the event. It *was* an event. Rows of wooden benches, neatly aligned, filled the courtyard itself. Formations of straight-backed, high-hatted troopers, their boots and buckles polished to perfection, awaited the execution with dull, soldierly patience. All along the walls of the fort stood the drummers, rigidly at attention, eyes staring directly forward, as if at nothing, as if they themselves were already dead, and merely bore back from the land of darkness the rhythm of sorrow and implacability, that maddening rattle of the drums.

And on the walls, and beyond the walls, in lampposts, hanging from windows of nearby buildings, clinging to the roofs and chimneys, waited the crowd, eager for the show to begin. *The rabble,* Selena thought, recalling Hamilton's mistrustful description of the common people. Perhaps he was right.

The benches in the courtyard were reserved for military officials and for people of rank. Except for a few late arrivals, or those delayed by the milling crowd outside the gates of the fort, all the benches were filled. An expectant hum rose from the audience. The men were in uniforms or formal morning clothes; the women were bright in their Sunday best. With sadness, Selena noticed a few of the women wearing gowns from La Marinda. That she herself should have created dresses that were to be worn on a day such as this. . . .

Gilbertus and Samantha Penrod were seated just behind the Bloodwells, and—bitter burden—Veronica Blakemore, the adventuress, was one row ahead of them, a bit off to one side of the bench. Veronica had no escort with her, but it was common knowledge that she had taken up with Lord Bailey, successor to Ludford. He was busy at the scaffold now, making last-minute arrangements for the execution, and would likely join her after the ritual was concluded.

Suddenly the drums ceased. It happened so abruptly that Selena started, as if someone had grabbed her from behind. Sean put his hand on her arm.

"All right?" he whispered.

She nodded, and closed her mouth tight, so that her lips would not tremble.

The iron door of the guardhouse clanged open and the condemned man was hurried along the few paces to the scaffold stairs, two men ahead of him, two men behind. They had almost to carry him up the steps, and Selena fought to hold back a moan as she saw what they had done to him. It hardly seemed Dick Weddington anymore, just a staggering, panting form that might once have been human. She saw the tortured twist of his mouth. Sean had told her. Manacled, his legs in irons, and no longer able to endure the torment, Dick had tried to commit suicide by biting off his own tongue, hoping to bleed to death. But he had been discovered. After that, a wooden block was placed in his mouth, like a horse's bit.

Now, with his escort, he reached the platform. He swayed unsteadily. One of the guards caught him before he toppled. Then he looked up at the beam and the noose rope which dangled from it. The crowd on the benches in the courtyard remained reasonably decorous, but Dick's glance at the noose served to release the tension elsewhere. A great sound, somewhere between a howl and a hoot of derision, went up from the spectators beyond the walls. Then, as if dazed, Dick looked down at the people directly below. He seemed to recover a bit, seeing the familiar faces. He gave no sign of greeting, but he met the eyes of many. He seemed to study Sean, then passed him by. Selena met his eyes momentarily. He looked directly at her, asking nothing, regretting nothing. Within her heart, she lamented unbearably the suffering and death of this bright young man, whose father had held her own in high regard. The moment ended. He looked away. And she knew that, in one sense he had been successful: somehow, he had not revealed her name.

Lord Bailey mounted the steps, then, followed by the hangman himself, a massively built man in black, wearing the black hood of his profession. Once again, the sight set the rabble to howling, quieted when Lord Bailey lifted his arm.

There was a moment of silence as they settled, waiting for the action to begin.

"By order of the offices of His Most Gracious Majesty,

George the Third," Bailey intoned, projecting his voice out over the multitude, "we here assembled shall witness the execution of Richard Allen Weddington, lawfully convicted of treason against King, Crown, and Country."

He paused a moment to let the weight of his words sink in. The hangman, meanwhile, sprang the trap a time or two and gave a good yank on the rope. It held his weight and snapped back. The crowd sighed.

"Do you affirm that you are, indeed, Richard Allen Weddington?" he asked Dick.

"I am." The voice was clear, extraordinarily strong considering the torment to which he had been subjected. He put his last strength into the effort.

"We shall proceed."

Guards moved Dick onto the trapdoor in the floor of the scaffold's platform. He did not resist. Instead, he seemed to be trying to stand a bit straighter, to meet the situation with whatever dignity he could command. It was considerable. The people, watching him, broke off yet another blood howl, becoming strangely silent. It would happen now, they knew. Death. They might cheer later, in a paroxysm of relief that, this time, death had passed them by. A collective shudder of the soul. But now they were silent, as if each person there present, for one moment, could not hold off the knowledge of his own mortality.

Bailey nodded, and the hangman stepped forward, slipped the noose over Dick's head, and adjusted the knot so that his neck would break quickly at the drop, sparing him the further torment of slow suffocation.

Selena watched the hangman in a daze. A hangman had saved her before. Was there, this time, no hope?

Satisfied, the executioner stepped back onto the corner of the platform and placed his hand on the lever that would spring the trap.

Dick stood straight, facing out onto New York harbor. He had a clear view of the harbor, the Narrows, and the open sea beyond. There are worse things to look upon, for the last time in your life. The eyes of the living were upon him. His own eyes were upon the distance, the future, perhaps, which in moments his spirit would know, and into which it would disappear. Suddenly—Selena felt it before she saw it—Dick's eyes began to glow. Something like a smile tried to curl his wounded mouth.

"According to the custom of the English-speaking peoples," Bailey was intoning, "according to the principles we all hold dear, the condemned man shall, if he wishes, have the right to say his final words on this earth. Do you choose to exercise this right?" he asked, facing Dick.

"I do," Dick said, lowering his eyes from the harbor to the crowd below. He looked at Selena again, that glow still in his eyes. She shivered. It was as if he had some unearthly knowledge that none of them could share, and yet at the same time he seemed almost amused.

"They've tormented him to madness, poor fellow," Sean whispered. "I hope this is over soon."

Veronica, grinning broadly, turned to face Selena.

I'll see you in hell, she told Blakemore with her eyes. *One way or another.* She felt a light touch on her elbow, and half-turned. Gilbertus Penrod was telling her to hold on. *It will be over soon. We will endure.*

"What I want to say . . ." Dick began.

The crowd tittered. He was a victim, they had decided. They could afford to make fun of him. Their transitory sense of death had passed, because it had been too heavy to bear. They *had* to make fun of him. Any one of them might well be exactly where he was right now, given different situations, and they knew it. So now, in a horrible, collective panic, they turned against the condemned, as if that turning might save them from the terrors of their own vulnerability. It is a principle as old as time: Courage is just a word until you have to show it. But when you do, people shrink away. Courage is a very threatening thing.

Dick Weddington waited a bit; he seemed to understand what was happening. But they quieted immediately at his next words: "Fellow condemned," he addressed them.

The silence was as eerie as the hooting had been profane.

Dick's gaze strayed again to the Narrows, and he seemed almost to smile. All eyes were upon him.

"You *are* all condemned, do you know that?"

Silence met him, and surprise. No one had expected this. The man was well known to have "succumbed to guilt," thus incapable of rational speech.

"Forgive my appearance today," he said.

Bailey was looking at the hangman, then at the crowd, clearly perplexed.

"They have altered me in some ways."

A slight laugh, but it was sympathetic.

"And while they tortured me, they laughed, and said they would feel no qualms about doing the same to anyone."

There was a stunned silence, and then something much like a growl. Anger, smoldering anger, its target not yet determined.

"Now let's . . ." Bailey began, stepping forward a little.

"*Aye! And what about the law?*" yelled a mighty voice from the top of the fort's outer wall. People turned, as did Selena. It was Will Teviot who had spoken, Will Teviot, his beard as bristly as that of old Rob Roy himself.

"Let him speak!" shouted someone else.

Lord Bailey glanced around, confused. The hangman's hand was on the lever.

"*Long live America!*" Dick shouted, with such surprising force that Sean seemed to shudder. His hand, which had been on Selena's to give her comfort, tightened reflexively. For the first time since she'd known him, Selena sensed that he was afraid. Instinctively, she wished to give him comfort and took his hand. She felt him take hers, a quick, reluctant pressure. Then he pulled away and sat up straight.

"You had best believe in America," Dick was saying. "Look what the King's men have done to me."

The sound was a rumble now, an angry, growling purr of sound, potentially deadly. It could not have happened in the space of a second, but it did. Dreamlike, Selena saw Dick Weddington's mouth open to speak again. Bailey's head was turning toward the hangman, and his arm was falling. The hangman moved only a little. And the moment stopped. Dick dropped like a shot through the sprung trap, jerked taut, and bounced on the end of the rope. He suffered no more; he was dead.

No one had the time to grasp it. Like apocalypse, in the same mighty instant, the entire sky was filled with roar and thunder. Behind the fort, a brick office building exploded into clouds of dust, flying bricks, and screaming people. And on the watchtower of the fort, a guard cried down,

"We're under attack! We're under attack! 'Tis a great black ship!"

There were more screams, and people rushed for the gates, trying to gain space. Clearly, the first shot had been off target. The cannoneers were going for the fort itself. Soldiers scrambled toward the big guns along the Battery, but were hindered by the crowds. Some of the soldiers were waylaid, beaten and trampled in the melee, recompense for Dick Weddington's death.

Sean grabbed Selena's arm. She was not afraid. In fact, she felt exhilarated, eager to get outside the walls, to catch a glimpse of the *Selena* even if it blew her away with the rest of them. She remembered Royce, directing his gunners in the attack upon the *Meridian,* and she rejoiced, in a strange and private way, for what she thought he must now be experiencing. The power of his body, of his will. His skill in slipping past the outer defenses of the harbor, and the risk involved. And now, finally, turning the might of his will and guns upon the fort itself, symbol of the enemy. Then Sean managed to drag her through the gates. They were running along the Battery. She saw the *Selena* there, just outside the Narrows, still with room to maneuver and to flee, turning to give a broadside. British ships in the harbor were frantically trying to spin toward the intruder. Battery cannoneers were furiously working. But Selena knew that, for this round at least, they would be too late. She was with Sean, running along the Battery, ducking behind a brace of heavy cannon. But she was also on the bridge of the black ship, and she could almost hear the savage, joyous cry, "TO THE HIGHLANDS! TO THE HIGHLANDS, FIRE!"

Three tiers of cannon thundered, and the *Selena* rocked back in the recoil. All of New York harbor was lost in smoke. Instinctively, Selena dove for cover, even as she rejoiced at the attack. Explosions rattled all along the harbor. Great holes were blown into the wall of the fort. Sean was gone . . . somewhere . . . she had lost his hand. Someone was calling her name. She could not hear because of the din and the screaming. She dove into a ditch— something more like a slight, grassy depression.

"I suppose Royce has come to save you," said the mocking voice. Veronica.

Out in the Narrows, the *Selena* turned from port to starboard.

"They've got him now. He can never get away this time," Veronica exclaimed. "Such a sad thing. Once he was bold, now he's only foolish. If you want to know the truth, I think you are to blame. You reached him in some way, and ruined him."

Several British ships were beginning to fire now, and along the Battery came the first great roar of the harbor guns. Sails were unfurling aboard the *Selena* as, simultaneously, Royce prepared to fire again and to flee.

"Isn't that strange?" Selena shot back. "I received the distinct impression that he's a finer man now than he ever was. . . ."

"Oh? You've seen Royce recently?"

Selena was trying to form an answer, when a cannonball, errantly fired from one of the British ships in the harbor, whined over their heads and crashed into one of the huge maples along the Battery, shearing it off. People ran in terror, and the tree crashed down, sending leaves and branches flying and raising the dust. Selena and Veronica dove to the grass and pressed against the earth. After a moment they raised their heads doubtfully. People were screaming and running about.

"So," Veronica exclaimed, following her suspicious train of thought, "you have, haven't you?"

"What are you talking about? For God's sake, people have been hurt and you're . . ."

"You've seen Royce, haven't you?" Veronica accused. "My, my. I bet you would confess many things if my friend Lord Bailey would be permitted to stretch you out on his rack. Anyway, you ruined a fine man when you ruined Royce's spirit. . . ."

"I did not. If anything, I made him stronger," Selena declared passionately.

Veronica Blakemore smiled her enraging smile.

On the water, the *Selena's* starboard cannons roared and thundered. Several British ships took direct hits. The air was full of flying timber, smoke, and the screams of the wounded. The *Selena* had already begun to move toward open sea. Battery gunners, taken by surprise, were having difficulty finding the range. The only remaining hindrance to which Royce would be subjected lay in the Narrows, but aboard the *Selena* the cannon were again being loaded. Selena doubted that he would be stopped now.

"I'm curious though," Veronica was saying, as the two women picked themselves up and brushed grass and dirt from their garments. "What did you do for him? Do you have a special way? Some secret form of lovemaking that you learned as a harem girl? What strange things can you do to his body, to have affected his mind so much?"

Selena realized that Ludford must have told Veronica about everything. Indeed, he had probably told her much more that was only suspected. She felt vulnerable and angry, yet triumphant. Royce loved *her,* not Veronica.

"I *love* him, that's all," she shot back at her tormentor. "And as for you . . ."

But, instead of anger, Veronica showed her teeth in a smile of satisfaction and delight. Not only had she successfully provoked Selena, her timing had been splendid. Selena looked up to see Sean standing there. He had heard what she had said about loving Royce. And it had hurt. Badly.

"Lady Blakemore," he said, nodding to Veronica. He did not smile.

"Why, Bloodwell," she said, omitting even the *mister* in order to demonstrate her assumption of superiority. "Did you enjoy the execution? I'm told you had a hand in it."

"Let's go, Selena," he said, and, taking her arm, he led her away from the Battery and in the direction of his office. The streets were crowded with people and horses. It was very noisy. Sean did not speak for a while.

"What I said to Veronica . . ." Selena tried tentatively.

"Don't speak of it," he replied, without looking at her. His face was bleak. "I feel badly enough already."

For a moment, Selena would have given all she had to have been born someone else, or to have been far away in a different land. Yet, for reasons as complicated as love, as obscure as the human heart, as simple as tenderness and gratitude, as fierce as passion, she could never get Royce Campbell out of her soul.

"I can see why you would admire him," Sean said, surprising her. "After what he did today, I must say that I

cannot help but admire him myself. But even so, we are left
with our problems . . ."

A big, glistening carriage, drawn by four white horses,
flashed past them, then drew to the curb and stopped. A
large golden *P* was emblazoned on the door. Penrod. Gilbertus put his head through the window. His face was as
round and ruddy as ever, but his eyes were sad.

"Let us give you a ride wherever you're going."

Sean wanted to be alone, and he thanked Penrod and
said he was going to spend some time at his Wall Street
office. He asked if Gilbertus might take Selena home. She
climbed into the carriage, taking a position next to Samantha. Sean went on down the street. The driver called to the
horses and the carriage began to move. Samantha, weeping
softly, reached and took Selena's hand.

"Sean is feeling badly?"

"Yes, terribly. He was caught in a dilemma when he
learned of Dick's espionage. He never thought it would be
handled as brutally as it was. Then, once Dick was under
interrogation, Sean was powerless to interfere because to do
so would have implicated me."

"We must be far more careful from now on," Gilbertus
said. "Hard times are upon us. Bailey will be far sterner
than Ludford was in dealing with rebel sympathizers." He
paused. "But, by God, when Royce opened fire today, I
nearly yelled for joy. I thought Bailey might arrest me then
and there. What was Sean's reaction?"

"He didn't seem to mind, particularly," Selena said. "He
even admitted to some admiration. I'm afraid Sean believes
he is finished now, at least insofar as his hopes for a title
go."

"And you, my dear?" Samantha asked.

"I don't know. I don't know . . ."

"No, Selena," Gilbertus said slowly, "I think Sean will
be able to resolve the matters that trouble him now. And,
in time, I think that you will be able to do so, too. No one
can tell you what to do. Your happiness is involved, but
also the happiness of others. It is a difficult choice."

He was speaking to her of her own intimate problems,
and she looked at him in surprise. His eyes were hard on
hers.

"You know?"

He nodded. "Several days ago, we planned Royce's attack. Royce himself, Hamilton, Will Teviot, and I. Royce is now leading the British out to sea, after which he will circle back and come to port at Sandy Hook, south of New York. He'll take on supplies and flee to Jamaica, in the islands . . ."

Selena felt the hollow feeling spread inside her once again. He was leaving!

The carriage was on Bowling Green now, driving past the mansions. Samantha was listening. Gilbertus paused, and then had done with it. "Selena, Royce asked my cooperation, and I agreed to give it. When he puts back in to shore, Will Teviot is to come to me and inform me of the landing."

"Yes?"

"And I agreed to come to you then, and tell you that I had a message for you. I did not ask what the message was."

Selena nodded. Her mind was spinning. The necessity of making a choice was imminent; in agony, she teetered on the precipice of decision. Royce would be asking her to come with him, and whatever she decided might be forever.

"When?" she heard herself ask.

"If all goes well, tomorrow."

Selena sighed with relief. She would have some time to think. *I won't have to decide until then,* she thought.

The carriage drew up to the curb outside her house. She saw Davina's yellow-topped head at the window, and the delighted wave of her chubby little hand. *Oh, God,* Selena thought, feeling ill, *what am I going to do?*

"Are you all right?" Samantha asked, leaning forward, a look of concern on her face. "You seem a bit unsteady."

"No, I'll be all right," Selena replied. But she wasn't sure about that, either.

THE MISTRESS OF COLDSTREAM

Selena was in agony, heart troubled, mind shrieking. The course of her entire life waited now, impatiently, for her decision. What now? She had to decide *now*. *Now* was all important. Heaven could wait.

Tension in the house was palpable. Servants pattered as soundlessly as they were able from room to room, making haste with their chores and errands, and, in the kitchen, speculating to one another in hushed voices. About what had happened. About what was happening. About what *would* happen. Traudl was gone now, having insisted upon resigning, and although Selena did not know for certain, she suspected that, in the manner of servants, whispered words of "another man" was the news beneath the stairs. Tongues were not stilled when Sean came late to dinner. Did he know about Royce Campbell and the expected message? It was possible. Veronica might have found out somehow, and told him. Veronica knew everything, Selena reflected bitterly, because of her connections. *Sleeps with everyone and knows everything. And is waiting for her revenge.*

Sean said little during dinner, save to rouse himself occasionally with a smile or a happy word for chattering Davina. The execution had affected him deeply, because of his part in it. And he now understood completely that Selena's views were fundamentally at variance with his own, and would always be. "Selena," he had once told her, "you are a natural force." Such a force would be inimical to change.

After dinner, he went into his study and sat for hours staring at the fire. Selena walked by his door from time to time, but he sat unmoving, staring into the flames, as if trying to find a solution to their differences, as if trying to divine some key, some masterstroke, which would allow them to regain what had been lost between them: an unquestioned trust. The love was still there; it was that pristine quality of trust which had flown.

Nor did Selena know how to help him. Even if she could erase Royce Campbell from her mind, how could she and Sean begin to resolve their differences of view? After the harrowing day, such reflection seemed too melancholy for words, and Selena collapsed in a soft chair in the bedroom, worrying, worrying, until sleep finally took her.

She awakened with shocked fright on the morrow, unable to believe her senses. Trumpets blared outside the house, and people were cheering and calling Sean's name. Drums were beating, but not with the doleful, ominous roll of yesterday. Today it was a march cadence, a soul-stirring boomboomboom-badada-boomboomboom, that measure of power and consequence.

She stepped to the window and pushed it open, and when the people saw her they brought forth a high-spirited cheer. Some of them called her name, too, and waved. Selena could not believe what was happening. There were several hundred people on Bowling Green. More were arriving by the minute. Already a row of carriages and horses lined the curb at the house front. Servants were running up and down outside the bedroom, calling out excitedly.

The music. The drums. The shouts. It was a festive sound, certainly. But why? Sean was not in the bedroom, nor had the bed been slept in. She was just about to go downstairs and ask him what was happening when little Davina came rushing in.

"'Ena, 'Ena!" she shrieked. "Daddy's a king! Daddy's a king!"

Then one of the servants appeared in the doorway.

"Best put on yer good things, mum. Somethin' big's afoot, an' 'tis all t' the good. The mister be at his ablutions right now."

Once more, Selena looked out of the window, standing back so that the crowd could not see her. And then she shuddered. It must be some terrible deception that was occurring. Lord Bailey was there, and with him Lord Howe, the conqueror of Philadelphia, and Admiral Howe, his brother, whose naval skill and speed of execution had landed British troops before Royce had been able to attack the convoy. Behind them, even more resplendently attired, was "Gentleman Jack" Burgoyne himself, victim of Benedict Arnold at Saratoga. The British had their Hamilton, too, a man who lost occasionally but who retained an inimitable style.

"Hurry, mum, the mister's callin' fer ye," said the servant, sticking her head in through the door again.

Selena selected a simply designed gown of pale green, and hurriedly put it on, brushed her hair, and raced downstairs. Sean was pulling on his morning clothes, which a servant had brought down for him.

"What is this?" she asked. "What are all those people . . . ?"

He looked at her for a long, silent moment. His face, his very being, were torn by deep emotion. She saw the unutterable joy in his eyes, but she saw, too, the look of a man whose joy is muted, who knows that there is a price attached to every gift. A moment passed, while the drums, the music, and the cheering paraded on outside the house. A festive delegation was clamoring on the front stoop.

"What is it, Sean?" she asked again, a little afraid of the expression on his face and of what it might mean.

"Lord Howe's at the door, sir," cried Sean's valet, rushing into the room. "You'd best . . ."

"Thank you," Sean said. Saying nothing more, he took Selena by the hand and led her to the front of the house. Lord Howe, Admiral Howe, Lord Bailey, and General Burgoyne were in the vestibule, in full military dress uniforms. They were smiling.

"Gentlemen, you do us honor." Sean bowed as, in turn, the men kissed Selena's hand.

"I should like," said Lord Howe, "to take you out before your fellow citizens. I have news for the city today, and, as I believe you are able to tell by the sound of the crowd outside, the news is not of a melancholy nature."

Howe was in a vibrant mood today, and he winked at Selena. What would he do, she thought, if he knew I tried to cause his defeat at Philadelphia?

He would hang you, Selena, answered the tiny voice.

Suddenly, in spite of the cheerful dignitaries and the

happy cheering, Selena began to feel that something was drastically wrong with this entire affair. But she had no time to consider it. The officials led Sean and Selena out onto the front steps, over which someone had hung the Union Jack, symbol of the Empire.

"*Daddy's a king*," Davina had said, but she was too young to know what was happening. Selena did not know, and as she and Sean became visible to the massed crowd on the Green, they were met by a welling roar, a tide of sound, and Selena felt vaguely frightened. She was reminded, incongruously, of the tattered, angry mob that had pursued them in Daman. Sean had rescued them that time. But now? If this was some kind of deception on the part of the military, she saw no hope of flight. They were trapped now, and must face whatever was to happen. She glanced at Sean, who seemed terribly agitated. It was unlike him, and that fact unnerved her further. Selena was quite alarmed now, without knowing why. The crowd was friendly, festive, with no hint of hostility. But the continuous outpouring of sound began to seem like the wild cry of a living thing that was greater and more powerful than the sum of its parts, and unpredictable as well.

She sought to calm herself by attempting to identify people in the crowd. This she did, and it was disquieting. Except for Gilbertus Penrod, who met her eyes frankly but revealed neither signal nor emotion, all of them were well-known loyalists. Even Veronica Blakemore was there, doubtless having arrived with Lord Bailey, after sharing his bed the previous night. In spite of her confusion, Selena felt a twinge of amused contempt for Blakemore. Veronica stood facing the crowd as if the cheers were for her.

But at last the sound diminished, and finally it faded. Lord Howe began to speak.

"I bring you news from the King . . ." he began. And, once again, a surge of cheering. Was the war over? Selena wondered. No. "As we are all aware, this is a time of war and crisis. Most of us do our duty as best we can. But some of us rise above the common station, contribute more than others to Crown and Empire. We are gathered here today to honor one such man . . ."

Later, recalling his words, Selena knew that she had already guessed what was about to occur. But then, standing next to Sean on the stairs, in front of the vast, ebullient throng, she heard Howe speak as if through a haze.

". . . my fellow citizens, word has reached us from London that the man who served us so well in identifying and bringing to justice the late, treasonous Weddington has been recognized and rewarded by His Majesty . . ."

The cheering again, wild now, raw-throated and passionate. These common people were sharing the thoughts of a king acknowledging the glory of a special man. Sean Bloodwell.

". . . I need not say how honored I am . . ." Lord Howe was saying.

The sound! The pounding roar of it!

". . . elevated to the peerage . . . called to London immediately, for installation at Westminster . . . family as well . . . reward for services given . . ."

A holocaust, a firestorm of collective ecstasy that beat against her ears.

". . . the dreadnaught H.M.S. *Lucifer* . . . waiting in the harbor . . . bring them to London before winter closes the North Atlantic . . ."

Selena's mind was spinning; she felt faint. London. England. Home. She felt hollow, incredulous.

"And now," Lord Howe raised his hands for absolute silence. It came. "And now, something I'm probably not supposed to mention, but why not?"

More cheers.

"As you know, in times past, the Empire has gifted its servants well, above and beyond the granting of title and peerage. Whole castles have been built for heroes. I recall the estate given Marlborough, in particular. And Lord Bloodwell shall be no exception. He can, in fact, take his choice of any of five estates, all in his native Scotland, estates which came into the hands of the Crown some years ago."

He turned toward Sean. "Which one shall it be, Lord Bloodwell?"

And then, as Selena was all but immobilized by disbelief, by a welter of contradictory emotions, and then by a sudden impulse to weep, Lord Howe inspected a small piece of paper. "Which shall it be?" he asked again. "You'd best decide by the time you reach London, so you know what to tell His Majesty. You have your choice of Kilmarnock or Inverness, Moray Castle, Kincardine or . . . *Coldstream,*" Howe finished with a flourish. "Are you familiar with any of them?"

The crowd was roaring again, great hurrahs for the new lord, whom they had known.

"Yes," Sean was nodding, his face blank and white. "One or two of them I know . . ." He was trying to turn to Selena, but people were pouring up the steps now, surrounding them, wild with congratulations and the sense of a celebratory day in the offing.

Selena had not yet begun to think. The impact of the news had been too sudden, too profound. To be returning, after all these years . . .

But it seemed that something was wrong. Gilbertus Penrod's eyes were on her, following her, burning her. And then she understood: the message. Torn between the impulse to run far away, to shut herself in a dark room, or to rush to Penrod, begging for his words, Selena stood rooted to the stairs, smiling, babbling inanely, as the congratulations came down upon her in a flood. She lost sight of Penrod then, and felt alternately exhilarated and terrified. But Veronica Blakemore's face stayed in her mind, even when the woman herself was lost in the crowd. Veronica's smile, even on this day, had been mocking and strangely triumphant.

After a time, a portion of the party moved indoors. The officers and their ladies, Sean's business friends, town dignitaries, and various gate-crashers filled all the downstairs rooms of the house. Outside, Sean had caused a dozen barrels of ale to be made available for the revelers on the Green. Inside, servants wove through the chattering throng, bearing trays of punch and whiskey, and, toward noon, platters of roast beef and cured ham. The servants were having a hard time keeping up with the work, since half of them had been assigned to pack the luggage for the trip to London. Even now, in New York harbor, the *Lucifer* was taking on water and provisions. A call from the King was not ignored, particularly as Sean's investiture to the peerage was to occur in London on New Year's Eve.

For his part, Sean worked furiously all morning, confer-

ring in his study with associates, bankers, and subordinates.
He did not now have time to do anything other than give
orders and delegate responsibility. It was already late October. The voyage to England was not likely to be completed
until early December, and, with winter coming on, it was
unlikely that he would be able to return to America before
April or May. He *would* return, he said, possibly to liqui-
date certain of his holdings before moving to Scotland for
good, possibly to sell his interests, or form long-term part-
nerships. The parlor, the front room, the dining room, the
corridors: everywhere the conversation was filled with
speculation as to Sean's future. He had talent and tact. A
shrewd but gentle man. If *he'd* been prime minister rather
than Lord North, he would never have provoked the rebels. He would have settled with them, sat down with them,
reasoned with them. There would never have been a war.
Such was the heady talk that day.

Here and there one man or another, of the nobility by
birth, would mutter, fueled by the courage of Sean's liquor,
that once a commoner always a commoner, and what was
the world coming to? But these were very much in the mi-
nority on that day of triumph. Selena realized once again
just how gifted Sean was, and how successful. He had made
his plans and carried them out. He had given his word and
kept it. He had loved her; she had loved him.

She realized that she was thinking of their marriage as if
it were already history. Then she knew why. Answering
again, for the hundredth time that morning, the question,
"How does it feel? How does it feel?" the image of Dick
Weddington appeared in her mind. He dropped dreamlike
from the gallows, jerked taut when the rope played out,
dead.

She knew, all right. *Dick Weddington's death had purchased Coldstream Castle.* True, Sean had done what he
believed to be right, but coin of the realm of restoration
must be of a far purer kind.

"What are you going to do now?" Veronica was asking,
with her honeyed voice and twisted smile. "You've been
taken off the hook nicely, once again. But don't worry.
Your nature will destroy you in the end."

"Oh? And what nature is that?"

"The same nature you passed along to Royce. A nature

which demands a purer world. No longer content to savor what you can grasp, the two of you are bound for sorrow. You just wait and see. Even now, with your precious Coldstream within your grasp, you will find cause to be unhappy with your luck. Something, however insignificant, will not quite suit you . . ."

"I would hardly call the execution of a friend insignificant."

"Don't be stupid, Selena. There are those who win and those who lose. You've won, for now, but only because you've had a man like Sean to look after you, to curb your impulses. Without him, you would already have made love to the end of a rope. At any rate, I do hope that you enjoy England once again, and Scotland, which is its fiefdom. I'll very much enjoy thinking of you there, a rebel married to a lord. Now, because of Sean's position, you *will* forever have to hold your tongue in check. My, but am I going to relish that thought."

Selena fled upstairs. She had to get away from the people below. It was a day of great triumph, but too many things were wrong. Just when the future should have been spreading before her, fate was forcing her to see what was inside her heart. The more she thought about her return to Scotland, the more she knew how wrong it would be, just now. Veronica's devilishly correct perception was only a part of it. There was also the memory of Dick Weddington. And there was her own heart.

Davina came rushing happily into the room, enchanted by all the bustle and the prospect of the trip.

"Coldstream," she said, throwing herself on Selena's lap. "Coldstream Castle." The words of her nightly prayer.

"And you go there for me," Selena said, holding the child tight against her body. "You go to Coldstream and be happy there. And someday—soon, I hope—I'll come to see you there. You can show me the castle yourself, then. There's such a fine, high tower, with ladders to climb up . . ."

She was rocking the little girl from side to side, as she'd done when Davina was just a baby, recovered from a village in the dark heart of India.

". . . and you can stand up there forever, higher than the birds, and across the North Sea . . ."

Brian and his sailboat, far out on the water. Father setting out to save him.

". . . you can even see as far as France . . ."

And in the vaults in the great wall of the castle, Mac-Phersons of past centuries watched for her, awaiting her return.

". . . and in the summer, Daddy will take you into the Highlands, where magic dragons live in the lochs, and if you look *very* quickly you can see them . . ."

The Highlands, and the call of the wolf, the hollow thunder of vanished horses, a remembered journey, mystic, inviolable, in the chambers of her heart.

"Dragons?" Davina chirped, with interest.

"Yes, darling, and . . ."

She meant to say something about a magic wolf that watched over everyone who loved it and believed in it, but Gilbertus Penrod appeared in the doorway.

They looked at each other, and Selena knew she had been correct. She had seen it in his eyes, outside. She had been running from him since then.

"I have a message for you," he said softly. "If you wish."

She was free to make her choice, and now she must do so.

LILAC NIGHT

They did not even touch each other at first. Somehow the moment seemed too electric. Danger, surprise, and the constant threat of observation hovered outside the small Brooklyn inn at which they met. The *Selena* was at anchor off southern Long Island, in Jamaica Bay. Royce, accompanied by Will Teviot, had ridden north to Brooklyn, disguised as common seamen. Selena had taken a hired hack as far as the East River, then a ferry across to Brooklyn village. She wore a plain, dark cloak. Her hair was covered by a shawl. At her home, the party was roaring into the afternoon.

Royce was already there at the inn, seated with Will at a table in the public room. Will gave her his abashed grin, then went out, announcing that he'd "keep an eye" on the street outside.

"Never can tell," he said too loudly. A couple of the reprobates and drinkers at the bar turned around and stared at them with sour calculation. *Rendezvous. Obvious. Man and wench, sneaking around.*

Royce, who had a bottle of sherry on the table, called for a glass and poured her a small measure. She took a sip, not tasting a thing.

"Selena, I have to leave America," he said. "The British Navy is coming after me every day with twelve or more men-of-war. I have to go down to the islands for the winter, and lie low for a time."

She said nothing, watching his face, her mind recording, recapturing the times they had been together in the past. In the early times, there had been tension, misunderstanding. His cynicism and apparent coldness, which she had grown to understand as the facade it was, had given way to the Royce she loved, still possessed of all his boldness and courage, but able now to be tender, too, able to offer his strength for a cause that was greater than himself. And to offer himself without compromise. She had taught him that, and now had need of the talent herself. And the other things he had taught her, in his arms, rose now with keen, piercing sweetness, in spite of the risk and danger with which they were surrounded.

"They're hunting me on the sea," he said. "And when I put ashore, agents seem to have a sixth sense as to my whereabouts. Of course, I doubt that my shelling the fort lessened their resolve to put me in chains."

He looked at her. "Do I have to ask? Should I ask?"

"I don't . . . I don't know."

"You aren't happy. You were not happy when we met. I knew. So I am here to ask you to come with me, difficult as that will be."

"I want to . . ." she began.

"But?"

"There is no 'but,' not really." And she told him about Sean's elevation to the peerage, and about Coldstream Castle.

"I'm happy for you, Selena," he said very softly. "It's everything you could have hoped for, everything you've always wanted."

"No, it's not," she said. "I want to come with you, too."

"Selena, Selena." He smiled sadly. "Coldstream is your life, your destiny . . ."

"Not yet," she said. "I cannot return to Coldstream, knowing Dick Weddington's death has bought me there."

"But *Coldstream*, Selena?" he asked once again. "If you come with me, life will be hard and dangerous. We will be on the run until the war is over, and we will be exiles longer than that. We may never be able to return to Scotland in our lifetimes. . . ."

"*We will return!*" she cried passionately, and the men at the bar turned to stare again.

"Out!" Royce ordered, looking at them. "You, too," he told the bartender. Their glances were hard and vicious, but they moved toward the door.

"Then we are one," he said, "and we leave together."

Will Teviot came stumbling in, a worried look on his face. "I do na lak it, Royce. There's British a-comin' o'er on the ferry fra' New York, an' what's worse . . ."

"Yes? Out with it, man!"

"Veronica Blakemore is here," he said, "an' she's brought a man wi' her."

Veronica entered, smirking in triumph. She was followed by Sean, whose face was pale with shock and anger.

"And there she is," Veronica said, pointing to Selena. "Just as I promised you."

She turned to Sean and smiled, as if expecting congratulations on having led him here, then said to Selena. "You really *must* be more discreet next time. I've been watching you for just this kind of escapade . . ."

"There isn't going to be a next time," Sean declared.

"Sir," Royce said, standing, "it would do little good to apologize or explain, and should you demand satisfaction, I will understand. But I want you to know that Selena has not . . ."

"I am afraid it no longer matters," Sean said.

Selena's very heart went out to him. It had been her fault, this hasty rush to see Royce. And, compounded as it was by Veronica's unerring instinct for inflicting humiliation, she could understand if Sean felt that his worst suspicions had been confirmed. But, true to himself, he surprised her. He surprised them all.

"You may go now," he told Veronica, very calmly. She started in surprise and did not move. "Go, you have done what your nature compelled you to do. That should be enough." He nodded toward Will Teviot, an abrupt gesture of command. "This gentleman will escort you to the door."

Sneering, but now unsure, Veronica acquiesced. Then Sean turned to face Royce. The two men stared at each other.

"I do love Selena," Royce said.

"I know that," Sean said. "So do I. And she loves both of us. But she loves you more, and in a way that is more natural to her, just as it will prove to be more dangerous to her."

"I have told her that."

"I expect you have. It is something that would be hard

to ignore, but it is something from which Selena has never been dissuaded."

Then he turned to face her.

"You have already made your decision, haven't you? Your presence here is proof of that."

"Yes," she said.

"It was Dick Weddington, wasn't it?"

"Sean . . . yes. Yes. I can't go back to Coldstream this way, not after . . ."

Sean's face was a mask of pain. "I did not know they would . . ." His voice trailed off. "You have to believe me."

She nodded.

"Selena," he said, "I shall always treasure what we had. But it is not there anymore. Perhaps we both destroyed it. Things happen. We changed . . ."

Again, he fell silent. Royce waited, not wishing to interrupt, but also aware that every moment spent in this public place increased the danger of capture. If Veronica . . .

Sean seemed about to speak again, then changed his mind. Instead, he leaned forward. He did not kiss her, but pressed his cheek to hers, and then withdrew. It happened so quickly that she had no chance to respond, and his skin on hers was as evanescent as the touch of a butterfly's wing.

"Good-bye, Selena," he said softly, repeating, too, the words of their parting in Kinlochbervie, long ago. "Ride fast, ride far, farewell."

And, turning, he was gone.

She opened her mouth to call him back, to tell him she was sorry, to say that they would meet again one day, perhaps at Coldstream, to tell him of her pride in his accomplishment, to affirm once more the love they had possessed. But he was gone. She turned to Royce and lost herself in his arms.

After a moment, they walked out into the street. Sean was making his way back to the ferry ship, ignoring Veronica, who hurried after him, trying to keep up. She felt their eyes on her and turned around.

"You are fools, both of you," she called. "The rebels are going to lose, and so are you."

"It's not possible," Royce called back. "You're on their side."

"Royce," Will Teviot worried. "Let's be a-movin', aye? Them Britishers is climbin' off that ferry now."

"So they are," Royce said. "Let's get the horses. We've a hard ride ahead."

There were three horses; Royce had been prepared for her decision. They galloped southward out of Brooklyn, through the rolling, wooded country of Long Island, toward Jamaica Bay and the great ship that bore Selena's name. It was soon apparent to them that they were being followed by soldiers on horseback. Royce, worried that the pursuers would deduce their direction and hence the location of the ship, decided on a ruse, and turned eastward, heading out onto the island rather than continuing their course toward the South Shore.

"We won't make the ship tonight," he said. "But I can't take any chances. We'll have to hope that tomorrow will be soon enough."

They were still riding when darkness fell. Royce called a halt in a blazing red-gold thicket of oak and willow. No hoofbeats sounded behind them any longer.

"They've given up on us for tonight," he said. "We'll rest here, and double back in the morning."

After a rude supper of bread, wine, and some hazelnuts Selena found on nearby bushes, Will Teviot left them and found his shelter for the night beneath other trees. Royce took the saddle blankets from the horses, and spread one of them on the ground, draping the other across several branches to fashion a small tent. Together at last, in each other's arms, their union seemed as natural as the night, and yet almost impossible to comprehend in the fullness of its wonder. The balance of their lives had hung upon the precipice of Selena's decision; the future lay invisible, like the heart of an orchid, beating within the petals of time.

"Oh, my love, my darling," Royce murmured, when he took her, "now we are forever."

"Yes," Selena told him. And, before she lost herself in the delight of their melding, she knew that her decision had been right. She had given up her dream of Coldstream, perhaps even her hope of returning to Scotland, to have this man whom she now held and pleasured with her body and her love. She had pledged even her hope of future peace to their love, and she and Royce were one now, irrevocably. *To part now would be almost to die,* she was thinking, but then the pleasure shook her, took him, too, and it was as it had been on the *Highlander,* when he had rescued her at sea. Except now she loved him better and understood him more. They climbed together, once again, the high ladder to heaven. The journey was as mystical as a prayer on the wing, and as immediate as the breathless joy he sorcered in her body. They took each other, then, and for the flashing instant of their mutual oblivion neither past nor future threatened. Even the present was but a pale shade left below on the spinning earth. They were together, came together, clung together. Protection enough, that free and fiery night in old October.

They slept later than intended, and the sun was climbing the sky as they rode over the rise of land near the ocean, hard by Jamaica Bay. The world glittered, pure and clean and safe. The Atlantic rolled blue and shining toward infinity. The *Selena* rested at anchor in the deep waters not far from the beach. Selena leaned forward in her saddle, surveying the clear horizon with a bursting heart, certain that the future beckoned where the sea met the sky.

But the very next moment fate was upon them, like an explosion. A band of uniformed horsemen came charging out of the hills to the north, shouting for them to halt, firing muskets and flintlock pistols.

"'Tis the beggars who were a-followin' us yesterday," Will cried. "They put their brains together an' figured out our plan."

They had barely absorbed this threat when another appeared. A watchman called from the *Selena*'s crow's nest, "Royce, 'tis a ship sailin' at us fra' New York, an' she looks a terrible danger to us now."

They looked, and saw the dreaded H.M.S. *Lucifer* approaching, sailing fast, surrounded by an escort of gunboats.

The three of them took off at a gallop, down across the dunes. Selena saw Royce's mount crash into the surf just ahead of her own. And, at the same time, she saw the bursts of smoke from the cannons of the far-off *Lucifer.* Sean and Davina were on that ship, she thought, bound for

Scotland and Coldstream and honor. She had no time to think about it anymore. Sails were unfurling all over the *Selena*, catching the wind, as crewmen worked feverishly to get the mighty vessel to safety on the high seas. It had already begun to move. Not a moment could be spared. The *Lucifer* slashed ahead at full sail, closing the gap. And the cannoneers were finding the range. Half a dozen cannonballs crashed into the water just off the *Selena*'s starboard, sending towers of spray forty, fifty feet into the sky, creating a series of powerful waves, through which Royce plunged his horse. He was near the ship, reaching for the boarding ladder, Selena was not far behind. But behind her, Will Teviot cried out in pain.

He had been hit by grapeshot, in the chest and shoulder. The pursuers were almost upon them now, riding down the dunes. The *Selena* was moving. Another shower of cannonballs exploded in the water, closing on target.

"Selena, my God! Hurry!"

Royce grabbed his pistol and fired at the horsemen onshore.

"Selena!" Will Teviot gasped, and fell from his horse into the sea.

The *Selena* was moving now. Great white sails stretched to embrace the free and riding wind.

"Selena!" Royce cried, his voice pure agony over the explosion of the *Lucifer*'s guns and the pounding of the sea.

Will Teviot's blood ran red in the surf; he lifted an arm, bidding her farewell.

Time stopped.

Teviot groaned in agony, struggling toward the shallows. Shouting horsemen reined their dancing beasts at the water's edge. And Selena reined her mount as well, and turned to help Will Teviot, who had saved her in the Highlands long ago.

"*Selena!*" Royce cried, one last time. The *Lucifer* fired, but missed once more, as the great black ship wrapped the wind of heaven unto itself and lanced upon the open sea. Royce was still clinging to the boarding ladder, one arm stretched out to her, in promise more than in farewell, his face a mask of horror and disbelief.

The soldiers looked at Selena, puzzled. She might have

made it to the ship and safety, but instead, at the last moment, she had turned back. She stared at them for just a second. A challenge. She dismounted and knelt in the cold surf, putting her hands beneath Will's neck, keeping his head out of the water. Blood poured from his upper torso, and she saw that the grapeshot had almost severed his arm.

Will gritted his teeth against the pain, but already there was in his eyes the glaze of death Selena had come to know so well.

"Ah, Selena, but ye didna 'ave t' do this thing," he gasped.

"Lady, let me help you get him onshore," said the officer who'd been in charge of the pursuing soldiers. He motioned to a couple of his men and began to dismount himself.

Will groaned. A word. Indistinct.

Selena bent her ear against his mouth. She was trying futilely to press her hands against his wounds, to stanch the flow of blood.

"Don't talk," she said.

But he made the sound again, more distinctly this time.

"Do na . . . Selena, do na let 'em touch me . . . please."

The soldiers were splashing through the surf, and one of them reached Selena and Will. "Here, lady," he said, bending down. He was a young man, little more than a boy. And he looked scared when he saw all the blood. He reached for Will. "Here, lady, let me help . . ."

"Don't you touch him!" Selena cried, her eyes burning with tears.

The young soldier drew back in surprise.

"Aye!" Will Teviot gasped, trying to smile. His cracked teeth were red with blood now, too. "Aye, Selena, there's the old fire I remember . . ."

He shuddered once. And he died. The soldier shivered in alarm, and looked to his mates for guidance.

Numb, angry, the world distorted and fantastic through her tears, Selena stood up. Will Teviot lay at her feet, washed in the sea. The same sea that now bore the *Lucifer* home to Scotland, on the high roads of the Atlantic. Several gunboats had broken away from the convoy and were now in pursuit of the *Selena*, which had all but disappeared to the south. The gunboats were light and fast, and very well armed. It would be a tight race, and there would probably be a battle . . .

The *Lucifer* sailed by, far from shore. Too far away for Selena to see any of her passengers, or even to make out the figures on deck. Nor would anyone aboard be able to identify Selena, standing there in the gentle surf, surrounded by redcoats. But she raised her arm in a farewell salute. *Love Coldstream,* she prayed to Davina, and, as Davi, the dark one would have done, she spoke with her mind to Sean: *I will never forget you; think of me kindly should you picnic one day on the banks of the Teviot River.*

She waved her hand one final time. She let her hand fall. The *Lucifer* rode proudly to the wind, bearing two whom Selena loved, homing on both the future and the past.

The soldiers were nervous and quiet. They realized that something of great significance had taken place here, but, aside from Teviot's death, they were not sure what it was. Then their commander spoke:

"We will have to get him out of the water, Lady Blood-well. Do you understand? You can understand that, can't you, Lady Bloodwell?"

She turned to look at him, and he seemed to start at the power of her gaze.

"I am Selena MacPherson," she said.

Then she looked again toward the southern horizon over which Royce had disappeared. Her father's words came back to her as clearly as on that golden day of childhood. Now she understood those words completely. She stood here on the shore and Royce was out there on the sea, where the horizon rose to meet the sky.

Selena, the sky begins here.

The Black Swan
by Day Taylor

is a dazzling, splendorous romance of fierce ecstasies, violent truths and wild dreams set against the terrors of the Civil War. The following is an excerpt from THE BLACK SWAN, to be published by Dell in July.

They rode across the cotton fields into the willow oak woods along the creek, following paths Dulcie knew well, and Adam had come to know, into the piney woods.

Dulcie reined in. She tore off her snood, shaking her hair until it spilled in a russet cascade over her shoulders. Feeling wild and free, she gazed at the towering pines, conical, spearing the heavens. She searched through the heavy boughs for sight of the wonder the forest promised, then her eyes lowered and met Adam's. They laughed in delight.

Around them the calm settled. Birds stopped singing and returned to nest, foxes sought their lairs, deer with folded legs snuggled into the brush, before the coming storm.

Adam dismounted. "All I can smell is your perfume. Just flowers." His eyes held hers, and his smile dimmed. He held up his arms, then she was off her horse and standing in front of him. He said her name only once. The rising wind soughed through dark green trees. His mouth came down on hers hard, his mustache coarse against her lips. With one vise-like arm he cradled her against him as though he would never let her go.

He drew his head away, his breath coming hard. "Dulcie. . . ." His lips met hers again and she was open to him. His hand moved under her jacket to the edge of her breast, unfettered except for the thin shirt.

She turned a little toward his hand, wanting him to touch her, explore her, know her fully.

In the distance a sharp crack of thunder rolled across the green-gray heavens.

Dulcie said breathlessly, "There's an old log house. . . ."

The wind rose swiftly, the tops of the pines bent and rubbed against each other in a melancholy music. Suddenly mobilized, he lifted her to her horse. They rode quickly down the seldom used forest path.

They tied the horses in front of a low door that sagged on its hinges. He held out his hand and Dulcie followed him. He pushed the door to, its primitive hinges protesting as he closed the world out.

He loved her. The thought rocked him, robbing him of the remorseless desire to take her as he had the others. "You're getting wet, Dulcie," he said, softly teasing. He put his hands out, motioning her to him.

"Oh Adam . . . Adam . . . Adam, hold me! Don't let me go . . . ever."

He buried his hands and face in her hair. She pressed her breasts, her loins against him, wrenching inarticulate sounds of love from the depths of him. With his tongue he forced her mouth open, seeking, and the flame swept Dulcie as it was sweeping him, making his arms tremble as he held her.

She stood quivering, resisting the impulse to hide her bared breasts from this large man to whom she thought to give herself. "Take off my shirt," he whispered. With shaking fingers she obeyed. He took her hand in his, placing it against his breast as he touched hers. His fingers burned against her flesh, sending an unbearable thrill through her.

"Touch me as I touch you. Let me feel you caress me, Dulcie." Hesitantly at first, her hands moved over the heavy muscles that mounded smoothly across his chest, feeling their taut contours with growing excitement.

Her voice shook as she said, "I . . . I came to you in the night, Adam. Last night, very late. I . . . was awake. I stood . . . unclothed . . . I wanted . . . to come to you. I stood outside your window. Oh, Adam . . . why didn't you know? I wanted to go on . . . but I was so afraid. . . . "

He kissed her and held her tenderly. "Are you afraid now, Dulcie?"

"A little . . . but I need you. . . . Adam, hold me."

"Dulcie . . ." He drew her hand down to his throbbing penis. His tongue went into her mouth, moving back and forth, probing, tantalizing. She responded, trembling, eager, caressing him through his trousers.

Dulcie looked into his darkened eyes, her own half closed, her nostrils flaring with passion. It was this she wanted . . . the touch of her lover's hands upon her secret flesh . . . the union of his body with hers . . . holding him within her as she had held no man. . . .

He placed her fingers on the top button of his trousers. His

574

lips were on hers, his tongue sliding against hers as she fumbled shakily with the tight fastening.

Adam moaned softly as he murmured her name. She jumped away from him, drawing in her breath in a screaming gasp. Rain and the wind whirled through the small room as the door let go of its hinges and crashed to the floor behind Adam. Then her heart exploded in her breast, leaving her without the means to breathe.

Wolf.

The torrential rain poured down on the overseer, funneling off his sodden hat down his neck, streaming down his filthy shirt and trousers. He smiled hungrily at Dulcie, a grimace of broken, tobacco-stained teeth, his face flushed with lust.

Adam instinctively moved toward Wolf. "Oh, God! You stinkin' *bastard!*"

"I been a-watchin' y'all," Wolf grinned.

"You son of a bitch. I'm going to kill you." Adam's voice was deep and grating.

"Cap'n," said Wolf in the burlesque of respect he loved to show his betters, "you ain't a-gonna kill me. Dulcie's treated me like dirt ever since she was a snot-nosed brat. Naow things is changed, ain't they. I seen her fer what she is. I ain't a-gonna fergit that. No sirree!"

Wolf moved out of sight. Quickly Adam picked up his coat. He wrapped it around her. She turned her face from him, shamed and horrified.

Adam sprang through the door. Wolf was mounting his horse. Adam, running, was almost on him when, with a hideous laugh, Wolf whipped his horse. The animal leaped forward, taking him out of Adam's reach. He reined in and turned around. "Cap'n . . . y'all ain't a-gonna do *nuthin'.*" He disappeared into the storm.

The rain pelted down coldly on Adam. In frustrated fury, he returned to the cabin. Dulcie cowered in the darkest corner.

Adam shuddered. "Oh, God, Dulcie." He wanted to erase the terrible moments by his presence, to hold her against him to stop her shaking and make her feel loved and safe once more.

She cringed at his touch. Her voice was high. "D-don't touch me!"

"Don't be ashamed, Dulcie . . . you . . . you could never be anything but beautiful to me, darling."

"Don't call me darling! Don't call me anything! Don't speak to me—ever!"

With a quick bend of her knees she grabbed for her pantalets. "Turn around!" she demanded. He heard the rustling of cloth as well as her hysterical commands. "Stay as you are! Don't look!"

"Dulcie, please—listen to me—"

She swept past him, running for the door. He grabbed her arm, spinning her around so she stood pinned against him. "What do you think you're doing? You can't go out there alone."

She struggled, then gave up, staring past him, her mouth set, her eyes fixed on nothing.

"It would have been an act of joy . . . not a thing to remember in shame—"

"Oh?" Her eyes flickered over his bare chest, raised to his mouth and to his eyes. Her gaze was filled with bitter self-pity. "Shall I undress for you again?

"Adam . . . if you had said once . . . just one time . . . that you loved me . . . even if it was a lie . . . But you didn't say it, did you?"

Adam hesitated too long, her hypocrisy choking him.

The tears spilled over. "You needn't bother, Captain Tremain," she said woodenly. "Your opportunity has passed. I no longer wish to hear . . . anything."

Adam said, "I'm going to carry you."

"You are *not!*"

He scooped her up, holding her so tightly she could not kick him. "Put your arm around my neck. Your horse fell. You hurt your back."

"I'm not going to lie—"

"You are, and I am. And if you must stay in bed for a day or two to preserve your reputation, consider it worthwhile."

It was a long distance across the fields to the house, and all the way Dulcie was forced to listen to the regular beating of Adam's heart.